THE FOLLY BEACH MYSTERY COLLECTION VOLUME II

THE FOLLY BEACH MYSTERY COLLECTION VOLUME II

BILL NOEL

Discord

Copyright © 2017 Bill Noel

Dark Horse Copyright © 2018

Joy Copyright © 2018 Bill Noel

Folly Beach Mystery Collection Volume 2

Copyright © 2018 by Bill Noel

Front cover photo and design by Bill Noel

Author photo by Susan Noel

ISBN: 978-1-937979-43-0

Enigma House Press

Goshen, Kentucky 40026

www.enigmahousepress.com

DISCORD

PROLOGUE

Midnight had come and gone. The Top Ten Bar had been stand-ing-room-only two hours earlier yet now was as quiet as a Baptist church on Tuesday morning. Rod, a tall, thin, thirty-something bartender, stood behind the distressed wooden bar wiping dry the last of the clean wine glasses; not difficult since most patrons were beer drinkers. The exhausted employee, who looked more like a history professor with his neatly-trimmed beard and glasses perched on his head, was forty feet from a couple of stragglers. Rod had pulled a double shift and the two customers were all that stood between his aching feet and heading to his girlfriend's condo where he hoped to find sympa-thetic coos, and with luck, a foot massage and more.

The female customer pushed an empty beer bottle aside and leaned against the table. "Think you can walk away after stomping on my dream?" She was seething and making no effort to hide it. "All your talk, your smiles, your empty promises. You've been lying through your freakin' teeth. You've taken my money. Buddy, let me tell you one thing you're not going to do." She hesitated, glanced toward the bartender who was ignoring her outburst, and turned to her tablemate. "You ain't going to get away with it."

The man shrugged. It wasn't the worst reaction from the customer sitting on the other side of the table from the tirade, but it was close. He grinned and things hit rock bottom.

The woman swept her arm across the table and the bottle tumbled to the cracked, beer-stained linoleum floor. The bottle exploded into hundreds of shards, and shattered not only the container but the eerie silence in the room. She shoved away from the table and stormed out of the bar.

The bartender's expression switched from boredom to irritation. The man who had been sitting across from the woman turned toward Rod, held his hands out. "I got it. I'll clean it up."

You better, thought Rod. He glared at the man, glanced at the door where the companion had stomped out, and reached for the broom and dustpan. He mumbled a profanity and faked a smile as he handed the cleaning tools to the customer. "Thanks, Kevin. I'd appreciate it."

Kevin had been a regular at Top Ten Bar, located a few blocks away from Lower Broadway, Nashville's epicenter of country bars and aspiring singers and songwriters, for the last year and had escorted a constant stream of young women to his evening "office." After the first few months, the bartenders had stopped paying attention to the ladies with Kevin and swore they couldn't recognize any of them even if the room had been lit by klieg lights. The inside joke among the staff had been that Kevin was either a talent scout in futile search for the next star, or a pimp plying his bevy of beauties with liquid encouragement before sending them out to enhance his coffers. Regardless, the less the bartenders knew about Kevin and his activities the better.

There was something else Rod didn't know about Kevin. This would be the last night he would be escorting anyone to the out-of-the-way Music City watering hole.

RoD COULD SPOT a cop within a millisecond of one entering his workplace, a talent he'd acquired from standing behind bars for a third of his life. It didn't take years of observation to tell him the two men walking his direction were on the payroll of the Metro Nashville Police Department. They weren't in uniform, yet their poorly-fitting navy blazers with conspicuous firearm bulges made formal introductions unnecessary. They flashed their creds at him anyway. Troy Rogers was the younger of the two; Wayne Lawrence, the more seasoned detective.

Detective Rogers unfolded an enlarged driver's license photo and slid it across the bar. "Recognize him?"

A dozen pre-happy-hour drinkers were spread throughout the warehouse-size room. They were more interested in their drinks than in the detectives.

Rod removed his glasses and laid them on the bar. He squinted at the photo and at the detective. "Sure, it's Kevin. Kevin Starr, at least that's what's on his credit card. What'd he do?"

Detective Lawrence ignored the question. "When was the last time you saw him?"

Rod glanced around the room. No one needed his services nor were paying attention to what was going on with the detectives. "Couple of nights ago. Why?"

Rogers took a notebook out of his jacket pocket. "What time?"

"Didn't see him come in. Had to be after eleven. I was busy. He sat over there." Rod pointed to a table on the far side of the room.

Rogers jotted a note and said, "He alone?"

"No. Had a woman with him. What's going on?"

"Know who she was?" Rogers asked.

Rod smiled. "Hell, I'm not Kevin's secretary. He has a

different woman every time he's here. Couldn't tell you one from another."

"So you don't know who she was?"

Ain't it what I said? Rod thought. Instead, he said, "Nope."

"Describe her?"

"I never got a good look. It was busy when they came in and Kevin came to me and got their beers. I was the only employee here. The damned waitress left sick an hour earlier leaving me with all this." He waved his hand around the room.

Rogers said, "Try anyway?"

Rod looked at the table where the couple had been sitting. "Average height. Didn't strike me as tall or short. Figure she was attractive because all of Kevin's *friends* are lookers." He shook his head. "She had her back to me. Sorry, that's it."

Detective Lawrence said, "Don't suppose she paid by credit card?"

"Don't you think I would have mentioned it? Besides, she didn't pay." Rod hesitated and grinned. "Not to me, that is."

"What's that mean?" Lawrence asked.

"Umm, nothing."

"Nothing?"

Rod looked at Rogers and turned to Lawrence. "Don't take this as gospel. Some of us thought Starr was a pimp. All those good-looking gals, you know."

"Any proof?" Lawrence said.

"Just gossip."

Rogers asked, "What time did they leave?"

"Twelve-thirty. Remember because they were the only folks here. Had to wait for them to go to lock up."

"Anyone else here that night who might recognize her?" Lawrence asked.

"Maybe, except I don't know who. I told you it was crowded when they got here. The waitress was gone. Don't know if they talked to anyone. Place was dead when they left; dead until he must've said something to piss her off."

The detectives leaned forward. "Explain."

Rod looked around to see if any customers were listening. "They added fifteen minutes to my already long night when she knocked a bottle off the table. Sticky beer and glass everywhere. I made Kevin clean it up."

"Accident?"

Rod grinned. "If flailing her arm around, knocking the bottle five feet from the table, and storming out of the room was an accident, sure."

Lawrence asked, "Know what she was angry about?"

"Nah, but Kevin was nice about cleaning the mess up. He kept mumbling about the chick not having to break the bottle. Something like he was doing the best he could."

"Any idea what he meant?" Lawrence asked.

Rod shook his head.

Lawrence jotted another note.

"Now your turn. What's going on?"

Detective Rogers glanced at his partner and turned to Rod. "We found the credit card receipt that showed he was in here two nights ago."

"So?"

"We found it on his body. Mr. Starr was murdered sometime Monday night or Tuesday morning."

1

I was in Cal's Country Bar and Burgers a block off the literal and figurative center of my slice of heaven on Folly Beach, South Carolina. The lunch crowd, if you call four people a crowd, had settled their checks and headed to the beach. The bar's owner and I were alone.

Cal folded his trim, six-foot-three frame in the chair and scooted up to the table. "Heard from them lately?"

The last four months, when anyone mentioned *them*, it was safe to assume they were referring to my best friend Charles Fowler and his girlfriend Heather Lee, the couple who had moved to Nashville so Heather could pursue her dream of becoming a country music star. Considering her singing voice, to put it gently, stank, the odds on her achieving the lofty goal were worse than me, a man in my sixties and allergic to exercise, running the hundred-meter hurdles in the Olympics.

"Last week," I said. "Charles called excited to tell me Heather made another appearance at open-mic night at the Bluebird."

"Got herself discovered yet?"

Cal, who was in his seventies, would know a thing or two about being discovered. He had a national top-twenty country hit, "End of the Story," that reached number one in his hometown of Lubbock, Texas. Unfortunately, he had reached his pinnacle of success in 1962 at the ripe old age of eighteen.

"Don't believe so."

Cal chuckled. "Suspect Michigan would've mentioned it if his gal had become famous."

Cal had a habit of calling people by their state of origin. Charles and I had come close to breaking him of it. He would occasionally backslide.

I nodded.

Cal continued, "Appearing at the Bluebird Cafe's a big deal. Back in my day, there weren't nearly as many places where someone could be discovered. Because they let Heather croon a tune there don't mean much other than she can say she did."

"She knows it. She's got her heart set on breaking into the music industry."

Cal pushed his ever-present, sweat-stained Stetson back on his head, looked at the front door where nobody entered, and back at me. "How many songs has she penned?"

"Two that I know of. Why?"

"How many times has she appeared at open-mic night at the Bird?"

"Several."

"Has she appeared anywhere else in Nashville?"

"Don't think so."

"Open-mic night at the Bird is for songwriters, not singers."

"I know."

Cal looked toward the stage at the far end of the bar. "My ears have suffered from hearing Heather warble through her two penned ditties many nights up there." Cal shook his head. "Now I'm no expert on the new-fangled country music. In my day, a songwriter hauled around a satchel with a hundred or more songs he, or sometimes a gal, had put to paper. Heather's two aren't much better than a dolphin could write and her singing's not as good as those swimmin' mammals can croon."

I knew how much Charles cared for Heather, and Lord knows, everyone who knew her understood how much she wanted to find fame and fortune standing behind a microphone. Cal was right. I started to tell him so when the door opened and I was surprised to see Preacher Burl Ives Costello peek his head in. He saw us and headed our way.

Cal said, "Afternoon, Illinois."

"A pleasant afternoon to you, Brother Cal," said the portly minister of First Light, Folly's newest, and most unusual house of worship. "And to you too, Brother Chris."

First Light should be called a place of worship rather than a house since it conducted most of its services on the beach. When bad weather descended, or in the preacher's words, the "Devil took to interferin' with the work of the Lord," the services were held in a storefront on Folly's main street.

Cal looked around the empty room. "Here to save someone? If you are, you're stuck with Kentucky, umm, Mr. Landrum here, and me. Don't see much hope for savin' us."

Burl was quite familiar with the aging bar owner and me. We had been embroiled in a deadly situation a couple of years back that involved members of his congregation, or as he called them, his flock. Burl had been the prime suspect in the death of several people, and just as quickly had almost become the victim of the real murderer. Since then, First Light had increased in popularity and its flock had grown, especially among those who were looking for a nontraditional worship experience.

Burl laughed. "My job's to not give up on anyone, although I reckon you might be right about little hope for you two. Truth be told, I wanted to sit a spell and enjoy a cold brew."

Cal tipped his Stetson. "That'll be a lot easier to rustle up than throwing out my demons." He smiled. "Bud, Bud Light, or Miller?"

Cal's range of drink offerings included three beers, and an equal number of wines: red, white, and pink. If he was pushed, which he seldom was, he could find you a glass of water or a Coke.

Burl patted his ample stomach and smiled. "Better stick with Bud Light to maintain my shapely figure." He pulled a chair to our table and lowered his *shapely* body on it.

Cal returned with the beer and held up the bottle before giving it to Burl. "Preacher, I hear rumors you preach about the sins of, what do you call it, the Devil's juice. Don't get this old washed-up singer wrong, I ain't trying to talk you out of sipping this brew and adding to my massive fortune. I'm wondering if this ain't what you preach against?"

Burl nodded. "Brother Cal, you're right … and wrong."

Cal rolled his eyes. "That explains it."

Burl chuckled. "I preach against excess, Brother Cal. Excess."

"Too much beer," Cal said, as if he needed clarification on the meaning of excess.

"Brother Jesus wasn't above sippin' wine. Heavens, if he was in here today, I believe he'd be tasting one of these." He held his Bud Light bottle in the air. "Moderation my friend. Moderation is the key to the good life. Excess is the work of the Devil. It includes this stuff." He hesitated and pointed at the bottle. "Or whiskey, or lovin', or speeding, or even consuming too many M&Ms. Excess, my friend."

"Got it, Preacher," Cal said. "Now if the theological lesson's over, can we commence drinking?"

"I can't help myself. To paraphrase Descartes, 'I preach, therefore I am.'" He chuckled and turned to me. "Brother Chris, my misquoting that French philosopher reminded me of our friend Brother Charles and the way he's always quoting presidents. Have you heard from him and Sister Heather?"

I was stuck on Burl knowing Descartes quote enough to paraphrase it, and asked him to repeat his question.

"Heard from them lately?"

I shared what I had told Cal, and Burl asked if the agent I didn't trust had found Heather any paying gigs. Heather's pilgrimage to Nashville had begun a little over four months ago, when she had been performing during Cal's weekly open-mic night. A man named Kevin Starr said he was in town meeting with record executives at the Tides Hotel and had walked to Cal's to get away from the boring discussions. He heard Heather, asked her to join him after her set, and told her he was an agent and owner of Starr Management, based in Music City. He offered to represent her and said he could get her appearances in Nashville's top venues for discovering talent. That was all it took. A few days later she had packed her belongings lock, stock, and guitar, and she and Charles had moved 560 miles to find her fame and fortune in the country music capitol of the world.

Burl sipped his beer and nodded or shook his head during my update on *them*. "Now I know Brother Charles and Sister Heather are your good friends, Brother Chris. I hope you don't take offense at what I am about to say. Umm …, I'm no expert like our friend Brother Cal here. From my untrained ears, I don't detect the qualities in Sister Heather's voice that would lead her to music stardom. Am I incorrect?"

Cal leaned closer to Burl. "If all those words mean you think Heather's singing sucks, you smacked the truth right on its noggin."

My phone rang before Cal could continue with his in-depth analysis of Heather's vocal talents.

I looked at the screen. "Speaking of the Devil," I said. "Figuratively speaking, Preacher."

2

"Is this Chris Landrum?" asked the voice on the phone. "You know, the aging, retired, guy who's bored because he went and shut down his photo gallery."

I grinned and thought of how much I missed my friend. "You got Chris Landrum and retired right. Hi, Charles."

"Nope, I got all of it right. As James Garfield said, 'The truth will set you free, but first it will make you miserable.'"

Telephone courtesies and greetings like *hello* are a thing of the past, or so it seemed. Instead of hitting the *End Call* button, I repeated, "Hi, Charles."

He mumbled, "You're no fun," followed by a moment of silence, and, "Okay, enough foolishness from you. I called to tell you about an epiphany I had in the middle of the night. Think it was brought on when Heather kicked me in her sleep, anyway, here it is—"

"Epiphany," I interrupted. "Who took possession of Charles Fowler's vocabulary?"

"Heather spends her time singing. I spend mine reading and grabbing a new word every once in a while; need them to talk to the intellectuals here. Stop knocking me off track, you want to hear my epiphany or not?"

I wanted to say "not," yet wasn't ready to incur the wrath of Charles; besides, I did wonder what could possibly have come to him because of being kicked. "I'm waiting."

"Good. It struck me that since you deserted the gallery you've become a retiredaholic."

"Have you thrown that word around those intellectuals?"

"Saved it for you. Stop interrupting. The point is you'll burn yourself out spending all your time retired—day and night, night and day, 24/7. After Heather kicked me awake, we talked about your precarious situation and came to a decision. You ready?"

Cal and Burl stared at me. I sighed. "Sure."

"You need to get away from retirement for a while and take a vacation. Hang on a sec, Heather's trying to say something."

I stared at the phone and realized I hadn't been aware how strenuous being retired was. I also realized Charles had finally gotten over me closing the gallery where he had been my unpaid sales manager. The few years it was open, the shop had done little but drain my net worth. It had given my friend a purpose in life and something he could take pride in. He was hurt, frustrated, and at times angry with my decision. The fact was, he hadn't been the one writing checks every month that exceeded the money I'd taken in.

"I'm back," he said. "Okay, the Charles and Heather Travel Agency have it worked out. This is Thursday, right?"

"Right."

"Take the rest of the day to pack. Tomorrow get in your little Cadillac ATS, set the handy-dandy navigation thingie for Nashville, Tennessee, and zip on over. Here's the best part. We have an extra bedroom—well, it's sort of a storage room. All the stuff in it can be put somewhere else, and you can sleep on the queen mattress the previous renter left on the floor. We won't charge you a single cent to stay here. See, we've already saved you at least a hundred bucks a night. Now get this. On Monday night, Heather will be performing at the Bluebird Cafe, and you can go with us."

"Charles, I—"

"I know, I know. You get a complete vacation package including room and entertainment for only the cost of gas and food. And, if you wanted to take Heather and me to supper to celebrate her Bluebird appearance, we know of a restaurant that has good food at cheap prices. We only have one bedroom left. Can we make your reservation? Besides, there's something important, a problem, we want to bounce off you."

Heather was laughing in the background and saying, "Please come. Please."

Cal and Burl continued to stare at me.

"Sure."

Heather must have been near the phone. She squealed.

Charles gave me the address to plug in my *handy-dandy navigation thingie*, where to park when I got there, and their apartment number. He told me to let them know when I was a few hours away. He said Heather wanted to be there when I arrived and would need time to reschedule some of her many appointments with music executives, and Charles might be at Starbucks reading a thesaurus.

I set the phone on the table, exhaled, as Cal and Burl said, "What?" They had heard my end of the conversation, so I filled in the blanks, omitting why I needed a break from being retired and Charles's made-up malady, retiredaholic, and his real, but totally out of character, word-of-the-day, epiphany.

"You moseying over?" Cal asked.

Burl said, "You miss him, don't you?"

"Sure, I do, Preacher," and realized how true it was. "He's my best friend. I told him I'd come."

Cal headed to the cooler. "Next round's on me. That'll help you pay for your gas."

Burl asked, "When are you going?"

"Tomorrow."

Cal handed each of us a drink. "Had a thought on the way back from the cooler." He took a draw on his beer.

I glanced at Burl and at Cal. He was waiting for one of us to ask about his thought.

Burl didn't disappoint. "Planning on sharing it?"

Cal looked at the preacher and pointed his Bud bottle at me. "Maybe I could tag along. It's been a bunch of years since I sauntered around Music City. I miss the good old days when I would hang around the Opry House; the real one, not the sterile one out by the hotel that's the size of Topeka, Kansas. Willie, Roger, Ernest, Roy—ah, the good ole days. Anyway, how about me going with you?"

I enjoyed spending time with Cal. He was entertaining and fun to be with, but, truth be told, I was more a loner. I wasn't sure I was ready to spend most of the day in the car with him, or for that matter, with anyone. And, I couldn't imagine that Charles and Heather's apartment had enough room for both of us. On the other hand, unless he went, he may never get back to the city that had meant so much to him.

"Sounds good, Cal." I shook my head. "But I couldn't take you away from your bar. I don't know how long I'll be there."

He frowned and looked down at his bottle. "Guess you're right. Wouldn't want to deprive my loveable drunks by locking them out."

Burl had been watching the exchange, and leaned closer to the table. "Perhaps I can offer a passable solution."

Cal said, "What might that be?"

"I mentioned this to Brother Chris a while back, but don't think you know, Brother Cal. Years back, when I was doing most anything—most anything legal—to make ends meet, I spent a year tending bar. I could fill-in for a week or so and you could have your part-time cook come in more shifts to fix food. Don't think your customers' stomachs would take kindly at me frying burgers."

Cal pushed his Stetson back on his head. "A mighty kind offer, Preacher. Now how would it jive with your preaching. Seems like it'd cause a passel of probs."

Burl smiled. "Can't think of a better place to find souls needing saving."

Cal leaned back. "Now Brother Burl, I can't have preaching in—"

Burl faced his palms toward Cal. "Kidding. I'd be glad to watch the bar while you're gone. No preaching, no plugging religion. Let's call it community outreach without the church reaching."

Cal looked at me, I shrugged, and he turned to Burl. "Sounds like a fine idea, Preacher. Not to sound rude and unappreciative, I'd take you up on it if you could do me one favor."

Burl smiled. "I ought to hear it first."

"When you're tendin' bar, would it be possible for you to refrain from calling everyone Brother or Sister. Don't think it sets the proper tone for my customers."

"You drive a hard bargain." Burl reached up and removed an imaginary hat from his head. "When I'm behind the bar, I'll take off my preachin' Panama and put on my beer-belchin' beret."

Cal grinned and stuck out his hand to Burl. "You've got a deal, bartender Burl."

And I had a vacation companion. To think, a mere thirty minutes ago, I hadn't known I was a retiredaholic in need of a vacation. I also wondered what was so important, such a problem, that Charles needed to bounce it off me. I'd known Charles for nine years and knew when he said problem he meant something most people would consider to be a disaster, or some other word Charles could find in a thesaurus.

3

Cal was silent the first four hours of our nine-hour drive. When I picked him up at his apartment he had said it was his middle of the night. Nights in the bar often lasted past midnight and during his forty-plus years travelling the country and singing most anywhere that would have him, his performances often didn't start until past dark. I was a morning person and encouraged him to put his seat back and sleep until he was ready to wake up. I didn't have to say it twice.

It wasn't until we were on the Interstate between Asheville and Knoxville that he showed signs of life. He stretched his arms over his head and said he was ready for a hearty breakfast. I reminded him it was noon and lunch would be more appropriate. He said, "tomato, tomahto," as I pulled in a Waffle House near Canton, North Carolina. The only tomatoes, or tomahtoes, I saw were when Cal slathered catchup on his hash browns.

Forty-five minutes later, breakfast/lunch was finished, and after Cal had started a conversation with everyone who walked by our table, we were back on the road; this time with Cal piloting. I tried to nap, though I would have had as good a chance reciting the first nineteen amendments to the US Constitution. Cal had his left hand on the wheel. His right hand fiddled with the radio controls trying to find the nearest country music station, singing along with each traditional country artist, and complaining about the stations that had the nerve to play contemporary country and hick-hop. Yes, Cal was awake.

Three hours later, we switched drivers at an exit between Knoxville and our destination. Cal grabbed his guitar from the back seat and serenaded me with 7,395 songs in the two hours it took us to get from the stop to the Interstate exit to downtown Nashville. If a country song had been recorded, oh, let's say, between 27 AD and 1975, Cal knew it. I'd heard what he said were the B side of many hits from that period, but when he started strumming B sides of songs he said had barely reached the top two hundred of the day, I was lost. I'm a country fan, although by the time we reached downtown Nashville, I was yearning for some Snoop Dog.

The navigation system did an excellent job of directing us to the address Charles had given me. The lot where he told me to park wasn't as easy to find. With the aid of Cal telling me each way *not* to turn, pointing out the Ryman Auditorium, and getting excited about a vacant building where he said he had performed "back in the day," we managed to find the narrow alley that led to the five-story warehouse that had been converted to apartments, and home of Charles and Heather.

I called Charles a couple of hours out and he said he'd have had Heather cancel any music appointments, except she didn't have any, so they would be home when we arrived. I put the car in park and Charles bounded out a windowless, rusting, steel door at the corner of the apartment building. At five-foot-eight inches, he was a couple of inches shorter than me, twenty pounds lighter, and had long, graying brown hair, mainly on the sides. He and I shared a near hairless top of our head. Instead of wearing one of his trademark long-sleeve college T-shirts, he wore a charcoal-gray Bluebird Cafe T-Shirt. He hadn't abandoned all traditions; despite being June, it was long-sleeve like his countless other shirts.

Charles had me in a bear hug before I closed the car door. If he'd attempted to shave in the last week, Heather needed to get him a new razor. Regardless of his shaggy face scraping my cheek, I was thrilled to see him. On the scale of world history, four months was merely a nano-speck. To me, it had seemed like an eternity.

Cal was feeling neglected and was on the passenger side of the car. He yelled, "Hey, Michigan, I'm here too."

Charles peeked around my head at Cal. "I ain't Ray Charles, I see you. Just haven't gotten around to huggin' you."

Heather scurried out of the building, made a beeline for the car, and squealed, "Yeah, they're here." Cal had come around to where the action was and Heather managed to put her arms around him.

She was approaching her fiftieth birthday and was a five-foot-six, bundle of enthusiasm. She greeted us with a wide smile and a giant hug. She's wholesomely attractive with her curly brown hair and freckled nose. She was seasonably attired in a dark-blue V-neck, short-sleeve Bluebird T-shirt, and tan shorts.

Heather moved to the rear of the car. "Let us help you carry your stuff."

Cal started to protest until Charles said they were on the third-floor. There was an elevator, although the old-time residents told him it worked about as often as Congress did something smart. The country crooner gave in to Heather's hospitable offer. I carried my suitcase and didn't start regretting it until I was between the second floor and our destination. I hadn't realized how far it was between floors in a high-ceiling, converted warehouse.

"Chuckie saw you pulling in the lot," Heather said as Charles unlocked the apartment. "We've got a great view of the parking lot from our living room."

What more could one ask for? I thought. "That's great."

My friend had spent most of his adult life riling when anyone called him anything other than Charles. Chuck, Charlie, and up until Heather came along, Chuckie, were like waving a Pepsi at a Coke sales rep. My friend would still correct anyone who made such a ghastly error, unless the person's name was Heather Lee. Love was not only blind, it was deaf.

The exterior of the building looked like it hadn't received attention in decades. Rust battled paint for control of most exposed steel surfaces; the fire escape looked like it would struggle to hold more than one person at a time; and, the brick walls had served as canvases to numerous graffiti artists. The stairwell didn't look much better, so I was pleased to see the interior of the apartment had a fresh coat of paint, the hardwood floors had been refinished, and from a glance in the kitchen, the appliances appeared new.

Charles hadn't been back to Folly to get his massive collection of books, yet he had already started a mini-library along one of the living room walls. Bricks that had come from the same era as the building were stacked three-high on each side of a four-foot-long board he had repurposed as a bookshelf. Approximately fifty books, many with library labels, stood at attention on the shelf. Fist-sized rocks served as bookends.

Heather waved her arms around the room. "What do you think?"

We had just entered the apartment and hadn't had much time to think. It didn't stop Cal from saying, "Honey, it's better than anywhere I've ever lived."

It wasn't saying much since Cal had spent much of his adult life living out of his 1971 Cadillac, and since settling on Folly, he lived in a run-down apartment building that had been swept out to sea during a hurricane, and was currently residing in an apartment which was a candidate for condemnation.

"I knew you'd love it," she said, responding to words which hadn't been spoken. "How about you, Chris?"

I moved to the corner of the room where I could look at the door leading to the bedrooms and glanced at Heather's black and silver karaoke machine and music stand, items I had helped her load in Charles' car the day they had left the beach. Crystals attached by a thin thread dangled from the top of a chrome picture frame that held a prominent place on a manicurist's table inside their bedroom. In addition to being a massage therapist and alleged singer, Heather prided herself on being a psychic. If true, a fact that's still unproven, her psychic abilities fall somewhere between her massage therapy skills and her singing. A forked, hazel twig, Heather's divining rod, leaned against the bookcase.

"What can I say, Heather, it's you."

"And me too," Charles said, as he leaned over and patted the bookcase. He didn't wait for a response. "Want the rest of the tour?"

Cal said, "You bet."

The entire apartment couldn't have taken up more than 700 square feet of Nashville's 504 square miles of land. The kitchen wasn't large enough for all of us, so I stood in the doorway while Heather pointed out each new appliance. I'm no expert in the kitchen, but had learned over the years what a refrigerator looked like. I was happy to see Heather so excited to show it to us. After moving her guitar case and wide-brimmed, straw hat she wore during most every performance, we were able to get in their *master bedroom*, as Heather proudly proclaimed. Cal and I nodded when she told us how grand the room was. She started to say something about the bed and mattress, when Charles interrupted and said it was time to see our room. She had inched close to *too much information*, and I welcomed Charles's interruption.

The best thing about the bedroom Cal and I would be sharing was it had a queen-sized bed and enough space for both of us to be in the room at the same time. Cal said, "Cozy," and we moved past the tiny bathroom back to the tiny living room. By Manhattan apartment standards, the room may have been considered spacious. It made my tiny cottage on Folly seem palatial. Cal and I squeezed together on the mini-couch, Heather sat in the only chair in the room, and Charles moved to the floor.

The awkward moments people experience after arriving at someone's house and having finished the tour, were beginning to set in. What do we talk about now? Heather came to the rescue.

"Are you ready to see our city?"

After spending the better part of the day in the car, I wasn't anxious get back in one, so I said, "Looked like there are lots of interesting things within walking distance. I'd like to see some of them."

Cal added, "I've got a couple of stories you wouldn't believe about things that happened to me right up the street."

Whether he did it on purpose or not, I was glad he kept us focused on a walking tour.

Heather grabbed her straw hat and waved us toward the door. "What are we waiting for?"

The temperature was mild for June and a walk would do my old muscles good. Tour guide Heather told us we were just three blocks from Lower Broadway, in her words, "The plum center of the country music entertainment universe." I'm sure many would disagree, but it was a major entertainment area in Nashville. We walked past the Ryman Auditorium, the former church that became the long-time home of the Grand Ole Opry, before the radio show and performing venue moved to its new home in 1974, and Cal started to tell us one of his stories we *wouldn't believe*. Heather would have none of it; it was her tour and we were moving on.

A half block more and we were standing at the corner of Fifth

Street South and Broadway. Across the street was the Nashville Visitor's Center and behind it stood the Bridgestone Arena that looked like a giant spaceship plopped down in the middle of a historic district.

"Ain't they something?" Heather said with a wide grin.

No argument from us.

"We're going this way." She turned left on Broadway.

We were standing beside a guitar on the sidewalk that was the size of a Boeing 747. Live music flowed across the street from the second-floor bar at Rippy's Ribs & Bar-B-Q, and from the loud sounds of electrified country from the open door of Legend's Corner fifteen feet away.

"Ain't this something," Heather repeated as we headed down the sidewalk, dodging tourists.

Charles tapped me on the shoulder and motioned for me to wait while Heather continued her tour. Heather stopped in front of Tootsie's Orchid Lounge, Nashville's most famous bar, and Cal finally got to tell one of his stories. He was telling Heather about having spent many late nights in there. "Most of the time in a booth, some on the floor. Ah, the good old days."

Charles took a couple of steps farther away from Cal's story and pulled me with him. He whispered, "Think we've got a problem."

I glanced at Heather who was focused on Cal's story, and asked Charles, "What?"

"Chuckie," Heather said, "you and Chris ain't baskin' in Cal's fascinating story."

She said something else, but was drowned out by "The Race Is On," the George Jones classic, being sung by an overweight, middle-aged man on the stage inside the front door of Tootsie's.

"Later," Charles whispered before he moved closer to Cal, Heather, and the George Jones semi-sound-alike.

Heather continued her tour pointing out the bars and live music venues along Broadway. She appeared cheerful and more in her element than I'd ever seen her. I was happy for her, yet conflicted knowing it would take something approaching a major miracle to convince her—and Charles—to move back to Folly.

We reached Second Avenue North and Heather guided us left where we walked three blocks and left again and back to their apartment. Cal said he needed a nap. He said his seventy-two-year-old body didn't quite have the "get-up-and-go" it had when he closed many of Nashville's bars "a while back."

His nap became our nap which flowed into bedtime. Heather said she and Charles were going to take in one more bar before "hitting the hay." We wished them well.

Cal's snoring woke me up at three in the morning; he also was occupying more than half of the bed. I stared at the dark ceiling and wondered what problem Charles and Heather had. Although we shared a lot of words after returning to the apartment, his "later" had not been among them.

4

Heather rattled enough pots and pans the next morning to wake Cal and me, and probably anyone living nearby. I suspected it was her intention, since she had fixed us a gourmet breakfast of Dunkin' Donuts with the consistency of Styrofoam. Nary a pot or pan was used in the preparation. She said the donuts would provide us energy for another day of walking around her town.

To a casual observer, our activities would have appeared to be a rerun of yesterday's tour. Lighter crowds and fewer live performances were all that separated the two days. She did listen to more of Cal's reminiscing about his days as a "big star," during his performances at the Grand Ole Opry House, his walking across the alley from the Opry to Tootsie's for a midnight brew, and staggering across Broadway to take in the live, midnight radio shows from the Ernest Tubb Record Store. Charles and I had heard most of it before. If Heather had, she fended enough enthusiasm for Cal to rehash his adventures.

Heather suggested we *check out* the Nashville landmark after hearing Cal's Ernest Tubb Record Store story. Charles said for Heather and Cal to go ahead, and he and I would stay and *shoot the breeze* until they got back. Heather seemed hurt we wouldn't be joining them. She got over it and grabbed Cal's hand and led him through the light traffic as they crossed Broadway.

I watched them and turned to Charles. "Is later now?"

"Good memory." He motioned me to join him on a bench in front of the Stage Bar.

Charles grabbed a hot dog wrapper from the bench and dropped it in a nearby trashcan while fifteen feet to our left, a street musician strummed on an old Yamaha guitar. From his straggly, age-stained attire, and equally straggly face, he appeared to be a permanent resident of a homeless shelter, and from the single, one-dollar bill in an open guitar case at his feet, he wouldn't be moving to the Hyatt anytime soon.

I turned back to Charles. "What's the problem?" We didn't have much time before Cal and Heather would be returning and I wanted to hear what Charles had to say.

He looked at a crumpled napkin on the sidewalk. "Kevin Starr."

I waited for him to pick it up and put it in the trash. He didn't, so I said, "What about him? He's still Heather's agent, isn't he?"

"Think he's ripping her off."

I had thought that from the moment on Folly after he'd heard her sing and said he'd like to represent her. Her bubbly stage personality made up for much of what she lacked vocally. I still didn't think it would be enough for her to be successful. Heather may be many things, and no doubt the best thing that had ever happened to Charles, but a singer, she wasn't.

A few days after Charles and Heather had arrived in Nashville he'd called me and said Starr wanted her to cut an expensive demo CD.

"Did she get the demo she paid for?"

Charles waited for a tour bus to pass before continuing. The smell of burnt diesel fuel washed over us.

"Yeah, the demo was pretty good. It showed Heather at her best."

"What's he done to make you suspicious?"

"Chris, we've met with the man four times. Each time was at a Starbucks over on Church Street. Yeah, it's convenient to our apartment, but each time Heather asked him if we could meet at his office, he told her he meets his artists in different public spots around town. Heather is in love with everything about Nashville and wants to add a trip to a real music agent's office. Starr always says something about how he likes his meetings to be convenient for the client." He paused and looked across the street to the record shop, and back at me. "I'm wondering if he has an office."

Heather and Cal were still in Ernest Tubb's. "Don't suppose he has to have an office. He could work out of his house."

"Maybe. That's not all. Heather's appeared at the Bluebird five times. Starr—*her agent*—said he'd be there each time."

"And he wasn't?"

He shook his head. "Plus, we've met other songwriters while we've been standing in line at the Bluebird. Heather's gotten to know a couple of them pretty well. They say Starr Management was handling them. It sounds good and impressive until they start talking and their stories are not a hair different than Heather's. None of them have been struck by fame."

A girl around nine dropped another dollar bill in the street singer's guitar case. The musician smiled and started singing "You Are My Sunshine." The child laughed and her parents stood behind her and smiled.

I waited for the song to finish, watched the parents applaud, and turned to Charles. "Have you confronted Starr?"

He shook his head. "You know I'm a detective, well, sort of, and I've—we've—gotten pretty good at it." He pointed at me and at his chest.

Now's when I wished Cal and Heather would run back across the street and interrupt the direction Charles was headed.

"We've been lucky," I said.

"You call it luck, I call it superior detecting skills."

"Whatever."

"Anyway," the faux-detective continued, "I thought since you were heading over anyway, we could talk to Starr. Then we could put our heads together and figure out if he's what he says he is, or if he's ripping us off."

Charles's reason for suggesting I needed a vacation was beginning to come into focus. This was as close as he would come to asking for help, and he was the best friend I'd ever had.

"What's Heather's take on Starr?"

Charles looked at another tour bus as it rolled by, at the singer, and finally at me. "She's trying to keep her head up and her cute little grin on her face."

"But?"

"She POed. She doesn't say he's conning her, although she wanders close to it. I've caught her balling her eyes out twice. She said it was Tennessee allergies. I didn't believe it." He glanced across the street. "She has a temper, you know."

She was high-strung and could be moody. I nodded.

"I think if Starr had come knocking on our door the day before you got here, he would have been greeted by a frying pan in his toothy smile. She's putting on a good front for you and Cal."

"Is she going to talk to Starr?"

"Don't know. On one hand, she's afraid he's taking advantage of her dreams, and she also wants to believe he's on the up-and-up and is going to make her famous. God, Chris, it tears me up seeing her hurt."

"I know. You're leaning toward him ripping her off?"

He nodded.

"Does she know about your plan to *investigate* the agent?"

"Umm, not yet."

"That's what I thought. When are you supposed to talk to Starr again?"

"He told her he was coming to the Bluebird Monday."

"He's said that how many times and failed to show?"

"I'm playing the law of averages. He's bound to show this time."

My law of consistency says *if he hasn't shown the last five times, he won't be there Monday.*

"What if he doesn't?"

"Tuesday morning we'll set out to find him. After all, I am a detective."

Heather and Cal made their way back from the record store.

Cal shook his head and pushed his Stetson back off his forehead. "Fellas, I remember back in the day when ETs was stocked out the door with records and people. Know what I couldn't find over there until your gal Heather showed me?"

My guess would have been records and people. I didn't want to spoil Cal's story, and said, "What?"

"It's chock full of books, CDs, DVDs, photos, songbooks, souvenirs, and a danged actual record section the size of Charles book shelf." Cal pointed in the direction of Charles and Heather's apartment. "To top it off, Heather and I were the only customers in there until a gal came in to see if they had guitar strings. Fellas, I'm dee-pressed." He shook his head again. "Should have let my memories do the walking over there instead of these old calloused feet."

Charles began humming "The Times They Are A-Changin'" but Cal was stuck in his memories and didn't appreciate, or hear Charles.

Heather convinced us we needed to spend culture-accumulating time a couple of blocks from where we were standing over a brew or two at the Tin Roof.

The Tin Roof called itself "A Live Music Joint," and looked a lot like a bar. A male-female duet was playing from the stage that had the front windows as its backdrop. The bar had a balcony, but we opted for a table on the first floor. We didn't want Cal's *old calloused feet* to walk more than they had to. As per Heather's suggestion, our brew became two, and we added Tennessee Hot Tops, another brew, and to honor my home state, Charles ordered Kentuckyaki Wings, followed by another brew. The band changed once, our conversation changed several times, and Heather changed from the venue's typical music fan enjoying the food and music, to a marketer when she asked the server what it took to get a gig playing there.

The mid-thirties, bearded server gave her a big smile and said, "Get in line, honey. Plum near every server, bartender, and taxi driver here is ahead of you to the line. We're all singers or song scribes waiting for our big break."

"You too?" Heather said.

"You bet." He pointed to the stage. "I was up there yesterday." He laughed. "Had my fifteen minutes of fame, but drug it out to two sets."

Heather looked at the stage and back at the bartender. "How do I get up there? I've got an agent. Can he contact someone here?"

The server nodded. "Could. It won't do much good. Word of mouth is the best way to get in the bars down here. We know who's good or not and tell our bosses; they tell other bosses, and time slots are filled. Word of mouth, honey."

Charles leaned close to me. "See. What good's Starr, even if he's on the up-and-up, which I'm doubtin', seriously doubtin'?"

The server told Heather he'd love to stay and talk but had other customers.

A new band had begun its set and Heather leaned closer so we could hear her. "It's what Gwen told me."

Cal said, "Who's Gwen?"

"A friend. Met her at the Bluebird. She's also a songwriter

and not a bad singer." Heather rolled her eyes. "She's also a client of Starr Management."

Cal asked, "Has Starr made her famous?"

"No. She's been his client for a couple more months than me. Claims he got her a couple of auditions on Music Row. Gwen said auditions meant getting to hand her demo to someone who acted like a receptionist more than someone important. They said they'd get back with her if there was interest. She's never heard a peep. That gal's pissed at Starr." She huffed. "Don't blame her."

Heather's dark side had made a brief appearance until more drinks followed. She cheered up, Charles asked about getting a Tin Roof T-shirt but declined when the server said they all were short sleeve. We called it a day.

5

Thunderstorms punished the area Sunday and we stayed holed up in the apartment most of the day. Cal was back in his comfort zone and regaled us with countless stories of his days hobnobbing with the "biggies" of country music. I had no doubt there was some truth in his stories involving Patsy Cline, Hank Snow, Roy Acuff, and of course, Willie, although I suspected his innate ability as a storyteller and songwriter, and years of retelling the tales added his personal spin—aka exaggeration. Regardless, Heather gobbled them up like a bat in a cloud of gnats.

Heather said eating three square meals a day was the key to her singing success, so she and Charles went to get pizza for supper. A bowl of corn flakes, a Velveeta cheese sandwich on stale whole-wheat bread, and now a cheese-laden pizza will be today's three squares. I wondered if they would improve her singing voice; truth be told, I wondered whether anything short of vocal cord surgery could improve it. While they were gone, I filled Cal in on what Charles and I had talked about.

He listened without interrupting, something I wasn't accustomed to having been friends with Charles for many years.

I finished and he said, "If Heather handing her demo to a secretary is the best Kevin Starr can do, she'd be better off having yesterday's server as her agent."

I told him that was what I feared.

Cal moved to the window with the scenic overlook of the parking lot, gazed out, snapped his fingers. "Tell you what, pard, hand me your phone and I'll try to track down my old bud Johnny Roman. He was a top-shelf A&R man in my day. If he's above ground, he may know something about Starr."

"A&R?"

"Artists and repertoire. It's the guy who handles stuff between the singer and the label. My friend goes by Johnny R and worked for several record labels. He was responsible for talent scouting, putting together songs with artists, booking the musicians and studios, and overseeing the development of artists. It's a big job."

I handed him the phone and he stared at it. "Now, how do I use this iThing contraption?"

Ten minutes later, numerous wrong numbers punched in, and finally a helpful electronic voice saying it would connect us to a number listed in the name of Johnny Roman, the phone was ringing. I handed it to Cal. I heard his half of the conversation and gathered Johnny R's daughter answered and her dad was in Oak View, a nursing home in Madison, nine miles north of where we were.

"Wonderful, we'll go see him," Cal finished and handed the phone back to me.

He filled me in on the other end of the conversation, most of which I had figured out.

"How long's he been in the nursing home?"

Cal looked at his hands like he was counting the years on his fingers. "She said nine years. He's a mite older than me, around eighty. Had a stroke and they had to put him in the home. His daughter bought his house and keeps his old phone number because he has so many friends who call. She wanted them to be able to find him."

A soaked Charles and Heather returned with pizza along with a six-pack of Budweiser and a bottle of cheap chardonnay, a concession to yours truly. Heather said it was still raining *felines and pups* and they weren't going out again.

THE NEXT MORNING, Heather was up before anyone else. I was next out of bed, awakened by the non-melodious voice of the girl singer, as Cal politically incorrectly calls her. She was standing behind her music stand, strumming a guitar, and practicing one of the two songs she'd written.

She stopped strumming and grinned as I came in the living room. "Practicin' for my big performance tonight. Didn't wake you did I?"

Why would she have thought a guitar playing and her singing as loud as she could ten feet away from where I had been sleeping may have awakened me?

Of course, I lied. "Nah, I was awake. Ready for the Bluebird?"

"Not yet." She shook her head. "I will come singin' time. My agent's going to be there. You'll get to see him again."

"Great," I said, not believing for a second that Mr. Starr and I will be shaking hands at Heather's performance.

She looked at her closed bedroom door, turned back to me, and whispered, "Got a favor to ask. I've got to get my head ready for tonight, gotta get my good Chi flowing and ready to channel Patsy Cline's voice." She looked back at the bedroom door. "It takes me all day before a performance as important as the Bluebird. Chuckie doesn't understand. He wants to talk or do things. He's trying to be sweet and doesn't know how he's messing with my Chi. Think you and Cal could get him out of the house? Go somewhere, anywhere, and let me do my thing?"

I was skeptical that a day of good Chi would make a difference. I wasn't a psychic or a singer, so what did I know? "We'll try."

Cal and Charles came in the living room at the same time—synchronized waking.

Cal rubbed his hands through his thinning, long hair. "What's for breakfast?"

I glanced at Heather and said, "I've got an idea. Why don't we go out and grab something to eat? I could drive and you and Heather could show us some of the sights outside downtown. It's been years since I saw Vanderbilt, or maybe we could go over to the Hermitage."

Charles looked at me like, "When did you take an interest in universities and historic sites?"

Cal said, "Good idea. I don't need to do any walking today." He lifted and wiggled his bare foot like it was nodding.

Heather said, "Great idea. I've already had breakfast. Why don't you boys go ahead and I'll hang around here and practice."

Charles didn't ask her what she'd found in the bare cupboards to eat, and said, "Sure, why not."

Waffle House fed our stomachs, a quick ride past Vanderbilt University fed our intellectual curiosity, and Charles making me stop at three used bookstores quenched his, and only his, need to stock up on books he didn't have. Cal asked me to drive by some of the publishing houses he had been familiar with during his times in Nashville. Several wrong turns later, I managed to find Music Row, an area southwest of downtown where Cal said hundreds of music-related businesses were located. Cal pointed out every house that had been converted to "publishing business-es," more traditional looking office buildings, and a few empty lots he swore used to be buildings where everyone knew him. I asked Charles and Cal to keep a look out for a sign indicating

Starr Management was in one of the structures. They said they would. I wasn't optimistic.

We were on Seventeenth Avenue when Cal pointed to a spot in the middle of the street. "Guys, remember when Heather met Starr in Cal's."

Charles said, "Sure, why?"

I said, "You were concerned that he didn't list the address of his agency on his business card."

"Your point, Cal?" said Charles.

"I said he didn't want every Tom, Dick, and nutcase singing wannabe knocking on his door."

Charles rolled his eyes and repeated, "Your point?"

"I remember back in the 1970s, not sure what year. My mind was a bit fluttered back then. Anyway, one of those wannabes wanted to get an appointment with Chet Atkins in his office right over there." Cal pointed across the street. "Chet was one of the biggest of the biggies in this town in those days, yes he was."

Charles said, "Cal."

"Hold your nosy nose, I'm getting there. Well the wannabe stood out in the center of the street, stripped jaybird naked, and stopped traffic until he got his appointment."

Charles said, "Did he get an appointment?"

"He sure did, got himself a ride in a Nashville police car, and an appointment with a judge. Don't think he ever got to show Chet anything other than his naked butt. That my friends is why many record agents and bigshots don't put addresses on their business cards."

I smiled, more at Charles's irritation than at Cal's story, and said, "Cal, thanks for sharing that bit of Nashville history."

After driving in circles, more accurately, rectangles, around the Music Row area for what seemed like hours, Cal said he was getting dizzy and suggested we park and "walk a spell." We walked two blocks down Music Square East and stumbled on a small park named for Owen Bradley. Cal shared that Bradley had been a songwriter, performer, and influential publisher. I wasn't particularly interested in Mr. Bradley, but was interested in the shade-covered benches in the park. I'd told Heather I would keep Charles and Cal away a few more hours, and was tired of driving.

Charles tapped his ever-present, handmade, wooden cane on the back of the bench. "Fellas, Heather's sure hyped you'll be there tonight. It didn't keep her tears from flowing after you hit the hay last night."

Cal asked, "Why?"

"She's afraid she's been snookered. After the server told her he didn't think an agent could help her get gigs at those restaurants and bars, she's wondering if Starr can do anything for her. That's if he's on the level." He looked over at a homeless man shaving on the next bench, and back at us. "If he's a fraud, she's afraid she'll end up like that poor guy." He nodded his head in the direction of the man shaving.

Cal pushed his Stetson back. "That's just one singing server's opinion. A good agent can work wonders."

A good legitimate agent, I thought.

Charles said, "I'm sure you're right, Cal."

"I know I am. Music's a tough industry to get a toe-hold in, and Nashville'll chew up and spit out thousands of aspiring youngins each year. Heather won't be able to make it on her own; she'll need all the help she can get. It don't come quick, no it don't."

"Cal," Charles said. "You're an expert on this stuff. Be honest. Does Heather have what it takes to make it?"

I looked toward the front of the park at the life-size statue of Owen Bradley seated at a piano and imagined his head shaking.

Cal took off his hat and set it on the bench, and took a deep breath before speaking.

Charles said, "Well?"

"There's a history of untalented folks making it here, not

many, but a few. Some guys and gals with limited talent have succeeded, again, only a few. And there are numbers too large to count of singers who have talent out their ears, and mouths, who never make it. Can I say your gal will? Absolutely not. Can—"

Charles interrupted, "But."

Cal waved his hand in Charles's face. "Let me finish."

Charles stopped in mid-interruption.

"On the other hand, can I say Heather won't succeed? Nope."

Charles waited for Cal to continue. He didn't and Charles said, "The odds are against it."

Cal looked the Bradley statue and at Charles. "A billion to one."

6

We returned to the apartment and Heather's moods swung from euphoric to morose and back again. One minute she was a few feet above cloud nine about her pending performance; the next, her expression said she was ready to bite the head off anyone who dared speak to her. Cal, who had been around performers all his life, understood her fluctuations and said he needed to get some fresh air and "mosey around lower Broadway." He told Heather he knew she had to mentally prepare and would rather be alone. She said it was a good idea and Charles, Cal, and I took a leave of absence.

"Heather ain't the Heather I knew," Cal said as we walked along Broadway. "I saw her every time she was in the bar and on the stage. Always happy, always bouncy. And, how about those times she'd sing at the farmers' market back when it was held in that parking lot beside The Washout restaurant. I can still see her standing by the restaurant's wall singing and strummin'. Her beaming personality charmed whoever stopped to listen."

I was glad he'd said it first. I had noticed the change in her moods and behavior. She was quieter, sullener, and did something I'd never imagined from her, she leaned toward the negative. She had been one of the most positive people I'd encountered. It was a big part of her endearing charm.

Charles stopped walking and pointed his cane at Cal. "You can say that again."

Cal grinned. "Heather ain't—"

"Got it," Charles said. "You're right. Half the time she's happier than a mouse in a cheese factory. She's lived all her life for this." He waved his cane at the bars on either side of the street. "Now she's pissed at the world."

"What's the problem?" Cal asked.

Charles lowered his cane. "Two words: Kevin Starr."

Cal shook his head and pointed at Charles's cane. "Don't hit me with that thing. It strikes me that it may be a couple of other words."

Charles said, "What?"

"Can't sing."

I took a step away from Charles and his wooden weapon. Instead of swinging it at Cal's head, Charles lowered his head. "I know. She's put all her eggs, and a lot of our bucks, in Starr's basket. Now it's up to more than six-thousand dollars. She thinks he can—"

"Whoa," I interrupted. "Last I heard you'd given him $2,900 for a demo."

"Yeah," Charles said. "I've been afraid to mention the other expenses. Knew you'd blow a gasket."

Cal moved closer to Charles, no longer afraid of his cane. "What'd it go for?"

"Full-service marketing campaign."

"What in Sam Houston does that mean," the Texan asked. "Marketing what? The gal ain't even got a record."

"Starr told us it was the latest in getting word around Nashville, heck, even getting to the music industry big-wigs in New York and Los Angeles. He said all the newcomers who make it bought the service. He told us because Heather was special, he could swing the deal for *only* $3,700. He said other agents charge more than five grand for the same thing."

"What's the pot load of money get her?" Cal asked. "I've been out of the business for a long time. I ain't ever heard of it. Back in my day, hawking singers meant an eight-by-ten glossy and a howdy."

Charles shrugged. "It gives Starr access to the inner-offices of the publishing and recording companies; gives him money to create marketing materials, mostly digital and electronic, called an EPK. For you newcomers to the music biz, that's an electronic press kit. It's to accentuate her strengths for the potential publishers and recording companies; and ..." Charles hesitated and looked around to see if anyone was listening. "To grease a few palms to get Heather past some of what Starr called *gate-keepers* who'd keep her out."

Cal leaned against the brick wall in front of Jimmy Buffett's Margaritaville Restaurant, glanced at me, and turned to Charles. "When I was growing up in Texas, we called that a crock of shit. Those things are what agents bankroll. Hell's bells, it's what agents do. I think we need to have a confab with this Kevin Starr."

"That's what we're planning to do tonight," I shared.

Cal said, "If the slime bucket shows."

THE BLUEBIRD CAFE hosted an open-mic night on Mondays and five times in the last three months Heather was, in her mind, the featured performer. Each week between thirty and forty aspiring songwriters have their three and a half minutes of fame in front of a packed audience. The event began at six o'clock so I wondered why we had to leave at three-thirty for the five-mile drive.

We weaved our way out of downtown and past churches, a residential section, and several suburban shopping areas, and pulled into the parking lot of a large furniture store near the Bluebird. I realized why we had to leave early. Two security guards stood in front of a faded blue awning with *The Bluebird Cafe* in script on it. If Charles hadn't pointed it out, I wouldn't have noticed the iconic venue in the nondescript strip center sandwiched between a Chinese massage parlor, and a hair salon. What I did notice was a line of thirty people standing in the parking lot.

Charles said, "Good, we beat the crowd."

"Are they here for open-mic night?" I asked.

"They sure are," Heather said. "In an hour, there'll be three times that many. Now we'll be able to get in."

Charles explained the Bluebird only held about ninety patrons and most every Monday there were more in line than its capacity. Charles also said since we were in the furniture store's lot a couple of us should do some furniture shopping or we'd get kicked out of the parking space. He said he and I looked the most like we could afford a couch so we went shopping while Heather and Cal got in line. None of the couches were to our liking, nor would fit in Charles and Heather's apartment, so we joined the others in the line which had grown in the short time we'd been couch hunting. The number exceeded the occupancy limit of the building.

"Hey, Gwen!" Heather shouted. She looked at the people near us and back at the woman at the end of the line. "Here we are. Get up here. What took you so long?"

I glanced at Charles who gave a slight shrug. The newcomer strolled past forty people in line behind us, and sidled up to Heather. The group behind us appeared far from happy at the line breaker.

Heather ignored those around us and said to the woman who

was around Heather's age, trim, and attractive. "You singing tonight?"

I thought the guitar case in her hand would have given it away.

The newest member of our group said, "You bet."

Heather said, "Meet my friends. You know my guy, Charles. That tall drink of water's Cal Ballew. He's also a country singer. Honest to God, he had a hit record."

"Cool," Heather's friend said. "Have I heard it?"

How would Cal know? I wondered.

Cal tipped his Stetson at Gwen. "It's called 'End of the Story,' hit number seventeen on the national charts."

Gwen said, "Don't recall it."

Heather leaned closer to Gwen and whispered, "It was before you were born."

Cal smiled. "A classic."

Gwen repeated, "Cool."

Heather pointed to me. "The other guy there is Chris Landrum. He's Chucky's best friend. Him and Cal are over from the beach for a few days. Drove all the way to hear me sing."

"Cool," said Heather's articulate friend.

Heather looked toward Cal and me. "Fellas, Gwen here— Gwen Parsons—is a friend of mine. She's written a whole basket full of tunes and is here as often as I am."

Gwen said, "Pleased to meet all of you."

Cool, I thought.

"Gwen is also handled by Starr Management."

Gwen's smile disappeared. "For what that's worth. You heard from him lately?" she said aimed at Heather.

"No, but he's supposed to be here." Heather hesitated and looked around the gathered group. "Got a few things to iron out with him."

Gwen looked at her guitar case at her feet and at the Bluebird. "I'd like to take an iron to his conniving skull. He'd better show."

"Hadn't made you a star yet?" Charles said, I suspect because he'd been ignored for three minutes.

"Chucky—umm, Charles—Starr's been my agent for going on half a year, and all he's done for me is charge me out the ear for a demo tape, tried to get me to buy a freakin' marketing package for more than I could sell my car for, and got me three gigs I later learned I could've gotten myself by asking the bar owners." She pointed to the Bluebird. "This here being one of them." She shook her head. "A star, right."

Gwen's ringing endorsement of her agent was interrupted when a short, chunky man in his thirties tapped Heather on the shoulder. "Yo, Heather, brought that guitar you wanted to try out." He held a guitar case in Heather's face.

Heather hugged the guitar wielding stranger. "Thanks, Joey. Hey guys, this is my friend, Joey."

Cal and I nodded, Charles said, "Hey, Joey," and Gwen looked irritated that he'd interrupted her rant.

"Would you mind putting it in my car?" Heather asked.

"No problem."

"It's the red Toyota Venza that's not supposed to be parked at the furniture store. The lock's broken so slip it in the back seat and cover it with the green blanket. Don't let the furniture guy see you."

"No problem," Joey repeated as he headed to the adjacent lot.

"Joey's a good guy, but not much of a songwriter. His singing's a bit on the weak side, too. You'll get to hear him tonight."

That's something to look forward to.

Heather said, "Seen Jessica?"

I assumed she was talking to either Charles or Gwen since neither Cal nor I would know Jessica.

"Don't think she's around. She usually beats me here. The last time—"

Gwen was interrupted again. This time by a man talking into a megaphone telling the group if they wanted to perform, they needed to sign a slip of paper he was handing out, and a drawing would be held to determine the order of their appearances. Several aspiring stars groaned when he said that since there was a large number of singers, each would be limited to one song. It seemed about every fifth person in line had a guitar case, so there would be a full complement of singers. Heather grabbed one of the sheets and put her name on it in big, block letters so there could be no mistake who she was.

The papers were collected and Gwen yelled, "There's Jessica."

We turned in the direction of a tall, thin woman, in her late-twenties walking toward us with a guitar case in hand and a scowl on her face.

"Seen Starr?" Gwen asked.

The woman standing behind us in line said, "Humph. No breaking line."

Jessica turned to her. "Hold your water, lady. I'm just talking to my friends. Somebody's holding a place for me in the back of the line." She turned to Gwen. "Starr was supposed to meet me yesterday at his *Starbucks office*. I waited two hours, made me late for my waitressing gig. He never showed."

Heather said, "Haven't seen him here."

"He'd better show," Jessica said. "I've got a piece of my mind to give him."

"Get in line," Heather said, not referring to the line to sing.

I suspected Jessica had similar experiences with the illusive and probable con-artist who pawns himself off as a music agent. I wondered how many more gullible wannabe singers and song-writers had fallen for his line. And I wondered how Heather's story would end with Starr. I couldn't picture it ending well.

7

Heather had drawn number thirty-six, Gwen twelve, and Jessica two slots ahead of Heather. Charles told me if songwriters who drew a high number didn't want to wait long to sing, they could have first shot at performing at future open-mic nights. Heather said "no way." Her beach friends were here to hear her and that's what she was going to do even if it took all night.

The door to the Bluebird was opened and the crowd filed in and was seated at vinyl table-cloth covered tables surrounded by wooden chairs. The space was tiny by bar standards and so crammed I doubted everyone in the room could exhale at the same time. A server was at our table as soon as we were seated and took our drink order. The menu was typical bar-fare except for edamame, something I'd never heard of. Charles, the trivia king, said it was young green soybeans in the shell. It sounded too healthy for my taste and I ordered a chicken-fingers basket.

Singer number one was called to the stage before our drinks arrived. She plugged her guitar into the sound system, said her name, her composition, and began singing. Over the next thirty minutes, a steady stream of songwriters moved to the tiny stage with assembly-line efficiency and stood, or sat at the keyboard and sang. Talking was close to impossible because of the music, and was discouraged out of respect for the performers. Charles tried to tell me about the photos along the wall, the history of the cafe, and what famous entertainers had performed before the packed-in audiences. I couldn't hear what he was saying. I nodded as if I understood.

I was surprised by the high quality of the performers and their songs, and was even more discouraged about Heather's chances. I was also impressed one of the songwriters was from Australia, two were from England, and one even from far-away, exotic Minnesota.

Gwen's number was called between our first and second round of drinks. She took the stage, gave her name, and said she was from McAlester, Oklahoma, and added it was the hometown of Reba McEntire. Her song was a lilting love song, her voice was pleasant, but nowhere near the quality of her fellow McAlesterian. Heather applauded when Gwen finished, with hopes it would be reciprocated when she finished her song some twenty-two performers later.

An hour and a half passed before Jessica's number was called. Heather, who was scheduled to sing two artists away, was having trouble containing her excitement and nerves. Gwen had stayed after her song to hear Jessica and Heather and applauded when Jessica finished. Heather took her guitar out of the case and bit her fingernails as the next singer performed an up-tempo song accompanying herself on the keyboard.

Heather took the stage, said who she was, and that she was from Nashville. I glanced at Charles who mouthed, "She is now." She sang one of her two compositions, a song I'd heard dozens of times. After three torturous verses, she strummed the last notes to the sounds of applause from everyone at our table, and from no more than four others in the room. Heather smiled as if she had received a standing ovation and thanked the crowd. My heart bled for her. She made it back to the table and received pats on the back from Gwen and Jessica. Charles reached over and gave her a hug. Cal said, "Good job, gal." I nodded and bought her another beer.

We filed out and stood in the parking lot looking at a line stretching past three stores in the shopping center waiting to get in the next show. Three of the people we heard perform were exchanging demo CDs. Two taxis were letting people out and a limo blocked the entrance. Heather stretched her neck to see if its occupants were famous or only people who had enough money to arrive in style.

Gwen and Heather were bragging on each other's set when Jessica approached and whispered something to the other two. They talked for a couple of minutes and Gwen grabbed her guitar case, waved bye to Charles, Cal, and me, and patted Heather on the rear and walked toward the McDonald's a block away.

Cal was telling us a couple of the people in the group, especially one of the "gals" in line before we entered looked familiar. He wondered if she was someone famous, and Charles said it was no telling who we might see taking in the show, when Heather came over to Charles and waved for Jessica to follow.

"Jess wants me to head downtown with her to a bar so we can "put back a few" and unwind after our performances. Wasn't she great guys?"

We agreed Jessica was great and Charles said if Jessica would have her, he'd let her borrow Heather for a while. Heather gave a wide grin, pecked Charles on the cheek, and handed him her guitar case and wide-brimmed straw hat to put in the car. She told him not to wait up, and headed off with Jessica *to put back a few*.

CAL WIPED sleep from his eyes and joined Charles and me in the kitchen. "What time did Heather mosey back to the bunk?"

It was a couple of hours after sunrise and I'd already taken a walk around the neighborhood. Charles was up when I returned and was trying to figure out how many eggs to put in an omelet he was struggling with. He said he'd made omelets although Heather was always around to supervise. She hadn't made an appearance.

"Could've been two-thirty, maybe three-thirty," Charles said without taking his eye off the stove. "Don't know for certain other than it had thirty in it."

Cal said, "Guess you didn't talk a bunch when she got here."

"Think I said 'ugg,' and she may've said, 'Go back to sleep.'"

Charles had finished making breakfast, the smell of burnt omelet filled the air, Cal and I had eaten it and commented on how "interesting" Charles's masterpieces of culinary delight had been and Heather still hadn't ventured out of the bedroom.

Cal glanced at the closed door to Charles and Heather's bedroom. "Think I need to go see my old bud Johnny R today. This Starr Management stuff's getting smellier and smellier. Don't take offense, Charles. It'd be best if she didn't go. No telling what Johnny R might say. He ain't known for beating around the burning bush."

"I'll stay here, and—"

The door of the bedroom creaked open. We turned toward the sound, which was fortunate since Heather whispered, "Morning guys," in a voice we wouldn't have heard unless we were looking. In muted voices, we agreed.

She walked to the table at about the speed of a snail, lowered her body on a chair, and sighed. "Any of y'all see the tour bus that hit me?"

Cal and I shook our head and Charles said, "Feeling poorly, sweetie?"

"If you call a headache that feels like I had three teeth pulled without any knock-out stuff feeling poorly, yeah."

Cal said, "Good show last night?"

Interesting use of the term show, I thought. Heather sang one song, so I suppose Cal was trying to get her mind off her headache.

Heather's eyes were bloodshot and her hand trembled as she lifted her coffee mug. "Thanks, Cal. You don't have to blow smoke up my, umm, posterior. I saw where the clapping came from. I thought I did pretty good, but other than y'all, I bet there weren't three people putting their hands together."

Cal nodded. "Believe you me, I know the feeling, H. Sometimes folks just don't appreciate good music. I've done shows where I thought I knocked it out of the park and the folks sitting out there must've been sitting on their hands."

Her face tried to smile. It was forced, looked painful, and didn't last long. "I'm frustrated Cal. I ain't giving up. I know it'll happen; just wish it'd get here soon."

"You never know, H," Cal said. "You never know."

I thought I did.

Charles looked at Cal, glanced at me, and turned to Heather. "The guys here want to do some sightseeing today, maybe go to the Hall of Fame. You and I could stay here while you're recuperating."

Heather blinked like that was too much information for her ailing head to comprehend. "No, Chucky, you go. You're a good tour guide and I could use some meditating time."

Cal smiled. "Thanks, H. He could show us the way around."

Cal had achieved his goal of visiting his friend without Heather.

The Country Music Hall of Fame and Museum was five blocks from the apartment so we walked rather than paying to park. According to Charles, the massive building complex with an exterior covered with symbolic images of music replaced the original Hall of Fame in 2001. Its windows mirror the configuration of piano keys and the overall façade seemed overwhelming. The sights and sounds inside were as impressive. Cal added his personal narrative to many of the displays. Walking through the museum with him felt like I was living part of country music history. The tour lasted two hours longer than necessary after we paused to hear each of Cal's "fascinating" stories.

We returned to the apartment and Charles checked on Heather before we headed to Madison to find Johnny R. She said she wasn't any better and for us to take our time. The nine-mile trip took longer than expected. A four-car accident had the road closed and we had to take a detour.

While Madison was easy to find, the nursing home presented a more difficult challenge since it was a mile outside town on a road that had befuddled the car's navigation system. Charles finally ran in Shoney's to ask for directions while Cal strummed on an imaginary guitar and sang Hank Snow's "I've Been Everywhere." It felt like a piece of the Hall of Fame had escaped and was sitting in a car entertaining the driver.

We walked through the double door of the nursing home that didn't look younger than its residents, and were slapped by the ever-present smell that must be sold only to nursing homes. Nothing about the odor said welcome. No one was at the desk, but a man sweeping the floor pointed us in the direction of Johnny R's room, smiled and said, "Get ready. He's having a mood."

Cal's friend must've been huge in his better days. He was lying on his side and the droopy skin of a three-hundred-pound man dangled from a body that couldn't have topped one seventy. Johnny R glanced at the visitors, dropped a copy of *People Magazine*, and smiled.

"Holy shit. I must have died and landed in the bad place. If it ain't my buddy Country Cal right here in Hillbilly Hell." He tried to sit, and fell back in the bed.

Cal moved to his side, bent over, and gave him a hug. They exchanged a couple of insults and Johnny R tilted his head my direction and asked Cal who his roadies were.

Cal introduced us to the man he'd told us was eighty, but looked to be pushing triple digits. "What'd you do horrible enough to my bud Cal to get him to drag you out here?"

Charles, in his best suck-up voice, said, "We're friends of Cal and were visiting the high points of Nashville. He said unless we met his good friend Johnny R our tour would've been wasted."

Johnny R looked at the stained ceiling, at me, and finally at Charles. "See why y'all are friends. You're as full of shit as Cal. You a singer? You have that beat-down look."

I figured he wasn't talking to me since I didn't think I looked beat-down. I answered anyway and told him we were from South Carolina and visiting a friend of ours.

"So why are you really in this old man's castle in the heart of Geezerland?"

"Johnny R ain't never been strong about editin' his words," Cal said in my direction. He turned to Johnny R. "Wantin' to pick your brain."

Johnny R chuckled. "Good luck with that. My old thought-machine's being starved in here. Not much left. Know what they won't let me do?"

Trivia-collector Charles asked, "What?"

"I can't smoke. The nicotine police say it's bad for my health. Do I look like I have enough health to worry about?" He hesitated and caught his breath. "And, get this, they won't let me have sex with the nurses. Can you believe it?"

None of us responded.

"They have more rules than the IRS. Anyway, I'm sure you didn't drive out in the middle of nowhere to talk about my sex life."

Cal knew what to say and how to say it, so we deferred to him. Cal shared that Charles's main squeeze had signed with

Starr Management and had become disappointed with the results. He didn't put it like that. That's my translation of his country-music insider lingo.

Johnny R waited for Cal to finish and continued to stare at him. "Cal, look around. Do I strike you like I'm in the center of anything related to the music industry? How in the name of Jimmy Rogers am I supposed to know anything about moon, planet, star, or whatever the guy's name is you're talking about?" Johnny R was getting louder by the word. "Hell, most of the people in here think Al Jolson just recorded 'Mammy.'"

"Don't blow a gasket." Cal put his hand on his friend's shoulder. "We knew you wouldn't know Starr, but I have a suspicion you still have contacts and maybe you could check around." Cal leaned closer to Johnny R. "You're the man. Think you can help out an old buddy?"

Johnny R leaned back in bed and smiled. "Give me a few days and a number where I can reach you. I'll see what I can find."

"Much obliged, my friend. Much obliged."

Cal gave his old friend his number and another hug. Charles and I shook his emaciated hand before we headed to the door.

Johnny R said, "On your way out, fellas, see if any of the nurses out there are hankering to have sex with me. There's one cutie, Mildred, couldn't be a day over seventy, but hey, I'm not above robbin' the cradle. Let her know I won't tell on her."

Cal said he would. To Charles and my relief, he didn't.

On the way to town, Cal said that in his heyday, there wasn't anything Johnny R couldn't find out. Charles astutely observed that Cal's friend didn't appear to be involved like he once was. Cal agreed, and said even though Johnny R seemed out of it, he probably still had more connections than some insiders. I doubted it, although Cal knew his friend and I didn't. Charles also suggested instead of waiting for Johnny R, we should call Starr and ask what he was doing for Heather.

Cal and I didn't enthusiastically jump at the idea. That didn't stop Charles for looking up the agent's number and dialing. He listened and instead of talking to someone or leaving a message, Charles hit *End Call* and shook his head.

"What?" Cal asked.

Charles looked at the phone. "Machine said the boy's message machine's full."

Cal asked, "What do we do now?"

"Head to his house, knock, and say, *Surprise, we caught you.*"

It was nearing my bedtime and I suggested we save the surprise for tomorrow.

Charles said, "Suppose we can wait." Cal said, "Halleluiah!" It was after ten when we traipsed in the apartment. Heather wasn't there but had left a note on the table telling us not to wait up.

I was exhausted and it didn't take a note for me to not wait up. I did wonder what tomorrow and a trip to Kevin Starr's house would bring.

8

The day started much like yesterday. Charles was in the kitchen attempting to fix breakfast. This time it was toast and scrambled eggs. I knew it was Charles's toast because I was familiar with the aroma of burnt bread as it drifted through the apartment. Also, as was the case yesterday, Heather was nowhere to be seen and her bedroom door was closed.

I looked at the clump of eggs in the skillet. "Heather teach you to do that?"

"Tried to teach me how to fix them over easy. I taught myself that when they plop out of the shell all a mess, I can slush them around and say they were supposed to be scrambled."

"Your secret's good with me." I scraped the blackened coating off the toast. "Heather sleeping in?"

Charles glanced at the bedroom door and back at the skillet. "Yeah. Don't know when she got in this morning. Didn't hear a thing." He again looked at the door. "Chris, I'm worried about her. She's moping around and on the verge of tears more often. Her temper's getting as short as a speck of dust."

"Think she's worried her dreams will never be more than dreams?"

Charles scraped the eggs on two plates, looked at his bedroom door and at the closed door to Cal and my room, and put the plates on the table. "Guess it's you and me feasting alone."

"There loss," I said as I wondered how Heather and Cal would survive without burnt toast and over-scrambled eggs.

"Think it's more about Kevin Starr than her dreams. She's growing a hate for that man, I'm afraid."

I had learned Charles's answers could come any time after a question. He'd gone days before getting around to the answer. Yet, if he asked something and the response didn't come before a breath could be taken, he'd be asking again.

"She's a lot like you," I said. "She tries to like everyone and looks for the good in the worst folks."

Charles took a bite of toast. "Yuck." He dropped it on his plate. "President Garfield said, 'I am a poor hater.' He and I agree. Heather used to be, now I'm afraid she's getting pretty good at hating."

"What's that about me, Chucky?" Heather's sleepy voice asked as she opened the door.

She had a smile on her face and wore a long red, white, and blue striped nightgown that looked like an American flag. She pecked Charles on the forehead.

"Nothing, sweetie. We were wondering if you got enough sleep."

She looked at his plate. "See you were playing Emeril LaChuckie again."

LaChuckie said, "Want me to fix you some?"

"Not hungry. Had some food late. What are we doing today, fellas?"

For whatever reason, Heather appeared to be either over or taking a break from hating and being depressed. I didn't know if

Charles had wanted her to go with us to find Starr, I deferred to him.

"Umm, Cal wanted to see Kevin Starr since he didn't get a chance to talk to him on Folly or at the Bluebird. They have a lot in common, being they're both in the music business."

Heather said, "Oh."

"Yeah," Charles continued. "Cal thought it'd be good to see if Starr was at home where they could talk without being interrupted."

"I'll be back," I said. "Got to get something out of the bedroom." I neglected to say I had to get to Cal before he talked to Heather so he'd know who he wanted to see today, along with why, and where. "Don't eat all my breakfast, Heather."

She turned up her nose at the eggs.

I shook Cal awake, told him *his* plans, and returned to the kitchen and my one-star breakfast.

An hour later, we were following the car's automated GPS directions across the Cumberland River and six miles away from the apartment through the East Nashville section of the county. Charles had finagled Starr's home address from someone he had met at one of Heather's open-mic appearances. Signs on a building indicated we had reached Five Points where, you guessed it, five roads converged. The navigation system led us through the confusing intersection and had us turn right at Three Crow Bar. From the looks of the small, well-maintained homes, East Nashville and Five Points was made up of a mix of artsy, and eclectic residents. Several of the houses were colorfully painted, a few had large sculptures in the yard.

"Cute as a cricket," Heather chirped, as she pointed to a yellow, converted VW minibus that was home to a hotdog stand named I Dream of Weenie. It wasn't open or Heather would have made us stop for lunch and would have forgotten about our destination. The mechanized voice from the navigation system wasn't impressed by I Dream of Weenie and led us another block before announcing: "You have reached your destination." A decorative wrought-iron gate greeted us in front of a light-green bungalow. It was situated on a narrow, deep lot. A concrete-block building was at the back of the lot with a swing set between the structures. The house and its surroundings were idyllic and looked like a set for a Hallmark movie. It was the last place I would expect to find a con artist.

Charles knocked four times and I was about to think we wouldn't be finding a con-artist, or anyone else at home. Heather had walked around the side of the house and returned and waved for us. We followed her toward the building where I heard a whooshing noise and what sounded like steel striking steel.

Charles, who'd never feared to tread most anywhere, looked in the open door. The rest of us stood behind him.

"Yo, hello!" he yelled over the loud whooshing. Heat rolled out the entry, adding to the already hot morning.

The hammering stopped and Charles stepped back. We were greeted by an attractive, petite woman. She was no more than five-foot-two, in her thirties, had her hair tied in a bun and wore a black, leather blacksmith apron over jeans and a white T-shirt. Black streaks mixing with perspiration covered part of her face. She had an oversized ball-peen hammer in her leather-gloved hand, and if she hadn't been so short and attractive would have looked like someone I wouldn't want to meet in a haunted house.

"May I help you?" she said in a throaty voice. "We didn't have an appointment, did we?"

Charles asked, "Are you Mrs. Starr?"

She glanced at the rest of us; her gloved hand tightly gripped the hammer. "Yes. Again, may I help you?"

I didn't blame her for being leery of four strangers at her door, particularly when one was tall and wore a Stetson, two others wore tan Tilley's, and the fourth person had on a yellow dress brighter than a caution light.

I stepped beside Charles. "Pardon our rudeness, let me introduce everyone." I proceeded to tell her who we were and that Heather was one of her husband's clients.

Mrs. Starr removed her leather glove, set the hammer on the ground, told us to call her Sandy, and shook hands. She said she was a blacksmith and sculptor and asked us to join her on the porch after saying the studio was too hot for normal humans.

"I've never met a blacksmith," Charles said, a statement most of us could make, as Sandy pointed to chairs on the porch. The porch was shaded by the house and more comfortable than her studio or standing in the sun. Neat and quaint were the words that kept coming to mind. Again, not the home of a con artist.

Cal asked, "What kind of blacksmithin' do you do?"

Sandy pointed at a medal table with a glass top in the corner of the porch. Its legs were wrapped in decorative, metal vines with leaves on them, and a framed photo with three children posed in white shirts and huge smiles sat on the glass top.

"That kind of stuff. Do mainly commission work for high-end builders. Stair railings and such, and tables for designers."

Heather pointed at the photo. "Them your youngins?"

Sandy looked at the photo. "Getting older by the day. Steve, Kevin Jr., and Dolly; four, five, and seven."

Heather said, "Cute as crickets."

I wondered what Sandy would have thought if she knew Heather had said the same thing about the hotdog stand.

Sandy smiled. "Thanks. I don't suppose you came out here to see what I make back there." She nodded toward her studio. "Or to hear about the kids."

Heather leaned forward in her chair ready to respond. Charles beat her to it. "No, but it was interesting hearing about your work, and your kids are adorable."

Sandy nodded. "But?"

Charles said, "We were looking for Kevin. Heather was performing a couple of nights ago at the Bluebird and Kevin was supposed to be there and was going to talk to us about her career.

We were worried when he didn't show and his phone message machine's full up."

Sandy's smile faded. "Oh, I'm so sorry. That must be why I got the other calls."

Charles tilted his head to the side. "Other calls?"

"Yes, two women called the last couple of days asking for Kevin. It was strange because all his clients have his cell number and he doesn't give out our home phone. Maybe he was supposed to meet them too. I asked if I could take a message and they said no."

"Did you get their names?" I asked.

"They didn't give them. One sounded young and the other older, about your age, Heather."

Charles asked, "Did you tell your husband?"

Sandy looked at her studio and at the floor. "No. He's, umm, been away for a few days and I haven't had a chance to tell him."

"Oh," Charles said. "Where is he?"

Sandy hesitated and looked at the porch floor. "Don't know. Haven't seen him since Sunday morning. I was working on a project for a builder in Franklin and had to get it done by Monday. The kids are with my parents over in Hendersonville, and to be honest, I didn't miss Kevin until that night."

Charles said, "Does he leave often?"

Sandy tried to smile. "There's a lot of travel with his business. Sometimes he has to go to Memphis, or up to Kentucky, and North and South Carolina to meet with potential clients and other music execs. It's a demanding business. I'd rather be pounding steel." She nodded toward the outbuilding.

"He doesn't tell you where he goes?" I said.

"I get caught up in my work and block out everything but the kids. He tells me, but it's in one ear, out the other." She chuckled. "He usually calls a couple of times when he's on the road."

"Not this time?" I said.

Sandy continued to look at the floor. "No. You don't even

know me and I don't want to burden you, but I'm worried. It's not like him to be gone three days without calling."

Cal asked, "Did he take a holdall with him?"

"A what?" Sandy asked.

Good question, I thought.

Cal said, "Suitcase."

"Oh, no. He keeps a travel bag in his car. Says he has to leave from downtown sometimes and doesn't want to have to come out here to pack."

"Tell you what," Charles said. "Let me give you my number. Give me a holler when you hear from him. In the meantime, we'll check around. We'll find him."

Sandy took the number, said she'd call Charles when she heard from him, and said she was sorry we missed her husband.

"Check around. We'll find him," I parroted Charles as we piled in the car.

Charles looked back at the Starr house. "Maybe the boy's not quite the rip-off, con man I thought he was. Nice wife, *cute as cricket* kids, maybe the boy's in trouble. Who wouldn't call them if everything was okay?"

"Now Chuckie," Heather said. "It's none of our business."

That'd never stopped Charles before. It wouldn't now.

9

On the drive to town, Charles, Cal, and I talked about where we could look for Starr. After ten red traffic lights, and a near collision with a garbage truck, we didn't have any more idea where to find him than we did finding an Eskimo in Nashville. Heather proved to be the smartest person in the car; she slept the entire trip.

"Got an idea," Cal said as he climbed the stairs with the aid of the handrail. "Got another buddy here, name's Vern Watson. I'll catch my breath, pop open a beer, and give him a holler."

That meant I'd have to find Vern Watson's number.

Heather declined a beer and said her headache had returned and she was going to catch more shuteye. The only name close to Vern Watson that directory assistance knew about was V. Watson, who turned out to be a woman named Veronica who worked at a Nashville bank and had never heard of Cal's friend.

"Got another idea," Cal said. "Vern's a retired steel guitar player, was in the Opry house band for a spell. The boy played steel guitar and the ponies—better at the guitar. I'll call the union and see if they still have his card."

That meant another number to find for my connected friend. The offices were closed so Cal would have to wait until morning. None of us wanted to, or had the energy to wander out, so we spent a couple of hours staring at the walls before heading to bed.

Cal managed to get a real person on the phone the next morning. The woman he talked to was helpful—sort of. Vern Watson was no longer in the musician's union; no longer a member because he'd gone to the great recording studio in the sky seven years ago. I could almost see the wheels turning in Charles's head where he was going to tell Cal that learning anything from Watson was a dead end.

A knock on the door prevented Charles from making the tasteless joke.

Cal was nearest to the door, opened it, and was greeted by two dour-faced men, one tall at around six-foot three, the other a half foot shorter, although he carried about the same weight except much of it drooped over his belt. Both wore dress slacks, wrinkled blazers, and cheap-looking ties. They weren't starving musicians.

"I'm Detective Lawrence," the tall one said. "This is Detective Rogers." Lawrence looked at a note in his hand. "Is this where Eileen Gordon Smith lives?"

"You've got the wrong crib," Cal said. "No Eileen—"

Charles stepped in front of Cal. "She lives here. Why?"

The detectives looked at each other and then Lawrence glared at Cal. "Need to get your story straight, cowboy."

Cal still had on his Stetson and started to speak.

"Cal," Charles said, "It's Heather's name. She stopped using it a few years back when she wanted to reinvent herself."

The shorter, and younger detective, held his hand between Charles and Cal. "Is Ms. Smith here?"

Charles turned to the detective. "Heather—Eileen—isn't up yet. Why?"

Lawrence looked at his watch. "Please get her. May we come in? You don't want us standing out here talking to her."

I didn't know why they were here, yet I doubted we wanted them talking to her in the hall or anywhere else. Charles opened the bedroom door and whispered something. A long minute later Heather walked in, blinked a couple of times, and wiped her eyes. Charles told her the two detectives wanted to talk to her and Detective Lawrence took the lead and introduced himself and his partner. Lawrence asked if she had a few minutes to talk. It was apparent she didn't have a choice. Heather nodded and kept glancing over at Charles. Lawrence suggested that he, his partner, and Heather have seats in the living room and the rest of us "might be more comfortable in the kitchen." Again, it wasn't a suggestion, and Cal, Charles, and I moved to the kitchen and gathered around the table.

Cal removed his Stetson and set in on the table and whispered to Charles, "What's going on?"

Charles looked at the door leading to the living room and shrugged.

There were many drawbacks to the tiny size of the apartment. One plus became apparent when we heard everything being said in the other room. Charles's chair was farthest from the living room and he scooted it around the table to be closer.

"Ms. Smith," Detective Lawrence said, "where were you Monday night?"

"I go by Heather Lee now. Think you could call me that?"

"But you are the Eileen Gordon Smith, in the system for grand theft auto?" Detective Rogers said.

Heather sighed. "It was a long time ago, and all I did was borrow my ex-boyfriend's car and it wasn't my fault that a deer ran across the road and I tried to miss it and ended up in the river. The car didn't even sink. The ex got himself pissed and called the cops and—"

"Enough," Lawrence interrupted. "The point is you are Ms. Smith."

"Umm, yes."

Cal leaned close to Charles. "You knew that?"

"Sure."

Cal turned to me and held out his hand. "You too?"

I whispered, "Yes. She likes telling that story and that she changed her name."

Cal looked at the ceiling. "I could've written a song about it."

"Shh," Charles whispered. "I'm trying to listen."

"To my question, Ms. Smith—Heather. Where were you Monday night?"

"That's easy. I was singing at the Bluebird Cafe. I'm a country singer and it was open-mic night. My friends in there were with me."

She must have pointed toward the kitchen. Cal and Charles nodded when she told the detectives where she was.

"When did you leave the Bluebird?" Lawrence asked.

"Let's see, it was going on nine o'clock. Why?"

"Then what did you do?"

"Oh yeah, I hitched up with one of my singing buddies and came downtown for a couple of brews. We were celebrating our performances."

Rogers asked, "Who was your singing buddy?"

Heather told them Jessica Sayre, the detectives had her spell it, and asked where they went. Heather gave them the name of a lower Broadway bar.

"What time did you leave the bar?"

"Ten-thirty or so. Jess got a call and said she had to meet up with someone, her boyfriend. I'm guessing it was him; she didn't tell me."

"Then where'd you go?"

"Why?"

Rogers said, "Answer, please."

"Okay, okay. I was still hyped from singing and walked around downtown a couple of hours or so. Not certain exactly how long. Everyone was asleep when I got back here."

"Anybody see you during that time?"

"Why sure. There were a bunch of people out and about."

Lawrence said, "Anybody who was able to vouch for where you were?"

There was a long pause before Heather said, "Don't reckon. I didn't talk to anyone. I stopped in a couple of the bars but spent most of the time walking around. I love this city, don't you?"

Lawrence asked, "Do you know Kevin Starr?"

"Sure. He's my agent."

"Did you see him Monday night?"

"No sir. He was supposed to be at my performance but didn't show. Are you looking for him too?"

"What do you mean?"

"Me and my friends went out to his house yesterday looking for him. Talked to Sandy, that's his wife, a cute little gal. Did you know she's a blacksmith? Can you believe that? Sandy said he'd been gone for a few days and didn't know where he was. Guess she told you. Whew, I'm glad y'all are looking for him."

There were a few seconds of silence and finally Rogers said, "When was the last time you saw Mr. Starr?"

"Must've been a week. Met him at Starbucks."

"You haven't seen him since?" Rogers said.

Charles was tapping his fingers on the table, Cal was leaning toward the door to hear everything, and I was getting a bad feeling.

"No sir. Any good leads on where he's gone to?"

"Your friends in there were with you at the Bluebird but not later, and they were with you at Mr. Starr's house yesterday?"

"That's what I said."

A few seconds later, Detective Lawrence stepped in the kitchen and asked us to join him in the living room. There was only room for one of us to sit so Charles and I deferred to age and motioned for Cal to take the chair. Lawrence waited for us to get situated and asked about Monday night, rehashing all the details he had covered with Heather. We acted like we hadn't heard their conversation and acted surprised by the questions. He asked about out trip to Starr's house. Charles did most of the talking and talked way more than the detectives wanted to hear about the kiln, the building behind the house, and Sandy's clients. Heather interrupted once to tell Charles to make sure he tells about the hotdog stand.

Detective Lawrence maintained eye contact but his partner kept looking around the room and appeared like he would be happier being somewhere else. Charles's trivia-infused conversations can have that effect on people.

"One more question," Lawrence said after Charles paused for a breath. "Whose idea was it to go to Starr's house?"

Strange, I thought, and turned to Charles who told the detectives it was his idea.

Cal pointed at the lead detective. "Now, Mr. Detective, I think we've answered all your questions. How about answering one for us?"

"What?"

"Where do you think Starr's gone? Seems strange his wife didn't know."

Lawrence glanced over at his partner and turned back to Cal. "I'm afraid he didn't go anywhere. Mr. Starr's dead."

"Oh, my God!" Heather shrieked. She started to stand and fell back on the couch.

"When? What happened?" I asked. "Car accident?"

"Afraid not, sir," Lawrence said. "Mr. Starr was murdered."

"Oh, my God!" Heather repeated.

The detectives stood and Lawrence handed Heather his card. "Thank you for your time. If you think of anything else, please call. And, please don't leave town."

Heather took the card and tilted her head toward Lawrence. "Am I a—"

Lawrence cut her off. "Again, thank you for your time."

And they were gone, sucking all the air out of the room with them.

"Oh, my God," Heather repeated for the tenth time after the detectives ruined our morning. "Do they think I had something to do with…with his murder?" she asked no one in particular.

From the line of questioning she was without doubt a suspect, if not the prime suspect. Instead of reminding her of the obvious, I said they were talking to anyone who had a connection to Starr, and that had to be many people.

"Especially if he was a con man," Cal added.

A tear rolled down Heather's cheek. "But he was my agent. He was going to make me a star. He was going to … now he's dead."

It was clear Mr. Starr had met his demise sometime Monday evening after Heather had left the Bluebird with Jessica. Since his wife didn't know anything about it during our visit, he must not have been found until yesterday. His death could have been mentioned in today's paper, on television, or the radio.

"Charles, where can I get a newspaper?"

He thought there was a stand by the coffee shop in the next

block, and I asked if anyone wanted to go with me. My question was met with blank stares.

I found the stand and grabbed a paper. A perusal of the Local section of the *Tennessean* made me realize we were probably the only people in town who didn't know about Kevin Starr's demise. The headline read: "Music Executive Murdered." I skimmed the article before taking it back to the apartment where I knew I'd be battling the others over it. The article revealed Starr was found yesterday morning in an industrial trash dumpster a block east of lower Broadway, no more than three blocks from the apartment. The body was found through luck and a habit of the worker emptying the dumpster. The truck driver said he had seen a television story a couple of years ago where a body was found in a dumpster. Since then, he'd been careful to watch the contents of the dumpsters he'd emptied into his truck. He said he couldn't live knowing he may have dumped someone without knowing it. The reporter speculated if it wasn't for an obsessed employee, Mr. Starr would have never been found. The article went on to tell about Starr's business and his wife and three children. My stomach sank when the article said the coroner revealed his death was caused by a gunshot wound and placed the time of death between late Monday evening and Tuesday sunrise. Much of that time Heather was with Jessica or walking around Nashville by herself. She'd told the detectives that she'd not been seen by anyone who would remember her.

All eyes were glued to the paper when I entered the apartment. I folded it so the article was on top and dropped it on the table. Cal, Charles, and Heather surrounded the table and started reading.

A couple of profanities later, and Cal saying something about excrement hitting a fan, Heather said, "I feel terrible about poor Sandy and those three chillins. What'll they do?"

Charles reassured her the Starr family would be okay, Cal said being stuffed in a dumpster was a terrible way to leave this world, and I wondered if everyone in the room—particularly Heather—realized the aspiring singer could be the prime suspect. A suspect with motive and no alibi.

Heather moved to the living room and plopped down on the couch and Charles sat beside her. Cal stayed in the kitchen and continued reading, and I moved to the window and stared at the parking lot three floors below. Charles had his arm around Heather and I heard him saying she hadn't done anything wrong and had nothing to fear from the police. I had known the psychic/massage therapist/country crooner since the day she and Charles had met seven years ago. She was as quirky as a one-armed, albino, one-man-band, as friendly as an Irish setter, and from everything I had seen, as harmless as a lady bug.

Then again, there had been a marked change in her demeanor since she'd arrived in Nashville. She was moody, shown an explosive temper I hadn't seen before, and while she masked it in front of Cal and me, was irate at Kevin Starr. Was she capable of putting a bullet in him and stuffing him in a dumpster? Capable, I suppose; likely, I honestly didn't know. What I did know was Charles was in no position to assure her she had nothing to worry about.

Cal was still in the kitchen when Heather grabbed Charles's phone and punched in some numbers. She waited a few seconds, and rolled her eyes, "Gwen, this is Heather. Listen, some cops just left. Did you hear someone killed our agent? Umm, there's more, call me when you get this."

She slammed the phone on the table. "Danged answering machines. The devil's gift to people who want to irritate other people."

Charles said, "You've got that right, sweetie."

She went in the bedroom, returned with a scrap piece of paper, and called the number on it.

"Hey, Jess, this is Heather … yeah. Did you hear about Kevin Starr?" There was a long pause and Heather flopped down on the couch. "Yeah, okay, the cops were here and said it happened after we left the Bluebird." Another pause. "Yes, it could have been after we split. Where did you say you were going after I left you?" A longer pause. "Oh, that's too bad. Seen him since then?" This time a shorter pause. "Sorry. What'd the cops ask?" A long pause. "Me too. Wasn't it scary when they told you not to leave town?" By now Charles was pointing to the phone and imitating someone talking into a megaphone; Charles-speak for put it on speaker. Heather ignored him. "They didn't." Another pause. "Oh, okay, talk to ya later."

She ended the call and flipped the phone in Charles's lap. "Shit."

I wasn't a psychic like Heather. I had heard enough to figure out Jessie had already talked to the police and was warned to not leave town. Not a good sign. I also didn't know what her alibi was, since from what I'd heard earlier, she was as unhappy with Starr as Heather was.

I asked, "Where did she say she went after you parted company?"

"Her boyfriend called and asked her to meet him at the Wildhorse Saloon but he wasn't there when she got there. Said she didn't wait and went home."

Charles said, "Isn't it weird he calls and asks her to meet him and doesn't show?"

"Not really. Her fella's kind of erratic. I think she ought to dump him." She sighed. "You know how blind love is."

If he wasn't there, I wondered what Jessica's alibi was for the time Starr was killed. "She live by herself?"

"She's got a cat. Cute little calico named Kitty."

I doubted her cat would be much of an alibi. "Anybody live with her?"

"Nah."

On the surface, Jessica would have had as much reason to kill

Starr as Heather had. What if the call she received was from Starr and not her boyfriend and she left Heather to meet the agent?

Cal asked, "Was the Jessica gal pissed enough at Starr to shoot him?"

Heather bowed her head and tapped her foot on the floor. She whispered, "Don't know, she was pretty angry. He was about all we talked about the other night. Could have, I suppose."

If that's the case, I wondered why the police hadn't told her not to leave town. Or did they?

My phone rang.

"Good morning, Brother Chris. Is this a bad time?"

The reference to Brother Chris and the polite way he asked if it was a bad time, told me it was Preacher Burl. I lied and said it was a good time.

"Good. Is Brother Cal in the vicinity? I'd like to speak with him."

I said he was five feet away and started to hand him the phone. Burl said I could listen if I wanted to, and he joked he wasn't going to say anything horrible about me. I tapped the speaker icon and told Burl that Cal was listening. So was nosy Charles, but I didn't mention that.

Cal said, "Hey, Preacher Burl. Is everything okay at the bar?"

"Fine. I tried your number—"

"Dead battery; forgot to charge it. Sorry. Is everything okay?"

"Yes, sir. It's busy. I—"

Cal held up his hand, and interrupted, "Not trying to convert my pickled patrons, are you?"

"Heavens no," Burl said, with an emphasis on *heavens*. "Everyone in last night said they were coming to the service Sunday and starting a choir. I think it was because they were reading the Bibles I put on each table, or maybe because I switched out all your old country songs in the jukebox with hymns."

"What?" Cal shouted.

I covered a smile with my palm.

"Kidding, Brother Cal. Preachers can have a sense of humor."

"Thank Go—goodness. You made my heart upchuck."

"Yes. Your customers don't have to listen to hymns. I turn the jukebox off during each evening's prayer meeting."

"Amen," Charles said.

"Hi, Brother Charles," Burl said. "I figured you'd be nearby. Is Sister Heather there as well?"

"I'm here." She smiled for the first time this morning.

Cal said, "Preacher Burl, you didn't call to stop my heart, did you?"

The preacher chuckled. "No, but doing so brought a touch of joy to my soul."

"Well?" Cal said.

"Brother Caldwell was in last night and wanted to know when you will be returning."

Caldwell Ramsey was my friend Mel Evan's significant other. I had known Mel, the owner of Mad Mel's Magical Marsh Machine, a marsh tour boat, for several years. He was a retired marine who found a niche in the tour business by taking groups of college students on excursions with the objective of his customers hiding out in the marsh and consuming alcoholic beverages. I didn't know Caldwell as well as I did Mel, but he seemed like a great person, somehow put up with Mel's rough edges, which encompassed most of his edges, and was a concert promoter in Charleston who worked with small venues and lesser-known bands.

Cal said, "Not certain when I'll be back. What's Caldwell want?"

"He didn't give me details but it has something to do with someone wanting to convert a failing bar to a country music location. Brother Caldwell said he wants to pick your brain about what would work best."

Cal said, "Hope the bar ain't on Folly."

"It's in Charleston. I don't picture it interfering with my nightly prayer meetings in Cal's."

"Funny. Tell him I don't know when I'll be back. It'll be in a few days, and I'll call him when I get there, and after I run the Holy Spirit out of Cal's."

"Funny," Burl said, with more enthusiasm than Cal had. "One more thing. This bartending, cleaning, opening and closing, and using my limited bouncer skills are taking a toll on this old, chubby body. The sooner you return the better."

"I'm working on it Preacher."

"Much obliged. I'll pray for your safe return during tonight's free beer and preaching at Cal's."

He ended the call, but it didn't stop Cal from mumbling, "Funny."

I woke the next morning to Cal strumming his much-travelled guitar and singing, "I'm So Lonesome I Could Cry." I yawned, opened the door and looked around the living room and only saw Cal. Heather and Charles's door was closed. Cal stopped strumming and asked if his singing was the reason I was up. I said no and asked if anyone else was moving around. The country crooner reported Heather was "sawing logs" and her Chuckie was "strollin' around Music City."

Cal looked at the closed bedroom door and waved for me to join him on the couch. "I do my best thinking when I'm singing songs that I've sung a few thousand times. My mind wanders out past the words to where they don't get in the way."

"What are you thinking about?"

He glanced again at the bedroom door and leaned closer to me. "Think Heather's in a cow pie field full of trouble."

Cal must be as psychic as Heather, and I wondered why it took singing to figure out she was in trouble. I also wondered what he was referring to, so I asked.

Cal leaned his guitar against the couch. "Let's see, first, she's got a pent-up load of anger at that so-called agent. Second, she thinks he ripped her off on the demo and the stupid-ass PR package. Third, out of all the nights she's finagled her way to the stage at the Bluebird, he's managed to show up zero times. And cripes, it almost slipped my mind, fourth, two cops showed up giving her the third degree." He looked at her door, lowered his head. "Chris, her alibi's holds as much water as a tennis racket."

"You think she killed him?"

"Don't matter a termite turd what I think. I ain't the police, judge, or jury."

"That didn't answer my question."

"Don't seem like Heather, but these old bloodshot eyes have seen stranger things. Tell you what I do know."

He paused. I figured I wouldn't have to ask.

"We've been here going on a week and I can't continue to impose on the good preacher to keep running the bar. I need to mosey back."

I hated to leave Charles with everything going on, but couldn't think of anything I could do to help. I offered to head home today if Cal was ready. He told me I didn't need to go and he could take a bus or hitchhike. I told him those were two of the dumbest ideas I'd heard from him, and said we'd leave once Charles returned and we could say bye to Heather.

He strummed and sang, "Thaaaank you."

Charles returned an hour later and said he loved the sweet aroma of stale beer along the sidewalks of Broadway. Heather made her appearance and I nearly saluted her in her patriotic gown. I shared that Cal needed to get home and I was taking him. Charles and Heather protested, yet I could hear relief in their voices. The apartment was barely large enough for the two of them, and houseguests, regardless how much we tried to stay out of the way, got old fast. Heather said she had another headache and said goodbye from the apartment and Charles walked us to the car.

Cal and I were on the Interstate headed to Folly by ten o'clock and pulled on the island a little before nine that evening. Burl had called for Cal when we were two hours out and said Mel and Caldwell were at the bar and since we were close, they'd wait for us. Cal would rather have gone home, but didn't want to disappoint Caldwell.

"Hallelujah, praise the Lord, I'm free at last!" Preacher Burl exclaimed as Cal and I entered Cal's.

I thought he was going to break into the chorus of Handel's *Messiah*. Instead, he rushed out from behind the bar and hugged Cal so tightly it knocked off his Stetson off. Cal and Burl exchanged a couple more pleasantries and Burl asked how Charles and Heather were. Cal told him about Kevin Starr's death and the visit by the police.

"Oh my." Burl's grin became a frown. "Why would the officials think she could have had anything to do with his graduation from this earth?"

Cal gave a vague answer and it appeared to alleviate the preacher's fear. Cal didn't get in a discussion about Heather's lack of an alibi and how angry she had been with the agent.

The conversation was interrupted by a growl and "Umm" from someone who had moved behind Cal. If I hadn't seen who it was, I still would've recognized the abrupt, rude interruption as coming from Mel Evans. The six-foot-one, bald, former marine wore a leather bomber jacket with its sleeves cut off even though it was in the eighties outside, camo field pants with the legs cut off below the knees, and a snarl designed to intimidate. I knew him well, so his expression was wasted on me.

Cal turned, smiled, and said, "MM, how in grouchy-world are you?"

"It's about damn time you got your sorry country ass back."

Cal opened his mouth to respond, when Caldwell Ramsey, who had been standing beside the former marine pushed him aside. "Give the man a break, Mel. He's been on the road all day." He turned to Cal. "Welcome back. We've been waiting for you."

"For hours," Mel interjected.

Cal ignored Mel, "Thanks Caldwell, it's been a long day."

Caldwell was three inches taller than his partner, was several years younger, and looked in as good a condition that he had been in when he played basketball for Clemson in the 80s. Mel had described their relationship as the twenty-first century version of the odd couple. In addition to being gay, Caldwell was African-American, polite, and didn't treat everyone he met with disdain, one of Mel's less popular but often displayed traits.

"Let me buy you and Chris a beer," Caldwell said. He twisted around and looked at bartender Burl, pointed at an empty beer bottle, and turned back to Cal. "There's something I'd like your advice on."

Burl said, "Go ahead, I'll get your drinks. Might as well finish my shift." He grinned. "Wouldn't want my boss to think I'm slacking off."

Cal tipped his hat to Burl and pointed to the ceiling. "Don't know about your boss up there, this one appreciates it. Much obliged, my holy friend."

Curiosity prevented me from wishing them well and heading home to a familiar bed. I joined the group at the table; one of only three with occupants. It wasn't a hymn coming from the jukebox, but close, as Johnny Cash sang "Sunday Morning Coming Down."

We settled around the table, Mel brought Cal and my drinks, and what appeared to be the fourth round for Mel and the second for Caldwell.

Cal turned to Caldwell. "What can I do for you, pard?"

Caldwell stretched his long legs out beside the table. "Need to pick your brain."

"May need a shovel to find anything in it tonight."

"I've got a client who has a bar on Folly Road near Savannah

Highway. Name's SHADES. The owner's done well with it. I've worked with her the last year or so finding entertainment on the weekend. The bands have been good; the crowds not so good. Most of the bands have leaned toward pop, occasional hard rock, some alternative rock. She's wanting to shake things up, completely remodel both the inside and the outside, and repackage the place."

"Don't blame her," Cal said. "That music can cause brain cancer and retardation."

Caldwell smiled. "Figured you'd say something like that. She has this bee in her bonnet and wants to switch to country. She thinks she could get it kick-started by having open-mic nights one or two nights a week, and bring in better-known country acts on weekends."

"She have the dough to do it?" Cal asked.

"Money's not the problem."

"What do you need from me?" Cal waved his hand around the room. "Don't think I'm the person to be asking about interior design."

Caldwell chuckled. "She has a designer to take care of the looks, and I can handle the acts, it's what I do. When it comes to open-mic events, I'm a fish out of water."

"I'm still confused," Cal said. "What's there to know about open-mic nights. Tell her anyone can show up, sing, and sit down."

"She's heard about places that have those kinds of nights and only terrible singers show up. It ends up like karaoke rather than a good draw. She wants an event that pulls audiences; not just relatives and friends of the singers. She's hoping to attract others who want to hear good music."

"And drink," Cal said.

"And drink. If she's available, can you meet me there tomorrow night so we can talk to her and see what she needs. Country's not my strong suit."

Cal turned to me. "Will you go?"

It wouldn't have been at the top of my priority list. Cal had spent a week with me, so it was the least I could do. I nodded.

Cal asked, "What time?"

Caldwell told him and Cal went to the bar to ask Burl if he could cover a few more hours. The preacher agreed and Cal said his brain, or what's left of it, and his broken-down body would be there.

Mel said, "Now can we get out of here?" He pointed to the jukebox where George Jones was sharing the downside of whiskey. "This country music moaning-and-groaning crap's giving me heartburn."

I got home a little after eleven. Other than a week's worth of dust and a temperature higher than I would have preferred because I had turned the A/C off before leaving, everything looked the same. I thought how soothing it would have been if an enthusiastic canine greeted me with a lick on my face, or a warm female body receiving me with an even more enthusiastic kiss. It was not to be. I loved most animals, while the selfish part of me couldn't handle their care and feeding. I lavished my animal appreciation on other people's pets.

The warm female issue was more complicated. I had been-there, done-that with a wife, but it was many years ago. Since I had been on Folly, I had been in three relationships not counting a few dates with Amber, none of which had approached fiancé level. I had dated Karen Lawson, a former detective with the Charleston County Sheriff's Office and daughter of Folly's mayor, Brian Newman, for four years before she took a high-paying position handling corporate security for a company head-quartered in Charlotte. I had shared a few meals with her when she was back in Charleston working with one of the company's satellite offices, until we both had realized a long-distance rela-tionship wouldn't work. Yes, I could have moved to Charlotte, but hadn't. That decision could have been one of the worst I'd ever made—or not.

Since Karen's been gone, I'd had three dinner dates with Barbara Deanelli, owner of Barb's Books which was in the space that had been my photo gallery for several years. Barb was close to my age, had spent much of her life as a practicing attorney in Pennsylvania, and because of illegal activities on the part of her ex-husband, she had given up law and moved to be closer to her half-brother, Dude Sloan, a good friend of mine and owner of Folly's surf shop. Barb was fun to be with, intelligent, and easy on the eyes. I didn't know where our relationship was headed, and neither of us appeared in a hurry to move it along.

With that said, it would have been nice to know someone was glad I was home. After a glass of chardonnay, I realized I had no business feeling sorry for myself. I had good friends on Folly and despite its shortcomings, I considered this island my heaven on earth. Besides, I was in a much better place, physically and emotionally, than Charles and Heather, Kevin Starr, and his wife and three children. I had much for which to be thankful.

1 2

After a twelve mile drive up Folly Road, Cal and I walked across a large parking lot to an attractive, stone building with a neon sign above the door that said SHADES with under it in script "Where you're always cool."

Cal said, "Stupid name."

I didn't think it was that bad. A handful of vehicles were in the lot.

The deep, thumping sounds of a bass guitar, eardrum pounding drums, and a vocalist who sounded like a cross between a screeching owl and a roaring tiger with a sore throat greeted us before we reached the entry.

Cal yelled, "Think this is the wrong place?"

"No such luck," I yelled and reached for the door. The handle vibrated in time with the "music."

Yellow and red strobe lights were doing their thing in time with the blaring sounds from refrigerator-sized speakers. Three couples were gyrating in time to the lights and music. To these old eyes, they seemed to be in excruciating pain or being attacked by killer bees. I assumed they were having a good time. The interior décor was as opposite to Cal's Country Bar and Burgers as a hummingbird to a Ferris wheel. The only similarity was the approximate number of customers. There couldn't have been more than a dozen people in the bar, and that included Cal and me.

Caldwell was standing beside the shiny, black and red-trimmed aluminum bar talking to a woman I figured to be the owner. She was tall, although a few inches shorter than Caldwell, trim, with curly-brown hair and appeared to be in her late thirties. The music promoter saw us and waved us over. Cal and I skirted the dance-floor and moved close to the two. Caldwell started to introduce us when the woman pointed to a door behind the bar and motioned for us to follow. She didn't have to ask twice since anywhere but this sound chamber on steroids would be an improvement.

We followed her to an office that would have been the envy of many CEOs.

"Room's soundproofed," she said and closed the door. They were the first words she said that I understood. "Only thing that keeps me sane. Excuse my rudeness, I'm Olivia Anderson, owner of this cornucopia of blaring bands."

Cal said, "If that means ear-splitting loud, I agree." He stuck a finger in each ear.

Olivia laughed. "You must be Cal. I looked you up on the Internet and saw where you had a hit or two a while back."

Cal tipped his Stetson. "That would be one hit, and it was probably before you were hatched."

"Maybe."

Cal told her who I was and she said something like it was nice to meet me. I had never had a hit record so she didn't seem to care about me one way or the other.

In the better light, I would guess her age to be older than I first thought. She looked more like a corporate executive than a bar owner. Her light-gray suit looked tailored, she wore expensive shoes, and her wrists must think God created them to hold bracelets. She had four, wide, gold bracelets on her left arm and three on her right wrist. On her left ring finger, a diamond sparkled, and if real, she should have an armed escort following her around.

She offered whatever we wanted from the bar and we declined. Her finely-appointed office had more chairs than I had in my house and we moved to the grouping on the far side of the room. Olivia excused herself to get a drink and I looked around the walls at the multiple photos of Olivia with a variety of people who I probably would have recognized if my musical tastes hadn't stagnated three decades ago. I was also drawn to two framed diplomas beside her large mahogany desk; both from Wake Forest University.

Olivia returned carrying a tumbler nearly overflowing with an amber liquid. "Don't mind if I drink, do you?"

Caldwell and I shook our heads. Cal said, "We're in a bar."

"Demon Deacons," I said and nodded toward the diplomas. I thanked Charles for that bit of trivia I'd learned from one of his college T-shirts.

She glanced at the diplomas. "Wake Forest. Best years of my life; worst years of my life. Got a degree in Latin and one in English. Means I couldn't get a job using either one of them, but I could read all the words on a dollar bill." She laughed at what I suspected was the often-told joke.

Caldwell laughed with her. He was here to get her business.

The name on the diplomas was Mona O. Alliendre, probably her maiden name.

"Gentlemen, why don't we get down to why you're here. Let me give you some background. Caldwell knows most of this."

Her husband opened SHADES four years ago. He had been a

successful businessman and wanted to "diversify his assets." He was a few years older than Olivia, and wasn't a fan of the hard-rock music the bar was known for, yet he was smart enough to know it was hot at the time. He died of a brain aneurism two years ago, and she was in a funk for the next year and walked through the motions without giving thought to changing anything.

Cal said, "Sorry to hear about your husband."

"Thank you." She paused and took a sip. "Sure you don't want anything?"

The room was soundproofed yet the thumping bass could be felt in the office. The sweet smell of a citrus candle on a mahogany credenza permeated the space. I thought how pleasant it smelled as compared to the stale beer and burgers aroma that greeted Cal's patrons.

We again declined.

"About a year ago, Edwina Robinson, mentioned redoing the place to me. She's one of the gals who sings here regularly and fills in when one of the other bands Caldwell books arrives late or is 'under the weather'—high, in other words."

Caldwell shrugged. "Musicians."

"Edwina's good," Olivia continued. "She prefers country but can rock with the best of them. The gal's going to make it big one of these days."

"Name sounds familiar," Cal said. "She ever sing on Folly?"

Olivia tilted her head toward Cal. "Don't know. She could have. Edwina started talking to me about redoing the place, calming the music down, and going country." She giggled. "As you can see from the crowd out there, a change couldn't hurt."

Cal smiled. "Got it."

Olivia waited for him to say more. He didn't. "I told Edwina it wasn't a bad idea and started working with a consultant on the changes and the concepts. That didn't work out, and Edwina said

I should talk to Caldwell who suggested that since you were in the country bar business, he'd see if you'd share your opinion. If I can get it off the ground, I'd like to expand to other cities, and maybe to Knoxville, Nashville, and Atlanta."

"I'll try, but I'm no expert on the business side."

Caldwell must not have told Olivia the only reason Cal now owned his bar was because he happened to be singing there when the man who owned it killed the co-owner, an action frowned on by the police. Cal took over by default and knew as much about the business end or running a bar as I did about the cholesterol level of a Jurassic dinosaur.

"I have a handle on the business," Olivia said. "Edwina said from what she's seen that a good way to get the crowds in early on would be to have one or two open-mic nights during the week and let Caldwell get us well-known entertainment on weekends. Edwina said she's played several of them, not only here but in other states, and they pack the venue. She also said her agent told her it was the way to go. So, Cal, how do I get good singers to show up? I don't want the ones who would be booed off the stage karaoke night. That won't bring in the type of customers I'm looking for."

Cal nodded. "Don't want the suckees."

Olivia took the final sip and grinned at him. "Couldn't have said it better."

Caldwell leaned closer. "Olivia's already scouted out a couple of open-mic venues in town."

The owner said, "I've been to the East Bay Meeting House where they have poetry and music and Parson Jack's Cafe."

I hadn't been to either. From what I knew of Cal's approach, they were probably better and had fewer "suckees" than Cal's attracted.

"Tell you what, Olivia," Caldwell said. "Let me work with Cal and I'll get back with a plan."

My phone rang before I heard her response. The screen said it was Charles and I interrupted and said I had to take the call. Olivia said for me to go out the back door where I would have some privacy and not be blasted by the music.

I would have been better off having the music burst my eardrums.

Charles screamed, "They took her!"

It took a second to realize what he'd said. "Who took who?"

"Cops. They took Heather. They just left. They got her. Gone, they—"

"Slow down," I interrupted. "Start at the beginning."

Charles was out of breath and struggled to breathe. I should have stayed in Nashville.

"Give me a second. Let me sit."

I heard a chair scrape the floor and a calmer voice. "They came pounding on the door an hour ago. Same detectives. There were two uniformed cops with them and the older detective handed Heather a search warrant; told us it was for the apartment and the car. I hadn't read all of it when they said for us to go downstairs while they searched the apartment." He sighed. "Crap, they had one of the cops go with us. What'd they think, we were going to try to run? It's horrible, Chris. Horrible."

"It's okay, Charles." I realized it was not only a lie, but a terrible response to his pain. "Go slow. What happened next?"

"We weren't down there a half hour. The cop got a call and

escorted us back to the apartment. Chris, they tore the place apart. Our stuff was everywhere. They even flipped through my books and threw them on the floor. Thank God we don't have much."

"Then what?"

"They told us to stay in the apartment; left a cop at the door like we were going to, I don't know what. They were gone a long time searching the car. Then the detectives came back with sour looks on their faces. The younger one stuck a clear plastic bag in Heather's face. He stared at her and said, 'Is this yours?'"

The pulsating rhythms of the sound system reverberated in the air. I waited for him to continue. After what seemed like an eternity, I said, "What was in it?"

"A gun."

I was stunned. I'd never known Charles or Heather to have a firearm. Charles hated them and would've been shocked if he'd known it was in their car. "Where'd they get it?"

"It was a little thing. The detective said it was a twenty-two caliber Derringer. I'd never seen it before."

"Was it in the car?"

"Said he found it under the registration papers in the glove box." I heard the chair scooting around and Charles taking a drink.

"Did you know it was there?"

"No." He paused. "Heather did."

"Oh."

"My honey looked at the gun, and said, 'That's mine.'"

The detectives stared at her. I nearly fell out of the chair. Chris, the cops hadn't even asked before Heather said her friend Gwen sold it to her a few weeks back. Gwen told her she wasn't in Kansas, or Folly, anymore and needed some girlie protection —it was her word, *girlie*. Gwen said it was more dangerous here in the big city and Heather needed something to keep her safe. Keep her safe. Now she's in jail. How damned safe is that?"

"I'm sorry. Then what happened?"

"The older detective took a card out of his pocket and read Heather her rights, and said she was … she was under arrest for the murder of Kevin Starr. Said she'd be able to call an attorney once she was booked. They made her put her hands behind her back and slapped cuffs on her." He hesitated. "Chris, they wouldn't let me wipe the tears off her face before they hauled her away."

My head began to throb in time with the music from the bar. "Charles, I'll leave now and try to get there in the morning."

"No. They said I could see her for a few minutes tomorrow. Let me talk to her before you come. You need to get some sleep anyway. Driving all night ain't going to do Heather any good."

I made him promise he'd call the second he left the jail.

I WAS BETTER off not leaving for Nashville last night, but not much. I couldn't have gotten more than three hours' sleep, for worrying about my friend, wondering what Heather was doing with a gun, and if the gun was the murder weapon. If it was, had Heather pulled the trigger? I also wondered why the police had focused on Heather in the first place. I knew of a few, and there were probably more, people who were mad at the agent. Someone was angry enough to kill him. What had Heather done to merit a search of the apartment and the car? Did the police know ahead of time about the gun? I also knew none of these questions would be answered in the middle of the night.

By six, I had given up on sleep and shuffled to the kitchen and fired-up Mr. Coffee, filled a Roasted mug with steaming hot coffee, and moved to the screened-in front porch. I watched a steady stream of traffic head to work, both on-island and headed to Charleston. One of my secret pleasures since retiring had been watching people go to work. This morning it wasn't the least bit pleasurable; it simply killed time waiting for Charles to call.

After three cups of coffee, a hundred or so cars passing the house, and a clock that read nine-thirty, the phone rang. Charles was calmer, but was again out of breath. I asked where he was and he said he had just left the jail and was sitting in the car. They only let him see Heather ten minutes. She looked like she hadn't slept, and was as scared as he'd ever seen her. She'd told the detectives she didn't think it was a good idea to talk to them without an attorney. They asked her if she had any money for a lawyer; she told them no, and they said a public defender would be assigned.

Charles hesitated. A large truck or bus moved past his car and he continued, "Chris, I have money I could give her. I don't think it would be enough to get a good lawyer. I also hate to have her fate in the hands of a public defender. Some of them are good. How do I know hers will be? Chris, how do I know anything?" There was a long pause. "Didn't even know she had a gun. What if it's the one that killed him? What do I do?"

"Let me get with Sean Aker and see what he says. Maybe he knows someone over there, or is able to find out more about the public defender she'll have."

Sean Aker was one of four practicing attorneys on Folly. A few years back, he had been accused of killing his law partner and Charles and I had helped prove him innocent. He said he owed us big-time, and we'd withdrawn from that bank several times. He was also a friend.

It wasn't yet ten o'clock and there was little chance he would be in. I called anyway. Marlene, his receptionist and only other employee in the one-lawyer office, answered and told me of course he wasn't there. "Chris, haven't you figured out after all these years, the boy doesn't start thinking or doing legal work until afternoon?"

I knew that. "I also know he comes in early some days so he can get a peaceful mid-morning nap."

Marlene laughed. "Yes, you do have him figured out. He's not in his opulent office snoozing. I can tell you where he is if you need him."

I told her that intel would be helpful.

"He's at the Dog, probably thinking he will be having a peaceful breakfast, until you show up. Be sure and tell him I wasn't going to tell where he was until you tortured me."

I assured her I would and thanked her for ratting him out. I wasn't in any mood to tease as much as I had, yet Marlene has a way of diffusing difficult clients who venture into Sean's office. She had brought a smile to my face, something I needed. Now I need to see if Sean can bring some advice to what had started as a terrible morning.

The Lost Dog Cafe was Folly's most popular breakfast spot and hangout for several locals and a must-visit restaurant for the thousands of vacationers who wander the streets and beaches of the barrier island each year. I had eaten countless more meals there than I had in my kitchen and had met and talked to more locals and learned more about the character and characters of the island than anywhere else on Folly.

Most days I found an excuse to drive rather than walking the short distance. Today, with the temperature in low seventies, nary a raincloud within a hundred miles, and feeling a need to continue the walking I had started while visiting Nashville, I hoofed the ten-minute trek. It proved to be a wise choice. There wouldn't have been a parking place near the restaurant and twenty people waited outside for a table.

Sean was at a table on the front patio. He spotted me heading his way, waved, and pointed to the empty chair across from him. I ignored the angry glare of two men in line and walked to the far end of the patio and opened the fence that led to Sean's table.

"Marlene told you I was here, didn't she?" said the thin, sickeningly handsome, and at age forty-six, sickeningly young attorney.

I nodded.

"Going to have to fire her." He rolled his eyes. "Again."

"She told me where you were. You invited me to the table."

He pointed to my chair. "So, it's my fault you're here?"

I nodded again.

"Since I'm stuck with you, are you going to ruin my peaceful morning?"

Nod number three.

Before he asked how I was going to ruin his morning, Amber appeared carrying a hot mug of coffee for me, and wearing her most endearing smile. Amber was five-foot-five, had long auburn hair tied in a pony-tail, and was a little older than Sean. She was one of the first people I'd met when I arrived on Folly and we had dated for a couple of years, and after that we'd remained friends. She was the best source of rumors, and occasional facts, on the island.

She turned her back to the glaring customers who were waiting for us to leave. "Hear you decided to become a country music star and went to visit Charles and Heather."

I grinned. "For being such a good rumor collector, you were led astray with the star story. Yes, Cal and I were over there."

"How're they doing?"

This wasn't the time and place to talk to Amber about Heather's problem and said they were adjusting to their new home.

Amber shook her head. "Hate to hear it. I miss the crap out of him. It's not the same without Charles clanking around with his cane, wearing those silly college T-shirts, and pestering me."

I told her she was right—again.

"Next time you talk to him tell him to get his sorry rear end back where it belongs."

She started to leave when Sean gently grabbed her arm and

turned to me. "Is this visit going to have me doing work and not getting paid for it?"

I nodded. If the reason for my visit wasn't so serious, this would be fun.

He let go of Amber. "Put my breakfast on his check."

I stopped nodding as Amber headed inside.

"Spill it," Sean said.

When he switched gears to lawyer mode, Sean was an excellent listener and was quick to assimilate what was being said. He didn't interrupt as I gave him an abbreviated version of why Charles and Heather had moved to Nashville, the trip Cal and I had made to their new home, learning about Starr's death, and the unsettling news that Heather had been arrested."

Sean, like most everyone who lived or worked on Folly, knew Charles but had only met Heather a couple of times.

He shook his head. "You never cease to amaze me. How do you manage to turn a simple life of retirement into a constant stream of murder, mayhem, and madness?"

"It's a gift."

Sean sipped his coffee, stared at the real estate office across the street, discreetly glanced at the throng of people waiting for our table, and turned to me. "What can I do?"

"Do you know any attorneys in Nashville?"

Sean grinned. "Darnell G. Edelen, Esquire, the best criminal defense attorney in Music City. I know he's the best because he tells me so each time I talk to him."

"Could he help Heather? I doubt her court-appointed public defender will do the kind of job she may need."

Sean took his phone out of his pocket and started scrolling through his contacts. "One way to find out. Darnell owes me." He tapped in the number. A few seconds later, he said, "Mr. Edelen, please." A short pause later. "No, but tell him his savior is calling." Another brief pause. "Not that one. That savior wouldn't call on the phone. Your boss will know who it is." Sean took a sip and I heard mumbling on the phone. Sean blew at the phone, and said, "Hear the wind howling? I'm getting ready to jump and thought of you. Want to come over and step out of a plane with me?" Sean laughed. "Okay, your loss. I need a favor."

Sean gave his friend a shorter version of what I had told him about Heather's situation, and answered a few questions. "Need I remind you about Chattanooga?" One more pause. "Great, here's my good friend Chris with details. Thanks, *amigo*."

Sean handed me the phone and I introduced myself to Darnell.

"Sean taken you skydiving yet?"

I said, "No," and thought it was a strange way to handle introductions.

He asked for Heather's name, Charles's name and phone number, name of the person she allegedly killed, and my number. He said he'd make a few calls and get with Charles. I thanked him and handed the phone to Sean who listened to something Darnell said, laughed, and ended the call.

"Sean, Heather can't afford the *best criminal defense attorney in Music City*, even if he exaggerates."

"Doesn't have to. Won't cost her a penny unless it goes to trial. If that happens, we'll figure something out."

I was stunned. "What'd you do, save his life?"

Sean smiled. "He thinks I did."

"Want to explain?"

"We went to law school at Alabama. Couple of years back, we had a class reunion and some of our buddies decided we needed to celebrate by skydiving. It sounded like a great plan at two in the morning after a night of, shall I say, enjoying the liquid fruits of our success."

I wasn't surprised. Sean was an experienced skydiver as well as a scuba diver and surfer.

"I reserved a plane at a skydiving school a few miles from the hotel and when we got there, Darnell was a lima bean shade of green. I figured it was from overindulging the night before. By the time the plane reached jumping altitude of twelve thousand feet, he was petrified. If he could've curled up and died, he would have. The other guys were stuck on themselves and didn't notice Darnell." Sean took another sip.

"What happened?"

"I fiddled with his chute, acted serious, and said there was something wrong with the way it was packed and he shouldn't jump. The other guys told him they were sorry he'd have to stay with the plane. Darnell told them he was disappointed. Lying's a skill we learned in law school. The rest of us jumped and caught up with him on the ground."

"He knew what you were doing?"

"When we met up after the jump, I was afraid he was going to kiss me; would've ruined my macho image in front of my classmates. Instead of a smooch, he said he owed me his life, the life that had a lifelong fear of heights. He thought he was over it until we got in the air. He said if I ever needed anything, he'd do it." Sean nodded. "I just cashed in."

I thanked him. He said he needed to get to the office before Marlene sent the police out after him, and I told him she was a good nanny. He joked I was nothing but trouble, and got serious. "Do you think she did it?"

"I'd love to say no. To be honest, I don't know. She's changed since moving. She was always kind, sweet to a fault, and found good in everyone. The Heather I saw in Nashville was angry, bitter, and depressed." I paused and shook my head. "She had motive, no alibi, and if ballistic matches her gun with the bullet, there'd be a strong case against her. Sean, I don't know."

He said he hoped not and told me to let him know what Darnell learns. I said I would and he left to incur the wrath of

Marlene, and I left so not to further incur the wrath of the line of customers drooling over the table.

Instead of heading home and pacing the floor, I stopped at Barb's Books, located on Center Street in a retail building that for seven years had housed my ill-fated photo gallery. My fine-art photos had never reached "necessity" status along with milk, bread, gas, and lottery tickets.

I was greeted by a smile. "Good morning. What brings you out this early? I know it's not to buy a book."

The store's owner, Barbara Deanelli, had short, black hair, hazel eyes, and was thin—almost too thin, although she said *too thin* was not possible. She had been slow to adjust to the laid-back lifestyle and friendliness of Folly's residents. After having a few months to experience us first-hand, she had warmed.

"Thought I'd stop and see my favorite bookstore owner."

"How many bookstore owners do you know?"

"Counting you?"

She nodded.

I held up my forefinger.

"Thought so. Interest you in coffee?"

I didn't tell her I'd had several cups and said sure as I followed her to the backroom and her ultra-fancy, single-cup Keurig coffeemaker—a major upgrade from the Mr. Coffee machine that had provided caffeine for visitors to Landrum Gallery.

We waited for the coffee to brew, and killed time talking about the weather, fickle vacationers, and the high turnover in the police department. She also shared she didn't know why she bothered to open on weekday mornings, and it seemed people who bought books stayed in bed until noon. I recounted some of my bad-old-days and said people who bought photographs must have never gotten out of bed.

She took a sip of some exotic coffee blend. "What really brings you in?"

I told her most of what I'd told Sean. Barb had been a successful attorney in Harrisburg, Pennsylvania, before giving it all up and moving to Folly. She understood what I was talking about without me having to explain.

"Kevin Starr. Didn't you say he was the reason Charles and Heather moved?"

"Yes."

"If memory serves, she met him when he heard her singing at Cal's."

I told her yes and that they only met one time before she moved. He had convinced her he could get her gigs in Nashville.

"What was he doing here?"

"He was at the Tides on a retreat with record executives. Why?"

"I find it interesting that he heard her sing, got her to move, and then she killed him. I never heard her, but from what I've been told, Heather's no Taylor Swift."

"Kindly put. I have no doubt he was ripping her off."

"Doesn't bolster her case, does it?"

I shook my head.

"You think there are other gullible hopefuls he was ripping off?"

"Yes, I met a couple in the brief time I was in Nashville."

"Other than Heather, any of them from around here?"

"Not that I know of. Why?"

"If he conned Heather into following her dream into his wallet, there may have been others from places he travelled. Just a thought."

I told her about Sean's friend who would be handling it and she seemed pleased it wasn't going to be a public defender. I asked what she thought about the case against Heather.

"Unless ballistics can tie her gun to the murder or someone saw her pull the trigger, a good attorney could throw enough crap at the jury to establish doubt. How much doubt will be the key."

I told her I hoped she was right and that the lawyer could throw whatever amount of doubt would reach the "reasonable doubt" threshold. Someone came in the front door and she started to see who it was.

"I also wanted to see if you wanted to have supper tonight?"

"Sure," she said and went to wait on the latest arrival.

I called Charles before I was to meet Barb at Rita's Seaside Grill. Good to his promise, Sean's friend had called and Charles said he felt a glimmer of hope with a big-shot attorney representing Heather. Darnell was going to meet with her this evening and try to find someone in the district attorney's office in the morning to see what they were basing the charge on. He had hoped my call was the attorney. I said I wouldn't tie up the line and that I wanted to know if the attorney had contacted him and to see how he was holding up. I told him I'd head to Nashville in the morning.

The temperature was still pleasant so I managed to commandeer the next to last vacant patio table. I wasn't nearly as obsessed about arriving early as Charles was, yet it was still fifteen minutes before I was to meet Barb. Since I'd moved to Folly, the restaurant had had three names and even more owners. Rita's had undergone a major remodel a few years ago, and featured one of Folly's most attractive outdoor seating areas, and arguably the best location on the island. It faced Center Street and the Sand Dollar, Folly's iconic bar; was directly across Arctic Avenue from the Folly Pier; and, catty-corner from the Tides, a nine-story hotel. The restaurant was often filled with conventioneers dressed in their best beachwear, sharing the patio with groups who had come directly from the nearby beach and were surf-attired in bathing suits and cover-ups.

I felt guilty. Charles was hundreds of miles away worrying about his girlfriend sitting in a jail cell and wondering when, or if, she would ever walk the sidewalks of her dream city as a free woman, while I was sitting on the patio, sipping a chardonnay, and watching a steady stream of people strolling along the sidewalks, and waiting to have a pleasant dinner with an interesting, attractive woman.

I saw Barb walking this way from her large condo complex on the far side of the hotel. She had on one of her trademark red blouses and tan shorts. She had gone home and changed for supper while I was sitting here in the same faded-blue polo shirt and shorts I'd worn all day.

I opened the patio gate so Barb wouldn't have to walk through the restaurant. She thanked me with a kiss on the cheek.

"Thanks for the invite," she said, as she sat and looked for the server. "I wasn't looking forward to cooking tonight. Today's been a bear."

"Grizzly or Teddy?"

She chuckled. "Folks talk strange here. Whatever bear it is when I've been as busy as a ticket-taker at a Bruce Springsteen concert."

"And you think we talk strange," I joked. "That'd be a black bear."

"I'll add that to my Folly vocab." Her smile faded. "Any news on Heather?"

I shared my conversation with Charles. She said she was glad the attorney was on it, and we glanced at the menu before Barb ordered the seafood Cobb salad, which explained her thinness; I ordered a burger, which by one look at me said it was my favorite food at Rita's.

"Speaking of Folly vocab," I said.

"Is that what we were speaking about?"

"Before food ordering got in the way. Have you seen Dude lately?"

Dude is Barb's half-brother and was as opposite of her as a duck was to a dandelion. He owned the surf shop, one of the island's most successful businesses. They had little contact during her years practicing law and had come back in her life when he suggested she move to Folly where she could escape her past. He had been wrong about that. It nearly got her killed a few months ago, when she crossed paths with her past. The best thing that had come from the traumatic events was Barb had reconnected with Dude and I got to know her.

"He stops in the store occasionally. I love him to death, but we don't have much in common, and as you know, his conversational skills are only exceeded by his ability to flap his arms and fly."

Dude was known to murder, mangle, and shred the English language, or as Charles had said, "The old surfer had never met a sentence he couldn't screw up." To Dude's credit, he would also never use twelve words ten words when one would do—almost. Understanding him was an acquired skill.

Barb was in a cheerful mood, one that was appreciated after what I had been dealing with. After what seemed like only minutes, I realized the sun had set and most of the tables around us had changed occupants. It was Tuesday and open-mic night at Cal's so I asked Barb if she wanted to go. She said she'd never been in Cal's, which didn't surprise me, and that she'd love to, which was a surprise.

The good thing about Folly's main business, restaurant, and bar district was it would fit inside the Georgia Dome with room left over for a cattle ranch. Barb and I walked two blocks to Cal's and were greeted by the smell of fries and sounds of a long-haired, tat-covered, forty-year old standing behind an antique mike on the stage singing a passable version of John Anderson's "Would You Catch a Falling Star."

Cal's wasn't nearly as crowded as Rita's, and we had no trouble grabbing a table against the wall.

Barb looked around. "Retro."

I waved toward the furnishings. "Yard sale."

Cal arrived at the table at the same time, tipped his sweat-stained Stetson at Barb. "Chris, I see you managed to lasso the most fetching bookstore owner on Folly for a night of good singing and hospitality." He smiled and tipped his hat again in case Barb missed it the first time. "Welcome Miss Barb. First drink's on the house."

Barb returned his smile. The singer belted out "Okie from Muskogee," and Barb said, "Only bookstore owner."

"You'd still be fetching even if there were fifty bookstores. What's your medicine?"

"Got Corona?"

"Miss Barb, I'm from Texas. We fought a war many moons ago so we wouldn't have to be drinking Mexican beers. How about a Bud?"

Barb grinned. "My second choice."

"Good, because it's all I got. Gotta introduce a girl singer. Be back in a jiff."

Cal headed to the mike and Barb turned to me. "A character, isn't he?"

I watched Cal thank the singer for sharing his talents and called for the next in line to head to the stage.

"Never heard him call anyone fetching. You must've charmed the crooner."

"He's been in three times asking if I have songbooks. Gave him the same answer each time. Seems like a nice fellow."

"One of the best."

"Ladies and gentlemen," Cal's Texas accent blared through the sound system. "Put your hands together and welcome one of the finest gal singers around. Edwina."

The bar was about one-third full so the applause for the newest aspiring star didn't quite reach deafening proportions. It didn't stop her from covering Tammy Wynette's "Stand by Your Man."

Cal returned with Barb's second-choice beer and a chardonnay for me.

Barb looked at the stage and leaned close to Cal. "Is she really one of the finest singers around? She sounds okay, not great."

"She's not bad," Cal faced the stage and said. "She's only been in once or twice and is far better than most. I say they're all *fine* singers when I introduce them. It's the only good thing most of them ever hear about their singing coming from someone other than tone-deaf relatives. It takes guts standing up there and a good word won't hurt any of them." He turned back to Barb. "What're you doing out with this old codger?"

Asked Cal, who was four years older than this old codger, and Barb was only a couple of years younger than I.

She punched Cal in the forearm. "Figured he needed someone to lean on after the long walk over. You know how old folks are."

Cal saw more humor in it than I did.

The Tammy Wynette imitator finished "Stand by Your Man," and moved right into Lea Ann Womack's "I Hope You Dance."

Cal leaned over and put his arm on Barb's hand. "Better drink it up quick and get another one."

"Why?"

"Next guy up. Good country songs are played with only a few chords. He's so bad, I call him *discord*; not to his face, of course. Don't say I didn't warn you."

She patted his hand. "Think I'll have another Bud."

"Wise decision, Miss Barb."

Barb watched Cal head to the cooler and leaned against my shoulder. "Bet he was a charmer back in his day."

"He thinks his day's still here."

She squeezed my arm. "Don't think so."

"At least he was right about you being fetching."

"Thank you," she said, and "Thank you," the singer said, after Cal introduced him as David, "one of the finest guy singers around." He went into his version of "Behind Closed Doors." He will never be confused with Charlie Rich, nor will he get rich from his singing.

Cal returned with our drinks and we listened to David struggle through two songs, before Barb said it had been a long day and she had listened all the *finest singers* she could stomach.

I walked her to her condo. She thanked me for the escort home, gave me a lingering hug, a kiss on the cheek, and said we needed to do it again. I said I'd like that.

My phone rang while I was on my way down the stairs. I stumped my toe on the next step as I glanced at the screen and saw it was Charles.

"So, here's the story," he said. There was no one around and I sat on the last step leading to the parking area under the condos.

For several years, I had been on a futile campaign to encourage my friends to start phone conversations with openings like, "Hello," or "Hi, Chris." I might as well have been trying to teach them how to build a nuclear reactor with LEGOS.

"Let's have it," I said, in the spirit of his opening statement.

"The whole thing sucks."

"Okay." Clarification would follow—I hoped.

"I talked with the attorney?"

"Public defender or Sean's friend?"

"Darnell G. Edelen, Sean's friend, thank God. He met with Heather and talked to the district attorney. It sucks, Chris."

"What did he learn?"

"Heather's gun killed him."

"You're right, that sucks."

Charles sighed. "There's more. They have a witness who saw her arguing with Starr the night he was killed."

"Is the witness positive?"

"Almost. The cops showed him photos of several women, including some of Starr's clients, and he picked Heather."

"Where were they arguing?"

"In a bar in an old warehouse a couple of blocks from the action on Broadway. The witness tends bar there. Edelen says he doesn't think he has a chance at getting her bail, something about Heather being a flight risk, not being in Nashville long, and her record." He hesitated. "Chris, she's not going to get out."

"What can I do?"

"Come back. Please."

I reminded him I was leaving in the morning.

"Thank you," he mumbled, and then dead air.

I detoured from my path home and returned to Cal's to see if he wanted to go with me. He was on stage introducing another *fine singer*.

"Come back to pick up another chick? One's not enough?" Cal said as he waved to the near empty room. "Past bedtime for old gals who'd be attracted to you."

"Funny." I told him about Charles's call and asked if he wanted to return to Nashville.

He said he would, but didn't want to ask Burl to man the bar again. He said the preacher had done a good job, although he didn't bring quite the country flavor the bar needed. Cal said he was afraid some of his "serious sinners" stayed away because of having to buy beer from a preacher and they were his "biggest booze buyers." He made me promise to call every day with the lowdown.

1 6

The distance from Folly Beach to Nashville was identical whether Cal was in the car or not, yet with only my satellite radio to entertain me, it felt about seven thousand miles farther. It didn't help that I was awake most of the night. I saw too many hours on my clock as I tossed, turned, and wondered if Heather was guilty. And if she wasn't, how was her gun, the gun that none of us knew she had, the murder weapon? All I concluded was that trying to think at three in the morning was futile.

Somewhere on the west side of Asheville, I remembered something that could have explained her gun being the murder weapon. When we had been outside the Bluebird, someone had loaned Heather a guitar. She told the man to put it in Charles's car and he wouldn't need a key because the lock was broken. I suppose someone could have taken her gun, shot Starr, and returned the weapon to the unlocked car. If true, how would the killer have known about the gun and broken lock?

A hundred miles later, my mind wandered from the road and the radio, and I rehashed my overnight thoughts about someone identifying Heather arguing with Starr. If they'd been arguing, it still didn't prove she'd killed him, yet Heather had denied seeing Starr that night. If she argued with him, wouldn't she have admitted it? Could the bartender have been mistaken? Could Charles and I find the bartender and see how sure he was?

To say I was exhausted when I knocked on Charles's door would be an understatement. I was tired, my eyes felt like if they had to look at another Interstate sign they would beg for cataracts, and my arthritic hands ached from gripping the steering wheel. I thought I was in bad shape until I saw Charles. His long-sleeve, gray Vanderbilt T-shirt had a pancake-sized mustard stain on the front and his shorts looked as though he'd slept in them. His hair, never poised for a model shoot, looked like a mouse had taken up residence. His eyes were red and his expression would have made a Basset Hound look gleeful.

I wrapped my arms around my friend and felt his body go limp. I helped him to the couch. He sat, put his head down, and tears rolled down his cheeks. I moved beside him and didn't say anything. I felt helpless. He sat motionless for fifteen minutes. The sounds of traffic three stories below and someone walking in the apartment directly above us, broke the silence.

"Chris, she killed him." He didn't raise his head.

"You can't be certain."

He glanced at me. "She did it."

"What makes you so sure?"

He slowly stood and walked to the window. "She's not the Heather I fell in love with."

"In what way?"

"You know she's always been as strange as a drunken, red-eyed tree frog. She was always a loveable goofball, and as sweet as a Hershey bar floating in a bowl of maple syrup." He paused. "No more."

I had no idea how strange a red-eyed tree frog was much less a drunken one. I was aware of Heather's loveable quirks, and knew when Cal and I were here, she was moody and angry. Was that all he was talking about? Moody and angry don't equal murder.

"How so?"

He continued to stare out the window. "You know how depressed she was when you were here, and she was being good because she had company. Before you got here and after you left she was in a funk. She seldom slept and was up all hours."

That was still nothing that would make her a killer. "Anything else?"

Charles returned to the couch and looked everywhere but at me. "She left the apartment several times and was gone for hours. Day and night. Never knew where she went, and when I asked, she stomped around and wouldn't say. I also heard her on the phone with her friends, the ones who were supposed to be represented by Starr. I couldn't hear what the other person was saying, but Heather moaned, groaned, and bemoaned how Starr had screwed them. How he was the incarnate of evil." He faced me. "I heard her telling one of the friends, I'm not sure which one, that something needed to be done. She was furious."

"You think she meant killing him?"

He hesitated and nodded. "Yeah."

"You know her better than I do. We know she was angry with Starr. Doing something about it doesn't mean shooting him. She could've meant going to the Better Business Bureau or reporting him to some agency that regulates what he does. When we get mad we often say things we don't mean."

"You didn't hear the way she was talking. You didn't see the hate in her eyes. She did it, Chris."

After the long drive, I needed to stretch my legs and thought it would do Charles good to get out of the apartment. I suggested a walk.

He looked around the room like he had something to do there. He finally said it might help. He grabbed his cane, smoothed his hair back with his fingers. "Where are we going?"

I said nowhere in particular and suggested we get some fresh air.

He whispered, "Whatever."

The neon lights from the downtown bars gave the appearance of an amusement park rather than a city street. The sounds of country music ranging from traditional country, bluegrass, and contemporary country, which sounded more like rock, leaked out of the bars and restaurants and often melded into conflicting beats. Charles, the consummate observer of people, began to relax as he watched the steady stream of tourists jamming the sidewalks.

We'd walked three blocks when I remembered that Charles said the witness who claimed to have seen Heather arguing with Starr worked in a bar a couple of blocks off Broadway.

"Charles, do you remember where the bar was where someone saw Heather with Starr?"

He stopped in the middle of the sidewalk and a man carrying a guitar case stepped on his heel. Charles said, "Sorry," and the musician said the same and went on his way. He reminded me of Heather doing the same thing on her quest for stardom. I hoped the man had better luck.

Charles reached in his pocket and pulled out a folded piece of paper. "Notes I took when talking to her lawyer," he explained. "Let's see. Yeah, the Top Tan, no, Top Ten Bar, three blocks off Broadway." He looked around and pointed to the opposite side of the street from his apartment. "That way. The bartender's name's Rod, umm, can't read my writing on his last name. Doesn't matter, bartenders don't need last names."

"Let's get a drink."

The festive sights and sounds on Broadway faded as we walked the three blocks. Lively, music-filled venues gave way to an empty lot, a medical supply house, and a vacant ware-house with a for sale sign in front that looked like it had been there forever. The Top Ten Bar was in a deteriorating brick building with the name Top Ten painted on the brick. It didn't get its name for being one of Music City's top ten watering holes.

We stepped in the cave-like dark building and once my eyes adjusted to the near-black environment, I was surprised how large it was. In its previous life, it must've been a storage building or factory. The structure wasn't wide, but was deep. A rustic bar was along the back wall and we had to walk past fifteen tables before reaching it. I thought Cal's Bar had seen its better days, but it was ultra-modern by Top Ten standards. This place's better days hadn't been in the last twenty years. I was also surprised to see how many customers there were. It was nowhere near the constant flow of visitors to the city, but there must have been fifty people enjoying libations and the rock music blasting from the speakers.

There were nine bar stools in front of the waist-high bar; three were occupied. The bartender had his back to us and was pulling beers out of a large cooler. We sat at the stools farthest from the three men and Charles swiveled back toward the tables we had passed on the way to our seats.

"Why in holy Hell would Heather have been here with Starr? For that matter, why would Starr have been hanging around this dungy place?"

I was wondering the same thing and told him I didn't know.

The beanpole-thin, six-foot-tall, mid-thirties bartender gave the beers from the cooler to a bored looking, middle-aged woman who appeared to be the sole server. He came over and asked what we needed. Charles said Budweiser and since I didn't figure there was an extensive wine list, I said white wine. He brought the drinks and said his name was Rod and for us to yell if we needed anything. Charles sat up straight and started to say something. I grabbed his arm and turned to the bartender. "Thanks, we will."

Rod left to do bartender things, and Charles leaned closer.

"Why'd you stop me? I was going to make him say he was lying about Heather."

I looked at Rod who was at the far end of the bar and turned to Charles. "That's why I stopped you. We can't come off strong or he'll clam up. Give it a few minutes, order a second drink, and we'll strike up a conversation."

I sipped my drink and wondered what possible motive Rod could have for lying about Heather. Charles, as impatient as an expecting father in a maternity ward, huffed, took a gulp of beer, and said, "Drink fast."

I patted him on the shoulder and swiveled the barstool so I could get a better look at the rest of the room. The customers at the tables closest to us were in their thirties or forties. They were casually dressed and several shared something on their tablet computers with their tablemates. A few of them wore headsets attached to laptops. They didn't look like salespeople but seemed to be working. I squinted to see the rest of the people in the room but it was near impossible. The room was dark and a couple of the overhead lights were burned out making many of the customers silhouettes.

Charles finished guzzling his beer and waved for Rod to bring another. Impatience at its finest. Rod returned with a Bud for Charles and although I hadn't asked for it, another wine for me. The three men from the other end of the bar left cash on the counter and told Rod they'd see him later. He waved bye, took off his glasses and threw them on the back bar. He wiped his face with the towel he had over his shoulder, and said, "I hate those damned things. Sweat and eyeglasses don't mix."

Charles said, "Know what you mean, Rod."

To my knowledge, Charles had never worn glasses. In addition to impatience, he had an innate ability to mimic those around him, putting them at ease, and getting them to talk about things they wouldn't think of telling their priest. Heather had once said, "Chuckie would make a chameleon turn whatever color envy is with envy."

"This is our first time in," I said to break the ice. "Looks busy."

"Welcome. Music biz?"

"Tourist visiting my friend." I tilted my head toward Charles. "Most of your customers in the music industry?"

"Mostly." Rod wiped his eyes again. "Back of the house guys: production, engineers, songwriters." He chuckled. "Not quite Blake Shelton's go-to drinking spot."

"Why here?" Charles asked.

Rod put his elbows on the bar and lowered his voice. "They can get away from the tourists on Broadway—no offense—and far enough away from Music Row to be able to let their hair down, sip a brew, and get work done while doing it, without the suits looking over their shoulder."

Charles shook his head. "Was Kevin Starr one of your regulars?"

Rod gazed at the counter, frowned, and looked at Charles. "Tragic about what happened. Was he a friend?"

"Nah. Met him a time or two."

Rod leaned closer to us. "He was here right before he was killed."

"Wow," Charles said. "That had to feel weird."

"What's weirder, he was with the gal who killed him."

Charles hands balled into fists.

"How do you know?" I said before Charles could climb over the bar and grab Rod's throat.

Someone at a nearby table hollered for more beer. Rod said he'd be back.

"You hear what he said?" Charles said through gritted teeth.

"Yes, but we knew that. Stay calm. Let's see what else he has to say."

Charles sighed, relaxed his fingers, and nodded.

Rod returned. "Sorry about that. Waitresses are getting sorrier and sorrier, and that's if they show up at all. Where was I?"

"You were telling us how you knew the person with Starr killed him," I said before Charles went off on a tangent.

"The police figured it out. They knew Kevin was in here before he was shot. Suppose I was the last person who saw him alive—other than that gal. The cops came in with a fistful of photos, those publicity shots singers pass out. Some of them looked almost alike, real young, big smiles, long hair. Two were older, not as old as you, but maybe in their forties, maybe fifty."

Now I was ready to strangle him. "One of them was the person who was with Starr?"

"Yes sir. They were sitting back there, that table on the side of the room." He pointed to a table at the far corner of the room where three men were focused on a laptop.

"Did you talk to her?" I asked.

"No, it was crowded when they got here and the waitress got herself sick and went home leaving me with a crowd. Most of my customers are regulars and understood so they came up here when they needed drinks so I didn't have to leave the bar. Kevin got their drinks."

"You're certain it was the woman in the photo?"

"Looked like her. Why are you asking so many questions?"

Charles glared at Rod. "I'm—"

"We're curious," I interrupted. "It was good talking to you. How much do we owe?"

He told me and I paid and said we'd better be going. Charles gave me one of his patented evil looks and followed me to the exit. Sunlight assaulted my eyes and I had to squint to let them adjust from the darkness.

Charles barked, "Why didn't you let me make him say it wasn't Heather?"

"That's her attorney's job. You saw how dark it was. When we were sitting at the bar and he pointed to the table where Starr and Hea—where Starr and whoever he was with were. Could you tell much about the guys in there today?"

"Not really."

"He said he never went to their table and Starr went to Rod for their drinks, so he never got a close look at the woman."

Charles looked at me and back toward Top Ten. "He also hates his glasses and probably didn't have them on."

"It wouldn't do any good for us to try to get him to change his story. He has nothing to gain by lying. He saw what he thinks he saw. If Heather's attorney is half as good as Sean says he is, he'll tear Rod's testimony to shreds. If Rod sticks to his story, because Heather was there arguing with Starr, it doesn't mean she killed him."

We were back on lower Broadway, surrounded by groups of people walking, and smiling as they listened to sad songs coming from multiple bars.

"Nothing personal," Charles said. "This ain't as much fun as it is with Heather. Let's go home."

We were headed up the steps to the apartment when Charles stopped. "Chris, I can't shake it. I'm afraid she's guilty."

"I know. We can't give up. Until I hear her confess, I'm assuming she's innocent. Let's say we find out who did kill him?"

Charles asked an excellent question before we had settled in the apartment. "How are we going to find the killer?"

Since I had known him, he prided himself on being an amateur detective. He'd considered doing it as a career until he learned he would have to have formal training and spend years apprenticing under a licensed investigator. He said that seemed like overkill and he had received years of "observational train-ing" watching a plethora of TV detective shows and reading novels written by Agatha Christie, Arthur Conan Doyle, and Erle Stanley Gardner. His detective career was mainly in his warped brain, although he and I had stumbled upon several untimely deaths and through luck, and being at the right place, or one could argue, wrong place at the right time, had helped the police. He kept forgetting we nearly lost our lives more than once in the process.

Charles had usually been the first person who suggested, or demanded, we get involved in what should have been none of our business. Today, he was reluctant to, or incapable of, pursuing what had occurred. His surprising belief she was guilty clouded his need to prove otherwise. Charles and Heather meant too much to me to let that happen.

When he asked how we could find the murderer, I hesitated, and said, "Motive. We know Heather had a motive. He also agented other people Heather knew. Wouldn't they have the same reasons?"

"Yes, but they didn't have the murder weapon in their car."

I stood at the window and looked down at Charles's Toyota. "Your door lock's broken so anyone could have taken it out, shot him, and returned it."

"I guess," he said, with little enthusiasm.

"If Cal's right, Heather and all of Starr's other clients paid too much for their demos. Let's find out who the others were. Do you have the name of the studio where she cut the demos?"

Charles went in the bedroom and brought back Heather's business card folder and began thumbing through it. "Crap."

"What?"

"The card's not here."

"Can you find the building?"

"Maybe."

I reached for my Tilley. "What are we waiting for?"

"You mean now?"

"Why not?"

"What if it's not open?"

"What else do we have to do?"

Charles shrugged, grabbed his hat and cane, and followed me out.

He drove since he thought he knew how to get to the studio. The trip to the Music Row area of Nashville was only a couple of miles from the apartment. Because of a wrong turn and a one-way street going the wrong direction, it took us twenty minutes to find what we were looking for.

The studio was a bungalow style house on Eighteenth Avenue South. If it wasn't for the tiny *DK Studios* sign in the front yard, it could have been a well-kept middle-class brick house in most any city. The front yard was manicured and had three large landscape areas with shrubs and annuals which displayed their summer blooms.

We stepped on the wide front porch and I noticed something else that set it apart from most residences. There was a speaker box next to the door and a note under it that said to push the button and do not knock. There was a security camera looking down at us from the ceiling like a raptor eying a squirrel.

Charles saw me reading the sign "Noise from knockin' can mess with recording in here."

I looked at him.

He pointed to the door. "That's what the guy told me."

He pushed the button and was rewarded by a female voice asking if she could be of assistance. Charles said who he was, looked at the camera, and pointed at me and said I was his friend. He reminded her he had been there with Heather Lee.

The voice said, "One moment please."

I don't know the definition of moment, though I knew it should have been fewer than ten minutes, the time it took for the door to open.

We were greeted by a short, to be kind, full-bodied woman with long, stringy, gray hair, around my age. "Sorry for the delay. Got a phone call from one of our famous clients. Sorry, can't disclose her name. You know how stars are. Think they come first. I'm Dale, by the way."

I wondered if she said that to everyone who comes to her door so she can convey the feel of success. Regardless, she invited us in and pointed toward what once had been a living room. A residential couch and chairs had been replaced by what looked like used office furniture. Four side chairs bookended two tables holding copies of *Rolling Stone*, *Billboard*, and *Country Weekly*.

"Let me see if my husband's finished with his session so he can join us."

She was gone before she gave us a chance to respond. The most recent magazine was a year old and decades newer than anything else in the room. Charles shared that the studio was in the basement and they used the rest of the rooms for their offices and place for artists to rest while waiting to record. I heard several voices coming from the back of the house and a door slam. Dale returned followed by a man about her age. He was a few inches taller than Dale. What little hair he had left looked like it had been waxed with black shoe polish, and his face was pale like he had spent his life in a recording studio or a cave.

He introduced himself as Kelly Windsor, the *much worse half* of DK Studios. We smiled like we were expected to and Charles reintroduced himself and told them who I was and that I was visiting from South Carolina. We returned to our chairs and Dale and Kelly sat opposite us.

"Heather Lee, Heather Lee," Kelly said. "Remind me again who she is."

Charles frowned like he thought, *who could possibly not remember Heather Lee?* He held his thoughts and told Kelly that Heather recorded a demo there a few months ago. "Kevin Starr set it up. He's her agent."

Kelly leaned forward, his face turned red, Dale put her hand on his forearm, glanced at him before turning back to Charles. "Mr. Starr sends numerous singers to cut demos. I do believe I remember, Ms. Lee." She described her.

Charles nodded.

Dale said, "Starr—"

"Ms. Lee," Kelly interrupted, "had a rather distinct sound. If I remember correctly, she was here for our standard demo package with an electric guitar, bass, acoustic guitar, and drums. That's all I recall."

Dale's face had returned to an ashen pale. "What about her?"

Perhaps word of Starr's demise hadn't reached DK Studios. I turned to the Windsor's. "Are you aware Kevin Starr was found dead the other morning?"

Dale gasped and put her hand in front of her mouth.

Kelly made a slight nod and said, "Murdered, no doubt."

"Why?" I asked and noted that I hadn't said murdered.

Kelly said, "Because it's long overdue."

Dale said, "Now dear, that's terrible. What happened?"

"And what's it got to do with us?" Kelly said. "Why ask about this Lee person?"

Saddened about the death would be the opposite of how I'd describe Kelly's reaction. "Why do you think it was overdue, Mr. Windsor?"

"Call me Kelly, please."

"Kelly, what was wrong with Kevin Starr?"

He glanced at his wife and to Charles and me. "Let me make some guesses. Stop me if I'm wrong."

Charles started to speak I held out my hand and told Kelly to continue. I didn't want to cloud whatever he had to say with the thought Heather may be involved.

"First, I don't remember her well. I'll say Heather Lee wasn't from around here. I'd guess Starr 'discovered' her singing in some out of the way place and told her he'd like to be her agent. She moved to Nashville to follow her dream. Starr told her he needed a demo to get her 'unique vocal styling'—punctuated with air quotes—in front of the big recording companies. And, oh yeah, the demo would only cost a few thousand bucks." He paused and stared at Charles. "How am I doing?"

"Not bad," I said. "I take it Heather wasn't the first to go down that path."

"My friends," Dale said, "it's a path so worn and bumpy you couldn't ride a bike down it." She waved her hand around the room. "As you can see, DK Studios is not one of what would be considered Nashville's biggest or most-prestigious recording venues. Our bread-and-butter is demo recordings and an occasional limited pressing product. We've owned the building for years and keep our expenses down." She looked at Kelly, smiled, and once again put her hand on his arm. "Kelly gets riled when Kevin Starr's name comes up. Don't get us wrong, we're sorry he's dead, hmm, for more reasons than one."

"What are they?" Charles said, asking the kind of question only he can get away with.

Dale shook her head. "We are saddened by the premature death of anyone."

Kelly's face turned red, and he blurted, "The bastard owes us seven-thousand dollars."

"Why?" Charles asked, again skating on thin ice.

"Seven demo sessions he never paid for plus two big-ticket sessions, six musicians, hours of post-production, need I go on?"

Charles asked, "So you didn't get Heather's twenty-nine hundred bucks?"

Kelly laughed, not an ounce of humor oozed from his mouth. "Do you know what we charge for our standard demo package?"

Until a few seconds ago, I thought I had. I shook my head.

Kelly said, "Seven hundred twenty-five dollars. That beats most studios in town. In other words, not only did we not get what Starr charged her, but we never even got our paltry fee. Bet there was a line of wannabes waiting to kill the basta…the agent. I hope he had a whale of a life insurance police. Maybe we can get our money that way."

I asked, "Do you often let your customers build up such a large debt?"

"No. Our sessions were light and Starr had several artists lined up. He said he had a deep-pockets backer and he'd clear up the debt at the end of the month."

Charles asked, "You believed him?"

Kelly started to answer and Dale put her arm in front of him and turned to us. "Why are you here? Does Ms. Lee have something to do with Mr. Starr's death?"

I waited for Charles to respond. He looked at me.

I said, "Heather Lee has been arrested for his murder."

Kelly grinned. "Good for her."

"I'm sorry to hear that," Dale said as she stared at Charles. "I take it you and she were close."

Charles mumbled, "We're engaged."

"Oh," Dale said. She leaned close to Charles.

"We're trying to find out who else may have had motive to kill him," I said, like it was the most logical thing we could be doing.

Kelly said, "Too many to count."

"I've known Heather Lee for a long time," I said. "I don't believe she killed Starr." I paused and waited for Charles to pitch in. He didn't. "We came to ask if you could give us the names of Starr's other clients who recorded demos here. We'd like to talk to them and see if they knew anyone who would have been angry enough to kill him."

Dale's expression hardened. "Since this is a police matter, and you're close to the accused murderer, perhaps we shouldn't be talking with you. Our attorney would frown on it. I'm sorry we can't be more help."

Dale stood, nearly pulled Kelly out of his chair, and started walking to the door.

We had exceeded our welcome.

We walked to the car, and Charles stopped and looked back at the studio. "Don't know about Starr's clients, I now do hereby park those two at the top of my suspect list."

From what they, especially Kelly, had said, it would have been hard to argue with my friend. Kelly appeared angry enough to do it. Also, Kelly had said murder even though I'd only said Starr was dead. It seemed they had two things working for them being guilty. Seven thousand dollars would have been a chunk of change for what appears to be a struggling business. So first, how would they have had a chance to get paid from a corpse? Second, and the most difficult to explain, was how would they have known about Heather's gun, Charles's broken door lock, and how to get and return the gun to the car?

I shared my misgivings as we sat in the car. "Don't forget," Charles said, "Kelly said he hoped Starr had a large insurance policy. He would have killed Starr figuring the only way he could get his money was from that."

I conceded that point and asked how he figured the studio owners knew about Heather's gun and Charles's broken lock.

"Don't know, but they did."

I didn't remind him that hours earlier he'd been convinced of her guilt. Since I didn't think she was guilty, I wanted to push on with our unauthorized and amateurish investigation. Kelly and Dale didn't give us a list of Starr's clients, but we knew two of them.

"Charles, what're the names of Heather's friends from the Bluebird?"

"Gwen Parsons and Jessica something. Good point, they were both pissed at Starr. I think Gwen even said something about wanting to conk him in the head."

"Was she the one who left with Heather after their performance when we were there?"

"No, that was Jessica."

"Where we can find them?"

He didn't know. "Their phone numbers should be at the apartment.

Charles found Gwen and Jessica's numbers in Heather's note-book. He left a message for Gwen, had talked to Jessica, and we were on our way to meet her where she was a server at a Cracker Barrel near the Opryland Hotel.

We had maneuvered through the maze of items ranging from pottery, candy, clothing, and thousands of other knickknacks with our goal being to reach the nostalgia-bathed restaurant's hostess station, when Jessica appeared at our side.

"Got a fifteen-minute break. Let's go outside."

She had her arm through Charles's arm before he could get to a revolving book rack and was leading him out. I followed them past the row of rocking chairs, and around the side of the build-ing. Jessica was puffing on a cigarette as soon as we reached a shaded spot and a paint-chipped bench at the employees break area. She was not the only smoker who worked there. The ground was littered with butts and the smell of smoke hung in the air even though no one else was nearby.

"How's Heather holding up? Can she get bail? I feel terrible about telling those horrible detectives I left her the night he was killed. I figured I must've set them sniffin' after her. OMG, I feel sick about it." She took a deep breath and another drag on her cigarette.

She was so hyper I didn't know what question to answer first or if she would hear or understand them. Charles didn't have any reservations. "She's miserable and won't get out unless we find who killed Starr. Do you know who did it?"

I wouldn't have been that direct, although it did cut through a lot of other questions.

She looked toward the front of the building, lit another cigarette, and looked at her watch. "Heather."

That wasn't the answer I'd hoped for. "Why do you think that?"

"God, I hate to say this. I had to tell the cops, you know. She said she'd like to kill him. Honest, she did. She said it to me after we left the Bluebird." She lowered her head. "I hated to tell them. Honest to God."

I glanced at Charles who had closed his eyes.

I asked, "Was she serious or letting off steam?"

"I don't know. Like how do you know for certain if someone means something? She had hateful feelings about him, you know."

Charles tapped his cane on the ground. "So, did you?"

Jessica had started to her mouth with the cigarette, hesitated, and glared at Charles. "What are you saying?"

"We're not saying anything," I said trying to diffuse the situation enough to keep her talking. "We're trying to figure out what happened."

"Good luck with that one. He had a whole shit-pot full of people who wanted him dead. I don't think any of them did it. Sure, I was one of them, and I didn't shoot him. Your Heather did. She was pissed. She had the gun. The cops said she was with him before he was shot. Duh." She shook her head. "I've got to get back."

She pivoted, threw her cigarette butt on the ground, and stomped away.

Charles watched her and turned to me and shook his head. "That went well. Any other brilliant plans to get Heather off the hook?"

"When's his funeral?"

"Should be soon if he's not already planted. Why?"

"I thought we might go to the visitation."

"Of that SOB?"

"Unless you have better ideas. If we could talk to widow Starr, she might help."

Charles pointed to my phone. "Look it up on that thingy."

A search of the Nashville area obituaries revealed Kevin Starr's interment was still in the future; tomorrow, in fact. Visitation was to begin in an hour at a funeral home a couple of miles from his house. We were on that side of town and decided we were dressed well enough to stop by. I pulled in the parking lot of the white-painted brick funeral home thirty minutes before visitation was to begin; on time, per Charles.

Gwen Parsons returned my call while we waited. I put the phone on speaker, and after a minute of her expressing sympathy for Heather, I asked if we could meet and talk about Starr. She surprised me when she said no, that she was busy and didn't have time, and she said it after I'd said it could be a time and location of her choice in the next couple of days. I gave up on meeting and asked if she had any idea who killed him. She said there could have been any number of people who wanted Starr dead. She couldn't or wouldn't narrow it down. She wished she could help her "good friend" Heather, but didn't know what she could do. She again said she was sorry, and had to go.

"Quick question," I said and hoped she hadn't hung up. "Who else knew you sold Heather the gun?"

She was silent, and I figured the next sound would be the electronic buzz after a hang up. "You there?"

"Sorry, I was thinking. A lot of people know. It wasn't a big secret. We were at the Bird when I gave it to her, standing out front with a ton of people around. Umm, Jessica was there, so was, oh what's his name, Joey, and two or three other pickers I sort of know." She giggled. "The only guys who didn't know were the fuddy-duddy security guards. Didn't think it would be wise to wave it in front of them."

"Who's Joey?" I asked.

"Some guy letting Heather try his guitar. He's always trying to sell something. Says he needs the money to write songs, calls it plying his craft. Can you believe that?"

I remembered him from our visit to the Bluebird. "Was Starr his agent?"

"Nah, he doesn't have one. He wanted us to introduce him to Starr, but the son of…uh, he never showed up at our gigs."

"Are you sure—"

"Sorry, have to go."

Everything in the funeral home was muted: muted music from the funeral home version of Muzak; muted-color, thick carpeting muted our footsteps, through the muted corridors covered with muted wallcovering. What wasn't muted as we stepped into a viewing room, was the robust fragrance of floral arrangements. I sneezed and told Charles, in muted tones, of course, how much the smell in funeral homes bothered me and how it always got my allergies in an uproar. Charles, being the fount of everything trivial, proceeded to tell me that in the pre-air-conditioned, pre-embalming days, flowers at funerals were to mask the smell of the corpse. I asked him if funeral directors realized those days were long gone and he suggested this would be a good time to ask a funeral director. I said never mind.

Much to my relief, the steel-gray coffin housing Kevin Starr was closed. Open coffins bothered me more than the stench of funeral flowers. The room was near empty. I assumed because the visitation had just begun and people were still at work. A man in his late-sixties asked if we were friends of Kevin. We lied and said yes and he shared that he was Kevin's father. He didn't know any of his son's friends since he lived in California, and told us he was the reason the funeral had been delayed. He had been in Italy and got back in the country last night and flew to Nashville. We listened to his long-winded story until he started telling us about his "holiday" in Tuscany. I interrupted and said it was nice to meet him and that we wanted to pay our condolences to his daughter-in-law.

Sandy was in one of the chairs with a muted geometric pattern on the seat, and talking to a woman who appeared to be about her age. We walked over to them, and Sandy glanced up at us like she recognized our faces but couldn't recall from where. The other lady leaned down and gave Sandy a hug and said she's let her talk to the new arrivals.

The grieving widow stood and held out her hand. She wore a black dress that looked new. It was loose on her shoulders and I suspected was probably bought for her by someone else. Make-up covered most the red around her eyes. I told her who we were and reminded her about the visit to her house.

"Oh yes." Her voice was hoarse and soft. If the room hadn't been so empty, I wouldn't have heard what she said.

Sandy didn't give any indication that she remembered who was with us or that she knew one of the visitors to her house was accused of murdering her husband. I told her we were sorry for her loss. She nodded, and glanced around the room and noticed there was no one waiting to talk to her.

"I'm being rude," she whispered, and pointed to the chairs beside her. "Please have a seat."

I said, "How are the children?"

Charles glanced at me and gave an expression that screamed, "That's not why we're here."

Sandy looked toward the door to the corridor. "They're in a

little room out there where they have toys and books. Kevin's mom's with them."

She continued to look at the door, and hadn't answered my question. Perhaps she was in shock and didn't want to, or couldn't, deal with their condition. If I didn't know it was the same person, I never would have suspected this was the same lady we'd met pounding on red-hot steel in her blacksmith shop.

Sandy turned back to us. "I apologize. This has been rough, and I'm not thinking straight, please tell me again how you know —knew, Kevin."

Charles said, "He met my fiancé when he was at Folly Beach a few months ago. He heard her sing and wanted to be her agent,"

He hadn't used Heather's name.

"Folly Beach," Sandy said like she was rolling the words around in her mouth. "Where's that?"

She still hadn't put two-and-two together and connected us with Kevin's alleged murderer. I explained that Folly Beach was a tiny island near Charleston, South Carolina, and we had met— sort of met—Kevin there.

Sandy looked at me like I'd said we hooked up with her husband on the North Pole. "I'm sorry," she whispered, "I'm confused. Kevin's never been to Charleston, a least not since we met ten years ago."

And she was confused, I thought.

"It was five months ago," Charles said, like that would make things clear.

She shook her head and stared at him.

"He told my fiancé he was staying at the hotel and was meeting with record executives from New York. Think he said it was a retreat. He—"

Sandy pulled her shoulders back and clinched her fists. "I don't know why you think that. It couldn't have been."

I said, "When we met you at your house, you said he was

gone a lot." Today must be horrible for the young widow and I could understand how she may have forgotten. "You mentioned trips to North and South Carolina. Couldn't the trip to Folly have been one of those times?"

"No. I distinctly remember the two trips he made to South Carolina were to Columbia. I remember because that's where one of my best friends in college was from."

I didn't want to argue while she was sitting a dozen feet from her husband's coffin. I was certain I'd seen Kevin Starr in Cal's Bar, on Folly Beach. "I'm a little confused myself. You're certain he hasn't been there?"

"Kevin called me most every night he was on the road. He always talked to the kids if they were awake, and told me where he was." She hesitated, and continued, "He brought them souvenirs from each of the cities he visited. Nothing big, you know, little cheap stuff with the city's name on it." A tear appeared in the corner of her eye. "He did it so they would learn about other places and so … and so they'd want to visit the cities with us when they got older."

When we had been at her house, she'd told us about him calling from the trips. It wasn't many years ago that saying where he had called from would have meant something. Now, with ubiquitous cell phones, his calls could have been from anywhere. I was as certain as I was sitting here, if he called her that often, one or more of them had originated from Folly, regardless what he'd told her.

Sandy wiped the tear from her cheek. Her hands began to fidget, she shredded a tissue, and squeezed it in her fist. It didn't take a psychiatrist to see we had started a conversation she didn't want to be a part of. I started to excuse us when she snapped out of her reverie and glared at Charles.

"What did you say your fiancée's name was?"

"Heather."

Sandy pushed out of the chair, stood and looked down at us.

If she had her blacksmith hammer, I suspected she would have treated us like a lump of molten steel.

"The bitch who killed Kevin?"

A handful of others had arrived while we were talking. All conversation stopped, and Kevin's father started toward us.

"We're sorry to have bothered you," I said and eased Charles toward the exit. The only smell I detected on the way out was that of hate.

"What do you think?" Charles asked. We were driving through rush-hour traffic on the way to the apartment.

"She either had lied to us about knowing he'd been on Folly or he had lied to her."

Charles looked at his imaginary watch and at the traffic stopped in front of us. We had nowhere to be, yet he was in a hurry to get there. He sighed like we were going to be late. "She didn't throw off any vibes she was fibbing. I can't see any reason she would have for not admitting he'd been on Folly."

For the next fifteen minutes, we traveled five blocks in traffic that was more akin to stop-and-stop rather than stop-and-go. We talked about why he may not have been telling her the truth and what it could've meant to getting him killed.

Starr had made several out of town trips looking for talent or doing whatever he could to increase his business, so I didn't understand why he'd lie about being in the Charleston area. Why would it have been different than being in Columbia, or anywhere else? Could he have been having an affair? The simple answer was yes. If true, there could have been two more people who may have wanted him dead: whoever he was having the affair with and the lady we had just left wearing a poorly-fitting black dress. I couldn't see Sandy as the murderer. She was hurting, and her reaction when she found out about Heather hadn't been faked. Besides, no one could have mistaken her for Heather, not even in a dark bar. The person Starr could have been having an affair with was another story. If she was one of Starr's aspiring singers, he probably conned her into moving here and since we had no idea who she might be, she could have looked enough like Heather to have fooled the bartender in a dimly-lit room.

We pulled in the parking lot and Charles once again asked the question for which I had no reasonable answer.

"What about the gun?"

"I don't know."

"That's what I thought."

"What I do know is Starr had a reason for lying about being on Folly, a reason which may have gotten him killed. We need to find what it was. We also know the police aren't looking beyond Heather. I need to head home and see what I can learn."

"What time are *we* leaving?"

I told Charles we should leave in the morning. He asked why we couldn't leave now. I asked if he wanted to drive all night; he said on second thought, leaving in the morning was a good idea.

I COULDN'T HAVE BEEN ASLEEP MORE than an hour and wondered why the alarm clock was going off. It took me a few seconds to escape from the sound sleep and to realize I didn't have an alarm clock. It was the phone. By the time I was awake enough to answer, whoever had called had been sent to voicemail.

It was after midnight so whoever had called must have had a good reason for calling. I tapped the voicemail icon.

"Yo, Chris," Cal said. "It's—oh, oh—past your beddy-bye time. Sorry. Anyway, if you get this and aren't going to give me a scolding for calling late, call me back. The number is—hell, you know the number."

I wasn't going to rule out scolding, but knew it had to be important for him to call. I tapped his number.

"Hello," he yelled, above the sound of George Jones

bemoaning something from the jukebox, and a few patrons who sounded like they had consumed a few beers on the other side of sober.

I told him who it was and said it sounded like he was busy. He said something about overflow from a property-managers' convention at the Tides and said he was glad I had called.

"Didn't wake you up, did I?"

I said he hadn't and asked what was so important.

"Think I've figured out something about shyster Starr's trips over this way."

Someone in the background yelled, "Another round, cowboy." I heard other voices but couldn't tell what they were saying.

"You still there, Kentucky?"

I said I was and that I didn't catch what he'd said.

"When're you moseying this way?"

I told him Charles and I were heading to Folly in the morning.

"Hold your jackass," Cal shouted.

I told myself he was talking to a soused property manager and not me.

There was more mumbling in the background and Cal said, "Holler when you unsaddle at your bunkhouse."

I went out on a limb and assumed he meant for me to get with him when we got home. "You got it, pard."

It was another hour before I stopped wondering what he had learned and returned to sleep.

After one Starbucks' stop, a Dunkin' Donuts' detour, and yawns that made the inside of the car sound like a six-a.m. commuter train, Charles and I were on the Interstate headed to Folly Beach.

Between yawns Charles asked, "What do you think Cal wants to tell you?"

"Don't know. He doesn't call often, so it's important."

Charles nodded, took another bite of doughnut, and mumbled, "Maybe you ought to call him."

I explained that Cal didn't get home from work not that long ago. If he wasn't asleep, he should be. It could wait until we got back. Charles said I was right about Cal being asleep and I could wait another couple of hours to call. The *wait until we got back* part slipped past him. I pretended it was a good idea.

The trip was all Interstate and except for several miles of winding roads on each side of Asheville, was easy driving. My age and having made the trip so many times in the last couple of weeks was taking its toll on my aching bones and my posterior. Despite his constant babbling about things trivial and irrelevant, having Charles with me made it go quicker. I would have been less patient if I hadn't suspected he was trying to distract me, as well as himself, from thinking about Heather's problems. He wasn't successful. Several times he repeated his belief she was guilty and wondered how he had fallen for a killer. I still couldn't wrap my arms around her guilt and tried to tell him we would do everything possible to find the real killer. I tried to be convincing, yet wasn't certain he was wrong.

Two hours later, Charles remembered his brilliant idea for me to call Cal. Unless I called, I would hear it repeated each mile marker, so I had him punch in the number. He did and handed me the phone. I got Cal's brief voicemail message and left him an equally brief request to call.

Cal hadn't returned my call when we reached the bridge over the Folly River. I was exhausted and suspected Charles was too, yet he insisted we go to Cal's and find the inconsiderate crooner before doing anything else. I parked a block from the bar in an empty spot in front of Cal's classic Cadillac.

I smiled, albeit an exhausted smile, as I entered Cal's. I felt at home. The aging singer greeted us in his Stetson. In the spirit of Folly, he wore a faded, black Nike golf shirt, yellow shorts, and mismatched tennis shoes. Charles had done better in his orange Clemson University National Champions long-sleeve T-shirt, blue shorts, as he tapped his cane on the worn carpeting. As usual, I was the most boring and least Folly-attired of the three in my light-blue golf shirt and navy shorts. The familiar, welcoming smell of frying hamburgers and seeing Cal made the long, exhausting trip worth it.

There were a couple of dozen others in the bar, a good crowd for a weeknight. I knew several of them and they waved at us. We reciprocated and Charles lit into Cal.

"We called you a thousand times. Got your danged machine. You never called back. We could have been turned upside down on I-26 and you didn't even listen to our messages to save our lives." He paused and took a breath. "Well, what do you say for yourself?"

Cal pushed his hat back and leaned against the bar. "Well, former Folly resident," Cal said in a calm voice he'd perfected during his years entertaining in bars to defuse difficult situations. "Seems to this old-timer that if you were ass up on the side of the road, you would've been better off calling 911 than this old barkeep."

Charles huffed. "Not the point."

I thought it was a good point and hugged Cal and said it was good to be home.

He thanked me, walked behind the bar, got us drinks, and said, "Sorry, Charles, didn't know you called. Must've left my phone in the car. What'd you need?"

Charles smiled. "Apology accepted. Chris wanted to hear what you learned and couldn't wait until we got back to ask."

I must have forgotten that part.

"Think I've got it figured out. It's gonna get Heather off the bucking bronco, and lasso the real killer." He put Charles's beer on the bar, looked around and saw no one was waiting for a drink, "Hang on a sec. Let me get the phone before I forget."

Charles started to object. It wouldn't have mattered since Cal was already headed to the door.

Caldwell Ramsey moved up to the bar and stood beside us. "Hello, Charles, Chris."

"Howdy, Caldwell," Charles said and looked behind the music promoter. "Where's Mad Mel?"

Caldwell nodded toward the empty bar stool. "May I join you?"

I waved for him to have a seat.

He sat and looked at his watch. "Mel should be pulling in to the dock about now. He had a group of college students who wanted to enjoy the marsh, privacy, and a few drinks. I was supposed to meet a client here but she called and said she wasn't going to make it."

"So, you're slummin' with Chris and me."

Caldwell smiled. "I've spent time with worse." His smile disappeared. "Cal told me about Heather—terrible. How's she doing?"

Charles gave a sanitized update on Heather's condition, how she was handling jail, and about her lawyer.

Caldwell leaned his tall, trim body close to Charles, listened, and nodded, before saying in a low voice, "Please let me know if there's anything I can do."

"I will. Thanks for asking. Can we buy you a drink?"

Caldwell looked down at his watch again. "Think I could throw back one more." He looked around the room. "Where's Cal?"

"Went to the car to get his phone," I said. "Should be back soon."

Caldwell smiled. "Suppose I can wait a little longer for my beer."

John Anderson's "Swingin'" blasted from the jukebox and one of the patrons I didn't recognize, accidently elbowed me on his way to the bar. "Excuse me," he said with a beer-breath slur. "Where's the cowboy?"

Charles told him to cool his jets and the bartender would be right back.

Caldwell looked toward the door and at Charles. "Where'd he park, Mt. Pleasant?"

Charles looked at Caldwell, and at the other man who was staggering around waiting for another beer. "Let's check on him. He should've been back."

I wasn't nearly as nosy as Charles, and it felt good to be relaxing at the bar after a day on the road. I followed Charles outside.

We'd parked in front of Cal's car, so we knew where it was.

The area was poorly lit and from a distance everything looked fine; fine except no Cal.

"Where'd he get to?" Charles asked. He stopped and shouted, "Cal!" Charles pointed to a body on the ground beside the car's rear door. I was behind Charles and couldn't see who it was until I recognized our friend's unmistakable attire. Cal was on his stomach and splayed out on the sandy berm. His Stetson was upside down beside his arm and it looked like it had been stomped on. So did Cal's head. His long hair was covered with blood and a trickle of it ran down the side of his face.

I rushed past Charles and bent down to see if Cal was breathing. At first, I didn't think so, until I saw his hand twitch. Charles moved to my side and bent over to get a better view. He asked if Cal was alive. I said barely, and told Charles to run get a medic and a cop. City Hall was across the street from Cal's and housed both its police and fire departments.

Charles rushed off and I kept asking Cal if he could hear me. He didn't respond. I was afraid to move him so I yanked off my shirt and pressed it against the head wound. I prayed an EMT would arrive in time to help. Blood was still oozing from his head, but seemed to be slowing as I kept pressing on the shirt. I hoped it wasn't wishful thinking on my part.

I realized that whoever had hit him could be nearby. I craned my head around while maintaining pressure on his wound. Laughter from a group walking on the other side of the road was all I heard. I didn't see anyone else.

Charles must have made quite a ruckus at the public safety building. Two minutes later, he was back with two EMTs and two police officers. I stood and on wobbly legs stepped aside for the medics to do their thing. One of them asked one of the cops to call for an ambulance. He said he already had. The other police officer pulled Charles and me away from the life-saving efforts and asked what had happened. We said we wouldn't be much help and explained how we had been with Cal in the bar when he left to get his phone out of his car. Officer Kasper took our names, contact numbers, and told us a detective would be contacting us in the morning. He said that was all he needed and waited for us to leave.

I wasn't going to be dismissed. "Is his wallet on him?" Cal always carried an oversized wallet.

Kasper walked over to the paramedic who was watching his partner work on Cal and asked if there was a wallet. The paramedic bent over and felt the back of Cal's pants.

"Don't think so."

The officer shook his head. "Looks like a mugging. Thanks again, gentlemen."

I was polite but firm and told him Cal didn't have any relatives, Charles and I were his good friends, and we weren't going anywhere until he was on his way to the hospital. I also told him we would follow the ambulance. From our vantage point, it didn't appear Cal had moved since we'd found him.

We waited for the ambulance, and I grabbed a clean shirt from my suitcase, before realizing there was no one in charge of the bar. I called Preacher Burl who agreed to play bartender and close for the night. He said he would pray for Cal. I prayed he would be successful. After watching the seventy-two-year-old lay motionless on the berm, I wasn't optimistic.

I had spent so much time at the hospital in Charleston, I should have been given access to the doctor's parking lot and the employee's discount at the restaurant. I'd been here as a patient, and often had visited friends in varying degrees of medical distress. I was never comfortable with the annoying odor of the antiseptic cleaning fluids and the sad sight of sick and injured people in the emergency room.

"When are they going to tell us something?" Charles asked, for a third time. He had stopped pacing the room, and flopped down in a chair.

"When they know something," I said, for a third time.

It had been an hour since the EMTs wheeled our friend through the door into the bowels of the hospital. One of the medics who transported him told us he had a concussion, and had lost a lot of blood. His vitals were adequate, although nothing to brag about. I had asked if Cal would make it and was told it wasn't up to him to say.

Preacher Burl called to ask about Cal, when a middle-aged, overweight doctor with a face that hadn't seen a razor for a few days walked out of the treatment area, looked around, and plodded over to Charles and me. I told Burl I'd call him back and shook hands with the doc. His face didn't give anything away except fatigue.

I explained Cal didn't have any family and we were his best friends. He hesitated before saying anything, but said, "He's fortunate. His skull isn't fractured. His brain's taken quite a jarring. To put it in simple terms, he was hit with a heavy object, maybe a ball bat or piece of wood or metal." He hesitated and rubbed his temples. "The blow caused his brain to rattle around in his head. It bounced off his skull, causing bruising."

Charles stepped closer to the doctor. "Is he conscious?"

The doctor grimaced. "He's mumbling and not making sense. Is he in the music business?"

I said he was a singer and had been for decades.

"Country music?" the doc asked.

I nodded.

"Makes more sense. Mr. Ballew tried to sit up in bed and started talking to someone he called Roy about singing 'Wabash Cannonball.' Then he said something about seeing her in Nashville and how much he missed Patsy." He smiled. "My dad was a big country fan and was always talking about Roy Acuff and Patsy Cline. Figured that may've been who your friend was referring to."

"Is it normal for him to be talking about ancient history?" I asked.

"Not unusual," the doctor said, back in his medical-professional voice. "A head trauma can cause a plethora of distinct and nonlinear reactions within the brain. He may not be able to remember what happened tonight, while he's as clear as day about incidents fifty years ago. It's possible to confuse periods of time."

Charles said, "Will he be okay?"

"His vitals are strong for someone his age. It may take time, but the odds on a full recovery are decent."

"Can we see him?" I asked.

The doctor shook his head. "The fewer distractions he has over the next twenty-four hours the better. He needs to stay calm. Maybe tomorrow afternoon. Leave your number at the desk in case we need to get in touch with you. Sorry about whatever happened."

We thanked him and he headed back to the treatment rooms.

"He's fortunate to be alive," Charles said. "No matter what you say, being hardheaded's a good thing."

"Hardheaded and wearing a Stetson."

"Huh?"

"Did you see his hat? It was crushed; must have taken some of the steam out of the blow. If he didn't have it on, I bet he wouldn't be with us."

"Fortunate," Charles said. He turned his attention to two men entering the room.

One was in a sport coat but with no tie and the other in a white polo shirt. Regardless of their dress, their gait and the way they surveyed the room screamed official, detective official. It also didn't hurt the identification to see each had a holstered firearm attached to his belt. The emergency room was nearly vacant, a rare sight, so the detectives focused on Charles and me.

The one in the sport coat asked, "Are you the ones who found the guy by his car?"

I was irked by his impersonal attitude, and told him yes, we found "Mr. Ballew."

He introduced himself and his partner as detectives from the Charleston County Sheriff's Office, didn't bother to show identification, and said they had a few questions.

The other detective nodded toward the treatment rooms. "He going to make it?"

"The doctor said Mr. Ballew has a good chance of recovering," I said, with an emphasis on Mr. I also told them what the doc had said about visitors in case they'd planned to barge in the treatment room.

"Oh great, now we'll have to wait until tomorrow to talk to him," the first detective said, and hesitated like he had realized how callused he'd sounded. "Glad he's going to pull through. The cops on Folly didn't think he was going to live. They told us what you told them. Let's hear it from you."

"I doubt we can add to what you already know," I said, and repeated what we had told the responding officers.

"Before the vic, umm, Mr. Ballew, left the bar to get his phone, did you notice anyone paying particular attention to him or if anyone left when he did?"

"We hadn't been there long," I said. "I didn't see anyone paying attention to him. Did you, Charles?"

"There was a crowd. Would've been hard to notice anyone in particular."

"Anyone leave when he did?"

Charles rubbed his chin. "Can't say yea, can't say nay."

"So, you didn't see anyone leave?"

Charles glared at the casually-dressed detective. "That's what I said."

Charles had taken great pride in getting along with everyone. Heather's experience with the police was shortening his fuse when it came to law enforcement.

I said, "We didn't see anyone leave. Sorry." I hoped Charles wouldn't say anything else.

"Did he carry large sums of money?"

"Not unless he was taking home the night's revenue," I said. "He was going to the car to get his phone, so I doubt he had much."

"Did he have enemies?" the detective in the sport coat asked.

"Not really," I said. "Everyone got along with him."

"Other than robbery, can you think of any reason someone would want to harm him?"

For a second, I thought about Cal's comment that he had figured something out about Starr's murder. Could it have had something to do with that? I couldn't see how, and didn't want to get into the Heather/Starr situation with the insensitive detectives.

"Not really."

Charles nodded and kept his mouth closed.

The detectives gave us their cards and asked us to call if we thought of anything.

WE RETURNED to the island and swung by Cal's to see if Burl needed help closing. He had shooed the last customer out, finished a cursory clean-up, and was locking the door. We updated him, and thanked him for coming to our friend's rescue. He said he would open the bar tomorrow night, actually tonight, since it was well past midnight. I dropped Charles at his apartment and drove home. My eyes watered from exhaustion and staring at pavement all day.

"What a day," I said to myself as I fell into my familiar bed for the first time in several days. Ride ten hours with my best friend who was in the most depressed condition I had ever seen him in; find Cal motionless on the side of the road; spend two hours in the hospital, a building I had come to hate; and now I lay here, eyes wide open staring at the ceiling faintly illuminated by the green digital numerals from my bedside clock. Yes, what a day.

Did Cal know something about the murder? If he did, how could he have learned whatever it was? Would he recover enough to tell us? Then, why did Starr lie to his wife about where he'd been? Starr had told Heather he had been at the Tides with record executives from New York. That didn't sound like something to keep from his wife. Considering what had happened, I wondered if he'd even been at the hotel.

I didn't think I had, yet apparently, I'd fallen asleep somewhere in my thought process. Otherwise the loud ringtone from my phone wouldn't be waking me up. The green digital numbers I had stared at most of the night, now indicated it was seven thirty.

"Let's take a meeting with Cindy," Charles said. He sounded more enthusiastic than he had in days.

"Huh?" I said, with less enthusiasm.

"Sorry. You're not in the music business. That means let's give a holler out to Cindy and see if she can jabber with us."

Cindy LaMond was Folly's director of public safety, police chief to most everyone else, and top cop to the more verbally challenged. She was also a good friend, married to another friend, Larry LaMond, the owner of Pewter Hardware, Folly's pint-sized hardware store.

"I know what take a meeting means. The *huh* was for why?"

"I was sitting in the living room in the middle of the night and thinking about slime ball Starr and him fibbin' to his wife about being here."

"Not only do great minds think alike, so do mediocre ones."

"Whatever." He continued like I hadn't spoken. "We need to fill her in on what's going on. We need her coppy skills. We've got to get Heather out of that horrid place."

"I was already thinking about calling the chief. Maybe she can learn if Starr was staying at the Tides and who he was meeting. She—"

"So why are you wasting time talking? Call her."

It would have been pointless to tell him it wasn't yet eight o'clock and I would wait until there was a better chance of not getting cussed out by calling so early. I told him I'd let him know as soon as I talked to her.

I reluctantly selected Chief LaMond's number from my contacts list.

"Well, if it isn't trouble's lightning rod," came the chief's way too cheery voice.

I hated caller ID. "Good morning, Chief."

"Don't get all mushy with me. I'm sitting here at my super-duper, big-girl police chief's desk reading a report my officers filed last night. And whose name should appear in big almost illegible print right on this here piece of paper?" I heard paper crinkling in the background. "What in the big pile of pachyderm poop have you stepped in now? Whoa, don't answer. How's Cal?"

Cindy took a breath and I took the gap in her tirade to give her Cal's condition and said I would tell her all about the pile of poop if she'd meet Charles and me at the Dog. She said that's what she lived for and meeting with the two of us was right up there with spending a month in Paris with her hubby. The only Paris she'd ever seen was in her home state of Tennessee. I thanked her for the totally-insincere compliment and we agreed to meet in a half hour.

I called Charles and told him the plan. He told me he'd already figured that out and was on his way to the Dog. I had no desire to get in a car, so I walked the few blocks to the restaurant. It was already hot, and the humidity lingered in the air like smoke from a campfire. I dreaded the walk home. Charles was already there and sitting in my favorite booth in back, and was wearing a black, long-sleeve T-shirt with NYPD in large block letters on the front. It was one of the few T-shirts he owned that didn't have a college name or mascot on the front. He wore the NYPD shirt when he was meeting with the police.

Charles looked at his imaginary watch. "She's not here yet."

Empty seats had already given that away and I reminded my pre-prompt friend it wasn't time.

Charles said, "So?"

Cindy arrived before we had time to debate the merits of being early. The chief was in her early fifties, five-foot-three, with curly dark hair and most often a smile. Her smile was missing this morning. She rolled her eyes and gave a slight shake of the head as she lowered herself in the chair beside Charles.

"Welcome back, stranger," she said and pinched Charles's arm.

He smiled. "Thanks."

Cindy turned to me. "If it weren't for you two, I could lay-off half of my force and save the penny-pinching taxpayers a bundle." My several-year-long crusade to reintroduce civility to personal greetings and introductions continued to fail. "You're going to kill me with all the trouble you trip over. This bod's not meant to work this hard."

Charles patted her on the hand. "Ronnie Reagan said, 'It's true that hard work never killed anyone, but I figure, why take the chance?'"

She shook her head, this time with much more determination. "My crapometer says you and your quotes are full of it."

Charles held his hands out, palms facing Cindy. "Look them up."

"Like I have time, or care. Any news on Cal?"

I told her she knew everything we knew.

She nodded and turned to Charles. "How's Heather?"

Charles gave a brief, canned answer. He didn't delve into how she was adjusting to jail life.

"So, what's so all-fired important that you're going to buy me breakfast?"

Amber arrived at the table with coffee for the chief.

"Don't I get any?" I asked.

She patted my arm like she would a puppy. "Top cop first. You'll get yours soon enough." She leaned over and gave Charles an awkward hug. "Good to see you; sorry about Heather. You okay?"

"Not really."

"Poor baby."

The perceptive server saw Charles wasn't going to say anything else. "I'll get your coffee."

Cindy put her hands around the mug but left it on the table. "What questionable deed are you two hankering for?"

Charles and I tag-teamed her with details of the search of the apartment and car, the police finding the murder weapon in Charles's car, the other clients of Starr who would have had just as strong a motive to kill him, and the couple at the studio where Starr owed a boat-load of money, and details of how Heather had met Starr. We told her about talking with Starr's wife and how she said he'd never been to Folly Beach. And finished with what Cal had said about learning something about Starr being here.

Cindy finally sipped her coffee. "You think it had something to do with his mugging?"

I said, "It may have been robbery. My gut tells me it was something else. Add to that what Starr's wife had said about him not being here, and it seems to me there are too many coincidences."

"Ah, this is where you drag me into your little drama?"

"No wonder you're chief," Charles said. "Brilliant, beautiful, and willing to help citizens in need."

Cindy rolled her eyes. "Charles, now you've gone and blown the top off my crapometer." She turned to me. "What do you need?"

"Check with the Tides and see if Kevin Starr stayed there. Your clout as chief can get information from the hotel that we can't. If he was there, for how long; if he was alone, see if there were guests from New York at the same time, and if so, their names. If someone there remembers him, ask if they remember anything about his stay."

"Like who he was having an affair with?" she added.

Charles said, "Knew we could count on you."

"While I'm at it, why don't I see if Starr's little floozy told anyone at the hotel she planned to steal Heather's gun and kill him with it."

Charles said, "Your thinking's getting gooder and gooder."

Cindy rolled her eyes. "I'll see what I can do."

Charles pointed his cane toward the exit. "Now?"

"No way. I was promised breakfast."

I gave her the approximate dates Starr had been here and she waved for Amber and ordered the most expensive item on the menu. Charles and I ordered the lowest priced meal. For the next forty-five minutes, we ate, Charles relaxed and talked about how Heather was, and told Cindy about Heather's appearances at the Bluebird. Cindy said growing up in East Tennessee her dream was to be a country singer at Dollywood in Pigeon Forge. She said the only thing that held her back was she couldn't sing "worth a bent toothpick."

I thought, but of course didn't say, it hadn't stopped Heather.

Amber slid the check to my side of the table. Charles grabbed it and mumbled, "You're the greatest friend anyone could ever have. I owe you big time."

Cindy grabbed her cell phone and took a photo of Charles and turned to me, "Chris, got the number of the *National Enquirer*? Aliens have done taken over Charles's body."

Charles said, "Ha, ha."

I smiled, and Cindy headed out to make our six-mile-long, half-mile-wide slice of heaven safer.

It hadn't been the twenty-four hours the doc said Cal needed to rest. It didn't stop Charles from insisting we stand outside his hospital room until he *comes to his senses* and tells what he had learned about Starr's murder. The nurse said Cal had improved, was alert, yet he was still vague about recent events. She said the doc allowed two detectives to interview him earlier, and since we were already here, we could see him. She tapped her watch and said we could only stay a few minutes.

"See," Charles said on our way to Cal's door. "Told you he was okay."

I followed Charles into the room. The head of Cal's bed was elevated and he was watching television. His head was wrapped in gauze from his eyebrows up. I didn't need to see that to know he wasn't well. He was watching *HGTV* which was akin to me watching the *Food Channel*. That was proof his mind wasn't functioning properly.

He glanced away from an "incredible" bathroom makeover and grinned. "Hear you two rustled me up and herded me toward this bunk. My hat's off to you if I can remember where I left it."

albeit untalented musicians. Charles wasn't enthused about helping Burl. A few years back, Cal had asked him to "go under-cover" as a bartender and use his self-anointed private detective skills. Cal was new to the bar business at the time and had suspected someone was stealing from him. The plan would have been perfect if Charles could bartend, which he couldn't, and if he could detect, which he was inept at. Through the grace of God, a once-in-a-lifetime alignment of the stars, and pure luck, Charles, with the help of yours truly, had caught the culprit—sort of. That's a story for another time.

Cal's would be open beyond my senior-citizen, normal bedtime, and I was taking a nap when Cindy called.

"No one using the name Kevin Starr checked into the Tides on or before the dates you gave me."

"How about Starr Management?" I said, task focused.

"Gee, Chris. Why didn't I think of asking that?" She sighed. "Oh wait, I did. I'm not chief just because of my pretty face. Got the same answer."

"Did you happen to use your amazing police-chief skills and pretty face to ask if there was a group from New York staying around that time?"

"Yes and no."

I waited for more and finally said, "Yes you asked and no you didn't ask, or yes you asked and the answer was no."

"You've got it." Cindy chuckled.

"No New Yorkers."

"Two couples of geezers from Yonkers. That was it. Doubt they were on a music retreat or were singers meeting with an agent. Thickens your plot, don't it?"

"Not only was he lying to his wife, he misled Heather about where and why he was here."

"Sounds like it. Because he didn't check in under his name, doesn't mean he didn't stay there. Yell if I can break any more laws for you."

The Tides may not have had anyone named Starr as a registered guest, yet there was one person who would remember if he'd met the agent. Jay Vaughn was a friend and had worked at the Tides for years. No one seemed to know his official title, although everyone who had stayed at the hotel knew Jay, and he knew them. He was bellhop, unofficial greeter, provider of security, and information about everything Folly and most everything Charleston.

He was off Tuesdays, but I walked through the hotel's lobby on my indirect route from home to Cal's to see if other employees I knew might have remembered the agent. I was surprised to see Jay talking to two ladies dressed for a formal event in Charleston—or I hoped so, because if they went to any of Folly's restaurants dressed that way, they would have been as out of place as a cheeseburger at a vegan convention.

"Hey, Chris," Jay said when he saw me standing behind the women, "let me introduce you to two guests."

He proceeded to tell me who the ladies were, that they were on Folly to attend a high-school reunion, and introduced me to the women. I detected a slight *who cares* look in their eyes. It didn't stop Jay. They said they had to get to Charleston for the reunion and said it was nice meeting me and excused themselves.

Jay shook my hand and said he had heard about Heather and asked how she was doing. I wasn't surprised he knew since there wasn't much that happened on Folly that he didn't know. I told him she was doing the best that could be expected. He asked how Charles was taking it. I said he could be doing better and he asked me to give him his best then asked what brought me to the hotel. I told him he was the person I wanted to see, and I knew it was his day off, so I was looking for anyone who could answer a question. He was there because two employees called in sick, and asked what I needed.

"It has to do with Heather."

"I hope I can help."

I told him a little about Kevin Starr and how Starr said he was staying at the Tides the night he first met Heather.

Jay tilted his head and asked when that was. I gave him the date and he shook his head.

"I'm not great on dates," he said, "but I do remember that one because I had to take my car to the shop to have some work redone. To be honest, I was perturbed with the mechanic. Anyway, I don't recall anyone named Kevin staying here that night. Did he say how long he had been here?"

I told Jay I wasn't sure. From what he'd said, it could have been several nights.

"No, don't believe he was here."

"How about people from New York? I heard they were in the music industry and on a retreat that Starr was here for."

"New York," said Jay as he rubbed his chin. "The Lawrences, John and Louise, and a couple Carl and Missy, the Mosers, stayed three nights and were from somewhere near New York City. They're in their eighties and said they were on vacation. Doubt they're who you're looking for."

I agreed and seeing how much he had remembered about them, I was more sure that Kevin Starr wasn't a guest, or if he was, he didn't go by Kevin. I thanked Jay and he said if there was anything he could do to help Heather or Charles to let him know.

22

Cal's was packed. I was glad I wasn't there to sit and drink since all the tables were occupied. There was a smattering of guitar cases beside several of the tables. I noticed a few familiar faces, a couple of regular open-mic performers, and several customers I didn't recognize. Burl was behind the bar. His rotund body squeezed in a space made for someone several belt sizes smaller, as he tried to gather drinks for six men who were waiting. Charles was at the far end of the bar restocking the beer cooler. Kristin, a part-time waitress who had worked at Cal's since her junior year at the College of Charleston five years ago, was making her way among the tables trying to keep up with the demands of thirsty customers. She was falling behind because of the bottleneck caused by two amateur bartenders.

It was a half hour past the time open-mic was scheduled to start and two musicians were getting antsy and glaring at Burl. Kristin saw me, smiled, and shrugged her shoulders. I motioned to the bar so she'd know I wasn't looking for a table.

"Brother Chris," Burl said, "my prayers are answered. Please lend a hand. I have to get the show on the road."

I knew as much about bartending as I knew about skinning a porcupine, but figured I could move beer from the cooler to the bar or help Kristin clear empties off the tables. I waited for Burl to squeeze out from behind the bar before I took his place. Charles nodded and said he would tend bar if I could keep him supplied.

Other than grumbling voices coming from the guys standing in line to get drinks, the next sound I heard was Burl tapping on the antique mic on the stage sandwiched between the restrooms at the far end of the room.

"Hello, hello! Howdee." He sounded more like Minnie Pearl than a host. "Welcome to open-mic night at Cal's. I'm Preacher Burl…umm, just Burl, filling in for Cal. Some of you know he's over in the hospital in Charleston recovering from a blow to the head. Let's have a moment of silence for our dear friend Brother, umm, Country Cal.

The moment of silence was interrupted by clanking beer bottles and one patron yelling "What'd he say?" Silence wasn't silent, nor was it golden.

"Now," Burl said, "please silence thy communication devices."

I put my hand over my eyes. That was Cal's weekly opening to get his congregation to turn off cell phones during his Sunday services. I prayed he didn't expect the first musician to open with "Amazing Grace."

I was relieved when the next thing he said was: "Now we've got a bunch of singers tonight, so let's hold it to two songs each. Okay, let's make welcome our first entertainer, the young lady standing over there." Burl pointed to a mid-twenties woman dressed in a striped shirt and torn jeans. "Kera," she stage-whispered. "Kera," Burl said to the microphone.

Kera was well into Kacey Musgraves's hit "Follow Your Arrow" when Burl made his way back to the bar.

Charles patted him on the back. "Fine job."

Charles has a knack for saying what needed to be said, and Burl needed positive reinforcement for his MC duties. Despite his shortcomings, Charles had been better, or quicker, at selling beer and the line was down to two people. I offered to help Kristin clear tables.

She smiled. "You aren't going to hog into my tips, are you?"

I shook my head.

"Clear away."

And I did. Two more entertainers were standing beside the stage. Burl wasn't a great moderator, though he had learned to ask the singer's name before going to the microphone, and refrained from reading Bible verses between songs.

The next vocalist, a man in his forties, opened with a poor imitation of Darius Rucker's "Wagon Wheel," followed by an even poorer imitation of the classic "Kiss an Angel Good Morning."

I was facing the exit when Burl introduced the next singer, Edwina, who said she'd like to go back a few years for her song, Tammy Wynette's "Stand by Your Man."

I remembered her from her appearance during the earlier open-mic night I'd attended with Barb. The name also sounded familiar from something else but I couldn't remember where I'd heard it. I took a handful of empty bottles to the trash behind Charles and asked, "She a regular?"

Charles looked up from the cash register, and squinted toward the stage. "Looks familiar. Could be, not every week." He was distracted and grumbled about losing track of the money, so I didn't pursue it. If Cal had been here, he would have been quick with an answer.

Kristin leaned over the bar, and tapped me on the arm. At five-foot-one she struggled to reach me. "Chris, could I borrow you. Bottles are piling up."

By the time I had cleared two tables, Edwina had begun covering Dolly Parton's "Coat of Many Colors," and the crowed began tapping their feet to the classic. Edwina, in ample proportions or melodious voice, was no Dolly, although she performed an admirable rendition, and was better than most of Cal's regulars.

"I think I might remember where I saw her," Charles said as I dumped the empties in the trash behind him.

I wiped my hands on a bar towel and held them out for him to continue.

"Remember when we were standing in line at the Bluebird and Heather sneaked off to the bathroom at McDonalds?"

"Yes."

"I thought I saw Heather coming back." Charles looked at Edwina on stage. "The gal had on a yellow blouse like Heather's and her hair looked the same, but when she turned around it wasn't Heather." He paused and pointed to the stage. "I think it was her."

"Bro…. umm, Charles," interrupted Burl, "More Buds."

I turned toward the stage but couldn't picture her from Nashville, but remembered why her name sounded familiar. The woman Caldwell was working with to change SHADES from rock to country had mentioned that one of the regulars was pushing her to offer open-mic nights. Wasn't her name Edwina? Olivia had said Edwina had performed at several other open-mic nights. It seemed likely it was the same Edwina, after all, how many Edwina's could there be who were performing at open-mic nights? Was Charles right about her being in Nashville?

How do I find out without arousing suspicion? I gave it some thought as Edwina was leaving the stage and Burl was preparing to introduce the next singer. Instead of introducing the singer, Burl was doing a thirty-second commercial for First Light Church, giving his confused beer-drinking audience the when and where of his Sunday service. If Cal had known what Burl was doing, he would have disconnected himself from the medical paraphernalia, hijacked a car, and charged in here to give Burl the boot, figuratively and literally. Cal had no idea and Burl had now slipped out of preacher, pitch-man mode and introduced the next singer.

Edwina was by herself. She latched her guitar case, waved at a couple of women who had applauded the loudest at the end of her set, and headed to the exit. I opened the door for her and followed her to the sidewalk. She thanked me, and I said, "Edwina, that's a nice name."

She glanced at me. It wasn't a hostile look but more a *who's hitting on me now* gaze. I didn't blame her. I held out my hand. "I'm Chris Landrum, a good friend of Cal."

I thought she was going to ignore me, when she reached for my hand. Hers was damp and warm. "Hi. Nice to meet you." She smiled and started to walk away.

The smell of cigarette smoke mixed with the hot, humid air in front of the bar. A trickle of perspiration ran down my cheek yet Edwina looked as fresh as she had when she had taken the stage.

"A few days ago, I was with Cal and another friend, Caldwell Ramsey, at SHADES, and we were talking with the owner. She mentioned one of her regular performers was named Edwina. I was wondering if it was you."

She looked at her guitar case and at me. "Yes. Olivia's been good to me over the years. She lets me fill in when some of her scheduled performers cancel."

I didn't know where to go with the conversation, so I said, "Small world, isn't it?"

She stared at me like it was a trick question. "Sure is."

That didn't help.

"You play here often?"

"A few times. I try to go to as many open-mic nights as I can." She grinned. "Getting discovered is hard work."

"You must know Heather Lee. She played here most every week until she moved to Nashville."

"I see a lot of folks at these things. I might if I saw her."

How do I keep her talking without becoming suspicious?

"I think Olivia said you play out of state occasionally."

"Some."

"Ever played Nashville?"

"Been there a time or two."

"Heather plays the Bluebird."

"Good venue. Gotta be going, nice to meet you."

I ignored her dismissal. "You ever play there?"

"Tell Cal I hope he gets feeling better. That preacher guy's okay," She shook her head. "He's no Country Cal." She waved bye over her shoulder as she climbed in a black Mercedes SLK 350 hardtop convertible that looked more like it should be in a sci-fi movie rather than on the streets of Folly. It didn't look like Edwina needed to be discovered to get by.

The crowd was thinning as I returned to clear tables. There were only two other singers who had attempted to wow the audience. Both had failed. The good news was that the master of ceremonies had survived open-mic night. He had performed better than most of the aspiring singers. Charles, as he does with most things he attempts, had muddled through tending bar. And I was exhausted. Only Kristin appeared in good spirits and full of energy at closing and asked if we wanted to hit some of Folly's other bars before they closed. Charles, Burl, and I responded in three-part harmony: "No ma'am."

I didn't wake up until eight-thirty the next morning, late for me. I would have slept longer if the phone hadn't jarred me awake.

"Hey, pard," Cal said in his strong Texas accent. "You awake?"

I said I was now and asked how he was feeling. I wanted to ask why he was waking me up.

"The cute nurse who was holding my hand and taking my blood pressure a few minutes ago said my hard head was healing good."

"Great. How's your memory?"

"Ain't made it back yet. Still don't remember what happened that night and my last couple of weeks seem to be all twisted around. I do remember why I'm calling. Peppi, that's the cute nurse's name, she said it's French, anyway, she told me today's Wednesday and even as confused as I am, I know it meant yesterday was Tuesday, a big night at the bar. Was Burl there and did he handle the singers okay? They're a fickle lot, you know."

I told him everything was fine and Burl, with a little help

from Charles, was great and to not worry about anything other than getting well and getting out of the hospital.

"Be sure and thank the preacher man for me."

I told him I would.

"Oh yeah," he said. "Nearly forgot. When I was drifting off last night, my buddy Johnny R called. The old, cranky nurse that ain't French heard the phone on the table over there ring and gave me a scolding look. Anyway, we went to see Johnny R when we were in Nashville, didn't we?"

"Yes."

"Good, I'm glad that part ain't gone from my head. Last night he called and said he had a little something to tell me about the scoundrel Starr. I told him I was in the hospital and my memory was going through a fuzzy spell and I'd have you give him a call to see what he knew."

"Did he give a hint?"

"Don't think so. Nurse Ratched made me hang up, turn the ringer off, and go to sleep. Didn't get Johnny R's number, but he's in that home. I said you'd call him. Did I already tell you that?"

I said I'd give his friend a call.

"Well I'll be branded. Guess who just came a callin'?"

From the way he'd said it, I assumed it wasn't Nurse Rached. "Who?"

"My favorite bartending preacher. Better go and be nice to him. God may've followed him in the door. You'll call Johnny R?"

I said I would and to say hi to Burl. I'm not sure he heard all of that since he'd already hung up.

I waited another hour to call since Nashville was an hour behind us, and spent most of the time wondering what Cal's friend could have learned about the agent who was fifty years his junior. I also wondered when, or if, Cal would remember what he thought he had learned about Starr being in South Carolina.

After several rings, I was about to hang up when a pleasant, Hispanic sounding, female said, "Oak View, this is Sena, may I help you?"

I told her she may if she could connect me to Johnny R's room. She asked my name. I told her, and shared I had visited a few days ago and was calling for my friend Cal Ballew. Sena giggled. "Give me a minute. I will check and see if he is receiving calls, and if he is in the kind of mood in which you would want to talk to him."

I heard muted voices in the background and a mattress store commercial on a nearby television. It was closer to ten minutes before Sena returned and told me Johnny R told her any friend of Cal's was a sorry so-and-so. He didn't say so-and-so. He said that he could find a few minutes in his busy schedule to talk to you." She chuckled. "That means that his favorite soap-opera is not on yet. I will connect you."

Good to her word, the next voice I heard said, "You the boring looking one or the ragged dude in the long-sleeve T-shirt in two-hundred-degree weather?"

"Boring one."

Johnny coughed and said, "Like to picture who I'm talking to. Now, what in hell happened to my bud Cal. He said something about getting run over by a concrete mixin' truck before he got rolled over by a freight train." He coughed and caught his breath. "The old boy tends to push the truth, so I figured if all that happened to him, I wouldn't be sharing a conversation with him until after I bite the dust."

I gave him a shortened version of what had happened and didn't stray from the mugging theory.

"Good—glad he's going to make it. Not good he got smacked upside his thick skull." He coughed up a chuckle. "Bet his head busted whatever hit it."

I needed to move him along before he choked to death. "Cal told me you had information on Kevin Starr."

"Yep," he said, and gave another wheezing cough. "This old bird's still got a few connections in the business. Only a few. Most of my best friends, and even most of my enemies are already sitting around the campfire and trading tunes with Jimmy Rogers and Hank Sr." He paused again. "I got ahold of an old flame. Can't be much more than a flicker left now. I'm sure you're not interested in my prehistoric sex life."

I'm not, and imagined how many questions Charles would have had. "Starr?" I said, to get him back on track.

"Damn, you're impatient." He wheezed.

I couldn't think of an appropriate response.

"Okay. According to my gal friend you don't want to hear about, Kevin Starr is new on the block. He's big on ideas and piss-poor short on the bucks needed to make his ideas come to life. He thinks if he played the odds and signed every Tom, Dick, and Harriet one of them would strike it big and bring him enough money to sign folks with more than a dream of talent. Crappy singing by a bunch of suckers is still crappy singing. The boy's master plan's doomed from freakin' day one."

So far, there were no surprises and I hoped that wasn't all Johnny R had called to tell Cal.

"Anything else?"

He wheezed. "Young man, anybody told you lately you're impatient?"

"You."

He laughed. "Good memory. There's more. Give me time to get there. I don't get a chance to talk to many folks who're still haulin' their mind around with them."

"I appreciate your time."

"Damn better, it's valuable. Crap, I could be playing nurse with the nurses, but no, I'm wasting my time with the boring friend of my buddy Cal. You sure he's going to be okay?"

I told him I was and apologized for keeping him away from the nurses.

He laughed again. "I heard your buddy Starr's sinking in debt and the hole in his boat's getting larger, until." He wheezed and coughed, and then silence.

"Until what?"

"Until he found himself a backer, a moneybags, a sucker with deep pockets. The person either is going to, or had already pulled his wallet out of the fire. Rumor is the 'backer' just might be a gal friend."

"Did your source learn who the backer is?"

"No, she said she don't think anyone over here knows. There was a rumor the mystery person got turned sideways with him, royally pissed. It was only a rumor."

"Any idea why?"

"No." His hacking cough returned. "Think I've had all the talking fun I can take this morning. You tell Cal he better get himself well or I'll tell everything I know about him to one of those tell-all TV shows. That'll get their ratings up."

I told him I would and thanked him for talking to me.

He coughed one more time. "Oh yeah, I almost forgot. You're in South Carolina, aren't you?"

I told him, "Near Charleston."

"Thought so. My old flame said Starr's money-chick was from your neck of the woods.

Two things became clear. First, Johnny R didn't know that Starr was no longer among the living. And second, if Johnny R's friend was right, there was finally a connection between Starr and South Carolina that went beyond him being on Folly for a retreat and a connection where someone was "royally pissed." Was the person angry enough to kill? And a more important question, how do I find out who? Edwina Robinson came to mind. From the car she drove, she appeared to have money. Would she have had enough money and motivation to kill the agent? According to Olivia Anderson, Edwina was a regular at several open-mic nights, and had evaded my question about singing at the Bluebird. She and Starr were about the same age, had made music their life's focus, and she was attractive and talented enough to have gotten Starr's attention, although talent didn't seem to be a criterion. That was all I knew about her.

Caldwell may shed more light on Edwina, so I took the chance and gave him a call.

"Hi, Chris, nice to hear from you," Caldwell said in his well-modulated, calm voice.

Caller ID strikes again. Out of habit, I told him who I was and asked how he was. I heard music in the background as he said he was fine. I asked if he had a few minutes. He said he was leaving a meeting with a client and to give him a second to get outside where he could talk.

The background music subsided. "How's Cal?"

I updated him and he asked me to tell Cal he was praying for him. I told him I would.

"So, what did I do to have the honor of this call?"

I asked if he knew a singer named Edwina Robinson. He said the name sounded familiar, although he wasn't sure from where. I reminded him her name was mentioned when we were meeting with Olivia Anderson.

"Oh, yeah, that's the singer who's pushing Olivia to switch to country."

"Do you know her?"

"No, why?"

I shared what I knew and how it could possibly be tied to the murder in Nashville. Caldwell didn't respond at first, and finally said, "That's quite a stretch."

I said it was. It was all I had.

"Tell you what, I'm meeting with Olivia in the morning. If you don't mind some tedious financial talk about business, you can tag along. You can ask her about Edwina."

I told him it would be great and asked if I could bring Charles with me. Caldwell laughed. "Couldn't stop him, could you?"

THUNDERSTORMS ROLLED through Lowcountry early Thursday morning and took some of the sweltering humidity with them as they had moved out to sea. It looked like it was going to be a gorgeous day; a day I would rather walk along the beach or take a photo-stroll along the historic Battery in Charleston, more than *take* a meeting in a bar. I called Charles to invite him, and was again reminded the second he got in the car we had to do something to "spring Heather." Talking to Olivia was the best I could come up with. A walk on the beach or around Charleston would have to wait.

Caldwell and Mel lived near downtown Charleston so Charles and I met the music promoter in the bar's parking lot. Charles, to look more professional, wore a muted-yellow, long-sleeve T-shirt with a University of Tulsa logo on the breast pocket.

Caldwell said, "She doesn't know you're coming, so follow my lead."

Charles pointed his cane at the door. "Of course."

Right, I thought.

It was several hours before SHADES was to open, and the only vehicle in the lot was a red metallic Porsche Panamera that probably cost more than Charles's, Caldwell's, and my vehicle combined. Charles, the budding detective, detected the red mass of fine German ostentatiousness belonged to the bar's owner; a deduction that was verified moments later when Olivia opened the side door and invited us in. If she was surprised to see Charles and me, it didn't show. She smiled and shook our hands as Caldwell introduced Charles and reintroduced me. Today, she wore a navy suit with light gray blouse. Instead of the dress shoes she had on the last time we met, she wore a pair of black, Nike running shoes.

She caught Charles looking at her shoes and chuckled. "The shoes I wear when we're open kill these aging feet."

Charles smiled. "I was thinking how great those look. Hate dress shoes, as you can tell."

Charles pointed his cane at his torn, mud-stained, generic tennis shoes. Olivia smiled, not knowing how else to react.

Her gold bracelets clinked against each other as she motioned us toward her office.

"Hope you don't mind Charles and Chris tagging along," Caldwell said. "They had a couple of questions and I thought this would be a good opportunity."

"Not at all. If they don't mind a boring meeting with us discussing budgets and your recommendations on how we start the rebirth."

Charles leaned forward and said, "President G. W. Bush said, 'It's clearly a budget. It's got lots of numbers in it.'"

Olivia tilted her head and looked at Charles like she was studying an aardvark in the zoo. I suspected she was reevaluating her response to Caldwell's comment about us being here.

Caldwell said, "Charles is big on quoting presidents."

Olivia chuckled. "Well he's right about what the president said. My dearly-departed husband was the financial whiz. To me, budgets are as Bush said, *lots of numbers.*"

Charles sat back in the chair and grinned.

Olivia turned to me. "Questions?"

This was where it would get tricky. How do I ask what she knows about Edwina without arousing suspicion? I didn't know how well they knew each other or how much Olivia would tell Edwina about my curiosity.

"A couple of nights ago I was in Cal's bar on Folly and heard Edwina Robinson sing. She was good. We talked a little after her set before she had to leave. She told me she'd performed in Nashville." I tilted my head toward Charles, "Charles lives in Nashville and his fiancé Heather is a singer. Since Edwina was so good, I wanted to ask if she had an agent, or if she would have some tips I could give Heather."

"Glad you mentioned Cal," Olivia said, "I meant to ask, how come he didn't come with you. I like the old-timer. Makes me wish I had been in the business in the good old days."

Charles said, "He's a little under the weather."

"Sorry to hear it. Hope he gets well soon." She slowly shook her head. "Back to Edwina. She had an agent. His last name was

Starr. Since you were talking about Nashville, that's where he had his agency."

"Was?" I said, after she had said it twice.

Olivia bowed her head. "Tragic. He was killed a while back. The story going around is one of the people he represented shot him. Edwina's torn up about it. She didn't tell me. I heard it from another singer that Edwina had given him a lot of money to advance her career. The kid's had a hard life. She inherited a fortune from her parents who were killed when she was in her teens."

Charles leaned forward. "What happened?"

I cringed. Let her talk.

Olivia looked at her hand and at Charles. "They were coming home from a Christmas Party. Tipsy, I gathered. They ran a red light and were broadsided by a semi. Killed instantly. Thank God, Edwina wasn't with them. Don't know much else."

"I'm sorry," Charles said.

"Anyway, Edwina's got a lot of talent, but not much business sense. She spends her money like she's got an unlimited pot of it. I don't see her outside here." She waved her hand around the room. "She's always talking about her cars, boats, a big, upscale condo overlooking the City Market, singing lessons, and paying her agent whatever he said he needed to make her famous." She shook her head. "I love her to death. You know what, I'd like to shake some sense in her."

Charles asked, "Did she ever talk about meeting with this Starr fellow over here?"

"She did. She told me—I think I have this right—he heard her sing, over by the ocean, I believe. He was impressed and asked to represent her. Think he's been back a few times since then and I know Edwina's been to Nashville." She looked at the huge diamond on her left hand and at Charles. "She's devastated about his death."

"That's too bad," I said. "I hope she got whatever she paid him for."

Olivia frowned. "I think the bundle she gave died with him. She doesn't talk about it. I've been around her in here long enough to know she's more upset than she lets on."

I glanced at Charles, then at Olivia. "When I was talking to her, she had to leave before I could get her contact information. Do you have her phone number or e-mail address?"

She flipped through some papers on an expensive, black leather blotter on her polished mahogany desk, jotted down a phone number, and handed it to me.

Caldwell looked at his watch and glanced at me.

I took the hint. "Don't let Charles and me keep you from your meeting. Charles, let's take a walk and let these two get on with their work. It's a perfect day."

Curiosity may kill the cat, yet Charles was ready to kill me for suggesting we miss anything Caldwell and Olivia would say. No feline alive could compete with Charles when it came to curiosity—nosiness.

Charles groused as soon as we were outside. "Why leave?"

"I don't want Olivia thinking more about Starr's death. If she's been following it, she may have heard the name of the person who'd been arrested. I shouldn't have mentioned Heather's name. If Olivia puts two and two together she'll realize why Heather sounded familiar. I'm afraid she'll tell Edwina. Talking shop with Caldwell without us around may distract her enough to keep her mind off it."

"Wise," Charles said, somewhat mollified.

Forty-five minutes later, Caldwell called to say the meeting was over. Olivia had walked him to his car where Charles and I were waiting. We said our goodbyes and Caldwell asked us if we got what we were looking for.

I said yes. At the same time, I wondered what it meant.

Charles called Heather's lawyer while we were on the way back to the beach. The receptionist said the attorney wasn't in, and that if Charles called, to tell him there was nothing new to report. He slammed his phone on the console, and I spent the last few miles reassuring him the attorney was doing all he could. Charles said he knew it and it still didn't make him more patient. He suggested I could be more successful calling Edwina.

"What do you propose I say?"

"You're the smart one, figure it out."

"That helps."

"Say the same stuff you lied to Olivia about. Tell her how great she is. Ask about her agent. Ask if she has any tips she could offer Heather. Ask if she killed Starr."

I looked at Charles. "That's the kind of question only you could get away with."

Charles rubbed his chin. "Okay, leave out the last part. We can't learn anything if you don't call."

Except for asking if she killed Starr, his ideas weren't horrible and I didn't have a better plan. I motioned for him to punch in her number. He did and hit the speakerphone icon and handed the device to me.

Instead of a live voice, I received a recording that said, "You have reached the voice-mail of recording artist Edwina Robinson. Please leave a message at the tone."

I tapped *End Call*.

Charles leaned forward. "Recording artist?"

I nodded. "She recorded a demo."

"So did Heather. She could add that to her message." He hesitated and looked out the window. "When she gets out." He jerked his head in my direction. "Why didn't you leave a message?"

I explained I was afraid she wouldn't return my call. I'd rather catch her by surprise and play the conversation by ear. Charles agreed it was a decent idea—this time he didn't go as far as saying it was wise.

I had to promise I would continue calling until I reached the recording artist before he would get out at his near-empty apartment. We decided the best way for me to approach her would be to say she was so good I wanted to hear her sing and ask about her next gig. Maybe it would be soon, and nearby.

I reached Edwina on the third try. At first, she was reticent to talk; after all, I was a near stranger. When I told her how much I enjoyed her set at Cal's, she turned more friendly. She told me when and where she would be performing. My enthusiasm increased when she said it would be tomorrow night at one of the restaurants beside Charleston's historic market. I said I'd try to make it. She said wonderful, the same word Charles used when I called and told him about it. She said she'd look forward to seeing me again. Charles said, "What time are you picking me up."

I HAD ASKED Barb to supper, and met her at her condo where we could walk to the restaurant. She met me at the door, again wearing one of her trademark red blouses, and white, linen slacks. The temperature was still in the upper eighties so I suggested we go next door to Blu, the upscale restaurant in the Tides Hotel. She agreed and once we reached the hotel also agreed we should eat in air-conditioned comfort and not on the patio. We got the best of both worlds when the hostess seated us at a table beside the window overlooking the beach.

I hadn't seen Barb for a few days and asked if she'd heard about Cal.

"What about him?"

I told her about his encounter with a blunt object and where he was recuperating.

"That's terrible. I overheard some women talking about someone getting mugged. I didn't hear who it was. Who would do that to such a dear sweet old man?"

Cal would have liked her sentiment until she got to *old man.*

I told her the police didn't know but suspected robbery.

The waitress arrived and took our drink order. Barb watched her head to the bar. "Do you think it had to do with Heather?"

"Yes, he called me the day before. I was in Nashville and he said he knew something about why Starr was on Folly and wanted to know when I was getting back. I told him the next day and he wanted to tell me in person. He didn't get a chance."

"How would whoever hit him know he was going to tell you something?"

I sighed. "No clue."

"So, what did he know?"

"Don't know. Cal can't remember anything about the attack or what he was going to say. The doc thinks his memory will be back. The problem is no one knows when."

Our drinks arrived. We took a sip and gazed at the ocean as the shadows of the setting sun reflected off the rolling waves as they approached shore. There were still several people lounging on the beach and a couple of joggers weaved their way past the loungers.

"Let me bounce something off you." I began telling her about Edwina Robinson.

Barb leaned forward and interrupted. "Is that the gal we heard sing at Cal's?"

"Yes. I'm impressed you remember."

"Don't be impressed, it's not often I hear the name Edwina."

I told Barb that Starr was Edwina's agent, she had given him a substantial amount of money, and had gone to Nashville several times.

Barb listened and didn't interrupt which was one of her more endearing traits and unique among my gaggle of friends. She took a sip. "Any evidence she had something to do with Starr's death or Cal's run in with a blunt object?"

"No."

The server returned and took our order. Barb chose soup and asparagus salad, and I went with the pork chop, another reason she was thin and I was, well, not.

"Okay," she continued, not distracted by the interruption. "Did Edwina know Heather?"

"I don't know. She told me that she might remember her if she saw her."

"So, all you know from the woman in Charleston is Edwina's another wannabe singer pissed-off at Starr."

I nodded. "And she gave him a lot of money. Olivia didn't say how much although it sounded like more than it would take to cut a demo and to use his marketing services."

Barb said, "It's no telling how many other aspiring singers have done the same thing."

"True. I doubt there were many from here. And remember, Cal said he knew something about Starr being on Folly."

Barb paused, glanced at the ocean, and turned to me. "Not

necessarily that it had anything to do with Edwina or the murder. I hate to say this since I know you're close, but Edwina's not the only wannabe from here who's in Nashville."

"I know. Heather had the same motives as Edwina."

"Motive, no alibi, and it was her gun. Do you even know if Edwina was in Tennessee when Starr was killed?"

"Good question."

Our food arrived and we ate in silence as I thought about the facts Barb had so lawyerly pointed out. She, of course, was right, yet I still couldn't picture Heather killing anyone. Sure, she had changed since moving to Nashville. Had it been enough to lead her to murder? Were my views clouded, as Barb had said, by me knowing Heather and her relationship with Charles? Could be. The police had a circumstantial case, a strong one, but circumstantial none the less.

Barb broke the silence. "I don't know Heather, and little about Charles, other than he has read most every book written since Gutenberg. I couldn't speculate on what may have happened, but if I were the cops, I'd feel pretty good about my case."

"She—"

Barb waved her fork in front of my face. "If I was her attorney, I would keep pounding the jury with the fact the police have no proof. I would parade all the other singers who felt ripped off in front of the jury, and I would call his wife to the stand and keep hitting her about how angry she must have been about him lying to her about where he had been, and imply it happened all the time, not only when he was in South Carolina. I would plant in the jury's head that the wife could've killed him, any of the many aspiring singers could have pulled the trigger, the people with the recording studio had a reason to kill him, and he was a stealing liar with people lined up around the block to have a figurative and literal shot at him."

"Would it get her off?"

She shook her head. "Fifty, fifty. The gun's the problem."

"I know."

Barb looked at her fingertips. "Were Heather's prints on the gun when the police found it?"

"No."

"That's something else a good defense attorney would pounce on. If she was going to get rid of the gun, it would make sense to wipe it clean. Why would she do that if she was leaving it in her car?"

"The car's lock was broken so anyone could have taken it."

"Yes. Who knew she had it, where it was, and that the lock was broken?"

"I don't know."

She grinned. "You're going to find out, aren't you?"

I sat up straight and nearly strangled my fork. "My best friend's girlfriend is sitting in jail in Nashville. My good friend Cal is downtown in the hospital. Charles is devastated. And the police are convinced the case is solved. You bet I am."

She set her fork on her empty plate and stared at me. "How?"

Our server returned and asked if we wanted dessert before I could tell Barb I was clueless about how. We said no, and I asked Barb if she wanted to get another drink at the outside bar. She said no, smiled, and said we could have one on her patio.

It was comfortable with a steady breeze coming off the ocean. Barb poured each of us a glass of white wine and said for me to go on the patio while she changed into cooler clothes. Ten minutes later, she'd substituted white shorts for her slacks, and had put on a red T-shirt. I noticed red polish on her toes. Red was beginning to grow on me.

Barb lowered herself in the chair and looked at the Folly Pier. "It's a beautiful sight."

I nodded.

Evenly-spaced lights illuminated the pier and I could see the silhouettes of people strolling to the end and back of the thousand-foot-long structure. The sound of waves slapping the shore provided a soothing background melody, broken occasionally by the engine of a vehicle on the street behind us.

"What's next? How are you going to do what the police can't?"

I told her Charles and I were going to hear Edwina perform tomorrow night. She asked what we planned to learn, and I told her I didn't know. I was going to play it by ear, and hoped Edwina would say something that would help.

"Sounds like a feeble plan."

"I agree."

"Want me to go?"

I was surprised. "Thanks. It may be best if just Charles and I were there. I don't want her to think we were ganging up on her."

She looked out at the waves illuminated by lights from the pier breaking on shore and turned to me. "Here's a thought. It would appear more natural if you had a woman with you. Tell her I was your date. That might put her at ease."

It made sense. "You've got a date."

She smiled. "Have you asked Chief LaMond to check into Edwina? You and Cindy are good friends and she has access to more databases than you have. Edwina might have a record, and all the information you can gather the better."

I said I'd call Cindy tomorrow and tonight was a good time to simply enjoy the view and the company. After enjoying both for another half-hour, I took Barb's yawns as a hint, thanked her for a nice evening, and said I'd better be going.

She grinned. "If you must."

I didn't know about *must*. I told her it was late and she needed her sleep. She said something about a rain check, walked me to the door, gave me a hug, followed by a lingering kiss.

26

I caught the chief on her way to the office.

"You want me to do what?" Cindy shouted. "I just spent an un-fun filled breakfast with Councilmember Houston listening to him bitch and moan about what he called 'middle-of-the-freakin'-night hoodlums' disturbing the sleep of his dear sister who happens to live fifty yards from one of our fine imbibing establishments and thinks retired librarians should be patrolling the streets in front of her house to *shhh* everyone walking home."

"Life of a police chief. Ain't it grand?"

Cindy ignored me and continued to rant. "I suggested to our illustrious member of the city council I could post some of my officers in his sister's front yard so they could shoot everyone who passed by who made noises louder than a giraffe. I was teasing, by the way."

"Of course."

"And you know what the knucklehead said?"

"Tell me."

"He said the gunshots would make too much noise for his *stupid to buy a house by a bar* sister."

I stifled a laugh, and chuckled. "Wow, Chief, my simple request for you to run Edwina Robinson through your databases will be a snap compared to Houston's sister's horrific situation."

Cindy exhaled. "Chris, if you weren't such an endearing creature, and not such a good friend of my hubby, and I suppose a friend of mine, I'd have one of my guys save one of his bullets after shooting the noisemakers, and put it in your troublemaking brain."

"So, when will you get back to me with the information?"

"And I thought Charles was the biggest pest I knew. If I don't have to deal with any *real* police business when I get to the office, I'll let my fingers do the walking on my keyboard. I'll call you."

"You're an angel."

"Tell that to Councilmember Houston."

I HADN'T HEARD from Cindy when I picked up Barb at her condo and Charles at his apartment. Barb, to no surprise, had on a short-sleeve red blouse, but had switched from white linen slacks to tan chinos. Charles, also no surprise, had on a long-sleeve black T-shirt with Belmont Bruins in red on the front. Charles said since Belmont University was in Nashville it would get Edwina talking about her visits to Music City.

He leaned back in the back seat and confidently said, "It'll make Edwina cough up a big-ass clue."

Barb glanced at me from the passenger seat and raised her eyebrows.

"Yes," I said. "He's always like this."

She whispered, "Wow."

Charles said, "What?"

And I thought regardless how strange, and desperate the situation was, I truly missed him being here and, well, being Charles.

Rubino's was a block off King Street near the College of Charleston. The Italian restaurant with its nondescript front, was known by the college community as well as young professionals in search of reasonably-priced pizzas and eclectic music. Because of its popularity and small size, we were told we'd have a thirty-minute wait. That was fine since the postage-stamp sized, raised stage was occupied by an empty bar-stool. Edwina hadn't arrived.

There was one vacant stool at the bar and Charles nudged a boisterous twenty-something year old man wearing a College of Charleston T-shirt aside and motioned for Barb to be seated. A harried bartender, with sweat running down his cheeks, was quick to Barb who ordered Chianti and pointed to me. I asked for a glass of pinot grigio, and Charles bypassed the Italian drink options, and said *birra.*

The server looked at Charles like he was a termite. "Huh?"

"Beer, *birra.*"

The server rolled his eyes. I didn't blame him, though I was impressed with Charles's Italian.

We were halfway through our drinks when Edwina pushed the door open with her shoulder and lugged a black box the size of a carry-on suitcase around the crowded tables to the stage. She was dressed in black. If she had worn a straw hat and yellow blouse, she would pass for a younger version of Heather. She set the box on the stage and headed back outside.

A few minutes later, she returned carrying a guitar case with Edwina written in script on the side and a three-foot long narrow container, and a portable mic stand. A male student standing near the door took two of the cases out of her hand and helped get them to the stage. She rewarded him with a grin and started assembling the contents of the cases.

Ten minutes later, the portable Bose sound system was operational, Edwina was tuning her Martin guitar, and my phone rang. The screen said *Cindy.* I answered and asked her to hold a second while I walked outside where I could hear without having to strain my ears over the loud din inside the restaurant.

"Where are you, at a circus?"

I gave her a brief explanation of where we were and asked what she'd found on Edwina.

"Your gal must have some bucks. She lives in a ritzy condo overlooking the Market, not far from where you are now. She ain't a serial killer or terrorist, but she ain't Mother Teresa's good twin. Three years ago, she took a knife to a food fight, and not to butter the croissants or whatever you do to those flaky things. She was living with a guy who owned a hole-in-the-wall hamburger joint and learned he was Frenching more than fries with one of his cook-chicks. Sweet, two-timed Edwina took a hankering to slice-and-dice the cook-chick. Thirty-five stitches and a successful workers-comp claim later, the cook-chick was in court pointing her bandaged finger at Edwina, who was assigned to the local jail for a day short of a year. The prosecutor tried to get more temper-tantrum crimes admitted as evidence but the wise old judge said they were too far in the past to reflect on current events, or some such judgy proclamation."

"That it?"

"Isn't that enough? Oh yeah, there's one more thing you might find interesting."

The restaurant's door opened and three coeds came out, all talking at the same time, two of them on phones and the third either talking to herself or to someone through an earpiece. Edwina's powerful voice singing a Martina McBride hit echoed onto the sidewalk, and I couldn't hear Cindy.

"Say it again. It's loud here."

"Your old ears are giving out. Okay, remember the day you said the cops first interviewed Heather?"

"Hard to forget."

"Miss Edwina Robinson was pulled over on I-40 near

Crossville by the serve-and-protect Tennessee State Police. Seems she was tooling along just shy of the speed of sound."

"Heading toward or from Nashville?"

"Excellent question. Miss Edwina had her Mercedes SLK 350 pointed toward London, England, with an intermediary stop in South Carolina."

"She could have been in Nashville when Starr was killed."

"Yeah, but she could've been coming from anywhere west of where she was stopped."

"I'd put my money on Nashville."

"Me too. I don't have anything to prove it."

"What happened?"

"Nothing," said Cindy. "She charmed the cop into giving her a ticket rather than giving her a lift to the pokey. Listen, Chris, and I know this is going to fall on deaf ears, leave it alone. If Edwina had anything to do with Starr's death, she's trouble. And she knows her way around a gun and a knife. I'll do more digging. Remember: Me, cop. You, retired geezer."

I thanked her for the information and for reminding me of my status in the universe. What I didn't say was that I'd leave it alone.

I rejoined Charles and Barb who had been seated at a table in the middle of the room. Edwina was sitting on the tall bar stool on the stage, playing guitar and singing "Tennessee Waltz."

Barb said "Welcome back," and Charles grabbed my arm and said, "What'd she say?" He nodded toward the stage, "Did she kill Starr?"

Edwina picked up the tempo and dove into Jeannie C. Riley's "Harper Valley PTA." I pulled Barb and Charles closer and shared what Cindy had learned.

"See," Charles said. "She did it."

Barb leaned even closer. "Allow me to put on my attorney's hat. I didn't hear anything that would convince a jury to convict her. Sorry, Charles."

"Her quick temper," Charles said. "Willing to poke a knife in someone. Coming from Nashville. Represented by Starr. And... and, Heather didn't do it, damn it."

I sympathized with him, but agreed with Barb. I was also pleased Charles was more optimistic about Heather's innocence.

Edwina had finished Mary Chapin Carpenter's "Passionate Kisses," and was telling the few people in the room who were listening she was taking a break. We, for reasons Edwina would not approve of, were among those who were paying attention.

Charles said, "Let's grab her."

Barb put her hand on Charles's shoulder and watched Edwina put her guitar in its case. "Give me a few minutes and I'll see if I can get her over. It'll look more spontaneous."

Charles started to protest, sighed, and nodded at Barb. His approach would have been to go to the stage and drag her to the table, while slathering words of praise along the way.

Barb met Edwina by the stage. She shook her hand and leaned close and said something. Barb pointed to our table and said something else to Edwina, who looked at us and gave a weak smile.

Barb retuned and Edwina headed to the restroom.

"What'd you say?" Charles asked. "Where's she going? Is she skipping out on us?"

Barb looked at Charles and at the restroom. "Unless she's going to climb out the bathroom window, she'll be here. I told her my date remembered her from Cal's and was too shy to ask her over. I asked if we could buy her a beer. She looked over here and said she sort of remembered Chris, and asked who the straggly, street person was."

"The what?" Charles said.

Barb grinned. "Kidding."

My admiration for Barb soared.

"Hmm," Charles said. "So, she's coming over?"

Barb nodded, although she didn't have to since Edwina was

standing behind her and pointing at the empty chair. Barb told her to have a seat.

She did and pointed at Charles. "I remember you now. You're Cal's bartender."

"I was only filling—"

Edwina interrupted and nodded to me.

I said, "You talked to me outside Cal's, and when I called yesterday."

"That's us," Charles said. "We really enjoyed your singing and wanted to hear you again."

Edwina squinted and said with little enthusiasm, "It's kind of you."

Our act was clearly not being bought when Barb said, "Chris has been telling me how good you are and he may have seen you in Nashville at the Bluebird. I hear it's the place to be. Congratulations."

She smiled. "Thanks. I love playing there. We get over every opportunity."

Edwina's ego was greater than her skepticism, and confirmed she had played there. It was a fact she danced around when I'd asked her the same question at Cal's.

"My fiancé plays there on open-mic night," Charles said. "You probably know her. Name's Heather Lee."

Edwina looked toward the stage, and the server returned with her beer. I thought she was going to jump up and run. She surprised me when she said, "Yeah, I like her. Terrible that they arrested her, terrible. I knew her from the Bluebird, and we had coffee a couple of times at a place downtown near her apartment."

I wondered if she remembered telling me outside Cal's she wasn't sure if she knew Heather and she might recognize her if she saw her. Not only does she know her, but knows Heather is accused of killing Starr, and she and Heather had coffee together.

"Did you know—what's his name, Chris? The guy who was killed?" Barb asked.

"Kevin Starr."

"That's it," Barb said. "Did you know him?"

"He was my agent and a nice guy. Such a tragedy."

The server returned to the table carrying a large pizza Charles and Barb had ordered while I was talking to Cindy.

Edwina said, "Smells good."

Barb slid the pizza toward Edwina. "Have a slice."

"How long had he been your agent?" Charles asked. No way he was going to let Edwina get off topic.

She grabbed one of the plates and slid a slice of pizza on it. "Less than a year. Why?"

Charles took a slice of pizza. "Just wondering. He'd been Heather's agent for four months."

"Heather met him at Cal's," I said. "Did you meet him in Nashville?"

"No," Edwina said between bites. "He caught my set in Charleston. Said he was in the area meeting with music bigwigs."

Sounds familiar, I thought. "That's great. Did he get you any jobs?"

She took another bite and shook her head. "Not enough for the money I gave him. He got me a couple of gigs in Music Row bars and one on lower Broadway. Didn't get paid, but got all the drinks I could put away." She paused, looked around the room, leaned closer to the table, and whispered, "Don't blame Heather for shooting him. He sold a bigger bill of goods than he could deliver. He screwed a lot of people."

Charles jerked his head closer to Edwina. "Heather didn't kill him."

Edwina slowly shook her head. "Hope you're right. I like her. From what I hear, it looks bad. Wasn't it her gun?"

Barb gave Edwina a motherly pat on the forearm. "For the

sake of argument, let's say Heather didn't do it. Do you know anyone who might have been angry enough to want him dead?"

Edwina smiled. "Me, for one. And I could name four or five others I know personally. No telling how many more there could've been."

"You didn't do it, did you?" Barb chuckled. "Just kidding."

Edwina started to say something, hesitated, and smiled. "Should have."

I asked, "Were the other people you thought were angry enough to shoot him in Nashville?"

"Some of them. Look, I need to get back to work. Good talking to you, and Charles, if you see Heather, tell her I said hey and hope everything works out."

Barb touched Edwina's arm. "Even if a bunch of you were angry with him, it had to be terrible learning he was killed. Were you in Nashville when it happened?"

Edwina cocked her head in Barb's direction. "Nah, I was taking some time to clear my head. I was surfing over on Folly. That's how I get away from worrying about things."

"Sounds like fun," Charles said, the person I'd never known to wade into the ocean, much less surf.

"Yeah, it is. Thanks for coming." She took another bite, guzzled the last of her beer, and returned to the stage.

Edwina opened her set with Tanya Tucker's "Delta Dawn," we finished our pizza and drinks, and Barb said we needed to head out as well, since she was the only one in the group who had to go to work tomorrow. I agreed since it was already past my bedtime.

We spent most of the ride home in silence. Charles finally said, "Well, she didn't feed us a pack of lies, but there was one whopper, wasn't there?"

"That she was here when Starr was killed?" I said.

"Yep."

"She also told me a pretty big one when I was talking to her at Cal's the other night," I said.

"That she didn't think she knew Heather?"

"Tonight, you'd think they were best buds. Sounds like she knew her well enough to frame her."

Barb said, "Lies aren't proof."

Charles said, "Thank you, Miss Defense Attorney."

"They're enough for me to tell Cindy," I added. "She'll find it interesting."

"Interesting enough to share with the police in Nashville or enough to talk to Edwina?" Barb said.

"Hope so," Charles said.

I called Cindy before I headed to the hospital to spring Cal. She was in a meeting with the mayor and said she'd call as soon as she "agreed with everything His Honor said and followed all of his wise and perceptive wishes and commands."

"Brian's listening, isn't he?"

Cindy giggled. "Yes, Mayor Newman is finding this conversation both stimulating and interfering with his meeting with the best police chief that has ever been under his command."

"You mean *only* chief."

"I'll call."

Cal was in an equally good mood, as I would have been if I was escaping from the hospital. He said the doctor had been in and told him he could leave as soon as someone showed up to collect him. I commandeered a wheelchair parked by the nurse's station and had Cal in it and headed to the exit before anyone saw us. We had almost made it to the door when two nurses spotted us and rushed over. I was afraid they were going to herd Cal back to his room. Instead, they hugged him, said he was a delight to take care of, and wished him and his injured Stetson complete recoveries.

Cal patted his back pocket and looked from one nurse to the other. "Got your numbers. I'll be a callin' as soon as I'm back to full strength so we can get together."

The health-care providers smiled. I wondered if Cal was serious. I suspected he was.

We sat at a stoplight a block from the hospital. Cal gazed out the windshield. "More's coming back to me."

Traffic, like most mornings in the hospital district, was terrible and we spent more time stopped than moving.

"You remember what you figured out about Starr?"

"Not at all. Still don't remember anything about getting conked, but think I remember that gal singer Edwina, umm, Robinson in the bar a couple of days earlier, or maybe it was weeks, little vague on that. She could've been talking about Starr."

"Who was she talking to?"

"Some younger gal, don't recall seeing her before, but with my memory cells dying off, I could have. They were sitting at the bar so I was close enough to hear some of their yacking."

"What do you remember?"

"The young chick was POed about something. I didn't hear what. From what Edwina was saying, I figured it was about Starr. Something about taking a bunch of money, and Edwina said, and I do remember this, that the young chick didn't lose nearly as much to the conniving shyster as she lost, and she knew others who were suckered out of their hard-earned cash."

"Did she say how much or why?"

"May have, I didn't hear. Now here's the interesting part. She didn't use these words, but I had the impression Starr and Edwina may have been close, if you get my drift."

I did. "What makes you think that?"

Cal touched the bandage on his head, and turned to me. "I've been hanging out in bars since Noah parked the Ark. Been singing most of that time, drinking a few decades' worth of hours, and watching humans and their nature all my life. I've known more drunks than show up at an AA convention. Cheating and affair talk has its own ring to it, and it ain't a wedding ring. I know it when I hear it."

Clearly, I hadn't been around nearly as many bars as Cal, so I tried again. "Do you remember what was said to make you believe Edwina and Starr were lovers?"

"Not all of it. I recall her saying the other woman kept getting in the way. That's the problem with affairs; pesky wives complicate sinning."

All Cal could add before I left him at his apartment was his head hurt and he needed to "rest a spell" before relieving Burl at the bar. I said he should stay in bed and let Burl tend bar until Cal had regained his strength. He waved me off and said he needed to get back before the good Preacher turned the place into a branch of First Light Church and the only wine to be found was at communion.

"Whatever."

Cal turned and looked in the back seat like he'd just remembered it was there. "Where's my hat? You did pick it up from where I got smacked?"

I told him it was pretty mushed up and had saved his life.

"Knew I could count on it. Where's it recuperating?"

I told him it was at my house.

"That old thing's been with me through thick, thin, and thinner. I'd hate to part company with it now."

"I'll bring it by."

He tipped an imaginary Stetson. "Thanks, pard."

On Cindy's way to following Mayor Newman's wishes and

commands, she called and asked if I was buying her breakfast at Black Magic Cafe. I asked if breakfast was enough to get her to do a favor for me. She said, "Yes, if the favor doesn't involve taking time, energy, money, or breaking any laws."

I agreed even though I knew what I wanted would infringe on one or more of those things.

The Black Magic Cafe was less than a block off Center Street, located near the Folly's retail area, and three blocks from the ocean. It was closer than that to my house, so I walked. Cindy's unmarked, GMC Yukon was parked in front of the restaurant and she was waiting for me near the entry at a table beside a large potted plant. She was gripping a yellow Black Magic mug.

She held the mug up. "I couldn't wait. Meetings put me to sleep and your duly-elected mayor didn't offer caffeine. They're fixing my breakfast. Told them you'd be in soon to pick it up and pay. You can get yourself something if you want."

Cindy, like Charles, was generous when it came to allowing me to pick up the tab. Meetings with the mayor not only had put the chief to sleep, they whetted her appetite. She had ordered the chicken and waffles with a side of hominy grits and orange juice. I grabbed a cheese Danish and coffee and joined her on the deck.

"How's hardheaded Cal?"

I told her.

"How's Heather?"

I told her I hadn't heard anything in the last few days.

"How's Charles?"

I said he wasn't doing well, but was hiding it.

Cindy cut into her waffle and to the chase. "What do you need?"

"Edwina Robinson," I said and sipped my coffee.

"Her again."

I spent fifteen minutes telling Cindy what I knew, much of what I speculated, and everything I hoped about Edwina. To my surprise, the chief took notes and only interrupted twice. She had already heard some of it, and still listened as I repeated my thoughts.

"Is that all?"

I said it was.

She closed her notebook and stared at me. "Let me get this straight. You want me to traipse over to her fancy-dancy down-town condo, lock her in a windowless room, and browbeat a confession out of her?"

"Of course not." I smiled. "The room doesn't have to be windowless."

"Funny," she said, slobbering sarcasm.

"I don't know what you can do, Cindy. I know she lied about knowing Heather. According to what you told me, she lied about where she was when Starr was killed. She could've known about Heather's gun, and it's clear she was angry with the agent about taking her money. From her previous encounter with the law, she'd capable of violence."

"Chris," Cindy pointed toward Folly's main street. "I'm one insignificant police chief on one tiny island. I have no jurisdic-tion outside Folly Beach. What do you think I can do?"

"Talk to her. Apply some of your endearing pressure. She doesn't know what authority you have. Give it a try."

She pointed a fork at her half-empty plate. "If you think you're getting by with this itty-bitty bribe, you're dumber than an earthworm with a lobotomy. I'll give it my best shot, although I won't be able to do it for a few days. I promised Larry I'd go with him to Charlotte for a hardware store trade show. We're leaving in a couple of hours. He says next to the latest innovations in power drills, I'll be the most exciting thing there."

I smiled. "Such a romantic."

"He's a charmer. I used to be offended. Now I know how much he loves power drills, so I figure I'm swell. Anyway, it'll be a few days, and when I do talk to her, don't expect her to hand me a written confession."

"That's all I ask."

I spent the rest of the day doing what I often spent mindless hours doing: catching up on my bills, housecleaning, and rationalizing that my aching back, arthritic hands, and pain in my knees were caused by healthy, strenuous exercise rather than old age. I spent less time on the routine rationalization than usual and devoted more time to trying to figure out if there was anything I had learned that would get Heather off the hook.

The longer I thought, I realized I had moved past the belief she had murdered Starr and was convinced Edwina was the killer. So, how did she know about Heather's gun and where it was hidden? When did she take it, and return it? If she hit Cal, did anyone see her that night in the bar or the night when she could have overheard Cal telling me he knew something? Should I have taken my suspicions to the cops in Nashville rather than sharing them with Cindy who couldn't investigate in Tennessee? And, was I focusing on Edwina because she was one of Starr's clients and she had told us a couple of lies? I wanted to call Charles but figured he needed a day of rest and if he needed anything he knew how to get me.

Something had to be done and I didn't want to wait for Cindy to get back in town to talk to Edwina. I could stop by her condo. Other than looking like a stalker, what would I accomplish? I could call her again, and say what? Cindy had already culled whatever was available on the Internet and from police databases, so there wasn't any reason to try to go down that road.

I fixed a well-rounded supper of Velveeta cheese on rye and kettle chips, washed it down with a Diet Pepsi, and decided to walk to Cal's to see if the owner was there. I grabbed his sad-looking, mashed Stetson, tried to shape it to look more like a hat, was halfway successful, and headed to the bar.

It was early and there were only a handful of customers

spread around the room. Burl was in deep discussion with Cal who saw me—saw his Stetson—and his face wrinkled into a frown. I thought he was going to cry. He stepped from behind the bar and took the hat in his hands like he was lifting a baby bird with a broken wing. He flipped the hat over and looked inside the crown, and up at me and thanked me for returning it. I asked how he was feeling.

"Was feeling like a hundred-fifty-three bucks until I got here and that preaching dictator told me I should go home." He looked back down at his hat, and sighed. "I told him the joint's name was Cal's and not Burl's Bible Bar and I appreciated everything he'd done. I was just fine, thank you."

"What'd he say?"

"He'd pray for me to get better and if I kicked the bucket because I didn't take his advice, he'd preach my funeral. I thanked him and said that's what preacher friends are for."

If there'd been a bigger crowd, Burl would have been right, but the preaching bartender and I managed to get Cal to park his weak, thinner-than-usual body at a table near the door and serve as greeter while Burl and I handled the beer distribution. His part-time cook fried a burger or two for the few hungry patrons. Every so often, Cal sauntered to the jukebox at the corner of the bandstand and punched in some country classics. His halted movement and forced smile revealed he was more comfortable at the table than he wanted us to know. It was still good seeing him back and getting better.

Burl wanted to talk about two members of his flock and their earthly trials and tribulations, and I was happy to listen, since I didn't know what to say about Heather and Starr's murder. I wondered when Cindy would have a chance to talk to Edwina and what, if anything, she could learn that could help Charles's fiancé. More than anything, I was frustrated.

Fortunate for Cal, Burl, and me, we closed the bar around ten after the last two customers drifted off. Sleep came slowly as I kept thinking there must be something I could do to help Heather, and wondering if there was something I already knew that could tie Edwina to the murder.

Short hours later, I was awakened by the shrill sounds of my phone. I opened one eye and glanced at the clock that told me it was only five thirty-five. I shook the cobwebs out of my head, picked up the phone.

I heard sobbing and realized it was Charles. "She tried to kill herself. Gotta go back. Can…can I borrow your car?"

He was gasping for breath and I couldn't understand what he was saying. "Slow down, are you talking about Heather?"

"Yes. Gotta go back now…now!"

It wouldn't do any good to try to ask for details. "I'll drive. When do you want me to get you?"

"Now, Chris. She may be dead."

"I'm on my way."

2 8

Charles was pacing the gravel and shell parking area in front of his apartment when I pulled in. He wore a plain white T-shirt without any logos, so I knew he was traumatized. He slid in the passenger seat before I got out of the car. His eyes were blood-shot from being up all night or from crying. His hand shook as he threw his cane and clothes bag in the back seat.

All he said was, "Go."

He wasn't ready to talk and I didn't push. I had driven off the island and was in Charleston on the way to the Interstate before he spoke.

He stared out his side window. "Her attorney called at one-thirty." He hesitated and sniffled. I didn't think he was going to say anything else, until he added, "He didn't know anything—wasn't certain if she was alive. Chris, what will I do if she's…you know?"

"What did he say?"

"She wasn't adjusting to being in there. They wouldn't let me to talk to her much. Each time I did she seemed so … depressed. She wouldn't say anything. I just don't know."

That didn't answer my question. We'd be in the car for many hours and he would talk when ready. Before today he'd confided that she seemed down when he had talked to her. He hadn't hinted it was more than what anyone would experience if locked up.

Thirty more miles of silence and I started telling him about last night at Cal's and asking Cindy to try to talk to Edwina.

He turned from staring out the window. "Too little, too late," he interrupted before I told him my suspicions.

"We don't know."

He took the phone from his pocket and set it on the console. "Edelen's supposed to call when he learns something." He looked at the phone like it would ring if he stared at it. "They called him around one this morning. The person he talked to knew she had been taken to the hospital. Said it was serious and that was it." He smacked his hand on the dash. "I was numb. I wanted to call you and go then. I was shaking so bad I couldn't hit the right numbers on the phone. What's going to happen?"

I put my hand on his shoulder. "I don't know. Let's wait and see."

An hour later, the phone jolted Charles out of his funk. He stared at it like it was a poisonous snake and nothing bad could happen if he pulled away from it. Curiosity got the better of him and he grabbed it and cringed. "Hello."

I heard a muted voice on the other end and Charles said, "Yes."

The low hum of the tires on the Interstate kept me from hearing much. Charles finally said, "When will they know?" More silence. "What happened?" He moved the phone to his other ear and tapped on the armrest with his other hand. Finally, he said, "How could that happen?" His pause wasn't as long this time. "Yes, as soon as ... okay, yes." He hit *End Call* and closed his eyes.

I returned my hand to his shoulder. He looked at it. "She's alive, but …"

I waited. He didn't say anything. "What?"

He looked over like he just noticed me in the car. "They don't know if she'll make it."

"What happened?"

"He didn't know much. He thinks she sneaked a plastic water cup from dinner to her cell. She broke it in pieces and slashed her wrist with a sharp edge. They didn't find her for a long time and she lost so much blood that she was almost…you know." He paused and wiped a tear from his cheek. "They got her to the hospital …"

"She's alive."

"Yeah. Edelen promised to call when he knows more."

It took passing three exits before I convinced him he needed to eat. He kept saying he wasn't hungry. He had to be and I said I needed food and while we were at the Interstate McDonald's he should order something. He huffed then ordered two cheeseburgers and pushed me out of the restaurant so we could get on the road.

An hour later, he had chewed on the cheeseburgers and fidgeting less. He said, "I knew she couldn't handle a cell. She told me years ago, she almost didn't rent her apartment because she was claustrophobic and thought it was too tiny. She didn't have enough money to get anything larger. Chris, she still had to leave the bedroom door open all the time so she could see sunlight from the windows." He paused. "Every time she came to my place she had to sit near the window. It bothered her."

"Did she say anything about the cell?"

"Only every time. She shouldn't have been in there—not one day, one hour, one minute." He shook his head. "What did she do to deserve that? All she wanted to do was become a singer. What, Chris? What?"

We had reached the outskirts of Nashville and the attorney

hadn't called. Charles took the phone and hit redial. Edelen had called from his cell phone, so Charles didn't have to go through his office gatekeepers to reach him. Charles asked if there was an update and Edelen must have said no. Charles asked what hospital, paused for the attorney to respond, and said, "I'm going there anyway."

Charles slammed the phone down on the console. "Edelen didn't have anything and didn't think the hospital would let me see Heather." He hesitated, looked out the side window, and mumbled, "Let them try to stop me."

IF THE AUTOMATIC front doors at the hospital hadn't opened as fast as they did, Charles would have knocked them out of their track when he barged through the entry. I thought the elderly women sitting behind the information kiosk was going to fall out of her chair as he stormed up to her.

"Heather Lee. Room number?" he shouted at the startled woman, Hazel according to a name tag that also read *Volunteer*.

Hazel regained her balance and checked the computer.

"I'm sorry, sir. We don't have anyone by that name."

Charles stepped back like the women had rammed her fist in the stomach. "Oh, my God. She's dead."

I moved beside Charles, looked at the volunteer, and gave my best calming smile. "Hazel, would, by chance, you have anyone registered under the name of the jail?"

She looked at me like I was getting ready to spring a prisoner. I didn't pull a gun or flourish an IED, so she tapped more computer keys, glanced at Charles who was still traumatized, and turned to me. "Sir, if you go to the fourth floor, there should be a police officer near the elevator. He may be of assistance."

I smiled, thanked Hazel, and led Charles to the bank of elevators. A uniformed officer greeted us as we arrived at the fourth floor. Hazel must have called while we were on the way up.

The officer smiled—the practiced smile he would use when asking a speeding motorist for his license and proof of insurance —and pointed us to an empty waiting room. "I'm Officer Neil. May I be of assistance?"

Charles eyes darted around the corridor. "Is she alive?"

"Please be seated, sir."

Charles started to protest, and instead flopped down in the chair. I sat beside him.

"Sir," Neil said as he remained standing. "Are you referring to Ms. Lee?"

Charles hands balled into fists and he looked like he was going to pounce out of the chair. "Of course, I am."

"Sir, please dial it down. Are you related?"

Charles's fist tightened. I was afraid he was going to lash out against the man who was simply doing his job. Charles took a deep breath before saying, "She's my fiancé."

Neil must have decided that was close enough to a relative. "To answer your question, Ms. Lee is alive, but in critical condition. The doctor says it's touch-and-go. I wasn't here when they brought her in, but I've heard she'd lost a lot of blood. It was a long time before the jail's medical staff got to her."

Charles sighed, and yanked his head up and stared at Officer Neil. "Why in the hell did it take so long?"

"Again, sir. I wasn't there. No one can keep a constant eye on the prisoners. Your fiancé was in her cell several hours after supper between routine rounds. They don't know when she tried to…umm, when her injuries were sustained. I'm sorry, sir. It's all I know."

Charles said, "Can I see her?"

"I don't believe that will be possible, sir. Not for a few days."

"What—"

The officer stopped Charles. "Sir, her condition is critical, and even if she was able to have visitors, someone from the jail must authorize it. My suggestion is you work through her attorney. He or she will know the ropes and what you need to do."

Charles started to stand. "Is she on this floor?"

"Sir, I can't—"

I put my arm on Charles shoulder and pushed him back down in the chair. "Charles, why don't we go to your apartment and call her attorney?"

Neil said, "That would be a good idea, sir."

I was afraid I was going to have to drag Charles out of the hospital until he turned to putty and I helped him to the car. I kept reminding him Heather was alive. By the time we reached his apartment, he'd regained some energy, yet relied on the handrail to support him up three flights of stairs.

I got him a beer as he moved to the couch. "Think it's too late to call her lawyer?" he said, before taking a sip.

It was eleven o'clock. I told him it would be okay. I didn't want to hear him mention it a hundred more times, and besides if he didn't call now, he would want to make the call before sunrise.

Edelen must keep the phone by his side. He answered on the second ring. Charles, as usual, dove into the middle of the conversation before the attorney had time to ask who was calling. Charles switched on the phone's speaker so I could hear. To the attorney's credit, he didn't hang up on Charles, was sympathetic, pleased his client was still among the living, and assured Charles he would contact the jail first thing in the morning and see if he could get Charles approval to see Heather once she was out of immediate danger.

My friend was somewhat relieved and finished off his beer and hinted for me to get him another. I got him the second bottle without pointing out he was as close to the refrigerator as I was. He finished the second drink and I asked if he thought he could sleep. He said he doubted it and wanted to take a walk. I asked if he wanted me to come, and he said he needed to be alone. I was exhausted and didn't try to change his mind. Before falling asleep, I realized I hadn't finished telling Charles about Edwina's past and my increasing suspicion about her guilt. I also decided that since we were in Nashville, I should meet with the detectives and lay out my thoughts and what I'd learned. None of that would matter if Heather didn't make it through the night.

I heard car horns on the street below. I blinked a few times and glanced at the time on my phone. It was nearly nine in the morning. I padded to the kitchen and found Charles at the table staring in his coffee mug. His eyes were bloodshot, but alert. He wore a blue, long-sleeve University of New Haven Chargers T-shirt, tan shorts, and considering what he had been through, a close replica of a smile.

He held up his mug and tilted his head toward the Mr. Coffee machine. "Sleeping the day away?"

I fished through the cabinet and found a clean cup and filled it and refilled his mug. "Sleep any?"

"Not a wink."

I nodded toward his phone. "Any word?"

He shook his head. "Expect it to ring any second."

I wondered how many seconds he had been sitting here waiting for a call. "No news is good news," I said, and hoped it was true. Heather could have died, and I doubt anyone would have thought to contact Charles, and wouldn't have called her lawyer until a reasonable hour this morning.

"Please be right."

I didn't see anything good coming from me staring at Charles staring at the phone, so I began filling him in on what Cindy had found about Edwina and that the chief was going to interview her once she returned from the tradeshow.

I had his attention. "We've got to tell the Nashville cops. They've got to start looking at Edwina. Chris, she's the killer."

He said it so quickly that I wondered how much coffee he'd already had. Before I could tell him that it didn't prove anything, the phone rang.

He hit the speaker icon and said hello. The first thing Heather's lawyer said was he just got off the phone with the hospital and she was alive.

"Thank God. When can I see her?"

"Not so quick, she's not out of the woods. It'll be tomorrow, maybe later, before anyone could get in. I'll have to coordinate your visit. Let me call you around nine in the morning."

Charles leaned toward the phone. "Tomorrow, no—"

"Mr. Fowler," Edelen interrupted. "That's all we can do. They promised to call if there's any change. I'll talk to you tomorrow."

Charles slumped in the chair. "Okay."

He stared at the phone, walked to the window, and returned to stare at the phone. I wanted to do something to help, if only I knew what it could be.

He saved me when he said, "Let's call the detectives and tell them about Edwina. The sooner they figure out she killed Starr the quicker Heather gets out."

Charles jumped up and went to the bedroom to find the detective's card, and had punched the number in his phone before he was back in the kitchen. I wasn't certain we had enough to talk to the police about, but it would get Charles's mind off Heather's condition. Detective Lawrence answered and Charles told him who he was. It took the detective a few seconds to remember Charles, who then said he had some information that would help the police catch the "real killer." A few seconds later, Charles said, "Great, we'll see you then," ended the call, and smiled for the second time in two days. "He's on his way."

The detective wasn't in as big a hurry to get to us as Charles thought he should be. It was an hour before he knocked on the door. Charles had it open before the detective had a chance to knock a second time. He stepped in. Charles held out his hand to shake. The detective ignored it, and glanced around the room. I gave a halfhearted nod to the visitor.

"So, what's so all-fired important?"

Charles looked behind the detective. "Where's your partner?"

"Not here."

I figured that out, and I'm not a detective.

Charles seemed disappointed he didn't have the full complement of detectives to share his wisdom with. He got over it quickly and motioned for Lawrence to follow him to the kitchen.

The detective sighed, and took one of the chairs. "I heard about your girlfriend trying to kill herself. Hope she's okay."

Charles scratched the side of his head. "They say she's going to make it."

"Good. What's so important?"

"Chris and I just got back from South Carolina," Charles pointed to me. "We've learned some stuff that'll put you on the right track to find the guy's killer." He abruptly turned to me. "Tell him, Chris."

Thanks, Charles. "It's about a woman named Edwina Robinson. She's a singer from Charleston and Starr was her agent." I proceeded to tell him about her contact with Starr and how he ripped her off; her relationship with others in the Charleston area; why we suspected she was in Nashville when he was killed; how she could have been mistaken for Heather in a poorly lit bar; and, how she could have killed Starr.

Lawrence had started taking notes, set his pen on the table, closed his notebook, and glared at me. "Is that what you took me away from my job for?"

I thought finding killers was his job. Instead of pointing that out, I told him it was.

He turned to Charles. "I don't blame you. If I was in your shoes and my girlfriend was in jail, I'd do anything to get her out. I'd look for anyone with the most tenuous connection to the dead guy." He put both palms down on the table and leaned to within a foot of Charles. "Let me tell you what I see."

Charles leaned closer to the detective and said, "You've got the wrong—"

"What I see is the person who killed Starr is cuffed to a hospital bed. She has motive. We have a witness who has no reason to lie. Her gun shot him. And, because she was overcome with guilt, she tried to kill herself. Case open and shut. Unless you have something that means something, I'm out of here."

Lawrence grabbed his pen and notebook, pushed away from the table, smoothed out his sports coat, and headed the door."

Charles was quick to follow. "Assho—"

Lawrence pivoted and glowered at Charles. "What?"

I stepped between them. "Detective, my friend's upset. We apologize for any inconvenience. We thought you should have the information about Ms. Robinson."

Both Charles and the detective glared at me.

"I'll give him a pass this time. I'm sorry about the suicide attempt. She's guilty. Period." He slammed the door on his way out.

Charles walked to the kitchen and back in the living room where I was standing. "Thanks a hell of a lot. Couldn't you have given me a tiny bit of support. He's convinced Heather killed the son of a bitch, and all you offer is 'my friend's upset.'"

I reached out to pat my friend's arm. He jerked back, went into his bedroom, and slammed the door shut. I lowered myself on the couch, lowered my head, and massaged my neck.

3 O

Twenty minutes later, another knock on the door disturbed my feeling sorry for Charles, Heather, and to be honest, myself. I wondered if Detective Lawrence had second thoughts about what we'd shared, or if he had returned to either arrest or berate Charles for his mini-temper tantrum. What I didn't expect to see was Heather's friend Gwen.

"Oh, it's you." She looked past me into the living room.

Nothing like being welcomed. I invited her in and said I'd get Charles.

"Is the famous old guy here?"

"No, sorry."

"Me too. It's pretty thrilling to meet someone who was really, really big way back when."

I thought it was the same thing she could have said about a dinosaur, as I tapped on Charles's door.

"What?"

I opened the door a crack and told him Gwen was here. I closed the door and said he would be out and told her she could wait on the couch.

After a couple of minutes, I was afraid Charles wasn't coming out and I was running out of chit-chat. He saved me when he opened his door. "Hi, Gwen."

"Sorry to drop in like this. I didn't have your phone number and was down the street, so I took a chance you'd be here."

"That's, umm, okay," Charles made the switch from anger to hospitable. "Thanks for stopping by."

"I was worried about my friend sitting in a jail cell and wondering how she was doing."

Gwen wouldn't have known about the suicide attempt. I waited to see how Charles handled it.

Charles shook his head. "She's not happy about being there. She's doing as good as anyone would."

That's one way of dealing with it.

"It sucks that she's locked up. She's such a sweet gal. What do you think the cops have on her?"

Charles tilted his head toward Gwen. "The gun."

"That's all?"

Charles shrugged.

I knew there was more. Charles didn't want to elaborate, so I jumped into the discussion. "Gwen, let me ask you something. Do you remember a singer named Edwina Robinson? She performed a few times at the Bluebird. You might have been there when she was."

She rubbed her chin and gave a slight nod. "Don't know for certain. There're a lot of singers every week and they start running together. I might know who you're talking about. I think the gal's name is Edwina. I don't know her last name. The reason I remember the name is because Heather said she'd been meeting her for coffee. Why?"

I wanted to say, how many Edwina's could there be at the Bluebird. Instead I said, "Remember if she ever had anyone with her?"

"You're asking some mighty hard questions, Mr. Landrum."

"Sorry, it's important."

"Most of the singers have someone with them." She grinned. "Somebody's got to clap after they sing."

"Yeah, but did she?" Charles asked. He had stayed out of the conversation too long for his liking.

"I don't remember. Not saying she didn't; just don't recall."

I nodded and smiled to indicate we understood. "You said Heather mentioned having coffee with Edwina. Did she say anything about it?"

"No. Who's this Edwina?"

"Someone who knows something about Starr's death," Charles said. "The police want to talk to her."

Did he forget how he and Detective Lawrence had left their conversation?

"You know if there's anything I can do to help Heather I will. Do the cops have anything other than it being her gun? Think they're looking for other suspects?"

Charles sat straighter. "Nothing that proves she did it, because she didn't." He hesitated. "They're not looking for anyone else. They're convinced Heather's guilty."

"Her gun shot him," she repeated. "That's why she's in jail."

I wondered why she'd mentioned the gun a second time. I asked if she wanted a drink to keep her talking. I didn't know what she might know, but at this point, she was the only person we could learn from. She said she was fine.

I said, "Do you remember if Heather mentioned the gun to anyone?"

Gwen nodded. "Sure. She told her friends about it. I already knew since I sold it to her. She liked having it and wanted everyone to know."

"Where'd she keep it?"

"Most of the time in her purse. Wouldn't do her good if it was in here and she was out somewhere. When she was at the Bird she left it in the car because she didn't want it in her purse when she was on stage. Someone could steal it. She said even if the car didn't lock, it was safer there."

Charles said, "Who else knew that?"

"Where it was or that the car didn't lock?"

"Both," I said.

"Probably everybody who knew her. Wasn't a secret, you know." She looked at her oversized, colorful watch. "Whoops, have to go. Nice talking to you. Don't forget to tell Heather I said hey."

She was at the door and turned to Charles. "Don't know if it means anything, but I do think I remember someone being with Edwina."

Charles took a giant step toward her. "Who?"

"I don't remember seeing anyone, but I recall one time she was talking about not performing because some guy with her needed to get to something on the other side of town."

"And you didn't catch a name or see the other person?"

"Nope."

Gwen left and Charles stayed in the living room rather than holing up in his bedroom. He was thawing. He asked what we'd learned from Gwen's visit. I told him I thought it strange for her to drop by. He said he thought it was sweet. I didn't disagree, although something kept nagging me about how helpful she appeared to want to be; and how she kept asking if the police had any other evidence and if they were looking for other suspects.

Charles began pacing, and I asked what he wanted to do. He started to say something about trying to find Heather's other friends and see if they knew anything about Edwina. I asked if he had any of their phone numbers, when my phone rang.

Cindy asked, "Where are you?"

"Nashville, in Charles's apartment. Are you taking a survey of all your residents?"

"No."

"You still in hardware heaven?"

"Screw you, or maybe that's auger you. This hardware stuff's confusing."

"You're calling to tell me that?"

"No, it's about Edwina," The chief switched out of teasing mode.

"Did you talk to her? What did she say?"

"No, I couldn't talk to her."

"What do you mean, couldn't?" I said it with more of an edge than I had intended. "I know you're in Charlotte. You could've called her."

"I couldn't because—"

My frustration from the last two days was overflowing. I interrupted, "She's Heather's only hope. Come on, Cindy, you've got to—"

"Stop!" Cindy blurted. "I can't talk to her because she's dead."

"She's what?"

"I said Edwina Robinson's dead. A guy and his Dalmatian were renting a house out past the Washout and found her body yesterday morning floating in knee deep water. The dog was barking up a storm or the guy wouldn't have noticed her."

Charles was flinging his arms around and pointing to the phone. I took the hint and hit the speaker button.

"What happened?" I asked.

"They said she had on a bathing suit so it looks like she was swimming and got caught in a rip current."

I remembered Edwina had told me she liked to surf. "She was a surfer. Did they find a surfboard?"

"Not that I know of."

"When did it happen?"

"Best guess is she had been in the water for several hours, probably drowned day before yesterday, late afternoon."

"Why do they think it was an accident? That's a gigantic coincidence."

"First, there were no signs of foul play, and second, it's only a *gigantic coincidence* in your mind. You're the only person who thinks she was tied to Starr's murder."

"I do too," Charles cried. He leaned closer to the phone as if Cindy hadn't heard his outburst and repeated it.

"Hi, Charles. How's Heather holding up?"

Cindy hadn't heard about the suicide attempt. I didn't want to muddy whatever she had to say about Edwina with news about Heather. I put my forefinger to my lips and hoped Charles would take the hint and not mention Heather's current condition.

"She's doing the best she can."

I couldn't understand why Cindy didn't think Edwina's death was more than an accident. "What about Edwina's lies about knowing Heather, or what about her saying she wasn't in Nashville when he was killed? Or what—"

"Whoa. I'm not saying you're wrong. Just saying there's nothing concrete to follow up on. Sure, she lied. I'll tell you something I learned in cop world a long time ago. People lie all the time. It doesn't mean they're guilty of anything except skirting the truth."

I took a deep breath and rubbed my hand through my thinning hair. Charles stared at the phone and didn't say anything.

I leaned closer to the phone. "Cindy, you have good cop instincts. Anything suspicious strike you?"

"Not really. There were no obvious signs of foul play, no signs of a struggle. I'll call a little later and see if the autopsy showed anything out of the ordinary."

"What about no surfboard?" I was reaching. I couldn't get my mind around it being an accident.

"That might be strange if she'd been surfing. We don't know she was. Even if she had a board, it wouldn't be unprecedented for someone to find it with no one around and *borrow* it, if you catch my wave."

Cindy was right. "Thanks for letting me know."

"Before you ask, I'll call as soon as I learn something about cause of death."

I thanked her, ended the call, looked at Charles, and said, "Now what?"

He looked at the silent phone and at me. "Even if Edwina's death was an accident, she could have killed Starr."

"Or, did someone kill Edwina? I can't believe she went and accidently drowned when everything was starting to point to her."

Charles nodded. "If she was killed, was it because someone found out she killed the sleazy agent and was getting revenge?"

"Consider this," I said. "If Edwina didn't kill Starr, did someone murder her because she knew who had killed him?"

"Who?"

"Your guess is as good as mine. It could be Edwina had nothing to do with Starr's death, and drowned."

Charles shook his head. "No way. She was killed because she either killed Starr or knew who did."

I walked to the window and looked at Charles's car in the parking lot. Cindy said they hadn't found Edwina's surfboard; she didn't say if her car was nearby. I punched in Cindy's number and was sent to voicemail. I left a message asking about Edwina's car.

Then I remembered something Edwina had said. I had asked her if she ever played Nashville. She'd said *we've* been there a time or two. And, Gwen also said she thought Edwina had someone with her.

"Do you know where Heather's friend Jessica lives?" I asked.

"No, why?"

"How about her address?"

"Should be in Heather's book. Did you forget my question?"

"No. I wanted to drop in on her and see if she remembers Edwina and anyone she may have been with at the Bluebird. I'd rather see her reaction in person. If you don't have her address, a call will have to do."

Charles must have decided my answer was acceptable. He went to the bedroom to get Heather's book and returned without an address but with a number. I called and hung up when her machine kicked in.

I said, "Let's visit good ole Dale and Kelly Windsor."

"Same questions face-to-face?" Charles said and looked at his imaginary watch.

"What else do we have to do?"

"Nothing. Just wondering when the lawyer's going to call." He grabbed his Tilley, cane, and headed to the door.

WE GOT to DK Studio quicker than the last time and found a parking space in front of the building. It helped that I had learned the way and that it wasn't rush hour.

Charles looked at the studio. "So, are you going to first ask them if they killed Edwina or if they killed Starr and then Edwina?"

"Thought I'd start out more indirect and ask if Edwina had anyone with her when she cut her demo."

"Next, you can ask if they ever take vacations, like going to Charleston in the last few days. And, here's one, ask if when they were on vacation, if they happened to drown Edwina?"

"Did you forget the indirect part? Let me do the talking."

"Okay. I'll only butt in when you ask the wrong questions."

I rang the bell and smiled at the camera staring at me from near the ceiling. Our last visit ended on less than hospitable terms, and hoped Dale and Kelly would be more accommodating today.

I recognized Dale's voice from the speaker. "What now?"

"Hi, Ms. Windsor," I said in my cheeriest voice. "We'd like to ask a few questions about one of your customers."

"Who?" she said in less than a cheery voice.

I would rather have told her from the confines of the reception room. "Edwina Robinson. I believe she cut a demo here a few months back."

There was a long pause before she said, "I told you before we had no more to say to you or your friend there."

"We'd like to talk to you and your husband."

"Kelly's out of town and I've said all I'm going to."

"Yes, but Edwina—"

"Goodbye."

"That went well," Charles whispered as we headed back to the car. "They're back at the top of the suspect list."

"Don't jump to conclusions. Something has them agitated. Don't forget, they told us the last time we were here they didn't have anything more to say."

"Wonder why she asked who we wanted to know about before running us off?"

"Interesting."

"You're danged right it is. Did you catch that her hubby's out of town? Bet he's in Charleston. Let's go back and get her to let us in."

"I've got another idea." Anything to prevent him from storming the fort—or the recording studio. "Let's find out if the Windsors or Heather's other two friends were on Folly when Edwina *accidentally* drowned."

"So, your plan is to call each of them and ask if they've been on Folly lately. Oh, and if they had been, ask if they happened to drown Edwina while they were there?"

"Good idea, except I doubt it'll work. I'll call Cindy and have her check the Tides, and if she has time, a couple of the other nearby hotels. There are many places someone could have stayed in the area, so it's a longshot."

Charles stopped staring at DK Studios and hopped in the car. "Don't forget to add Kelly Windsor to the list. A longshot's better than no shot."

"Did a president say that?"

"Not that I know of, why?"

"Never mind." I punched Cindy's number.

"What?"

"And a pleasant hello to you, Chief LaMond. Are you still in Charlotte?"

"Bolts and a bunch of nuts running all over the place. What now?"

I shared our thoughts that some of the people we knew were angry with Starr and had killed Edwina. If so, he or she would have been in the Folly area at the time of the alleged accident.

"What am I supposed to do about that?"

I asked if she could check the local hotels. She huffed, mumbled a profanity, and asked for the names. I gave them to her and thanked her for considering it. Another profanity was uttered. I started to end the call.

"Hang on," the chief said. "I talked to the detective who's considering the drowning and told him your thought that it wasn't accidental. He asked if I agreed and I told him you were a prolific pain in the patoot, but were occasionally right. He said it looked like an accident. As a favor to me, he'll look at it again."

"Great," I said. "Did the detective find out if her car was nearby?"

"He's checking."

"Thanks."

"Once again, you owe me."

3 1

At seven the next morning, Charles was in the kitchen with both elbows resting on the table. He was staring at his phone. I resisted the urge to tell him a watched phone doesn't ring, and instead poured a mug of coffee.

"When's he going to call?" Charles asked as I joined him.

"It's early."

He turned away from the phone. "Abraham Lincoln said, 'If there is a worse place than hell, I am in it.'" He pounded his fist on the table. "It couldn't have been worse than waiting, wondering if she's alive, and if she is, getting convicted and spending the rest of her life in prison." Charles pushed away from the table and started pacing.

He wasn't helping himself, and I couldn't stand spending the day in here watching him suffer. "Let's walk."

"Nothing's open."

"Good, we won't spend much money. We could go to that coffee shop and get some breakfast. The alternative is for me to fix cereal with water since there's no milk."

Charles grabbed his phone, and started toward the door.

Combining a coffee shop breakfast, a brisk walk to the bank of the Cumberland River, sitting for an hour watching the meandering river and watching commuters cross the bridge to the city, and a slower walk seven blocks along Broadway, kept his mind off Heather's situation for three hours. Each time he started to bemoan the attorney not calling, I changed the subject. I avoided walking by the Top Ten Bar; he didn't need a visual reminder of why Heather wasn't with us.

I was as excited as Charles was when Darnell Edelen called. I could get away with distracting Charles only so long, and he was about to explode. I pointed for him to put the phone on speaker, as we moved off the sidewalk to a quieter spot in a drive between two commercial buildings.

"Have good and bad news, Mr. Fowler." I had never gotten used to hearing Charles referred to by his last name. "Ms. Lee's condition continues to improve."

"Thank God. Can I see her?"

"That's the bad news. The doctor told the officer who called he didn't want any distractions for his patient, and was prohibiting anyone visiting until tomorrow."

Charles gripped the phone so tight his knuckles turned white. He kicked the gravel drive. "If she's better, why not?"

"Mr. Fowler, I'm sharing what I was told."

"Then do something about it."

"Sir." Edelen's voice became louder and unsympathetic. "I will call you when I have been given authorization for you to see the prisoner—umm, Ms. Lee."

I leaned close to the phone and told the attorney who I was and thanked him for doing what he could for Heather.

"Please reiterate to Mr. Fowler that I will call tomorrow."

I did, and slid Charles phone in my pocket and put my arm around him. "That's all the man can do."

"I know, dammit." Charles pushed my arm away and started toward the apartment.

He was several paces in front of me, when his phone rang again.

Charles stopped and pivoted. "That's him calling back. We can see her today."

In Charles's parallel universe, it was possible. In the real world, it had only been a minute since we had talked to the attorney. The phone's screen read *Cindy*.

"Why's she calling me?" he asked as I handed him his phone.

He answered and a few seconds passed. Finally, he said, "Umm, yeah, here he is." He thrust the phone in my hand.

"Why in the hell didn't you answer your phone?" the chief asked.

I patted my pocket. Empty. "Sorry, must've left it in the room."

"You're getting so big for your britches you have Charles play secretary?"

"Cindy, I forgot the phone. Give it a rest."

"It appears you've been smacked by a bad mood."

"It's been rough here. Please tell me you're calling with news someone on the list was on Folly when Edwina was killed."

"Sorry, the only good thing about all those calls was it gave me an excuse to stay in the room while Larry drools over new sawblade technology. I couldn't find anyone who had knowledge of any of them staying in the Folly area. You know that doesn't mean much; there are oodles of places to stay I couldn't check, even if I had time."

Charles knocked me off balance while leaning close to hear Cindy's side of the conversation. I caught myself before falling and then a tour bus lumbered by and blocked her words from both of us, and filled the air with the rancid smell of burnt diesel fuel.

"Why did you call?"

"To tell you I just got off the phone with the detective on the case. After my pestering, he said Edwina's death may be accidental, although there were some bruises on the body that were, per the ME, curious. Still there were no overt signs of violence, and her lungs had saltwater in them, meaning she was alive when she went under."

"What now?"

"He said he would check her phone records and search her condo to see if anything seems amiss."

Before Charles knocked me in the street trying to get closer, I hit speaker so he could hear. "What about her car?"

"They found it a quarter of a mile from where she washed up. The door was unlocked and her keys were under the floor mat. It's not unusual for surfers to leave them there."

"Surfboard?"

"Nope. But like I told you before, it doesn't mean anything."

"Still—"

"Listen Chris, I'm doing what I can."

I wondered if she had been taking lessons from Heather's attorney.

"What now?"

"I made the strongest case possible the death should be investigated as a homicide. The detective said he would follow up. That's it."

We didn't hear from anyone the rest of the day. No news could be good news. You couldn't prove it today. Charles continued to mope, wander around the apartment, and glance at his phone like he could make it ring. My only relief came when he decided he needed another walk and said he'd rather be alone. It was fine with me.

He didn't return until ten o'clock, which had given me several hours to go over everything I knew about Starr, his murder, Edwina, her alleged accidental drowning, and the hours I had spent with Heather over the years. The simplest explanation for everything was Heather, in a moment of anger, pulled the trigger. It would explain her gun being the murder weapon, her not having an alibi for the time of his death, and for her attempted suicide.

After Charles returned, his conversation bounced from topic to topic. He avoided mentioning Heather. He shared trivia about the history of some of the lower Broadway bars, gushed about the singer in one of them, shared every detail about a conversation he had with a family from Ohio who had stopped him to ask directions to the Hall of Fame, and several other things I forgot the instant he told me. He finally wound down and we managed to be asleep by midnight.

The next morning started like a carbon copy of yesterday. I found Charles at the kitchen table staring at his phone. I chose not to remind him the attorney said he would call today, but only specified it would be when he heard from the police. Common sense told me it probably wouldn't be until late morning at the earliest. Other than both common sense and Charles beginning with the letter C, the two had little in common.

After two hours with Charles in the tiny apartment that felt like two of the hours from yesterday, the gods smiled down on us, and Darnell Edelen called. He said if Charles was at the hospital at one o'clock he could see Heather for fifteen minutes and not a second longer.

3 2

Charles, being Charles, insisted we arrive at the hospital no later than twelve fifteen for his one o'clock visit. He had driven, saying that since he lived here, he would know the way better than I. His navigation system knew the way better than either of us and because of its excellent directions and light traffic, we were in the hospital's parking lot a little after noon. I was surprised when Charles suggested we wait in the car until it was closer to the time.

His hands tapped on the steering wheel, he fiddled with the radio dial, and he kept twisting the air-conditioner vent. "Chris," he said as he wiped dust off the dash, "would you go with me?"

"Of course, although I doubt they'll let me." I didn't say Heather was a prisoner and Charles was fortunate to get to visit.

He continued to wipe the dash and rubbed his chin. "They may if you were her brother."

"You want me to lie to the police?"

He lowered his head. "Chris, I need you. I'm scared and don't know what to say to her." He looked at me. "Please."

We bypassed the information kiosk and took the elevator to

the fourth floor. No one met us at the elevator door like they had during our first visit. A corrections officer was seated outside Heather's door. We approached and he stood and gave us an intimidating stare.

Charles smiled. "Hi, officer. I'm Heather Lee's fiancé and was told I could see her."

The guard glanced at his watch. "Yes, in five minutes, and for a visit not to exceed fifteen."

The five-minute comment was anal. Charles didn't argue and said we would wait.

The officer looked at me. "Who are you, sir?"

Charles stepped in front of me. "He's her brother."

I didn't lie.

The officer looked at me and glanced at the door to Heather's room. "I was told only her fiancé would be visiting."

Neither Charles nor I said anything.

He shrugged. "Okay. Do either of you have any weapons on you?"

"No," we said, as I visualized us storming the room with guns blazing as we "sprung" Heather from the hospital.

The officer looked at his watch. "Okay, remember fifteen minutes tops. I will be watching through the window so don't try anything."

Heather was in the bed, her eyes closed, and her right hand cuffed to the bed rail. Her face was as white as the bandage on her wrist.

Charles tiptoed to the side of the bed. "Heather, it's me. You awake?"

Her eyes fluttered open and she quickly closed them. "Light. Bright."

Charles leaned close to and ran his hand through her curly brown hair. "How're you doing?"

Considering the circumstances, I thought it was a horrible question.

Her eyes opened and she squinted at her fiancé. "Chucky, I'm sorry. I'm so confused."

Charles continued to stroke her hair. "It's okay. It's okay."

I stayed back from the bed.

Heather's eyes had adjusted to the light and she looked around. "Hi, Chris. Didn't know you were here."

Charles leaned close to Heather's ear. "If the guard asks, he's your brother."

Heather blinked, looked at me, and at Charles. "He is?"

Charles whispered he had to say that so I could visit.

Heather smiled for the first time. "That's sweet." She exhaled, frowned, and repeated. "Chucky, I'm confused."

Charles glanced at me. I stepped closer. "You'll be fine."

She blinked twice and whispered something I couldn't understand. Charles leaned closer and asked her to repeat it.

"I killed him."

He leaned back like she'd punched him in the nose, and closed his eyes and moved closer to Heather. "Of course, you didn't. Why would you say something like that?"

"I don't remember what happened that night. It was my gun. I hated him." She paused. "Chucky, I saw me do it. I don't know if I was dreaming it or it's my psychic powers dragging me through it, helping me remember. I killed him … I must have."

Charles turned to me. His eyes screamed "Help!"

I stepped closer to the bed. "Heather, we believe we know a couple of people who may have killed Starr. You didn't do it. You could help us find who did."

Her eyes sprung open. "Really?"

"Really," I said and realized our fifteen minutes were almost over. "Are you up to a couple of questions?"

"Guess so."

"How well do you know Edwina Robinson?"

"How well? Don't know. Suppose better than some of Starr's singers. You know I even met her on Folly at Cal's. She said

Starr sold her the same bill of goods he laid on me. We talked some at the Bluebird and had coffee once, maybe twice. We bitched about Starr. Why?"

"Was she giving him more money than what you'd given him?"

"Let me think. God, it's so confusing. Yeah, she said something about giving him a bundle, whatever that meant. Edwina has lots of money." Heather hesitated. "Whoa, do you think she killed him?"

"Yes," Charles said.

Heather closed her eyes. I thought she was asleep, but she opened her eyes and said, "What about her friend?"

Charles looked over at me, and at Heather. "What friend?"

"Her friend was putting up bigger bucks than Edwina. Something about him going in partnership with Starr. Big plans. Could be confused about some of it. Could be—"

The door opened and the officer firmly said. "Time's up."

I ignored him. "Heather, who was Edwina's friend?"

"She never said, but—"

"Now," the guard barked and stepped between the two of us and Heather.

Now meant now, so Charles and I left Heather's side, thanked the officer for letting us see her. We left the building with more questions about the identity of the killer, and about Heather's mental state.

33

Charles had been too nervous to eat before we went to the hospital, so we stopped at a Subway. Charles said he wasn't hungry, but I convinced him he wouldn't be doing Heather any good if he starved. He soon forgot he wasn't hungry as he scoffed down a foot-long chicken sub and repeated, nearly word for word, Heather's disjointed conversation.

Charles swallowed the last bite of the sandwich. "Do you think she really doesn't know if she killed him?"

"She's confused. She was depressed enough to try to kill herself. She's still on meds, and look where she is, not to mention being cuffed to the bed. How would you be under those circumstances?"

"I'd know if I killed someone."

"I'm not certain. She's been drifting in and out of consciousness. Dreams and reality get muddled together, then when you add the trauma of being arrested, plus the suicide attempt, she must be confused. Give her benefit of the doubt."

"I suppose."

"Charles, I don't think she killed him. Edwina is tied up in it.

She either killed him or knew who did. Edwina said "we" went to Nashville, and now Heather said Edwina had a friend with her. We need to find out who he is."

"How?"

An excellent question, and one I didn't have an answer to. My phone rang.

"Well, well," Cindy said by way of introduction. "You fire your secretary?"

"I remembered the phone."

"Good, I didn't want to talk to Charles again."

"You didn't call to tell me that."

"How quick can you get here?"

"Why?"

"I'll tell you when you get back. Can you be here tomorrow?"

Strange. "Let me talk to Charles and call you back."

"Fifteen minutes, no longer."

"Cindy?" Charles asked.

I told him yes and what she asked.

"Why?"

"You know all I know. I don't want to leave you and Heather in her condition."

Charles looked out the large window overlooking the street. He took a sip of soft drink and turned to me. "No offense, but I doubt the chief misses your warm personality so much she's begging you to come home. Don't it make sense that whatever reason she has, has something to do with Starr or Edwina?"

"Yes."

"So, go. I need to stay here in case they'll let me see her."

"You sure?"

"Yes."

I called Cindy, waited while she asked what took me so long to call, and said I'd be there by sunset tomorrow.

I was pleased when I got up the next morning and did not find

Charles at the kitchen table staring at his phone. His bedroom door was closed and I hoped he was getting much-needed sleep. I was on the road before rush hour, and on the Interstate headed to South Carolina before the sun had peeked above the tree-lined roadway.

Seven hours, four coffee stops, one meal stop, and three restroom stops later, I called Cindy to tell her I'd be home in two hours and asked for a hint about why she needed to talk to me. She said it could wait and to meet her at her office. Other than having my curiosity on high alert, I didn't know more than I did when I talked to her yesterday.

I parked a block from City Hall and headed up the steps to Cindy's second-floor office. I had visited her there several times. This was the first time I'd knocked on her door and she wasn't alone. She stood, gave me what seemed like a forced smile, and introduced me to Detective Marshall Grolier, Charleston County Sheriff's Office.

The detective was a few years younger and a few inches shorter than me, had a military buzz cut, and wore a black suit. He reminded me of a mortician. He shook my hand. His expression gave nothing away.

"Chris, Detective Grolier has a few questions. I'll leave you two to talk."

Grolier directed me to one of the chairs in the corner of the room, and he took a seat opposite me. Our knees touched. A notebook appeared from his inside coat pocket, and he flipped through a few pages. "Mr. Landrum, may I call you Chris?"

I nodded.

"Chris, I'm looking into the circumstances surrounding Edwina Robinson's death. I believe you are aware her body was found on the beach."

"Yes, it wasn't an accident, was it?"

"Let me ask the questions, Chris." He scooted to where our knees didn't touch. "How well did you know Ms. Robinson?"

"A little. I only met her a few times. She was a friend of a friend of mine, Heather Lee, and I saw her singing once at Cal's, at Rubino's in Charleston, and maybe at the Bluebird Cafe in Nashville."

"That's all?"

"Are you thinking she killed Kevin Starr?"

Grolier ignored my question. "Chief LaMond tells me you believe Ms. Robinson had something to do with the murder of Starr and you're, umm, nosing in police business."

"Not nosing, asking questions."

"Are you familiar with Olivia Anderson?"

I hesitated. "Yes."

"Have you been to her place questioning her about Edwina Robinson?"

I started wiggling in the chair. I saw darkness enveloping the island outside the chief's large windows that overlooked the Surf Bar. Was it my imagination that it seemed to be getting darker in the office as well? "I did ask if she knew if Edwina had appeared in Nashville."

"And you only had a few conversations with Ms. Robinson, is that correct?"

"Yes."

"What makes you think she had something to do with Starr's death?"

"This may be a bit convoluted, but I know Heather Lee wouldn't have killed him, so I was trying to figure out who might have. Starr had ripped off several aspiring singers and I figured one of them could have done it."

"What ties it to Folly Beach? He was killed in Nashville and from what the police there tell me, he had several enemies. Why here?"

I recounted what Starr had told Heather and Edwina Robinson about why he was on Folly. I shared how he hadn't been at the hotel where he had said he was; how he had lied to his wife about being here.

He put up his hand for me to stop. "You talked to Starr's wife?"

I told him about the meeting at her house and the discussion at the funeral home. The detective jotted a note and told me to continue. I finally told him it appeared to me that someone had framed Heather—another Folly connection. The detective listened. Again, I couldn't tell from his expression if I was making headway.

"Can you explain why she had a note in her apartment that said, *Meet Chris Landrum. Time?*"

"Who?" I asked.

"Edwina Robinson."

I found it hard to swallow. My mouth was dry, but I managed to say, "No."

"Were you supposed to meet her?"

"No."

"What do you think the note meant?"

"I don't know. Could be she wanted to talk about me seeing her perform again."

The detective nodded and wrote something in his book. He touched the pen to his lower lip, paused, and pointed the writing instrument at me. "Where were you the afternoon she died?"

It took me a minute to absorb the question, and a few more seconds to try to remember the answer. "I'm not certain."

"Try."

I looked at my hands griping the armrest, and at the detective. "I was here. The next day I want back to Nashville. I may have gone to the store—really, I don't know."

"Is there anyone who could vouch for your whereabouts?"

My stomach was now in knots. I mumbled, "No."

"Do you have a boat, Chris?"

That I knew the answer to. "No."

"Have you used anyone else's boat lately or have access to one?"

I shook my head. "I suppose I could borrow my friend Sean Aker's boat if I wanted to. I've never asked. Why?"

He was staring at me. "And you're sure you weren't with anyone that afternoon?"

I nodded.

He closed the notebook and stood. "That's all—for now. One more thing, Chris. Don't leave the area."

3 4

I was numb as I walked down the stairs and gripped the handrail. I was afraid my legs might give way.

Did he think I killed Edwina? I was the only person who was raising a red flag about her death. Why would he think I'd do that if I had killed her?

Cindy was on the sidewalk and motioned me to follow her across the street to the Surf Bar. It wasn't crowed, but the customers were spread out enough so there wasn't a vacant spot where we could be assured of privacy. She pointed to the door leading to the patio. There was one vacant table and I grabbed the chair facing the street. Cindy sat opposite me and we were joined by a college-age server who told us she was Lizzy and would be taking care of us. Cindy told her that her friend wanted a chardonnay and shrugged and said that she was on duty and ordered sweet tea.

Lizzy had gone and Cindy looked around to make sure there was no one close enough to hear. "What did he want?"

I shared Grolier's questions and how it seemed that he was accusing me of killing Edwina.

Cindy lowered her head. "I'm sorry, Chris. I had no choice. He came by yesterday and asked if I knew where you were. He knows we're friends. I told him that when I started pushing for him to start looking at the death as murder and not a simple accident. I told him I wasn't sure where you were and that I'd call you." She pointed across the street to her building. "He was there when I called, so I couldn't say anything. After I hung up he told me he had some routine questions and didn't want you to know ahead of time. He didn't beat around the bush about ordering me not to tell you he wanted to meet. I doubted his questions were routine. I knew you didn't have anything to do with Edwina's death, so I figured it wouldn't hurt for him to talk to you cold. Sorry."

Lizzy was back with our drinks and asked if we wanted to order. I told her I wasn't hungry. Cindy wasn't to be discouraged. She ordered a cheeseburger for me and a house salad with chicken for herself. It reminded me of doing the same thing for Charles when he'd said he wasn't hungry. She told Lizzy I needed the food and if she wanted, she could stand and watch the weight fall off the chief with each bite of salad. Lizzy smiled, like she would at any inane customer remark.

I watched the waitress leave and turned to Cindy. "It's okay," I said, even though a heads-up would have been appreciated. "What I don't understand is why he thinks I had something to do with Edwina's death and then push for him to investigate. He'd already decided it was an accident."

Cindy sipped her tea, said yummy, made a gagging motion, and turned serious. "All I can figure is he started becoming suspicious before you began your crusade. If that's the case, he might have thought that by you saying it wasn't an accident, you were trying to appear not guilty. I know it's circle-like thinking— your buddy William would say circuitous. Since I'm from the hills, I don't know those big words."

She was trying to cheer me. I was having none of it. "Edwina

Robinson was murdered. I knew it and now the cops believe it. Cindy, you know I didn't kill her."

The chief hesitated. I hope she wasn't going to make some smart remark about not knowing I didn't kill Robinson. "So, who did? And, did Robinson kill Starr?"

Our food arrived and Lizzy asked if there was anything else we needed. Cindy said I needed more wine. I declined and Lizzy moved to a family of four on the other side of the patio. The smell from my cheeseburger made me realize Cindy had been right about me needing to eat.

I scarfed down two bites and took a deep breath. "Cindy, I'm still confused. Until Edwina's death, I was convinced she had killed Starr. She may have, so what reason would anyone have to kill her?"

I would love to say Cindy and I solved the various mysteries while I devoured my cheeseburger and pounds fell off her as she grazed on her salad. All we managed to do was to talk in circles —circuitously, in William-speak—and sated nothing except my appetite.

I WAS EXHAUSTED after the drive, my brief, disconcerting conversation with Detective Grolier, and the fruitless discussion with Cindy. The thought of going home and worrying had little appeal, so I headed the short distance to Cal's where I was met by the aroma of stale beer, burnt burgers, and Cal singing his much-performed cover of Hank Williams Sr.'s "Hey Good Lookin'." He was in full stage regalia in his rhinestone-studded coat. His long, gray hair flowed off his shoulders around the sides of his misshaped Stetson.

The room was two tables shy of full and I suspected the busy weekday crowd had inspired Cal to do an impromptu set. He was more comfortable standing behind a microphone than tending bar. His part-time cook was at the grill and Kristin, the waitress, was scampering around the room trying to keep up with drinks. I didn't recognize many of the patrons and assumed most were from a convention at the Tides since they were dressed like they had come from a meeting rather than from the beach. I did recognize a couple sitting at a table near the back of the room. It would have been hard not to recognize Caldwell's six-foot-four frame towering above others in the room. In addition, he was seated with his partner, Mel, whose bomber jacket and camo attire stood out like the Goodyear blimp at a funeral in contrast to the bright-colored golf shirts worn by most of the customers.

Caldwell saw me in the doorway and waved me over and before I lowered myself in one of the two vacant chairs, he asked, "How are Charles and Heather?"

I didn't know if he had heard about Heather's suicide attempt, so I kept my answer generic and said they were both doing as well as could be expected.

"I hope everything gets sorted out soon," Caldwell said.

That told me he hadn't heard about Heather's health.

Mel, not being a big fan of being left out of a conversation, leaned forward. "I'm no stranger to being cornered and crapped on by cops, so I know Charles's little lady can't be doing well. What can we do to spring her? I got it! I could make a couple of calls and get a slightly-used shoulder fired rocket launcher. That ought to do it."

I assumed Mel was teasing, or not. I told him it was up to the lawyers.

Mel waved his hand around and pointed to two or three of the tables. "Don't take me for one of these paper-pushing bureaucrats who don't know a jib from a jellybean. I know it's somewhere in your screwed-up genetic structure to catch whoever killed that scumbag agent and get Heather out of the pokey."

I didn't want to tell him I didn't know what a jib was other than something on a boat, and said I had been looking at suspects.

Two tables of *paper-pushing bureaucrats* sang along with Cal as he began the chorus of Merle Haggard's "Okie from Muskogee". Kristin delivered a glass of chardonnay without me having to ask, and I quickly forgot I was tired.

Mel's chair nearly toppled over when he leaned back; its front legs were off the floor. His crusty, permanently-affixed frown broke momentarily into what I knew was a smile, others would think he had gas. "Told you, Caldwell. I knew Chris'd be on killer patrol."

Caldwell put his arm behind Mel and pushed him forward until four of the chair's legs were where they were designed to be. "You were right."

"Damned right I'm right."

"Anyway," Caldwell said as he turned to me. "You really think Heather's innocent?"

"Yes." I remembered our visit to SHADES and wondered if Caldwell could recall what Olivia had said about Edwina. Perhaps she had said something I had forgotten. I also realized Caldwell and Mel might not know about the drowning. "Caldwell, remember when we were at SHADES?"

"Sure."

"Do you remember Olivia talking about Edwina?"

"Yes, the lady who talked her into trying open-mic nights."

"Did she say—"

"Howdy, Kentucky," Cal interrupted. He had finished his set and was standing over our table. "How're Charles and Heather?"

I gave him the same evasive answer I'd rehearsed on Mel and Caldwell.

"It'll be fine; know it will."

"Is your jukebox broken?" I asked, knowing it provided most of the weeknight entertainment.

Cal grinned. "No pard. I'm doing two sets by popular

demand. Couple of these here conventioneers said they heard me last year and said I could sure do the whole group a heaping favor if I'd share my talents with them."

Mel pointed at Cal. "Crap, Cal. Why don't you do this old jarhead a *heaping favor* and sing some good music, like some funky James Brown. Your prehistoric country songs give me the runs."

Caldwell channeled all of us when he smacked Mel on the arm. Cal nodded to Caldwell, and Mel grinned. No one grabbed a camera quick enough to capture the historic moment.

I figured we had suffered enough foolishness. "Cal, how's your head?"

"Hard and empty," interrupted Mel.

Cal ignored him. "Thanks for asking, Kentucky, it's better."

"Remember more about that night and what you wanted to tell me?"

"It's not all there yet. You'll be the first to know." He looked at the empty stage and over at the bar. "Gotta grab a drink and get back to my fans. Tell Charles and Heather I said hey when you talk to them."

I told him I would.

"What about Edwina?" Caldwell asked, taking advantage of a music free bar.

"Have you heard what happened to her?"

Caldwell said, "What?"

"Why would I care?" Mel asked.

I turned to Caldwell. "She's dead. Drowned a few days ago at the Washout."

Caldwell gasped. "My God. What happened?"

Mel blurted, "Rip current?"

Mel had come close to dying in a rip current more than twenty years ago, and was saved by my surfing-buddy Dude. The two had been the most unlikely of friends ever since, and Mel had rip currents on his mind whenever anything bad happened to anyone in water—ocean, river, or bath.

"That's what the cops said at first. Now they think she may have been killed and someone tried to make it look like an accident."

"I suppose you're trying to solve that one too," Mel said.

I wasn't about to tell them that I was a suspect. "I think she may have had something to do with the music agent's death. Caldwell, that's why I was wondering if you remember anything Olivia may have said about her."

Cal was back on stage. He thanked the group from the hotel for coming and told them to be sure and tip Kristin for all her hard work, and started singing "Rose Colored Glasses."

Mel shook his head. "Where're the Doobie Brothers when you need them?"

Never in Cal's, I thought.

"Remember anything else, Caldwell?"

He looked at his beer bottle and at the stage. "Not really. Olivia and I talked about what she would need to change and I was leaving most of the open-mic stuff up to Cal."

My exhaustion from everything that had happened during the last twenty-four hours was catching up to me. I told my table-mates I was heading home, waved bye to Cal, and the only thing I remembered after falling into bed was the sun shining in the window at nine-fifteen the next morning.

35

I'm no fan of telephones even though they served a purpose, and though I try never to be away from home without mine, I would rather have my conversations in person. I also wasn't ready to drive back to Nashville, so I grabbed my much-maligned phone and punched in Charles's number.

"It's about time you called. Did you run into a bison on the Interstate; run out of gas; throw your phone out the window? Well, I'm waiting for a great explanation why you didn't let me know you made it home."

I held the phone away from my ear and took a deep breath. "Charles—"

"I'm not done. What'd Cindy want?"

"Done?"

"For now."

I told him I had a bison-free trip, had plenty of gas, and still had my phone since he was talking to me on it. I told him about my meeting with the detective, wishing I had hit a bison instead, and about talking with Mel and Caldwell.

"You couldn't find ten minutes in all that to call?"

"Could, but didn't. Sorry."

"Your sincere, heartfelt apology is accepted. Now why in Neptune's name do the cops think you drowned Edwina?"

"Because I pushed Cindy to have them think beyond accidental drowning."

"That doesn't make a lick of sense."

I agreed and shared Cindy's theory that I may have thought the cops would decide it wasn't accidental and by drawing attention to it, would make me look less guilty. Charles said he didn't think the sheriff's office was that smart, and I changed the subject and asked if he was going to see Heather. He said the slow-moving attorney was working on it. I asked him to let me know.

"Like you let me know you made it home?"

The phone went dead.

The temperature was still tolerable, yet was supposed to reach the upper eighties by mid-afternoon. My legs needed to stretch after yesterday's marathon drive, so I headed towards a couple of blocks to the Folly Pier. Over the years, the Pier had become my prime thinking spot, or that's the excuse I used for visiting the Folly landmark. Puffy white clouds were overhead and a gathering of storm clouds loomed inland. I didn't remember the forecaster mentioning rain, although this time of year pop-up showers could appear anytime.

As with telephones, I was also not a fan of symbolism, but I couldn't help think about how my life since retiring was like the unexpected storms. I was happily retired, living what most would consider the good life, and more often than anyone should be exposed to, I'm confronted with death—death of a friend, or a death where one of my friends was accused of being responsible. These were situations only the police should have to deal with. Did I have to get involved? Of course not. When one of my friends was touched by a tragedy or accused of murder, I was touched as well. I'd nearly been killed on more than one occasion because I stuck my nose into a situation I had no business being involved in. Had I regretted getting involved? Absolutely not.

Here I was again, trying to keep Heather from being convicted of a crime I was convinced she hadn't committed. Not only trying to find out who killed an agent who probably had been killed because of his unethical behavior, but now I find myself the focal point of an investigation into the death of a singer I barely knew. What now?

I didn't know what to do and was relieved when the phone rang and the screen said *Ramsey Promotions*.

"Chris, this is Caldwell. Is this a good time to talk?"

I was pleased someone in my circle of friends could still be courteous on the phone. I told him it was and I was glad to hear from him.

"I just got off the phone with Olivia at SHADES. Thought it was interesting since we were talking about her last night. Anyway, it looks like all my work, and Cal's thinking, are for naught."

"Why?" I asked and watched three surfers riding a medium-sized wave to shore.

"Don't know the details. She'll fill me in when I meet with her in a little while. It sounds like she may have to postpone the remodel and the switch to country. Too bad. After you left last night, Cal finished his set and told me he had come up with a list of things she could do to attract the best open-mic performers around. Some of his ideas were good. The old boy surprised me."

"I learned a few years back not to underestimate Cal. Why's she postponing?"

"Said she's made a bad investment and it was coming back to haunt her. Thought you'd be interested since we were talking about her."

"Thanks, and tell Mel I said hi."

Caldwell laughed. "It'll have to wait. Mel said he can't hear anything because his ears were bleeding from the thorny country cactuses stuck in them at Cal's."

I chuckled and said Caldwell could write him a note. He said he would, but then he'd have to teach Mel to read. I put the phone in my pocket and watched the surfers. I wondered if one of them could be riding Edwina's surfboard.

The storm clouds were inching closer to the beach. I thought about what Caldwell had said. Was it possible Starr was Olivia's poor investment? She had said Edwina gave Starr a lot of money, and hinted it was more than the cost of the demo tapes and marketing promotions. Olivia may be able to give me insights into Edwina's relationship with the promoter. And even if she didn't, at least I'd feel like I was doing something; something to help Heather. Caldwell said he was meeting with her. If I tagged along with him, I could ask some of the questions without looking like I was accusing her friend of doing anything bad. And, it would be safer with Caldwell present.

I called him back. "Hello, Chris. Seems like I just talked to you."

I laughed and said it was because he had. I asked when he was meeting Olivia. He said in an hour and told him I was wondering if he minded if I tagged along. He hesitated, said that I could, and didn't ask why. It was refreshing not to have to explain.

A half hour later, I was barely off the island. Blue sky was to my left, but the black clouds were overhead and doing what heavy rainclouds were known for. Rain pelted the windshield. Another couple of miles and the rain had ended as quickly as it had begun. The more I thought about what Caldwell had said, the more I wondered if Olivia could be tied with Starr more than I had imagined. When we'd visited Heather in the hospital, she said a friend of Edwina had given Starr more money than Edwina had. Hadn't Heather said "he" when referring to Edwina's friend? Heather had also said she was confused. Could the person's gender be one of the things she was confused about? At the first stoplight, I called Cindy.

"Yes, my favorite troublemaker?" the chief said.

I should have Caldwell conduct a seminar on phone courtesies.

"Got a favor to ask."

I heard her exhale. "Of course, you do."

The next voice was Larry in the background. "Hi, Chris."

"Tell Larry hi," I said. "Where are you?"

"Making Larry take me to Harris Teeter. He hates grocery shopping and I'm torturing him for dragging me to hardware hell. What's the favor? It's not legal for a change, is it?"

"Would I ask you to do anything illegal?"

"Yes. What is it?"

"See if Olivia Anderson, may be using her maiden name, Mona Alliendre, or if Dale or Kelly Windsor, possibly going by DK Studio, stayed at the Tides in the last few months."

"I already checked on the Windsor's, remember?"

"Yes, but maybe Kelly checked in as DK Studio."

"Gee, okay. Want me to see if the president, the pope, or the Easter Bunny stayed there too?"

"Not yet."

Cindy mumbled something and said for me to hold my nosiness while she got something to write on. It sounded like a glove box clanking closed and she returned. "Okay, names again. I told her and she reminded me she was a simple country girl and asked how to spell Alliendre. I gave it my best guess and she said she would be "seriously starved" after she got the answers. I told her I was on my way to meet Caldwell at SHADES and I'd trade supper for information. "You're danged right you will," she said and was gone.

A couple more miles down the road and I remembered something Cal had said when he was speculating Edwina had been having an affair with Starr. He said Edwina had been angry about

Starr taking her money and he had taken much more from someone else. She also said something about *the other woman*. Cal thought it was Starr's wife and how "pesky wives complicated sinning." What if Edwina had been referring to Starr's relationship with Olivia?

If Olivia was involved with Starr, could she have drowned Edwina. If so, why? Was she romantically involved with the agent and after learning Edwina had killed him and then killed Edwina out of anger? Did Olivia learn Edwina was going to do something to implicate the bar owner and was killed to prevent it? Could Olivia have killed both Starr and Edwina? Or, was I jumping to farfetched conclusions to get Heather off the hook? There was nothing I knew that could prove any of this. Could I learn anything by talking to Olivia? The one thing I was certain of was there was zero chance of learning anything if I didn't.

I pulled into the SHADES lot armed with a full quiver of questions and a serious dose of apprehension. Caldwell hadn't arrived and the Porsche Panamera was the only vehicle there.

I parked and was waiting for Caldwell when the phone rang and *Ramsey Promotions* appeared on the screen.

"Hi, Caldwell."

"Chris, got a problem. Mel called and asked if I could pick him up at the Chevy dealer. His car was running hot and the service department said it'd take several hours to get the part from the parts house before they could fix it. I'm going to have to reschedule my meeting with Olivia. Hope I didn't inconvenience you."

I told him it was okay and he said he would call Olivia to reschedule as soon as he picked up Mel to keep him from blowing a gasket at the service department. I said that if Mel was going to blow a gasket, the service department would be the best place to do it. Caldwell chuckled and said he'd let me know when the meeting was rescheduled.

Over the years, I had stumbled into a few dangerous situations and had even been ambushed, but never went into a situation that could turn lethal without someone covering my back. It would be foolish to talk to Olivia by myself so I shifted the car to reverse when the bar's side door opened and Olivia stuck her head out. She squinted at my car, seemed to recognize me, smiled, and waved for me to join her.

I cringed and turned off the ignition.

She looked past me toward my car. "I was expecting Caldwell."

She seemed satisfied I didn't have Caldwell with me and waved me in. I told her about his situation and that he would be calling to reschedule and that I was supposed to meet him here.

She wore tight-fitting jeans and a lightweight sweatshirt, much differently attired than in her tailored suit. Lines around her eyes were accentuated by the sunlight and she looked gaunt as she offered me her hand. I gave it a brief shake. Her wrist was still a bracelet collector.

She glanced outside and closed the door. "Why were you joining him?"

Good question, I thought. "He told me he was meeting you and since I had a couple of questions about one of your customers, I asked him if I could tag along. Sorry for the intrusion."

"That's fine. I was here catching up on paperwork. Want something to drink?"

"No thanks."

"Wish you would've brought that charming old timer with you. I loved meeting Cal. It's not often that someone gets to meet a legend."

Legend? I wondered if she'd confused Cal for someone else.

She didn't elaborate and said, "Which customer?"

"Edwina Robinson."

She moved behind the desk and pointed for me to take a seat in one of the two chairs in front of the desk. She sat and shook her head and looked at the black, leather memo pad. "The ocean is so unforgiving. It was a tragic death." She paused and looked at me. "What do you want to know about her?"

"She was a friend of yours, so I hope you won't be offended by what I'm going to say. I think she may have killed Kevin Starr."

Olivia's eyes widened, she leaned forward, but didn't say anything.

I continued. "I was wondering if she'd said anything to you that could help the police figure it out."

Olivia leaned back in her chair and twisted a pen in her hand. "Do the police think she killed him?"

"Not really. That's why I'm asking for your help."

"Back to your question, I'm not offended at all. I didn't know Edwina that well. She was in the bar often. I think I told you that she performed several times, and she wanted me to go country. She considered herself an expert on open-mic nights." Olivia smiled. "She sang at enough of them" Her smile faded. "She had a good voice and was here when I needed her. She'll be missed." She set the pen on the desk. "We weren't friends though." Olivia smiled. "Are you sure you don't want something to drink?"

I declined a second time and was beginning to relax. The more I thought about it, the more I was convinced Edwina was guilty.

"I think I'll get something. Last chance?"

I shook my head as she headed toward the door to the bar.

I was curious if I'd been correct when I spelled Olivia's name for Cindy. I walked to the wall and looked at Olivia's degrees. I grinned when I saw I had the correct spelling, and headed back to my chair when I noticed one of the many photos of Olivia with various people she had hung in groupings around the room. I had been focused on the Wake Forest diplomas during my first visit and hadn't noticed the photo.

The photographer had focused on a group of three people

standing on the bow of what appeared to be an expensive, ocean-going craft. Olivia was next to an older gentleman who had his arm around her shoulder. She wore a bikini with a flimsy cover-up that failed to live up to its name. Edwina Robinson was on the other side of the SHADES owner. Edwina held a beer, had a smile on her face, and was leaning against Olivia. Hadn't she just told me she wasn't friends with Edwina? Sharing time on a boat with Olivia appeared to be something more. I had a sour feeling in my stomach. Was I wrong about Edwina? Was Olivia the killer? I need to make a graceful exit and call Cindy.

Olivia startled me when she returned and coughed to get my attention. I stepped away from the photo and returned to the chair. Olivia smiled but glanced at the photo before returning to her seat.

If Olivia's return hadn't startled me enough, I nearly jumped out of the chair when my phone rang. The screen indicated that it was Cindy. I held up my forefinger for Olivia to give me a second. I wanted to leave the room to take the call, but was afraid it'd make Olivia suspicious.

"Yes, ma'am," I said to the chief.

"Ma'am? What Boy Scout possessed your body? Never mind," she continued without taking a breath. "I hate to admit it. You finally got something right. A woman with the highfalutin name of Mona Alliendre was a registered guest at the Tides for five nights, which happened to be over the same timeframe that the slimy agent *discovered* Heather. And yes, he of guessing right for a change, Ms. Alliendre had stayed there two other times over the last twelve months."

"Interesting."

"Interesting. That's all you can say. I think you're on to something. Sounds like your smarmy agent and Ms. Alliendre, aka Olivia Robinson, were, umm close."

How do I say I need help without coming out and saying it? I hesitated, and said, "Oh, I see."

"Chris," Cindy whispered. "Calling me ma'am, thinking what I found about her was only interesting. Is Olivia there?"

I smiled at Olivia, and with as calm a voice as I could muster, told Cindy, "Yes."

"At SHADES?"

"Thanks for calling. Yes, you're right. Go ahead and have them repair it. Know when they'll be done?"

"Are you in immediate danger?"

"Don't know. See you soon. Bye."

"I'll be there in fifteen minutes."

I hit *End Call*, glanced at my watch, smiled at Olivia, and said, "Sorry for the interruption. They've been having trouble finding a part for my air conditioner." I rolled my eyes. "It's finally arrived."

Olivia didn't smile. My smile ended when I realized she had substituted a handgun for the pen she had had been twirling. She wasn't twirling the gun. It was pointed at my head.

"Chris, we have a problem."

I couldn't have agreed more. I looked at Olivia but the image of the gun burned into my retina. I wasn't certain how she had planned to solve the problem. What I did know was unless I could stall until Cindy arrived, the outcome wouldn't be to my liking.

I tried to slow my breathing and gave her my best smile. "Olivia, what's going on?"

"You know the answer." She shook her head. The direction of the gun never wavered. "Did you think you could just waltz in here and trick me into telling you I killed Starr?"

"I don't know what you mean. I told you Edwina killed her agent. He had been ripping her off and she had to do something?" I nodded at the gun. "What's that about?"

"And I suppose you think Edwina got careless and drowned?"

"That's what everyone thinks. Isn't that what happened?"

"It would've been if you hadn't appeared at the door. Why'd I let you in? Why'd I leave the room and let you nose around?

Why'd I leave that damned picture on the wall? And, why'd I lie to you about how well I knew Edwina? Stupid, stupid, stupid."

I didn't see any upside by acknowledging her questions or agreeing with her about it being stupid, yet had to keep her talking. "You killed both."

She grinned.

"Why?"

"One, I wanted to." She shrugged. "Two, I had to."

A brief answer like that wouldn't kill enough time. "Tell me about it."

"Why should I tell you anything?"

"Why not?" I said, and nodded toward the gun. "You have no intention of letting me out of here."

"You're not that stupid after all."

I nodded and looked around for a weapon. The large executive mahogany desk between us was too heavy to shove into her. The leather letter tray on the desk was outside my reach. Her Gucci briefcase was beside the desk and out of reach.

She watched me looking around. "Kevin Starr," she said. "He walked in here a year ago. Had a rock band blaring out there and I was working the room. He sat at a table by himself, had a half glass of Maker's and water in front of him. Thin, full head of hair, nice looking guy, clean cut, well dressed. Was little younger than me." She shrugged. "He wasn't the kind of patron I normally get." She sighed. "Was a light crowd and I returned to his table and asked if he needed anything else." She stopped and looked down at the gun.

"Go on."

"He said I could join him for a drink. I made the biggest mistake I've made in years. I sat down. He told me he was a music agent out of Nashville and was developing a chain of bars across the South—he called them nightclubs, sounded classier, I suppose. I had a decent amount of money from my husband's estate and was getting bored with this." She waved her free hand around the room.

I nodded. "And he said he was looking for partners to open these, umm, nightclubs?"

"See, more proof you're not stupid. Yeah, and I fell for it hook, line, and heart. He gave me a sales pitch that could convince a mouse to adopt a pet cat. He came back the next night. In fact, it was the night he met Edwina. He listened to her sing and signed her on the spot. I was happy for her." She hesitated. "Also, I was a little jealous about the attention he was lavishing on her."

"What happened?"

"To make a long story shorter, let's say he and I became much closer over the next few months. I didn't want to take him to the house—I'm old-fashioned about that. Besides, I'd been dating a guy who was so jealous if he got a hint I was seeing someone else, there'd be big trouble. I started getting Kevin and me rooms over on Folly. He liked going to some of the bars there, said he was fishing for talent. Anyway, he brought some partnership papers over and I gave him three hundred thousand dollars—a big chunk of all I had."

I glanced at my watch and realized it had only been five minutes since I'd talked to Cindy. The last thing I wanted was for Olivia to make the long story shorter. "What was he going to do with it?"

"Said he was going to expand the agency. He needed some of the money to provide services for his clients he couldn't do now. Said he should pay for the demos instead of having the clients foot the bill, and wanted to pay off some debts. He would use some of the money to open a Nashville bar. Said it would be bigger and better than anything there."

Some of it was now beginning to make sense. "Did you and Edwina go to Nashville?"

"Several times. Kevin wanted us to get a feel for the city's successful bar business, and he wanted Edwina to start performing at some of the venues."

"The Bluebird?"

"Yeah, that's where Edwina met Heather Lee. She got to liking Heather, and I started getting bad vibes about Kevin."

"Why?"

"I kept asking about the partnership agreement I'd signed. He tried to charm his way around telling me he hadn't filed it yet. He gave some feeble excuses, legal mumbo-jumbo."

"He had your money?"

"And I had nothing except a lying lover."

Her gun hand began to shake. I was afraid she was going to squeeze the trigger. "That's too bad," I said, hoping to calm her.

"Yeah."

"Is that when you decided to kill him?"

"Yes. I had to figure a way to set someone up for it. If the police started looking deep, they'd find a money trail that led to me. I couldn't have that, could I?"

"Heather?"

"It was perfect. Edwina kept dragging me over to Nashville and insisted on appearing at the Bluebird. She was convinced fame was going to be staring at her from the audience. I stood in line with her some of those times. It didn't take a detective to learn Heather had a gun—think someone named Quinn or Gwen gave it to her. Everyone knew it; knew she kept it in her car, the car with the broken lock."

"You stole the gun."

She nodded. "I wanted to give Kevin one more chance to make good on his promises. I met him at an out of the way bar so no one he would know would see us."

"Top Ten Bar?"

"Yeah. He tried to slather his charm on me. I'd had enough of it and told him so. All he did was shrug. That did it. I stormed out."

"And shot him with Heather's gun and put it back in her car."

"The perfect crime, or so I thought."

My phone rang again and I thought Olivia was going to pull the trigger. Instead, she said, "Let it ring."

After five rings, it kicked to voice mail. A minute later an icon indicated that I had a message.

Olivia looked at the screen and said, "Put it on speaker."

We heard Cal say, "Chris I … whoops you ain't real. Danged machine. Anyway, good news. Something finally came back to this ancient, pickled brain, something you need to know. When I was talking to you on the phone about what I knew about Starr's killin', guess who was in the bar and close enough to hear me say I needed to tell you? Never mind, you don't have to guess. It was that lady who has the rock bar we went to. Think that's a clue? Well, call when you get this and I'll tell you more. There's not much else to tell. Crap, you don't have to call; that's all I know. Have a great day."

"What more can happen?" Olivia asked. She rubbed her eyes with one hand but held the gun steady with the other. "Now I've got to take care of him."

"You saw him leaving Cal's and bashed his head in?"

"Yeah, thought I'd killed him. Damned hard head. I was in there when he called you and I overhead him saying he knew something about Starr and Folly. I didn't know what it was. Whatever it was it could lead to me. I was supposed to meet Caldwell at Cal's the next night and saw the cowboy coming out when I was headed to the door. There was a scrap of wood next to the building. I grabbed it and smacked him and left. I didn't think anyone saw me. I couldn't take a chance of staying around to make sure he was dead."

I glanced at my watch. It'd been nearly twenty minutes. Where was Cindy? Olivia was getting antsier and I didn't know how much longer I could stall. If Cindy barged in now, what would I do? I could drop down in front of the desk out of Olivia's sight.

"He lived," I said.

"Now I have to do something about that."

"Why kill Edwina?"

"Hated to do it. She was a good kid and always wanted to help. Kevin had made the mistake of screwing her over. He took more money from her than he should have. She got riled and threatened to kill him. Too many people heard her, and the police started to look at her."

"But Heather was already in jail."

"Yes. Some busybody"—she pointed to me with her empty hand—"started asking questions. I was afraid the cops would start questioning Edwina. She knew too much about me. I couldn't wait to see if she'd fold."

"Did she know about your, umm relationship with Starr?"

"She wasn't stupid."

"How'd you kill her?"

"It was tricky. It had to look like an accident. I told her I was going out on my boat and wanted her to go with me. Said we'd swim in the ocean. She loved the water and jumped at any chance to get in it."

"That's how you got her in a bathing suit?"

"Yes. Pretended like the engine was acting up and I told her something was stuck in the prop. She went in the water in to see what was wrong. She's a good swimmer so I had to keep pushing her away with a paddle; she'd swim away and I'd go after her and hit her again. We were far enough out that no one was around and nobody could see us from shore. She finally wore down." She sighed. "It took forever. I had to pull her on board and dump her close enough to the beach so she'd wash up and be found. I figured the cops would figure the cuts and bruises were from her being tumbled in the waves and on the rocks."

"They almost did."

"Yeah, until you started waving red flags and the cops found the note in her room with your name on it. They started after you but I knew they couldn't make anything stick."

"How'd you find that out?"

"County cops are in here all the time and one of them knew Edwina had been a regular. Didn't take many drinks for him to tell me—hush, hush, he said."

"How did you—"

She smiled. "Enough. I think my short version of a long story has gone long enough. Now if you'd please stand, you need to head to the restroom. I'd hate to mess up my office."

I didn't know what'd happened to Cindy, but couldn't wait. I started to stand and flipped the leather blotter up at Olivia's as she started to stand. The pistol jerked up as she pulled the trigger. A bullet burrowed into the ceiling.

She grabbed the edge of the blotter and flung it out of the way and lowered her gun hand. I dove sideways and reached for the letter tray. If I could get to it, I could throw it at her.

She fired another round. The bullet ripped through my sleeve but missed my arm. I lunged at her. My stomach rammed the desk. I gasped for breath.

Olivia stared at me, a bemused look on her face. And again, she pointed the weapon at me. I grabbed for it.

Olivia yanked it out of my reach and tripped over the chair. She fell backwards. Her head slammed the credenza. Her eyes rolled up and she slumped to the floor. At the same time, the door leading to the bar exploded inward and Cindy stumbled through the shattered door and tripped. Her knee hit the floor and she screamed a profanity.

Olivia didn't hear her. She was out cold.

I pushed backwards and slid off the desk and collapsed in the chair I had been sitting in. Cindy regained her balance and pointed her service weapon at Olivia who hadn't moved.

"Are you okay?" the chief asked, as Larry came in the room.

I nodded, caught my breath, and said, "What took you so long?"

"Don't go there," She was rubbing her knee and taking deep breaths. "Is she okay?"

"Don't know, better call an ambulance."

Cindy looked around and spotted her phone that had been jarred out of her pocket when she slammed into the door. She dialed and muttered some police-speak into it and turned back to me. I was still in the chair. "We've been here several minutes. Both doors were locked. Didn't figure knocking would be a good idea. The lock on the front door must have been made by a high-school shop student, one who should've flunked. Thank God. Larry had it picked in seconds. I figured you were in here, and I put my ear up to the door." She pointed to the door she had stormed through. "Couldn't hear anything."

"She soundproofed the room so she didn't have to listen to the music from the bar."

"Sound proofers would've earned an *A* in their shop class. Couldn't hear a damned thing. That changed when a gun went off. That's when I decided a quick entry might be wise. And as your buddy Dude would say, 'Rest be history.'"

With the soundproof door in pieces, we heard sirens. Cindy kept her gun drawn, gave me a quick hug, mumbled something about being pleased I was okay, and flopped down in one of the other chairs where she could see the unmoving Olivia. Larry seconded it and went to welcome the troops.

Cindy still had her handgun drawn and another gun was on the floor beside the supine murderer. The first officers to arrive took a moment to evaluate the situation before deciding what to do. It wasn't made any simpler when they asked if the unconscious female had been shot and Cindy said no that she had been attacked by a leather desk blotter and a mahogany credenza. One of the officers asked if the chief would hand him her weapon. Cindy smiled, handed it over, and made another call. The officer smelled the barrel to determine if it had been fired, waited for Cindy to finish her call and returned her service weapon.

The next officer to arrive recognized Cindy and put her on the side of the angels. The first officer to arrive had bent over Olivia and after feeling for a pulse, announced she was alive. Neither cop paid much attention to Larry or me since we were sitting motionless with no weapons in sight.

An ambulance arrived and two paramedics peeked in the shattered doorway before entering. They decided it was safe and headed to Olivia. Cindy rubbed her knee and watched the medics do their thing. She wouldn't admit it, but I knew she was in pain and reeling from her encounter with the door.

The medics were wheeling Olivia out on a stretcher with a police escort when Detective Grolier strolled in, looked at the totaled door, and gazed around the room.

"Chief," he said, and looked at me. "Mr. Landrum." Only four of us were left in the room and Grolier asked Cindy what had happened. She introduced Larry and started to tell the detective what had happened, hesitated, turned to me, and said, "Chris, from the beginning?"

And I did. Nine thousand questions later, I finished my story that started when my best friend followed his girlfriend to Nashville to find fame and fortune and ended with Olivia Anderson confessing to two murders—one that Heather was currently being incarcerated for, and the other where I had been the prime suspect.

Because of those connections, my story would have had little credibility. That was until Detective Grolier called in the crime techs who thoroughly searched Olivia's office. Fortunate for both Heather and me, Olivia was a packrat and had kept copies of the partnership agreement between her and Kevin Starr, and in her business folder, copies of gas receipts that showed she bought gas in Nashville the same day Starr was killed, along with restaurant and hotel receipts showing where she had eaten and stayed, again around the date of the murder.

The receipts and agreement didn't prove that she had killed Starr, but they were enough for the police to go to the DA in Nashville and get Heather a new bail hearing scheduled for next week.

From the hospital and with her hand cuffed to the bed, under advice from her attorney, Olivia refused to talk to the police. She wasn't stupid.

Three days later, the police searched Olivia's boat and discovered blood in a corner of the deck. It would still be several more days before a definitive DNA match could be made, but since it was Edwina's blood type, all bets were on it being hers.

On the same day, Rod, the bartender at the Top Ten Bar, was shown two photos of Olivia and said he may have been mistaken about Heather and that Olivia, "Sure looks like the gal with Starr the night before he got himself kilt."

A WEEK after my near-fatal visit to SHADES, I was on the road to Music City USA. Charges had been dropped against Heather and she and Charles had walked hand and hand out of the jail. Charles begged me to come over so the three of us could celebrate with a night on the town.

Heather opened the apartment door and greeted me with a lingering hug and "thank you." She wasn't as enthusiastic as she had been on my first visit to their apartment, but she had to be exhausted. She was pale and had lost weight, but smiled, something I hadn't seen in quite a while. Charles was behind her and stepped forward to give me an equally long hug.

I threw my overnight bag on the couch and followed them in the kitchen where there was two unopened beers and a bottle of white wine beside a plastic wine glass. The wine bottle was sitting on a square hat box with a red top with STETSON on the side and a rendering of a cowboy herding cattle. The bottle was anchoring a blue string attached to a red balloon floating above the table. It said *CONGRATULATIONS!*

Heather pointed at the balloon. "That's from Chucky."

Charles popped open the beers. "It's a new hat for Cal. It's an old hat, but hardly been worn and it'll be new to Cal. Found it in a consignment store."

"He'll be thrilled," I said and unscrewed the top on the chardonnay.

Heather said, "Best screwed up bottle of wine seven bucks can buy."

We sat around the table sipping and telling each other how great it was Heather was here and not having supper with thirty-seven women, all dressed alike. Charles asked how everyone was on Folly.

Heather said, "Later. Let's go eat."

"Where?" I asked.

Heather stood and straightened her yellow blouse. "Don't know. I know where we ain't going. Ain't going anywhere there's singing or strummin'."

Next to Charles buying Cal a hat, the biggest surprise came when Charles said we were eating at The Capitol Grille, one of the city's most expensive restaurants, and that he was paying.

After a terrific supper, I saw the bill and told Charles he didn't have to pay. I'd pick up the tab.

"No way, Chris. Heck, I'm flush. I figure I saved a million dollars by not having to bail my sweetie out of the pokey."

It was great hearing Charles joking after what he and Heather had been through.

Heather raised her hand like she wanted to ask a question. "Something else I wanted to say. Think your friend William can give me the name of his, umm, counselor?"

William Hansel had suffered a nervous breakdown a few years ago, and since then had regular counseling sessions and had been pleased with the results.

"I'm sure his counselor could recommend someone over here."

Heather giggled. "Well that's the thing." She turned to Charles. "You tell him, Chucky."

Charles patted her on the hand and turned to me. "Sweetie's decided she'd rather be a big fish in a small pond instead of a minnow in the ocean. Nashville's a wonderful place, got a lot of good stuff going for it."

I held my breath as Charles paused.

"Cept it ain't got an ocean; ain't got our friends. We're moving back to Folly."

I stood, waved the server over, and said, "I'm buying the champagne."

DARK HORSE

1

I was enjoying a sandwich for lunch and halfheartedly watching a Live 5 newscaster ramble on about what was going on in the Charleston, South Carolina, viewing area. The talking head's report of multiple shark sightings off nearby Sullivan's Island was sound clutter, until I heard her mention a dead body and Folly Beach, my retirement home for a decade, in the same sentence. My sandwich took second place to me staring at a young reporter standing outside the entrance to the Folly Beach County Park, with the lights of three police cars alternating between red and blue in the background.

I didn't catch the beginning of the story but the reporter now had my attention as he said, "I've been told a body of a female was discovered in a gray mid-sized sedan you can see behind me." He dramatically turned his head and faced the gathering of police vehicles behind him and turned back to the camera and continued. "The body was found at approximately ten-thirty this morning by a Folly resident who was walking to the end of the island with a metal detector in search of elusive valuables lodged in the sand. Instead, he found something far worse—the body of the woman in the car."

The station cut to a taped interview with Folly's Director of Public Safety, better known as Police Chief Cindy LaMond, who said, "The body of a white female in her early forties was found in a gray Chevrolet Malibu with South Carolina plates this morning along West Ashley Avenue near the entrance to the Folly Beach County Park." Cindy paused.

Reggie, the interviewer, filled the void, "Do you know her identity and cause of death?"

Cindy nodded. "We know who she is but won't be releasing more information until next of kin has been notified."

Reggie interrupted, "Cause of death?"

The chief sighed. "It is being treated as a death investigation and there is nothing else to be said at this time. Thank you." She turned and walked away from the camera.

Cindy and I had become good friends after she moved to Folly from east Tennessee eight years ago and joined the city's small police force. She had been appointed chief a few years later, by the former chief who was now the mayor. Cindy was funny, excelled at her job, and had no use for reporters of any ilk.

The tape ended and Reggie started to say something but paused as he waited for the talking head in the studio to ask him a question. She didn't disappoint. "What else can you tell us?"

Reggie did disappoint, "That's all we know at this time."

Enlightening, I thought.

"To repeat," the newscaster said. "A body was found this morning in a car parked along the street outside the Folly Beach County Park. We will bring you updates as they become available." She went on to say we should check with the Channel 5 website for more information and to read all the latest news we should download the Channel 5 app to our smartphone and tablet. In other words, she stuck a commercial for her station in the middle of the newscast. One more reason I'm not a big TV watcher.

Folly Beach is an island located in the shadows of Charleston. It's small, only six miles long and a half mile wide, with the Folly Beach County Park anchoring the west end of the barrier island. News of anything happening on the island was big news to its roughly two thousand residents, so I wasn't surprised when the phone rang before the newscaster could say more than it was going to be a late August scorcher and to get the sunscreen ready.

"Hear about the dead bod at the County Park?" Charles Fowler said before I got to the "o" in hello.

Charles was one of the first people I met when I moved to Folly. For reasons unknown to anyone with a sense of logic, we became best friends. I worked most of my professional life in the human resource department of a large Midwestern healthcare company; Charles retired from his life of paychecks at the ripe young age of thirty-four and hadn't received a payroll check in the last thirty-one plus years. He was single, his financial needs minimal, and he met them by providing an extra set of hands to contractors, cleaning restaurants during busy season, and delivering packages for our friend Dude's surf shop. His picture can also be found in the dictionary beside the word "nosy." Don't look it up; that was an exaggeration, but only a slight one.

I said, "Just saw it on the news."

"Who was she and what happened?"

I told you he was nosy.

"How would I know?"

"You mean you haven't called Cindy yet?"

"Charles, what part of *just saw it on the news* don't you get?"

"So, you're going to call her now?"

The wise thing to do was to say yes, hang up, and call the chief. When it comes to Charles, I don't always do the right thing, so instead of agreeing, I said, "You have a phone. Why didn't you call her?"

"The poor, misguided police chief thinks you are smarter and more sensible than yours truly. She'll tell you more than she'll tell me. Go figure."

"Charles, if I was all those things, I'd have better sense than to call the chief who's probably still at the park."

"See," Charles said, "I know none of those things are true, so that's why you should call her now. Besides, if she's still with the body, she'll be able to tell you more."

I once again asked myself why I didn't do the wise thing in the beginning. I told him I give up and hung up.

"Chris Landrum, what in the hell took you so long to butt into police business?" Chief LaMond said.

I hated caller ID. "Good morning, Cindy."

"Don't give me that morning cheery voice. My day went to hell before I had my second cup of coffee. I'm standing in the middle of a sandstorm. I've got a dead lass sitting in a car about ten feet from me. And now I must take time from my underpaid, overworked job to talk to one of my city's biggest nosy nellies."

I heard several voices in the background and the sound of a heavy truck engine. "Did I catch you at a bad time?"

Cindy laughed. "Really? You really asked that? What do you think?"

She hung up before I could respond. The answer to my question was yes.

Fifteen minutes later, the phone rang again. Gee, give me a break, Charles.

I was wrong, it wasn't Charles but someone who started with, "I saw this big hair, little brain news chick on TV jabbering about a death on your island. Who was she? What happened?"

For years, I had unsuccessfully tried to get friends to start phone conversations with pleasantries like "good morning" or with their name. Bob Howard was the perfect example of you can't teach old dogs new tricks. During his more than seven decades on this earth, the successful realtor had perfected rudeness, overbearingness, obnoxiousness, and most every profanity. Despite his drawbacks, almost too numerous to mention, he was a friend.

"Good afternoon, Bob. What do I owe the honor of this call?"

"Crap, Chris. You make sugar taste sour. Now answer my questions."

"How would I know who she was and what happened?"

"Shit, because you butt in anything weird that happens over there. Figured you'd have your nosy nose in the middle of this."

Before moving to Folly, my life could best have been described as staid, solid, and yes, boring. I went to work in a large, bureaucratic company, lived in a middle-class house in a middle-class subdivision, drove a middle-class car, had married my high-school sweetheart and we had stayed together for twenty years, childless, but had participated in most middle-class activities. Somehow when I moved across the Folly River to the city I now call home, my life turned upside down. Through luck, mostly bad, and being at the wrong place at the wrong time, I had stumbled into the middle of a murder, helped catch the killer, and while accumulating a cadre of characters, had helped the police solve several other unnatural deaths since then. In fact, Bob Howard had aided me more than once in bringing a killer to justice.

"Bob, all I know is what I saw on television; the same thing you saw. It has nothing to do with me. I'm not involved."

Bob cackled. "Not yet!"

2

I flicked off the TV, finished my sandwich, moved to the living room, and smiled about how both Bob and Charles assumed I would know something about the body found fewer than two miles from my small cottage. A few years ago, it would have never entered my mind to give more than a few seconds of thought to what happened. Yes, I had stuck my nose where it didn't belong a few times, but I only did it at the urging of Charles or when it involved a friend. While growing up and throughout my many years in Kentucky, I had paid a premium on friendships. I didn't have many close friends, two at the most, but not until I moved to Folly, and I suppose had matured and gotten a better perspective on my world, did I hold friendships as close as I do now. Seeing those friends in danger or in pain tugged at my heart and I knew unless I did something to lessen that danger or their pain, I was a failure. It led me to a few situations that I could easily have lost my life over, but I've never regretted getting involved.

A glance at the clock revealed I must have dozed. It was after three in the afternoon and my neck hurt from sleeping in the chair. I stood, stretched, and walked to the screened-in front porch. Several cars were parked in the small lot in front of Bert's Market, my neighbor on the right, and two large construction vans barreled past the house on Ashley Avenue, Folly's longest street that ran from the shuttered Coast Guard Station property on the east end, to the site of the death on the west.

To the left of my cottage was Brad and Hazel Burton's house. In a move that must have had the god of irony doubled over with laughter, the Burtons moved in next to me two years ago. Brad had been a thorn in my side for the five years before that when he had been a detective in the Charleston County Sheriff's Office. He accused me of murder my first month on the island and despite me helping the police catch the killer, he had been angry with me ever since. Every time I stuck my nose in police business, which was far more times than I had hoped to, Brad was on my case. For a time, he was partnered with Karen Lawson, the detective I had dated for several years, and I got better acquainted with the incompetent detective. To the elation of most of his colleagues, he had retired and moved next door. When he bought the house, he didn't know I would be his neighbor. When he found out, it was too late to back out and he had avoided me ever since moving in. For that, I was thankful.

Brad and Hazel's late model Chryslers were usually the only vehicles at the house, so I was surprised to see two Ford Crown Vics in the drive. I was even more surprised when I recognized the dark gray one as Chief Cindy LaMond's unmarked car. Several questions rushed through my mind. Was something wrong with one of the Burtons? Unlikely, since there were no emergency vehicles at their house, and if there had been an emergency call, members of the Folly Beach Department of Public Safety who served the dual role of police officers and fire fighters would have responded. So, no sirens, no flashing lights, no emergency. Could it have something to do with the death near the park? Was Cindy there to get retired detective Burton's help?

That seemed remote, since she hadn't felt much better about Burton's competency as a detective than I had—which was next to none. Then, who did the other vehicle belong to? It could simply have been a black Crown Vic, unrelated to law enforcement. Brad and I were far from being best buds, so I wasn't about to knock on his door and ask. Let's hope Charles didn't see the cars there.

∽

THE OFFICIAL-LOOKING vehicles were gone when I walked to Bert's to get supper. Eric, an affable employee, nearly ran into me as I walked through the double doors into the iconic grocery. He was carrying a stack of boxes and apologized for nearly running me down. He was stopped, so I asked if he knew what the chief was doing at the Burtons. Bert's is the go-to store for everything from beer to bait and was open twenty-four hours a day. If anyone wanted to know what was going on nearby, Bert's or the Lost Dog Cafe were the places to begin. They were hangouts for locals and nearly every vacationer who set foot on the island. I was surprised when Eric said he didn't know and hadn't noticed the cars, nor had Chief LaMond been in Bert's this afternoon. It made more sense when he said he had been in the back and this was the first time he'd seen daylight in the last three hours. He offered to ask around and let me know if he learned anything. I thanked him and said it wouldn't be necessary. My culinary skills were slightly lower than my skills at splitting the atom, so I grabbed a frozen pizza and a cheap bottle of Chardonnay. My cable television had inadvertently landed on the Cooking Channel a month ago, and in a fit of boredom, I spent a half hour watching some famous chef show how easy it was to fix some exotic recipe using the microwave. Perhaps old dogs could learn a few tricks, especially if they were easy, and I was now proficient in using my microwave. I had switched the television off before I was tempted to use my oven.

I figuratively patted myself on my back for mastering heating the pizza, took the last bite which was now cold and tasted a lot like a piece of cardboard slathered with ketchup and called Chief LaMond.

She answered on the third ring and said, "I win!"

"Win what?" I said, skipping my preferred greeting of "Hi, Cindy."

"Larry bet me ten bucks you wouldn't call until tomorrow. I said you'd be pestering me before the night was over. Poor boy will never learn."

Larry was Cindy's husband of six years and owner of Pewter Hardware, Folly's best—only—hardware store. I had known him since before he'd met Cindy and considered him a good friend.

"Congratulations, I suppose."

"Wonder when the little squirt will start believing everything I say," she said, and repeated, "Poor boy."

Larry weighed one hundred pounds, more or less, and was five foot one, but only Cindy could get away with saying anything about his diminutive size. And heaven forbid anyone use the word squirt around him unless they were referring to a toy that shoots water.

"Guess he's a slow learner," I said.

"You've made my night, Mr. Perceptive Nosy Resident. Wait until I tell him what you called him."

"I'll deny it. Now could we get to why I called?"

"Sure. I know you geezers are always afraid you'll die before you get to ask all your questions."

Since I had now reached the second half of my sixties, I consider geezer status not beginning until I reach my nineties. Cindy was still in her early fifties, but I didn't see any point in debating her.

"What were you doing at the Burtons this afternoon?"

"And I thought you called to invite Larry and me to supper, or here's another thought, you wanted to know the details about the body."

"I'll have my people check with your people about supper, and of course I want to know about the body, but…"

"The seriously deceased person happened to be a Ms. Lauren Craft, age 41. She had been in her most recent state of dead for two hours when found by a nearby resident headed to the park and its beach to find his fortune in the sand. Looks like a drug overdose, heroin would be my guess. There was a used hypodermic needle on the floorboard below her right hand."

"Are you sure it…"

Cindy interrupted my interruption, "I'm not finished."

"Sorry, proceed."

"That's more like it. I'm a big fan of citizens apologizing. Anyway, it appears Ms. Craft had been in and out of drug rehab facilities several times. My guys checked her address on East Ashley Avenue and were greeted by her two roommates. Umm, give me a sec." I heard paper rustling and Larry's voice in the background and Cindy said, "Sweetie, get out your wallet. Yes, it's Nosy Chris. Yes, I'm serious. Ten bucks, now." The phone clanked against something and Cindy said, "I'm back. The late Ms. Craft had two roommates, Candice Richardson and Katelin Hatchett. Candice works as a clerk in a Real Estate office in downtown Charleston; Ms. Hatchett said she's 'between jobs' which probably means she got fired from her last one. Think her former career was in the waitressing field."

"What did Lauren Craft do?"

"Other than take drugs and kill herself?"

I exhaled and didn't say anything.

Cindy took the hint. "Seems she didn't work. One of the roommates said they didn't know where she got her money. She never had a lot, but they said she didn't have a job."

"Are you sure it was an overdose?"

"Chris, to you every death is a murder. Gee, can't people die on their own? You don't need to get involved in everything."

"Just curious."

"Yeah, right. Anyway, it appears that way, but we won't know more until the autopsy is complete. Now to your first question, you know the one about me being next door."

"I remember, Cindy. I'm not so old that I'm forgetting everything."

"It wouldn't be hard to find some folks who would disagree. Anyway, here's the sad news. Lauren Craft was Brad and Hazel Burton's daughter."

3

Other than being on the high side of nosy, Charles felt that if any of his friends learned anything he might have the slightest interest in knowing, the friend must tell Charles within a nanosecond of learning it. So the first thing I did after talking with Cindy was to call my friend.

After a dozen rings, I hit end call. Up until several months ago, Charles failing to answer was the norm. He had a phone in his apartment and unless he was there the call would have been wasted. He didn't have an answering machine and didn't own a cell phone until he and his long-term girlfriend, Heather, had moved to Nashville so she could pursue her dream: a career as a country music singer. She had been talked into moving to the country music capital of the universe by an agent who had heard her sing at an open-mic night. No one had ever compared Heather's voice to her idol Patsy Cline; truth be known, no one had ever compared it to the melodious singing voice of a snapping turtle, but nothing could deter her from trying. To say Heather and Charles's move to Nashville was a disaster would be a gross understatement. The highlights of the trip included

Heather being arrested for killing her agent, her attempting to kill herself, and me nearly being murdered. I'll save the details for another time, but suffice to say, only two good things came from their move: Charles's cell phone purchase and Heather deciding they should move back home to Folly where she could pursue singing in front of far less discerning audiences. I hit redial and gave Charles one more chance to get the latest news. No luck. You can lead Charles to a phone, but you can't make him answer.

I tried again the next morning with better luck. Charles answered, and I began telling him what I had learned about the body in the park.

"Whoa!" he interrupted. "When did you find out?"

"Last night."

"Last night! That was hours ago. And you waited all those many hours to tell me? Why didn't you call me?"

I rest my case!

"Charles, I tried. I called twice but you didn't have your phone on."

"Excuses, excuses. Hmm, maybe I was sort of with Heather. We were…"

"More than I need to know. The point is I tried."

"Okay," Charles said. "Apology accepted. What'd you learn?"

I must have missed the apology; regardless, arguing with him would be like arguing with a jellybean. I told him the details Cindy had shared and who Lauren's parents were.

He hesitated and said, "You're kidding."

I assured him I wasn't.

"I didn't know he had a daughter."

"I didn't either," I said, "but I also don't know much of anything about him other than he was a terrible detective, he can't stand me, and he lives next door."

"When are we going to go pay our respects?"

"Never, would be my first choice," I said.

"He's your neighbor. Because he hates you is no reason not to tell him, especially his wife, that you're sorry about their loss."

Charles was right, at least this time, and I told him we should probably wait until this afternoon or tomorrow. Charles said he had to make some deliveries for the surf shop and wouldn't be available until late afternoon. I thought the later the better and suggested tomorrow. He asked what time this afternoon would work. I sighed and said around six.

"I'll be at your house at five."

Charles hasn't owned a watch since I've known him, but time was one of his many quirks. He considers on time to be thirty minutes earlier than most mortals do and seldom fails to point out how late people were if they showed up on time. When he said he would be at the house at five, I assumed he thought it would take us a whopping half hour to walk from my house next door so we could arrive by five-thirty instead of six o'clock like I had suggested. Charles was Charles, love him or leave him. Until moving to Folly, I had been under the misunderstanding that appointed times equaled appointed times. I had adjusted to Charles time.

As sure as clockwork, I stepped out my front door at five o'clock and was greeted by Charles. It was in the upper eighties, but he wore a long-sleeve, navy blue T-shirt with a gold NYPD logo over the breast pocket. His usual attire included a long-sleeve college T-shirt or sweatshirt with a logo of the college mascot adorning the front. He didn't say it, but the NYPD shirt was his way of showing respect to Brad Burton, the former cop. For reasons I had not been able to determine, the shirts were always long-sleeved, and he carried a handmade, wooden cane. Charles, at five-foot eight, was a couple of inches shorter than me and a few pounds lighter. He had shaven for today's sympathy visit, but still had stubble on his chin and with his unruly gray hair, could have been mistaken for a street person. Today he looked his best.

"Well, I see you're looking boring as usual," he said and pointed his ever-present cane at me.

My green polo shirt was adorned with nothing, and I had on light-weight tan slacks, and boat shoes. Most of my work life had required a coat and tie, and I seldom wore a message on my chest. Charles considered it boring, and to him it was, but it was me. The one thing that did surprise me about Charles was that he was carrying a clear vase with several flowers in it. They looked suspiciously like blooms from a landscaped area in the yard next to Charles's apartment.

"You didn't have to bring me flowers," I said.

"Ha, ha. They're for the Burtons."

As if I didn't know that. Regardless of their origin, it was a thoughtful gesture, but I wasn't about to acknowledge it.

"Want a beer?" I asked since I was in no hurry to visit my nemesis.

Charles looked at his watch-less wrist. "Guess we have time."

"Do they know we're coming?"

"No."

I chose not to comment further about having time and waved him in. He set the flowers on the front porch and followed me to the kitchen, grabbed a Bud Light from the refrigerator, took a large sip, and plopped down in one of the chairs at my kitchen table.

"Hear anything about Lauren's death?" I asked and poured a small glass of Chardonnay.

In a community of numerous rumor collectors, Charles was among the best. If he put half as many hours in something that paid as he does cajoling information—both fact and fiction—out of others, he would be one of the city's wealthiest citizens.

"Heather said she heard from one of the hairdressers at the salon that Lauren was dating someone over here."

In addition to being an aspiring singer, Heather was a psychic, or so she said, and made a living as a massage therapist at Milli's Salon.

I took a sip of wine and asked, "What's interesting about that?"

"The hairdresser has known Lauren for several years and while she's dated several guys, this was the first serious one."

"Who is he?"

"The hairdresser didn't know."

"Hear anything about her death?"

Charles looked at his wrist. "That's one of the reasons we're going next door."

Charles prided himself on being a private detective. That's using the terms loosely since he had zero training in the field and wouldn't qualify as a private detective in South Carolina, or any other state that had a semblance of qualifications for the profession. His rationale for being qualified was that he had watched countless police shows on TV and had read countless books involving private eyes. Charles was a voracious reader and owned more books than many small-town libraries. His imaginary profession had been bolstered over the last few years because he and I had stumbled, bumbled, and fell into several murders and through pure luck and a little skill, had helped the police catch some killers. Which brought me back to Brad Burton and why he had such strong negative feelings about me, and probably Charles.

I nodded. "And I thought it was to express our sympathy to Lauren's parents."

"That too," Charles took a sip of beer, clinked his can down on the table, and pointed his cane toward the front door. "We're late."

I shook my head and followed him out.

$$4$$

The Burtons had lived in their home for a brief period, but during that time they improved the exterior, both house and the landscape. Hazel spent hours planting flowers, rearranging landscape beds, and supervising a landscape company as it cut the grass on a regular basis. I had never seen Brad in the yard other than when he was showing a painting crew what he wanted done to the exterior. And, I never saw anyone visit. I would have sworn they didn't have any children, or at least none who lived nearby.

It only took us a couple of minutes to make the trip from my cottage to the Burtons' newly painted, attractive ranch house. It was larger than my cottage, and I had wondered how the Burtons could have afforded it on a detective's retirement. Charles knew my feelings about Brad and on the walk over suggested that the retired detective had mellowed since turning in his badge. Charles was an eternal optimist but was often eternally wrong. As we stepped on their recently painted concrete front porch, I hoped he was right, but didn't think there was a chance.

I took a deep breath, motioned for Charles to join me on the porch, knocked, and prayed Brad wasn't home.

Hazel opened the door and smiled. Her smile appeared sincere, but her bloodshot eyes told a different story. She was a few years younger than her husband, but the shock of the last twenty-four hours had aged her. She wore a black blouse and a dark gray skirt.

"Hi, Chris," She didn't appear to know what to do next. She added, "Umm, come in."

I reached out and gave her a hug. "I'm so sorry about Lauren."

She mumbled, "Thanks."

"Do you know my friend Charles Fowler?"

Charles stepped to my side and held out the vase.

Hazel glanced at the flowers and up at Charles. "Umm, we've not met. I have seen you around town.

Charles handed Hazel the flowers and looked like he didn't know if he should try to hug her or shake her hand. It was one of the few times I'd seen my friend indecisive. He said hello and expressed his sympathy.

Hazel smiled. "Gosh, I'm being rude. Please come in. Can I offer you something to drink, or perhaps something to eat? God knows we have more food in here than we could ever use. People are so sweet."

That was a sentiment I doubted her husband had ever uttered. I declined and said we didn't want to interrupt anything and wanted to say how sorry we were.

Charles looked at me and at Hazel. "A glass of something cold would be nice."

I gave him a dirty look as Hazel headed to the kitchen. I realized I had already forgotten his second reason for wanting to visit. As we waited for Hazel to return I looked around. The floors were a highly-polished, light colored hardwood and there were two colorful nautical-patterned area rugs covering much of the floor. The furniture was even a shade or two lighter than the floors. Two whitewashed chairs had bright blue and green cushions and a large side table had two large, pink and white conch shells in the center. The furnishings looked more like a high-end condo package rather than the furniture in a retired couple's house. A 56-inch flat-screen television sat on a chrome stand against the far wall. It was oversized for the room. Everything was neat, cheery, and nothing reminiscent of the rumpled, poorly attired detective I had come to dislike. In addition to the two conch shells, there were two photos in silver frames on the table. One was of a smiling couple with a young girl probably no more than six years old, the other of the same girl playing on a swing. I looked around and didn't see other pictures.

I heard Hazel saying something, and Brad responding in a louder voice. Hazel interrupted him and a moment later appeared in the doorway. "Chris, Charles, come on in. Brad would like to say hi."

I knew things were going too well. Charles said, "Sure," smiled and followed Hazel to the kitchen. I followed.

The blinds were closed and although the sun was shining, only filtered rays penetrated the room. If it wasn't for an over-head light, the room would have been dark. I was able to see new stainless appliances. On the granite counter there were three small cakes, a basket of fruit, two plastic bowls covered with aluminum foil, and a bundle of flowers in the sink. Hazel had been right about the kindness of people. A coffee pot was on the back of the counter and the aroma of day-old coffee lingered.

Hazel saw me staring at the flowers. "Several of Brad's former colleagues have already visited and brought the flowers and food. Are you sure you don't want something to eat?"

The kitchen was tiny for the size of the house and Brad was seated at a small, glass-top table within inches of us. He hadn't looked up or spoken.

We again declined food as Hazel handed Charles a Coke and offered me one. I said yes, mainly so I wouldn't appear rude.

I felt strange being this close to the retired detective without acknowledging his existence, and said, "Hi, Brad."

He gripped a coffee mug like it was trying to escape. He had always looked old to me but appeared much older today. His shoulders slumped, his hair, always unruly, was a mess, and his white dress shirt was untucked, wrinkled, and raveled at the cuffs. I felt sorry for him, until he spoke.

He pointed his mug at me. "What the hell are you doing here?"

Hazel interrupted, "Now sweetie." She put her hand on his shoulder. "Chris and Charles were kind enough to stop by to express condolences. And look, they brought flowers." She held the vase in front of her husband who was still seated.

"Crap, Hazel, just what we need, more damn flowers. Our daughter's gone, and we get flowers."

Hazel squeezed Brad's shoulder, I wanted to bolt out of the house, and Charles said, "You have a lovely house Mr. and Mrs. Burton."

Hazel smiled, and Brad looked at Charles like he wanted to put a bullet in his head.

"Brad," I said, "we're neighbors and when I heard the young lady who … umm, was found dead was your daughter, I was heartbroken. Charles and I wanted to say how sorry we were."

Brad tightened his grip on the mug and twisted around to stare at me. "You mean the woman who offed herself with a drug overdose. You probably think it's funny. The old cop who spent his life putting bad people in jail has … umm, had a damn kid who kills herself doing something her law-and-order dad hated, despised." He looked down at the table. "The kid who's been in and out of drug rehab facilities. The kid who … oh shit, please get the hell out of here. Leave me alone."

Hazel let go of Brad's shoulder. She moved toward the door and motioned for Charles and me to follow. I wanted to say something else to the grieving father but knew this wasn't the time. We followed Hazel to the living room.

She shook her head. "Gentlemen, I apologize for my husband. Brad's grieving, or the best he can do. He's torn up. He's never handled emotions well. And when it comes … came to Lauren, he … well, you saw how he is."

"We understand," Charles said.

Hazel looked toward the kitchen. "The minute Brad retired, we sold our house in North Charleston and moved to Folly because Lauren lived here. Brad thought if we were closer we may be able to help her. She'd just got out of a horrible marriage from Sebastian Craft and was a mess." She looked at the ground and then up at me. "At first we thought we were helping. With the drugs, and everything. We thought we were helping." She faked a smile. "Anyway, Brad didn't mean anything personal in there."

I doubted that, but said, "That's okay, Hazel. We understand. Thanks for the drinks and again, we are so sorry. Let me know if there is anything you need."

She said she would and saw us out.

On the way to the house, Charles said, "Well, that went well."

That wouldn't have been my take, but I didn't say anything. Charles said he had a date with Heather and I was glad to hear it was at a barbecue restaurant on Folly Road about five miles from the island. Until Charles and Heather moved to Nashville earlier this year, neither had a vehicle that used anything other than pedal power. Before they moved, Charles bought a used Toyota Venza and now that they had returned to the island they should have never left, he had rediscovered the world of restaurants, shops, and sights off island; locations to which I had previously been his primary chauffeur. I encouraged him to explore without me. I was glad he didn't ask if I wanted to go since I had planned to meet Barb when she got off work and knew she would be exhausted and wouldn't want to go anywhere off island. Before he left, he told me I'd better call if I learned anything about Lauren's death. He held up his cell phone as if I wouldn't know how to let him know.

5

I'd met Barbara Deanelli six months ago under less than ideal circumstances. I happened to stumble on a body splayed out in the alley near the back door to Barb's Books. Things tumbled downhill from there. First, Barb moved her used bookstore into the space I had rented for several years while trying to make a go of Landrum Gallery, a shop featuring my photographs. As hard as I found it to comprehend, the fine citizens of Folly and the thousands of vacationers the island attracted each year failed to appreciate the fine artistic images that I had for sale. Oh sure, many said they liked the photos and some bought a few, but overall, they decided they would rather spend their hard-earned money on luxuries like rent, gas, electric, taxes, cell phones, and the latest iWhatever. Go figure.

Even though I had closed the business before Barb came to town, I resented her from before we'd even talked. And when we met I found her aloof and appearing, for lack of a better term, snooty. Add to that the fact many suspected her to be the murderer. As is the case with many things on Folly, appearances don't tell the whole story. After several conversations leaning toward the cold side, either she had begun to warm toward me, owing to my charm, I hoped; more likely, it was because I'd saved her life and managed to catch the person who was willing to stop at nothing to kill her. Regardless, we started seeing each other on a semi-regular basis. We enjoyed each other's company, and if I was honest with myself, it was great to be able to enjoy time with someone other than Charles.

I met Barb for supper at the Folly Beach Crab Shack, one of several popular restaurants on Center Street, the island's six-block long primary commercial district. Charles's time obsession had rubbed off on me. I arrived at the colorfully painted Crab Shack fifteen minutes before Barb said she could get there. I was seated at the last vacant table on the deck overlooking the street and the variety of pedestrians taking in the sights and sounds of the island.

Barb spotted me as she turned the corner to the restaurant's entrance and headed my way. She wore tan shorts and one of her trademark red blouses. She weaved her way through the restaurant and out the door to the patio. Her hazel eyes gleamed as she pointed to the container of peanuts I put in front of her chair. I envied her metabolism. It seemed like she could eat all she wanted and remain thin. She was my height at five-foot-ten and looked younger than her sixty-four years. Her short black hair was also in contrast to my rapidly balding, blond turning gray head.

I stood and pecked her on the cheek; she grabbed a peanut and looked around for someone to order a drink. Elizabeth, one of the restaurant's personable employees, was nearby and Barb ordered a beer.

"Rough day in the book selling business?" I asked as Barb cracked open the peanut shell.

"You know how much I can't stand romance novels."

I nodded.

"About 11,000 customers stomped in today and 'just had to

have' something by Danielle Steel, Barbara Taylor Bradford, Nora Roberts, or blah, blah, blah. My head started thumping by three o'clock."

I laughed. "You're complaining to the wrong person about 11,000 customers. I would have been thrilled if eleven customers had ever graced the door in one day during the time your building housed Landrum Gallery."

She reached across the table and petted my hand. "That's probably because you didn't have photos of Danielle Steel."

"True," I said as the waitress set a bottle of Budweiser in front of Barb. It didn't stay on the table long.

"Enough about my day. What's happening in your world?"

"Glad you asked," I said. "Did you hear about the body they found near the county park?"

"Between requests for Judith McNaught and Julia Quinn gooey romances, someone mentioned it. Something about a drug overdose." She flipped a peanut shell in a blue pail in the center of the table. "Why?"

I explained about who she was and who her father was.

"You've mentioned him. You're not his biggest fan, right?"

"That's an understatement," I said, and proceeded to share some of my history with the retired detective.

Barb was an attorney but had given up a lucrative practice in Pennsylvania and a husband that went with it when he was arrested for bribing state officials. She didn't know anything about his illegal activities and was exonerated of any wrongdoing but felt the need to leave that world behind and moved to Folly. She used the listening and questioning skills she had learned in law school and had honed through her practice. She interrupted a couple of times with questions, but listened, something I wasn't used to from my other friends.

I shared much of today's conversation with Brad.

"Not the kind of reception you would have liked, I suppose."

"Hazel was as sweet as could be, considering the circumstances. Brad was an ass. I thought since he was retired and my next-door neighbor, he'd have mellowed."

Barb grabbed another peanut, deposited the shell in the bucket, and started to pop the peanut in her mouth, but hesitated and pointed the nut at me. "Did you ever think he was angry at the world and not only at you? People close to suicide or drug overdose victims often feel guilty. They think there must have been something they could have done to prevent it. He could also be embarrassed about what happened. He'd been a cop, yet he couldn't prevent whatever happened to his daughter."

"I suppose that's …"

Barb interrupted. "One more thing. While he lashed out at you, it may not have been personal. You were a handy target for his emotions."

"Barb, those are good points, and I would like to give him the benefit of the doubt, but with our fractured, and often hostile, history, it's hard to do."

Barb smiled. "Give the man a chance. You never know."

I returned her smile. "Okay."

"Now with that out of the way, are we going to order food or are you going to sit there and watch me shrivel up and blow away?"

There was little chance of that happening, especially if there was an unlimited supply of peanuts, but I got the waitress's attention and we each ordered a fried fish basket and another drink.

I realized my stomach was still in knots from thinking about my history with Brad Burton and how my recent conversation with him had dredged up the memories I had mostly put out of my mind. Time to change the subject.

"Heard from Dude lately?" I asked.

Jim "Dude" Sloan was Barb's younger stepbrother, and owned the surf shop, one of Folly's stores catering to the significant population of surfers and surfer wannabes. He was a long-time resident of Folly and had encouraged Barb to move here after her divorce.

"He called a couple of nights ago. Said he was wondering if I was still doing okay, of course he didn't use those words. I think his quote was, "Fractional-sis be OK?"

Dude was as opposite from Barb as a magnolia tree was to poison ivy. Both were living things, but that was about it. Dude had never met a sentence he couldn't mangle. He treated words as if they were gold and shared as few of them as he could. Charles had sworn—partly in jest—that Dude had come to Earth from another planet, and I think he was disappointed when Barb confirmed Dude, in fact, was from Earth, more accurately Altoona, Pennsylvania.

"Did you tell him that you be good?"

She rolled her eyes—a motion of endearment, or so I wanted to believe. "Sort of."

"He say anything else?"

"After I said I was fine, he said something in surfer talk that I think meant good and hung up."

Our food arrived, preceded by the strong aroma of frying fish. Barb had taken a bite before I reached for my fork. Eleven-thousand customers heightened her appetite.

"I know you don't want to talk more about Brad and the death of his daughter," Barb said between bites, "but let me ask you one more question. Is there a possibility the death could have been more than an accidental overdose or suicide?"

I was surprised by her question. "Why do you ask?"

"No reason. From my experience, most deaths like this one are treated as if there could be more than the obvious. I know you have connections with the police and would probably know how they were looking at it."

"Cindy, Chief LaMond, told me it looked like an overdose, but wouldn't know more until she had the coroner's report. I'll let you know when I hear anything."

Barb cocked her head. "You don't talk like you're convinced it was accidental."

I gave a slight nod. "It probably was, considering her history with drugs. Besides, the police will figure it out. It's none of my business."

She looked up from her plate. "Um hum."

Honest, I thought.

I walked Barb to her condo in the Oceanfront Villas complex and slowly walked home. I stepped in my living room when my cell rang. I was surprised to see Brian Newman's name on the screen.

"Good evening, Brian."

"I'm beginning to see why you hate caller ID," he said.

I started with something polite and appropriate, not like most of my friends who feel they must start phone conversations with … oh well, never mind. "To what do I owe the pleasure of hearing your voice?"

"I wish more of your fellow citizens had your attitude. You know how many bitchy, complaining, irritated calls I receive?'

"Mr. Mayor, you want me to guess?"

"No, but it's a bunch. When I was police chief, I had a staff to hand off most of the complaints to. As mayor, the buck stops here."

"Public service," I said, still not knowing why the mayor had called. But I also knew him well enough to not push.

"Listen," he said, "I hate to call so late. It's almost your bed time but wanted to know if you could meet me in the morning for breakfast."

"Sure," I said. "Where and when?"

"The Dog, 7:00 o'clock."

"I'll be there."

He said thanks and was gone. And I still had no idea why he had called. What I did know was that it was important.

6

The Lost Dog Cafe is a block off Center Street and most days it was the epicenter of early-morning activity on Folly Beach. It was cool for August, so the mayor was inside. His hands were wrapped around a coffee mug as he was reading today's newspaper. Amber, my favorite waitress, had her back to me and was leaning over Brian's shoulder and looking at the page he was holding. I had known Amber since my first week on the island and we dated for a time. After we stopped dating, she remained a good friend and one of the best sources of information—fact and fiction—about most anything Folly.

I patted her on the shoulder and she jerked back.

"Sorry I startled you," I said.

"Chris, you gave my old heart a scare."

Old wasn't a word I would use with Amber. She was approaching fifty but still looked in her early forties. The only person I'd ever heard referring to her as old was Jason, her nineteen-year-old son; but to him, everyone over forty was about ready to kick the bucket.

"A bit jumpy this morning?"

"Brian was showing me this story about that guy who killed three members of his own family. Can you believe that?"

"Sorry. Yes, it was terrible."

"Hmm!" interrupted Brian. "Umm, Chris, I'm here too. Remember me, I'm the person who asked you to breakfast."

"Sure," I said and put my arm around Amber's waist. "But, she's much better looking."

"You're still my favorite mayor," Amber said as she leaned over and kissed the top of Brian's head. "I'll leave you two to your confab. Chris, coffee?"

I said, "Duh!"

Amber headed to the kitchen and past the nearly countless dog photos that dotted the walls of the restaurant like spots on a Dalmatian. Brian motioned for me to sit at the other side of the table. The tall, trim, and confident mayor leaned back in the chair and looked around to see who was nearby. With short black, but graying, hair, he oozed military which made sense since he had been in the armed forces before retiring after thirty years.

"Thanks for joining me."

"Glad you called."

"I suppose you're wondering why I asked you here."

I shrugged. "It did enter my mind."

Brian looked around again. No one appeared to be paying attention to us. "Chris, I'm going to run for reelection."

That was no surprise. He was in his early seventies but had unwavering enthusiasm for his job and the island, and although he was thrust into the position when his predecessor had slinked out of state after some untowardly information was revealed, the role fit him like a wetsuit. I was however surprised by how early he was making the decision.

"That's great but isn't the election next April, what, almost eight months from now?"

Amber arrived with my coffee and asked if I was ready to order. I ordered French toast, my favorite Dog breakfast item, and Amber shook her head but said she'd get it started. She had been on a one-person crusade to get me to eat better but had conceded defeat.

Brian watched her go, and said, "I know that's a long time from now, but rumors are that there will be at least one well-financed opponent, and maybe a couple more. If I want to stay on the job, I need to get an early start."

"Who's running against you?"

"Do you know Joel Hurt?"

"The landscape guys?"

Brian nodded.

"I've seen him a couple of times at Bert's and it seems like Hurt's Landscape trucks are always running around town."

Brian took a sip of coffee and said, "He has more than a landscape service. He owns the three Lowcountry Garden Centers, the one on Folly Road near the cutover to Charleston, one past Mt. Pleasant on the way to Georgetown, and one in North Charleston. He also owns a large nursery."

"I didn't know the garden centers were his."

"Not many do."

"Sounds like he's successful."

"Very. Not only will he throw a lot of his personal wealth to the campaign, but he'll have the support of several well heeled locals who want to run off our more, let me say, bohemian residents, and especially the college students who flock to the beach on weekends and during the summer. *Sanitize the island* is a phrase I've heard some of his supporters are whispering about."

"Take the folly out of Folly."

Brian nodded, and Amber arrived with my unhealthy breakfast. I thanked her, and she rolled her eyes when she said, "Enjoy."

"Chris, I know Folly's not perfect. We all know in season there are many weekends, and now an increasing number of weekdays, when more and more people swarm to the beach than there's room for their vehicles. I'm not blind to the fact that inconsiderate day-trippers flagrantly violate the law against drinking on the beach, throw their trash in yards, and don't hesitate to share their loud opinions of most anything. Hell, when I was police chief, I dealt with it every day."

"True."

"I'm not defending anyone who commits a lawless act or infringes on the personal space or property of others, but I don't want our small slice of heaven to become a Kiawah Island or a place where a visitor needs a passport and a good conduct medal to be allowed to enter. Our island has a long history of being tolerant of people of all shapes, sizes, colors, and views on life. We have always been inclusive, and I don't want that to end."

It sounded like a campaign speech and still didn't tell me what he wanted me to do, so I said, "I agree."

Brian took another sip of coffee and I took a bite of French toast. I waited for him to say something, but when he didn't, I said, "Brian, you're respected, have done an excellent job as mayor, and are popular. Does Joel have a chance?"

"Many will call him a dark horse candidate, but he scares me. He and his supporters have the money to make a difference. You know the local races usually don't involve mega-bucks." He looked down at his mug and chuckled. "In past elections, some of the council candidates have considered it obscene if they had to spend more than pocket change and they stuck a few God-awful looking yard signs in some yards, and that was it."

"Don't remind me of that yard clutter."

"This is going to be different. Rumors are Joel is holding hush-hush meetings with potential supporters and getting commitments from them to use their influence to get as many people as they can to contribute to his campaign, and these people have money. Understand, I don't have anything against Joel Hurt. In fact, I think he's a nice guy and from what I can see, he's sincere. I think we could be friends even though we have drastically different ideas about what's good for Folly. Unfortunately, some of his supporters and donors have more drastic, and I believe harmful, ideas about what Folly should become."

Brian tilted his head and stared at me like he wanted me to say something.

"So, what can I do?"

"There's one more thing," Brian said, sidestepping my question. "I'm not the only one with a target on his back. They're going after Marc and Houston."

Marc Salmon and Houston Bass were two long-term council members. They were on the council when I moved to Folly. I didn't know Houston well, but was more familiar with Marc. The two met daily in the Dog, and I was a little surprised they weren't here now. Marc tried to tell those who happened to ask that he met Houston to discuss city business, but from what I could tell, their main goal was to gather as much gossip as possible. Marc would pass on facts, but gossip was his forte.

"Why them?"

"The misconception that they vote for anything I tell them to."

"Who'll be running against them?"

"No idea, but you can be assured whomever it is will have money behind them."

"Great."

The Dog was full, and the sounds of happy diners seemed louder than usual. Brian looked around and again, no one appeared to be paying attention to us.

"Now to your question. One of my biggest flaws as a candidate is asking for money." He laughed. "I suck at it. I know it's important, but so far, I haven't had to go far down that road. That's changing and is the reason I'm starting my campaign early."

I wasn't wealthy. In fact, my failed photo gallery drained a sizable chunk of my life savings, but unless I live to reach triple digits, I should have enough money to live if not comfortably, at least adequately. Brian knew this, so I wondered what could be coming next.

"Bottom line, Chris, is I need to raise far more than I ever have needed to win reelection. I'd like your help."

"Brian, I'll contribute what I can."

"Thanks, you don't know how much I appreciate that, but I'd like to ask more."

"What?"

"To host a couple of fundraisers."

I started to laugh, but saw he was serious. Before retiring and moving to Folly, I had attended a few political fundraisers. The events were usually held at the homes of some of the wealthiest people in my hometown. Most of those in attendance were recognizable and were some of the wealthiest leaders in the community. I was invited because I worked for one of the city's largest employers and was expected to make contributions to candidates the company felt could help their business. I had a good salary and could contribute without cutting too far in my savings. But even then, my contributions were limited to the lower end of the amounts expected.

"Brian, you know most of my friends well enough to know they're not rolling in dough."

He laughed, "You mean Charles, Cal, and Mel don't have gold bars buried in their back yards?"

"Brian, they don't even have back yards."

"True, but you forgot to mention your successful real estate buddy Bob Howard. And how about Barb, that lovely lady who for some strange reason has decided to date you? Then, despite outward appearances, Dude, your other good friend who has more money than probably all the rest of us combined."

He had a good point, although I had never looked at it like that. A few of my friends could probably make significant contributions. Brian had also never asked me for anything and if I could do something, however minor, to help, I would.

"Okay," I said. "I'm in. Let's talk about it."

And we did. Brian had already given it a lot of thought and we decided two distinctly different events would be best: one on Folly with my closest friends, and one in Charleston, and hopefully at Bob Howard's house where some of the wealthier donors could be invited. All I had to do was to convince Bob. Brian agreed it would be no simple task but appreciated that I would try.

Brian relaxed after he made it through the part of running for office that he was most uncomfortable with, so I took the opportunity to get into another difficult topic. "Now that that's out of the way, have you learned anything new about the death of Brad Burton's daughter?"

His smile turned to a frown. "No, why?"

"Curious. Charles and I visited the Burtons and it was still on my mind."

His eyes narrowed. "Everything points to an unfortunate drug overdose. Tragic, but it happens. Is there some reason you think it may be something more?"

"No, like I said, I was curious."

"Yeah, right. You're not planning on sticking your nose where it doesn't belong?"

"Of course not. There's no reason for me to get involved, there's nothing to get involved with."

Brian took the final sip of coffee and shook his head. "Chris, you need to get some business cards that say: *I'm not going to get involved.* On the other side: *Kidding.*"

7

I spent most of the time on the six-block walk from the Dog to my house trying to figure out how Brian had convinced me to organize not one but two fundraisers for his campaign coffers. The answer simply came down to friendship. Many island residents had befriended me, and I had reciprocated. Finally, I came to the realization there weren't many things more important than true friendship. Granted, it had nearly gotten me killed on more than one occasion, but my deep bonds with a handful of people were worth it. My thoughts were transitioning from the theoretical to the tasks necessary to pull together the fundraisers when I bumped into Hazel Burton on the sidewalk in front of Mr. John's Beach Store.

"Sorry, Hazel," I said and stepped aside.

She looked better than the last time I saw her, but her eyes were still bloodshot and her cheeks had a slight red tone from crying.

"That's okay, Chris. I was walking and not paying attention to where I was going."

I smiled. "That makes two of us."

"Thanks again for stopping by the house."

"Sorry it was under such terrible circumstances."

"Are you in a hurry," she said.

"No, just had breakfast and was heading home."

She looked in the direction I was going and turned back to me. "There's something I wanted to tell you. Care to walk?"

Since she put it that way, even if there was somewhere I needed to be, I would have gone with her.

I moved in step beside her, wondered where she was going, but didn't say anything. She had a need to talk and that was okay with me. I thought she was going to the Dog, but instead she turned into the small park beside the combination library and community center and led me to a bench overlooking a nicely landscaped area. The bench was shaded so the temperature was comfortable. I waited.

After an awkward silence that felt like it had lasted for hours, she looked at the Lost Dog Cafe located on the adjacent property, and said, "Nice place. Brad and I like eating there."

I agreed and said it was where I had had breakfast. I didn't think she brought me over here to say that, so I waited for her to continue.

"How long have you lived here?" she asked at the end of the long pause.

"Almost nine years."

"Oh yeah," she said, "I remember Brad telling me about meeting you. Out at the end of the island overlooking the lighthouse, wasn't it?"

I nodded. "A bad day. I stumbled on a man who'd been shot. Detective Burton, umm, Brad, and Detective Lawson were investigating."

Hazel looked at me and grinned. "Brad thought you were the killer."

I told her more about my unpleasant encounter with her husband and tried to make light of a traumatic and sad occurrence. She listened but seemed distracted. I ended the story as quickly as possible and hoped she'd get to her reason for us being here.

Hazel looked at the ground. "I'm not going to tell Brad I talked to you."

I nodded but didn't ask why.

"To be honest, Chris, my husband doesn't take too kindly to you."

Duh, I thought.

She chuckled, "He thinks you're a nosy, busybody who can't help but stick your nose into anything bad that happens."

I smiled. "Looking from his perspective, I see where he's right. I have been way too involved in several situations that should have been handled by the police, but most of the time, I'd been sucked in by friends, and to be honest, the police weren't always doing their best to solve the crimes."

"That's what Brad said."

I was surprised her husband would admit the police weren't being effective.

I started to say something about it, but she held her hand up and motioned for me to stop. "When Lauren was a little girl up through much of her teens, Brad was always working. He was trying to prove he could be a good cop and I suppose it paid off since he was promoted to detective. He missed most of her school activities. She was a cheerleader and acted in several school plays, but Brad only made it to one play, and seldom got to see her cheer." Hazel blinked a couple of times and looked at the ground. "He feels guilty about not being there .... umm, he really does."

"A lot of men go through the same thing," I said. "I can't imagine what a demanding job being a cop can be. And the family almost always suffers."

"Lauren got hooked on pills while she was in high school. I was married to a cop, but I was sheltered from the serious stuff that goes on in the world. Chris, I didn't know anything about her drug abuse until the school principal called me to come get her. She had been in a math class and started acting strange. She gave me a story about someone giving her one pill to take and that she didn't know what it was. Said she'd never done anything like it before. Brad was working a double homicide and didn't get home that night. Stupid me, I bought her story and didn't tell Brad the next day."

"You wanted to believe her," I said.

"Mistake number one," Hazel said. "And that was only the beginning. Her use—abuse—got so bad we had to place her in an outpatient rehab program. We didn't want to disrupt her life more than we had to. That was mistake number two. She was getting therapy, but she was still in a toxic environment with her friends. Temptations were too strong. Poor Brad kept kicking himself. Kept saying he was in the business of catching the bad guys and trying to make life safer for everyone, and in his own house he had a daughter who was using and probably laughing at him behind his back. It tore him up. It hurt his home life; screwed up his work life. I'm embarrassed to say it almost broke up our marriage."

I remembered Chief LaMond had said Lauren had been in and out of rehab facilities, so I knew the answer to my next question but wanted to hear it from Hazel.

"What happened then?"

Hazel wiggled her hand back and forth. "We thought things were getting better. I suppose they were, but it didn't last. She graduated from high school and was trying to take classes at the community college. She had a waitressing job and managed to rent a small apartment. A patrol officer pulled her over in the middle of the night. Her car was weaving all over the road, and … Christ, Brad would kill me if he knew I was telling you this. The cop was certain Lauren was under the influence of something, but instead of hauling her in, he called Brad who dragged himself out of bed and picked her up where the patrol officer was waiting. Brad brought her home and we got her car the next day. By now she wasn't even trying to lie about what was going on. We got her committed to a residential facility through a contact Brad had with the director."

"Did it help?"

"For a while. She stayed with us a few weeks after they felt she was in good enough shape to be out on her own. She said the people who were a bad influence on her were in Charleston and she persuaded us she needed to get a little farther away and had met some women who rented a house over here. It wasn't six months later that the cycle began all over again. That's when Brad decided to retire, and we bought the house next to yours, so we could be closer to her. To make the story a little shorter, she went back in rehab, stayed until they felt she was better, and moved back in with the girls over here." Hazel hesitated and stared into space. A tear rolled down her face. "We thought she'd kicked it. We moved here, were able to see her every few days, and she seemed better than she had in high school before it all began. Chris, we thought she'd kicked it."

"I'm sorry."

She wiped the tear away and tried to smile. "Sorry to dump this on you. All I wanted to do was apologize about the way Brad treated you when you came to visit. The thing is, he feels responsible, he feels guilty, he's angry with himself, and took it out on you. It wasn't anything personal. I want you to know that."

I understood how Brad must be feeling and didn't doubt it was taking a toll on him, but I thought she was wrong about me. It was personal, but I didn't see any benefit of getting into it.

"I understand and again, I'm terribly sorry about what both of you are having to deal with."

She reached over and gently touched my arm. "Thank you. You're easy to talk to; I didn't mean to spill this on you. Thank you for listening."

"No need to thank me. Please let me know if there's anything I can do."

"I will."

"Would you like me to walk you home?"

"Thanks, but no. I'm going to walk around some more before I head home. There is one thing you could do. Please don't let Brad know we had this talk."

You can bet on that, I thought, and said I wouldn't.

8

I hadn't given much thought to the Burtons or their daughter's untimely death since my conversation with Hazel three days ago. The routine chores of life had taken much of my time. I had written my check for homeowners' insurance and went through my annual rant about how it was three times more than I had ever paid in Kentucky. I spent an additional hour praising myself for the wise decision to move to the ocean, or as some would say, my rationalization for the excessive cost of insurance. I also remembered how thankful I had been to have insurance when a hurricane had nearly ripped my home off its foundation a few years ago. Then there was grocery shopping, an exhausting event that I do at least once a month, whether I needed to or not. That ate up a couple more hours. Finally cleaning the inside of my cottage, something I don't do as often as I go grocery shopping, took up another half day. The total of hours I spent on these activities didn't add up to three days, but it seemed like it. If I admitted it to myself, reaching the latter stages of my sixties added more hours of rest and naps to fill the time I had to do other things during earlier years. Many of those hours had been taken up with my career, so regardless how I look at it, I'd chosen retirement and aging, naps, and exhaustion came with it.

I realized after I had wasted three days with the mundane chores of life, that the autopsy results from Lauren Burton should be available, and I hadn't heard from Chief LaMond. I put my broom in the closet, told it I'd see it again in a month or so, and punched Cindy's number in my phone.

"Thought you were dead," the chief said as way of a pleasant greeting.

"Don't think so."

'It's been three days since you've pestered me about Lauren Craft's death. You already cost me the ten bucks I won from Larry. I went double or nothing with him that you would've been on my case two days ago. You owe me big time."

I smiled thinking how great it was to have friends like Cindy. "Okay, I'll buy you a cup of coffee the next time I see you. It should—"

"Cup of coffee?" she interrupted. "You mean a meal."

"Okay, so have you—"

"With dessert."

"Okay, okay."

"Good. Now if you're interested, I have the autopsy results."

I waited for her to continue.

"Aren't you going to ask what they are?"

"Didn't think I had to."

"You better be glad I'm in a good mood, Mr. Nosy Citizen. You can thank Larry for that, and no, it's none of your danged business why." She chuckled. "You do know nowhere in my job description does it say I have to give confidential information to you?"

"An obvious oversight."

She sighed. "You want to hear what I know or pretend that

you're back being an overpaid HR bigwig writing job descriptions?"

"I'd love to hear what you learned, Chief LaMond."

"That's better." I heard papers rustling and Cindy continued, "Ms. Craft has joined Janis Joplin, River Phoenix, John Belushi, and Philip Seymour Hoffman with a common mode of demise, an overdose of heroin. She also had enough alcohol in her blood stream to pickle a bull elephant."

"No surprise there," I said, more to myself than to Cindy.

"No, but while that's the official cause of death, it still doesn't answer how or why."

"Doesn't a needle found on the floorboard answer how?"

"Sort of," Cindy said. "The OD was administered with that needle, but did she squeeze it into her vein willingly? Was it an accident or did she know what she was doing? Was she so drunk she only vaguely knew what was going on."

"Suicide?"

"Possibly."

"What's that mean?"

Cindy said, "Could someone else have injected her or made her inject herself?"

I was confused. "Were her prints on the needle?"

"Good question. Yes."

I was still confused. "Why would there be any question about her doing it?"

"A couple of things. Want to guess what, Mr. Faux Detective?"

"That's Charles, not me."

"If you say so. Guess anyway."

"Where her car was found isn't near where she lived. Do we know if she drove to where she was found?" I asked.

"Excellent question. We think she did."

"Were her prints on the steering wheel or the door handle?"

"Even better questions. The answers are yes and yes."

I was beginning to feel like I was on a quiz show and about to lose a zillion dollars because I didn't know the right questions to ask. What was I missing? There had to be something or Cindy wouldn't be playing 20 questions.

"Were there prints on the passenger side door?"

"Bingo!" the chief said.

"No prints."

"Clean as, as … umm, something really clean."

"So, no prints?"

"There were some smudges, but no clear prints, no dirt, hell, no bird crap, no nothing," she said.

"Was the rest of the car clean?"

"Not dirty, probably had been washed recently, but there was dust on it." Cindy paused. "You can't park where it was in the sandy berm without some grimy ocean crap landing on it."

"So, you think it was wiped clean which would mean someone may have been with her when she died and skedaddled before she was found?"

"No way to prove that. It's possible the EMTs rubbed their hands on it when entering the car."

"If they did, would it have been as clean as you found it?" I asked.

"Don't think so, but it's possible since they wore those cute blue gloves. It's also possible someone may have stumbled on the car, looked inside, saw the highly deceased Ms. Craft, panicked and wiped the handle clean, before hightailing it so he, or to be politically correct, she could avoid being questioned. That seems unlikely to me."

"Are you thinking she was killed and someone wanted it to look like an overdose?"

"That's a possibility, but it could also mean someone was shooting up with her and when she accidentally overdosed didn't want to get caught. We coppers look askance at our fine citizens shooting heroin along a city street, especially if they're found sitting beside one of our former fine citizens."

"True. You said there were two things that raised questions."

"The other thing might not mean anything, but it strikes me as odd. Lauren had apparently been in and out of rehab facilities several times, all for heroin use."

"So, her death shouldn't be a surprise."

"I agree, but the medical examiner said the fatal needle mark was the only recent mark on her. It'd been a long time since she'd used, or at least injected."

"Couldn't she still have misjudged the strength and taken a fatal dose?"

"Yes, but from my experience with addicts, they have to be mighty high to make that mistake. All I'm saying, Chris, is that it seems strange."

"What happens next?"

"It's in the hands of the Sheriff's Office. They'll be conducting an investigation, if there is one."

Folly Beach is in Charleston County, and the Charleston County Sheriff's Office is charged with investigating major crimes on the island. Cindy's staff is limited in size and experience in dealing with most deaths but handles most other infractions and the daunting task of traffic, particularly during vacation season.

"Do they agree it seems strange?"

"They're giving lip service to it, but their plate is full, and I wonder how much actual investigating they'll be doing. It's still an open case and Detective Ken Adair is working it."

I knew Detective Adair from another death I got stuck in the middle of. He considered my friend Mel Evans as the prime suspect in a murder, but Charles and I stuck our noses in the case enough to prove Mel wasn't guilty. I almost got killed in the process, but that's another story. Other than that error in the detective's judgment, he appeared to be a good cop. But, I also knew his workload, as it was for all detectives with the office, was overwhelming.

"So, what are you doing?" I asked.

"Keeping my eyes open, talking to everyone who knew her here, and praying."

9

I also hadn't heard from Charles the last three days. Since he has a mode of transportation that didn't depend on pedal power, he had spent hours exploring the many sights of interest in and around Charleston. I know because he felt the need to tell me about every place he visited, including its location, historical significance, and mound of trivia surrounding it.

He answered on the third ring.

"Well, well," he said. "Have you returned from the dead?"

"You been talking to Cindy?"

"No. Why?"

"Never mind. Available for lunch?"

"Depends."

"On what?" I said and realized I had nearly forgotten why I'd called.

"Where you're buying."

"Yogurt, Kangaroo Express."

"Shucks, Chris, my calendar's crammed full."

"Fish sandwich, the Grill."

"Whoa, look here, a spot just opened up. Noon. Bye."

That meant eleven-thirty and I surprised myself when I arrived at the Grill and Island Bar five minutes before Charles-time. The Grill was on Center Street and was one of the small island's largest restaurants. I was a regular at its Thursday evening performances by the Folly Beach Bluegrass Society, a collection of talented bluegrass musicians who converge on the restaurant to share their love for traditional bluegrass music with enthusiastic audiences. There was no live entertainment today, but the smell of fried flounder greeted me and made me realize I hadn't eaten.

I was seated on the patio overlooking Folly's main drag when Charles rounded the corner from his apartment three blocks away. He wore a gold, long-sleeve T-shirt with the outline of a buffalo and UC in the center.

"See you're on time for a change," he said, making me wonder about the wisdom of inviting him to lunch in the first place. He continued, "It's Ralphie, University of Colorado's mascot. Most think it looks like a dude buffalo but it's a chick."

"Fascinating," I said.

"Thought you'd think so. I love learning new stuff," he said, not catching or simply ignoring my sarcasm. "John Quincy Adams said, 'Old minds are like horses; you must exercise them if you wish to keep them in working order.'"

Another of Charles's quirks was quoting U.S. Presidents, or he claimed they're actual quotes. Of all my priorities, verifying the source would be at the bottom of my list next to doing the backstroke in boiling motor oil.

"Good to see you, Charles," I said, trying to interject civility into the conversation.

"Guess where I was this morning?" he asked as he threw his Tilley hat on the bench seat beside him and carefully placed his cane on the concrete floor.

"Lisbon, North Dakota."

Charles tilted his head and gave a slight nod. "Close. Went to check out Charles Towne Landing. Neat place."

I didn't want to tell him that even though I'd lived here for years I'd never been to the historic landing.

"Did Heather go with you?"

"She had to work, but that's okay. She's not much into history stuff. She says all of it's old. Can you believe that?"

I could, since I wasn't into it either, but again, I didn't want to remind him. A waiter appeared before I had time to respond. We each ordered grilled tuna sandwiches, Charles ordered a Budweiser and I chose the house chardonnay.

Charles watched the waiter leave and pointed his index finger at me. "So, why the lunch invite?"

I smiled. "Maybe I've missed you the last few days."

Charles shook his head. "Of course, you have, but that's not why we're here."

"You're right."

"Of course," he interrupted.

"I talked to Cindy this morning and wanted to let you know what she'd found about the death."

"What's stopping you?"

Nothing, so I shared the information. My sharing was only interrupted about seventeen times. Charles had to know every detail, most I didn't know, but that didn't stop him from asking.

After I'd finally finished, and the waiter had delivered our lunch, Charles took a bite and mumbled through a mouthful of food, "What do you think?"

"Everything points to an accidental overdose. She was drunk and didn't know she was shooting too much heroin. She had a long history of drug abuse, and other than the passenger door handle being clean, nothing points to anything other than an overdose."

Charles watched two SUVs slowly roll past us on Center

Street, gazed at the three other tables of diners on the patio, and turned to me.

"No offense, but that's a crock of bull hockey."

Charles may lack many things but opinions were not among them. "Why?"

"Didn't you hear Cindy? She said poor Ms. Craft's death was murder."

"Charles, I must have missed that. Refresh my memory, what exactly did she say that meant murder?"

"I have to explain everything, don't I?"

I shrugged.

"First, she said Lauren had kicked the drug habit, so an overdose of something she wasn't doing would be impossible. Then she said someone wiped fingerprints off the passenger door and was trying not to leave any evidence of being there. And, the most important thing was when she said she was praying. Don't you see, she's praying for us to get involved and help her solve the terrible murder." He slammed his hand on the table. "So there."

That may have been how Charles loosely translated what I said, but I'd learned over the years, his reality often doesn't mesh with the real world. I also learned that arguing with him was as big a waste of time as trying to teach a turtle to type.

"I don't think that's exactly how she meant what she said."

He grinned and shook his head. "Chris, oh Chris, when am I going to teach you how to read between the lines. Of course, that's what she meant. And the cherry on top of the hot-fudge sundae was when she said it was still an open case and Detective Adair was working it. They don't have detectives working things that aren't crimes. I rest my case."

"It's something to think about," I said as insincerely as possible and knew it was time to change the subject. "Brian Newman met with me the other day."

I knew Charles wouldn't leave his opinions about the death

on the table, but his insatiable desire to know what was going on would delay more murder talk until he learned what there was to know about my talk with the mayor.

"Without me?" he said, like me meeting with the mayor without my sidekick was one of the most ridiculous things he'd heard.

I nodded.

"Let's hear it."

I shared that Brian was concerned about a heated race for the office and there were big money citizens lining up behind the potential opponent. I was surprised when Charles asked who the opponent was. With his ear to the gossip of the community, it seemed unlikely he wouldn't have already known.

"Joel Hurt. You know him?"

"You're kidding. Joel, the landscape, garden center guy?"

Charles was already shaking his head when I said yes.

"Crap," Charles said.

"I know. I hate anyone running against Brian."

Charles shook his head faster and said, "That's not what the crap was about."

I shrugged.

"Guess who Joel Hurt was dating?"

From the look on Charles's face, it wasn't much of a leap when I said, "Lauren Craft."

"Yep."

"How do you know?"

"Heather heard about Lauren's death when she was giving a massage to Mrs. Teeter. Heather said that Old-Bitty Teeter— Heather's not one of her fans—rambled on about how sad it was about Lauren being a druggie and how rough her death must be on her wonderful, handsome, charming boyfriend, Joel Hurt."

"Did Old Bitt … Mrs. Teeter say how she knew Lauren?"

"Teeter cleans beach houses for some of the frou-frou folks with more money than interest in cleaning their big houses.

Heather says she's the snootiest cleaning lady she's ever known. Anyway, Teeter heard Lauren was friends with some of the kids of the frou-frous and their parents were always talking about how the younger generation was going to hell in a helium balloon— drugs, drink, and sniffing around things where they shouldn't be."

I nodded. "Heather got all that from one massage?"

Charles smiled. "She's learning information gathering techniques from me. A quick study, I must say."

"How to be nosy?"

"Some less-enlightened folks might say that."

"Did Heather know Lauren?"

"Said she never met her."

"Do you know Joel?" I asked.

"Said hey a few times but never got beyond that. He seems a little standoffish. I see his trucks around town and stopped at his garden center a couple of weeks ago."

Charles lived in a small apartment with no landscaping, and I don't recall him ever mentioning growing anything other than a scruffy beard. "Why?"

"Was driving by and saw a big orange sign out front saying SALE. Thought he might have some cheap books on gardening. There's a big dead patch in my book collection in the gardening area."

I smiled at the thought of Charles buying anything related to gardening. "Have any?"

"Not a one, well they had some, but they weren't on sale and the ones they had cost as much as my cell phone monthly payment; you know, the cell phone you made me buy and's breaking me with the bill."

I suspect Charles could roll out a president's quote saying something like *history is determined by who is telling it*, but since I couldn't care less about what old, probably dead, presidents had said, I would remind him I had never insisted he enter the current century and buy a cell phone. He and Heather had decided they would need one when they moved to Nashville. I ignored his comment.

"Was Joel in the store?"

"Didn't see him. So, what does Brian want us to do?"

I didn't recall Brian saying anything about *us* but told Charles that the mayor had asked if I could hold two fundraisers. Charles asked the same question I had posed to Brian about who I knew who had any money and I gave him the same answer Brian had given me.

"Well, what're we waiting for? Let's get raisin' dough to keep Brian governin'."

I wanted to ask Charles if we should start raising money before or after he caught the person who had murdered a person no one thought had even been murdered. Before I could, Charles's phone began an instrumental version of "Crazy," Heather's favorite song.

"Yes, sweetie pie," he answered and after listening for a few seconds, said, "Of course I'm on my way. Just around the corner."

He hit the end call icon, took a deep breath, and looked around the patio for the waitress.

"You gotta go?"

He rolled his eyes. "How could I have forgotten about the big toilet paper sale at Walmart?"

"The one you promised to take Heather to?"

He shook his head, grabbed his Tilley and cane. I said I'd get the check, something I would have had to do anyway. He thanked me and rushed out. I was thankful Charles had found someone he could rush to a toilet paper sale with and that he had finally bought a car, so I wouldn't have to take him.

10

I didn't have a sale to get to, toilet paper or otherwise, so when the waiter returned to clear the table, I ordered another glass of chardonnay and leaned back in the booth and thought about Charles's opinion that Lauren had been murdered, all from what I'd said about Cindy's comments that he—we—were supposed to help the police catch an alleged killer. I pondered how big a coincidence it was that Brian's opponent had been dating Lauren. My phone rang before I was able to make sense of any of it. A glance at the screen indicated that it was Bob Howard.

"Hello, Mr. Howard."

"Humph, don't be all cheery with me, caught the killer yet?"

"Bob, no one said anyone was—"

"Never mind," he interrupted. "That's not why I'm calling. Are you going to buy me supper?"

It would have been useless to ask why, besides, whether he would admit it or not, Bob wouldn't have called unless it was for something important.

"When and where?"

"Six o'clock, Rita's."

"See you there."

He had already hung up.

Three hours later, I was sitting at a table on Rita's patio. It was hot and muggy, but I would rather be outside enjoying the late summer breeze blowing off the ocean than inside. Rita's sat on a prime piece of property and since I'd lived here, had been three different restaurants, and was previously the site of a bowling alley. It was at the corner of Center Street and Arctic Avenue, catty-corner from Tides, the nine-story oceanfront hotel; directly across Arctic from the iconic Folly Pier; while directly across Center Street from the Sand Dollar, a popular members-only bar.

Bob didn't share Charles's penchant for promptness, for that matter, he didn't have any of Charles's proclivities, so he saw nothing wrong when he barreled onto the patio fifteen minutes late. My realtor friend was as oversized as his profane vocabulary. He stood six-foot tall but carried the weight of a seven-footer. He wore a four-day old beard, a flowery Hawaiian shirt covering his ample stomach, and bright green shorts that looked as stylish on him as a lampshade on a pig. He turned sideways to get past two tables on the way to me, bumped the chair of a man sitting at one of the tables, and mumbled something to the man that, depending on Bob's mood, could have either been, "Sorry, my fault" or "Get the hell out of my way." I lowered my head as if not to notice the interaction.

"Well, well," Bob said as he reached the table. "See nobody's killed you yet."

I didn't think I needed to confirm his observation, so I pointed to the empty chair on the other side of the table.

He plopped down, pointed to my glass of wine, and said, "Where's my beer?"

I held up my wine and said, "If I'd ordered your beer when you said you'd be here, it'd be hot by now."

"I suppose that's your damned subtle way of saying I'm late."

I smiled. "If the shoe fits."

"Crap, Chris, if I'd wanted a lecture on being tardy, I would've brought Betty."

Betty was Bob's wife of nearly forty years, and in my opinion, should be a candidate for sainthood for putting up with Bob

"What brings you to my island?" I asked.

"Maybe I wanted to have supper with my good friend."

I stared at him.

"Okay, that and I'm meeting a couple to show an overpriced house on the ocean that's about the size of the Pentagon. There'd only be two of them living in it so they need that big of a house as much as I need shingles."

"Don't suppose you'll share your astute observation when you show it to them."

"Hell no. It'll be the perfect damned casa for them. There'll be room for each to have their private space, and with seven bedrooms, and enough bathrooms for a senior citizens' center, the resale value will be off the charts. The perfect house." He paused and bellowed at a waiter who was at a nearby table, "Beer!"

The waiter, who wasn't assigned to our table, smiled his best faux smile, and scurried away.

Bob wiped perspiration off his forehead. "So, enough about me—for now. Who killed your neighbors' kid?"

"You know everything I know about what happened."

"I bet your street-person buddy thinks it's murder," Bob said as our waitress set a bottle of Coors in front of him.

"Yes, Charles does," I said, while Bob attacked his beer. "The cops are still looking at it, but they're not sure if it was anything other than an accidental overdose. I don't know more than that."

Bob's beer bottle was half empty when he said, "But I damned well bet you will find out more."

The waitress returned before I could deny it. Bob fanned his face with the menu and said, "Don't confuse me with your overpriced specials, get me the biggest damned steak you have back there." He pointed the menu at the kitchen.

I pictured a big hit to my checkbook and ordered a burger and fries. Bob told her to add two orders of fries with his steak.

"Takes a lot of fuel to keep this fine-tuned machine running at its peak. Especially to con—umm sell—tonight's overpriced mansion to the sweet young, more money than sense, couple." He fanned his face again. "Speaking of fine-tuned machine, there's another reason I wanted to talk to you."

I motioned for him to continue.

"It's about Al."

Al Washington owned a small, tired, bar in Charleston. Bob and Al were as different as black and white, a fitting analogy since Al was African American and Bob was as white as snow, but not anywhere near as pure. Regardless of their cultural and upbringing differences, the two bonded years ago and had been friends forever. Bob once confided he considered Al a true hero, both of the Korean conflict where he had saved seven soldiers from certain death and because Al and his now deceased wife adopted nine children, giving them love, and a solid upbringing.

"What about him?"

"He's been having health problems."

Al was eighty and spent most every day, and late until the evening, at his bar. Except for a part-time cook, it was a one-man show. I wasn't surprised.

"What's wrong?"

"You know he's had damned heart problems for years and his arthritis in his knees has him moving about the speed of a slug on Ambien."

I was aware and nodded.

"The last time I was in there, I was surprised to see Tanesa talking to him. Think it was the first time I'd seen her in her dad's bar. I asked her what a lovely ER doc was doing in a dump like Al's. I think she's got a crush on me, all my charm, good looks, and wit. Think she sees our forty-year age difference as sexy."

I rolled my eyes. Bob stepped out of his fantasy world, and continued, "Anyway, she walked me to my table while her dad went back to the grill to get a burger for someone. She said she was worried about him. Said because of his heart condition, the countless hours he's in the bar, and his age, that he's the perfect candidate for either another heart attack or blood clots that could scamper from his legs, up his veins, to his heart or lungs, or something like that. She said all of it in doc-speak, too complex for this old dullard to understand. The part I did catch was when she interjected dead into the description."

Bob was anything but a dullard. After knowing him for nearly four years, I had learned he held an economics degree from Duke University, in addition to being a highly successful realtor. An even bigger surprise after noticing his outward appearance and listening to him, he had a heart that was bigger than many ministers and would do anything to help people in need.

"Sorry to hear that," I said.

"You're not kidding," Bob said and shook his head. "If he's dead, where will I get the best cheeseburgers in the world?"

I slowly shook my head. "That's touching Bob, so caring."

"You know I'm kidding. I'd do anything for Al."

I did know and told him so.

"That brings me to what I wanted to talk to you about. Al won't admit he has a problem. He needs to hire help but can't afford it. He's still paying on some student loans a couple of the kids have. He's getting later and later paying his damned rent. So, guess what?"

I told him I had no idea what.

"Your highly-successful realtor buddy is riding to Al's rescue on his white elephant, or whatever animal is large enough to carry this fine-tuned body. I'm buying the bar."

I'm glad I didn't try to guess. "You're what?"

"Crap, have you turned deaf in your senior, senile years. I said I'm buying Al's."

I started to laugh, but saw that Bob was serious. "Really?"

Our supper arrived, and Bob grabbed a steak knife and sliced into the beef. I slowly took a bite of burger and pondered what he had said.

Bob took a bite and looked around the restaurant, before turning his attention to me. "Chris, I'm seventy-six years old. I owned my own commercial real estate firm for a quarter of a century and have had Island Realty fifteen years. Real estate has been good to me, but I'm getting damned burned out with it. I think I used up my quota of customer smiles a while back, and if you ever repeat this, I'll deny it and break your big toe, but I feel bad about convincing folks to buy houses they can barely afford. They seem to think they need to buy the most house that some greedy bank will finance. They never think life changes and expenses go up, but their incomes usually don't go up as much. That's not necessarily a bad thing for realtors." Bob smiled. "Hell, we get to sell the house again." His smile faded. "But that's not right." He took another bite.

"You're retiring?"

"Isn't that what I said?"

Not exactly, I thought. "I understand about you retiring, but buying Al's?"

"Betty said I could do whatever I wanted to do, but she doesn't want me around the house. Something about me being a pain in the ass, and if she had to put up with me more than she already does, she'd either kill me or move to Switzerland."

"That I can understand."

"Al needs me."

"No offense, Bob, but what do you know about running a bar and restaurant?"

Bob pointed at his stomach. "Do I look like I should be

running a fitness center? I'm the perfect shape for a bar and burger joint owner. Besides, all I need to do is hire a cheap cook and use my charm to bring in the customers."

And I thought Charles's logic lacked something. Now a more delicate topic. Bob had never been known for his political correctness, and with roughly ninety-nine percent of Al's customers being African American, I could see problems abound.

"Do you see a problem with you buying a bar serving mostly black customers?"

Bob sighed and shook his head. "Shit, Chris, I've seen some of the same customers in Al's for years. Some even talk to me; okay, they mostly mumble about me, but they know I don't like blacks. They also know I don't like whites, browns, reds, and even those starchy white-faced Scandinavians. I'm an equal opportunity disliker. Hell, I can count on one big toe the people I like." He grinned. "His customers will love me."

"What's Al think about it?"

"Are you going to let me finish my food or keep asking stupid questions?"

"I've never known you not to finish your food, and everyone else's around you, besides you brought it up."

"Al tried to protest, but it was feebler than his feeble body. He started with *no way*, but that became, *are you sure*, and ended with *thank you*. He's deeper in debt than he'd let on." Bob looked down at the table and in a deep voice—low for Bob— said, "He started crying and put his thin arms around me. Chris, I love that man."

I suspected Bob would regret showing me his kinder, gentler side, so I didn't say anything except, "That's great. I know you mean a lot to him, and he has to be relieved."

"Yeah, well shit, now you know it. So, what's going on in your life?"

"Hold on, you can't leave it there. When are you taking

over?" What I meant to say was who would give him a crash course in restaurant/bar management and where would he get a suit of armor big enough to protect him from being attacked by customers he would insult, irritate, and drive to violence.

Bob said, "Sort of already have."

"Sort of?"

"Do I have to spell out every damn thing to you?"

"Yep."

"And everybody says you're so smart. Okay, listen well, I asked Al to give me a list of his debts, the longest past due first. He did, and I wrote him a check to cover everything. Chris, please keep this confidential, but he had some bills that were a year old. The landlord had already begun eviction procedures." Bob shook his head. "It's no wonder why the poor man is in such bad health. Anyway, I have my lawyer working on all the damned paperwork to make the purchase official. When he finishes milking me for as many billable hours as he can, I'll write Al another big ole check and voila, the business will be legally mine, lock, stock, and all those damned worthless tables, chairs, and a stinking grease-filled kitchen that must've served soldiers in the Revolutionary War."

The only reason Bob was buying the business was to save Al, an extraordinarily generous gesture, but one Bob would never admit to.

"What's Al going to do?"

"First, the broken-down, ancient, geezer's going to the hospital and get a bunch of God-awful expensive tests run to see if he's about ready to croak. If he makes it though that poking and prodding, he said he'd stop by the bar each day and check on how I'm doing. He didn't say it, but that means making sure none of his regulars have threatened me with bodily harm. He said he could sit by the door and do the Walmart greeter thing."

It was a clever idea and I told Bob so.

"Guess I can waste a chair for him to plop his bony ass down on."

That was Bob-speak for *I'd love to have him around. He's a great guy, and I'll need all the help I can get.*

"Good idea," I said.

"That's enough damn talk about that old man and his—umm, my—bar. What's going on with you?"

That was probably the first time he'd ever asked about me, so I knew he was embarrassed about what he had shared about Al and the bar.

"Glad you asked," I said as he stuffed a large bite of steak in his mouth and waved for the waitress to get another bottle of beer. "The election for Folly's mayor is in April."

"That's a half year away, and why the flying flip would I care?"

Bob was back to normal. I proceeded to tell him about Brian's opponent and why Brian needed to raise more money than usual to have a chance at winning.

"So, back to my flying-flip question. Why would I care?"

Bob liked Brian and in the last election had supported him with the maximum individual donation allowed. "Because Brian would like you to host a fundraiser?"

I gripped the side of the table and readied myself for a flurry of expletives.

Bob took a sip of his new beer, stared at me, and nodded, "Okay. Where and when?"

I pictured a gaggle of aliens taking over Bob's body and sucking out all his hate brain cells. I was shocked, but slowly regained my composure as he took another bite.

"Your house and as soon as possible."

"Okay," he repeated.

We discussed some details and he started naming realtor friends he could invite and some of his best customers over the years and joked he could have his new gourmet restaurant cater the event. I assumed he was joking. He said, "Anything else? I've got to meet the rich suckers."

"One more thing," I said. "I don't think it's related to the mayoral race, but I heard Joel Hurt had been dating Lauren Craft."

Bob raised his eyebrow. "The dirt-digging, landscape guy turned mayoral candidate, and your best-bud, Brad Burton's dead daughter. And you, the person who doesn't believe in coincidences, don't think that's related?"

"I don't see how."

"Hmm."

Bob pushed away from the table and on his way to the door told the waitress I was getting his check and to be sure and add a humongous tip.

That was more like the Bob I knew, I thought, and looked out the window. Could Bob be right in thinking Lauren's death may have something to do with Joel?

11

I stopped at Burt's on the way home to grab something for breakfast. It was one of the store's prime beer-buying hours and
several customers were milling around. Three men I had seen in
the store many times were in deep conversation in front of the
beer cooler. An elderly woman I only knew as Mary was at the
counter holding the collar of her large collie and talking to Eric. I
smiled when the dog jumped and placed its front paws on the
counter hoping Eric would give it a treat.

I weaved my way to the side of the store, grabbed a
cinnamon Danish and turned to head to the cash register when I
nearly ran into Brad Burton. I barely recognized him. I thought
he'd looked bad when Charles and I visited his house to offer my
condolences, but compared to now, he'd looked like a television
star that day. His brown eyes were sunken, and he had on the
same wrinkled white dress shirt he'd worn during our visit but
with added food stains on the front. He was carrying a loaf of
bread and his hand trembled and I was concerned he would drop
the bread.

"Landrum," he said and gave a slight nod.

"Burton," I responded and gave a weak smile.

"I see you're shopping," he said and nodded toward the Danish.

I started to make one of my patented smart-aleck comments like, "I see why you were a detective," but first, I had learned years ago he didn't appear to have a sense of humor, and second, I was feeling something I had never thought possible: sympathy. I limited my response to, "Breakfast."

Our awkward conversation was interrupted by Chester Carr who patted Brad on the back and said, "Brad, I was sorry to hear about your loss."

I had known Chester for several years and got to know him much better a couple of years ago when he had dated Charles's aunt who had spent her last few months on Folly before succumbing to cancer.

Brad turned to the newcomer and thanked him for his concern. I took the opportunity to move away from Brad. Chester stopped me. "Hey Chris, see you and Brad here are becoming friends. Glad to see it, you being neighbors and all."

"Good to see you, Chester. I was sharing my condolences with Brad. How are you?"

Chester smiled, said, "Good," and looked at the carton of milk he was holding. "Better be going. Need to get this home." He glanced back at Brad, said he was again sorry for his loss, and headed to the cash register, leaving Brad and me staring at each other in awkward silence.

I was saved by Eric who apparently had to go to the shelf behind us to find something for a customer. He handed the small jar of pickles to the appreciative woman and turned to Brad and me.

"How are my favorite detectives?"

Clearly, Eric hadn't heard as much about Burton and my ongoing disagreements as had Chester.

I was surprised when Brad chuckled rather than going into a

rant about how terrible I was. He patted Eric's shoulder and said, "You've got that wrong. I'm a has-been detective." He tilted his head toward me. "And he never was one."

Eric stroked his long beard. I smiled and said, "Brad's right about me, but he may be retired but was a top-notch detective for years."

Brad gave me a sideways glance, probably because he knew I was lying about what I thought of his skills. I would have looked at me that way too and was surprised I had said it.

"Anyway," Eric said, "it's nice to see you neighbors gabbing, and Brad, I'm terribly sorry about Lauren. She seemed to be a nice gal."

Brad nodded and Eric said he had to run. "Got to help keep our fine citizens lubricated."

Brad remained at my side and twisted the tie on the bread wrapper.

What do I say now? No words were necessary. Brad looked at the concrete floor and muttered, "I did appreciate you and your friend stopping by the house. I know I treated you badly when you were there. I'm sorry."

"I understand. It must have been terrible on you and Hazel. If there is anything I can do, please don't hesitate to ask."

He looked at me. "That's kind. You have no idea how horrible this has been on Hazel."

I didn't know about him, but it felt strange for the two of us to be carrying on a civil conversation in the middle of the busy store after years of such an acrimonious relationship. It seemed like he wanted to talk, so I said, "You walking home?"

He looked toward the register and said he was. I followed him to pay and walked beside him as he went out into the humid night air.

"We moved here to be closer to Lauren and somehow try to help her," Brad said as we reached my yard.

Hazel had told me that, but since she'd requested I not let

Brad know she had talked to me, I didn't let on I'd already heard it.

"I'm sorry you weren't able to help." I pointed to my front step. "Want to sit?"

He glanced next door to his house and at my step. "Okay."

We sat on the concrete step and shared another awkward silence.

Brad took a deep breath and said, "I was never there for her when she was a kid. Don't try to deny it because I know you think I was a horrible detective." He paused, and I quickly decided silence was my best response. "When Lauren was little, I was a great cop. Before I got promoted to detective, I ran rings around the other beat cops. I wasn't the smartest guy on the force, but I wanted to make a difference and the only way I knew how was to put in as many hours as possible." He hesitated and smiled. "Some of the guys swore I was bucking to be police chief. I wasn't, but I did want to be the best I could be. What I became was the worst dad in the world. I can count on one hand the total number of concerts, plays, games, activities, and whatever my little girl participated in that I attended. And Chris, she was in everything. She played the violin in the school orchestra, acted in every play, was cheerleader for both football and basketball, and still found time to get straight A's in class. Her mom was there for everything; I let the damned job dominate my life."

I knew that wasn't unusual at the time when Brad was raising a family, but I also didn't think Brad needed me to tell him so.

"I'm sure she knew you loved her."

He looked over at me. "I'm not."

I waited for him to continue.

Brad stared as two trucks sped past the house, and he said to me, "During her junior year of high school, she got mixed up with the wrong crowd. Alcohol and pot. I didn't learn about it until months later. Me, the big-time cop who was always out catching criminals, and helping others, couldn't even see that my own kid…. If I had spent more time looking out for my little girl instead of being gone and worrying about everyone else, things … things could have been different. Chris, she would still be with us."

"Brad, you don't know that. Over the years, I've known several parents who were perfect with their kids, did everything with them, doted over them, and did whatever possible to keep them away from bad influences. Despite those efforts, some of their kids ended up being the kind of people you spent years catching."

"I know that, but I still failed her. You know what's so strange? The last year I thought she'd turned her life around." He glanced at his house again. "We had her over to eat several times. She seemed fine. She had a job. She was dating a successful, well-liked guy. Sure, she still had bouts of depression, but nothing like how it had been when she was a regular at rehab." I followed Brad's gaze as he looked down at his hand. It was shaking, and he grabbed his knee to stop the shake. "I know the ME is still futzing around with the cause of death, but I know it was an overdose. It had to be."

"Brad, you said she still had bouts of depression. Is it possible she had, umm, intentionally overdosed?"

He let go of his knee and his hand balled into a fist. "Suicide?"

I nodded.

He unclasped his fist and sighed. "If I saw it once, I saw it a thousand times. When I was a cop, some guy would be found in his room hanging from the ceiling, or someone in a bathtub with her wrists slit. Obvious suicides, but the family swore it couldn't be. They'd say maybe it was an accident, or someone murdered the poor soul to make it look like suicide. Basically, the relatives couldn't handle the guilt associated with their loved ones killing themselves. I've thought about it every waking moment since it happened, could I be doing the same thing and wanting it to be accidental for the same reason." He paused and shook his head. "Chris, it was a damned, horrible accident. She'd been off heroin for a while and somehow overdosed when she got back into it. It was; it had to be."

Perhaps it was, but I couldn't shake how strange it was that there were no prints on the passenger side door. I was feeling uncomfortable with Brad's deteriorating mood and wanted to change the subject.

"Brad, you mentioned she had been dating someone. Was it Joel Hurt?"

His head jerked toward me. "How'd you know?"

"I heard it somewhere around town. Have you talked with him since, umm, her passing?"

"He stopped by the house to bring us food and a plant. I don't know him well, but from what Lauren says, said, he was a nice guy and seemed good for her. Hazel likes him. Why?"

"Nothing. I heard he was going to run for mayor."

Brad seemed surprised. "Against Brian Newman?"

"Yes."

"That's news to me. Brian's a good mayor. For someone who had been a cop most of his life, he's maybe a tad too soft against vagrants and some of the other bums who hang around Folly. Brian's popular so I don't see how anyone could beat him." Brad looked at his watch. "Better get home. Hazel will start worrying. She knows I'm not handling this too good and is afraid of what I might do."

He thanked me for listening, stood, and headed home without turning back.

1 2

Since the first day I'd met Brad Burton some eight years ago on that hot, sandy path to the beach overlooking the Morris Island Lighthouse, he'd been a pain in my side, and I suppose, I to his. I still think he'd only been going through the motions his later years as a detective, but I suppose he was honest about how he'd done his job at first. When he had moved next door, I doubted we'd ever have a pleasant conversation, and for his first year there, my doubts had been confirmed. Now I didn't know what to think. Sure, I knew he was torn up about the death of their only child, and could understand how that might alter his behavior; but I couldn't get over how much he felt comfortable confiding during our strange conversation on the porch.

I awakened the next morning thinking about it; not only thinking about how funny it felt to have had a real, and emotional, conversation with Brad, but how I couldn't shake my uneasiness about the missing prints on the car door. I had reached for my phone to call Chief LaMond to see if there was anything new with the case when the phone rang.

341

"Chris," came a vaguely familiar voice through the speaker, "this is Wayne Swan."

Wayne was a successful contractor specializing in home remodels. It's rare to drive more than a few blocks on Folly without seeing one of his job signs. He had a reputation for quality work, on time, and at reasonable prices—all rare qualities in today's construction industry.

I had known him five years, since he was one of my regular —unfortunately, one of only a few regular—customers when I had owned my photo gallery. I couldn't keep the shop open with only a few, a very few, regular customers, and truth be told, not that many irregular ones as well, and was forced to close it a year ago. In addition to buying prints, he had an interest in photography and would stop in to talk cameras. I enjoyed our conversations. He also invited me to a couple preview parties he held upon completion of major projects. He'd paid for the events which were hosted by the happy homeowners who were anxious to show off their remodeled spaces.

"Morning, Wayne. Inviting me to a party—I hope?"

He chuckled. "Not this time. Have you heard Joel Hurt is planning to run for mayor?"

"Think I heard something about it," I said. I avoided telling him I hated the idea.

"Good. He's asked me to be his campaign manager and I've got a favor to ask."

"Congratulations, I suppose."

Wayne's chuckle turned into a laugh. "Condolences would be more appropriate. Kidding aside, I'd like you to meet with Joel."

"Wayne, if you don't already know, I'm a good friend of Brian Newman and will be supporting him in the election. Why would Joel want to meet with me?"

"Yes, I know about your connections with the mayor, but Joel said he didn't know you other than in passing, and since you're a well-respected member of the community, he wanted to at least share his vision with you." He laughed, again. "We're not asking you to wear a *Hurt for Mayor* button or stick a sign in your yard, just to give my candidate a chance to share his ideas. How about it?"

I was still absorbing that someone thought I was a *well-respected member of the community*. "Let me think about it and get back with you."

Wayne hesitated, and said, "I go way back with him, Chris. I think you'll like Joel. He's a great guy with some progressive ideas for *your* island."

"Got a question, Wayne. Do campaign managers ever say anything negative about their candidates?"

"Hmm, give me a sec." Another chuckle. "Got it, Joel chews his fingernails."

"I won't tell anyone."

"Good. And get back to me soon. Joel wants to talk to as many community leaders as he can before officially announcing."

I said I would, hung up, and thought *community leaders!*

WHAT WAS Joel's real reason for wanting to meet with me? I had been on Folly for several years and had been thrust into notoriety because of a few horrific events, but I didn't for a second believe the *community leader* and *well-respected member of the community* baloney. And if he thought he could win me over, there wasn't a chance in Vegas for me making a significant donation to his campaign. And, if I did meet with him, would it look like I was being disloyal to Brian?

Instead of spending time pondering these unanswerable questions, I called Charles.

"Caught the killer yet?" Charles said, instead of a common courtesy.

I told him there wasn't a killer so I couldn't have caught him.

"If you say so. Anyway, guess where I am?"

"Getting a facial."

"Yuck. Try again, never mind, I'm at Office Depot looking at computers."

Charles had never owned a computer, not surprising knowing that he didn't have a cell phone or an answering machine until a few months ago. When I had the gallery, he considered the computer there as his.

"Why?"

"The times they are a changin'. I might need to look something up, and besides, Heather says she can use it to watch videos of her favorite singers. Think about it. If she's using my computer, she'll need to be at my apartment. If she's at my apartment we can—"

"Got it," I interrupted. "Want to know why I called?"

"Thought you wanted to know where I was, what I was doing, and what Heather and I would be doing while she was at my apartment."

"That too, but figured you'd be interested in knowing who I got off the phone with." I told him about my conversation with Wayne. Charles was being unusually attentive, and not interrupting, until I told him what Wayne had said about me being a community leader.

Charles laughed so loud that I held the phone away from my ear. "He said you were what?"

I repeated it, and Charles said he'd heard me the first time, but couldn't imagine anyone uttering those words when referring to me. I assured him Wayne had.

"A politician couldn't find the truth if it squawked in his ear and bit him on the nose."

"Did a president say that?"

"Why?"

"No reason other than you're always quoting presidents."

"Nope, this time it'd be little ole me being profound. So, when are you going to meet him?"

"Don't know that I am. I think it'd look bad since I'm supporting Brian."

"Wrong," said Charles. "Of course, you are. You have to."

"Why?"

"Data gathering, spying, reconnoitering, surveilling; come on Chris, get with the program. Look how helpful this will be to Brian. Oh yeah, make him buy you a meal, order two desserts, and bring me one."

I wouldn't have gone as far with the purposes, but I saw how it may be helpful in knowing what Joel disliked about the job Brian was doing. And, in the back of my mind, I was thinking about Lauren. Perhaps Joel could share insight into her mental state.

"You win, I'll meet with him."

Charles made a clicking sound with his mouth. "Wise man. Keep listening to me and there's hope, albeit slight, that you could grow into a community leader."

I called Wayne Swan and told him I was willing to meet with Joel. Thirty minutes later, Wayne called and said Joel was available and wanted to know if I could I meet him tomorrow evening at BLU, the upscale restaurant in the Tides Hotel. I told him I thought I could fit it in my busy schedule and we agreed on a time. I spent the next day running some routine errands and continued to wonder what Joel really wanted.

13

Wayne was waiting for me as I walked through the automatic doors at the Tides ten minutes before I was to meet with Joel. He looked the part of a professional campaign manager with his navy blazer, blue button-down shirt, and gray slacks. I looked the part of a retired executive with my faded red golf shirt and wrinkled khakis. He and I were about the same height but unlike my blond and graying hair, he had dark hair with a bald spot on the back of his head. My bald spot had spread over most of my scalp. Wayne was also two decades younger than me.

Wayne reached out and grabbed my hand like he was on a mission, which, of course, he was. "Chris, glad you could make it. Joel is eager to meet you. He's already got a table. Hope you don't mind eating inside; it's too steamy for Joel on the deck. He has to work in this heat and humidity every day at the nursery, so he likes to get inside whenever possible."

I said it was fine and followed him to BLU's nautically-themed indoor dining room. I was surprised to see Joel seated at a small table beside the window looking out on the outdoor bar and the Folly Pier.

"Aren't you joining us?" I asked Wayne as we approached the table set for two.

"Afraid not, got another appointment. I wanted to be sure the two of you got together and then head out."

Joel saw us and stood. He was roughly three inches taller than Wayne, slimmer, and his sun-bleached, blond hair contrasted with his campaign manager's. Other than those differences, Joel was dressed exactly like Wayne, with his blue blazer, light blue shirt, and gray slacks. He greeted me with a quick smile and a strong, confident handshake.

"Thanks for agreeing to meet with me, Mr. Landrum. I know you must be busy."

The handful of times I had talked with him previously, he'd called me Chris. He was now in political mode. I told him it was my pleasure.

Wayne put his arm around my shoulder and said, "I'll leave you two to talk. Again, thanks for agreeing to this meeting, Chris."

Wayne turned to the exit and Joel motioned for me to be seated opposite him. A waiter was at the table before I could place the black napkin in my lap and asked if I wanted anything to drink. There was a half-empty white wine glass in front of Joel and I said I would have the same.

"I'm terribly sorry that your gallery closed. I should have been in more often, but you know how work sometimes gets in the way of what you would like to do. Wayne told me wonderful things about your talent. I know he's purchased several photos."

Since Joel had never been in the gallery, I thought *should have been in more often* was over the top, but I appreciated his kind words.

"Yes, Wayne was a regular. I know his wife wanted to paint some of the photos and he enjoyed talking photography."

"Again, I am sorry you were forced to close. That's one of the key issues that precipitated my desire to run for mayor. Small businesses have a challenging time staying viable on Folly. The island is inundated much of the year with hordes of what I call non-spenders—college students, adults with little disposable income, others who can only afford enough beer to get them through the day, and even then buy the drinks before arriving here. A business like yours was a perfect example. Forced out because of that kind of people. It galls me."

My wine arrived, and my only thought was that the "successful," local resident sitting across from me had never stepped in my gallery, yet he was blaming outsiders for its demise.

"I apologize for hopping on a soapbox," Joel said and leaned back in the chair. "I'm passionate about the topic, and I sometimes get carried away."

I took a sip of wine, and lied when I said, "That's okay. Is that why you're running?"

He shook his head and frowned. "Over the last few months, I have been approached by numerous residents who have shared their dissatisfaction with the happenings in City Hall. I can't divulge their names at this point, but am certain you would know most of them, either personally or by reputation. They have offered their support, monetary and otherwise, if I would run." He paused and finished his wine and held the glass up for a refill. The waiter was quick to the table and said he would take care of it. Joel turned back to me. "I considered their requests with mixed feelings. I do agree with their position, but I believe Mayor Newman has been an exceptional leader. He brought a wealth of experience to the job. He has a good handle on the city departments. He's considered to be fair to his employees and presents a professional appearance to his constituents. Honestly, I like the man."

"But?" I said.

"Shall we order supper first? It's on me, of course."

The waiter returned with Joel's wine and waited for us to order. Joel either had studied the menu before I had arrived or was a regular. I had neither advantage and perused the menu while he ordered a tomato and crab salad and I decided on a Caesar salad. Joel told the waiter we would decide on our entrees after the salads arrived.

"But?" I repeated after the waiter headed to the kitchen.

Joel smiled. "Mayor Newman has given most of his life to public service. He was serving our country before I was born, and I admire and praise him for that. He's a true patriot. And, he has spent more than twenty years serving our community as either director of public safety or mayor." Joel's smile faded. "But sadly, his ideas for governing and his views about the future of Folly are stale and outdated, or so I believe as those who have asked me to run also believe."

I wanted to challenge him but knew this wasn't the time.

"Chris, I know I'll be a dark horse candidate. I know I'll be going up against lethargy on the part of many voters, the vast experience of Mayor Newman, and the current establishment, but I feel I must, as do those who support me. There are also council members we feel should be replaced."

Our salads arrived, and Joel quickly told the waiter he wanted the crispy snapper and I settled on the grilled Mahi Mahi. Joel nodded as if he had approved my selection. That was probably the only thing we would agree on tonight.

"What are you proposing? What's your platform? What will you do differently?" I asked.

"First, we must crack down on those who flaunt the law. Drinking on the beach is illegal, yet you can go out there any day and find violators. Public drunkenness is illegal yet walk down Center Street any night of the week and see people under the influence of alcohol or other substances. It should go unsaid, but littering not only is unsightly, but a health hazard, yet, look how many yards of our fine citizens are dotted with trash daily. And we must do whatever we need to keep bums and college students away who have no reason for being on our beach other than to drink and cause trouble."

I could point out that everything he mentioned had been discussed, addressed, over-and-over since I had moved to Folly, and from what I had heard, that had been the case for many years prior to my arrival. I had several conversations with Brian Newman about each of these issues. Yes, they were concerns, but the city didn't have the budget to hire enough law enforcement officials to stop it, and so many of the times the violations were marginal and could go either way. Folly was a beachside community, open and welcoming to everyone, and some inconveniences associated with that were part of what makes the island special.

"What do you propose to do to stop the violations you've mentioned?"

Joel looked out the window at the Folly Pier. "I'm not naïve enough to believe there are simple solutions, but innovative approaches must be tried."

"For example?"

"We must dissuade outsiders from using our beach community as their debauchery location of choice."

His platitudes were beginning to irritate me. "How?"

Instead of becoming angry, he smiled. "It will take time and dialog among many constituent groups. And that leads to one of the reasons I wanted to have this candid talk. I would like your support and for you to become part of one of my small groups of advisors who can work toward solutions."

Our food arrived, and my first bite gave me time to craft my answer. "Joel, I appreciate the supper invitation and the chance to hear your concerns. I suspect you also know Brian Newman and I are friends and I supported him in the last election. I think you have the same concerns that have been addressed numerous times, many of them by Mayor Newman himself. To be honest, I haven't heard anything that would make my support for the mayor waiver."

"Chris, I didn't come into this meeting blind. I am aware of your connections with the mayor and doubted I could persuade you to change horses over one meal, but I also thought it was important you got to hear my ideas first hand. There's an old saying that it's funny how the people who know the least about you, always have the most to say." He took a bite of his fish and laughed. "Maybe if you know me a little better, you won't say too many bad things about me."

I smiled. "I believe you also said there were a couple of council members you felt needed to be replaced. Who are they?"

"Houston Bass and Marc Salmon?"

"Why?"

"Again, it's nothing personal against either man. They have been on the council for years; they've devoted countless hours to the city's business, and quite frankly, I like each of them. But, they appear to be puppets of the mayor rather than effective leaders. To make the kind of changes that I will be promoting, I need support and forward-thinking council members. That would not include Marc and Houston."

I thought of Charles's comment about me needing to spy on the opponent. "Who would run against them?"

"I'd love to say, but I'm sworn to secrecy. But again, you'd know them."

"What do you think your chances are of winning?"

"As I mentioned, I'm the dark horse candidate, as will be the new candidates for council, but I like to look at it like I would crabgrass in my business. It—like the mayor and council—are deeply rooted and difficult to eradicate but can ruin a yard. It will not be easy to overcome the past and the harmful decisions being made, but that's why I am starting my campaign earlier than has been the tradition. Several treatments of herbicides are often needed to kill crabgrass and it will take several months, and way more than several dollars, to unseat the current mayor and the two members of the council." He paused and smiled. "But I believe I can be successful."

Not if I have anything to do with it, I thought, but returned his smile.

He nodded and gave me a serious look. "I've talked a lot, but what I wanted to do was give you a chance to ask questions you may have."

"I have a good idea of what you want to do as mayor," I said, although I didn't. I wanted to get him off the crabgrass analogy. "Tell me a little about who you are. I've seen you around town and your landscape trucks seem to be everywhere, but I don't know much about you."

He chuckled. "Yes, my gasoline bill lets me know how much the trucks are driving around Folly and James Island." He gave me a capsule version of his businesses—nothing I didn't know.

"Are you married?" I asked, already knowing the answer.

He bit his lower lip and gave an almost imperceptible shake of his head. "I've reached my mid-forties without finding the right lady. Came close a time or two. Recently I had been dating a wonderful young lady until … umm, no, to answer your question, I'm single."

I felt Charles channeling through me. "Until what?"

He looked at me and I was afraid he wasn't going to answer, but then he said, "Have you heard about the woman who died of a drug overdose near the county park the other day?"

I said, "Sure."

"Her name was Lauren Craft. She and I had been dating."

I acted surprised. "Oh. I'm sorry."

"She was a wonderful person. I knew she had a history of drug abuse, in fact, she'd had a couple of stays at rehab, but I thought she'd kicked the horrible habit." He paused and shook his head. "I believe drug use and the horrible consequences of it is one of Folly's biggest problems—quite frankly, that's not only on Folly but everywhere in this country, and I want to make it a big part of my campaign. And then something like this happens. I knew Lauren had become distant lately, and had avoided me on several occasions, but it wasn't until a few weeks ago I learned she was using again." He hesitated. "Using heavily."

"Heroin?" I asked.

"Yes. The last time I saw her—I guess a couple of days before her … umm, her death, she confided she was back where she had been a year ago, struggling with staying away from the evil drug. She was avoiding me, and, well, allowing the drug to kill her."

"Sorry," I repeated.

"Two days before she left us, I talked to her into going back in rehab. She said she'd think about it. That was the last time I saw her."

I thought about what Cindy had said about there being only one needle mark on Lauren.

"Joel, you're certain she was using?"

He cocked his head and looked me in the eye. "She said she was. I had no reason not to believe her. Of course, I never actually saw her shooting up, but the last time I saw her she was grabbing her cell phone out of her purse and I saw a couple of needles in there. God, what a tragedy." He turned and stared at the beach.

"Yes, it was," I said, not knowing what else to say.

We finished our entrees and Joel turned back to me. "Chris, I didn't mean to get into any of this about Lauren. I apologize and hope I haven't dissuaded you for considering my candidacy over such a tragic event regarding Lauren."

I told him it hadn't, but I also didn't tell him I wouldn't have considered supporting him regardless what he'd told me. He said he wasn't in the mood for dessert or an after-dinner drink, but I was welcome to have some. I declined, and he asked for the check. I usually was the one who was stuck with paying, and it felt good to see him pulling out a credit card.

He thanked me for taking the time to meet with him and hoped I would consider supporting him. I lied and told him I would consider it.

After he had gone, I headed to BLU's outdoor dining area, leaned on the wooden bar, and stared at the waves rolling in as they were illuminated by the amber colored lights from the Folly Pier. I thought back on tonight's conversation and could see how Joel could be a viable candidate. He was likable, more likable than I had anticipated. He would be well financed. His platform, while short on answers, would resonate with a sizable portion of the voting public. And he was starting his campaign early enough to pull together a significant amount of support. He might be a dark horse candidate, but he had a shot.

14

Heavy thunderstorms cascaded through the area overnight and steam rose from every wet surface as the sun peeked over the horizon. The slight smell of sea air oozed in the house through cracks under the front door. The temperature was supposed to reach triple digits and combined with sky-high humidity, it would be a great day to stay in air-conditioned comfort. Besides, I had nowhere to go or to be. Retirement was a wonderful thing, and my only regret was I couldn't have begun it years earlier when I had energy and a stronger desire to travel and experience more new things and places. So, instead of booking a flight to Tahiti or rushing out and buying a jogging suit so I could start training to run a marathon, I sat at my kitchen table, gripped a mug of steaming-hot coffee, and replayed much of last night's conversation with Joel.

He had been clear and outspoken about wanting change both in the position of mayor and two of the council members. He was clear about what he saw as Folly's problems. Clarity ended when asked what he would do to solve them. And, when I had asked him about himself, he had shared little. In fact, he didn't tell me anything I didn't already know about his businesses. The one thing he had said that threw me was about Lauren. Joel said he knew she had begun using heroin again, that she had told him so. Yet there was only one needle mark on her body when she was found near the park. Why would she have lied to him? Or, why would he have lied to me. If he hadn't told me the truth, could there be other things he might not have been as forthcoming about?

Perhaps the most world-altering invention that had been created in my lifetime was the personal computer, more specifically, the Internet. The extraordinary tool provided everyone a window into worlds, information, and opinions previous generations could have only imagined. I moved to my spare bedroom that served as my office and turned on the computer and Googled Joel Hurt.

A downside of the Internet was it often provided too much information. In fewer than three-seconds, I learned there were more than 25,000 references that mentioned Joel Hurt. Many of them were about a Joel Hurt who was an influential businessman in Atlanta. I used my brilliant power of deduction to eliminate him since he died in the 1920s. After limiting my search to South Carolina, I started finding references to the Joel Hurt I had shared a meal with. He was a more successful businessman than I had been led to believe. There were lists of charities he had donated thousands of dollars to, everything from childhood diabetes to Alzheimer's research. There were a dozen photos of him at various charity events dressed in a tux and smiling at the camera. There were four different young ladies latched onto his arm in the various photos; none of whom were identified as Lauren Craft.

Other than learning he liked to party, dress well, give to charities, and share the special events with various women, I didn't learn anything significant. I was about to turn the computer off when I noticed the cutline on one of the earlier photos that read: *Joel Hurt, and his date Samantha Forest. Mr. Hurt recently moved to South Carolina from Lafayette, Louisiana.* I had assumed Joel was a native South Carolinian. Out of boredom and my continuing lack of desire to go outside, I added Lafayette, Louisiana, to my Google search criteria, and a half-dozen references to Joel Hurt popped up. Two were about a Joel Hurt who had died at age eighty-four after a long bout with cancer, the other four were about a young landscaper who had bought a well-established garden center from the owner who was retiring after fifty years in the business. A head and shoulder photo of the landscaper showed a younger version of the Joel Hurt running for mayor.

I quickly forgot the other articles when I found the last mention of Joel Hurt. It was in an extensive obituary for the daughter of a prominent Lafayette attorney. According to the article, the daughter was a junior at the University of Louisiana at Lafayette and had "succumbed to an accidental overdose." A sentence at the end of the obituary read: *At the time of her tragic death, she was engaged to Mr. Joel Hurt.*

I stared at Joel's name and reread the obituary. The only mention of cause of death was the benign *succumbed to* statement which didn't indicate an overdose of what, most likely the wording dictated by her father, the influential attorney. Joel was mentioned briefly, but that was enough. It didn't take much imagination to see the similarities between the death in Louisiana and that of Lauren. A coincidence, possibly, but to me, a highly suspicious one.

I grabbed the phone and punched in Cindy's number.

"You saved me a call," the chief said before I could say anything. "Just got the ruling on Ms. Craft's death."

"Murder?" I said and crossed my fingers.

"Was that a guess or are you psychic?" Cindy said.

"Guess. Why?"

"Then you're a sucky guesser. The coroner determined it was an accidental overdose of heroin."

"But—"

"Let me finish, sucky guesser. He said there were no signs of a struggle and her blood alcohol level was almost off the charts. She was drunk and misjudged the dose. Tragic, but accidental. Now you can add *but*."

I sighed. "But what about the lack of prints on the passenger door handle? And, wait until I tell you what I found this morning."

"Hang on. I'm from the hills so you know I can't multitask. Let me answer your question first."

Despite Cindy's self-deprecating comments about where she was from, she was one of the brightest people I knew. "Yes, Chief, answer away."

"Detective Adair speculates one of the EMTs grabbed the handle and since he wore gloves, it wiped off any prints that may have been there. And before you ask, yes, the detective did talk with the EMTs and one of them said he did open that door to get a better angle on Ms. Craft, and that he could have rubbed the door handle. It could have also happened if someone saw the car, grabbed the handle to bend down and look inside, saw the late Miss Burton, panicked, wiped the handle clean so no one would tie him or her to the scene, and ran like … like someone running fast."

"Do you agree with him?"

"Seems unusual but does make sense."

That didn't answer my question, but thought it was time to tell her what I'd learned and that might help make up her mind.

"Ready to hear why I called?"

"Do I have a choice?"

"No."

"That's what I thought."

I told her about my Internet search and what I'd learned about Joel's *fiancé*.

"Chris, right up there with piss-poor insurance reimbursements, and damned medicine commercials on television, do you know what doctors complain about the most?"

"No, but I bet you're going to tell me."

"It's their competitor: Dr. Google. Seems most of their patients come to their office certain they know what's wrong with them. They've looked up some of their symptoms on the Internet and are ready, willing, and able to tell the docs who have wasted all those years in medical school when all they had to do was look it up and write a prescription for whatever Dr. Google said they needed."

"You made that up," I said.

"Gee, give me some credit, Mr. Citizen. I read it in that highly respected medical journal, *People Magazine*."

I smiled but didn't let Cindy know I found it amusing. "So, what's that have to do with Joel?"

"So, you're going to take an accidental death, stir in a little ancient history off the Internet about some chick from somewhere in Louisiana, and leap to the conclusion Ms. Craft's death—her *accidental* death—had something to do with Joel Hurt. Oh yeah, did I mention *accidental* death?"

"Cindy, all I'm saying is it seems like a large coincidence. Don't you?"

"Yeah," she said.

"So, what are you going to do about it?"

"I'm going to hang up, go to a meeting with our mayor that I'm five minutes late for, say 'Yes sir, yes sir, whatever you say sir,' leave the meeting, and call Detective Adair and share your harebrained coincidence. Then when he says it's absurd and asks what idiot came up with it, I'm going to tell him it was you, and hang up on him before he calls me names."

"Thank you," I said before she could hang up on me.

It may not have sounded like it to anyone who may have been listening to our conversation, but I knew Cindy had heard me, was taking it seriously, and would follow through with Detective Adair. What I didn't know was how seriously he would take it.

15

I barely had time to ponder if the Charleston detective would take my information seriously when the phone rang.

"Good," said Bob Howard. "Glad I caught you alive. Meet me at Al's at noon."

Sorry Bob, I'm busy. Why, Bob? Good morning, Bob. How are you today? All were responses I would have liked to share with the realtor, but I couldn't because he'd already hung up.

Al's Bar and Gourmet Grill was located a block off Calhoun Street, a main road that crisscrossed downtown Charleston, and three blocks from the hospital district. It was in a section of town Realtor Bob referred to as being in its pre-gentrification period. After three beers one night, he'd revised his terminology and classified the houses surrounding Al's as being slummy dumps still standing because termites were afraid to live there. It shared a dilapidated, concrete-block building with a Laundromat.

Bob was already in the bar, and probably had been for some time since his deteriorating dark-plum colored PT Cruiser was parked in front of the door. Bob had been driving the convertible ever since I had known him. It looked more like the vehicle an underpaid short-order cook would be driving than a successful realtor. Bob had once told me he drove it, so his clients would know he was only out for their best interests rather than making money off them. I didn't agree but trying to argue with Bob was like trying to convince a rhinoceros to play Scrabble.

I was greeted by near total darkness as I stepped from the sunlight into the bar. I was also greeted by Al who looked as worn as the exterior of the building and the yard-sale tables and chairs that filled the room. His skin, somewhere between deep brown and light black, appeared paler than usual and his handshake weaker than I had remembered. What hadn't changed was his high-wattage smile as he hugged me.

"It's great to see you, Chris. It's been too long."

Bob had told me about Al's declining health, and it'd only been a few weeks since I was in, but the change in his appearance was distressing. The Four Tops were belting out "Reach Out I'll Be There" from the jukebox, but not loud enough to mask Bob's voice coming from a booth near the back of the bar, "Dammit old man, stop huggin' on the boy. Let him get over here and buy me lunch!"

Three tables of diners stopped their conversations and glanced at Bob who was spread out on one side of the booth he had staked a claim to years ago and grumbled if anyone else had the nerve to sit in it. They turned to Al to see how he would react to the burly, bag of hot air.

Al pointed at Bob, smiled, and said, "Shut up and stick a fry in your face."

Bob and I were the only Caucasians in the room, so Al's generous smile had probably prevented a race riot. Two of the diners whose ages approached Al's clapped and some of the others in the room laughed and hoisted their beer bottles to Al.

Ray Charles was singing "Hit the Road Jack" and I wondered if I should follow his advice, but instead I told Al I was glad to see him and weaved my way through the tables and squeezed into the seat opposite Bob.

He waved his hand around and said, "See, they love me."

Not exactly my interpretation, but I let it go, and said, "Al is looking bad."

"Isn't that what I already told you?"

I said it was but didn't realize how bad until now. I glanced back and noticed Al was leaning heavily on a chair and appeared to be breathing heavily.

The music from the jukebox had switched from R&B to Connie Smith singing the country classic *Once a Day*. As a concession to his friendship with Bob, Al, to the consternation of many of his regular customers, had salted his jukebox with several country music tunes, which Bob had often and loudly proclaimed to be the only kind of real music.

"Thank God, my ears will stop bleeding now," Bob said, loud enough for all to hear.

I leaned closer to the table and said, in a voice I didn't want anyone other than Bob to hear, "Does everyone know about you buying the bar?"

"You talking about everyone, like all the monks in Tibet and whoever those short people are who live in Australia, or are you limiting it to Al's customers?"

I stared at Bob.

"No," he finally said, "Al wants to wait until the damned lawyers get all the I's dotted and Q's sliced before announcing it." He tilted his head toward the door. "And speaking about the damned old codger, look who's here?"

Al was three feet from the table and leaning on a rickety chair.

"Park your bony ass, old man," Bob said.

Al moved from leaning on the chair to the space beside me and said, "How could I pass on such a nice invitation. Chris, I went ahead and told my cook to fix you a cheeseburger and to bring you a glass of white wine. Hope that's okay."

I told him it was perfect but was surprised that he was having the cook bring the burger and wine to the table. Al had always taken pride in delivering the food.

Al took a deep breath. "Heard about the big corporate takeover?"

"Yes, if you mean your buddy here purchasing the best cheeseburger restaurant in South Carolina."

Al chuckled. "That's the one. Tubby here said he was going to keep the name of the place Al's. He said—"

Bob interrupted. "Thought about changing it to Bob's Burgers but figured that was too classy a name for this dump and that Al's had just the right dumpy ring to it."

I ignored Bob, a talent one must acquire to be able to spend time around him. "I hear you've agreed to help him."

Al shook his head. "I'll stick around, but don't know how much help I'll be."

Willie Nelson crooned "My Heroes Have Always Been Cowboys," my cheeseburger and wine arrived, and Bob said, "He'll always be welcome and is a tremendous help."

I was pleased by Bob's admission. I knew he felt that way about Al but figured it would take a mule train to pull it out of him with Al close enough to hear.

Al waited for me to bite into my cheeseburger, and said, "Blubber Bob here told me the other day that you're sticking your nose into another strange death on your island. He said you were suspicioning that it may be more than an accident, something about lack of prints or something."

"Not really," I said. "The police are saying it was an accidental heroin overdose. There wasn't any evidence it was forced. I took an interest because the woman's parents live next door to me."

Al slowly nodded. "Yes sir, I hear that. Her dad's that detective you called lazy and incompetent."

"A worthless sack of dog dung," Bob added.

Al's physical health may be fading, but there was nothing wrong with his memory. It had been a year or more since I'd said anything to him about Detective Burton.

Al rolled his eyes at Bob and said, "I was telling Tanesa about it. She said she's seen way too many ODs in the emergency room. I asked her if someone could force another person into sticking themselves and squirting enough H into the system to kill them. She said if the person had enough to drink, it'd be possible."

Cindy had said Lauren had been drunk. "That's true I suppose, but I think there's bigger news around here than what's happening on Folly. Al, I'm glad you'll be getting help with the bar. I know—"

Bob interrupted, "Bar *and Grill*. This ain't only a drinkin' dive. It serves the best cheeseburgers in the civilized world. I see great things happening when I sprinkle my dining-extraordinaire marketing talents to the business. This fine establishment will be reeling in five-star reviews. I can picture the Food Channel broadcasting live from here and that famous chef who goes around the country getting stomped by local chefs and chefettes when he tries to fix their specialties." Bob tapped his forefinger against his temple. "Before you know it, that TV channel will want to pay me, I mean us, a zillion dollars to host a series on their soon to be famous network."

Al laughed. "I can picture it too, Bob. You'll stand out front and when anyone sees your ample stomach they'll figure you must be an expert on cheeseburgers. Then you'll slop on the charm you're famous for and look at the potential customers—umm, excuse me, Food Channel audience—and woo them with something like, 'Get your damn ass in here and eat one of these famous burgers, or get out of my face.' Yes sir, I can see it now."

I leaned back in the booth, gazed at Bob as his face turned red, and ramped-up my admiration for Al another hundred percent.

Instead of exploding in a patented Bob rant, he grinned and leaned his *ample stomach* against the table to get close enough to reach Al's hand. Bob patted the thin, bony hand and said, "Great idea, former owner, and soon-to-be official greeter."

Bob and Al continued to exchange brilliant marketing ideas, I enjoyed the rest of my cheeseburger and especially my wine, and from the jukebox, Freddy Fender's accented voice reminded us what would happen "Before the Next Teardrop Falls."

1 6

Over the last few days, I'd noticed Brad Burton walking past the house on his way to or from Bert's. I suppose he had made the walk many times, but I had never paid attention to him until the tragic death of his daughter. I had been tempted to step outside and say something to him but knew there wasn't anything to say. He was devastated and there was nothing I could say that would lessen his misery.

Who I talked to several times in the last forty-eight hours leading to tonight's fundraiser was Dude. We had more telephone conversations than during the entire eight years I'd known him. A week ago, I shared with him the idea of him hosting a fundraiser for Brian. After listening to him vacillate between laughter and fear about hosting the event, he finally said, "Okee-dokee. Dude be kingmaker."

The closer we got to the event, panic had overcome any enthusiasm my surfer friend had for the fundraiser. One of his nonnegotiable conditions for holding the event was that it must be catered by Cal's. I hadn't argued, but having the singing cowboy cater anything was like having Bob as the keynote speaker at a Weight Watchers convention. Regardless, Dude asked me to negotiate the catering with Cal who had reluctantly agreed to have his staff of fine culinarians—one underpaid short-order cook—prepare hors d'oeuvres, which when he said it, sounded like *horse nerves*, under the condition he would be able to sing a few songs. He'd reminded me that, "Political types always have music at their shindigs."

I thought it was a small price to pay for having *fine culinarians* catering the event.

I picked Charles up and headed to his girlfriend's apartment building a short distance away. Charles told me to keep driving and that Heather wasn't going. I was surprised since they had been nearly inseparable over the last couple of years.

"Is she feeling bad?"

Charles stared out the windshield and I wondered if he'd heard my question.

"Charles?"

"I heard you," he mumbled. "She's been down, up, and down, since we got back from Nashville. More downs than ups. I've tried everything, but she seems immune to being cheered up."

I knew she had been depressed and while in Tennessee had attempted to take her own life after being arrested for a murder that she hadn't committed. I had been with the two of them three or four times since they had returned from chasing her dreams in Nashville but hadn't seen evidence of continued depression.

When they returned, I shared the name of a counselor who had helped William Hansel, another of my friends after he'd suffered depression. "Has she met with the counselor William recommended?"

Charles turned toward me. "Don't think so. She keeps saying she's going to make an appointment, but I'm not sure she means it."

I asked if there was anything I could do to help. He said he wished there was but didn't know what it could be. He returned to staring out the windshield as we approached Dude's small, elevated house located a couple of blocks east of Center Street. It would've been hard to miss. His light-green, rusting, 1970 Chevrolet El Camino was parked in the front yard. A four-foot by four-foot sheet of plywood was propped up between two concrete blocks in the vehicle's bed. The plywood was painted white and hand lettering said *BRIAN'S CASH BASH* in fluorescent red paint with a red arrow pointed at the house.

"Dude be subtle," Charles said, mocking the surfer's command of the English language.

The party—cash bash—wasn't to start for another half hour but there were already a half-dozen cars parked in the front yard. I found a spot a block away and was sweating before we made it to Dude's front steps. It was in the low nineties, with high humidity. The only saving grace was thick, black clouds looming overhead. Rain was predicted.

There was a note on the front door that read *IF YOU BE DONATIN' BIG BUCKS, COME IN.*

"Yes, subtle," I said.

I had never been in Dude's house but after knowing the surf shop owner for several years, I was prepared to not be surprised by anything. His décor didn't disappoint. The door opened to the living room that looked like a museum devoted to the 1960s. Bright-green shag carpet covered the floor and the seating grouping consisted of an orange, a green, and a yellow beanbag chair. Three framed photos of a much-younger Dude standing beside other surfers were hung on the wall in an erratic pattern. After my eyes adjusted to the colors, I looked through the door leading to the kitchen and a large wooden deck. This was clearly where the action was.

Dude was waving his arms, his multi-colored tie dye shirt flapped in the breeze, and the subject of his gyrations, Dennis, Cal's short-order cook, pointed to an aluminum pan holding what looked like mini-hotdogs wrapped in dough, covered in freezer-frost.

"Fine chef and host be disputin' something," Charles said.

I elbowed him and headed to the patio. The Doors were screaming "Light My Fire" from an eight-track tape player on a table at the corner of the deck. And Dude was also screaming something about lighting a fire, but for the mini-hotdogs. Cal was standing stooped-shouldered behind his cook and nodding at everything Dude was saying. Five classic surfboards were hanging vertically on the wall by the door.

About that time, Mother Nature added her two-cents to the conversation in the form of a torrential downpour. Dude, the cook, Cal, and three other early arrivers grabbed their drinks, the eight-track boom box, and what was left of their dry clothing, and scampered inside.

Dude was in his early sixties, about five-foot seven, thin, and with his long, mostly white, stringy hair, looked like a shorter, thinner version of the folk singer Arlo Guthrie. He shook his head like a dog and noticed Charles and me.

"Whoa, cool T," he said and nodded toward Charles's long-sleeve T-shirt.

I made a conscious effort years ago to ignore the many long-sleeve, predominantly college logoed, T-shirts that Charles felt compelled to wear. Many others chose not to ignore them. Tonight, he had on a gold T-shirt with the word *Gauchos* written in script on it.

Charles smiled. "University of California at Santa Barbara."

Dude returned his smile, and said, "*Numero Uno* bestest surf college in US of A."

Okay, I couldn't resist asking, and turned to the host, "How do you know that?"

Dude looked at me like he'd seen me for the first time. "*Surfer Magazine*, duh!"

How had that fact slipped by me?

Dude and Charles's enlightening conversation was interrupted by the arrival of three more people who I assumed were here to be *donatin' big bucks*. Todd Livers, who I'd met last year, and was a surfer friend of Dude's, shook the rain off his ball cap and looked around the room. Behind him stood Stephon, one of Dude's employees and a perennial candidate for the East Coast rudest employee of the year. Both men were half my age. The third member of the trio of arrivers was much closer to my age. Mel Evans, better known for reasons that quickly become obvious as Mad Mel, shoved his way past Stephon, waved his camouflage hunting cap in the air throwing water in all directions, and glared at Dude, "Why in the hell didn't you have this shindig on a dry night, you damned, draft-dodging, hippy, druggy?"

Dude appeared nonplussed and nodded. "Welcome Melster. Crack a grin or skedaddle."

I saw Todd look around, probably to grab anything breakable before the earthquake hit. There was no need when Mel laughed. Mel and Dude had become friends more than two decades ago when Dude had saved Mel from being pulled out to sea in a rip current.

Dude looked behind Mel. "Where be Caldwell?"

Caldwell Ramsey was Mel's significant other and a music promoter in Charleston.

"Said he couldn't think of a single reason he wanted to see you tonight. Decided a colonoscopy would be more fun."

Dude shrugged. "He be sorry."

"Doubt it," Mel said. "He sent a check."

"Be better if Caldwell be here, better than have camera stuck up in butt. You send a check, if it no bounce."

The Doors sang "People Are Strange" from the boom box Cal retrieved from the rain. I agreed, and Brian Newman, the reason for the gathering, stuck his head in the door.

"Yo, Mr. Mayorster," Dude said. "Welcome."

As if on cue, Dude's Australian Terrier, Pluto, stuck his head out of a red, tiny, domed, camping tent, with a glow-in-the-dark peace symbol on the side, and barked.

"Be saying howdy," Dude translated for the pup that looked like a shorter version of the surfer.

Brian looked to see who was in the room and, like all good politicians, leaned down and let Pluto lick the side of his face. There were no babies to kiss.

If anyone else arrived, we would be standing on each other's toes, so I was happy to see that the rain had stopped, and rays of the setting sun filtered through the window. Dennis was putting the thawing hot dogs in the oven, and Mel was rooting through the tub holding the beer. I suggested we should migrate back to the deck. Cal took the hint and said he'd begin singing as soon as a crowd gathered outside. Mel rolled his eyes and grabbed the beer tub and hauled it outside. Others followed, most likely following the beer rather than the country crooner. Dude told Stephon to wipe the rain off the chairs. Mr. Rude snarled at his boss but grabbed a dry rag and started slapping the ponded water to the deck.

Barb arrived next. She looked lovely in one of her red blouses and linen slacks. She had a bottle of white wine in her hand, winked at me, and said it was for emergencies in case Dude didn't have any of my drink of choice. I kissed her on the cheek and thanked her for the care package. She asked if I knew everyone at the fundraiser and I said yes, some better than others. I took it as a hint and introduced her to Mel who acted civil and said he'd heard a lot about her and her bookstore. He backslid a bit when he asked her what she was doing with such a stuffy, prude like me. She said all the charming guys were taken and I was all that was left. He said all the charming straight guys may be taken, but there was one charming gay guy in the room. I looked around to see who he was referring to, he said, "ha ha," and moved away to pester

Dude. Barb already knew Stephon and Todd from the surf shop.

A younger version of Barb came around the corner. She was thin with stylishly-cut, short blond hair, wearing a white and light-blue sundress and looked more like she was going to a cocktail party than anything at Dude's. She spotted the host and headed his way without stopping to talk to anyone. Barb asked me who she was, and I told her I didn't know.

"Then let's find out, shall we?"

Barb was normally reticent to meet strangers and had a reputation among those who didn't know her well of being standoffish. I followed her to Dude and the stranger who had knelt and was petting Pluto.

"Howdy, Barbstress," Dude said and shook her hand. Barb gave it a brief shake and hugged the host.

Dude smiled and said, "Woe, make me woozy."

Barb returned his smile, didn't comment on her level of wooziness and thanked him for inviting her.

"Me be invitin' all big-buck peeps. Need to keep el mayor mayor."

Pluto drifted toward his food bowl and the newcomer stood and looked at Barb. "Book store lady, right?"

Barb said she was right and said, "And you are? I don't recall seeing you around."

"I'm Katelin Hatchett." She stuck out her hand. "Dude invited me. We met in the surf shop. He's a nice old hippie."

"Whoa," Dude said for the second time. "Me be hippie, but young compared to age of rock—stone one, not rock and roll one."

He said something else, but I didn't catch it—not that rare an occurrence. I was trying to remember where I'd heard her name. It struck me about the time Cal struck the first notes of "Hey Good Lookin'" as he channeled Hank Williams Sr., one of his idols. Katelin was one of Lauren Craft's housemates.

Cal tried to get everyone in the spirit of Dude's house and sang "Surfin' U.S.A." His rendition fell under the category *it's the thought that counts*. Country music was in his blood and in his voice. His vocal range began and ended there. He finished, and Dude applauded and said, "Boss!" The only reaction from everyone else was to look at Dude and, I suspect, wonder what music he was listening to. Cal slid back into his genre and began Ricky Van Shelton's "I'll Leave This World Loving You," and the rest of us continued our conversations. I tried to think of something to say to Katelin, but she moved away to talk to Stephon before I had a chance.

I was surprised to see Brad Burton at the back of the patio. He must have arrived while I was talking to Katelin. He was looking around like he didn't know anyone, so I sighed, and as much as I hated to admit it, felt sorry for him and wandered his way and said it was nice seeing him.

He continued looking around the deck, and said, "I've always liked the mayor and Hazel said I should make an appearance to show our support." He hesitated and smiled. "And give him a check."

The only positive encounter I had with the former detective before he'd moved here was a couple of years back when he had shared with me some damning information about the unpopular previous mayor, and I used it to get him to resign, thus opening the door for Brian to be elected.

"It was nice of you to come. I know how difficult this must be."

Brad saw Brian Newman talking to one of the surfers. "That's why I'm going to say hi to the mayor, leave my check, and get out of here. Excuse me."

I again thanked him for coming and watched him move to Brian.

I looked for Charles but instead saw William Hansel peeking in the door. He looked around and smiled when he saw me. The sixty-four-year-old professor at the College of Charleston had been one of the first people I'd met when I got to Folly. We were about the same age, and even though he'd lived on Folly for more than ten years at that time, we in many ways had been outsiders. I was new to the community and William was African American, one of only a couple of handfuls residing here at the time. He had made a few good friends since his wife died seventeen years ago. I was honored to count myself as one of them.

"Chris, I am heartened to see you among the guests at this event."

William's navy-blue dress slacks and tan, button-down, dress shirt were as formal as his speech. He could be as difficult to understand as was Dude, but for the opposite reason.

"Glad you could make it," I said. "Brian will be pleased to see you."

William looked around the room. "It appears I am amid several people to whom I am unfamiliar."

I pointed out he knew the mayor, Charles, Barb, and Dude, and offered to walk with him to the bar.

"That would be appreciated."

Charles had seen William and ended his conversation with Mel and met the two of us at the drinks.

"Evening, Professor," Charles said and nodded in my direction. "Couldn't find anyone better to hang with?"

William chuckled. "Mr. Fowler, you were in deep conversation with Mr. Evans and I didn't want to interfere with your social intercourse."

"If you mean that Mad Mel was blabbing on about how great he was, you're right."

Cal finished "On the Other Hand," and waved Dude to stand beside him and said, "Guys and Gals, Dude here invited us to share in this gala, so we could support the reelection of our mayor. So, let's give Dude a big hand and let him say a few words." Cal smiled. "And if I know Dude, it'll be very few words."

Applause for Dude wasn't quite as strong as was the laughter at Cal's remark. Either way, Dude moved to where Cal had been standing.

"Thanks for coming. Lay oodles of dough on getting the mayor reelected." Dude gave a bow like he'd recited the Gettysburg Address and stepped aside.

Brian put his arm on Dude's shoulder. "Thank you, Dude, for hosting this event, for giving me a chance to share why I am running for reelection, and for your, umm, words of encouragement."

Barb had moved to my side and was surprised to see Katelin and Stephon on my other side. Brian began by sharing what he considered his main accomplishments since being in office and a little about his background as police chief. He told us since there was an opponent—a well-financed opponent—who had already started his campaign, that Brian needed to start early. He confided he hated asking for donations, but he would have to get over it since it appeared that record amounts would be spent on the election.

"Now don't get me wrong," he said. "My opponent appears to be sincere, with the best of intentions." Brian was following the current political strategy of not mentioning his opponent's name. "Many of us already know him through his businesses. He's telling everyone he's a long shot or a dark horse in the race, but don't believe it for a second. He's got money and a message that sounds better than it is. I believe he is a fine man, but we simply have different visions of what Folly should become."

"Fine man, shit," mumbled Katelin, louder than she had intended.

I glanced around and no one else appeared to have heard her.

Brian continued with how he differed with his opponent, and ended by asking for our support and turned it back over to Cal.

"Now friends and neighbors," Cal said, and pointed to a small table by the door "I hear there are empty envelopes back there on that table. Before y'all leave, grab one, stuff it full of cash, checks, gold nuggets, whatever, and fill out the pesky paperwork. Our mayor, Brian Newman, needs our support." He picked up his guitar and back in the spirit of Dude, he started strumming and poorly singing "Fun, Fun, Fun."

The day after the fundraiser, I was having breakfast at the Dog, joking with Amber, and watching Marc Salmon and Houston Bass arguing about a parking ordinance the council had been debating. Were they as worried about the upcoming election as Brian was? I also replayed parts of last night's fundraiser and what I had told Charles about how Katelin had reacted to Brian's complimentary comment about Joel. Charles had been so distracted about Heather that he failed to do what he does best: ask thousands of questions about what I was telling him, most of them irrelevant. I hate to admit it, but I missed his interruptions.

I had noticed a change in Charles since he and Heather had returned from Nashville. He had been one of the most upbeat people I'd ever come into contact with from the day I'd met him until the day they loaded up his car and moved to Music City. Folly had been his home for years and he had embraced it and had become one of its biggest supporters. To be honest, Charles was the walking, talking personification of the kind of person the island I had fallen in love with represented. He liked almost everyone, could find good in the most obnoxious resident, and was a chameleon when interacting with the wide range of personalities with which he came in contact. And I knew from personal encounters with evil that he would put his life on the line for his friends. Charles had said he was glad to be back after their move to Tennessee, and at times I recognized the Charles of old, but while others had said he was the same, I knew differently. I hoped time would bring out the old Charles, for both his and my sake.

Amber had refreshed my coffee when Katelin stepped into the crowded restaurant, glanced around, and headed in my direction. She looked exhausted. Her stylish attire from the fundraiser was replaced by ratty shorts and a wrinkled, black T-shirt with Nike written below the company's iconic swish.

"Mr. Landrum, umm, Chris, could I join you?"

I nodded toward the seat on the other side of the table. "Of course. Want coffee or something to eat?"

Amber had seen Katelin arrive and was quick to the table.

Katelin started to answer me but looked up at Amber. "Maybe some coffee, yes, coffee please."

Amber headed to the kitchen, and Katelin tapped her fingers on the table. "Pretty day, isn't it?"

"Beats last night's weather," I said. I wanted to jump into the reason she was here, but it'd be better for her to get there at her own pace.

She looked at the framed photos of dogs on the wall beside me. "Lots of dogs in here."

I agreed as Amber returned with Katelin's coffee and a second refill for me. Amber asked if Katelin wanted something to eat. She said no, and Amber moved to the next table to share her endearing smile and helpful attitude.

"Umm," Katelin said, "saw you talking with Lauren's dad, umm, Mr. Burton, last night and figured you were friends."

I acknowledged that we were *acquaintances* and had been talking at the fundraiser.

Katelin took a sip of coffee. "Well anyway, I wanted to tell him something, but he disappeared before I could get to him."

I told her Brad wanted to support the mayor and wasn't there long.

She looked in her coffee mug and in a lower voice said, "I was afraid he'd be mad at me, or try to blame his daughter's death on me."

"Why would you think that?"

"I'd only talked to him a couple of times when he came to the house Lauren and I shared. He didn't say anything bad, but I could tell from his expression that he didn't approve of where we lived. I figured he thought I was a bad influence on Lauren."

I wanted to repeat "why would you think that" but didn't and nodded for her to continue.

"I don't know if he knew it or not, but I had gone through rehab with Lauren a couple of times." She shook her head and frowned. "We shared some rough patches. If she told her dad about our history, he probably would've thought I was bad for her." She looked up from the mug. "Chris, I wasn't bad. Lauren was good and most of the time real clean. I was sort of between waitressing jobs a while back and we had more time to spend together. She had a good heart and was funny, not jokes funny, but said funny things about what was going on around her, if you know what I mean."

"I think I do. You said she was clean most of the time."

Her head dipped, and she returned to staring at the coffee mug. "Umm, I hate to admit it, but over the last two months, she relapsed. She was back on H big time. It was so sad. I tried to talk to her, remind her of all the, excuse me, shit we'd gone through getting off the stuff. She wouldn't listen."

I thought about what Cindy had said about only one needle mark. "Are you sure she was using again?"

Katelin sighed. "Yeah, I'm certain. She was shooting up

worse than ever before; shooting up right in the living room, not even trying to hide it. Drinking heavy too."

"Do you know why?"

"She never said it, but I'd put money on her a-hole boyfriend, Joel."

"Why?" I asked, and decided I was becoming nosy Charles.

"He's not good for, umm, not good for Lauren. He had a way of putting her down. Condescending, I think that's what you call it. One minute he was all lovey-dovey and the next he was saying he was ashamed of her, hinting that her drugging was going to give him a bad name."

I also remembered how Katelin had reacted to Brian Newman's remark about him last night and wondered if his treatment of Lauren was what precipitated her strong reaction.

"Last night I saw how you reacted when the mayor was complimenting Joel and saying he was a good guy."

"I was afraid you might have heard me. I couldn't help it, just blurted it out."

"Was it because of how he acted with Lauren?"

She glanced around the room and at me. "Sort of."

"Sort of?" I said.

Her face looked like she'd been sucking on a lemon.

"I dated him before she did." She shook her head. "No, that's not accurate. He dated both of us at the same time and I didn't know about it. Joel and I were getting serious, or so I thought. I was working a lot of double shifts and wasn't ever home." She sighed. "Crap, I don't know why I'm telling you any of this." She paused and looked at me like she was expecting an answer.

"It's okay," I said.

That seemed to satisfy her. "Anyway, Joel's a lying two-timer. He was trying to juggle both of us. Can you believe that? We were housemates. The only reason he dumped me was I found out about him and Lauren. He blew a gasket. I was afraid he was going to hit me." She gripped her fist so tightly I thought her fingernails were going to draw blood. "Thank God, he didn't. He seems so sincere, even sweet, but the more I got to know him, I realized he would lie about anything. It was my good luck that he dumped me. Enough about that. I wanted to tell Mr. Burton I was sorry about Lauren, that's all."

"Katelin, do you think her death was accidental?"

"Sure, why? Do you think she killed herself on purpose?"

"I'm not saying anything. You knew her better than most anyone, maybe better than everyone, so I thought you might have an opinion. Just asking."

"If she killed herself, it was over Joel. She thought they were close but was wondering more and more where he was when she thought he should be with her. That shouldn't be reason enough to harm yourself. Should it?"

Good question. I wish I had an answer. I told her I didn't think so and it seemed to satisfy her.

"Chris, do you think Mr. and Mrs. Burton would mind if I stopped by their house to tell them how sorry I am?"

"They would appreciate it."

She took another sip of coffee and clunked her mug down on the table. "Think I'll try to do that now while I've got my courage up."

I told her I thought it was a good idea and said I'd pick up the tab on her coffee.

"Thank you for letting me mouth off. I hope the mayor got enough money last night to stomp Joel. If you excuse my French, he's an asshole."

She pushed away from the table and was gone before I had time to excuse her French.

1 8

I called Charles twice over the next two days. Each time, he was abrupt and said he was busy making deliveries for the surf shop and would call me when he had time. He didn't ask if I knew anything new about Lauren's death or Brian's candidacy. His behavior was so un-Charles-like that I wondered if I'd gotten the wrong number. It sounded like I was talking to a stranger, and he never called back.

I hadn't heard from Charles and the fundraiser at Bob's house was this evening, so I called to see if he was going. When the topic of fundraisers was originally discussed, he had said nothing could keep him away, but he knew the event was tonight and hadn't said anything about it recently.

"What?"

"Good afternoon," I said. "Are you going—"

"No," he interrupted.

"You don't know the question; how can you say no?"

"You're going to ask if I'm going to Bob's thing."

I hated him knowing what I was going to say before I said it. "So, you're not going?"

"That's what *no* meant," he said, without a hint of warmth.

"Charles, what's wrong?"

"Nothing, I'm busy, that's all."

"Busy?"

"Okay, not that busy. It's just Heather says she doesn't like to be around all those hoity-toity rich people, and she's been in such a sour mood I don't want to leave her tonight." He hesitated, and said, "Sorry I've been short with you."

I was surprised. "She thinks rude, obscene, politically incorrect Bob Howard is hoity-toity?"

"Okay, you got me there. Not him, but she means the kind of people Bob will invite. For reasons I can't figure out, he does have some snooty friends. Even if he doesn't or if none of them show up tonight, Heather thinks they are and flat out won't go. I need to stay with her."

There was no sense in trying to convince him otherwise, so I wished him luck with Heather and he told me to let Bob know he wasn't there because he hated Bob's guts. I knew that was one-hundred percent incorrect but said I would share his sentiments. On a more pleasant note, Barb had said she had to work late, but would join me at Bob's.

ON THE SHORT drive from Folly to Charleston, I realized I had never been to Bob and Betty's new house. They'd moved about three years ago from James Island to a ritzier section of Charleston a few blocks west of King Street and three blocks north of Broad Street. My navigation system still managed to lead me to their house even though it'd also never been there. The predicted late-afternoon showers failed to appear, and the humidity was lower than usual as I pulled up to the address. I knew Bob was a successful realtor, but was still impressed by the large, two-story, Georgian style home that had Bob's street address beside the front door. I was more impressed when a college-aged gentleman, dressed in a red blazer, and black slacks waved for me to pull to the curb between two orange cones—illegally placed there by Bob, I suspected—and said he would valet park my car.

"This is Bob Howard's house?" I said, feeling more like I'd parked in front of the White House.

"It is the residence of Mr. Howard," said the polite valet. "I'm not certain of his first name."

I said I supposed it would have to do and left him with my car, and hoped he wasn't an industrious car thief.

I took a moment gawking at the house and passed through a decorative, traditional Charleston wrought iron gate and walked up a pea gravel path to the front steps where I was greeted by a grey-haired, older gentleman wearing a white server's jacket, black slacks, and black shoes so highly polished that they could've been made of glass.

"Welcome, Sir," he said, and honest-to-goodness, he bowed.

I was now certain I was at the wrong house, but he reassured me it was indeed the residence of Mr. and Mrs. Robert Howard, the "fine couple who are hosting tonight's political gathering." I was starting to agree with Heather.

"Other ladies and gentlemen are gathered on the back patio," said the doorman. "Please allow me to aid you in finding your way."

I did. On the walk through the hallway I peeked in the formal living room on the right and formal dining room to my left, before we arrived in the larger, and more casual, family room. All the rooms were filled with antiques and fine furnishings that made the house look more like a museum than where real people lived. The one hint of reality was a flat screen television on the wall of the family room. The set was the size of an Interstate billboard. I suspected that was Bob's decorative touch.

Two sets of French doors led from the family room to an

expansive brick patio that sat on a more expansive manicured lawn. Twenty people were milling around a six-foot-tall version of the distinct Pineapple Fountain located in downtown Charleston's French Quarter. Most of the attendees were all smiles with a drink in one hand while trying to balance a china plate of finger foods in the other.

Of the group, I only recognized a half dozen and was tempted to turn and leave when I heard Bob yell, "Well it's about damned time you got here."

He scurried—more like a slow walk for most everyone else—around a couple of the guests and headed my way. He had made major concessions to his normal attire since he had on long pants instead of shorts, and his extensive Hawaiian flowery shirt collection had given way to a yellow dress shirt. I nearly reached for my phone/camera to record Bob in sartorial splendor, truly a historic event, but he had already put his arm around my shoulder. "Where's piss ant Charles?"

You could lead Bob to a classy event, but you couldn't make him classy, or something like that. I explained Charles was staying with Heather and she'd been a little under the weather. I doubted he'd believed me, but he didn't press it. A waiter arrived about the same time Bob had and offered me a glass of Champagne. I took it, thanked him, and gave Bob a sideways glance.

"All Betty's idea. You'd better enjoy that damned drink. You know they don't even sell that stuff in boxes?"

I told him I didn't know that, but I thought it was classy. He told me she made him hide the beer cooler behind the shrubs that were aesthetically placed around three sides of the patio.

A second waiter magically appeared carrying a silver tray with a selection of finger foods that looked more colorful than appetizing. I took one that looked familiar and thanked the smiling waiter.

Bob waved his hand in front of me. "Don't even think about

asking me what that crap is. I can tell you it costs more than a new Dodge Dart."

I told him that I appreciated his fiscal analysis, and turned more serious, and thanked him for the generous offer to host the event.

"Don't thank me," he said as he turned to look at the group gathered near the outdoor bar. "Betty said if I didn't make this a memorable shindig I'd better have one of my builder friends start on an oversized doghouse."

I didn't catch everything he'd said about the doghouse; I was stuck on him having friends, builders or otherwise. I also knew he was doing little more than blowing smoke, because he would have done anything for Brian.

"It's still kind of you. So, who are these people?"

"Most are realtors who spend all their time slinking around looking for potential clients. Free booze and little clumps of food that no normal person can recognize drew them in." He chuckled. "They also have money and with the right twist of the arm can be convinced to give a chunk of it to the right political candidates."

"And that would be Brian Newman?"

"Hell, Chris, they don't have a rat's turd idea who Brian is. They do know me, and if I suggest they donate to him, they'll smile and take the duct tape off their checkbooks and scribble out a check for the legal maximum amount."

I smiled. "I didn't know you had that many good friends."

"I don't. Half of them work for me, and most of the others work for people who owe me favors. You're beginning to bore me, so let's go, I'll introduce you to some of them."

I was once again reminded why he didn't have many good friends. Bob told me I wouldn't have to remember any of the names since most of the realtors had money and since I was old and broke I wouldn't see them again. He was wasting his words since names and I had never been on remembering terms.

He dragged me over to a couple of gray-haired men in deep conversation. Bob, being Bob, was oblivious to what they were talking about and shoved his way between them, told me the taller one was Gordon something, and the "skinny, malnourished little twerp" was Lawrence Brockman. He said they were two of his employees which apparently gave him authority to interrupt and insult to his heart's content. Bob told them I was a good friend of tonight's guest of honor, Brian Newman. They smiled and pretended to care who I was and probably who Brian Newman was.

I held their smile and looked around to see if the *guest of honor* had arrived, but he either wasn't here yet or was hidden behind some of the other guests of lesser honor. Bob told the two realtors that he'd love to stay and talk longer but had to mingle. They didn't appear to be sad to see us go.

A violinist, not more than a teenager, was plying her trade on the other side of the patio. Her eyes were closed and she was lost in the music. That was good because I doubted anyone could hear her because of the water splashing in the fountain and the din of several people talking over each other. The succulent smell of late-blooming flowers flowed through the air.

Bob pointed at the musician. "I wanted a fiddle and guitar, so we could have real music—country music—but Betty vetoed my brilliant idea. There's no king at this castle. Betty rules with a firm skillet."

Our next stop was one I did look forward to. Al and his daughter Tanesa were standing by themselves near the violinist. I realized it was only the second time I'd seen Al outside his bar/restaurant and the first time I'd seen Tanesa in something other than her medical scrubs. She wore a knee-length yellow and white sundress that contrasted nicely with her coco-brown skin and black, curly hair. She looked more like a doctor's daughter rather than the highly skilled ER doc I knew her to be.

Al had on a black dress shirt, gray slacks, and an expression that screamed *I'm uncomfortable as hell.*

"Well if it ain't beauty and the damned ugly old beast. Hope none of my fine Caucasian neighbors saw you two sneaking in," said Bob, warmly welcoming the Washingtons to his house.

Tanesa ignored Bob's comment, smiled, and gave the burly politically incorrect realtor a kiss on the cheek. Al also smiled, his coffee-stained teeth contrasting with Tanesa's gleaming white ones.

Bob looked at Al and took a step back. "Don't you even think about kissing me, old man." He looked around and waved one of the waiters over. "Get this old man some of those food clumps before he dies of starvation right on Betty's manicured lawn."

Bob made a few ruder remarks, hugged Al, showing a glimmer of his true feelings about his friend, and said, "Gotta spread more joy among the others, so I'll leave so you can talk about me."

Al and Tanesa thanked him for inviting them, Bob mumbled it wasn't his idea, and left the three of us. Tanesa suggested her dad may want to sit on one of the stone benches along the perimeter of the yard. Al didn't pretend to argue with her and moved toward the closest resting spot, leaning on Tanesa's shoulder the entire way. And yes, we did spend some time talking about our host, but regardless what Bob might think, it was all positive.

After talking about Bob and how lovely his house was, Tanesa said she wanted to get another drink and asked if I would walk with her to the bar. I didn't want to leave her dad, but figured she wasn't asking just to have an escort so I said "sure."

"He's not doing well," she said once we were out of earshot of her dad. "You don't know how thrilled I am that Bob bought the bar. Dad wouldn't say it, but we all knew he was on the verge of bankruptcy. The bar means everything to him and if he lost it that way it'd kill him. I just hope—never mind, I hope he'll be okay."

"But you're worried?" I said, to keep her talking.

"He needs a good checkup, he's getting weaker. I can tell that from how much he's having to lean on me, and how much trouble he's having catching his breath after taking a few steps."

"What does he say?"

"He laughs and blames it all on his arthritis and age *sneaking up* on him. He seems to forget he helped pay my way through medical school. His problem is much worse than age and arthritis, but it'd be easier to get Bob to lose 100 pounds than to get dad to the hospital."

We'd reached the bar and grabbed three more drinks and headed back to Al. His eyes were closed and for a second, I thought maybe he was sick, or worse. He opened his eyes, smiled, and thanked Tanesa as she handed him his drink.

I saw Brian come through the French doors onto the patio. He was dressed in a sports coat and tie and I started to head his way, but Bob, who had been talking to and probably insulting a man and a woman I didn't recognize, cut off their conversation and headed toward the guest of honor. I would let him handle the introductions since I still didn't know many of the guests. Barb was next through the French doors. I wasn't going to let anyone, especially Bob, greet her and excused myself from Al and Tanesa and walked around the fountain to meet Barb. She had on another of her red blouses but wore a white, linen jacket over it. She smiled when she saw me and gave me a hug as she looked around the patio.

"Just like Dude's party," she said with a large dose of sarcasm.

"Hard to tell the two apart," I said.

She stared at the fountain. "I knew Bob was successful, but you never mentioned he lived in a palace with a fountain he must have stolen from a square in Rome."

"If it wasn't for someone who is the most patient woman in the world, Bob's wife, Betty, he'd be just as content living in a three-room shack at the beach, that is if the shack had air conditioning, cable TV, and a refrigerator stocked with thirteen cases of beer."

Barb looked around. "Where is Saint Betty?"

"Bob said something about it taking her longer to put on her face than it took him, and she'd be making a grand entrance at any moment."

"In honor of our host, I'll refrain from commenting on Bob's face."

I nodded, and Bob yelled for everyone to pay attention to what he was about to say. The violinist stopped, the smattering of conversations stopped, and all that could be heard was the fountain. Bob glared at the flowing water like it should have obeyed his command. It refused his order, he faked a smile and introduced the person the fundraiser was created to assist.

Brian thanked Bob and stepped on a nearby stone bench. "First, let me thank Mr. and Mrs. Bob Howard for hosting such a magnificent event." Betty had stepped out on the patio and waved acknowledgment to Brian. The rest of the guests applauded, but not as loud since most of their hands were holding food and drink. Brian gave nearly the identical speech he had shared at Dude's house.

He finished his remarks and Bob tried to step up on the bench and failed. He mumbled something about the bench being too high and "reminded" those gathered that there was a table near the door to the house, and there were several empty envelopes on it, and said, "As you know, our insightful, helpful lawmakers have dictated the maximum amount individuals can donate to Brian Newman's reelection campaign is a mere thousand dollars. I know all of you carry more than that in your wallet and consider it petty cash. So, I expect—I repeat, expect—you to slip your measly thousand bucks in an envelope before you leave."

I wondered how many of us had that much in our pockets. I know I didn't, but I also didn't know the rest of Bob's friends that well, so they could have. There was a smattering of applause, most likely because Bob was finished speaking, and the host drifted back to the couple he was talking with earlier.

Barb and I walked around the edge of the lawn as she admired the weed-free flower beds. She asked if I knew what kind of flowers had such a pleasant aroma. I told her I knew as much about flowers—and trees for that matter—as I did about the founding of Finland. She smiled at my ignorance, something she was learning I had no shortage of, and started to say something. Bob, often oblivious to conversations not involving him, interrupted as he dragged the couple he had been talking with over to us.

"Lovely Barb and, well, not so lovely, Chris, meet Lisa and Jeff Holthouse. They're a husband and wife realtor team who're always trying to steal my listings. Despite their larcenous ways, they're not bad blokes."

In Bob-speak, that meant the middle-aged couple, whose last name seemed quite appropriate for realtors, who I had seen him speaking to earlier, were friends. Lisa nodded to Barb and me, and Jeff held out his hand for each of us to shake.

"Enough bonding," said Bob after I shook Jeff's hand. "Jeff's got something to tell you about the ball of crap who's trying to knock Brian out of office. Well, don't stand there, Jeff, tell him."

Who wouldn't want to be friends with such a charming guy?

Jeff was around six-foot three and leaned toward me and glanced around before speaking. "Lisa and I specialize in high-end properties."

"Try to steal them from me," Bob interjected.

My thought that Bob and Jeff were friends was confirmed when Jeff ignored Bob and continued, "High-end residences, of course, are slower to sell than smaller homes with a much-more palatable price point."

Bob interrupted again, "Cheaper."

"Anyway," Jeff continued, "because they are often on the market so long and are occasionally vacant, we contract with a lawn-care company to do the routine yard work, and if the exterior needs sprucing up, the company adds additional landscaping or cheers up the tired existing landscape."

"We call it exterior staging," Lisa added.

Bob threw up both hands. "Get to the damned point before Chris and Barb fall asleep."

Jeff glared at Bob and turned to me. "For the last three years, we've contracted with Joel Hurt's lawn service company and garden centers. He and I are graduates of the Citadel and met at a cocktail party hosted by the alumni association. Nice fellow, or so I thought."

"Now to the point," Bob said, as he pointed at his watch.

"The point is I met with him last week at a residence on Tradd Street that needed extensive exterior staging. The owners had moved to Arizona and thought their house was worth more than I had estimated it to be worth. They told me to do whatever I needed to do to bring it close to their expectations."

I was ready to join Bob in asking what the point was but waited for Jeff.

Jeff put his arm around Lisa's bare shoulder. "Lisa was with me and after we walked through the property we were cooling down on the lanai when—"

"Cripes, Jeff, it's a damned porch. You gotta dumb-it-down for Chris."

"I know what a lanai is, Bob. Jeff, you were saying."

"I was *trying* to say that Joel started talking to us about running for mayor of Folly Beach. He wanted us to donate to his campaign. But the funny thing was how he started badmouthing the current mayor." Jeff paused and nodded his head toward Brian Newman who was standing near the fountain and talking to Betty. "You have to understand, we barely know Joel, only talked with him at the cocktail party and at six or seven work sites, and he starts mouthing off about the mayor we had never heard of. Thought it was strange and inappropriate."

I waited for Bob to interrupt, but he remained silent, so I said, "What kind of things was he saying?"

Lisa moved a step closer. "Joel said everyone knew Mayor Newman was taking bribes from bar owners, so his police would look the other way about under-age drinking. He said Mayor Newman often played favorites for his friends. Even said Mayor Newman had been a suspect in some horrible murder when he was in the military police and stationed in Europe."

I was shocked. "Are you sure Joel was talking about Brian Newman?"

Jeff answered for Lisa. "No doubt. He kept saying Newman."

I thought back to my meeting with Joel when he praised Brian for the job he had done as mayor and for his stint in the military.

"It didn't bother us too much," Lisa said. "Politicians are always saying terrible things about their opponents, but what surprised me was we didn't live on Folly, couldn't vote in the election, had never heard of your mayor, and barely knew Joel. He wanted our money, but he didn't have to be so, how shall I say it, umm, vile about his opponent." She turned to Jeff.

He took the handoff. "When our friend Bob invited us to this gathering, we wanted to come to learn more about the devil incarnate you have as mayor. Then, as Bob can often do, he screwed up everything when he told us a little about Brian and how good a guy he was. Bob said you were a friend of the mayor and an inquisitive gentleman—"

Bob interrupted, "I said damned nosy, not inquisitive."

Barb didn't say anything but put her arm around my waist.

"Since you were the mayor's friend and *inquisitive*, Bob suggested we tell you what Joel had said."

Lisa looked at her husband. "Jeff, tell him what Joel said about the police chief and those other council members."

"Joel went on to say the police chief wasn't even from the area and the only reason the mayor had hired her as chief was because she would do anything he told her to do—legal or not. Joel said she had to go, before she made even a bigger mockery of law enforcement over there."

"The other elected people," Lisa prompted.

"Two council people, names I don't remember, had to go. Joel said they were nothing but puppets of the mayor."

"Houston and Marc?" I said.

"Think that's them," Jeff said.

Lisa nodded.

Bob held up his empty glass. "Enough boring political talk. We need to get back to the bar. Anything else?"

Jeff and Lisa said that that was it and repeated how unprofessional they thought it was that Joel was telling them what he thought about Brian. Bob had heard enough and herded the couple toward the bar.

Interesting, I thought, and wondered if it had meant anything other than a politician doing what many of them do so well—lying.

19

The rest of the evening was a haze. The roar of water from the fountain mixed with the soothing violin music; conversations from those I didn't know melded into the words from Betty, Bob, and Brian. I told Barb I had spent as much time socializing as I could without pulling out my remaining hair. Al and Tanesa had already departed, so I said my goodbyes to Bob and Betty, and Barb and I headed to the front of the house to ask the smiling valet to collect our vehicles.

Barb asked if I wanted to have a drink on her balcony, I agreed and followed her back to Folly to her condo overlooking the Atlantic and the iconic Folly Pier. On the drive, I mulled over the thought that if Joel had been telling such blatant lies to people who had no interest in the election, what could he be telling people who could make a difference? I tried to push it out of my mind and focus on the lovely evening with a lovely lady.

It was warm on the deck but the breeze off the ocean made it tolerable. Barb said for me to fix each of us a glass of wine while she changed into something more comfortable. My culinary skills were limited, but pouring wine was one of my specialties, perhaps my only one. Moments later, she returned and had changed into tan shorts and a red T-shirt with the cover of *The Great Gatsby* printed on the front.

"You're not going to start competing with Folly's 759 stores that sell T-shirts, are you?" I asked and handed her the wine.

She glanced down at the shirt and said, "No, but because I have a bookstore, a wholesaler from Virginia wants me to. This was a gift, bribe, to get me to carry their famous books and authors' collection. I think *Le Petit Prince* would have a tough time competing with *I'm not awesome; I'm awe every day!*"

I agreed and told her that when it came to selling books, she had little competition. She joked she had nearly as many books in her store as Charles had in his apartment. My friend had more books than a small-town library, so Barb wasn't far off although she was teasing—or so I thought.

We watched the lights from a shrimp boat gently bob in the waves a few hundred yards off shore, and three people carrying flashlights walking on the beach.

"Changing the subject," I said, "what do you make of what those two realtors said about Joel?"

She turned from watching the trio on the beach and stared at me. "I think the guy running against your friend was doing what politicians have done since the beginning of democracy in Athens during the sixth century B.C.: lying about their opposition. Nothing more, nothing less."

"Sixth-century B.C. You learn that in law school?"

"Sixth grade studying Greece. I was interested in history then slept through most things related to it in law school. What's your take?"

"You make a good point, but it galls me. I sat across from Joel the other day and listened to him go on and on about how nice a guy Brian Newman was. He praised his military service, his service as chief of police, and even his work as mayor. He was convincing. Now I hear what he told those realtors, the opposite of what he told me."

Barb nodded. "You're taking it personally. You can't do that with politics. Could your feelings have something to do with learning Joel had been dating Lauren? Could it be clouded because of what her roommate Katelin had said about Joel dating both of them at the same time and her anger toward him?"

I turned my attention to the Folly Pier. "And now Lauren's dead."

"And the only reason to think Joel had anything to do with her death could be because she may, and I emphasize may, have been distraught over their breakup when she killed herself."

"But what if her death wasn't accidental or suicide? What if—"

Barb jerked her head my direction and interrupted, "It wasn't long ago that I heard your friend Bob accuse you of sticking your nose in every death over here regardless if it was caused by someone else's hand or natural causes." Her voice rose with each word. "I thought he was kidding, but I'm beginning to wonder."

"Barb, I'm only trying to see how the pieces fit together. I don't know that they do."

She sighed. "You said Detective Adair was looking into Lauren's alleged OD. You said he was good at his job. You said your friend Cindy was a good police chief and wouldn't let go until she got to the truth. Right?"

I knew I was being backed in a corner. "Yes, it's in good hands. I know Lauren's death looks like an accidental overdose or suicide. Her friend Katelin said she was using again and drinking. I know all that and so do the police."

"Then let them do their job." Her voice was calmer, and she put her hand on my arm. "Chris, I don't know where our relationship is going. I doubt you do either, and that's okay. I'm still not over what my ex did, and it gave me a sour taste in my mouth for men, a taste that I thought would last for a long time." She stopped talking and returned her gaze to the pier.

I understood what she had meant and decided to wait her out and sipped my wine and stared at the pitch-black horizon.

She lowered her voice and said, "You screwed up my plan to avoid the opposite sex. My ex was great at the law; he sucked when it came to listening to me. It took him being hauled off in cuffs for me to realize that he was as devious as hell. So I got here, avoided any interactions that would make it appear that I had any interest in a man, and then that damned body was found behind my store and you stumbled across it and shot my plans to hell."

I nodded.

She continued, "I know I'm not making much sense, but what I'm trying to say is you came along and seemed about as opposite from my ex as one could be. You listened to me. God, I appreciated that." She broke a smile. "And unless you're a much better liar than I think, you're as open and honest as anyone." Her smile faded, and she squeezed my forearm. "Chris, I like you and I'm scared. Bob may have exaggerated, but you have an innate sense of right and wrong and for some reason you feel the need to right as many wrongs as you can. I don't think it was, but if Lauren's death was murder rather than accidental or suicidal, have you thought about what that means?"

I nodded. "It means there's a murderer out there."

"Yes, and the person sitting next to me is wondering if it could be Joel."

"Not really," I said. "It's that he might have a reason to want her out of the way."

"I'm no expert," Barb said, "but murder is a huge leap from breaking up with someone."

"I know. What do you think I should do?"

"At the fundraiser, you learned Joel was a liar, but that's all you learned. If you told that to the police, and to a cop who doesn't know you well, he would probably say, and rightly so, 'So what? What's that have to do with Lauren's death?' You and Cindy are close, so tell her. It may mean nothing, but you'd have told someone, someone in a position to do something about it."

"And then?"

"And then drop it. It's none of your business. You didn't know Lauren."

She was right. In the past when I'd become involved in things that should have been left to the police, the only reason was because I had witnessed the murder or it had touched a friend of mine. Lauren's parents were my neighbors, but I had no allegiance to Brad Burton. But I couldn't shake the feeling something wasn't right.

I put my hand on Barb's shoulder. "I'll tell Cindy what the couple at Bob's said about Joel."

"Good."

What I didn't say was I would drop it.

20

I called Chief LaMond the next morning to share what I had heard at Bob's house. From the voices in the background I knew she wasn't alone.

"Hello, Mr. Landrum, how may I be of assistance?"

She didn't begin with an insult, so I knew she was with someone who didn't know about our friendship and she couldn't speak. So, instead of getting into what I had called about, I asked if she could call me when she had a free minute.

"Sir, I will pass that message along. Thank you for calling."

The mayor had been trying to get his chief to act more *chiefly*, as Cindy had called it. For that brief conversation, I would say Brian was succeeding. *Too bad*, I thought.

Five minutes later the phone rang, and I was glad Cindy had gotten rid of whomever she had been talking with. My happiness was short lived when instead of the chief, Charles was on the other end.

"I need to hear about the party, every detail. I'm on my way to the Dog. Will probably beat you there." He had hung up.

I wondered how difficult it would have been for him to ask if

I could meet him; and I wondered why I had wasted my time wondering about it. Coming from my life in a boring, bureaucratic work, and truth be told, life environment, I must admit Charles's quirks were some of his most endearing qualities. If I'd given it more than a cursory thought, the same applied to most of my friends on this enchanting island. Regardless, this was not the time to think about it, and wouldn't dare tell any of them. Instead of going down that path, I started down the path—more accurately, road—to the Lost Dog Cafe, knowing when I arrived, my friend would scold me for being late. Maybe his quirks weren't that endearing after all.

Charles had secured my favorite booth along the back wall and was in conversation with a distinguished looking, white-haired gentleman at the nearby table. I slid in the booth opposite Charles and he introduced me to Alex, a "young man" from Gravenhurst, Ontario. He quickly went on to say Alex had recently retired and he and his wife Hilary were travelling along the east coast and had been on Folly for the last week. Alex only nodded as Charles rattled on about his *friend* like he'd known him for years. It may have been my imagination, but I thought I could detect a Canadian accent as Charles, the chameleon, went on to say that Hilary had slept in this morning and they were going to visit a couple of Charleston's plantations this afternoon.

Amber stood to the side as Alex said he had to be going and how nice it was to meet Charles, and me, and headed to the exit. She set a mug of coffee in front of me and asked if I was ready to order. I asked her to give me a few minutes.

Charles lifted his Tilley hat that was sitting on the seat next to his cane. "Alex liked my hat."

I smiled, and nodded toward his gold colored, University of Minnesota T-shirt. "What'd he say about that goofy-looking gopher on your shirt?"

"Didn't mention it. He probably sees a lot of these shirts in his neck-of-the-Canadian-woods. Enough about my fine taste in attire, let's hear about last night. Everything about it."

I knew he meant it when he said everything, so I started from arriving and the valet parking. After that I had to tell him the color of the cones that had been reserving space along the street, what the valet had been wearing, and if the house had a single or a double door entry. Finally, he let me tell about entering the house. My coffee was cold before he let me catch my breath, take a sip, and regret not insisting he accompany me to the fundraiser. Amber returned to see if we were ready to order and Charles told her not yet because he didn't want me to slow up my story by sticking food in my mouth. I did manage to nod toward my mug and Amber said she'd get me coffee. I continued my narrative of everything—everything—that had happened at Bob's.

I was telling him in chronological order, so I had shared almost everything when I got to the part about meeting the Holthouses and what they had said about Joel.

Charles raised his hand. "Whoa, let me interrupt a sec. When you're done, I've got something to tell you about Joel."

Interrupt a sec, I thought. He'd already interrupted my story 7,000 times. I said okay and continued sharing up until Barb and I left the party, and changed directions, something my friend had mastered decades ago and that he'd tutored me in.

"What about Joel?"

"I decided to get a laptop computer instead of one of those with that big black box attached. The guy at the store said the black box ones are obsolete and I can take mine everywhere and even can get Internet access with its Y-fly."

"Wi-Fi," I corrected.

"Whatever."

"About Joel?"

"I'm getting there. Be patient."

I didn't think he knew the word *patient*, and I knew he'd never followed it. "Go ahead."

"So, while you were hobnobbing with all the snobs at Bob's and before I spent the, umm, evening, yeah, the evening, with Heather, I was at the Surf Bar doing what you're supposed to do in a place with surf in its name. I was surfing the web from their free Y-fly—Wi-Fi."

"And?" I tried again.

Charles sighed. "John Quincy Adams said, 'Patience and perseverance have a magical effect before which difficulties disappear and obstacles vanish.'"

I stared at him. "Chris Landrum said *what did you learn about Joel*?"

"Chris, you're beginning to sound like me. There's hope for you."

I chose to follow the axiom, regardless who'd said it: Silence is golden.

"Anyway," he said, "Teri came in and asked where Heather was."

"Teri?"

"You know, Teri, the hairdresser at Milli's."

I didn't, but said, "Okay."

"I told her I'd see Heather later and she asked if I could give her a message. Guess what she told me?"

"Do you want me to guess?"

"No. We'd be here all day. She told me she was talking to Katelin yesterday in the shop and she—Katelin, not Teri—said Lauren told her she was afraid of Joel."

"Did she say why, and why did Teri want to tell Heather?"

"She said Heather had been asking everyone who worked at the salon about Lauren. Teri said she figured I had put Heather up to it, because everyone who knows Heather knows I'm a pretty good detective and have helped the police crack some of their most difficult cases." Charles chuckled. "Heather had told them I was so good I'd cracked cases that weren't even cases."

That was the same Heather who thought she was a good country music singer!

"Why was Lauren afraid of Joel?"

"That's where it gets convoluted, if that's the right word. It seems Lauren told it to the other housemate, Candice Richardson. Candice didn't think anything of it but after Lauren turned up dead, she told Katelin, who told Teri, or maybe she told it to one of the other hairdressers who told Teri. Anyway, the story is Joel was angry about Lauren getting back on drugs. And get this about the heartless, selfish Joel, he wasn't upset for Lauren, but was worried her drugging would be bad for his campaign. I guess he's going to hang one of his campaign promises on being anti-drugs."

Amber returned and each of us ordered French toast, my breakfast of choice.

"I'm shocked," she mumbled as she headed to the kitchen.

"Did she say anything else about Lauren or Joel?"

"Nope."

"Was Teri, or Candice, or Katelin implying Joel might have something to do with Lauren's death?"

"After she decided she wanted an order of fries to go with her beer, Teri said she wanted to tell Heather because she knew Heather and I were close. Then she decided I didn't have to tell Heather because the only reason to tell her was, so she could tell me, and since Teri already told me, I didn't have to tell Heather."

It took me a moment to follow the trail of who told who what, and I said, "Do you think Joel could have been responsible for Lauren's death?"

"Good question. Could have been. He could have split with her over the drugs and she decided she didn't have anything to live for and took the overdose. That would make him responsible, I suppose."

"Do you think he could have killed her?"

"Like on purpose?"

I nodded. "Yes, Mr. Detective."

"Since they'd been dating, she would have let him go with her that night." He paused and rubbed his chin. "She was drunk and could have been out of it enough for him to inject her. That could explain why there weren't prints on the door. It's something to think about."

"You're sure Teri didn't say anything else?"

"Other than *another beer barkeep* and a few burps, nope."

"I was going to tell Cindy what I learned from the realtors last night. Think Teri would mind if I give the chief her name? It sounds like what she said was consistent with Joel's character."

"Tell away."

"How is Heather?"

I had wanted to ask earlier, but he was too intent on hearing about the fundraiser.

"To be honest, I don't know."

Breakfast arrived, and Charles took two quick bites before he pointed his fork at me and started to say something, but instead shook his head and looked down at his plate.

"You don't know?" I said, prompting him.

He took a bite, rubbed his forehead, and said, "We had a good time last night. She brought up a couple of funny things that happened after we moved to Nashville. We laughed at some stuff she couldn't kid about when it happened. She talked about the singing buddies she met at her gigs at the Bluebird Cafe and that she missed them but was still able to laugh about not being there." He hesitated. "Yeah, we had a good time."

The look on his face told me there was more. "But?"

He moved his head from side to side. "Can't put my pinkie on it. There's something she's not telling me. She says she's glad we moved back. She says she's enjoying working at Milli's. She says she's happy that she can get back to singin' at open-mic night at Cal's. Umm, don't know what it is. I don't. Just a feeling."

Charles, along with being one of the quirkiest people I know, was also one of the most perceptive. He managed to see through the smokescreen that many people throw up when they're trying to mask their feelings. He recognized insecurities in others that most of us can't see and bolstered their positives. He could bring out good traits in others even if they couldn't see them in themselves. So, when he said it was just a feeling he had about Heather, I knew he was right. What did surprise me was he couldn't define it.

"Help me understand, what gives you the impression there's something she's not telling you?"

Charles looked around the crowded room and toward the outside door. I followed his gaze and didn't notice anything unusual. There were several people waiting for tables, but that was not unusual this time of day. My friend dropped his fork on the plate, waved for Amber to bring the check, and said, "Let's get out of here."

I paid and followed him out the door. He ignored the group milling around and walked past two large dogs drinking out of a water bowl provided by the restaurant. I knew something was wrong when Charles didn't bend down to let the dogs welcome him with slobbery licks—kisses.

2 1

I followed Charles across Center Street to the Folly River Park where he flopped down on a picnic table under the small covered pavilion. Unlike the area around the restaurant, the park was deserted, and Charles stared at the steady stream of traffic on the bridge. Two good-sized fishing boats motored past on their way upstream. The temperature had to be approaching ninety and the shade felt good on my aging bones.

Charles finally turned towards me. "You know how off-the-wall Heather is. She blurts out whatever's on her mind regardless how it may be taken." He chuckled. "She's stuck her foot in her mouth so often that if she was a cow she'd have hoof-in-mouth disease."

I nodded and smiled. "I'll be sure to tell her you don't think she's a cow."

"Ha, ha," he said and turned serious. "There've been more and more spells when she won't say anything; stretches of time that before she'd fill with who knows what. Silence is something she'd never taken kindly to. Chris, she gets this look in her eyes like she's staring into another world. She says she's a psychic,

408

but before when she'd go into psychic mode she didn't stare that weird. I don't know what's going on."

"The other day you said she hadn't met with the counselor. Has she seen him yet?"

"Funny you asked. Last night when I was trying to figure out what was wrong, I asked the same thing. She would've reacted better if I'd asked her to go in the kitchen and slice her thumb off with a steak knife."

"Sorry. Does that mean she hasn't talked to the counselor?"

Charles looked at the ceiling of the gazebo. "Don't recall her saying no, but she left the room and slammed the door so hard I thought it'd knock the paint off the wall. I may've missed her answer."

"Sounds like no," I said and patted him on the shoulder.

Charles turned and looked toward Center Street. "Speaking of the devil."

We weren't, but with Charles it didn't matter. I looked in the direction he was facing and saw Chief LaMond's unmarked car parked in a parking spot parallel to the road. Cindy walked our way.

Charles said, "Howdy, Chief. What brings you out on such a lovely day?"

"Got a complaint about a couple of old, really old, farts hanging out and doing no-telling-what in the park. Figured I needed to earn my astronomical salary paid by the good citizens like the one who complained and came to check it out."

She stifled a smile, so I said, "You made that up."

"Yep, especially the astronomical salary part. I was riding by and saw you and thought there was no time like the present to share a nugget of news."

I patted to the empty space on the bench. "Join us."

"Thought you'd never ask." She pointed toward town. "You get kicked out of a restaurant or a store?"

"Us, kicked out," Charles said in mock exasperation. "We

were at the Dog and they begged me to stay to add some class to the joint, but Chris insisted we come over here, so we could enjoy the sweltering, miserable heat."

Cindy rolled her eyes. "Then let me suck some of that enjoyment out of your day. Got off the phone about an hour ago with Detective Adair. Chris, I told him what you'd said about Joel and Kristin."

Charles interrupted, "What'd he say?"

"He said he didn't see how that changed anything. Said as far as he was concerned, the case was closed. He was confident Lauren had accidentally or intentionally overdosed. Said there's no way to tell which it was."

I was surprised. "It didn't matter that Joel had a reason for her death?"

Cindy watched a beer truck cross the bridge and turned to me. "Guys, I'm as frustrated as you are, but the case is with the Sheriff's office and I'm stuck with their conclusion. But tell you what, if you hear anything else, let me know. No guarantees that it'll do any good, but I'll try."

I said we would. She stood and said, "Gotta go stir up some crap in my office. The guys will think I'm goofing off if I'm not on their case about something. The mayor says it's superior administrative oversight."

We watched her pull back in traffic and Charles turned to me. "Why didn't you tell her what Katelin said to Candice, who told Teri, who told me?"

"And then you told me, and now wanted me to tell Cindy."

He nodded.

"I might later, but for now that's too many *who tolds* to hit Cindy with."

Charles shrugged. "If you say so. I've got to make a delivery for the surf shop, so I'll leave you here to ponder ... well, to ponder whatever you want to ponder."

He grabbed his cane and left me to ponder.

It was hot, humid, and the sun was out at full force, so I decided the shade of the pavilion was as good a place to ponder as any. At least, it beat walking anywhere.

I was amazed Charles didn't know what was going on with Heather. They were a perfect couple, or as close to perfect as a couple could be in this imperfect world. They were quirky beyond definition. They both marched to the beat of a different drummer, or guitar in Heather's case. They were kinder than ninety-nine percent of the people I'd ever met, and on the surface, it appeared their main interest was making the other one happy. I vacillated between telling myself that whatever was bothering her was none of my business and trying to think of what I could do to help them through whatever was going on.

All I accomplished by trying to figure it out was giving myself a headache, so I tried thinking about something else. What jumped to the forefront was Lauren and what had happened. Why was her death bugging me? The police were convinced it was either accidental or a suicide. Why couldn't I let it go at that? Since I had been on Folly, I had been involved in several murders. Was I beginning to see all deaths as being nefarious? There was no evidence of foul play, so why was it still on my mind. Sure, the lack of fingerprints on the passenger's door could seem suspicious, but there were logical explanations. Was Joel angry enough to want her dead? Possible, but it was also possible—maybe even probable—that I was looking at him through bias-tinted glasses. He was running against a friend and that could be clouding my opinion.

I took a deep breath, shook a couple of random thoughts out of my head, leaned back against the picnic table, and watched three trucks and a scooter cross the bridge. When I had gotten dragged into previous murder cases it was because of one of two reasons: I was nearby when the death occurred, or the murder involved one or more of my friends. So why now? I never knew or met Lauren Craft, and the only connection between her and someone I did know, was her father. Technically Brad and Hazel Burton were next door neighbors, so there could have been a friendship connection, but Brad and I were as far from being friends as were a worm and a catfish. There was no reason for me to get involved. No, not a single reason.

So why was I having to convince myself?

I HEADED HOME. After two blocks, I realized how wise I had been to stay under the shade provided by the park's shelter. Two more blocks and sweat was running down my face. I approached my house and saw Brad Burton sitting on his front step; a sight I hadn't seen since he had lived there. It was even stranger when he saw me approaching, smiled, and waved. For a moment I thought I was hallucinating from the heat. I returned his gesture and walked past my house to his yard.

Brad stood and shook my hand. I apologized for it being sweaty. He said his was too and asked if I wanted to join him. The front of his house shaded us from direct sunlight and I sat next to him. I didn't know what to say so I asked him how he was doing and realized how stupid a question it was. He had lost his only child, and by being nice to me indicated something was wrong with him. He glanced over at me and I imagined him saying something like, "How do you think I feel, you idiot?"

He started to speak, thought better of it, and lowered his head. I watched a squirrel foraging around in the side yard, before Brad finally said, "Chris, I've spent my entire professional life staring at dead bodies. After so long, I became calloused to the sight, smell, and revulsion. I had to do that, or I couldn't do what I was paid to do; find the person responsible and bring justice and some small degree of closure to the families of the deceased. At first, I took the images of the horrible transgressions home with me. I'm afraid I burdened Hazel with my gut-wrenching feelings. She was an angel to put up with it; nearly didn't … umm, well, I finally was able to block it out." He hesitated, watched a plumbing truck roll by, and again lowered his head.

I waited in awkward silence.

"I thought I could handle anything, but Chris, I was wrong, damned wrong." He hesitated again. "Lauren was such a sweet little kid. When I came home from work before she knew or could understand what I did for a living, she'd ask me how my day was. I'd smile, hoped she didn't smell death on my clothes, and told her I was great now. Those days became fewer and fewer. I was working all hours, but even then, and after she knew what my job entailed, she would still break out in a big smile, and ask about my day." He shook his head. "Most of the time I lied and said, 'great.' She was so sweet."

"It's got to be terrible for you and Hazel."

"My heart pained for her when she married Sebastian Craft. She was looking for someone who could be there when she needed him; something I couldn't do for her. I knew it was a mistake. I never felt good about him, but Lauren couldn't see it. I hold him responsible for her spiral into drink and drugs." He shook his head. "I'm just as responsible. Anyway, she ended the abysmal marriage, but couldn't end the debilitating habits that came with it. Chris, I thought we could help her by moving here. I thought we had. God, I was wrong, horribly wrong."

"You did what you could."

"I tried, and so did her roommates."

"How well do you know Katelin and Candice?"

"I only met them a couple of times when Lauren was … before her death. She spoke highly of them and they seemed like nice gals. Yesterday I went to the house they rented to pick up Lauren's possessions." He put his head down and put a hand on each side of his head. I waited silently. "Umm, Katelin was there and talked a lot about Lauren. She didn't say it, she talked around it, but I had the impression Katelin knew Lauren was back on drugs. I didn't want to press her."

"Did you find anything in Lauren's things to give you that impression?"

He raised his head and turned to me. "Chris, I've spent countless hours rooting through people's stuff, both at murder scenes and when searching houses of suspects. I know where to look and what to look for. There wasn't anything there, not a thing. But, that doesn't mean much." He shook his head. "I'll tell you what I did find. There were copies of online job applications from several stores in Charleston, and a couple of handwritten ones for places over here. They were recent, two were filled out the day before she … left us. She was hot and heavy on a job search." He looked at me, but with the such intensity that he was staring through me. "I can't fathom how she turned from hope to hopelessness that quick."

"How well did you know her boyfriend, Joel Hurt?"

"Hardly at all. He seemed a lot nicer than that shithead she was married to." Brad bit his lower lip and wiped perspiration off his brow. "I only met him once. I ran into him and Lauren in Bert's. He seemed okay and told me that meeting Lauren was the best thing that'd happened to him since he moved here."

I knew what I'd learned on the Internet, and wondered what Brad knew about his past. "Did he say where he'd moved here from?"

"No. I asked him, and he laughed and said something like, 'Somewhere that's not as nice as Folly.' I started to push him, but Lauren said they had to get going, they were late to something, and rushed out."

A motorcycle roared past and we watched it speed toward the Washout. Now would be as good a time as any to broach a delicate topic. "Brad, is it possible Lauren didn't take her own life?"

"Why would you say that?"

"Simply curious."

"Chris, there's nothing that makes me think that. And remember, I'm a retired homicide cop." He hesitated and stared at the road where the motorcycle had been seconds earlier. "Sorry, I can't go down that path. It's over. My little girl died … died of an accidental overdose."

Brad looked around, patted his knee, and said he'd better be getting inside. Our relationship was so precarious that I wasn't comfortable pushing him somewhere he didn't want to go. I told him it was nice talking to him, that again I was sorry about Lauren. I told him to let me know if he needed anything. I knew he wouldn't.

2 2

The next morning began as a cool wave passed through the Lowcountry. The temperatures were still going to be in the eighties, but the humidity levels dropped. Over the years, I made half-hearted attempts to get in better shape, and while most failed, I convinced myself that walking was my best route to success. Anything more strenuous seemed like work, misery, and for me, unsustainable. Walking without direction also struck me as nonproductive, so most of my walks occurred on my way to or from restaurants where I usually defeated the benefits of walking by eating unhealthy foods. I'd convinced myself that the walks counteracted the evils of my diet. Exercise was one of my greatest weaknesses; the art of rationalizing was near the top of my strengths.

I was thinking about what to order and nearly ran into Dude who was dressed, well, dressed like Dude, carrying the latest issue of *Astronomy* magazine, and standing in front of the surf shop.

"Whoa, Chrisster. Where be daydreamin' off to?"

"The Dog."

"Boss! Birds of a feather, think like together. Me boogie with you."

Correcting Dude's expression would be as productive as trying to teach his dog Pluto to learn Konkahi, so I said, "I'd be honored."

He pointed the magazine toward the restaurant and skipped along beside me. On the three block walk he shared the latest updates about Dude's other favorite Pluto, the dwarf planet, from an article he'd read in the magazine, and about the latest tricks that his much smaller, and a zillion miles closer Pluto had learned. We reached the restaurant, and I thought how Dude was the perfect companion for me to get my mind off Brad and Lauren.

Amber was standing on the patio and asked if we wanted to sit outside or inside. Dude said, "Wherever the Amberster say."

The Amberst…., umm, Amber, pointed to a table she had finished cleaning and Dude and I moved to the vacant table.

Amber pet Dude on his long, stringy hair, and said, "How come you brought this old dog with you. Where's Pluto, the cute one?"

Dude shook his head, sat down, and glanced at me on the other side of the table. "Stray. Felt sorry. So, here he be."

Maybe I would have been better off thinking about Brad and Lauren. I smiled and told Amber it was good to see her too. She kissed the top of my balding head and said she would return with menus.

Dude watched Amber head inside and turned to me. "You be jabberin' with Kategal?"

"Katelin, Lauren's housemate?"

"That's what me said."

Close, and said, "Not recently. Why?"

"Thought you be detectin'. Fishin' for clues."

"Charles is the detective, remember?"

"Okeedokee, me not report what the Kategal said."

"You win. What did Katelin say?"

Dude grinned. "See, you be detectin'." He nodded like he'd discovered the secret of removing wrinkles. "The Kategal likes to gander in surf shop—not buy, just gander. She be in last daytime."

"Yesterday?"

"What me said. She be rantin' about her dead roomie. She be pissed."

"What'd she say?"

"Details not clear. Something about always discord in house. Temper tantrums. Two chicks pullin' at dirt guy's arms."

Where was Charles my Dude Translator when I needed him? So, I had to resort to guesses. "Lauren and Katelin were fighting about Joel Hurt?"

He nodded and probably wanted to say, *What me said,* but instead said, "The dirt guy dumped Kategal like load of monkey manure. He be Superglued to dead gal before Kategal knew she be dumpee."

Amber returned with menus and we quickly glanced at them and ordered Chicken salad croissants. Amber mumbled something about my order almost being healthy. I told her I'd get over it, and she left smiling.

"Dude, did Katelin say anything else about Lauren or Joel?"

Dude rubbed the stubble on his chin. "Squawked some about drugs, but drug words go in one auditory organ and wiggle out other." He patted his left ear, so I would know which auditory organ he was referring to.

As far as I could tell, much of Dude's past was filled with voids. If I were a wagering person, I'd lay a few bucks on him having more than a passing encounter with the drug culture of the 1960s. During the time I'd known him, he had the reputation as someone who could bridge the gap between the bohemian residents, surfers, and the more well-heeled citizens and law enforcement.

"Do you know the third housemate, Candice Richardson?"

"She be petite Barbie." Dude pointed at his eyes and out the door. "She be with other two once, she and me never shared words." He hesitated and rubbed his chin. "Heard something from Kategal. She—Kategal, not Candygirl—say third roomer never at house. Kategal say that's why Candygirl be good housemate. Three pay rent, two share air."

"Did Katelin ever say anything about Lauren being depressed or being back on drugs?"

"Not recallin' anything."

"Know anything about Joel Hurt?"

"Other than two-timing two chicks?"

"Yes."

"Got more faces than Lernaean Hydra."

"The Greek water monster with many heads?" At some point, I must have paid attention in school.

Dude rolled his eyes. "How many other Hydras you know?"

"Good point. Do you say that because of some of his comments about our mayor or about Lauren and Katelin?"

"All."

"Is that everything you know about Joel?"

"He and his waterfowl friend moved here mucho full-moons ago."

Wayne Swan was the first waterfowl that came to mind, mainly because I had remembered that Joel had said he and Wayne went way back. "Wayne Swan, his campaign manager?"

"You know more waterfowl than you know Hydras?"

Some comments deserve nothing more than being ignored. Our food arrived, and Dude took two bites and started telling me something about the next solar eclipse. He was finished talking about dead citizens, politicians, waterfowl, and multi-faced mythical creatures. I also had stopped listening until he said that the third roommate, Candice Richardson, Candygirl in Dudes-peak, had worked for Joel and had been fired from one of Joel's garden centers. At least that was my understanding of what Dude had said. He used fewer than half that many words, so something could have been lost in translation.

"Anyone say she was fired?"

"Official reason, stealin'."

My understanding was she now worked for a real estate office in Charleston. If that was the reason for her termination, I was surprised she got the new job.

"Dude, you said official reason. Do you know that it was for something else?"

He nodded. "Rumor."

I nodded. "What?"

"Story spread like PB & Jelly on bread that she caught dirt man plantin' bod part where not belong, if you get my drift."

I did, and if true, could be how she got a positive reference for her next job. I doubted Joel, the dirt man, would have shared the real reason with someone asking for a reference. It also struck me that if mayoral candidate Joel Hurt was sincere about getting elected, he would have a reason for all three of the women to be silenced—one way or the other.

Instead of elaborating, Dude started talking about the dwarf planet Pluto, a topic he spent more time on than the rest of the Folly's citizens combined. I doubted he could shed more light on Lauren's death, but before I could ask him, the phone rang.

Bob Howard's voice bellowed out of the speaker. "Here's your deal of a lifetime. Be at Al's at one thirty tomorrow afternoon and I—yes I—will buy you lunch. And, don't call the television stations to tell them about this historic event. If they show up, I'll say *me buy, shit no! Where'd you hear that damned rumor?*"

Bob's offer to buy was historic. I didn't need Heather's psychic powers, or Charles's detective skills to know that there was no such thing as a free lunch waiting for me at Al's.

I found a vacant parking spot much closer than on my last visit and stepped from blinding sunlight into blinding dark with minimal illumination coming from rays of sun sneaking over the top half of the front window. The lower half was painted black to keep nosy eyes from staring in the building. Budweiser neon signs provided a bit more light and a jukebox that appeared as old as the eighty-year-old proprietor, added a glimmer of colorful light to the corner. The lunch crowd had either come and gone or hadn't come at all. The bar was two diners shy of empty, and I was one of the two.

My first surprise was when I saw Al beside the front door sitting in a chair that belonged to the nearest dining table. He saw me enter, grinned, and leaned forward and used his hands to push himself out of the chair. Other than his visits to our table when the bar had few or no other patrons, I had never seen Al seated. And, even in the poor lighting, he looked worse than he had at the fundraiser. From the jukebox Jerry Lee Lewis was wailing about someone shaking his nerves and rattling his brain, so it was difficult to hear what Al had said, but words weren't needed as he wrapped his emaciated arms around me and squeezed.

I told him it was good to see him and started to say *you're looking good*, but he would have known I was lying. He looked horrible.

He leaned closer, so I could hear and said, "Thank the good lord you're here. Fatso's been asking every five minutes why you weren't here yet."

I glanced at Bob—Fatso—and leaned closer to Al. "He told me to come at one-thirty. Has he been talking to my buddy Charles?"

Al smiled. His coffee-stained teeth were illuminated by the neon signs. "Charles, the thirty minutes early to be on time, buddy?"

I said, "Good memory," and patted him on the back.

"Get on over there to shut him up," Al said. "If I had any customers he'd be running them off."

Jerry Lee Lewis finished his piano riff, but Bob's voice would have been heard over it if it was still playing, "Welcome fine customer! Come join me."

"Extreme Mouth Makeover," Al said as he shook his head and lowered himself back in the chair. "Bob says his charm will bring in the customers by the boatload."

Lawrence, Al's part-time cook, laughed and asked if I wanted a cheeseburger. I told him of course and headed to the table. Bob was stuffed into his side of the booth, a normal sight, but what was not normal was a two-by-four-inch brass plate screwed into the top of the table facing the room and Bob holding a screwdriver—the tool, not the drink.

"What are you screwing up now?" I said before I was close enough to read what had been inscribed on the brass addition.

Bob said, "My first action to add a touch of class to this dump."

I slid into the other side of the table, no simple task because

Bob's ample stomach had pushed the table to my side of the booth. I looked down at the shiny plate and read: *BOB'S BOOTH. WARNING: Sit at your own risk.*

I smiled. "Class?"

Bob followed my eyes. "You're not making fun of the person who's buying your lunch, are you?"

I continued to smile. "Of course, I am, Bob. I didn't think you were going to be here until later."

"Don't remind me," he said. "Was supposed to show a frou-frou couple a three-million-dollar shanty south of Broad." Some of Charleston's most majestic homes were in the area between Broad Street and the Battery. "They called a little while ago and said they were going to 'reassign their resources to other opportunities,' whatever the hell that meant. If you ask me, which I'm sure you were about to do, they couldn't afford the house and probably had to reassign their resources to buying food to feed their two gigantic Mastiffs."

I stifled a smile and said, "Sorry."

"They damned sure are." Bob turned toward the grill. "Where in the hell's this damned ingrate's food? Snap, snap!"

Tanya Tucker's "Delta Dawn" drowned out normal conversation, but the cook uttered what appeared to be a string of profanities.

To try to prevent an employee revolt, I said, "So what's up?"

Bob harrumphed in the direction of the cook and turned to me. "Why can't I invite a friend to lunch? Why does it always have to be something?"

"Could be because in the eight years I've known you, you've never offered to buy me lunch, or anything else, for that matter."

Bob shrugged. "To quote that song written in 1964—which happened to be the last year any good music was written—by Bobby Dylan, "The Times They Are a-Changin'.""

Bobby Dylan, I thought, and showing more maturity than I possessed, I repeated, "So what's up?"

Bob pointed his thumb at Al who was slumped down in the chair by the door. "Anything look normal about that?"

"I was surprised to see him there when I came in. Is he okay?"

Lawrence, who was a couple of decades younger than Al, delivered my cheeseburger and glass of chardonnay and asked "Mr. Howard" if he needed anything. Bob told him he was Bob and not Mr. Howard and not to forget it. He also requested—demanded—another beer. Lawrence faked a smile at his new boss and scooted away.

Bob watched me take a bite and said, "Al called last night to talk about bar business, something about ordering from another vendor and an electrical issue with that doohickey that cooks the fries."

And I thought Bob wasn't an expert on owning a bar. "And?"

"Then he started repeating himself, but before that, he asked me something I had answered a few seconds earlier. The old man tried to laugh it off and said that he was testing to see if I remembered what I had told him. Chris, he laughed, but there wasn't a damned thing funny about it." Bob glanced back toward Al. "He lost his train of thought; not once, but several times. He started talking about something that happened in here in 1957 like it was last week, and he—"

"You talking about me?" Al said as he leaned against the back of a chair at the next table.

I moved over and waved for him to join us.

"Hell yes," Bob said. "Chris was saying you looked like you just stepped out of a coffin. I told him to stop making fun of you." He shook his head. "You know how cruel some white customers can be—especially those young whippersnappers like Chris."

Al flopped down on the seat, wiped sweat off his forehead with a bar towel, and stared at Bob. "Don't know about customers, but cruel's talking too kindly about a white bar owner."

I smiled and kept my mouth shut, something Bob couldn't find it in his DNA to do. "That's no way to talk to your good buddy and person who singlehandedly will save this decrepit old bar and its more than decrepit former owner."

Al looked at the brass plate and at me. "Chris," he said and pointed an arthritis ravaged finger at Bob and at himself, "if there's only one thing this old, shriveled up, bar man can teach you, it's that friends, not the fair-weather kind who are with you when things are going well, and dump you like chewed gum when things go sour, but true friends will stick with you no matter what. They'll stand behind you and keep you from falling; they'll go to the ends of the earth to help you in your time of need. They'll do anything for you, yes they will."

Bob interrupted, "Get to the point, old man. The boy's burger is getting cold while he's waiting with bated breath for whatever you're trying to say."

Al continued to look at me and waved his hand at Bob like he would shew a fly. "I'm nearly there, Chris. The point is that cranky curmudgeon over there is the best friend this old man's ever had. Lord knows why; I sure don't. But anyway, he is."

In a move uncharacteristic for Bob, he reached across the table and touched Al's hand. Tom T. Hall's "Old Dogs, Children, and Watermelon Wine" flowed from the jukebox. And I felt like I was infringing on one of the most poignant moments in Bob's long life. Neither man spoke until the mood was broken when three boisterous middle-aged men entered the bar.

Al looked their way and said, "Done shirking my greeting duties. Good luck, Chris, with putting up with the tub of lard."

Bob watched Al head to the door. "And that's my friendly greeter."

I turned back to my cooling cheeseburger and Bob returned

to his no-telling-what-number beer, when I heard a chair hitting the floor and Lawrence scream, "Oh shit!"

Bob moved quicker than I had ever seen him move. He was out of the booth, slammed two chairs out of his way, and was standing beside the prone shape of Al on the floor. One of the three men who had entered was bent down and checking for a pulse. He calmly looked up and told Lawrence he was a doctor and to call 911.

I grabbed a handful of bar towels and the doctor put them under Al's head. "Is he alive?" I asked.

The doctor ignored me and started CPR. My friend's eyes were closed, and I couldn't see signs of life. Bob stood back and muttered a plethora of profanities. I felt helpless. Had Charleston lost a true hero, and had I lost another friend?

2 4

The doctor ordered us to step back and give Al air as he continued to press on his chest. Bob had given the doc a dirty look and I was afraid he was going to ignore the order and move closer, but instead he nodded and plopped down on a nearby chair. The two men who had accompanied the doctor had gone out front to make sure the ambulance found us, and Lawrence had turned on the overhead lights giving the doctor a better view of Al. It was the first time that I'd seen the inside of the bar with the lights on. It had always looked tired and rundown; now it looked exhausted and on its last legs. Lawrence had moved behind the bar and bowed his head. I didn't know if Lawrence was praying, but I was.

It only took a few minutes for the ambulance to rush the three blocks from the hospital, but it seemed like an eternity. Two paramedics walked in the room. They appeared confident, listened to what the doctor who had been administering CPR said, and focused their attention to Al. The doctor stepped aside and one of the paramedics took over the CPR. The other paramedic leaned over Al's head, but his body blocked my view, so I couldn't see what he was doing. Regardless, I felt Al was in good hands; all irrelevant if he was no longer with us.

It was then that I glanced over at Bob at the table beside me. His head was resting on the table and his breath was coming in gasps.

I scooted my chair over to his table. "Bob, are you okay?"

He didn't answer, and I moved around to see his face. Sweat was rolling down his face, his arms were shaking, and in the harsh fluorescent light he looked whiter than a bar of soap, and his skin looked as waxy.

I yelled to the doctor who was standing beside the paramedic administering CPR. He glanced over, took a quick look down at Al, and rushed to Bob's table. Bob had opened his eyes and mumbled, "I need air ... air." He tried to raise his head, but it fell back to the table. I moved back from the table and the doc took my place. He leaned close to Bob and asked if my friend could hear him. Bob said yes, and the doc asked him what he was feeling.

I closed my eyes, took a deep breath, and felt helpless. I was surprised to see Lawrence at my side offering me a glass of water. His hands trembled as he handed the glass to me and he never took his eyes off Al, still unmoving on the floor.

I don't know who called them, but a second set of paramedics burst through the door. One of them pushed a gurney and stopped at Al and the second one came over to Bob, conferred with the doc, and leaned down to talk to Bob. I wasn't close enough to hear what was being said, but it looked like Bob was responding to the questions; a good sign, I assumed. I walked across the room to be closer to Al and heard one of the paramedics say they needed to get him to the hospital stat.

I may have been fooling myself, but I took that as a good sign—he's alive. But, he hadn't moved, and his eyes were closed as they were loading him on the stretcher and wheeled him out the door. I turned back to Bob and watched the EMT take his blood pressure and continued to ask him questions. Bob was becoming more animated.

He jerked his head back and looked over to where Al had been. "Where's Al? Is he okay?"

The paramedic told him Al was on the way to the hospital, he was in good hands, and Bob needed to stay calm for them to figure out what was wrong with him. Bob mumbled a profanity. I smiled and thought he was getting back to normal. Bob became more agitated when the paramedic said they were going to take him to the hospital. Bob insisted there was nothing wrong and he was just upset about his friend.

"That may be, sir, but we've got to check you out. Keep taking deep breaths and we'll wheel another gurney in and give you a ride to the hospital."

I expected an expletive-filled explosion, but instead Bob lowered his head to the table and closed his eyes. Maybe his condition was worse than I had thought. Bob's gurney arrived, and the two paramedics maneuvered it around to get Bob's large body situated on it and to wheel him out. Lawrence and I moved three tables out of the way so they could get Bob to the ambulance.

I watched the ambulance as its siren stopped traffic as it made a U-turn and headed to the hospital. I wanted to rush to the ER but from experience with some of my friends who had made similar trips, knew it would have been fruitless. It would be a while before anything was known, or at least before the medical staff told me anything. The doc and his two friends were sitting at one of the tables and Lawrence was wandering through the room with a lost look on his face.

I thanked the good Samaritan for everything he had done. He gave me a sad smile and said, "All I wanted was a cheeseburger."

Lawrence heard him, hurried to the table, and asked what everyone wanted. He now had a purpose, something he could do. I didn't know if the men worried about how Lawrence would fix their food in his current state of mind or were no longer hungry, but two of them said they didn't need anything and the doc said they had a meeting to get to. Before they left, I asked the doctor how he thought Al and Bob were.

He nodded toward the table where Bob had been. "I think he had a panic attack. His vitals were normal—normal for an over-weight diabetic. He'll probably be okay. The other gentleman is another story. Don't take this as gospel. I didn't have enough time or information to know for sure, but he was barely holding on when he left. Sorry."

Lawrence moved beside me and heard the prognostication. "Oh Lord, please help Al. He's such a dear sweet man. God, he's lived your wishes. Please help him."

I seconded that and realized I should contact someone from Al's family and Bob's wife, Betty. I also realized Tanesa, an ER doctor at the hospital, was the only member of Al's family that I knew. She had given me her cell number a couple of years ago; I was glad, since I doubted Lawrence, in his state of shock, would have been able to find it.

I was afraid Tanesa wasn't going to answer and had almost hung up when she answered. She was off work for a couple of days but said she'd head to the hospital and would be there in fifteen minutes.

I wasn't as lucky with Bob's wife. After six rings, I got Bob's cheerful, warm, friendly voice mail message that said: *What? If you haven't figured it out, we're not here. Leave a message and we might call you back.* I left a message for her to call me and kicked myself I didn't have her cell number.

Lawrence asked if I needed anything. I was tempted to say a liter or two of wine, but instead said I was fine. The part-time chef and I were the only two left in Al's and Lawrence stood behind the bar and stared at the door like he was expecting Al to walk through it. I moved to Bob's table and looked at the brass nameplate. I hadn't done anything but felt exhausted. My legs were weak as I plopped down in the booth. The jukebox was silent, and I missed the bickering between Bob and Al about the musical selections—Motown versus country. Al asking Bob if he liked any music created since Kennedy was president; Bob responding by asking Al if he liked any singers who had skin lighter than his. I smiled thinking how Al had salted the jukebox with songs only Bob would like and the harassment he had endured from most of his African-American customers.

I also remembered the countless words of wisdom that flowed from the bar owner; wisdom he hadn't gotten from formal schooling, for he had little, but from his many years of living in a world that many of us couldn't endure and the sacrifices he had made for the nine children he and his wife had adopted before her death several years ago.

And I thought about what Al had said only a little while earlier about friends and how the true ones would do anything for you. Bob and Al, each from a different world, were perfect examples of that. I hoped I could be that good of a friend to my friends. I was never big on symbolism, but as I sat and listened to silence coming from Al's jukebox, I prayed that wasn't telling me Al would never be punching in another song—Motown or country.

I turned my head, so Lawrence couldn't see the tears streaming down my cheek.

25

Tanesa was waiting for me as I entered the hospital. She forced a smile and motioned for me to follow her to an empty row of seats off the side of the packed lobby.

"Is your dad—"

She squeezed my arm. "He's alive." She hesitated, and then continued, "Probably a heart attack, but with his declining health it could be complicated with any number of things. His vitals are sucking wind."

I didn't know what to say other than I was sorry.

Al's daughter stared at the double doors that led to the bowels of the hospital. She gave a slight nod and mumbled, "There's always hope." She looked up at me. "Chris, if that doctor hadn't been in the bar, we wouldn't be having this conversation." She grinned. "Dad always said he'd take luck any day over something going right just because people tried to do their best. It was pure luck that man was there."

I asked if she'd seen him. She said briefly but was moved out of the medical team's way. She knew she was too close to the patient to be much help.

"He's a stubborn man," I said. "If anyone can make it, your dad can."

She tilted her head in my direction. "Stubborn, you're not kidding, but with everything else going wrong with his aging body, stubbornness may not be enough." She snapped her fingers. "His—your—friend Bob Howard's in much better condition. There's nothing wrong with his heart." She hesitated and smiled. "Other than dad saying that he doesn't have one. Anyway, it was a panic attack. They're hanging on to him for another hour or so then kicking him out. He'll be fine."

I told her I was thankful for that, and I felt sorry for whoever was back there having to deal with him. She looked back at the double doors and chuckled. "Yeah, he told the poor nurse who was trying to take his blood pressure to 'take that damned squeezy thing off my arm and get the hell back to saving his good friend's life.'"

I smiled. "I'm surprised they haven't thrown him out."

"Folks back there are used to insults, abuse, and malcontents who frequent the ER. Bob'll fit right in. Has anyone called his wife?"

I told her I couldn't reach her and didn't have her cell phone number. She said she'd go back and see if Bob had called her or wanted me to. I suspected Tanesa wanted to see if there was anything new to report on Al.

She was gone longer than I had hoped, when I heard him before I saw him.

"I'll break his scrawny neck if he bothers Betty. Push faster!"

The doors to the treatment area swung open and out came a wheelchair being pushed by Tanesa and stuffed with the ample rear end of Bob. He glared at me. "Does Betty know I'm here?"

I returned his glare. "Not that I know of. What are you doing out here?"

"Hospitals are for sick people. I'm as healthy as a horse."

Substitute jackass, I thought. "So, they kicked you out?"

Before Bob responded, Tanesa said, "They wanted to keep him a couple more hours, but your friend here told them that unless they let him walk, roll, out of here in the next ten minutes he was going to call the cops and report he'd been kidnapped."

Bob uttered a profanity and repeated, "Hospitals are for sick people." He started to stand, but slowly lowered himself back in the wheelchair, took a deep breath, and said, "Now are you going to take me to my car or not?"

"Not," I said. "If I take you anywhere other than the psych ward, it'll be to your house. Take it or leave it."

Bob looked over his shoulder at Tanesa who was standing behind him and said, "See the insolence I have to put up with." He turned to me. "What in the hell are you waiting for? Get your car so sweetie pie here can wheel me to the door."

Sweetie pie, Tanesa, should have smacked him, but instead ruffled his already disarranged hair and kissed him on the cheek. Ten minutes later, I had helped Bob in the front seat and started to close the door. He held up his cell phone and said, "Tanesa, you promise, swear, and whatever else is holy to you, that you'll call me the second you hear anything?"

She said she'd call both of us and I headed to Bob's house. He closed his eyes and I thought he was asleep, but instead he said, "I've always been overweight, even when I was in grade school."

Where had that come from, I wondered, and nodded.

He stared straight ahead, and said, "Kids made fun of me but not nearly as much fun as they made of Jacob."

"Jacob?" I said.

"Jacob Bishop, only negro in my class. You may have noticed I'm an irreverent, loud, some might say, smart ass."

He could say that again, but I didn't say anything and waited to see where he was going with the story.

"The shit I say doesn't compare to what some of the kids said about, and to, Jacob. Cruel, damned cruel."

"Kids can be cruel, especially to someone who's different from them."

"Don't get all damned sociological or psychological on me. It's my story."

What's not to love about Bob?

"Anyway, I figured Jacob needed a friend and what better person to be that friend than chubby Bobby; yes, I was called Bobby way back then. I started palling around with him." Bob closed his eyes and nodded. "That was decades before that politically correct crap reared its damned ugly head. Jacob called me Fatso Bobby, and I called him Nigg—umm, Negro Jacob. We became best buds and the damned bullies had a harder time picking on Jacob or me. Bullies lose their bulliness when there is more than one person to pick on. I was the only kid in the school who knew Jacob was a great kid. He was funny, kind, and smart as a whip, whatever the hell that means. We spent hours together, having fun, and still insulted each other every chance we got. It was our way of saying we liked each other without getting all gooey about it." Bob's eyes closed again.

"What happened to Jacob?"

"Hell if I know. We went to different high schools and lost contact." He shook his head, "Oh God, please let Al be okay."

His story had begun to make sense. If anyone who didn't know him watched how he and Al had traded insults and talked about each other, it would have been hard to understand how they had been friends. I was wondering if I should ask him more about his childhood friend as we pulled in front of his impressive house.

He looked at me. "If Betty's here, keep your damned mouth shut. I'll do the talking. I don't want to worry her."

I agreed, as if I had a choice, but needn't have worried. Betty wasn't home. Bob settled in an oversized, leather recliner in the family room and asked me to get him a beer. I asked if he should have one, and he repeated, for the third time as I recall, that he was not sick. I returned with his beer and a bottled water for me.

Bob had his eyes shut but opened them when he heard me returning, and said, "Think we did well at Brian's fundraiser."

"It was a great event. I know Brian appreciated it."

"I know a few more realtors whose arms I can twist for a few more bucks for the campaign. They don't know Brian, crap, they're so uppity they don't know that Folly Beach exists. One of them—goes by Norvell, real name's Norm—has perfected a snooty British accent when he says Kiawah or Isle of Palms." Bob shook his head. "The guy's a jerk but has made oodles of bucks."

I was beginning to realize Bob was talking about anything but his friend Al. He was worried, and from what Tanesa had said, he had reason to be. We talked more about the fundraiser as Bob finished the beer and asked me to get him another. I wondered when Betty would get home and relieve me of Bob sitting.

Before I returned with his second beer, his strong voice blurted. "So, who killed Lauren?"

I delivered the beer and said, "Don't know."

He took a gulp, rested the bottle on the armrest. "Why the hell not? You're trying to figure it out, aren't you?"

"Bob, the death has been ruled accidental or self-inflicted. There's nothing to figure—"

"Blah, blah, blah. I didn't ask for the police version. I've known you too long for you to slide that crap by me. I'm not as good at it as Charles's gal Heather but let me slip on my psychic hat." He moved his hand to his head like he was putting on a hat. I swallowed a laugh as he continued. "Slimeball Joel Hurt was dating dead Lauren, correction, was dating the live Lauren. Slimeball Joel is running against your bud Brian. My colleagues the Holthouses told you that Slimeball Joel was badmouthing

Brian. Some ancient proverb, said before even you were born, said the enemy of my enemy is my friend. The Holthouses were pissed at how Joel was talking which made him their enemy so Slimeball Joel is your enemy. Therefore, he must have kilt his gal friend Lauren."

Bob's psychic revelation or confusing lesson in logic held water up until he jumped to the conclusion that Joel must have killed—kilt—Lauren. Logical or not, it was what I was thinking based on more information than Bob had been privy to. "He may be my enemy, but why the big leap to him being a murderer?"

Bob smiled. "Nothing. Correct me if I'm wrong, you think her death was more than a mere overdose and Slimeball Joel jumps out as the best suspect. Does he have an alibi for when she was offed?"

Bob's question made me realize I hadn't heard, or if I had, didn't remember when she died. "Don't know. I'm not certain when she died."

"And you call yourself a detective. This old, chunky realtor knows that's important if you're going to solve the crime."

"Bob, I don't call myself a detective, and no one knows if there was a crime committed."

"Whatever. But when you wake up in the morning and put your britches and detective clothes on, check the alibi."

I wasn't about to admit it was a good idea, not only to check on Joel, but to eliminate my suspicions about Katelin, or possibly even Candice.

"I'll do that," I said, more to get him off the subject.

It wasn't necessary since Betty, Bob's angelic wife, came through the back door carrying two grocery bags and a bag from Walmart.

Betty glanced at Bob reclined in his chair and smiled at me. "Chris, did you pick up a runaway and bring him home?" She turned to her husband. "Where's your car?"

Bob stood and gave Betty a hug. I didn't want to be there when Bob told her about his trip to the hospital and told her I was late for a meeting. She didn't question who I could be meeting. Bob told her he would explain after "that little twerp skedaddles."

Before the fireworks began, I skedaddled.

The first thing in the morning, I called Cindy to see if she had the timeframe on Lauren's death. The chief answered with, "Hello, Mr. Landrum, how may I be of assistance?" It was her way of saying she was meeting with someone important and don't pester her. I asked her to call when she got a chance, and she said, "Of course." I hadn't received an update on Al and had waited as long as my patience would allow. I called Tanesa but it went to voicemail, so I said I was worried about her dad and asked her to call me if she got a chance.

I was O-for-two, so instead of pacing the floor waiting for the phone to ring, I walked next door to Bert's Market to grab a Danish and a cup of coffee. Two construction workers were ahead of me in the coffee line and Eric was waiting on a teenager dressed in a red bathing suit and a fisherman's vest. I grinned as I thought of how out of place that would have appeared most anywhere in the country. I poured my coffee and waited for Eric to wait on the customer in front of me, paid for the Danish, and said, "Eric, got a question."

"Make it simple. This morning's been a bear."

"Has anyone mentioned Lauren Craft's time of death?"

He tilted his head and ran his hand through his beard. "Might I assume you question her manner of demise?"

"Curious, that's all."

"Um-hum, whatever you say. To answer your question, asked out of curiosity, I heard it was around nine o'clock the night before they found her."

My phone rang before Eric could tell me he didn't believe me.

"Chris, this is Tanesa. Is this a good time to talk?"

That's the way to start a phone conversation, I thought, and realized why she had called. I tensed up but managed to say it was.

"I don't have much to report. He's still in critical condition. His vitals show hope, and then regress. From my perspective, that he's still alive is a good sign. The next twenty-four hours are critical. Sorry I can't offer more."

I told her I was pleased she had called and that he was still among the living. I asked if she was getting any rest. She said no, chuckled, and said that wasn't unusual for an ER doc. I thanked her for calling and she assured me she would let me know if there was any change.

Eric had overheard my half of the conversation and gave me an inquisitive glance. I shared what had happened with Al and a little about Bob. Eric had never met Al but knew Bob from a couple of encounters in the store. He told me he was sorry and that he'd pray for Al's speedy recovery. I said I would be satisfied for recovery, speedy or otherwise.

I still wasn't ready to go home and worry, so I walked around Bert's looking at various food items, items I would never buy, but were providing a distraction. I was further distracted when I saw Wayne Swan. He saw me and headed my way.

Wayne gave me a strong handshake and at the same time a

politician's pat on the back. Instead of the navy blazer look from the previous two times I'd seen him, he was dressed like the construction worker that he was. He wore torn jeans, scuffed work boots, a tan T-shirt and his dark hair was speckled with sawdust.

"Good to see you, Chris. I was going to call you yesterday but got tied up with a challenging rehab on East Huron."

"You were going to tell me that your candidate was dropping out of the race and supporting Mayor Newman."

Wayne laughed, louder than necessary. "No such luck, my friend. I wanted to ask you to meet again with Joel."

"Sorry, Wayne, I don't see where it—"

He held his hand in front of my face and interrupted. "Come on, Chris. What harm could it cause?"

I was distracted and thinking about Al and Bob and didn't have the time or mental energy to play games with Brian's opponent. "Harm, none, but what good could it do? I've already said I was backing Brian."

"I know, I know," Wayne said, and looked around the store. "But Chris, if you give Joel a chance, I think you'll like him and his ideas for improving the community that you play such a critical part in."

Sucking-up at its best, I thought. "Wayne, I like Joel. He seems to be well-respected and I'm sure he has innovative ideas, but—"

Wayne interrupted. "No buts, Joel knows it will be hard to convince you to switch allegiance. He knows he might not succeed but asks to talk to you again about his ideas. You never know."

"Wayne—"

"One more thing, Chris. We know Dude Sloan held a fundraiser for Brian Newman. I've known Dude ever since I moved here, so I was surprised. Think it's the first thing he's done anything politically in all those years—yes, surprising.

Anyway, I was in the surf shop talking to my good friend Katelin Hatchett when Dude came over. I took the opportunity to talk to him about Joel. Dude said he liked Brian and was supporting him, but after we talked a little about Joel's ideas, and about his deep-seated support of local businesses, Dude met with Joel. They sat down the next day and after it was over Dude said he liked some of Joel's ideas and might switch to Joel." Wayne smiled. "Of course, Dude didn't use those precise words, but I think that was the drift of what he'd said."

I guess Wayne did know Dude, at least how he talked. I doubted Dude would support Joel but had no interest in arguing with Wayne.

"I still don't see not supporting Brian, but I appreciate your efforts."

"Chris, I've known Joel for many years and would do anything for him. For him to have a chance, I must convince some of Mayor Newman's supporters to listen to Joel's platform. Give it one more chance, please."

I kept looking at my phone and wishing it to ring with updates on Al or Bob. Wayne was keeping me distracted, but not in a positive way.

"Okay, I'll meet with him," I said, more to get away from Wayne than to agree.

He shook my hand again and said, "Great, I'll talk to Joel and let you know when he can meet and I'll get back with you." He nodded like he'd won a major battle. "Better get back to my job site and keep my guys plugging away."

Hallelujah, I thought, and lied, "Nice talking to you."

"Havin' a political rally back there?" Eric asked, as I walked to the door.

"More like an arm-twisting session."

Eric laughed. "I don't recall there being so much politicin' this far before an election. If sheer persistence can win, Mayor

Newman better keep an eye on Joel Hurt and his good bud Wayne."

I started to tell Eric it wasn't going to work with me when Cindy returned my call.

"When in the hell were you going to tell me about Al, and that damned, blustery, foul-mouth, fat realtor that for reasons beyond my comprehension you call a friend?" she said as way of a pleasant introduction.

"How'd you hear about them?"

"I'm the freakin' police chief. Give me a break. Besides, all I had to do was walk in the Dog and one of my bosses, Councilmember Salmon cornered me before I got coffee—a serious mistake, in case you're interested—to tell me. And no, I don't know who told him. Remember, I hadn't had my coffee."

I gave her an update, as sketchy as it was, and she said she was sorry and hoped Al made it. She didn't say the same about Bob, but to give her the benefit of the doubt, I assumed that was because he was already at home.

I thanked her for her concern and for returning my call and she thanked me for not calling her a dozen times after my first call. I asked if she had an estimated time of death for Lauren. She asked me why I wanted to know. I said I'd tell her after she gave me the time of death. She uttered an East Tennessee profanity, mumbled something about me being the death of her yet, but only if I didn't get killed first, and then got around to saying the coroner estimated the time of death being between seven and ten the evening before her body was discovered. Eric was right again.

"Now, why did you want to know?"

"I'm still thinking her death wasn't accidental."

"Chris, when are you going to get a life and stop butting in to police business? Crap, never mind, I know the answer is never. So, what's her time of death got to do with anything?"

"Have you checked Joel Hurt and Katelin Hatchett's alibis for that evening?"

There was silence on the other end of the line, and then Cindy mumbled something I couldn't understand, and said, "Gee Chris, I started checking everyone who lives on Folly's alibis but only got through the last names starting with *G*. Was going to start on the *H* this afternoon."

She finished ranting, and said, "Why in the holy blue blazes should I check their alibis? What aren't you telling me?"

"From what I've heard, their relationship with Lauren was fractured at best. Joel had dated Katelin and Lauren at the same time—seldom the formula for a healthy life. They each have said things about Lauren's drug use that contradicted the autopsy's findings."

"So, the motive was Katelin being jealous? That's all you have? What about Joel? Why would he want his girlfriend dead?"

"Cindy, they each lied about Lauren."

"Everyone lies."

"Maybe, and I don't have a better reason for either of them to have killed her. I don't know if she was murdered, but all I'm asking is someone checks their alibis."

"The sheriff's office has already ruled out homicide. What reason would I have for opening that can of sardines?"

"Because you're so wonderful, because one of your favorite citizens asked you to, because—"

"Enough, enough!" she interrupted. "I'll do it to shut you up." The phone went dead.

Cindy was right. There was no evidence the death was anything but an accidental overdose or possibly suicide, but it still bothered me. Was I projecting my distrust for Joel to Lauren's death? Did I want him to be a killer because he was running against Brian Newman and had lied to me about liking him? Why had both Joel and Katelin lied about Lauren getting back into drugs? And was a door handle without prints enough to think something sinister had taken place?

My phone rang and distracted me from my game of twenty questions. I was almost afraid to answer for fear of bad news about Al but was relieved to see Barb's name on the screen. I was more relieved when she asked if I wanted to meet her for supper. I said yes and figured it would be the perfect distraction.

2 7

I met Barb a block from her condo at Locklear's Beach City Grill. We were given a table inside but it had the same incredible view of the Folly Pier as did the outside seating. She wore light gray shorts and a red blouse. I complimented her appearance and she said that makeup could hide a plethora of ills. I told her I should try wearing some. She laughed and said, "No need." The optimist in me decided that she'd meant I looked good enough without it. The realist in me knew better.

I started to tell her about Al and Bob but didn't want to ruin what I had hoped was to be a pleasant, refreshing, and peaceful evening. She shared a couple of stories about some irritating customers in her bookstore and she told me a joke that a preteen girl had told her while the girl's parents perused the used collection. The joke was more silly than funny, but Barb seemed to need cheering up as much as I did.

She switched directions when she asked, "Heard anything more about Lauren's death?"

I was surprised she'd brought it up and asked her why.

"No reason," she said, and looked out the window at the pier.

I cocked my head to the side. "No reason?"

"Curious, I guess. Council member Salmon's wife was in today and said her husband was worried about Lauren's boyfriend and the slate of council candidates he was putting together. Marc complains about being on the council, but he still loves being there. I knew you were questioning Lauren's death, and hearing about Joel made me think about her."

This wasn't quite the distraction I was hoping for. "I still have bad feelings about it, but there's nothing specific to point to anything other than an OD or suicide."

She reached across the table and put her hand on my arm. "Good, you don't need to be worrying about something like that. Besides, you didn't know her?"

"True, but—"

"And you don't like her dad, and from what you've said, the feeling's mutual."

"Yes, but—"

"And you don't like Joel because he's running against your friend, so that makes you suspicious of him."

"Also true," I said and waited for her to interrupt.

She didn't have to, a waitress did when she asked if she could get us something to drink. We each ordered, and Barb still didn't say anything.

"I'll tell you what does bother me," I said. "Joel, and for that matter Katelin. Each of them lied to me about Lauren's drug use. Why would they have said she was using again when the coroner's report said there wasn't evidence of recent use except for the overdose in her system?"

"I don't know," Barb said. "But everyone tells less than the truth on occasion. Have you thought that they may have truly believed she was using?"

I shook my head. "That doesn't make sense. I don't know about Joel, but Katelin has been a user, she'd even been in rehab with Lauren, so she'd know the signs. On top of that, there's Joel lying to me about liking Brian and going behind Brian's back and telling near-strangers how horrible the mayor is."

"Chris, when I was practicing law in Harrisburg, I dealt with several politicians—which was several more than I wanted to—and learned that lying came as easy to some of them as breathing did. Yes, Joel might be a liar, but that doesn't mean he had anything to do with Lauren's death."

I agreed with Barb and saw her point, but it still bothered me. Besides, there was no point arguing with her. There were several people walking along the pier and pointed it out to Barb and said how good a time they seemed to be having. I was determined to have a peaceful evening and wanted to get away from talking about Lauren.

Barb followed my gaze and said it was great seeing people having a good time. Our food arrived and she took a bite and looked at me. "So, when were you going to tell me about your friends Al and Bob?"

There went the pleasant, peaceful evening.

"How did you hear?"

She pointed her fork at me. "You know the hardest thing I've had to adjust to since moving here?"

I didn't figure she wanted me to guess. "What?"

"You probably don't remember, but the first time I met you we were in the Lost Dog Cafe. Either you or I, I'm not sure which, said something about one of their menu items, and a woman at the next table leaned over and said how good it was. I'd never seen her before, and to my knowledge, she'd never seen me."

"I remember." How could I not have remembered? It was one of the most traumatic mornings of my life. I had stumbled on a dead body in the alley behind Barb's Books and the foul-weather sanctuary of First Light Church.

She continued to point the fork at me. "My point is this is the first place I've lived where everyone seems super friendly. It's a bit disconcerting." She hesitated and smiled. "But it's endearing, I suppose endearing is the right word, regardless, that trait is beginning to grow on me."

"Good," I said, but still didn't know what that had to do with Al and Bob.

"What's slower to grow on me is how so many people figure it's their mission in life to share everything they know about everyone. Seems that boundaries are often crossed. I know I'm a bit off track, but where I'm going is that in addition to Marc Salmon's wife telling me about Joel and the candidates he was putting together to run against Marc, she told me since you and I were dating, she wanted me to know she was sorry to hear about your friends. She said Marc told her, and he'd heard it from Dude, who'd learned about it from Charles, who, may or may not have been with you when poor Al collapsed. Or something like that." She put the fork on her plate and stared at me.

I looked out the window and then at Barb. "To be honest, I was hoping I'd be distracted tonight and not have to think about Bob and Al. I haven't spent as much time with Al as I have Bob, but I consider both good friends." I updated her on their condition. I also apologized for not bringing it up earlier and repeated why I hadn't.

"I'm terribly sorry about your friends," she said and reached across the table and squeezed my hand. "I've become jaded from years of practicing law. I was always having to look past what people said and try to figure out what their angle was, what they wanted, and not what they said they wanted. It was exhausting. I was so sick of fake smiles, fake feelings, fake damned near everything." She shook her head like she was throwing out those thoughts. "Chris, one of the first things you told me was that newcomers to Folly either loved or hated it here. I didn't tell you, but at the time, it was looking like I was one of the haters. The world I came from was as different from Folly as, umm." She hesitated and looked at her fork. "This fork is from an ant colony.

You'll never know how many times I wanted to pack up my belongings and slink out of town under the cover of darkness."

"You didn't appear happy, but I didn't know how bad it was."

She set the fork on her plate and grinned. "Know what turned me around?"

I smiled. "My charm, good looks, and wonderful personality?"

Barb laughed, not the reaction I had hoped for, but it looked good on her.

"You better add sense of humor to that list," she said.

I wasn't certain if it was an insult or compliment, but either way, her laughter went a long way to improving my mood.

She stopped laughing and said, "Dude."

"Dude what?"

"Dude turned me around. For being my brother—step-brother—we're as opposite two people can be. But, in his word-challenged way, he pointed out the good around us. I wasn't ready to listen at first, but I started seeing examples firsthand. Kindness I'd never experienced before appeared around every corner." She stopped and turned to the window.

"Folly is filled with wonderful people."

She nodded. "And when Rocky gave his life protecting me, a near stranger, I was rocked to the core. Chris, that poor man didn't know me from Eve, but out of blind devotion to Dude, he put himself between a bullet and me. That's a level of friendship I'd never seen or experienced." Rocky had been one of Dude's two snarky employees who had learned that Barb's life was in danger and, because of his dedication to Dude, sacrificed his own life to save Barb. "From what you've said, Bob has little in common with Al, but they've been friends for years. And if what Marc's wife said was true, it was a friendship that was so strong that when Al suffered his heart attack, it affected Bob so much he had a panic attack."

"That's true," I said, not knowing anything to add.

We finished eating in silence and Barb suggested that we walk to the end of the pier. I felt the tension slipping away as she held my hand while we strolled past several visitors looking over the side toward the sun as it slid down behind the island.

We were seated on one of the wooden benches at the end of the pier when she said, "I'm glad I didn't slink away."

"Me too."

The rest of my tension left after she suggested I spend the night in her condo.

2 8

I was about to let the entire situation go, but it still bothered me that both Katelin and Joel had lied about Lauren using drugs. I wasn't ready to talk to Joel again, but figured it couldn't hurt if I asked Katelin one more time about Lauren's relationship with Joel. I didn't have her phone number, but she'd said she was between jobs so there was a chance I could catch her at home.

I parked in front of a large, wood frame house Katelin, Candice, and Lauren shared on East Ashley Avenue. I was surprised to see the house was new and large by Folly standards. It had a two-car garage, another rarity on the island. A red Mazda was in the drive so I figured someone was home.

Katelin met me at the door. She saw me and blinked a couple of times. I couldn't tell if she was just waking up or was leery of me being at her door. She hesitated and opened the door half way and looked past me toward the street.

"I hope I'm not intruding," I said. "I had a few questions to ask and didn't have your number. Could I come in?"

She glanced back in the room. "Umm, sure, I was surprised

to see you. Come in." She was wearing cut-off jeans, an over-sized T-shirt, and was barefoot.

I stepped in the large entry hall and glanced into the living room on the right. She saw me looking, said for me to go in and have a seat, and asked if I wanted coffee or something else to drink. I had already reached my coffee limit and said I was fine. She said she still needed a cup and would be back. I sat in a wingback chair across from a large upholstered couch. The furniture was old but appeared to be high quality. I heard what sounded like floorboards creaking from the second floor but couldn't tell if it was someone up there or the wind that had picked up, rattling a shutter or some loose wood outside.

She returned and was taking a sip from a Black Magic Cafe mug and sat on the couch across from me. She had slipped on sandals and crossed her legs. "Questions, Mr. Landrum?"

I wished I had given more thought before I'd arrived to what I wanted to ask. "Again, Katelin, I'm sorry about Lauren. I know it must be difficult for you to lose a roommate that way."

She looked in her mug and shrugged. "Yeah. You know, I was afraid something like this might happen. She did it to herself, but I blame Joel for pushing her back to drugs and the dark path where they led."

"Why blame Joel?"

"You mean other than he's a complete asshole? You mean something other than because he was dating both of us at the same time—lying out his freakin' mouth to both of us and pretending it was our imagination? Or because of what happened to Candice, our other roommate?" She jumped off the couch. Some of the coffee sloshed out of her mug as she went to the window and looked toward the street. "Did you see anyone out there when you came in?"

"No. Are you expecting someone?"

Her hand trembled and I was afraid she was going to drop the mug. "Umm, no. Just wondering." She moved back to the couch and plopped down.

I didn't know which of her questions to respond to first but felt like I was walking on egg shells and didn't want to set her off more than she already was. I also wondered if she was on something.

"I was curious about what you'd said about Lauren being back on drugs. Someone said that she wasn't and I was confused." I didn't want to tell her that the someone who said Lauren wasn't on drugs was the coroner.

She stared at me and shook her head. "I thought the last time we'd gone through rehab together that she'd kicked it for sure. She was finally getting her life together, think she wanted to get closer to her parents." She looked back in her mug. "Then Joel came along and screwed both of us up. He got her back on drugs, I know he did. And now he wants to be the mayor. What a crock."

"Do you think he could have had something to do with her death?"

"Of course, he did. He got her hooked. She found out about him two timing her. He got her the drugs. What more could he have done to lead her over the edge?"

"I understand, but do you think he could have been more directly involved. Could he—"

Katelin interrupted. "You mean like killing her on purpose?"

I nodded.

"You don't think her death was accidental?"

"I don't know. I'm just looking at the possibility."

She looked at me and tilted her head. "What do the cops think? Do they think it was intentional? Oh my God, really?"

"I don't think so. They're working under the assumption it was either an accidental overdose or suicide."

Katelin exhaled and looked at the floor. "That's what I think happened."

"Overdose or suicide?"

"Crap, I don't know. Either way, it was Joel's fault. God, I wish he had never moved here."

"Why do you think Joel would have intentionally hurt Lauren?"

"Anti-drugs, anti-drugs! Isn't that Mr. High and Mighty's big campaign pitch? Isn't he telling everyone if elected mayor he'll crack down on illegal drugs and all the dastardly things they cause? How will it look if his little girlfriend's an addict? He had to get her out of the way before he started politicin' big time. The day before she died, I hear he was telling some people he'd broken up with her and their relationship hadn't been serious anyway." She pounded her mug on the coffee table. "Hadn't been serious, hah! He dumped me for her and had the nerve to say it wasn't serious. Let me tell you, I could say some things about him that'd keep him from getting elected to dogcatcher, much less mayor."

"You think he killed her so she wouldn't hurt his campaign?"

"Wouldn't surprise me one iota." She jumped up from the couch again and looked out the window. "You sure no one was out there?"

Wasn't paranoia a possible side effect of drug use? Did her bizarre behavior indicate Katelin was on something? I said, "Do you think someone's out there?"

She jerked her head around and glared at me. "They have been. Are you sure .... Never mind. Do you have other questions? I'm busy."

I remembered she had said something about the third roommate, Candice, but figured this wasn't the time to ask. My time was up. I thanked her for her time and saw myself out. I glanced back and saw her staring out the window. I walked to my car and looked around to see if there was anyone out here. I didn't see anyone.

Now what, I wondered as I drove to the house. Was Katelin

being paranoid because of drugs or had someone been watching her? Were her comments about Joel being the reason for Lauren's death legitimate, or was she a jilted lover thinking the worst about Joel because he'd left her? Did Joel tell someone he had broken up with Lauren and that possibly caused her to end her life? Then another possibility struck me. Could Katelin have killed Lauren in hopes she could get Joel back, and because he didn't respond the way she wanted him to, she was throwing him under the bus?

I pulled in the drive, let the motor continue to run, and stared at my steering wheel. An hour ago, I was ready to accept the police version of what had happened. Yet now, I thought I could make a good argument that Katelin or Joel could have been responsible for Lauren's death. But, had she killed herself, either accidentally or on purpose, or had one of the others murdered her?

I would get yelled at but took the chance and called Cindy. Instead of getting voice mail where I could ask my question without her yelling at me, she answered.

"Yes and no," she said as way of a greeting.

It was now a tossup on which I hated the most: Caller ID or cryptic responses.

"Yes, that you think I'm the most wonderful person in the world," I said. "And no, even though you'd love to, you won't ditch Larry and run off with me."

"You calling from the psych ward?" Cindy laughed. "You've done gone loony."

I was glad I got a laugh out of her rather than one of her patented rants. "I'm calling from my driveway, and some may call it a psych ward."

"No argument from me," she said.

"Yes and no?" I said.

"It's been almost twenty-four hours since you asked about

alibis, so I figured you couldn't wait a second longer before you started pestering me about them. Right?"

"You got me there."

"Of course, I did. So, the yes is I found out if Joel had an alibi, and no if Katelin had one."

I waited for her to elaborate, but her small amount of revenge was to force me to ask. "Yes, you found out about Joel, or yes he has an alibi?"

"Joel was holed up with his campaign manager during the timeframe we were given for Lauren's death. Unless he could be in two places at the same time, he's as innocent as baby Jesus."

"Did you confirm his story?"

"Golly, gee, Chris, why didn't I think of that?"

"I suppose that means you did."

"Of course, I confirmed it, numbskull. Remember, I'm the brilliant police chief. According to Wayne Swan, he and Joel spent several hours that evening working on a brochure for his campaign. And before you ask, no, Joel didn't leave Wayne's house that entire time. You can mark Joel off your list of imaginary killers of Lauren Craft who you, and only you, have imagined being killed."

I ignored the last comment. "What about Katelin?"

"I haven't talked to her yet. The phone number I had for her has been disconnected, so I'll try to catch her at home."

I told Cindy I'd left Katelin's and a little about her reactions to my questions and her thinking that someone was watching her. Cindy proceeded to express in strong, unkind words how stupid it was of me to visit Katelin, and I needed to learn to mind my own business. I crossed my fingers and told her she was right and that I would butt out.

Before the phone went dead, she responded like a highly-trained chief of police would by saying, "Liar, liar, pants on fire!"

The next morning I was drinking coffee and staring at my refrigerator as if I expected words of wisdom or a clue to what was going on to appear on it. None appeared but the phone did ring. It was barely seven o'clock so I tensed; seldom did good news come this early.

"Chris, this is Tanesa. Did I wake you up?"

I took a deep breath and closed my eyes expecting the worst. "I was awake."

"Good. With my screwy shifts around here, I lose track of when normal people get up. Anyway, I wanted to give you an update."

She sounded upbeat. *So far, so good*, I thought—I hoped. "How is your dad?"

"The best I can say is he's alive but still in a coma."

"I thought he had a heart attack. Can that cause a coma?"

"Without getting too technical, yes, he had a cardiac arrest and that led to a lack of oxygen to the brain which in turn caused the coma."

"Tanesa, I hate to ask, but what's your best guess about his chances?"

"To be honest, it doesn't look good. Even though he's alive, his body is frail. If he was thirty years younger, I'd have hope, but … well, I don't know."

That's what I was afraid of. "I'm sorry."

I heard her sniffle and there was a long silence before she said, "But I'm not giving up. I've seen people come through these doors who didn't seem to have a chance in the world of surviving. Miracles can happen. Everything is being done medically that can be, but it'll take more. Even if he pulls out of the coma, he could have serious disabilities. It'll all depend on how long his brain was deprived of oxygen. Please pray for him."

"I will, Tanesa. He's lived through some terrible times. He's strong."

"And as stubborn as hell."

I chuckled. "I think he'll pull through just to be able to sit back and watch Bob battle with customers at Al's."

"He'd love that. I hope you're right."

I asked if she wanted me to come to the hospital and she said it wouldn't do any good. She'd let me know if there was any change and I thanked her for calling. She asked if I'd call Bob and fill him in.

I'd wait a couple of hours to call Bob. His mornings didn't start until around ten. Calling sooner would be like waking a bear out of hibernation, but more profane. Instead of incurring Bob's wrath, I walked to the Dog for breakfast. There were three vacant tables on the front patio, but I didn't need any of them. Charles was at a table and bent over exchanging kisses with a Labrador retriever attached to a leash held by a man at the adjacent table. I pulled out the chair opposite my friend before he noticed me. Nothing stands between Charles and a dog.

"Whoa, where did you come from?" Charles said after he bid

farewell to his new canine friend that was following its master to the exit.

I was distressed about Al's condition, so I resisted offering a smart-aleck remark, and asked if I could join him for breakfast.

He stared at me and squinted. "What's wrong?"

"Why do you think something's wrong?"

"First, in the zillion years we've know each other, you've never asked if you could join me, and second, you passed up laying a smart remark on me when I asked where you came from."

He knew me too well. I told him about my conversation with Tanesa.

"Does Bob know?"

"Don't think so. Tanesa asked me to call him."

Charles put his hand over his face. "Make sure I'm a couple of miles away when you make that call."

A food delivery truck stopped in front of the restaurant and I couldn't hear what Charles said next. I doubt I missed much. The truck, and its loud diesel engine moved down the road and Charles was saying something about Marc Salmon. I asked him to repeat it.

He tilted his head toward the inside dining area. "I said, Marc said that one of his supporters told him Joel is holding fundraisers in West Ashley to get money for his council candidates to, as Marc put it, 'stomp my ass.' Marc said he'd never had to resort to begging for money to run for council, but if he wanted to stay on the job, he'd have to do something."

"I'm afraid Joel's going to do whatever he needs to do to beat Brian and to get his candidates on the council."

Amber appeared at the table with coffee for me and asked if I wanted granola and yogurt; I said French toast. She smiled and headed to the kitchen.

"Speaking of Joel," Charles said as if Amber hadn't been

here, "you still think he had something to do with Lauren's death?"

I glanced around to see who was nearby. "I did, but now I'm not sure. Not even sure her death was anything more than what the coroner has ruled."

Charles started to say something but paused as a Folly Beach patrol car blasted down Center Street with its siren blaring. Seconds later, the distinct siren of one of the city's fire engines started dogs howling as it pulled out of the station a couple of blocks away.

Charles looked in the direction of the fire station, and said, "Don't suppose you want to call Cindy and see what's going on?"

I may have the smart-aleck gene, but Charles had the nosy gene in spades. "No but speaking of Cindy." I took a sip of coffee and shared my conversation with her and what she'd said about Joel's alibi. Before Charles interrupted with a hundred questions, I told him about my visit to Katelin and what she'd said about Joel.

"So, you figured Joel killed Lauren and Cindy blew it all by coming up with such a good alibi for Joel." Another patrol car's siren could be heard in the distance. "Sure, you don't want to call Cindy?"

"I'm sure."

Charles shrugged. "So, Wayne was Joel's alibi?

I nodded.

"That's the Wayne who's running Joel's campaign; the same Wayne who's Joel's good friend. Was there anyone else at this brochure-creating meeting?"

"Cindy didn't mention anyone."

"So, this could be the same Wayne who would be the only person on earth who could vouch for being with Joel when Lauren met her maker."

I nodded, again, and said, "And could be the same Wayne

who's such a good friend of Joel that he might lie about Joel being with him?"

Charles pointed his knife at me. "Now you're catching on. Lauren and Joel were dating, so it would make sense he would be with her that night. It had to be someone who knew her and that she trusted."

"Not necessarily. I've given it some thought. Anyone could have stuck a gun to her head and made her drive out there. And Charles, that's assuming she was murdered, which it seems that only I believe."

"Add me to that short list. Oh yeah, there's one other person who needs to be added."

"The killer," I said.

"Yep, and that could be the person you went to see yesterday."

"Katelin did seem intent on pointing fingers at Joel at the same time she was painting a picture of Lauren falling back into drugs."

"Throwing around stuff that would deflect attention from her. What's her alibi?"

"Cindy's still checking."

Amber arrived with my breakfast and Charles had taken the last bite of his eggs. "And you'll let me know the second you find out, right?"

I told him of course, and he said he had to meet Heather. She'd said she needed to talk to him, and when Heather calls, Charles jumps. I was impressed by her control over him.

There was one other table occupied on the patio, so I decided to call Bob and get that unpleasant task out of the way. I was surprised when Betty answered Bob's cell phone. I told her who I was and asked if Bob was okay.

"Oh, Chris, I'm glad you called. I don't exactly know how to answer your question. I think his health is okay, or at least he hasn't complained since yesterday about feeling bad. And when it comes to his health, he's a big baby and will moan and groan about a splinter like someone was cutting his hand off. Anyway, I'm not worried about that, but I don't recall ever seeing him so down about anything as he is about Al."

"I'm sorry to hear it. Anything I can do?"

"Short of waving a magic wand and making Al well, I don't know what it could be."

It wouldn't help his mood, but I felt I needed to tell him what Tanesa had said. "Is he there now?"

Betty said yes, but he was still asleep. She was surprised he had slept that long but didn't want to disturb him. I shared what Tanesa had told me and asked if she wanted me to tell him when he woke up. She hesitated, but finally said it might be better if she told him. I deferred to her judgment and ended by saying I was sorry about Al and wished her luck in telling Bob. She said she'd need it.

Amber brought a refill on my coffee, looked around, and sat where Charles had been earlier. She said, "Are you okay?"

"Sure, why?"

She tapped her fingers on the table. "Because you look like someone stole your car and burned your house down. You may be able to fib to other folks, but remember, I know you better than anyone here. So, what's wrong?"

I told her about Al and Bob. She reached over the table and put her hand on my hand that was holding the mug, and said, "Oh Chris, I'm so sorry. I know how much friends mean to you, and I know they're two of your best. Anything I can do?"

I smiled, thanked her, and said she was doing it.

The couple at the other table waved for Amber to bring them the check. She nodded in their direction and said to me, "Let me know if you need anything, you hear?"

After she left, I started thinking about what she had said about friends. Would Wayne have lied about Joel's whereabouts? And I tried to remember what Katelin had said about her friend, and roommate, Candice. Wasn't it something about Lauren possibly killing herself because of what happened to Candice? I was busy trying to figure out Katelin's relationship with Lauren and why she may have killed her and didn't catch what Katelin had meant about Candice. All I knew about the third housemate was she was seldom home and Dude had said she had been fired from one of Joel's garden centers allegedly for theft but the rumor was that was actually because she had learned something about Joel that he didn't want known. She was now working at a real estate office in Charleston. Would it help if I talked to her to get her take on what happened to Lauren? Possibly, but I didn't know where she worked.

Instead of sitting at the Dog and asking myself questions, that I knew I had no answer for, I decided to go back to Katelin and Candice's house to see if Candice was there. I'd like to get her take on Joel and Lauren, and with luck, more about what had happened to her job at the garden center.

A block before I got to their rental, one earlier question was answered—an answer I didn't want to know.

Three police cars, two fire trucks, and an ambulance were parked at all angles in front of Katelin's house. Yellow crime-scene tape blocked the entrance to the open garage door and a glimpse of the rear of Katelin's Mazda was visible under a blue tarp on the other side of the tape. A gaggle of area residents were milling around the yard next door. One of the Folly Beach Public Safety officers was waving his arms at cars to keep moving on the busy street. One of the fire trucks blocked most of the garage as I slowly drove past the house so I parked in the next empty drive and walked to the group of people standing as close to Katelin's house as the police permitted.

It was easy to spot my friend, Chester Carr, in the group. Charles's late Aunt Melinda had said he was a "spittin' image of Mr. Magoo", and she wasn't far off. I'd known him for several years.

I asked him what was going on.

"Don't know much," he said and pointed to a woman on the other side of the group, "Marge said they found a body in that red car in the garage. I just got here, was on my way to visit a friend who lives out past the Washout."

I was afraid I knew the answer, but asked, "Anyone know who it was?"

"Suppose the cops do, but I don't."

There was a black Ford Focus in the drive. "Know whose car that is?"

Chester turned his Coke bottle thick glasses my direction. "Chris, I just got here, and I ain't a reporter."

"I know, but I thought you—"

He stuck his hand in my face and said, "Hold on." He turned and waved for the woman he'd referred to as Marge to come over. She smiled at Chester, gave a quick glance at the garage, and walked over.

"Marge," said Chester. "You know Chris?"

She shook her head and Chester introduced me as the guy who used to have the photo gallery where Barb's Books is now located and that I've helped the police catch a few killers. I wished he'd left out the last part. She shook my hand and said she was Marge Monroe and lived in the house across from Katelin's. She was in her eighties but had a strong handshake and bounced on the balls of her feet with energy I hoped I had when I reached her age.

Chester pointed to Katelin's. "Marge, know who's dead?"

"Suspect it's one of those girls who lived there. Think her name's Katelin something. That's her red car and the EMTs hauled somebody out of it. Couldn't see much since they strung that blue tarp over the car."

That's what I was afraid of. "Know who the black car belongs to?"

Marge looked at the Ford Focus and back to me. "Candice Richardson, she's the third gal who lives there. My goodness, that makes two of them dead. Hope nothing happens to Candice."

"Marge," I said, "how well do you know Candice?"

"Better than the other two, I suppose. She's seldom there, but I've run into her a couple of times in Bert's and she liked talking about flowers. I have a flower garden behind my house and Candice had planted some over there, so it was something we could talk about."

"Have you seen her since all this happened?"

"No, but I guess she's in the house since her car's there." She smiled and patted Chester on his bald head. "Gotta get back home. My hubby'll be wondering what happened to me. He's bedridden and I can't be gone long. Nice meeting you, Carl."

I told her it was nice meeting her as well. I didn't correct my name.

A patrol car was parked directly across the street from where we were standing and Officer Allen Spencer was walking to it from Katelin's house. I had known the six-foot tall, muscular officer since I had moved to Folly. He was new on the force at that time, and I was new to Folly so we had something to talk about. I excused myself from Chester and intercepted Allen as he reached the car door.

"Hey, Chris."

He'd always been cordial, polite, and helpful, characteristics that not all police had shared.

I shook his hand and said, "What happened?"

"Looks like suicide. Young lady who lived there." He glanced at something he'd written on his palm. "Her name's Katelin Hatchett. She was in her locked car in the garage, motor running."

"Who found her?"

"Housemate."

"Candice Richardson?"

Allen stared at me. "How'd you know?"

I told him a neighbor said the black car in the drive belonged to Candice and I knew she was the other housemate.

"Tragic," Allen said. "Such a young lady, so much life in front of her."

"Are you sure it was suicide?"

"That's what the EMTs said. No signs of foul play and the car was locked. She did have a big bruise on her forehead, but the guys think it was caused by the steering wheel her head hit when she passed out." He hesitated, looked at the name on his palm, and back at me. "Do you think it was something else?"

"Did you know Lauren Craft was a third housemate?"

"The woman found dead near the County Park?"

"Yes," I said. "Doesn't it seem strange both died this close together, both were found in their car, and both could have been suicides?"

Allen nodded. "I suppose. I'm sure the detectives from the Sheriff's office will get it sorted out. One of them should be here any minute."

"Do you know who's coming?"

"No."

I nodded toward the house. "Is the chief over there?"

"Yeah, she's waiting around for a detective. Chris, I've gotta run. I'm supposed to be on patrol."

I thanked him for the information, and he repeated they'll figure it out, before pulling out to make my island safer. I hoped they would figure it out but didn't have as much confidence as did Officer Spencer.

There wasn't anything I could do here but knew there was one thing I had to do, and that was to call Charles and let him know what'd happened. I would incur enormous quantities of grief if I didn't tell him within seconds of when I learned something important. Even then, I would be surprised if he didn't say, "What took you seconds to tell me?"

"Got something important to tell you," Charles blurted as way of greeting upon answering my call.

"So do I," I said.

"Not as important as what I have. I'm home, come over. It'll blow your mind away."

Since he didn't bombard me with questions about what I had to tell him, I figured whatever he had to say might blow my mind away. Besides, with everything cluttering up my mind, it wouldn't take much to make it explode.

CHARLES HAD BEEN WATCHING for me. He opened the door before my car had come to a stop in the gravel and shell parking lot of his small, book-filled apartment on Sandbar Lane. He wore a crimson and blue Samford University, long-sleeve T-shirt, navy shorts, and a wide smile.

"You're not going to believe my news," he said as I stepped in the book-filled living room.

I didn't waste my breath by saying something like *Hi, Charles*, nor did I step in the middle of his story to tell him about Katelin's death. I said, "What's the news?"

He raised both hands over his head. "I'm getting married!"

He's right; I didn't believe it. I headed to the kitchen that, if possible, was smaller than his tiny bathroom, and poured a glass of white wine out of the double-bottle he kept in his refrigerator for me. I asked if he wanted a beer. He said yes and told me to get back in the living room so he could tell me more about his nuptial plans.

I handed him the Budweiser and said, "Is that what Heather wanted to talk to you about yesterday?"

He took a sip, clinked the can down on a stack of books beside his chair, and scratched his stringy hair. "Sort of."

A couple of years back, Charles had proposed to Heather. Their marriage had been the final wish of his aunt before she'd succumbed to cancer. The proposal was more an emotional response to his aunt's request than something he'd thought out, and he'd later decided he wasn't ready for marriage, and may never be. Heather said she'd understood, but I was never certain she had accepted it.

"Sort of?" I said.

"She didn't come right out and say we should get hitched, but wanted me to know she wasn't getting younger, and now her dream of becoming a country music star had been stomped on, she was feeling like a failure. You know I can't do anything to make her a star, but I can help her meet her need to be married."

"Did you propose?"

"No. Most of the time she talked about feeling like a failure and something had to happen. I spent most of the rest of the time reassuring her she was a wonderful person and far from a failure. Besides, popping the question and making her Mrs. Charles Fowler came to me in the middle of the night. I can't imagine why she'd want to be that, but I'm going to make it happen. Chris, I'm excited."

"When are you going to ask her?"

"Tomorrow, and you're going to be there."

"Whoa," I said. "Why? That's a private moment between you two."

He shook his head. "Wrong. I've been reading up on this. The latest thing in marriage proposals is for the groom to invite his friends and sneaks around and invites her friends and family to be wherever the question's to be popped. They even video the big knee-on-the-ground moment. Can you believe that?"

I couldn't, but didn't say anything before he continued, "You're my only friend, and I don't have any family left, and I couldn't figure out if Heather had anyone she would want to be there, so it's you. Yep, you'll be with us."

"Are you sure you want to propose, and if you are, about me being there?"

"Gerald Ford said, 'I know I am getting better at golf because

I'm hitting fewer spectators.' I'm going to get this proposal thing right this time; yes, I am. I'm definitely positive that I'm sure."

"Okay. I'd be honored to share the moment with you." I also wondered what Heather would think about me crashing their intimate moment.

Charles took another sip. "Now with that settled, what's so important that you had to barge into my home and drink my wine for?"

No, I didn't remind him he'd invited me and the only reason he had wine in his apartment was for me. I did tell him where I'd been and what had happened.

The first sign he was distracted by his marriage plans was when he didn't chastise me for waiting so long to tell him. He also didn't ask who was there, what everyone watching the police action had said, and if any of them had their dogs with them.

"Strange," he said.

"That's all you have to say?"

He took another drag on his beer and said, "Think I need to get a ring before I pop the question?"

I said no, asked what time tomorrow, and where. He said eleven o'clock in the morning, and that he wanted to "pop the question" on the Folly Pier because it provided a great view of the beach and that it was where he'd said his farewells to his aunt. He'd spread her ashes in the ocean from the end of the pier. I said I'd meet him there, and said I'd better be going.

I echoed his comment as I walked to the car. "Strange."

31

"Okay, nosy one, this is your duly appointed, highly competent, plum near able to walk on water police chief."

I may have missed a word or two from her telephonic wakeup call since I glanced at the window and saw it was dark outside and looked at the bedside clock and saw it was five thirty.

"Good morning Cindy."

"I figured since you're the one who wakes the roosters up each morning, that I'd catch you awake. You were, weren't you?"

I lied and said, "Of course. What have I done to be honored with your call?"

"Damned near nothing, but I figured you'd want to know what happened out on East Arctic yesterday since it involved someone you've taken an interest in."

I opened my sleep-filled eyes wide and said, "Katelin Hatchett's death?"

"You've already heard?"

472

I told her I was one of the inquisitive citizens at Katelin's house.

Cindy sighed, "Why am I not surprised? Then I can go about keeping your island free of crime. Adios."

"Cindy," I said, hoping to stop her from hanging up.

"What now?"

"Was it suicide?"

"Everything points to it."

"Did she leave a note?"

"No, but that doesn't mean anything. Less than half of suicide victims leave notes."

I carried the phone into the kitchen and started to fix coffee. I knew what Officer Spencer had told me, but asked Cindy anyway, "Were there any signs of a struggle?"

"What part of suicide don't you get? Not really. She had a bump on her head but it was probably caused by it hitting the steering wheel when she first passed out."

"Could she have been hit hard enough to knock her out?"

"Chris, how the hell would I know that? Tell you what, let me come over there and smack you on the head and see how big a bump it'll take to knock you out. A bump's a bump. But, I get your point. I'll check with the ME."

"Thanks," I said. "I hear her housemate found her."

"Yeah, Candice came home, changed clothes, and started to fix something to drink when she heard Katelin's car running in the garage. At first, she thought Katelin had come home, and Candice didn't hear the garage door open. She said she realized that she parked blocking the garage and her housemate couldn't have gotten around her car. She went to check, and the rest is history."

"Bear with me a second, Cindy. So, it's possible Candice could have been home long enough to set it up to look like a suicide."

"Stop and hold your jackass. Why would Candice kill Katelin?"

Instead of answering, I asked, "Did you check if Candice had an alibi for when Lauren was killed?"

There was a moment of silence on the other end of the phone. "Not yet. Crap, I could have asked her yesterday, but had a more immediate death on my hands. Are you saying she killed both housemates? And I guess more importantly, I'm looking at one suicide and one either accidental overdose or possibly suicide. Why the bee in your Tilley about them being killed?"

"Cindy, I'm only asking questions. I have no idea what's happening. But don't you think it's mighty strange that they died so close together?"

"Yes, but because something is strange doesn't raise it to the level of homicide."

She was right, but I wasn't ready to let it go. "Could you do me one big favor?"

Another sigh on the other end of the line. She said, "What?" It sounded like an exclamation more than a question.

"See if Joel Hurt has an alibi for when Katelin was killed, umm, died."

The next thing I heard was a dial tone. I assumed that meant, *"Of course I will, Chris. Good suggestion."*

CHARLES HAD SAID ELEVEN O'CLOCK, so I knew that meant ten thirty, so I arrived at the pier a little after ten. It was a gorgeous day with light billowy clouds overhead and a temperature in the mid-seventies. The pier was busier than usual. Several men had cast lines and were waiting for the fish to grab the bait for an early lunch. Two children were giggling and pointing to three birds that were fighting over a potato chip the children had accidentally—on purpose—dropped on the deck. And an elderly couple leaned over the edge and watched a group of college age men playing volleyball.

My phone rang and I was surprised that Cindy was able to get back with me so quickly. There was no need to be surprised since it wasn't her.

"Thank god, you answered," Charles said, sounding out of breath. "Come to Heather's apartment. Now!"

For the second time this morning, I was hung up on. But Charles sounded much more distressed than Cindy. I was pulling up in front of Heather's dilapidated apartment building ten minutes later and saw Charles's car parked in front. Heather's apartment door was open but I knocked before entering.

Charles came out of the kitchen waving a piece of paper in his hand, and said, "She's gone. Everything's gone."

I glanced around and didn't see any of the knickknacks that had dotted every surface in the apartment. "What do you mean gone?"

He handed me the paper, flopped down on the couch, and bowed his head.

The note was in flowing script and read: *Chuckie, dear. I wanted to tell you this in person but chickened out. Sorry you must find out this way. My dream of singing is busted. It was squashed like an elephant stepping on an ant. My hopes of becoming your wife seem as far away as Spain. And I feel like I'm in one of those straitjacket things. I must leave. Honest to god, I must. I may be making a big mistake, but it's what I want to do. I'm taking all that I can carry. You can do whatever you want to do with the rest. I'm getting a cab to the bus station and by the time you read this, I'm long gone. PLEASE do not try to find me. Chuckie, this isn't your fault so don't start blaming your-self. xoxo forever, Heather*

Charles's hands covered his head. For the first time, I noticed he had on a white, long-sleeve T-shirt unadorned with any logos or school mascots.

"I'm sorry," I said, and felt helpless.

"No matter what she said, it's my fault. I couldn't do anything about her singing, but why didn't I go through with marrying her the first time, and why didn't I say something about getting hitched when she was feeling so bad the other night? Why, Chris, why?"

"There're no easy answers, Charles. Getting married had to be right for both of you. The last time it wasn't."

"I know, but was I being selfish, wanting everything my way?"

"You were wonderful to her and she knew it. Don't kick yourself. Any idea where she's headed?"

He looked at the door. "I don't know. Could be anywhere—except Nashville. She never mentioned wanting to be somewhere else." He put his head back down. "If she'd waited one more day, one more measly day, my proposal …"

I didn't say anything for a couple of minutes. Charles was deep in his thoughts and didn't need to be disturbed. I finally said, "Want to try to find out where she's going?"

He looked back at the door and at the note I still had in my hand. "She said for me not to. Chris, I've got to honor her wish. I've go to."

Tears formed in the corner of his eyes and he looked away.

And I felt helpless.

32

I'd tried every way I knew to help my grieving friend. Nothing worked. He said he needed to be alone. I didn't want to leave him, but his words had an edge of finality, so I told him to call me day or night if he needed anything. He said he would, but I'd be shocked if he did.

I called Bob on my way home and asked how he was doing.

"My best friend is about dead. I'm old and the idiot doctors tell me that I'm falling apart. I own a damned run-down bar that's losing money. And Betty said that unless I get my sorry butt out of the chair and do something worth a damn, she was going to put me in the wheelbarrow and dump me at the curb for the trash collector. How the hell you think I'm doing?"

I coughed to mask a giggle and said, "Poor little Bobby Howard."

"You're damned right, for a change."

Enough foolishness, I thought, as I pulled in my drive. "Any news about Al?"

"I called Tanesa an hour ago. She told me yesterday that she'd call me if she learned anything, but I was damned tired of waiting. Anyway, she said there's slight improvement. He's still in that damned coma but his heart sounds stronger this morning."

"That's good news."

Bob said, "I suppose."

I debated whether to tell him about Katelin's alleged suicide and about Heather leaving but decided that Bob didn't need more unwelcome news.

"He's still alive, so that's good."

"Yeah," Bob said. "Betty yelled something, so unless you want to hear me bitch and groan more, I'd better go see what she wants. She's not that good with the wheelbarrow."

"Tell her I said hi."

For the third time today, I was hung up on. Fortunately, I'm not paranoid. What I did realize was that I was hungry and didn't feel like facing people in a restaurant. I walked next door to Bert's to grab whatever doughy delights they had in stock. I was pleased that they had a cinnamon Danish, but what I was not pleased to see was Wayne Swan heading my way.

"Chris Landrum, the person I wanted to see."

Wayne Swan, the last person I wanted to see, I thought but didn't say it. "Hi, Wayne. What'd you need?"

"Listen, Joel and I are going to be in the bar at Loggerheads this afternoon around four. Could you join us?"

I gave my best faux smile and said, "Why?"

"Joel would love to meet with you one more time. He has some things that might help you change your mind about supporting him."

I wanted to scream, "No!" but thought it may be a good idea to meet with Joel, so I said that I'd be there. I didn't tell Wayne that while I'd be there it wasn't why they wanted to meet me. What better chance to learn more about Joel's relationship with Lauren and Katelin?

Home was my next destination, and I reached it without having to get in an extended discussion with anyone else. I thought about calling Tanesa, but after she'd endured a call from Bob, she probably needed peace and quiet. I'm not a big nap person, but after Cindy's early morning wakeup call, I managed to sleep for an hour before waking up regretting that I'd agreed to meet with Joel. What could I learn about his relationship with the two deceased housemates? I waffled between thinking he would reveal something that would lend support to my belief that he was responsible for their deaths, and that whatever he'd tell me couldn't be believed.

I had a hard time focusing on anything other than Charles and Heather. My friend was in pain and there was nothing to do to help. How would things have been different if Charles had proposed earlier? I had known him for a long time and on numerous occasions he had confided that he was afraid of marriage. And he and Heather had lived together during their short-lived, ill-fated move to Nashville. It would have been the opportune time to see if marriage would be right for him, yet he never mentioned the possibility while they were there or after their return to Folly.

Nothing was being accomplished by my analyzing Charles's situation and Joel's believability, so I walked to Loggerhead's. It was a half-hour before I was to meet Joel and Wayne and I smiled to myself as I headed up the steps to the elevated outside bar. I was becoming more like Charles than I ever imagined possible. The temperature was in the mid-eighties and a gray cloud-cover kept the sun from being intolerable, so the large outdoor seating area was packed. I wondered how long we would have to wait for a table when Ed, half of the husband and wife team owners of the restaurant, put his arm on my shoulder, welcomed me, and said that he was expecting me. I smiled and asked how he knew I'd be here.

He pointed to a table by the railing. "They said you were coming and if I saw you to point you their way."

Joel and Wayne were at a table that had the best view across the street to the Oceanfront Villas. A sliver of the ocean could be seen through the gap between the parking lot and the elevated condo complex. They leaned toward each other and appeared in deep conversation.

I thanked Ed, told him to give my regards to his wife Yvonne and weaved my way past the standing room only crowd to Joel's table. Wayne was flailing his arms around and saying something about not going to do it when Joel spotted me.

Joel waved his hand in front of Wayne, stood, smiled, and said, "You're early. You caught us discussing the landscaping on a big project Wayne is working on."

From the way Wayne was acting before I arrived, I would have used the word arguing rather than discussing, but whatever. I returned his smile and shook his hand. Wayne took a sip of his beer from a plastic cup and waved in my direction. He remained seated as I sat in the plastic chair facing the bar.

Joel looked at Wayne who hadn't spoken and turned back to me. "I've asked Wayne to join us, hope you don't mind." He gave me a politician's smile, baring all his teeth. "He can help keep me on track; I have a way of wandering in my conversations."

"Fine with me," I said, although I wanted Joel to wander.

A waitress had been at the table beside us and Wayne touched her back to get her attention. She pointed at the near-empty cups in front of Wayne and Joel. "Another round?"

Wayne said yes and ordered a glass of white wine for me. I was impressed that he knew my drink of choice but irritated that he ordered without asking if that was what I wanted. After the waitress had headed to the bar, Wayne said, "Sorry, Chris, I should have asked before ordering for you. Was that okay?"

Partial redemption. I said that it was.

Wayne looked at Joel and turned back to me. "I'm being rude. Sorry. Joel and I were debating an issue about a remodel. The owner keeps changing what he wants but doesn't want to spend more money on it. We're trying to see how to cut costs while giving him what he's asking for."

That wasn't my impression of what they were arguing about, but I mumbled something about how it must be difficult to meet everyone's needs.

Joel interrupted. "Neither here nor there. Don't want to bore you with our work. I'm thrilled you agreed to meet with me again. Have you given more thought to supporting me in my Quixote-like quest to unseat Brian Newman?"

"A little," I said. Most of my thought has been trying to figure out how to prove he killed the two women but didn't think it would be wise to mention it.

"Good," Joel said. "I was afraid you were so deep in his camp that I wouldn't have a chance with you. And, before you say anything, I know that two of your friends have had fundraisers for Brian and you attended each of them. I understand friendship and am not a stranger to loyalty. In fact, I admire it, but I also know that you have the reputation of doing what you believe is right, regardless of what others may think. I also know about you getting involved in death investigations, often involving perilous situations." He chuckled. "I've even heard you're asking questions about the tragic death of Lauren Craft. I admire your gumption, although I'm afraid it's misplaced with Lauren. The poor girl couldn't handle the horrific dangers of drugs and overdosed." He paused, shook his head, and said, "So sad."

I couldn't decide if he was continuing to suck up to me or fishing to see how much I knew, or suspected, about Lauren's death. Either way, I saw this as an opening to the real reason I was here.

"It was terrible about her death. I offer my deepest condolences. I know you and she were close and her loss must be painful."

He glanced across the street toward the ocean and at me.

"Yes, it is terrible, but we weren't that close. We went out a few times but it wasn't serious. Of course, I liked her, but didn't see it going anywhere, and when I learned about her renewing her affair with drugs, I had to sever our relationship. As you know, I have a strong anti-drug stance; I see the use of illegal drugs and the misuse of legal prescriptions as being one of the biggest problems facing our country, and yes, infiltrating our community. I cannot tolerate it. I believe that is where our current elected officials and I differ, and—"

I wasn't ready to listen to a campaign speech and interrupted, "I'm surprised. I was under the impression that you and Lauren were much closer than that."

The waitress returned with our drinks.

"See, Wayne," Joel said and pointed to me, "he doesn't beat around the bush. He doesn't hesitate to challenge things. I admire that." He smiled and turned back to me. "You and I have a lot in common, and that's why I'm asking you to support me."

The waitress returned with our drinks and I noticed how much louder it was than when I had arrived. The crowd had increased and groups were speaking louder to be heard over other groups.

I wanted to steer the conversation back to Lauren but didn't want to be obvious. "Joel, I'm honored that you are spending so much time with me and I think you have a lot of promising ideas, but I've known Brian Newman for a long time. I like and respect him. He's not been perfect, and I don't agree with all his positions, but he's been good for our community, and I will continue to support him."

Wayne was fiddling with his napkin and turned to Joel. "My friend, I don't think you're going to win Chris over. We should let him get on his way."

I wasn't ready to pass up this opportunity to pump Joel for information. "That's okay, Wayne, I'm not in a hurry, besides it's great to be outside."

Joel said, "I agree and even if I can't twist your arm, it's good getting to know you better."

I snapped my fingers like I'd thought of something. "Have you heard about Katelin Hatchett?"

Wayne glanced at Joel who gave a slight nod and said, "Just heard about it this morning. Can't imagine what would cause someone to end his or her own life."

"She was one of Lauren's housemates," I said. "Did you know her?"

Joel rubbed the side of his nose, and said, "Umm, we'd gone out a couple of times."

"Oh," I said. "Before you dated Lauren?"

"Yeah," he said and took a sip.

I didn't think he would say that he was at the same time. Might as well go for broke. "Her housemate found her. That must've been horrible. Her name's Candice something. You knew her, I hear?"

Wayne leaned toward the table. "Don't believe I do."

Joel mimicked Wayne's move. "Yeah, I knew her a little. She'd worked at one of my garden centers for a while. She found a better paying job, something where she could use her degree in accounting. Why?"

"Curious," I said. "It's amazing how rumors get started." I smiled.

"Rumors?" Joel asked.

"I heard that Candice had stolen money from your garden center and that she was fired, but now that you said she got a job in accounting, that couldn't be true or she wouldn't have gotten a good reference."

Joel laughed, but his hands were gripping his cup so tightly that I was afraid it would break. "You're right about rumors. No truth to that as far as I know, and since they're my businesses, I'd know."

I nodded like I believed him and decided to go for broke.

"Speaking of rumors, I heard that Katelin's body was found yesterday morning, and someone said it was around dusk. Do you know when it was?"

"Don't know," Wayne said. "Didn't hear about it until today."

"I don't know for certain," said Joel. "But it was probably late morning when we heard sirens coming from everywhere. Wayne and I were a couple of blocks from here. I was pricing the landscaping for one of Wayne's new clients. He tore down an old shed and wants to extend his garden around the back of his house. We'd been there way longer than we should have been for the size job."

Wayne said, "That's probably what that racket was about."

"Enough about death," Joel said. "It's too pretty a day to be talking about depressing things."

Wayne agreed and we drifted into a benign discussion about the weather, the new restaurant on Center Street, and how much both were looking forward to fall and cooler weather. Joel said that he had to be going and we went our separate ways.

As I walked home, I thought about what I had learned. Joel had continued to lie about the depth of his relationship with Lauren, the reason that Candice had been fired, and adroitly avoided the subject of dating Lauren and Katelin at the same time. But the most significant revelation was that if it wasn't for Wayne, Joel wouldn't have had an alibi for the times either of the ladies had died. Interesting.

33

It'd been more than twenty-four hours since I left Charles. I hoped that he'd reach out to me, but that was not to be, so I made the first move and called. Instead of hearing his voice cheery or otherwise, I got his message: *This is Charles. I won't return your call, but if you want, leave a message in case I change my mind.* I almost yearned for his pre-Nashville sojourn when he didn't have a phone or answering machine. Should I go and knock on his door? No, if he wanted to talk, he knew how to reach me. He needed time to absorb Heather's departure and what it had meant, and more important, how he was going to proceed from here.

It had been even longer since I'd heard from Al's daughter, but was determined not to pester her. She'd said she would let me know if there was any change. It had also been a couple of days since I'd talked to Cindy. As chief of police, she was pulled in countless directions, her priorities changed minute by minute depending on what her department was involved in: vehicle accidents, burglaries, inappropriate actions of inebriated citizens and visitors alike, calls from irate residents, and the never-ending issues related to illegal parking. And that's not considering the wishes and desires of the city's elected officials. I decided to call and remind her of a couple of items I'd asked her to check into.

"No, Chris," were the first words out of her mouth.

"No what?"

"Don't know, but I figure whatever it is, the answer is no."

"Couldn't I be calling to wish you a pleasant day?"

She made a noise that sounded like a braying goat before she said, "Umm, no."

"So, alibis: Joel for when Katelin died and Candice for when Lauren died."

"I haven't talked to Joel yet, but Candice says she doesn't remember what she was doing when Lauren bit the dust."

I knew what Joel had told me about where he was and wished Candice could have been more specific with Cindy. I was mulling that over, when she added, "But, I did talk to Detective Callahan. He caught Katelin's case and is convinced that her death by asphyxiation was of her own doing. The coroner said the knot on the head was consistent with contact with the steering wheel and Callahan said that was good enough for him."

Detective Callahan and I had a few encounters, of which most were negative, when he investigated the death of a member of First Light Church. Callahan was young, but proved to be competent, although a bit stuffy.

"So, he's closing the case?"

"Yes and no," Cindy said and paused.

"Which means?"

"I shared the same questions you'd asked when you thought I wasn't paying attention. He agreed that having two deaths that close together, involving housemates, and with both having a history with Joel, seemed an unlikely coincidence."

"Good," I said.

"But, he didn't see enough evidence to conclude anything other than Lauren's death was either accidental or suicide, and that Katelin's was a suicide. Before you get all huffy, he said that before he moved on to the latest crop of murders, he would talk to Joel and anybody else whose name came up. He's doing that as a favor to me."

I thanked her and she said that whether I believed it or not she had more to do than take calls from a bald, nosy, senior citizen. I told her to spend my tax money wisely, and she reminded me that I was retired and was taking rather than paying tax money. She giggled and then was gone.

I started to check on Bob but decided that I had already endured enough grief for the day, so instead, I walked three blocks to Cal's for a late lunch and an earful of country music. Cal had owned the bar since taking over for its former owner who now resided in prison, the permanent address he'd earned after killing an attorney and framing my friend Sean Aker who was a law partner with the deceased attorney. Cal's could be described as the perfect country music bar. An antique Wurlitzer juke was full of country classics, the ambience included the strong smell of stale beer and burnt burgers, and tables and chairs that had seen their better days—a decade ago. It also included another country classic, Cal Ballew, who'd had a hit record, although it was popular before most of his customers were born.

From the jukebox, Barbara Mandrell was singing about "The Midnight Oil" as my eyes adjusted to the dim lighting. The bar was half full, or in the eyes of its owner who had to pay the bills, half empty, so I didn't have trouble finding a table nor finding a glass of wine. Cal had my drink to the table before I looked around to see who was there.

Along with the wine came the questions: "How's Al? How's Bob? Did you hear about that gal who offed herself in the garage? How's that neighbor you don't like since his kid overdosed?"

I took a sip and waited for the gangly six-foot-three Texan to finish his litany of questions, and when he stopped to take a breath, said, "You forget to ask, 'How's Chris?'"

He smiled. "Don't think so, so how's Al?"

He must have figured that I was okay, so I gave him the meager update that I had been given and told him that Bob was fine. I ignored the questions about Katelin's death and about Lauren's parents.

"Since you're short on news, let me tell you what happened this morning."

Randy Travis's voice filled the room singing about what happened in "1982," and I nodded for Cal to tell me what happened more recently.

"When I'm in the mood to open for lunch, I come in at ten-o'clock. Figured there wouldn't be too many people in today so I let my cook have the day off. I can fix the customers anything they want to eat as long as it's a burger and fries. Most only want to drink beer."

I knew he was headed somewhere with the story and I didn't have anywhere else to be, so I let him ramble at his pace. Once again, I nodded for him to continue.

"I stuck my key in the lock when I saw Michigan by the side of the building leaning on his cane. He looked at his wrist and told me I was thirty minutes late. I asked him late for what, and he said I should've been here earlier."

One of Cal's less than endearing habits had been calling people by the name of their home state. Charles and I had been trying to break him of the habit and had come close to succeeding—but only close.

I smiled. "That sounds like Charles. What'd he want?"

"First he wanted to give me a hard time for being late. I didn't let it take, so I asked him one more time what he wanted. He followed me in, helped me turn on the lights, and straighten up the chairs from last night's non-interior-design-oriented customers, and said he wanted to have a party."

"What kind of party?"

A customer two tables over called for Cal to bring him another drink.

Cal unfolded himself from the chair and said, "Hold that question, I'll be back."

Jim Reeves's mellow voice was singing "He'll Have to Go," and Marc Salmon lowered his body in the chair previously occupied by the country crooner—Cal, not Jim Reeves.

"Mind if I join you?" he asked.

He was already seated so I thought the correct answer would be I didn't mind, and said, "My pleasure."

Cal had started back and saw Marc in his chair. He frowned and then put on his happy proprietor face and asked Marc if he could get him anything.

"Hi, Cal. How about a fish sandwich?"

Cal nodded and bit his lower lip like he was thinking, and said, "How about a hamburger?"

Marc said, "That the special of the day?"

"Only choice of the day," Cal said.

Marc said, "Sounds good."

Cal tipped his Stetson to the council member and headed to the grill.

Marc watched Cal go and said, "Heard any gossip about the election?"

Gossip and politics were to Marc like hydrogen and oxygen were to water.

"Nothing you don't already know, I suspect. What's the latest?"

He looked around the room and leaned closer like he was getting ready to divulge a state secret. "We don't have much formal polling over here, especially this far out from an election, but I was talking to a couple of local political tongue waggers who said that unless something drastic happens between now and the election, Brian's a shoo-in to get reelected."

I hoped that was the case, told Marc so, and asked what his tongue waggers, if there was such a word, had to say about the council races.

"They didn't say it, but it seems to me that if Brian wins reelection by a large margin, I should be okay. He and I don't always agree, but on most issues we're on the same page."

"What'd they say about Joel?"

Marc shook his head. "The newcomer's spreading manure about our mayor. If you listen to him, you'd think Brian's a serial-killer, rapist, who hangs around the barnyard with amorous intentions." Marc smiled. "Other than that, Joel thinks the world of our current leader."

"Any talk about Joel and Lauren or Joel and Katelin?"

Marc leaned close and whispered, "Why?"

I didn't think his question was worthy of a whisper. "Seems strange that he dated both and now they're dead."

"Don't the police think your neighbor's daughter's death was self-inflicted? And the latest gal killed herself, right?"

"That's what they're saying."

Marc leaned closer. "You don't think he had anything to do with their deaths, do you?"

I shrugged. "If you hear anything about Joel that involves them, let me know."

"You got it," Marc said as Cal slid a burger in front of the council member.

Cal pulled the chair out that was beside Marc and started to sit when another customer called for him.

"Hold your pony," Cal said, huffed, and headed to the demanding customer.

Marc took a large bite out of the burger and tilted his head. "Forgot to ask, how's your friend Al?"

There was a reason Marc had the reputation of being the biggest repository of news and gossip on the island. To my knowledge, he'd never met Al, and I wasn't certain that he knew that he existed. I asked how he'd heard and he said something vague like *word gets around.* I shared what little I knew and he expressed his sympathy and wish for a speedy recovery.

Marc looked at his watch. "I'm late for a meeting at city hall."

He looked around for Cal who was busy playing chef. I said I'd take care of the tab. Marc thanked me and rushed out, and I sat and reminded myself that everything he'd said about Joel was consistent with what I'd heard.

Cal returned mumbling something about pesky customers whittling into his fun time. He took off his Stetson, wiped his brow, and mumbled something else about chefin's hard work. He took a deep breath and said, "Where were we?"

I said he was about to tell me about Charles's party.

"Ah, yes. The boy said he wanted to have, let's see, what did he call it, oh yeah, a *happy journey party* for Heather. Cripes, I didn't even know that she was heading out on a journey, and he told me not only was she heading out but had done gone. I was flabbergasted."

I agreed. "Did he say why he wanted to hold it?"

"This is where it gets sad. The poor boy said that he hadn't done enough to keep her here, and the least he could do was to wish her the best on her journey to wherever. He told me that he didn't know where she was headed. Ain't that the pits?" He shook his head. "Not that I'll miss her singing in here, but I sure as hell will miss her bubbly personality, and it didn't take a psychiatrist to see how happy she made Charles. No, it didn't."

"When does he want to hold the, umm, party?"

"Saturday."

"That's the day after tomorrow."

Cal held out his hand and looked at his fingers like he was counting the days. "Sure is. Seemed soon to me, but that's what the boy said. I even asked if he didn't think that was too soon to put together a proper party."

"What'd he say?"

"Said he needed to do it soon before he chickened out."

Another customer demanded Cal's time and I called Charles, although I wasn't optimistic that he would answer. I was right. He did have a new message: *If you insist on seeing me, I'll be hosting a big Happy Journey Party for Heather at Cal's Saturday night. The shindig starts at eight.*

George and Tammy were singing about "My Elusive Dreams" as I left Cal's, sadder than when I arrived—and that was going some.

I left Charles a couple of phone messages the next day and true to his word, he didn't return my calls. I also knocked on his door early Friday evening in hopes that he would acknowledge my existence. His car was there so I assumed he was holed up among his books. I called Tanesa and she was at work but in clipped, hurried phrases told me that there was no change in her dad's condition. I had no better luck when I called Bob and Betty answered and said that her more-cranky-than-usual hubby was taking a nap and if she'd learned one thing over the years it was not to awaken him unless she was ready to suffer the conse- quences. I told her I was calling to see how he was and she said, "Gruff, antsy, irritable, and boorish."

"So, he's back to normal."

Betty laughed. "You know him way too well."

"I share your pain. Let him sleep and if he wakes up in a good mood, tell him I called."

I had better luck when I called Barb, Dude, and Preacher Burl to invite them to Charles's party. Each said they'd be honored to attend—actually, Dude said, "Cool," which I assumed meant he'd surf over to the wingding.

Charles's message said the party was to start at eight, so I was outside Cal's at seven-thirty under the assumption that Charles would arrive around then. I wanted to see if there was anything I could do before he made it inside. Consistent with his normal behavior, I saw my friend approaching the bar at seven-thirty on the dot. He wore a long-sleeve University of Arkansas T-shirt and cargo shorts. Instead of his crooked smile, his face was squished up in a frown that would have been appropriate at a funeral. His shoulders were bent down and he leaned on his cane more than I had seen before.

"Hello, Chris," he said.

That ordinary by most people's standards salutation told me that he was hurting more than he would let on. I put my arm around his shoulder and asked how he was doing. He said fine which I knew was a lie. I asked if there was anything I could do to help.

"I wish there was," he said, and looked at the sidewalk.

His eyes were bloodshot and his hand on the cane was trembling.

He looked at Cal's door and pointed his cane to the vacant lot beside the restaurant and bar. I took the hint and followed him around the side.

"Remember how I told you Heather was so sad the other night?"

I told him that I did.

"She told me about a vision that she had, but I didn't pay much attention to it then. She said it came to her through her psychic powers."

"Has she done that often?"

"Not much, well not much as I remember. Some of the stuff she says is so far out that I sort of tune some of it out. I'm not as big a believer in her psychic powers as she is." He stared at the light pole across the street.

"What'd she say?"

That jarred him back to the here and now. "She said it came to her when she was half awake, half asleep, and half in psychic mode. I didn't want to get in an argument with her about math, so I tried to do what you do. I nodded and told her to go on. She said that she was a baby bird, well, not that she was the bird, but seeing whatever was going on through the eyes of a bird. Apparently, the bird had a bad wing and somehow got separated from its mother. Heather, or the bird, felt lost in a large clump of trees near a river. She said, it may not have been too large a group of trees, but to a baby bird it seemed humongous."

"What was her mood when she was telling you this?"

"Strange. It was sort of like she was telling me about a show she saw on TV. She didn't seem happy or unhappy when she was talking. But the more I think about it, she could have been sounding all factual like so she wouldn't get swept into the vision, or whatever it was."

"I didn't mean to stop you. What else did she, umm, see, dream, or think?"

"Said the little bird knew it was supposed to be somewhere else doing something, but it didn't know what. It saw other birds fly away, but because of its bad wing it couldn't follow. Some of the other birds fluttered down and sat on one of the trees and tweeted like they were as happy as—happy as a lark. She didn't say lark. A couple of them came down and sat by the lame bird. They were nice, but the baby bird knew they couldn't help it fly." He looked down and back at me. "Chris, to be honest, I didn't hear everything she was saying. It didn't make sense, and I tuned some of it out. I started paying attention again when she said the one-wing bird saw a stubby log floating down the stream beside where it was sitting. The log was moving fast and the little bird decided to hop on and float wherever it was going. There was room on the log for the little bird, but not enough for any of the others. Suppose the big question was whether the little critter should get on the log and float away."

"What did it do?"

Charles smiled for the first time since he'd arrived. "Don't know. Heather woke up when the little thing was about to decide."

I said, "And you think Heather saw herself as the bird and decided to let the log take her away?"

He tilted his head toward the ocean. "There wasn't room on it for me."

"And you're blaming yourself for not understanding her vision, dream, whatever, and for doing something about it then."

"Yeah," he mumbled.

"Charles, there was no way to know she would leave."

"I should have. She takes her psychic stuff seriously."

Cal's front door opened and sounds of George Jones singing "The Grand Tour" laid a blanket of country sadness on us.

Charles looked at the building and offered a weak smile. "Nothing like George's moaning to cheer up a hurtin' soul."

As strange as it seemed, I understood. I said, "Time to get your party started," and ushered him to Cal's front door.

35

It was still ten minutes before the party was to begin and there were already a dozen patrons in the bar. Each table had a balloon floating above it attached to a string that was held in place by a fist-sized rock. A variety of messages were printed on the multi-colored balloons. One read *Let's Celebrate*, three read *Bon Voyage*, and the rest read *Happy Birthday*. Cal met us at the door with a strong handshake and a pat on Charles' back. He was attired in his traditional, sweat-stained Stetson, his rhinestone-studded, white jacket, and in the spirit of Folly, red knee-length shorts.

The bar owner waved around the room. "What do you think, Charles?"

Charles faked a smile and said, "Festive."

"Yep," Cal said, "Tried to get all *Bon Voyage* balloons but the store just had three. I figured after a few drinks, nobody'll be able to read them anyhow. Got the rock idea from a party I sang at a few decades ago. They covered bricks with shiny paper and used them to hold down the balloons. Didn't have any shiny

497

paper or bricks." Cal laughed. "Now I can say this ain't only a country bar, but a rock bar."

Charles smiled, sincerer this time. I told Cal it looked like he'd thought of everything.

Vern Gosdin was singing "Chiseled in Stone" from the jukebox and Cal said he would grab our drinks and for us to join the party. Dude was leaned against the bar talking to Preacher Burl. We walked over and Charles patted the back of Dude's tie-dyed T-shirt.

Dude smiled and said, "Here be the guest of honor. Aloha."

Preacher Burl took the more conservative route. "It's good to see you, Charles. Thank you for inviting me to this significant event."

"Glad you're here," Charles mumbled.

Cal handed Charles a beer and a plastic cup of wine to me. There were two men in deep conversation on the next two bar stools. I didn't recognize them, so I caught Cal's eye and nodded their direction.

Cal leaned close to me and said, "Couple of salesmen staying at the Tides. They're not part of our shindig, but I let them buy beer anyway."

Cal was generous like that. There were a few others in the bar I didn't recognize and figured they were also here for the drinks and not, as Cal had put it, our shindig.

Cal had pulled a couple of the tables together in the center of the room, covered them with a Happy Birthday paper tablecloth and had placed a large bowl of chips in the center. Two smaller containers held salsa. Chester Carr was munching on a chip and talking to Cindy LaMond and her husband, Larry. I started to walk over to talk to them when Dude said, "Where be H?"

I had wondered how Charles would handle questions about Heather's departure.

Charles looked around the room and back at Dude. "I don't know, but I wish her well wherever it is."

So far, so good, I thought.

Dude nodded. "Me be praying to sun god for H to have boss surfin'."

Preacher Burl took a step closer to Charles. "My prayers are with her."

I suppose he didn't want his god to be left out. Barb walked in with Amber. They headed to the chips, and I asked Charles if he wanted to greet the latest arrivals. He told Dude and Burl he'd get back with them and followed me to the center of the room where he was mobbed by the chip munchers. Cal reached the group at the same time and asked who wanted drinks. The Charles lovefest was put on hold while everyone told Cal what they wanted. Fortunately, everyone said beer, so Cal could handle the orders. Amber hugged Charles; Barb gave me a peck on the cheek and was next to hug Charles. The chief hugged him next, and the men in the group forsook hugs and shook his hand. Charles thanked them for coming and from the jukebox the piano genius of Floyd Cramer played "Last Date."

Several more of Charles's acquaintances came in while he was with the salsa group. I knew most of them, but a couple were strangers; but since they seemed to know the others, I assumed they knew Charles and weren't here just for drinks.

I moved away from the group and Cindy followed me. The decibel level increased with everyone talking over the music. The chief and I moved to the quietest corner.

"Talked with Joel about his alibis," she said and took a sip of beer.

"And?"

"Cool your jets, impatient one. Give this chick a chance to enjoy Cal's generosity." She took another sip, and continued, "Joel, a charming snake that boy is. Know what he told someone whose name I will not divulge?"

I had no idea, so I shrugged.

"Said the first thing he would do as mayor would be to fire

the director of public safety. Since that's the highfalutin title on my business card, I didn't take too kindly to it. But, you'd be proud of me. When I was talking to him about his alibis, I didn't once pull my gun and shoot him in the, let's say, male body parts. I was tempted but figured it could possibly look bad on my record."

I rolled my eyes. "Alibis?"

I didn't think it possible, but the room was getting noisier. Several more of Charles's friends arrived and gathered around him. It looked like a herd of cattle surrounding a food trough—figuratively speaking, of course. I moved closer to the chief to hear what she was saying. Nearby, Chester Carr was talking to David Darnell, an insurance agent who had moved to Folly a couple of years ago and was a member of a walking group Chester had formed around that time, but they weren't as loud as most of the others in the room.

Cindy repeated in great detail what I had already known about Joel and the strategy session he was holding with Wayne at the time Lauren had died.

I wanted to move her along. "What about when Katelin was murd … umm, died?"

"Take a patience pill," she said and sipped her beer. "That's where the story gets a bit fuzzy. Joel said he had three yard crews working on the island that day. Said he spent most of the time going from crew to crew. Also said he may have been at one of his buddy's remodeling job sites working on a landscaping bid."

"Wayne Swan?" I asked.

Cindy nodded. "He wasn't sure exactly when he and Wayne were meeting, nor when he was with his other crews."

"Times that couldn't be accounted for?"

"Yes, but don't get all suspicious about that. I think most days, most of us would have a tough time accounting for every hour."

"True," I said. "But it still doesn't get him off the hook. I wish it'd been more definitive."

"Chris, I agree. Heck, I'd like to plant a little-ole chip in everyone's head so we could track every movement around the island, but the mayor keeps throwing in my face that pesky thing called the Constitution and says I'd better stick to catching crooks the old-fashioned way. Bosses!"

As often is the case, she got a smile out of me, and said she'd better get back to her hubby before he started boring everyone with hardware store gobbledygook. Cindy moved away to save the non-hardware store obsessed public and Chester told David that he'd talk to him later and moved in front of me.

"Chris, I'm not the nosy, busybody type, but I couldn't help overhearing parts of your conversation with the police chief."

Chester was right. Among my friends and acquaintances, he was one of the least nosy—the key word being least, which, of course, still made him nosy.

"And?" I said.

"Did the chief say something about Joel Hurt meeting with someone during the time that poor Brad Burton's daughter died?"

"Yes, he was meeting at Wayne Swan's house, something about working on a campaign brochure."

"Funny."

"Why funny?" I asked.

"Maybe I have the time she died wrong, but I'd asked a couple of people and they said it was between eight and ten o'clock."

I said, "I was told between seven and ten, but you're close."

"Where does Wayne live?"

"Somewhere near the Washout. Why?"

"That night I was sitting on my front porch talking on the phone to a cousin in Maine. Name's Sally. I seldom get to talk to her, see we're not close. Anyway, I saw Joel's big truck speed by the house like a bat out of hell, can't miss it, it's got all that writing on the door bragging about his company. You know I'm less than a block off Center Street and it gets crowded that time of night."

I interrupted. "What time was it?"

"Oh yeah, I hadn't mentioned. Exactly nine-fifteen, Sally's favorite show came on at nine-thirty and she only had fifteen minutes to talk. Anyway, I was irritated Joel was driving that fast; could've killed someone walking up the street. So, if he said he was meeting all that time with someone in the other direction, he's not telling the truth."

"You sure?"

"Yes, sir. I remember it was the next day that all the police cars and two television trucks went right in front of the house on their way toward the County Park and poor Brad Burton's daughter." Chester looked toward the entrance. "Speaking of Brad."

I turned and was surprised to see Brad and Hazel Burton stepping into the bar and looking lost. I told Chester I'd talk to him later and went to the door to greet the Burtons.

"Brad, Hazel, thanks for coming."

Hazel stepped in front of her husband and reached to shake my hand. Her hand was warm and clammy. Brad stayed behind her and gazed around the room. He looked as comfortable as a typewriter in an Apple store.

Hazel reached back and pulled Brad forward, turned to me, and said, "I was in Mr. John's Beach Store yesterday and got in a conversation with a young lady buying a beach towel. She told me about this party and how the community sticks together whenever something bad has happened. Said everyone fights like dogs and cats unless there's a crisis. She said she didn't personally know Charles or Heather, but her boyfriend did and they were going to come out tonight to support Charles."

"That was nice of her," I said.

Hazel nodded. "So, I told Brad it was what we'd experienced since, umm, losing Lauren and maybe it'd be good if we came tonight. If for no other reason than getting us out of the house and not think all the time about our loss. Isn't that right, Brad?"

Brad smiled and said yes, but he still looked like he'd rather be somewhere else.

I pointed toward the bar. "Follow me, and let's get you something to drink."

Hazel followed and Brad lingered a couple of steps behind us. Cal was quick to hand each of them a beer and Hazel said she saw the woman from Mr. John's on the other side of the room and she and Brad should go over and thank her for inviting them.

Gene Watson was singing "Between This Time and the Next Time," the smell of beer and burnt hamburgers filled the air, and I stood beside the bar and agreed with Hazel's new acquaintance about the community gathering together in time of crisis or need. I also started thinking about what Chester had said about seeing Joel during the time he was allegedly with his friend working on the campaign. Did it prove he had something to do with Lauren's death? Not really, but what it did was say he was a liar, and that was something I already knew.

The jukebox went silent, and Cal tapped on the softball-sized, silver microphone in the middle of the small stage. "Attention," said the bar's owner. "Y'all focus up here for a few."

Most of the conflicting conversations ended but three people leaning against the bar kept talking. Cal tapped the mic again, and Brad, who was grabbing a second beer at the bar, grabbed one of the talkers by the shoulder and motioned for silence. It was probably a hold Brad hadn't used since he was with the Sheriff's office. It worked and Cal had everyone's attention.

He held his forefinger in the air. "First, I want to thank all of you for coming out. It's only been two days since my buddy Charles there," Cal pointed at his buddy, "approached me about having this party. He's going to say a few words in a minute, but I wanted to hog the stage for a few first." Cal gave a stage grin. "For those of you who have been begging me to sing a few hits tonight, Charles said it was okay and I'll croon a few later. But now you need to know why we're gathered. As I suspect most of you know, Miss Heather's not only a singer; heck, she'd used this here mic many a night to entertain many a happy customer, but she's also a psychic. Now I know some of you aren't believers in what psychics do, but I know Heather, and she's a powerful believer. She's not with us in body tonight, and I'm not certain where she is. But what I am certain of, is wherever she is, she's using her psychic power to learn about this here big party in her honor, and knows all our good thoughts," Cal paused, looked at Preacher Burl, and continued, "and our prayers go with her on her journey. And Miss Heather, you're missed a heap here and are welcome back anytime."

Cal stopped and looked out on the gathering like he was waiting for a response. I wasn't certain what response would be appropriate, but Dude must have. He applauded, and everyone followed his lead.

Cal nodded. "Thank y'all. Now Charles, want to say a few words?"

Charles was standing directly in front of the bandstand, whispered something to Cal, and Cal stepped back to the mic. "Charles'll say a few words to us a little later. Drink up."

And we did.

36

Hazel was still talking to the woman who told her about the party. I had seen her working in Mr. John's but didn't know her name. Brad grabbed a third beer and looked around the room and headed my way.

"I had no idea how many friends Lauren had here," he said as he stopped beside me. "You wouldn't believe how many people have come by the house or stopped Hazel or me on the street to offer condolences. Most of them I'd never seen before. Know what else surprised me?"

"What?"

"Every one of them expressed everything from surprise to shock about Lauren overdosing. Now some of them did say they knew her back when she was using, and even they said she'd kicked drugs and became vocal about not using whenever the topic came up. Two of her friends said that she swore to them there was no way she would ever use again."

"I'd heard that too."

"Chris, you and I have never seen eye to eye on, well, most

everything, but the one thing I keep hearing about you is that you're loyal to your friends and can keep a secret."

"I like to think so," I said wondering where he was going with this.

"I was a cop for a long time, way too long a time," he said and closed his eyes. "During that time, I investigated numerous suicides. Kneeling down and looking at a body with half its head blown away or looking up at someone who'd hanged himself… or herself…was no picnic, but you know the hardest part?"

I guessed. "Breaking the news to their loved ones?"

Brad nodded. "Nearly every one of them swore the death couldn't have been suicide. Their dear sweet daughter, son, husband, wife, or whatever couldn't possibly have done it. It had to be something else, usually murder, and I as a cop had better find the killer and find him quick. Regardless how obvious the cause of death, they were in total denial." He looked around and said, "I'll be back," and headed to the bar for beer number four.

What he'd said didn't surprise me, but why was he telling me? He was back with a fresh beer in hand so I didn't have to wait long for an answer.

He took a deep breath and sighed. "Chris, when I heard about Lauren, every one of those notifications flooded my mind. I was determined not to fall into the same state of denial as did all those family members. So, even after her friends said she was clean, and the coroner found little, if any, drugs in her system, I told myself not to do what those other people had done. I bought into the suicide or accidental overdose explanation." He hesitated and looked at the floor. "I think I was wrong."

"I do too," I said to the top of his head.

His head jerked up. "Really?"

I said yes and told him what I had learned about Joel from Chester, and about my suspicions about him having something to do with Katelin's death. Brad's hand gripped the beer so hard his knuckles turned red. He took a step toward the bar but turned and came back to me.

He pointed the empty beer bottle at me. "First thing Monday, I'm going to contact my friends in the Sheriff's office and push them, push them hard, to pursue her death—her murder."

From the comments I had heard from his colleagues, I'd be surprised if he had any friends left in the office but was glad to hear someone felt as strongly about it as I did.

"Good."

"If they don't want to do their job, I'm going to figure it out myself. Damned if I'm going to let my little girl's killer get away."

My phone rang before I could respond. The screen indicated it was Tanesa. I excused myself and moved to the sidewalk where I could hear better. I noticed my hand shaking as I touched the answer button. Please let this be good news.

"Chris, this is Tanesa. Can you talk?"

I said I could.

"I wanted to tell you Dad has pulled out of his coma."

"Wonderful," I interrupted.

"Yes, he's talking some, but not making any sense. That's not necessarily bad. It's understandable that his brain's a bit scrambled after what he's been through."

I told her I remembered how a couple of months earlier Cal had confused timeframes after he awoke from his coma after being hit in the head. It took him a couple of weeks to get back to normal—Cal normal.

"I hope that's the case," Tanesa said. "But it'll be a while before we know if dad has suffered permanent damage. The flow of blood had been restricted for a long time, and some, hopefully minor, damage is likely."

"The good news is he's still alive."

"Where there's life, there's hope," Tanesa said, sounding more like a philosopher than an ER doc.

I agreed, thanked her for calling, and asked if he could be having visitors anytime soon. She said she'd let me know, but it might be a while. I asked if she had called Bob to let him know. She said no and she had to get back to work and asked if I'd call him.

I made a quick call to Bob before I returned to the party. I felt I was talking to a total stranger rather than Bob. He was civil, almost polite, thrilled about Al, and for the cherry on top of the soda, he thanked me for calling. I hit end call and glanced at the screen to make sure I had called the same Bob Howard I had learned to love, despite himself.

I returned to the bar and found Barb to tell her the good news. She was talking to her step-brother Dude and from the slice of conversation I overheard they were sharing a story from their childhood in Pennsylvania.

I heard Dude say, "You be weird sis."

Barb laughed and said, "You calling me weird's like a frill-necked lizard calling a rabbit weird."

Dude looked at her and ran his hand through his long, stringy hair. "Me no know what naked lizard be."

Barb chuckled, "Frill-necked lizard. Take my word for it, it's weirder than a rabbit."

Dude rubbed his hair again. "Me take word of lawyerster even weirder."

Barb said, "I'm no longer a lawyer; I'm a simple bookstore owner."

"Cool."

I'd heard enough about weird and moved closer to Barb and put my arm around her waist.

Dude said, "Ewe, mushy. Me leave and let you mush-away."

I watched Dude move in Charles's direction and asked if Barb needed another drink.

"You had to ask if I wanted more beer after you saw me talking with Dude?"

I smiled and headed to the bar to get her another beer and refill my wine. Brad had another beer in his hand and was leaning on the bar; to be closer to Chester Carr who he was talking to, and to stay balanced. I heard him slur something about murder and going to catch the killer. I also saw Hazel headed his way, hopefully to rein him in.

I handed Barb her drink and told her about my call from Tanesa. She said that was great and pointed the neck of her bottle at Brad. "See you and your good bud have been powwowing."

"Good bud, no; powwowing, sort of. He's coming around to believing his daughter's death was not by her own hand." I told her what I had learned from Chester that shot down Joel's alibi. Barb asked if I had told Chief LaMond. I said, "Not yet."

She gave me a stern look and tilted her head in Cindy's direction. "You haven't asked my advice, but if you had, I'd tell you to tell the police what Chester told you and then butt out." She held out her hand before I could respond. "I know, I know. The odds on you doing that are as great as Dude playing Hamlet in a theatre production in town. So, please be careful. I'm getting accustomed to spending time with you, time with you alive."

"To show how much I pay attention to your advice, I'll tell Cindy now."

I started toward Cindy and Larry when Cal tapped on the classic microphone. I stopped and returned to Barb's side.

"Okay ladies and gentlemen," said Cal in his Texas accent. "Here's what you've been waiting for. Charles, come on up."

Charles looked at Cal, and turned to look at the crowd, before stepping behind the mic. He wiped the back of his hand on his shorts and gently touched the mic with his other hand and said, "I want to, umm, I want to thank ..." He lowered his head and coughed back a tear. He wiped his eyes and said, "Thank you for coming." He stepped back and Cal rushed over to him, put his arm on Charles's shoulder and leaned toward the mic.

"Folks, Charles wants to thank all of you for being so kind to him and to Heather before she left. He knows with all your fine thoughts she's bound to be okay, wherever she is. Now before some of you drift off, and before I sing a tune or two to honor Heather, let's all move closer to the stage."

Cal grabbed one of the chairs from the front table and set it behind the mic. He had Chester bring a long-handled, silver flashlight to the stage and told him where to stand with it. Cal asked Larry to hit the light switches so the only illumination in the room came from the neon beer sign over the bar. The room became eerily silent and Cal said something to Chester who turned the flashlight on and pointed it at the empty chair.

Cal said, "This is for you, Heather. Safe travels." He started singing Heather's favorite song, and one she had sung at every performance in Cal's. "Crazy."

I began to feel like I was at a funeral, and in some way, I suppose I was.

3 7

Cal's tribute was well intentioned. He had a huge heart and wanted to do everything in his power to smooth Heather's departure and to show Charles he and many others cared. Unfortunately, it had the opposite effect on my friend. After Cal's flashlight moment, he slid into a set of traditional country songs, and Charles came close to sliding off the stage. Even before the lights were turned back on, I saw Charles slump and grab his knees. I rushed to the stage and gave him a shoulder to lean on as he moved to the nearest table. He was hurting. I got him a glass of water and asked if he was okay to walk. He didn't need to stay in the bar any longer. I motioned for Barb to help me clear the way to the exit and Charles walked, with the aid of each of us, out the door where he sucked in the fresh air and regained his composure. Several people who had come for the sole purpose of supporting Charles saw us, wanted to say something to him, but instead respected his privacy as we left.

Charles had driven the seven blocks from his apartment to Cal's, but said he'd feel better if he walked around a while before walking home. I asked if I could go with him, and I was pleased when he said yes. Barb headed to her condo, and Charles and I inched our way to the Folly Pier. It was in the opposite direction from his apartment, but I could tell he wanted the peaceful walk to the end of the structure. It was in the mid-eighties but a brisk breeze blew off the ocean and made the walk comfortable. I didn't know what to say, and Charles seemed caught up in his thoughts and didn't speak.

We reached the end of the pier, Charles flopped down on one of the wooden benches, and I sat beside him and waited for him to start the conversation. No words came as we both stared at the lights of the Tides Hotel and the large Charleston Oceanfront Villas condo complex beside the hotel. A few small groups of people walked along the beach swinging flashlights toward the sand as they went along.

"Nice tribute Cal put together," Charles said, the first words he'd spoken in fifteen minutes.

"It was," I said.

"Wouldn't be surprised if Heather didn't see it however she gets the vibes. Hope she did."

"She knows we all care."

Charles stared at the shore and said, "Chris, I thought I was as messed up as a person could be after Melinda died two years ago." He turned to me. "I didn't know what screwed up was until now. Why didn't I ask Heather to marry me earlier? Why?"

No answer would be adequate, so I said, "Sorry. You know she did what she had to do. Maybe she'll come back. You never know."

He shook his head like he was flailing out bad thoughts. "Heard anything about Al?"

I was glad he'd changed the subject. What else could be said about Heather? I was also glad to tell him about Tanesa's call and Al's improved condition.

He sat up straighter. "When were you going to tell me?"

Charles was getting back to being Charles. I told him this was the first opportunity. He didn't agree or disagree; he huffed.

"Want to know what I heard about Joel's alibi for the time Lauren Craft died?"

"Duh!"

I told him about what Chester had said and that I was going to share that information with Cindy in the morning. I hesitated and told him what Barb had said about me about me butting out. Charles asked why? I said because I didn't know how I could find out more and was leaving it to the police.

He looked at the Tides and at me. "Teddy Roosevelt said, 'Whenever you are asked if you can do a job, tell'em, *Certainly, I can!* Then get busy and find out how to do it.' You've got to find out how to catch that sleazeball who killed Lauren, and who's trying to stomp Brian's chance of getting reelected."

"Tomorrow," I said. "I'll deal with it tomorrow."

Charles nodded, and said, "Think I need to get this weary sack of bones home."

"I'll walk with you."

"Out of your way, besides, I need to be alone."

Charles stood, grabbed his cane from the deck, and left me seated on the pier.

The faint sounds of music coming from the bars on Center Street combined with an occasional slap of waves against the pier's pilings were the only sounds I heard. Most of the noise came from thoughts and questions rattling around in my mind. Tonight's party, even though it was the creation of Charles himself, showed him how much support he had and how much everyone missed Heather, but I was afraid that instead of cheering him up, it put him deeper into a funk. Charles was hurting and there was nothing I could do for him. I would be there for him if he asked for anything, but was that enough? Al had broken free from his coma, but could have significant brain damage, a condition possibly worse than if he had died. Bob now had a bar to run; a career change that would tax anyone, so no telling how it would affect my burly, aging, iconoclastic friend. There were way more downsides than positives. And I still had the nagging feeling Lauren's and Katelin's deaths were at the hands of the person who was trying to unseat my friend as mayor, instead of suicide or resulting from an overdose.

It was too late to call Cindy and tell her what I'd learned about Joel. Too late to do anything to help Charles. And there was nothing I could do to help Al. I started to tell myself things couldn't get worse but reminded myself that every time I had thought that, I was proven wrong. The wisest thing for me to do would be to go home, get some sleep, and contact Cindy first thing in the morning.

For once, I did the wise thing.

A LIGHT RAIN was falling the next morning as I crawled out of bed. My head was fuzzy from having more wine at Cal's party than food or sense. I was hungry and certain there was nothing in the house to eat; or at least, nothing intended to be eaten this early in the morning. I wasn't ready to face anyone in the Dog, so I walked next door to Bert's to grab coffee and a muffin. I was half-asleep as I left the house, but the steady rain served the same purpose as a shower, and I was fully awake as I stepped through the double door of the iconic store.

"Hear there was quite a bash at Cal's last night," boomed the cheerful voice of Eric as I headed to the coffee urn. "Suppose you were there." He threw the hand towel he'd been using to wipe crumbs off the counter over his shoulder and walked my way.

Somehow, our conversation had passed the *good morning* phase, so I smiled and said, "Yes, it was nice."

"How's Charles? Must have been a mixed bag for him."

I said he was pleased that so many people had turned out but was still in shock about Heather leaving.

"Sorry to hear it," Eric said, and tilted his head in the direction of my house. "Also hear your neighbor showed a side we haven't seen around here."

"Brad Burton?"

"That would be the one."

"What'd he do?" I asked.

Eric smoothed out his beard and nodded. "Let's see. First, I hear he tried to drink Cal's dry. Came close, from the word that's been spreading around here."

I looked at my watch. It wasn't yet eight o'clock, fewer than seven hours after the party ended. "Who'd you hear that from?"

"Chester Carr about a half hour ago, and Janice, she left right before you came in. That's all so far. I also hear he was nearly screaming before his wife dragged him out."

"Screaming about what?"

Eric looked around and even though we were the only two in the store, he leaned closer and said, "Screaming that Joel Hurt killed his little girl and he was going to prove it and make sure Hurt burns. You were there, didn't you hear him?"

I explained that Charles and I had left before it was over and missed Brad's outbursts.

"By now, you're probably the only two on Folly who haven't heard about it." Eric waved his arms around. "Speed of light and speed of rumors are about the same."

Eric was right and I told him so, when Preacher Burl strolled in, saw Eric and me, and gave a big Sunday morning smile. He wore a wrinkled white shirt, black suit slacks, and a food-stained tie.

"How is my favorite Bert's employee and my favorite retired, former photo gallery owner this fine Sabbath morn?"

Eric told the preacher he was "as fine as frog hair," a simile I understood, but had never been a fan of since frogs don't have hair, fine or otherwise. I simply said I was okay.

"Brother Chris, did you and Charles leave the gala early? I looked for you and no one seemed to know where you had gone."

"Charles needed fresh air, so we walked to the pier." Not quite the whole truth, but close.

"I thought it was as such. Brother Charles didn't appear chipper after Cal performed his moving rendition of Heather's favorite song. Is Charles okay?"

Eric excused himself to wait on a new customer.

I lowered my voice and said, "I'm glad you asked, Preacher. It might be helpful if you'd talk to Charles. He's pretty torn up about Heather leaving. I think it's worse than he was when his Aunt passed away."

"I will try to engage him in conversation after this morning's service. Of course, that's if he attends. Looks like we'll have to meet in the foul-weather sanctuary rather than on the beach. Will you be joining us?"

I hadn't planned to but couldn't think of a good excuse not to. "I hope to."

"Excellent, and I will do whatever I can to help Charles. He's lucky to have such a good friend as you. Of course, true friendship goes both ways."

"I agree, Preacher. I don't know how I would have survived over here without Charles."

Burl smiled and said, "I wish I had such close friends during my times of need."

"One question," I said, "did my neighbor, Brad Burton, say anything, umm, unusual after I left the party?"

Burl looked down at the concrete floor. "Now, Brother Chris, you know I'm not prone to gossip and am uncomfortable saying anything negative about someone, especially after the tragic loss of his daughter."

That said enough. "I understand Preacher."

"I need to prepare for this morning's service. See you in church."

I nodded, more uncommitted than affirmative.

3 8

The rain intensified and I rooted through the hall closet to find my seldom-used umbrella before I headed out to First Light Church's harsh weather meeting spot in a former storefront on Center Street. Preacher Burl had come to Folly from Indianapolis and founded the church under the sun and over the sand on the beach close to the Folly Pier. Because of its unique location and endearing personality of its minister, First Light had grown and met needs of residents the city's traditional houses of worship failed to attract. Charles was a regular, and I, for lack of a better term, had become an irregular in attendance.

I shook water off the umbrella and set it inside the door. The rain, combined with meeting in the least popular of the church's sanctuaries, had taken its toll on attendance. There were fewer than a couple of dozen people gathered around the lemonade cooler in the front corner of the storefront. Charles was talking to the preacher but before I could speak to them, Burl moved to the school lectern that served as his common-man's pulpit.

"Please take your seats and silence thy portable communication devices," Burl said, using the words that had started every service. I joined Charles on the second row and looked around. I was surprised to see Joel Hurt moving to the front pew. He had a *look at me, I'm important* smirk on his face and took his time being seated to make sure everyone saw him.

I must confess—something that's wise to do in church, but not the best route in the courtroom—that I didn't pay much attention to Preacher Burl's Bible readings and homily. My thoughts kept going back to Lauren, Katelin, Joel, and how devastated Brad and Hazel Burton must have been and Brad's outburst that Chester Carr had told me about. Something else kept nagging at me, something I couldn't put my finger on, but something that seemed important at the time. What was it?"

As Burl's flock, as he called us, stood to sing one of my favorite hymns, "How Great Thou Art," to conclude the service, I still couldn't get my mind off Joel and my hostile feelings toward him.

"Chris, earth to Chris," Charles said and tapped my arm.

"Sorry," I said. "What?"

Several of the worshippers had left and Charles and I were standing beside the pew. "Burl wants to talk to me, but I told him you and I were heading to the hospital to sneak in and see Al."

It was the first I'd heard about "our" plan. "We are?"

He answered my question when he said, "Ready to go?"

The ride to the hospital on the edge of downtown Charleston was miserable. The rain was so intense that layers of water covered more of the roadway than remained clear. Charles stared out the side window and didn't say anything about last night's party. He never mentioned Heather and had the defeated look of someone wallowing in misery. My focus was on keeping the car from sliding off the road.

I wasn't any more optimistic as we entered the automatic front doors of the hospital. I couldn't imagine that they would let us see Al, making the trip a total waste. My fears were partially realized. Outside the intensive care unit, a harried nurse stopped us and said there was no way Al Washington could have visitors. I asked her if Dr. Tanesa Washington was on duty. She said she didn't know but was kind enough to check and told us Al's daughter was in the hospital and for us to go to the ER and ask if Dr. Washington was available.

We had waited fifteen minutes before Tanesa was able to meet us in the corridor outside the emergency room. Her shoulders were slumped, her eyes bloodshot, and it looked like she'd aged a decade since I'd seen her last.

She managed a smile and said she was glad to see us. I asked if she was okay and she said, "Not really. We lost someone on the table." She bit her lower lip and shook her head. "Not a damned thing I could do to save him."

I told her I was sorry and she said it was part of the job. I didn't know how she did it and told her so.

"Thanks. I suppose you came to see Dad."

"You bet," Charles said. "How can we sneak in?"

"It's better if you didn't. He's in bad shape, still not making sense. Sorry."

I told her we were sorry as well and were praying for him.

"I'll tell you something you can do," she said.

Charles asked what.

"Bob Howard was over a couple of hours ago. I told him the same thing I told you about seeing Dad. He was on his way to open the bar. He's been a godsend and allowing him to keep his pride and joy open. The bar's been Dad's life, and Bob's truly been Dad's savior." She hesitated and scraped her shoe on the tile. "But, umm, how can I say it, I worry about the, umm, cultural differences between Dad's customers and, umm, Mr. Howard."

"Got it," I said and smiled.

Tanesa returned the smile. "I know Lawrence, Dad's cook, will be there and helps more than Dad would admit, but, well, you know."

I did and told her getting a cheeseburger was next on our agenda.

She thanked us and said she needed to get back to work. She shuffled back into the ER and we left to make the short three block drive to Al's Bar and Gourmet Grill.

The sounds of Marvin Gaye singing "I Heard It Through the Grapevine" reached us before I reached for the door to the tired bar. We stepped in the dark room and waited for our eyes to adjust before trying to find Bob. From what I could see, the crowd appeared as sparse as it had been at the First Light service. There were groups at three tables and two men leaned against the bar. Lawrence was facing the grill and the most unlikely bar owner in the United States and probably on the continent leaned against the wall beside the grill.

Bob had on frayed navy-blue shorts, a sweat-stained Hawaiian flowery shirt, and a frown the size of a football. Sweat rolled down his cheeks.

I smiled as I approached him. "See you have everything under control."

Bob wiped the sweat from his cheeks. "You're a damned smart ass."

"Is that anyway to address your fine customers?" I said.

"Hell no, and if a fine customer ever comes in, I'll treat him different."

Charles couldn't stand being left out, even if it was a conversation of insults. "How are things going, Bob?"

Bob pointed his chubby forefinger at the jukebox where Stevie Wonder was singing "Superstition." He pointed to his ear. "Is blood pouring out?"

Charles studied Bob's ear like it was an archeological find. "Don't see any."

"Damned sure feels like it. That frickin' crap these deaf-eared customers call music is making my head explode."

"What happened to all your country classics Al had added to the jukebox?"

Over the wishes of most of the bar's regulars, Al had added several of Bob's favorite country songs to his Motown-oriented jukebox. Bob and Al's friendship defied all logic, but it was real, "damned real" according to Bob.

"When you came in, did you see a damned picket line in front? Did you see angry, hungry hordes flinging signs around and chanting 'Down with Country Music!?'"

We said no.

"Know why you didn't?" Bob asked.

I played along. "Why?"

"Because that damned Al's afro, black, negro, African American, or whatever they want to be called today, customers said unless I kept the jukebox playing good music and not country crap, they were going to picket. Chris, I've been in here less than a week and have already had to squelch a damned race riot. Hell, I had one former Black Panther member scoot in on a walker and threaten to punch me in my happy, smiling, ivory-colored face."

And I'd wondered why Tanesa was worried!

Lawrence delivered burgers to the nearby table and came over and asked if we wanted anything to eat.

I started to answer when Bob said, "Lawrence, get your bony butt back to the grill. You're messin' in my job."

I was surprised when Lawrence smiled. "Yes, Master Bob, whatever you say." He walked away.

"He's a good guy," Bob said. "I'm thrilled he's here."

"And it shows," I said, oozing sarcasm.

"Yep," Bob said. "I'm a natural at this customer and employee relations schmoozing." He looked around the room like he didn't know what to do with us. Finally, he said, sit anywhere and don't mess up anything. Cleaning's not my strength."

Not like customer and employee schmoozing, I thought as we moved to the booth with Bob's plaque on it.

"Think he'll make it?" Charles asked.

"Al or Bob?"

Charles looked toward the grill. "Bob. Al's in good hands."

"If someone doesn't kill him first, he has a chance," I said.

"Those two opposites would do anything for each other," Charles said and shook his head, more in admiration than anything negative.

I tapped my fingers on the table. I realized what had been nagging at my unconscious: Joel's alibi, more accurately, his alibis.

"Charles," I said, "What were you doing three days ago in the middle of the afternoon?"

"Don't know, why?"

"That's the point."

"What on earth are you talking about?"

"If someone asked me what I had been doing let's say last Thursday at two o'clock, I would have been hard pressed to remember. You just said you couldn't remember three days ago. I suspect that'd be true if you asked most people about a day and time farther back than yesterday. Times get muddled, the order in which we do things can get turned around, and whether we admit it, much of what we do is so inconsequential that we don't remember it."

Charles looked down at the table and blinked twice. "Yeah, a couple of days before Heather wanted to talk to me—you know, before she decided to leave, I thought about talking to her about marriage. I forgot all about it and look what happened. She's gone."

That wasn't what I had meant, but my friend was having a tough time focusing. What had happened with Heather was weighing on him. I tried again, "My point is we forget our actions quicker than we think that we do."

He said, "True, so what?"

"Joel told Cindy that he had been meeting with his campaign manager at the time Lauren died."

"Yes."

"And Wayne confirmed Joel's alibi. That means—"

"So?" Charles interrupted.

"Let me finish. When Katelin allegedly killed herself, Joel told the chief he was with one of his landscape crews, or possibly pricing a landscape job at one of Wayne's remodel sites, or he could have been driving between some of those locations."

"Come on Chris, I've got a headache. One more time, so what?"

Lawrence brought our cheeseburgers before I got to the *so what*. The soothing aroma from the still-sizzling burgers made me realize how hungry I was and I took a bite before continuing. Charles ignored his food and stared at me. Waiting was not one of his strengths.

"So, Joel has one airtight alibi, and one that wouldn't hold up in court. If the police had suspected that Katelin's death wasn't a suicide, Joel would be the prime suspect. He may be a liar, but he's not stupid. He would have known he would be a suspect and would have concocted a better alibi."

"I don't follow," Charles said and waved his hand in my face. "Got a question, do you think Heather heard how good everyone was talking about her at the party?"

Charles was able to change direction on a pinhead, but whenever we had been talking in the past about something as serious as murder, he was the first not to let the conversation drift.

"I'm sure she knows how much everyone there loves her," I said, hoping that satisfied his concern.

"I think so too. Sorry, what were you saying about Joel's alibis?"

I repeated what I'd said and Charles looked toward the door, before he said, "Are you still thinking Joel killed both?"

"He's obsessed about getting elected mayor. He's started an aggressive political campaign much earlier than anyone ever has. He's proven himself to be a liar and backstabber. And one of the foundations of his campaign is to stamp out illegal drugs on Folly."

Charles made eye contact. "And his girlfriend's thought to be a druggie, not quite the poster child for his campaign." Charles nodded. "So, Joel killed Lauren and Katelin, we already suspected that."

"But," I hesitated, "I don't think he did. He could have killed Lauren, or maybe he didn't."

Charles continued to ignore his lunch, but took a long draw on his Budweiser, and said, "So let me see if I have this right. You think Joel killed Lauren because he had an airtight alibi during her time of death. And that he didn't kill Katelin because he didn't have a good alibi? What am I missing?"

"Yes and no. What if we're looking at it backwards?"

Charles shook his head. "I feel like I'm talking to Dude. I know my mind's been operating at half-speed, but what in the hell are you talking about?"

The country sound of Roger Miller's "When Two Worlds Collide" flowed from the jukebox, and a chorus of groans came from two tables when Miller started singing. I glanced over at Bob who was standing by the door. He had a huge grin on his face.

I turned back to Charles. "In the last week Burl, Cal, and someone else have made comments about how good friends do anything for each other. Look at Al and Bob, or Cal and Burl; and, you don't look that far, how about you and me. I'd do anything for you, and suspect you'd do the same."

Charles nodded but didn't say anything.

"I think it was Wayne."

"Whoa, Wayne. Why?"

"He and Joel have been friends long before they moved to

Folly. Wayne is Joel's campaign manager and is as intent on getting Joel elected as Joel appears to be. Wayne alibied for Joel, but it also provided him an alibi at the same time. And, as far as I know, we don't know what Wayne's alibi is for the time when Katelin died, was killed."

Charles closed his eyes and tilted his head left and then right. "I still don't get why it was Wayne instead of Joel."

"Joel would have created a better alibi if he killed Katelin. From what everyone said, he was closer to Lauren than he let on after her death. I simply don't think he would have killed her."

"But you think Wayne could have because he wasn't close to her."

"Yes. I think my feelings about Joel have been biased because he's challenging my friend Brian."

Charles looked at his cheeseburger and at me. "I'm not convinced."

"I'm not sure I am either, but it makes more sense to me than the other way around."

"If Wayne did it, wouldn't Joel have known since he was Wayne's alibi?"

"Known maybe, suspected possibly. I don't know."

"So, what are we going to do about it?"

"I'm going to find Cindy after we leave here and tell her what Chester said about seeing Joel driving by his house when he was supposed to be with Wayne."

"And tell her your suspicions about Wayne?"

"Maybe."

I had been so intent on convincing Charles about the possibility of Wayne being a killer while trying to keep his focus off Heather long enough so we could discuss the killings, that I didn't notice Bob until he scooted into the booth and shoved me against the wall so he would have enough room to fit his ample rear on the seat.

Bob looked at Charles's plate and said, "What's wrong with your food? Hell, I didn't spit on it."

I knew Charles was in no mood for kidding, but Bob didn't.

Charles gave him a nasty look. "It's fine. I'm not hungry."

"Well excuse my helpful ass," Bob said and wrinkled up his nose. He turned to me. His shoulder rammed into my arm as he turned. He said, "Forgot to tell you something. I got a call last night from Jeff Holthouse."

"Jeff Holthouse?" I said.

"You getting senile? You met him and his wife at the fundraiser at my mansion."

"The realtors," I said.

Bob nodded. "Anyway, Jeff called to say he had met with Joel Hurt again about the landscape job he told you about at the party. Joel started talking about how corrupt your buddy Brian Newman was. Joel had told him the same thing earlier, and Jeff wanted to change the subject and said something about hearing about the woman who killed herself in the garage and wondered if Joel knew her. Know what Joel told Jeff?"

I wondered how I would have known. "What?"

"Joel told Jeff he barely knew her, but his best friend had dated her but dumped her because she was crazy."

"Did Joel say who his best friend was?"

"Damn, Chris, do I have to do everything for you? I figured that might be a clue but I don't know a clue about what. And don't say you're not getting involved in whatever's going on over there. You always say that, but you get sucked in anyway."

I started to thank Bob for whatever, when one of the customers at a table by the window yelled, "What's it take to get another beer around here?"

"Hold your damned horses!" Bob said and mumbled something I couldn't understand.

"Customer schmoozing, Bob," I said. "Customer schmoozing."

He cocked his head in my direction. "Smart ass." He pushed himself up from the table and ambled to the thirsty customer to do some customer schmoozing.

"Interesting," I said to Charles.

Charles watched Bob go and said, "Don't suppose Joel's best friend is Wayne."

"I'd put money on it."

3 9

There was no break in the rain as I headed back to Folly. There was also no break in Charles's despondency. I tried to talk about Joel and Wayne and anything either of us may have heard that would help point a finger at one or the other, but I would have had better luck talking to Bob's customer who wanted another beer. I understood Charles's pain, but didn't know what I could say to help. I decided silence was the best approach and listened to the wipers slapping against the windshield as they rhythmically moved back and forth, barely keeping up with the downpour.

The rain had eased as I pulled in Charles's parking lot. I asked if there was anything I could do for him and he mumbled something about nothing could be done. I reached over to pat his arm, but he opened the door and hopped out of the car before I could say anything else. He opened his apartment door and went in without looking back, and I sat in the car staring at his closed door.

I couldn't do anything to help my friend but did have some thoughts I wanted to share with Chief LaMond about the two deaths. I called her cell phone and was rewarded when she answered. I asked if she had a few minutes to spare. She said no, but it had never stopped me from interrupting her in the past so she didn't see any reason for me not to interrupt now. She was at her office and said she was stuck under a "three-foot high pile of elephant poop" and I could stop by and help her dig herself out. I assumed she'd meant it figuratively, and said I was surprised she was at the office Sunday evening.

"Twenty-four seven, twenty-four seven," she said and I said I'd be there in a few minutes.

Her office was on the second floor of the relatively new police and fire addition to the back of the coral-colored city hall. I knocked on her door and she yelled for me to come in. I was relieved to see that the three-foot high pile of elephant poop was a foot of file folders and loose papers.

She looked up. "There'd be less paperwork if we shot everybody who got drunk or parked the wrong way on the streets." She threw a piece of paper in the air. "I'm stuck in report hell."

"The glamour of chiefdom," I said and moved a pile of file folders off the chair in front of her desk and sat. I looked out the large window behind her that looked out on the Surf Bar. The rain had returned and the expression on Cindy's face was as gloomy as the weather.

She moved the stack of folders to the side of the desk and said, "Okay, this ain't national *invite yourself to the office day*, so why are you here and how are you going to ruin what's already a crappy day?"

Bob and Cindy could use a lesson, or two, or a million, in schmoozing, but I didn't figure this was the time to start. Instead, I began telling her what I had learned from Chester about Joel's alleged alibi.

She stuck both palms out like she was stopping traffic. "Halt! If you're going to try to get my brain working by spinning some convoluted story, I need bourbon." She rolled her eyes. "Since I'm stuck in report hell, coffee'll have to do. Want some?"

I said yes and she scurried out of the office and left me staring at the rain and wondering what I was going to say next that could possibly convince the chief I hadn't lost my mind. She returned before I'd figured it out and was carrying two white mugs with FB in blue letters on the outside and steaming hot coffee on the inside.

She handed me one of the mugs, lowered herself in her chair with a sigh, and said, "Let's hear it."

I spent the next ten minutes telling her everything I knew and everything I suspected. She shifted from exasperated bureaucrat to attentive police chief and even took notes during my monologue. I finished and realized I hadn't convinced myself of Wayne's guilt, so I doubted Cindy had been swayed.

The chief nodded, looked down in her coffee mug, and then back at me. "Chris, I've known you for a long time, going on eight years if my finger counting is accurate. During that time, you and your collection of quirky pals have defied all odds and have stumbled into some terrible situations and even more odds defying have helped catch some really, really bad people."

I shrugged.

"You've also accused folks of dastardly deeds who were as innocent as, umm, I don't know any spiffy analogies, but they were innocent."

I couldn't argue with that. I nodded.

"We've had two tragic deaths in the last few days, and both were investigated by the Sheriff's office. You know, I don't take too fondly to some of the sanctimonious, egotistic, know-it-all folks in that office, but most of the time they're right. They say one of the deaths was suicide and the other either a suicide or a self-inflicted drug overdose."

"I know, but…"

Cindy interrupted. "Hold that but. Here's my but. I tend to

half-way agree with you, a practice that will be the end of me yet. I believe their deaths were caused by someone else, but I think it was Joel. Before you say it, it's not because he wants to kick me out of this high-paid, sexy, all-powerful, fun-filled job, but because, if Chester is right, Joel loses his alibi and he had the most reason to want Lauren out of the way. I don't know what happened with Katelin, but suspect she knew something about Joel and he was getting antsy about whatever it was getting out."

I couldn't argue with Cindy's logic, but still felt Joel would have done a better job establishing his alibi.

"You may be right, but could you at least check to see if you can pin down Wayne's whereabouts at the time Katelin died? And, I believe Chester did see Joel during that time frame. If he did, that means Wayne's story about being in a strategy session with Joel is bogus."

Cindy fumed, hemmed and hawed, and mumbled a couple of profanities, but in the end, agreed to talk to Chester, and again with Wayne and Joel. I thanked her and headed to the door before she changed her mind.

I wasn't quick enough. "Hit the brakes, troublemaker."

I stopped and turned back to the chief. She ruffled through a stack of papers and pulled one from near the bottom. She slipped on reading glasses and said, "Think you'll find this interesting. At zero two hundred—that's two this morning to you civilian types—Officer McCormick stopped a *Caucasian Male, age sixty-five, walking in a staggering pattern, along the two hundred block of East Arctic Avenue.* I'll skip the rest of the professional police jargon and'll dumb it down for you. Officer McCormick said the man was clearly inebriated and while staggering isn't against the law public intoxication is. The staggerer was alternating between mumbling and yelling words that sounded like, 'I'll get the son of a bitch if it's the last thing I'll do.' That may not be an exact quote, but it conveys the message."

"Who?" I asked.

"Chill. I'm on my way there. Now, if we arrested every citizen who's walking the streets, sidewalks, and beach under the technical definition of intoxicated, we'd have to rent the Tides to hold all of them in. For that reason, and another less ethical one, Officer McCormick ushered the individual far off the roadway and out of the way of moving vehicles and let him off with a warning."

"Then why the report?"

"Good question," Cindy said, and turned the report face down and slid it back in the pile of papers. "Officer McCormick, being an astute officer and one who didn't want me to be caught with my pants down—figuratively—thought he'd better write it up and give it to me. To shred or not to shred, that is the question."

I was ready to reach over the desk and grab the report, but Cindy decided she'd teased me enough. "You want to know who it was?"

"Of course."

"I believe you know him. After all, he's your neighbor."

"Brad Burton?"

"Bingo."

I shared how I'd mentioned at the party what I'd learned about Joel's alibi falling apart, and how Brad had reacted. Cindy said it must have eaten on him the more he'd thought about it. She also said Officer McCormick had taken extra time patrolling near where he'd stopped Burton. Her officer knew who Burton was and wanted to extend as much "fellow officer courtesy" as possible, even though Burton was retired. She ended with saying McCormick only saw Burton one more time, and he appeared to be near his house. I thanked her for letting me know and left her office. This time she didn't stop me.

The rain was stronger than it had been on the ride back to Folly and I had left the umbrella in the car. I was soaked before I reached the dry confines of the car. What now? I agreed with

Cindy's need for a bourbon, or wine in my case, but decided it was too early for that and headed home. Besides, I needed to get out of these wet clothes.

I pulled in the drive and looked over at Brad and Hazel's house. I had only a few conversations with Hazel, and although I had spent much more time than that with Brad, we weren't friends. He was hurting and I was surprised by his early morning behavior after Charles's party. I could understand his anger, but he'd never struck me as someone who would become that agitated. Common sense told me I should butt out. I had shared what I had learned with the police chief. It was up to them to follow up. But Brad was my neighbor now, and wasn't checking to see how he was the neighborly thing to do? Maybe, but most neighbors didn't have as strained a relationship as I had with the former detective. But, that was in the past, and in the last few weeks he had confided some things in me he wouldn't have broached in the past. And, I kept coming back to the fact he was my neighbor.

So what harm could come from changing into dry clothes and walking next door to see how he was doing?

Had I only known!

4 0

It was still raining as hard as ever, but this time I had my umbrella, as I walked through the wet grass and hopped over a couple of puddles on my way to the Burton's door. I figured someone was home since I could see the rear of Brad's car sticking out from around the side of the house. I couldn't see if Hazel's vehicle was there. After three knocks, I was beginning to doubt my initial assessment. Perhaps Brad had gone somewhere with Hazel.

I heard what sounded like a piece of furniture hitting the floor, and the sound of a door slamming at the back of the house. I rushed around the house and saw the back of a man jogging toward the yard behind the Burton's. More accurately, I saw Wayne Swan running away.

Do I chase him? Do I see what had happened in the house? He had a head start and twenty years of youth on me, so the odds on me catching him were minimal. And what would I do if I caught him? I turned and headed to the back door. It was standing open a couple of inches.

I started to knock, but instead pushed the door the rest of the way open and yelled, "Brad, Hazel?"

The rain was making so much noise that I didn't hear anything, so I stepped in out of the deluge and yelled again. I was in the kitchen and everything appeared normal. There were a couple of supper plates in the strainer beside the sink and two magazines open on the small island on the far side of the room. "Brad, Hazel?" I tried again.

This time I heard a faint noise on the other side of the island that sounded like someone moaning. I moved around the island. Brad on the floor, on his side, his arm was bent over his head, and a trickle of blood oozed out from under his arm. His left leg moved—he was alive.

I knelt beside him and asked if he could hear me. He mumbled something I couldn't understand and I leaned close to his head and asked him to repeat it.

"Hazel," he said, "shit … call." He mumbled something else, but again, I didn't understand.

I stood, careful not to move Brad, and grabbed a dishtowel off the island and moved his arm away from his head wound. It was bleeding but the flow had eased. I covered the wound with the towel and moved his arm back over it.

"Brad, put pressure on the towel. I'll call for help."

"Hazel," he mumbled.

I pulled my phone out of my pocket and tapped in 911, as I looked around the kitchen for Brad's wife. I told the professional sounding 911 operator where I was and that she needed to dispatch an ambulance and the cops. She told me to stay on the line until help arrived; I said I'd try, but finding Hazel was more important than maintaining phone contact.

I told Brad not to move and that help was on the way. He didn't respond and I didn't think there was anything I could do for him, so I headed to the other rooms to find his wife.

The two small bedrooms were on the left side of the house

and I did a quick canvas of each of them. No Hazel. The bathroom was between the bedrooms and again, no one was there. I had glanced in the living room on my way to the bedrooms and hadn't seen anyone but had to look more closely. After all, I wouldn't have seen Brad hidden by the kitchen island if I hadn't heard him.

In the living room, I looked behind the couch and the two chairs. I heard the sirens from the emergency vehicles heading in our direction as I concluded Hazel wasn't at home. I started back to check on Brad when I noticed a red, nylon NIKE backpack in front of the couch. It had to have been there when I first looked in the living room, but I didn't notice it. I wouldn't have now if it didn't seem out of place. I couldn't picture either of the Burton's taking long walks, much less backpacking anywhere.

I knelt beside the backpack and unzipped the top zipper. What I saw made me thankful I had a strong heart. Five sticks of what looked like dynamite were wrapped together by duct tape. Taped to the top was a small digital clock with a display that showed minutes on the top and seconds in smaller numbers at the bottom.

The hour and minutes display read 0; the second display clicked from 59 to 58. Crap!

Now what? The wires attaching the clock to the dynamite were taped so I couldn't see them; and even if I could, I had no idea which ones to try to unhook.

The seconds display read: 53. Probably not enough time to take the backpack to anywhere safely. The emergency vehicle sirens were closer, but not close enough to do anything.

I had to get Brad out of the house.

47 seconds!

I ran to the kitchen and leaned down over Brad. "Brad, can you hear me?"

He moved his arm and moaned.

"Can you get up?"

No reaction, and there wasn't time to ask again. I grabbed him under the arms and tried to pull him toward the door. He wasn't a large man but lifting him was like lifting three sacks of concrete. It was all dead weight. I managed to slide him around the island and to within a few feet of the back door.

He moaned louder and I was afraid I was hurting him, more than he already was. The alternative was worse, so I ignored his moans and dragged him to the door. I stepped off the back porch and yanked him out the door and into the yard. He gave a loud guttural sound and opened his eyes and gave me a look like he thought I was killing him.

I ignored him and continued to drag him away from the house. My back felt like it was on fire and my arms were numb. We were twenty feet from the house when all hell broke loose.

I was facing the house with my arms wrapped around his chest. It looked like a bolt of lightning. The white flash blinded me, before the shock waves from the explosion slammed into us. I was knocked on my back and Brad didn't move. The kitchen window shattered into a zillion particles and covered the yard like a hailstorm. The door flew off its hinges and landed three feet to our left. Everything happened at the same time and I couldn't comprehend it. I think I saw the back-wall buckle and fall; part of the roof fell with it.

The sound of the explosion was deafening—literally. I saw parts of the house flying around but didn't hear a thing. The rain was joined by pieces of the house pelting down on the yard. It wasn't until someone held a large golf umbrella over our head, that I realized others were there.

The entire back half of the house was demolished. There was little fire after the explosion, but the fire department was hosing down the house. I don't know why it came to me, but I smiled thinking the hoses weren't needed; the rain was doing a good job of soaking everything.

I slid out from under Brad and two paramedics began

working on me. One of the firefighters asked if I was okay. He pointed to my head and said I was bleeding. Other than feeling like I had been run over by one of the fire engines, I said I was fine, but he insisted one of the EMTs look me over. He also asked if anyone else was in the house. I said no but wondered what Brad had meant when he kept saying Hazel.

Cindy arrived next and shoved her officer out of the way so she could get to me. I assured her I was okay, and told her what had happened, and who I had seen running from the house moments before the explosion. She asked if I was sure. I nodded, and she stepped away and called someone on her radio.

Brad was loaded on a stretcher and they were loading him in the ambulance. I was concerned about Hazel and saw Brad talking to the EMT. Thank God, he was okay—or close. I tapped the medic on the arm and asked if I could ask Brad a question.

"Make it quick."

Brad's eyes were blinking and his head was wrapped in gauze. He saw me and said, "What happened?"

"I'll tell you later. Where's Hazel? You kept mentioning her name when we were in the house."

"I wanted you to call her. She'll worry."

"I will, but, where is she?"

"The mall. She's buying drapery for the living room."

And we had nearly gotten ourselves killed because I spent so much time looking for her.

Brad reached over and squeezed my arm. I leaned closer, and he said, "I think we'll need more than drapery."

41

It had been eight days since the Burton's attractive wood-framed cottage had become a pile of kindling; the same number of days that it'd been since Hazel Burton arrived home with three sets of tan and green drapery and nowhere to hang them.

Six days had come and gone since Joel Hurt, faced with charges of murder, decided he would rather flip on his long-time friend, to avoid a long, protracted trial. While Mr. Hurt admitted that Wayne Swan had concocted an alibi for each of them for the time of death of Lauren Craft, he swore he didn't know Swan had killed Ms. Craft until Swan told him so, the day he decided to leave town.

Five days had passed since Trooper Marcel Samuels of the Massachusetts State Police pulled over a late model Dodge Ram Pick-up truck near Worcester and with a hand on his firearm asked the driver if he was aware the folks in the Charleston County, South Carolina's Sheriff's office had a keen interest in talking to him. In fact, the interest was so keen Trooper Samuels asked the driver, identified as Wayne L. Swan, to step out of the truck where he was cuffed and taken into custody.

Two days had passed since Al Washington had started speaking in coherent sentences and asking about how Bob was doing running Al's Bar and Gourmet Grill. I had gotten to see him for a few minutes and joined in a lengthy line of visitors who had lied to him about how wonderful things were at the bar but were truthful when we said he was sorely missed.

And, it had been twenty-four hours since Bob decided to hold a party at Al's bar to celebrate Al rejoining reality. Another reason became apparent when he said, "Since I've got to be at that damned run-down shack anyway, I want some of my friends suffering along with me."

I hesitated for several hours before calling Charles to see if he wanted to go with me. I had talked to him once since the explosion and had left three messages he hadn't returned. In the off-kilter spirit of Folly, apparently four times was the charm instead of three. Charles answered the phone. It was three in the afternoon but he sounded like he had been asleep. I told him about Bob's misery loves company party, and was surprised when he said, "Sure, nothing else to do."

It was Monday, a traditionally slow night for bars and restaurants, and Al's wasn't bucking the trend. Four elderly gentlemen were seated around the table closest to the door. Each held a beer bottle and a hand of cards. There was a pile of matchsticks on the middle of the table that I suspected had some value other than cheap wood. Two other tables were occupied with couples. I had seen most of the diners in Al's but didn't know their names. Bob had told us the party was to begin at eight, so of course, Charles insisted we arrive by seven-thirty, so, other than Bob, we were the only partygoers present.

Lawrence greeted us at the door. "Thank God, some of Bob's white friends finally got here. He's been pestering me ever since six wondering if anyone would show."

I told him that Bob told us the event started at eight.

Lawrence held out his hands. "Don't tell me anything about him. Lord, he's your friend. He only inherited me."

The only sound in the room was laughter coming from the card players. Bob looked over at us and walked to the side of the jukebox and hit some buttons. Willie Nelson began his version of "Faded Love," and an audible groan arose from the men at the card table.

Bob yelled over Willie's singing, "The party's on. Drinks are on me!"

That immediately stopped the card game and three of the four men raised their hands for more beer.

The door opened and Cal, followed by Chester Carr, stuck their heads in and stepped the rest of their bodies into the room, deciding it was safe. Cal had on his Stetson, his rhinestone-studded jacket, and jeans. Chester wore a navy blue, starched, dress shirt and gray dress slacks.

Bob saw them enter and said, "Look everybody, it's Hank Williams Sr. himself. And they thought you were dead."

The regulars had learned how much credence to put into anything Bob said; they ignored him. Rickey Van Shelton and "Somebody Lied," followed Willie on the jukebox and I heard one of the men at one of the other tables say something about grabbing the picket signs. Bob laughed, and Lawrence brought each of the newcomers a drink. It didn't look like the party's host was going to do it, so Charles and I pulled three tables together and slid chairs up to them.

It was Chester's first visit, and he looked around and took the chair closest to the back of the room. "How's Al doing?" he asked, to no one in particular.

Bob smiled and said, "He'll be back sitting over by the door in a couple of weeks. We'll try to find a chair for him or make him bring his own if we're crowded."

Right, I thought.

The Four Tops began "Reach Out I'll Be There," and an

on-key chorus of Hallelujah came from the card players. Bob made a choking motion and asked Charles how he was doing. Charles mumbled a neutral response and then Chester asked him if he knew anything about what was happening with Joel and Wayne.

"According to Marc Salmon, Wayne doesn't have a snowball's chance in that fryer over there." Charles pointed to the small kitchen. "And, while there isn't much to pin on Joel, he started his campaign as a dark horse candidate, and now would have a tough time finding a snail to ride to the polls on."

Bob had moved behind Charles. "That mean I can have my campaign contributions back?"

"No," I said.

"That's okay, my commission from finding the Burtons somewhere to live after Chris blew their house up will make up for it."

Cal tipped his Stetson in Bob's direction. "I hear finding them a house was easy. Didn't four people volunteer somewhere for them to live?"

"So, what's your point?" asked the Realtor.

Cal smiled. "My point is Folly has the kindest, most giving folks in the world and the Burtons are lucky to live there."

Chester didn't want to be left out. "And Chris is mighty lucky too. He ain't got Brad Burton next door anymore."

"Until they rebuild," Charles added.

Thanks for the reminder, friend.

Lawrence brought a second round of drinks to our table, and no telling what round to the card players. From the corner of my eye, I saw one of the players head to the jukebox and another member of the group move behind Bob.

The Four Tops blared, "Can't Help Myself," the man behind Bob twisted him around and walked him to the center of the room, where they were joined by the man who had gone to the jukebox.

Sugar pie honey bunch I'm weaker than a man should be, sang the man on each side of Bob.

Bob smiled and blurted out, *"I can't help myself, I'm a fool in love you see."*

I found myself somewhere between shock and amusement—not a bad place to be.

Can't help myself, no I can't help myself.

JOY

A FOLLY BEACH CHRISTMAS MYSTERY

1

Barb Deanelli was waiting for me in front of her condo building on West Arctic Avenue. It was a little after sunrise on a cold, mid-December morning, and she had on black skinny jeans, a black down jacket with a texture that looked like bubble-wrap packing material, black boots and a black wool beanie cap. She looked like someone planning to break in someone's second-story window.

Barb folded her five-foot-ten-inch trim frame into the front seat of my car and gave me a peck on the cheek. She was sixty-four years old, three years younger than me, yet looked much younger.

"You look more ready to climb Mt. Everest more than hunt shark teeth," I said and leaned closer to receive another kiss.

I was rewarded with an eye roll from the woman I'd been dating for six months. "After last-night's storm, I didn't know what to expect. Besides, the wind's kicking up and from previous trips to the County Park, I knew that there was nothing to block it from chilling my bones."

The Folly Beach County Park anchors the west end of the

small South Carolina barrier island and is a mile-and-a-half from Barb's condo. The park doesn't open to vehicles until ten, so I navigated the turnaround in front of the locked gate and moved to the nearest spot where I could pull off the road and park.

Barb was wiser than I was since I didn't have a down coat and had to get by with a lightweight jacket over a long-sleeve denim shirt. I'd never admit that I was cold and on my way to freezing in the brisk wind.

The park consists of more than a hundred acres of mainly flat, sandy terrain, and its beach covers more than four-thousand feet of ocean frontage. There's a picnic area, boardwalks, showers, dressing areas, and restrooms, but we appeared to be the only humans making our way from the deserted parking area to where she hoped to find shark teeth along the receding tideline.

"Tell me again why you decided to drag me out here this morning," I said as I put my arm around her waist to help block the wind. Block it from me, not from her.

"One of my customers, Michelle, makes shark teeth jewelry. I asked where she bought the teeth and she said she found them on the beach, and the best time to find them is after a storm stirs up the surf and extracts them from deeper water. I suppose I've led a sheltered life and didn't know that you could find them here."

"Thinking about making and selling jewelry in the store?"

Barb moved to Folly a year ago from Pennsylvania and opened a used bookstore on the town's main drag.

"No, it takes more patience than I have. I told Michelle I'd carry hers. She did pique my interest enough to ask where she found the teeth. She said anywhere along the beach, and the County Park was a good location, especially before others traipsed along the waterline and grabbed them." She waved her arms toward the ocean. "And, here we are."

Residents and visitors spend hours scouring the beach hunting the teeth that can date to prehistoric times, but in the decade that I'd lived here, I'd never found any. Someone once told me that you don't find shark teeth, they find you. Fortunately, no teeth still attached to a shark have found me, nor have any teeth from their ancestors. I didn't know about shark teeth, but yesterday and last night's tumultuous storm brought some of the largest waves I'd seen in years. Regardless, it was fun spending the morning with Barb.

Then it ceased being fun.

Barb pointed to something at the shoreline a hundred yards in front of us. It looked like a surfboard with someone splayed out on top. My hunch was confirmed as we got closer. The surfboard was barely out of the water and the body of a woman was partially on the board with her arms wrapped around it. Long, black hair either flecked with gray or mixed with sand was spread out and covered part of the white board. She had on tan khaki slacks, a red sweatshirt, and was barefoot. I wasn't optimistic about her being alive since the water temperature was in the low-fifties and prolonged exposure to it could be fatal. The top of her sweatshirt was dry, but the lower half was wet as were her slacks.

I bent down to feel for a pulse when her left hand grabbed my wrist. The sudden movement startled me, and I fell backwards in the damp sand. She let go and pushed up off the board before falling back. Barb moved to the other side of the board, knelt, and whispered something to the woman. The sky was getting lighter, and I noticed the woman's arms shivering.

I removed my jacket and covered her back. Barb laid her heavier jacket over the woman's legs before wrapping her arms around her to provide body heat.

I leaned back and punched 911 on my phone and told the dispatcher where we were and what we found. I suggested that along with medical help, she send the police. I didn't know what had happened but was confident that it wasn't a surfing accident.

Barb was talking to the woman, who'd turned on her side and faced my friend. A good sign.

The screaming siren of a police cruiser could be heard a few blocks away, and the distinct sound of one of the city's fire engines followed the cruiser. Help was on the way. The car's siren shut off, and it took another minute for its occupant to open the park's gate and continue to the parking area near where we were huddled.

"Chris Landrum, is that you?" yelled a Public Safety Officer, the official name of Folly's police officers.

I turned toward the voice and recognized Officer Allen Spencer. I'd met him shortly after he and I arrived on Folly ten years ago. At the time, he was in his mid-twenties, six-foot-tall, and at least thirty pounds lighter. We crossed paths often and had a good relationship.

"Allen," I said and stood to shake his hand.

We shook, and he nodded toward Barb. "Ms. Deanelli."

Barb acknowledged the new arrival and Officer Spencer shifted his attention to the person Barb had her arm around and who was sitting on the surfboard. Spencer saw how much she was shaking and added his heavy jacket to mine and Barb's.

The fire engine pulled beside Spencer's vehicle and two fire-fighters hurried over. One carried a heavy blanket and wrapped it around the woman. The other firefighter, who on Folly doubled as a certified EMTs, started taking the woman's vitals.

She was in good hands, so I stepped away from the medical team. Spencer followed and looked up and down the shore and then toward the parking area. "Chris, what happened?"

I said I had no idea and this was how Barb and I'd found her. He asked why we were here, and I shared Barb's story about hunting shark teeth. One of the EMTs returned Barb's coat and offered me my jacket.

Spencer watched him go back to his patient and asked me, "Did she say anything?"

"She mumbled something to Barb, but I didn't hear what it was."

Barb was standing back and watching the EMTs work on the woman. Spencer waved her over and asked her the same thing he'd asked me.

"She asked two questions. She said, 'Where am I?' I told her on Folly Beach." Barb looked back at the woman and shook her head.

I said, "The second question?"

Barb looked at Spencer. "She asked, 'Who am I?'"

2

The sun had begun warming the air while Barb, Officer Spencer, and I stood back and watched the EMTs load their patient in the ambulance that had arrived from nearby Charleston ten minutes after the first responders from the fire department. The three of us moved to the surfboard to see if it held any clues to what had happened.

Spencer flipped the board over and glanced at its underside. "This isn't a crime scene, so it doesn't matter if I disturb it," he said, more to himself than to Barb and me.

I knew as much about surfboards as I knew about the Harappan civilization. "Learn anything?"

"Not really. It's a Channel Islands New Flyer. Popular and common. Board of the year a few years back."

Officer Spencer spent many off-duty hours sitting on a surfboard waiting for the perfect wave, so I wasn't surprised with his knowledge of the vehicle that transported our mysterious lady to shore. I suspected that's where his knowledge about the event ended.

The first firefighter to the scene had loaded his equipment on his vehicle and came over to the three of us.

Spencer said, "Len, is she going to be okay?"

"I didn't see any signs of physical trauma. She has hypothermia and if you hadn't found her when you did, she might not have made it. Did you notice the red marks around her ankles?"

I said I had.

The firefighter, whom I'd never met before today, said, "It's not uncommon to see something similar caused by a surf leash attached to the ankle. Never around both ankles. She also has marks around her wrists."

"Think she was restrained?" I said.

"That'd be my guess. Don't hold me to it. It's for someone else to determine. Gotta get back to the station."

Spencer said, "Len, before you go, did she say anything about who she is or how she got here?"

"Nothing that made sense. Her speech was slurred, and she didn't appear to know where she was or why. Allen, don't read too much into it. Those are symptoms of hypothermia. She'll probably be fine in a few hours."

"Did you ask her name?"

He nodded. "She couldn't remember."

Len repeated that he had to get back to the station and walked away as a silver Ford F-150 XLT pick-up truck slid to a stop in the sand behind Spencer's cruiser. Cindy LaMond was named Director of Folly Beach's Department of Public Safety two years ago, and I'd known her since she joined the police force six years before that. She was a good friend and married to Larry LaMond, owner of Pewter Hardware, Folly's only hardware store.

The five-foot-three, well built, bundle of energy didn't waste time getting to us. In her endearing style, she said, "Hi Barb, what's that old fart Landrum dragged you into this time?"

I didn't recall dragging Barb into this or similar situations, but I'd inadvertently been ensnared in a few horrific situations since retiring on Folly after a peaceful, a.k.a. boring, life as a bureaucrat in a large insurance company in Kentucky.

Barb didn't know Cindy as well as I did, but knew her enough to ignore her comment. "Hi, Chief. Chris and I were looking for shark teeth and instead found a damsel in distress."

"Crap, Barb, you're beginning to sound like the old fart." The chief turned to me, "Okay, spill it. What in the hell have you stepped in now?"

We shared everything, which wasn't much, about what we'd found.

Cindy gazed out to sea, and said, "My highly trained, police brain tells me that the person who rode in on this board didn't surf from Wales. Any boats out there earlier? Any evidence she was at the park before ending at water's edge?"

"No and no," I said.

Spencer said, "It's possible she came from Kiawah."

Kiawah was another barrier island, and a gated resort fewer than two miles across the Folly River and the Stono Inlet from the County Park.

Cindy sighed. "It's also possible she was dropped out of a space ship and landed on our lovely slice of earth. Officer Spencer, contact the powers that be on Kiawah and see if they have any missing person reports. I'll do the same here."

I said, "Anything I can do, Chief?"

"Yes, you and the lovely lady standing beside you, the one I can't figure a reason in the world why she'd want to hang around with you, continue your search for shark teeth." She snapped her fingers. "Oh yeah, one other thing. Don't, that's do not, get the slightest inkling to butt in police business."

"Cindy—"

She interrupted, "I know, I know." She waved her hand in my face. "There's a better chance of you sprouting wings and flying to the Bahamas than minding your own business. Give it a try, for once."

"Of course, Cindy."

If she noticed my crossed fingers, she didn't let on.

Barb and I made our way to the car and were savoring heat pouring out of the vents. Our jackets were damp from covering the woman and Barb's teeth chattered.

"What do you think happened?" she asked as she rubbed her hands together in front of the vent.

"I don't think she started from the County Park, so Kiawah or from a boat seem like the most logical explanation. Another possibility is that she drifted to the ocean from either the Stono or the Folly River which means she could have gone in the water from several places. I hope someone reports her missing. That'd answer most of the questions."

"Hypothermia can cause temporary memory loss. If the EMT is correct, there's a good chance she could answer questions fairly soon."

"I hope so. One thing I'm certain of is that she didn't decide to go surfing dressed like that. Something happened, something bad."

"I don't disagree." She hesitated, and then in a lower voice said, "Are you going to follow Cindy's advice and leave whatever's happened to the police?"

Barb was aware of my knack of accidentally stepping in piles of problems, occasionally including murder. Less than a year ago, and with the aid of a few friends, I'd helped catch a killer who was seconds away from ending Barb's life.

"I'll try."

She smiled. "Thanks for not lying and saying that you wouldn't get involved. I'll take an *I'll try*."

I returned her smile and said what I wanted to do now was get her home so she could get in warm clothes and so I could do the same. I let her out at the gate to her condo complex and she left me with, "My next search for shark teeth will be at Mr. John's Beach Store."

I thought it was an excellent idea.

MY BEST FRIEND since I arrived on Folly, correction, my best friend ever, is Charles Fowler. We met during my first week here and it didn't take long to learn that he and I were as different as a blue jay was to a blue whale. Charles retired to Folly at the age of thirty-four. Since then and now, as he approached his sixty-fifth birthday, he'd never held a steady job. He picked up enough money to live modestly in a tiny apartment by providing an extra set of hands for local contractors, helping restaurants clean during vacation season, and delivering packages for our friend Dude Slone, owner of the surf shop. I'd spent those same years working in boring jobs while living a boring existence. Charles has quirks too numerous to list. Despite our many differences, we overcame the law of averages, and became closer than brothers. One of his quirks should be mentioned. If I learned something he'd consider interesting, such as discovering a beached lady at the County Park and didn't share it with him in the first seconds after learning it, I would be subjected to a glare, reprimands, and being chastised unmercifully.

I wasn't in the mood to be harassed and called him on my way home.

"Charles, good morning. I just left the County Park with Barb where we found an unconscious woman on—"

"Meet me at the Dog in fifteen minutes."

He'd hung up. It'd been more than a few seconds since we'd found the woman.

The Lost Dog Cafe was less than a block off Center Street, the figurative center of commerce on the half-mile-wide, six-mile-long island. I and many others consider it the best breakfast spot on Folly. My kitchen was used as often as a wood pencil in the BIC factory, so I'd spent countless mornings enjoying a warm breakfast, the company of my favorite server Amber, and conversations with various friends and acquaintances. It was named the Lost Dog Cafe, although there were approximately a zillion photos of dogs, none of them lost, attached to most every vertical surface in the restaurant. Its two outdoor patios were dog friendly and often occupied by more than one canine. Festive Christmas lights were strung around the railing around the front patio.

"Morning, Chris," Amber said as she met me at the door. "Your regular table?"

Amber was the one person on Folly who I'd known longer than Charles—two days longer. She was on the verge of her fiftieth birthday, five-foot-five inches tall, with long auburn hair, often tied in a ponytail while she was at work. She's funny, insightful, and one of Folly's rumor-collecting-champions. She and I had dated for a while and after that remained good friends. December was one of the few times of the year when the Dog wasn't packed and my favorite table along the back wall was vacant. I told her yes to my seating preference.

She pointed to the table and said, "Go ahead. I'll grab your water."

Two city councilmembers, Marc and Houston, were seated at their preferred table in the center of the room. They had been on the council as long as I'd been on Folly and weren't in danger of losing their elected positions anytime soon. Another position they weren't in danger of losing was as the town's unofficial gossips, especially Marc. To stretch the tree falling in the forest question, if something happened on Folly and Marc didn't know about it, did it really happen?

I said hi to the councilmembers, received pleasant grins, and from Marc, "Hey, Chris, what's new?"

I wasn't ready to throw the events from the County Park into the gossip mill. "Not much, how about you, Marc?"

"Same old, same old."

I smiled and nodded at the phrase I never understood since I wouldn't have a way of knowing what the same was with Marc, much less how the same had happened again. The smile was because I was surprised that he hasn't heard about the woman. I didn't have time to savor that knowledge since Charles barreled through the door and pointed at the table with his handmade wooden cane that he carries for no apparent reason. I nodded again, this time without the smile, and he made a beeline to the table.

At five-foot-eight, Charles was a couple of inches shorter than me and unlike my balding head, his graying hair always appeared to be in search of a comb. He wore a long-sleeve, gray and crimson, Washington State University sweatshirt, jeans that were too large, a canvas Tilley hat, and three-days of unshaven stubble.

He slid in the booth before I could get there, smiled, and said, "What took you so long to get here?"

I didn't take the bait but did take a sip of water from a Ball jar that Amber had slid in front of me.

"Spill it."

I figured he meant the story about the woman and not the water, so in a voice low enough not to reach the gossip-gathering ears of Marc and Houston, began rehashing the trip to the County Park. As with sharing most stories with Charles, I didn't get far before he interrupted.

"Who was she? Did her sweatshirt have a logo on it? Is she going to be okay? Did she have a dog with her?"

"Don't know. No. Don't know. No."

"I'm confused."

I'm usually the one with that feeling. "About what?"

"Which question I asked first?"

Amber returned with water for Charles, one of her endearing smiles, and the question, "What can I get you for breakfast?"

I said, "French toast."

"Lordy, Chris. One of these days you're going to order something different and my little-ole heart won't be able to take the shock."

Charles patted her on the arm. "Don't worry, Miss Amber, your heart's safe. And, if you're interested, I'll have the Loyal Companion."

She ruffled his unruly hair and said that she was always interested in him, pivoted and headed to the kitchen to order my French toast and bacon and eggs for Charles, a.k.a. the Loyal Companion.

"Okay," Charles said, "I'll start over. Are you sure she didn't tell you her name?"

I shook my head.

"I hate calling her *the woman*. Let's go with Jane Doe."

I nodded.

"Could Jane have gone in the water at the Park?"

"It's possible, although unlikely. There was nothing nearby that indicated that she'd been there before she washed up."

"No one goes surfing in khakis and a sweatshirt."

I didn't think that astute observation merited comment. I waited for him to continue.

"If Jane fell off a boat, she wouldn't have landed on a surfboard. Dressed like she was, it's unlikely that she would've willingly stepped in the water off Kiawah or somewhere back in the river. You're sure there was no evidence that someone smacked her in the head and dumped her in the Atlantic?"

"Sure, no. There was nothing obvious."

"She could've been drugged."

"It'll be up to the docs and the police to figure what happened."

"Chris, I was thinking."

Always scary when it came to Charles. I took a deep breath and said, "What?"

"Luck, karma, fate, predestination, whatever led you to Jane. She could've died if you weren't there. You saved her, so it's destined that you must figure out what happened."

"Charles, you know—"

He waved his hand in my face. "Here's the best part. I'll take time out of my busy schedule to help. Great news, right?"

For reasons unknown to anyone, Charles had decided a few years back that he was a private detective. Did he have a law enforcement background? Not unless you count being on weed patrol when he worked for a landscaper fifty years ago in his hometown of Detroit. Did he have private detective training? Absolutely not. Was he a licensed private detective? Nope. he was, however, a voracious reader with an apartment filled with more books than a Barnes & Noble store. He'd claimed to have read every mystery novel written since Gutenberg invented the printing press. That was an exaggeration, although not by much.

"That's a kind offer, considering how busy you are." I hoped he grasped my sarcasm since he didn't work and from what I could tell, had a blank calendar.

"Where do we begin?"

I sighed. "Charles, we don't know anything about her or what happened. I'm sure Chief LaMond will solve it."

He grinned. "See, Chris, Cindy LaMond is your friend. You found Jane. Your involvement is meant to be." He picked my cell phone off the table and handed it to me. "Go ahead, call and see what she's learned and tell her we're on the case."

That wasn't going to happen for more reasons that I could count. "Charles, she hasn't had time to learn anything. I suspect Jane is still at the hospital being evaluated."

"You're right again. Call me this afternoon after you talk to Cindy."

If I wanted to eat in peace, I knew what I had to say. "Sure."

Charles didn't get a chance to pin me down on what time I'd call him. He looked up and saw Burl Iven Costello standing by our table with a smile on his face.

"Good morning Brother Charles and Brother Chris," said the five-foot-six-inch tall, portly man with a milk-chocolate colored mustache who was standing beside the table.

Burl, known to most as Preacher Burl Ives Costello, arrived on Folly two years ago after founding and for several reasons closed churches in Mississippi, Florida, and Indiana. He began First Light, a non-denominational church that met most Sundays on the beach near the Folly Beach Fishing Pier. I'd become better acquainted with him when he became the prime suspect in the murder of two of his followers. Charles and I helped the police catch the killer when he tried to add Preacher Burl to his list of victims.

"Join us Preacher," Charles said, as he slid to the end of the seat to make room for the newcomer.

"If you don't mind."

He slid in beside Charles, not waiting to hear if we minded. He looked around the room and turned to Amber who was quick to the table to see what he needed. Charles told him to order anything he wanted because I was picking up the check. Charles was in the holiday spirit with my wallet. Burl said coffee was all since he'd had breakfast.

"Preacher," Charles said, "any trouble with the nativity this year?"

First Light Church had an impressive nativity scene squeezed on a narrow piece of land between the Folly Beach Post Office and Pewter Hardware Store. Last Christmas someone stole a valuable, hand-carved baby Jesus from the display, nearly sucking the Christmas spirit out of the island. A miracle in the form of two teenagers averted a disaster by finding the missing figurine Christmas Eve.

"Brother Charles, it's been perfect this year. Praise the Lord." He smiled. "Baby Jesus won't be making an appearance until Christmas Day and will be under the watchful eyes of members of our flock."

"Wise move," I said, and since he wasn't here to eat, asked, "What brings you out this morning?"

"Excellent question, Brother Chris. I was looking for Brother Taylor, one of my residents."

The residence Burl referred to was Hope House, which loosely could be described as a halfway house that the preacher had started nine months ago. A wealthy and generous member of First Light donated a six-bedroom house on East Erie Avenue under the condition that Burl would rent to people he felt needed the assist to get back to productive members of the community. Rent was based on ability to pay and ranged from zero to a few hundred dollars a month, with most residents near the zero end of the scale.

Charles looked around the room. "Don't suppose he's here?"

"No, Brother Charles."

"Why are you looking for him?" I asked.

"I learned of an outstanding job that I believe his skills would make him a perfect candidate."

"That's great, Preacher. How's the house doing?"

"Most of my prayers have been answered, although we've had a few challenges," Burl said, and nodded like he was praying. He then turned to me and smiled. "Our benefactor said that the house needed a couple of cosmetic improvements. I didn't realize a new electrical system qualified as cosmetic." Burl chuckled. "At least when the power was off, the residents didn't know that the air conditioner was also, how shall I put it, under the weather."

"What's going to happen?" Charles asked.

Burl looked toward the ceiling like he was checking with God for an answer. "Brother Charles, I'm leaving it in the hands of the Lord."

"Preacher, I don't think—"

"Worry not, Brother Charles, the Lord already sent an electrician and an HVAC specialist to address the issues. The Lord sent them, and Brother Edward sent a check to cover the expenses."

"Brother Edward?" I said.

"Edward Bancroft, the wonderful man who donated the house."

"That's great," Charles said. "How many residents are there?"

"Four, each is blessed with a private room although two of the rooms are so large that we could put two people in each if need be." Burl glanced over my shoulder. "Ah, there's my resident. I would like to stay longer but feel the necessity of sharing with him the good news about the job." He stood, said, "May you have a blessed day," and headed to the door to meet his resident.

Charles watched Burl put his arm around the shoulder of the man as he escorted him to an empty table. He then turned to me and glanced at his wrist where most people wore a watch. His was bare. "Isn't it time for you to call Cindy and find out about Jane Doe?"

I took a sip of coffee, regretted it immediately since it had turned cold, stared at Charles, and said, "No. She hasn't had time to learn more than she would've known fifteen minutes ago when I told you that I'd call her this afternoon."

Charles sighed. "Worth a try. You're going to call me as soon as you hang up with the Chief?"

"Yes, oh patient one."

IT WAS TWO HOURS LATER, and if I didn't call the Chief soon, Charles would be on my doorstep wondering why I hadn't let him know what she said.

"What took you so long to pester me about Joyce?" Cindy LaMond said when she answered the phone.

I would have preferred something along the lines of, "*Hi, Chris. How are you this afternoon? How may I help you?*" I also would have preferred to be twenty pounds lighter, thirty years younger, and have a full head of hair. The odds were equal for any of those events happening.

"Who's Joyce?"

"How quickly you forget, Mr. Senior Citizen. You found her this morning."

"The person we found said she didn't know her name. Is her memory back?"

"Nope."

I sighed. "How do you know her name's Joyce?"

"Superb detective work, an incredibly high level of training and experience, use of all of my Super Chief skills."

"And?"

"And, Joyce was printed with a laundry marker pen on the label in her sweatshirt."

"Wow. No wonder you're Chief."

"True, oh so true, Mr. Senior Citizen."

"Did your superpowers tell you if Joyce was her first or last name?"

"First, I assume. Who ever heard of Joyce as a last name?"

I wasn't a big reader and had seldom paid attention in literature class in school, but it didn't take a scholar to have heard of James Joyce. I shared that tidbit.

"How about anyone with that last name in our lifetime?"

"None I can think of."

"Then I'm sticking with it as her first name."

"Cindy, has she said anything about what happened?"

"Very little. She thinks she remembers being on a boat, a storm, and then in the water clutching the surfboard. Her next memory is of some old geezer staring at her."

"Old geezer?"

She shrugged. "I added that part. Anyway, she claims she doesn't know anything else."

"Had she been injured? I didn't see any sign of physical injury."

"She's at the hospital getting a complete checkup. They're planning on having a head-doc talk with her to see if she understood what happened. They'll hold her overnight and if nothing pops up, release her in the morning."

"Then what?"

"Then I'll see if her memory is back. I'm having my guys check if there's a missing person report matching her description."

"And, then what?"

"Heck if I know."

"Can she have visitors?"

There was an audible sigh. "Chris, is Charles rubbing off on you?"

"What's that mean?" I said, knowing exactly what she meant.

"Are you going to start playing detective like you half-wit friend?"

"Of course not. Barb and I found her and so I wanted to see how she was doing."

"Yeah, right. To answer your innocent sounding question, yes, she can have visitors."

Cindy gave me the room number and a warning that if I started nosing in police business, she'd have me arrested for impersonating an officer, for gross stupidity, and for giving her ulcers. She hung up before I could thank her for being so kind to one of her constituents.

4

Barb said she felt a connection to Joyce and offered to accompany me to the hospital. She also hinted that since we'd be in Charleston, it would be a great night to have supper at one of the city's many fine restaurants.

Joyce was barely recognizable as the person from the beach. Her hair that had been mixed with sand and in a state of disarray was now combed and while not styled, was passable. She looked to be in her forties and had healthy color in her cheeks as opposed to the white with a blue tinge they had on the beach. The look of confusion she gave us when we entered the room was replaced by a radiant smile of recognition.

"They tell me that you saved my life," she said, before we could speak. "Thank you."

Barb moved close to the bed and rested her hand on Joyce's shoulder. "We were worried about you. It's wonderful seeing you doing so well. I'm Barb and my friend is Chris."

I moved beside Barb and reached out and shook Joyce's hand. She let go and grabbed the television's remote and muted a game show that had an infuriatingly loud studio audience.

"Nice to meet you. Please have a seat."

There was only one chair, and I motioned for Barb to take it. I stood beside her and leaned on an over-bed table at the side of the room.

"I hope you don't mind us visiting," Barb said. "We were wondering how you were doing."

"Heavens, no. It's great seeing familiar faces. I wasn't at my best the last time I saw you."

"How are you feeling?" I asked.

"Fortunate. I have scrapes and bruises but nothing to complain about. They did an MRI on my brain, so I suppose I have one, although it's a bit scrambled. The main problem was hypothermia, and they had me drinking hot tea and wrapped in warm blankets. I'm fine now and told they're going to kick me out in the morning unless I take a turn for the worse."

I said, "Your name's Joyce?"

She lowered her gaze and in a faint voice said, "That's what they say."

"You don't remember?"

"No."

"It's none of our business," Barb said. "You don't have to tell us anything if you don't want. I was wondering what you remember."

"Like I told that lady police chief and a psychiatrist who visited me right before you got here, all I remember is being on a boat. Don't know where, what kind of boat, or who else was on it. There was a storm and the next thing I remember was being in the water. Freezing water. I was holding on a surfboard for dear life. I remember seeing the words Ocean Pacific on the board. They said that's the brand. It's funny that I remember that. The next thing I knew was you leaning over me." She shook her head. "Barb, Chris, that's all, I mean all, I remember." She closed her eyes and whispered, "I didn't know my name was Joyce."

Barb said, "Was the psychiatrist helpful?"

"She was nice and listened. Helpful, I don't think so. She said I have amnesia, she called it a word I can't remember."

Barb said, "Retrograde."

I glanced at Barb and didn't say anything.

"That's it. Said it was caused by a trauma." She closed her eyes and Barb nodded toward the door.

"Joyce," I said, "we'd better let you get some rest. It's great seeing that you're doing so well."

Her eyes opened. "Thanks for coming. That was kind of you."

Barb and I patted her on the arm.

Joyce smiled up at us, and said, "What now?"

I wish we had an answer.

BARB WAS UNUSUALLY quiet as I maneuvered through downtown Charleston on the way to Fleet Landing Restaurant and Bar, one of many nice restaurants in the city known for fine dining. Barb had never been there, but I'd been twice. The restaurant over-looked the Charleston Harbor and is near the Historic City Market with half of the eatery over water. Christmas lights deco-rated the entry and from our table we could see other seasonal lights from buildings along the waterfront.

Our server asked if we wanted drinks and an appetizer. We each ordered the house Cabernet while Barb scanned the menu. She added, "An order of Fleet Landing Stuffed Hush Puppies would be good."

Barb had the metabolism of a hummingbird and could out eat people twice her one-hundred-twenty pounds while never gaining a ounce. It was irritating. I had no idea what was stuffed in the hush puppies despite the menu saying it was a veloute of lobster, rock shrimp, and leeks. The server left, and I asked Barb what a veloute was.

"Clueless. Figured anything with hush puppies has to be good."

Her ignorance made me feel better, sort of. It was good hearing her speak after being unusually quiet since we'd left the hospital.

It was dark outside, and Barb nodded toward a row of lights from across the bay as they reflected on the calm water. "That's beautiful. I'm glad we came here."

I agreed, and in a lesson learned from Charles, she changed direction on a dime. "What do you think of her story?"

"I know little about amnesia. After Cal got hit on the head back in the summer he forgot recent events for a few days. The doc called it amnesia, but he could remember things from his past."

Cal Ballew was a friend who owned Cal's Country Bar and Burgers.

Barb said, "That was anterograde amnesia, where the person can't remember current information. His was caused by a brain trauma, the blow to the head. Joyce has retrograde amnesia which is the opposite of anterograde. There are several other kinds of amnesia, but those are the two most common."

I nodded like I understood, which was partially true, and said, "You sure you didn't go to medical school rather than law school?"

She chuckled. "I had a client whose husband suffered from retrograde amnesia resulting from his mother's sudden death. The father died a few years earlier. There was a ton of money involved and my client had been told by her mother-in-law that the bulk of it was to go to her grandchildren and the humane society. The husband with amnesia said he couldn't remember but *knew* that wasn't true and that he was to inherit, and it was up to him to decide what to do with the estate. This is the kind of legal crap you step in when there's no will."

"They didn't have one?"

"No. My client's in-laws were in their fifties and thought they had plenty of time to worry about things like wills. Wrong. Anyway, I researched amnesia to represent her. One of the hardest things I did as an attorney was become an expert on oodles of things in which I had no interest."

"What happened with your client?"

"Other than me using my superior Penn State Law training to win a victory?"

"That goes without saying."

"Perhaps, but I like saying it. The other critical development was when my client's husband regained his memory and found a notarized letter he'd hidden that his mother had given him telling that he would get everything."

Thinking of Joyce, I said, "How long did it take for him to regain his memory?"

"Four months of legal wrestling and delaying depositions."

I smiled and turned serious. "Cal's amnesia was caused by the smack on the head. Joyce didn't have any apparent physical injury other than a few bruises and scrapes. What caused hers?"

"Most likely, a form of retrograde called psychological amnesia, also referred to as dissociative amnesia. It can be caused by a multitude of things, being the victim of a crime, child abuse, witnessing a traumatic event, on-and-on. Basically, any intolerable life situation that causes psychological stress can cause it. It's rare."

"Thank you, Doctor Barb. Any idea how long she could've had it?"

She smiled. "No. I missed that class in law school."

Our drinks arrived along with the appetizer. The server said the bar was backed up or we would've had our drinks sooner. Barb told her it wasn't a problem. Barb ordered shrimp and grits for her entrée. Grits were on my list of least favorite foods and I stuck with the chicken piccata. The server left, and Barb took a bite of the appetizer.

I thought about the causes of psychological amnesia, and said, "The first thing Joyce said she remembered was being on a boat, so wouldn't it make sense that whatever she suffered from occurred around that time?"

Barb held up a finger and pointed to her mouth. Talking with a mouthful of food wasn't unheard of among my friends. Barb had more class than most of my them, so I waited.

She finished chewing, took a sip of water, and said, "Don't know."

I'd waited for that.

"Cal's doctor said that time was the best cure for his amnesia. It was a week before he regained most of his memory. It was scrambled at first, but finally returned to his pre-traumatic head bashing. What treatments are there to help Joyce?"

"Time is the best. If there are underlying physical or mental disorders, psychotherapy could help. Family support is also critical. Orientation aids such as photos, familiar smells, and even music can speed up remembering the past."

"That's if the police find her family."

"That could be awhile unless someone reports her missing. She could be from anywhere." Barb turned to the large windows that overlooked the harbor. "Look how beautiful the flickering Christmas lights look on the surface of the water."

That was her way of saying we'd talked enough about Joyce. We spent the next hour enjoying the scenery, each other's company, and a wonderful meal. She told me about Troy and Nate, two men from Canada, who'd rented the condo next to her for a month and how much they were enjoying the "balmy" December weather on Folly. She crossed her arms and made a shivering motion as she said it.

Several units in Barb's condo complex were vacation rentals, and she never knew from week to week who some of her neighbors would be. That would bother me, but she said it was interesting seeing who was staying there, and besides, the high turnover meant the more books she'd sell in her store.

The ride to Folly was peaceful and quiet, and I couldn't help smiling at the brightly lit crab, dolphin, turtle, and sand dollar decorations that adorned light poles at each intersection along Center Street. I also couldn't stop thinking about the first or last name woman named Joyce. And, that she was going to be released tomorrow. Released to go where?

5

I sat up in bed and wondered why I hadn't thought of it earlier.
I'd slept later than usual, and the low December sun filtered
through the blinds. Was it too early to call Chief LaMond? Over
the years, I'd called her several times before eight o'clock and
she'd berated me for pestering her before her work day began. I
smiled, picked up the phone, and recalled that she'd also berated
me for calling during work hours, after her work day, and on
weekends and holidays.

"What in the Elf on the Shelf are you pestering me about
before I've had time to enjoy a hot brew of hazelnut coffee with
my adorable hubby?"

"Elf on the Shelf?"

"You know, Santa's danged scout elf that parents use to trick
their kids into being nice rather than naughty before Christmas.
Hate that thing, hate ads for it, hate seeing it sneaking around
the house."

I was vaguely aware of the Elf, but never considered it a
four-letter word. "Did Larry put one in your house?"

I didn't think she was going to answer. She finally said, "If I hear one word about it from anyone other than you, you will not live long enough to get a lump of coal from Santa. Now, in case your feeble mind forgot, you called me. Would it be rude to ask why?"

After the elf talk, I'd almost forgotten the reason. I stifled a chuckle, and said, "Any word on who Joyce is, or what happened to her?"

"Double no."

"That's what I was afraid of. Barb and I stopped by the hospital to see her. She was doing well and said they might release her today. Where will she go?"

"For being such an infuriating pest, you occasionally come up with a good question. That's one of them. My answer is one I give more and more. I don't have a freakin' clue. The hospital has a case worker who'll work with her. Joyce isn't in medical distress, so the options are limited."

"What if I have a possible solution?"

"Hence the reason for this ungodly early call?"

"An astute observation, Chief LaMond."

"Any chance you would share it?"

"Yes." And I did.

She said my idea wasn't horrible, which I took to mean she thought it was great. She asked me to let her know the results. I said I would, and she asked if she could get back to her coffee and peaceful morning. I said yes, and she hung up before I could add anything to spoil it.

My next call was to Preacher Burl Costello who answered in a better mood than had Cindy. I asked if it was too early to call and he laughed and said no that his residents were up and clanking around all hours of day and night. I asked if he was entertaining visitors and he said he was if I was the visitor.

Fifteen minutes later, I pulled in the gravel parking area in front of the large, wood-frame house. A massive live oak butted up to the house on one side and smaller trees and shrubs were grouped on two other sides. The structure was at least fifty years old and its north-facing wall was covered with moss. Despite its unkept appearance, the house had weathered many a storm and was sturdier than most of the houses surrounding it. White, LED Christmas lights were strung around the door frame and along the roofline.

The front door was open and a man in his mid-thirties and cut-off jeans despite the temperature in the forties was on his knees and working on the lock. I asked if the preacher was available and he said for me to go in and yell.

I stepped in the narrow hallway and didn't have to yell. Preacher Burl saw me, shook my hand, said he was waiting for me, and asked if I wanted coffee. Chief LaMond could learn hospitality skills from the preacher. He led me through a long, center hallway. The wallcovering reminded me of a rainforest with its various shades of green and a dark overcast feel. It was ripped in a couple of spots and gave a depressing feel to the house. At the end of the hall, Burl turned left, and I followed him to the large kitchen, the kind in country farmhouses.

A woman was taking something out of the stove and was startled by our entry. "Sorry, Sister Adrienne," Burl said, "Meet my friend, Brother Chris. Brother Chris, Sister Adrienne was the first person to move in when Hope House opened. She's a great cook and we're fortunate to have her."

Adrienne was probably in her fifties, paper thin and wore her graying black hair in a bun. I told her it was nice meeting her, and she said likewise although I didn't detect a great deal of sincerity. Burl poured two cups of coffee while I was having my awkward conversation with Adrienne, and suggested I follow him to the living room.

"Adrienne's not great with people, especially men," Burl said, as he pointed to the brown vinyl-covered sofa with chrome legs that'd look at home in a doctor's waiting room. He lowered his voice. "Her husband left her for his massage therapist. Poor

Adrienne took solace in alcohol before finding the Lord and First Light Church. She now works for a landscaper and by the grace of God, will be moving to an apartment all her own come summer. The move will be wonderful for her, bad for our quality of meals." Burl patted his stomach.

The waiting-room-style sofa was out of place in a residence, but various Christmas decorations warmed the room. A seven-foot-tall pine tree stood in the corner and was wrapped with colorful lights, and adorned with silver and gold ornaments, plus a few homemade, cardboard decorations. A dozen or so colorfully wrapped packages rested on the tree skirt. I smiled at how cheerful the room was. Burl took a sip from his mug and leaned back on the sofa. Adrienne's story was interesting, but time was important, so I wanted to share the reason for my visit.

"Preacher, the other day when you were in the Dog, you said you had four residents and six bedrooms. Has the number of residents increased since then?"

"No. The house was not created to be a permanent home for its residents. Since I've opened, we've had several come and go. In addition to Adrienne, we have Taylor Strong, the gentleman working on the broken lock on the front door, Rebekah Leachmen, she's at work at Black Magic Cafe, been there going on six months and doing well. You just missed her. Then there's Bernard Prine. You're the reason Brother Bernard is here."

I'd met Bernard a year ago. He was homeless, and I learned he'd been a war hero, had received a serious head injury in Afghanistan, and suffered from PTSD, or PTSS as it's now called. He'd been kicked out of several homeless shelters because of his temper and when I told him about Preacher Burl, Bernard sought him out and the two were good for each other. I thanked Burl for all he'd done for Bernard.

"Brother Chris, I don't suppose you're here to take an inventory of my residents."

I told him no, and that I was there to see if he could provide lodging for Joyce.

He said that it would be his Christian duty, and that, "It would be a joy to do so. In fact, if acceptable with her, I will call her Joy." He made an exaggerated nod. "Tis the season of tidings of comfort and joy."

She didn't remember her name was Joyce, so I told him I doubted she'd mind him calling her the shortened version. I also said I didn't know if the hospital would release her to him. He smiled and said one of his flock, which is what he called members of First Light, had been in the hospital, and he got to know someone in the discharge department, and would call her. After he brings Joy to Hope House, he said he'd contact Chief LaMond and tell her, so she would know where to reach Joy if her identity was discovered. I appreciated that he was willing to take-charge of these tasks and asked that he let me know what happens. I also told him how admirable I thought it was for him to have opened the house and asked if it was too much for him to shoulder alone.

He laughed. "I've thought that several times a day. Sister Lottie volunteers when I need extra help, which is often. As I shared with you when we first met, I have carpentry skills and they're being utilized more than I ever imagined. Three of the windows leaked when it rained, and there are more holes in the drywall than I can count. One of my previous residents was a finish carpenter and a tremendous help, a gift from heaven, you might say. I was happy for him and saddened for Hope House when he was offered a high-paying job in Summerville and was able to afford an apartment. It was a sad day indeed when he left. Regardless, Lottie does the best she can, and is especially good with the women."

Lottie was the first member of First Light and after some of us had pestered Burl about it, he realized that she wanted more than a preacher/member relationship. They've dated several months and the rumor among members of the flock was that they might soon be seeking another preacher. More specifically, a preacher to perform their wedding ceremony. I hoped it was true.

"That's good." I looked out the window. "Any static from neighbors about this type of establishment in the neighborhood?"

"Some looked askance at first, but I have strict rules and any violation is cause for immediate removal. Most of the folks who end up here are temporarily, shall I say, disenfranchised, and find their way back to a productive member of society. Or, they have been to this point."

"Preacher, there's one other thing I should mention. All that Joyce, Joy, remembers is being on a boat and then in the ocean clinging to a surfboard, before Barb and I found her."

"I was aware of that, Brother Chris."

"Then you know it's possible something happened on the boat that could've caused her amnesia. Something bad. Whoever was on the boat may not know that she survived. Or, they do, they may try something."

Burl nodded. "In other words, the fewer people who know she's here the better."

"It'd be best if no one knew."

"My guests will know, and I feel I must tell Lottie since she's good with the women."

"That's fine. If we can keep it to those few along with the police, it'd be best."

Our conversation ended with a sales pitch from Preacher Burl for me to attend his Sunday service and his special Christmas Eve service. I told him I'd try. He didn't appear convinced. Neither did I.

6

I hadn't told Charles what I'd learned from Cindy, or from the visit to the hospital. I called, and he suggested that our conversation would best take place over an early lunch at the Crab Shack. The popular restaurant was halfway between Charles's apartment on Sandbar Lane and my cottage on East Ashley Avenue. The temperature was still in the forties, yet I decided to walk. The exercise would do me good.

"About time you got here," Charles said, as he grabbed a peanut out of the cardboard container in front of him. He wore a red and blue Walters State long-sleeve sweatshirt, and jeans. My friend has one of the largest collections of college and university logoed sweatshirts this side of Dick's Sporting Goods. I'd tried to find out why he has them and where they came from. The best answer he'd come up with was, "Here and there." I stopped asking years ago, although it never stopped him from sharing trivia about the shirts.

He pointed to his chest. "I know you're wondering, they're the Senators. It's in Morristown, Tennessee."

See?

"Good morning, Charles," I said, ignoring his comment about me being late and the college highlighted on his torso. I picked a nut out of the container and cracked it open.

He sighed. My disinterest annoyed him, but I knew what I was going to share next would hold his attention.

"Barb and I visited Joyce in the hospital. She—"

He grabbed another nut and pointed it at me. "Who's Joyce?"

I realized I hadn't told him about yesterday's conversation with Cindy.

"Chief LaMond found the name in the sweatshirt of the woman Barb and I found on the beach."

His eyes narrowed. "When did you talk to Cindy?"

"Late yesterday," I said, a slight time-shift.

"You didn't call to tell me like you said you would, and then you called Barb and invited her instead of me to visit Jane Doe, umm, Joyce, in the hospital. Oh, and then you got home and instead of calling me, you did whatever you did at home. How am I doing?"

"Time got away."

And, I haven't even mentioned meeting with Preacher Burl and what's going to happen next. Before I could dig a deeper hole, Kaylee, the server, appeared and asked if we were ready to order. She glanced at the container of peanuts and added, "Something other than freebees."

We took the hint and ordered flounder crunch sandwiches and refills on the water she'd added to our table while we were gorging on peanuts.

Kaylee's timely interruption took the steam out of Charles's rant.

He leaned back, slowly shook his head, and said, "You went to the hospital without me?"

I thought that was self-evident but understood where he was going. "Yes. I thought about asking if you wanted to go but figured Joyce wouldn't be comfortable with two strange guys visiting."

"Barb and I could've visited while you stayed in the car. After all, I'm the detective. I could've found out…. Never mind, what'd you learn?"

"Nothing more than I told you the last time we talked. She has retrograde amnesia and doesn't remember anything before being on a boat, and even then, she doesn't remember what happened."

"That's horrible. When will she be well enough to get out of the hospital?"

"Could be today."

Charles leaned his elbows on the table and stared at me. "Where's she going? If she can't remember anything, what'll happen to her?"

I tightened my grip on the plastic water glass and prepared for rant number two. "Preacher Burl said he would see if he could get her released to Hope House. If he can, then—"

Charles leaned across the table and waved his hand in my face. "Whoa. When did this happen? How do you know?"

"That's why I called you as soon as I left Burl," I said, emphasis on *as soon as*.

Food arrived along with more questions. "When's her memory coming back? Will Burl be able to take her to Hope House? Do you think she's still in danger?" He hesitated and took a bite of his sandwich, and then with food in his mouth, said, "How're we going to find out who she is and what happened?"

Instead of saying, "I don't know?" four times, I shrugged and stuck a fry in my mouth.

I was seated facing a colorful mural featuring the Ferris wheel that once towered over Folly and Charles was facing the entry. He jumped up and headed toward the door. I turned to see what'd grabbed his attention and saw Chief LaMond talking to the hostess. Charles joined them and pointed at our table. I imagined that Cindy was thinking she'd chosen the wrong restaurant for lunch. I smiled as Charles put his arm around her shoulder and escorted her to the table and pulled out the chair beside his and motioned for her to join us.

"Hey, Chris, look who wanted to sit with us."

Wanted to turn and run out the door as soon as she saw Charles, would've been my guess. "Glad you could join us."

She glared at me like it was my fault she chose the wrong restaurant for a peaceful meal.

Charles pretended not to see Cindy's glare, and said, "We were talking about the lady Chris and Barb found surfing. He was getting ready to call you and see if you learned who she is and what happened." Charles turned to me.

Cindy glanced at me. "Hmm, is that right?"

"Have you found out who she is?" I asked, skirting Charles's claim that I was going to call.

Kaylee returned to the table and asked Cindy what she wanted for lunch.

"I'd like three bourbons and a liter of gin to put up with these troublemakers. Instead, how about water and whatever they're having."

Cindy shook her head as Kaylee headed to the kitchen. "No, I don't know who she is. There are no missing person reports fitting her description, and her prints aren't in the system. She's still Joyce Doe or Jane Joyce, depending on if Joyce is her first or last name."

I was tempted to tell her that Burl had shortened it to Joy. Instead, I told her of my conversation with Burl and that he was contacting the hospital to see if she could stay at Hope House. Rather than Cindy getting mad at me, and I suppose Burl, for butting in, she said she was glad. She'd be closer when her memory starts returning.

Her food arrived. I'd observed over the years how much

quicker a police chief gets served than other mortals. Cindy took a sip of water and a bite of sandwich.

Charles took the break in her talking to ask, "Learn anything else?"

Cindy looked at Charles and rolled her eyes. "Yep, two things."

"Well?" Charles said.

"First, to case the inside of a restaurant before coming in. Peace, quiet, and a relaxing lunch don't go with Chris, Charles, and your pestering."

"Second?" Charles said.

"Do you know Jamison and Renee Caulder?"

I said, "Don't think so."

"I know Renee." Charles said. "Met her walking her dog Bowser. Adorable Pekingese pup, originally from China, Pekingese dogs, not Renee. They're also called lion dogs because they look like the Chinese guardian lions that—"

"Enough," Cindy interrupted.

I silently seconded that.

She continued, "The Caulders are a nice couple. Jamison retired early from a highfalutin, high-paying job, and bought a house out on Tabby Drive that backs up to the river and the marsh. They've got a walking pier that goes from their deck to the river. The last few days they've been up in Asheville visiting relatives and spending some of their oodles of dollars. They got home late yesterday and guess what was missing from their nice little walking pier?"

I didn't know, but knew it was interesting or Cindy wouldn't be telling the story. "What?"

"Their cute little eighteen-foot Tahoe Q4i runabout."

"Do they know when the boat was taken?" I asked.

"Nope, and neither did their neighbors. The people in the nearest house were in Phoenix until yesterday. They're the ones who noticed it missing and told Jamison when he got home."

"Don't suppose anyone's found a lost eighteen-foot-long boat?" Charles said.

Cindy smiled. "Finally, a question I can answer. Yep."

"Someone found it?" I asked.

She nodded. "Not far from where it was taken. It was tied to a pier, a piss-poor knot, I might add. It was behind a deserted house on Seacrest Lane. Some guy a couple of houses away saw it and didn't think anything of it until his wife who likes to stick her nose in everyone's business—like you, Charles—said it didn't belong there and made him call us."

I said, "I don't suppose you found any prints on it."

"Only Jamison and Renee's. Also found an ignition that'd been mangled and hotwired. Want to guess what we didn't find?"

"Not Bowser, I hope," Charles said.

Cindy sighed, and said, "He went with them to Asheville."

"What didn't you find?" I asked.

"Jamison's surfboard."

"Let me guess," I said. "Ocean Pacific?"

Cindy smiled. "You win the opportunity to pay for my lunch."

"Chris always wins the good stuff," Charles said, through smiling teeth.

I ignored him. "So, you think someone hotwired the boat, somehow and somewhere got Joyce on board, and took her out in the ocean to what?"

"A theory is that it was to get her far enough off shore to throw her overboard. Mind you, that's mere speculation. Until her memory returns, we don't know anything other than the boat was stolen."

"What about the surfboard?" Charles asked.

"Charles, did you miss the part where I said, way back thirty seconds ago, that all we know is that the boat was stolen?"

Charles stuffed a fry in his mouth, nodded twice, and said,

"So, Chief, what do you want us to do to help figure out what happened out on the deep-blue sea?"

She looked up from her plate, glared at Charles, and said, "In the spirit of the big guy in the red suit coming next week to visit all little chillins, and big chillins like you, Charles, I say Ho, Ho, Ho! In case that's not clear, it means I'm laughing at your suggestion and the best way you can help is to stay out of our way. Leave the coppin' to cops."

Charles took the hint, or decided it wasn't time to argue, and said, "That's a good idea, Chief."

I'd known Charles for a long time, knew his moods, knew his approach to most everything. I also knew he was lying through his teeth.

7

There was a good chance that Joyce had been on the stolen boat, yet several questions remained. Those questions kept me awake most of the night. Who was Joyce, be it her first or last name? What trauma erased her past? Will her memory return? If she's from the area, why hadn't someone reported her missing? And, if she'd been on the stolen boat, why?

I must have fallen asleep at some point. The phone jarred me awake at seven-thirty.

"Brother Chris, did I awaken you?"

I lied and said, no.

"Good. I was excited and wanted you to be first to know. I have been given authorization to collect Joy and bring her here. Praise the Lord."

"That's great news, Preacher. Do you know when she'll be released?"

"They said I could come over now, and they'll discharge her when I get there."

"Great," I repeated.

"Brother Chris, might I ask a huge favor?"

"Sure."

"Would you go with me? You're a familiar face to her. I know she'd appreciate you being there."

"I'd be glad to."

Burl's granite-gray Dodge Grand Caravan pulled in the drive fifteen minutes after I'd agreed to go, and thirty minutes later we were in the hospital visitor's lot.

Burl stepped behind me as I approached Joyce's door, and said, "Since she knows you, why don't you go in first?"

The patient was sitting on the chair. Her hair was pulled in a ponytail and she wore a long-sleeve, blue T-shirt and the same slacks she had on when we found her. Someone must've given her the shirt and had the slacks cleaned since they were sand free and pressed. She smiled when I entered. The smile lessened when she saw the man behind me.

"You look great," I said. "Ready to get out of here?"

"Yes, but I don't have anywhere—"

"Good morning, Sister Joy, I'm Preacher Burl Costello."

Joyce glanced at Burl and quickly turned to me. "Chris, what's going on?"

I smiled and hoped it put her at ease. "Joyce, Preacher Burl is a friend and the minister of First Light Church on Folly Beach. Part of First Light's ministry is a large house where several people live. Preacher Burl talked to one of the hospital administrators and he agreed to let you stay there until you can get on your feet and your memory returns."

"But, I don't have money. I can't afford—"

Burl took a step closer to Joyce and said, "Sister Joy—"

"Sir, who's Joy, and what's this sister stuff? I'm not your sister... I don't think."

"Joyce," I said, "Preacher Burl calls those who attend First Light either brother or sister. Your name's Joyce, so he thought Joy was a pretty sounding name."

Burl added, "Christmas is right around the corner, so I

thought calling you that would be reflective of the joy you will bring to us all."

"Preacher, no offense. I don't know you, crap, pardon my language, I don't even know me. What makes you think I'll bring joy? For all you know, for all I know, I could be a serial killer, or I don't know what."

I wondered the same thing and waited for Burl's response.

He rubbed his hand through his bristle-brush mustache. "Joyce, I hope you don't mind me calling you Joy. As you can tell from looking at this rough-hewn face, I've been around the block a time or two. I've seen evil up close. Regardless, I believe the good in people. Yes, there's a chance that you might not be a saint." He chuckled. "The Good Lord knows I'm not. I see a lady who's suffered a terrible fate. I can't imagine how horrific it must be to not remember the past. I see a lady who needs a break or two to get back on her feet. And, I see someone I, even with my meager resources, can provide a comfortable bed, decent meals, and others who can share with you their hopes and dreams. I would be honored to have you as a part of Hope House for as long as you need, or want, to be there."

She gave a faint smile and said in a faint voice so that Burl and I had to lean closer to hear, "That's kind of you, sir, but I don't have money. I can't afford to pay."

"Ah, Sister Joy, you're in luck. You qualify for the special close-to-Christmas rent of zero dollars a week. And, for no additional charge, Chris and I will provide transportation to your new home."

"Are you certain, Burl, umm, Preacher?"

"Absolutely."

She gave Burl a tentative hug, and whispered, "Thank you."

I gave a sigh of relief.

After what seemed like an eternity getting Joy discharged, the ride to Folly was awkward at best. Burl tried to explain how he founded First Light two years ago and how it met most

Sundays on the beach near the Folly Beach Fishing Pier, and during inclement weather, in a storefront on Center Street next to Barb's Books. I shared how I met the preacher when my photo gallery occupied the space where Barb's is now. I didn't get into the deaths that surrounded First Light's first few months in existence.

Joy alternated between listening to Burl patter on about First Light and staring out the window with her mind wandering. Burl didn't notice the difference until he asked if she would be interested in attending his Sunday service in two days.

"I'm sorry, Preacher. What?"

He repeated the question.

"Preacher, are there other churches on Folly?"

"Excellent question, Sister Joy. There are three other wonderful houses of worship on our tiny island. The Baptist, Catholic, and Methodist churches are within sight of each other."

She turned from staring out the window to Burl. "Why start another one?"

"Another excellent question, my dear. First Light is nondenominational and attracts men and women who, for whatever reason, are not attracted to the more traditional denominations." He laughed. "Some of the first to attend were surfers who'd been on the beach waiting to ply their skill in the waves. I'd love to say that my wonderful, spiritual, and inspirational message drew them in. They finally told me that they were bored waiting for, as they said, 'boss' waves, and enjoyed the group singing."

Joy said, "That must've been disheartening."

Burl patted her on the arm. "To the contrary. As I often share from the pulpit, God works in strange and mysterious ways. That day, He provided a flat sea to prevent the young people from surfing and provided members of the flock singing at the top of their lungs to attract those nearby. Several of the surfers have attended religiously, pun intended, since that glorious day."

Burl pulled in my drive and I said it was nice seeing Joy

again and that she would find Hope House and Preacher Burl to her liking. I had no idea if that was true, but wanted to reinforce the decision for her to stay there. In a less than convincing tone, she said she hoped so. Our conversation ended with her thanking me for coming with Burl to pick her up and for me to say hi to Barb.

The first thing I did when I got in the house was call Charles to let him know the latest on Joy. I was pleased when he didn't scold me for waiting to tell him. He added that he was planning attend First Light's next service. I said I might see him there, emphasis on might. I was an irregular attender which meant I attended more often than Christmas and Easter, but less, far less, than weekly.

Charles thought he had my commitment to attend, then asked if Joy had regained her memory and shared with what had happened on the boat.

"Charles, don't you think if that happened, I would've led with it?"

"Does that mean she doesn't remember?"

"No more than the last time we talked."

"Doesn't give us much to work with finding out what happened, does it?"

"We're not trying to find out, remember?"

"Good Ole Abe Lincoln said, 'How many legs does a dog have if you call the tail a leg? Calling a tail a leg doesn't make it a leg.'"

Another of Charles's quirks was quoting United States Presidents, or he said they were actual quotes. I had never taken the time to research their origin. As Chris Landrum said, I don't care an atom if they are. That sentiment was shared by others who knew my friend, although it didn't stop him from spewing them.

"Your point is?"

"The point, my friend, is whether you say you are or not, you along with the help of your trusty sidekick are on the case. You can deny it to Cindy, to Burl, to anyone who will listen, and to the Caulders' dog Bowser. That still don't mean you ain't trying."

"Whatever."

He laughed, and the phone went dead.

8

Moving to a strange house, surrounded by strangers, and not knowing who you are, where you came from, or anything about your past, had to be traumatic. I decided to drop by and see how Joy was adjusting. I didn't have anything encouraging to offer except a face that she'd known longer than anyone there. I hoped that would be enough.

It took three knocks before Bernard Prine opened the door. I hardly recognized him. When we'd met a year ago, he had stringy, dark-brown hair, a week-old beard, and wore a faded army jacket and gray dress slacks two sizes too large. Now, his hair was neatly trimmed and combed, he had on a long-sleeve, yellow dress shirt, black jeans, new tennis shoes, and a smile he'd seldom shared a year ago.

"Well if it isn't my friend, Chris Landrum," Bernard said in a Southern drawl. "Welcome, sir."

We'd had little contact since last Christmas, so I was pleased that he'd referred to me as a friend. He shook my hand with a grip powerful enough to open a stubborn food jar.

"It's good to see you, Bernard. How do you like it here?"

He smiled. "One of the best things that ever happened to me was last Christmas when you told me that I could talk to Preacher Burl about my issues. He's a godsend. Crap—whoops, Preacher doesn't like me saying crap—umm, phooey, even if he wasn't a preacher, I'd still say he's a godsend. He's provided room and board, lent me a few dollars when I've needed them, and best of all, he's been there when I sort of threw a couple of temper tantrums, the kind that got me kicked out of homeless shelters. Preacher put his arm around me and took me aside and talked me through whatever inspired me to make an ass, umm, a fool out of myself. I'd do anything for that man."

"I'm glad to hear it. Is your newest resident around?"

"Yes, sir. We were in the kitchen having coffee with Preacher Burl. How about joining us?"

He was leading me to the kitchen before I could answer. We passed one of the female residents, Adrienne, I believe. She was dressed in a light jacket, jeans that were no stranger to manual labor, and calf-high, leather work boots.

Bernard said, "Off to work?"

Adrienne lowered her eyes when she saw me, and mumbled, "Yes."

She headed to the door, and Bernard leaned close and whispered, "If you ask me, she's housing a herd of secrets."

Coming from Bernard, that was something. I remembered how many times Charles and I tried to get him to tell us where he was living when we first met. He never would.

"What kind of secrets?"

He rubbed his chin and stared as Adrienne exited. "If I knew, they wouldn't be secrets. Reckon it's a feeling I get when I'm around her." He shrugged.

Burl was pouring coffee in a mug in front of Joy, and she was laughing.

He saw me in the doorway and without skipping a beat, grabbed another mug, filled it, and handed it to me.

"Brother Chris, if you'd arrived a half hour earlier, you could have joined us for breakfast."

"Yes," Bernard said, "we had crepes, blackberry-mint scones, arugula and pistachio pesto quiche, and, oh yeah, crumpets."

"Really?" I said.

Burl laughed, and said, "Brother Chris, we had a bowl of Raisin Bran and orange juice."

I had forgotten Bernard's sense of humor. "Sounds good."

Bernard glanced at Burl and said, "I must've been thinking about yesterday."

Joy ignored the factual and fictional breakfast menu, and said, "Chris, it's nice to see you again."

"You too, Joy. How do you like it here?"

"It's far better than the room at the hospital. Preacher Burl gave me a choice of two bedrooms and I picked the one with two windows instead of one."

"Brother Taylor moved out and looks like Sister Rebekah will be leaving soon. She's doing well at her job at Black Magic and will be moving to her own apartment after Christmas."

"It's great that your residents find places to live," I said.

"They're blessed, yet I'm always sad to see them go."

Bernard pointed his mug at Burl. "Don't worry, Preacher. I won't leave you."

Burl chuckled. "You have a home here as long as you wish."

Bernard took the last sip and excused himself saying that he thought a walk would do him good. He headed out the back door, and I told him it was good seeing him again.

Joy whispered something I couldn't understand. Apparently, Burl couldn't either and asked her to repeat it.

She stared in her mug and said, "What if I have a house somewhere? What if I have a husband, children? Brothers, sisters, parents? What if…" She held out her hands palms up and repeated, "What if?"

Burl reached out and hugged her. I didn't know what to say and sipped coffee.

A minute later, Joy stepped back from Burl and said, "If you gentlemen don't mind, I'd like to go to my room."

Burl said, "Joy, this is now your home. Feel free to come, go, and do as you please. I lock the doors each night, but I'll give you a key. And, I'm here if you need anything."

She nodded and left the kitchen.

Burl watched her go, and said, "Christmas is a week away and the best gift in the world for Sister Joy would be her memory. I can't give that to her."

"None of us can. What you are giving are some of the greatest gifts possible, a place to call home and a loving environment."

"Yes," Burl said, "I'm afraid that isn't enough when it comes to Sister Joy. My other residents know where they've been yet are uncertain of their future. That's why most end up under this roof. Without knowledge of her past, Sister Joy can't determine whether staying here is a good or a bad thing. She had no perspective on her reality."

"Did she share anything beyond being on the boat?"

He shook his head. "Nothing like a direct memory, but here's something. I was showing her around upstairs and she pointed to a couple of places where I needed to repair the wood trim. She said she could help."

"Perhaps she has construction experience."

"Maybe, although not necessarily," Burl said. "I told her I'd worked construction back in the day. She could've wanted to help and figured I'd show her what to do. She wants to help."

"True. Did she say anything else?"

"No."

"What did you tell the others about her?"

"Nothing other than she's been in the hospital and would be staying here until she got back on her feet."

"Did you say anything about her memory?"

"I told them that she was foggy about the past."

"How does she get along with them?"

"There's been little contact. She stayed in her room most of time. She talked for a while to Bernard, but little to the others."

"Preacher, I'm still worried that there is someone who may want to harm her. Have you told everyone that it's important that they don't talk about her with anyone outside this house?"

"I told Sister Adrienne and Brother Bernard. I haven't had a chance to talk with Rebekah. I will when she returns from work. More coffee?"

I told him I was okay, and he said, "Now, a question. Have the police learned anything about what happened?"

I told him about the stolen boat and surfboard.

"They're certain that the surfboard was the same one you and Sister Barb found with Joy?"

I nodded.

"Have they checked the boat for fingerprints?"

"Chief LaMond said there weren't any except those of the owners."

I told him I'd better be going and asked him to call if Joy said anything that would help the police.

He said he would and ended with, "I look forward to seeing you at tomorrow's worship service."

How could I say no to that?

9

A clear, pollution-free sky greeted me as I left the house to walk to the morning service at First Light. The temperature was flirting with the upper thirties, so I headed three blocks to the church's inclement weather sanctuary. Attendance was lower when the service was indoors, and approximately twenty people were standing around a coffee pot in back of the room. It was easy to spot Preacher Burl. He was wearing a white robe crafted from a bedsheet and pouring coffee in a Styrofoam cup. Lottie was nearby. I was reminded of the first time I'd seen her. She was in this building and helping Burl and a few others refinish discarded church pews to use in the sanctuary. She wore over-sized clothes hiding her attractive figure and had a self-cut hair-style. Today she looked and acted the part of a preacher's wife, something I hoped she'd soon become. She handed coffee to William Hansel, another friend of mine and a regular at First Light.

Joy was in the corner in animated conversation with Bernard. She had on a tan blouse and dress slacks, clothes I assumed donated by one of the other residents. It was good seeing her socializing. Amber and Jason, her nineteen-year-old son, were in the front of the room talking to a woman I didn't know.

Charles was huddled with Mary Ewing and her girls, Jewel, seven, and Joanie, three. Mary had been homeless until Preacher Burl learned of her plight a year ago and worked with her to find a house to share with two women, and to get a job at Bert's Market. Charles saw me, glanced at his bare wrist, and shook his head like he was scolding me for being late.

I was on my way to talk to Charles, Mary, Joanie and Jewel, when Lottie whispered something to Burl and he moved to an old lectern that'd spent its better years in a high school gymnasium. The preacher cleared his throat, and said, "Please repose thyselves." He pointed to the pews.

A couple of older ladies I didn't know moved to the front row and reposed thyselves. They were followed by three more members who heeded his charge. The others either weren't ready to stop socializing or didn't know what the preacher meant. I knew because he announced the beginning of many services with those words, so the regulars who hadn't moved, weren't ready to.

Burl tapped his hand on the lectern and repeated his "call to worship," and gained the attention of the remaining talkers. Dude Sloan, was among that group. He'd seldom attended First Light until earlier this year when one of his employees was killed attempting to save Barb from the hands of a man trying to kill her.

I was going to see if Joy wanted to sit with me, but she was already seated beside Bernard. I slid in the pew next to Dude as Preacher Burl was saying something that began each service. "Please silence thy portable communication devices." Most did, and Burl asked William Hansel to lead the group in singing "Away in a Manger" from the songbook made from sheets of paper stapled together. The songs had been photocopied from a church hymnal.

William had a phenomenal voice and most of us, including

me, knew that unless we could improve on the song, he shouldn't try. We mouthed the words as we listened to him sing. Burl's flock was kind, considerate, and many other good things, but except for William, singers we were not.

Burl was in his element, standing in front of *his flock*, sharing a lesson from the Gospel, and reminding us of the historic and spiritual events leading to Christmas, seven days away. Joy was staring at the preacher, and I wondered what was going through her mind.

Burl announced two services for next weekend. He called the first a Christmas Eve midnight service while at the same time saying it'd begin at seven o'clock. He joked—I assume he was joking—that it would be held then instead of midnight because his message would be more meaningful if his flock was sober, and there was a better chance of that at seven. He then said the Christmas morning service would be at the regular eleven o'clock time. Today's service concluded with William singing "O Come All Ye Faithful" with a few of us humming along and the rest mouthing the words.

Charles was on the sidewalk talking to the two women who'd been on the front pew. I stood aside until he patted each of them on the back and they walked away.

"Who're they? I don't remember seeing them before."

Charles watched the ladies go, and said, "You have to come to the service to see who's here."

Touché. "So, who are they?"

"Dixie and Martha."

"Dixie?"

"Doubt it says that on her birth certificate. That's all I've ever heard her called. She lives in the three hundred block of East Arctic across the street from Martha. Dixie's an ubergardener."

"A what?"

"A super-duper gardener. Her back yard is full of plants,

flowers, herbs, and other growing things. Rumor is she has name holders beside each plant with the name, both the common name and the Latin name, printed on them."

"Why?"

Charles rolled his eyes. "Why do you wear boring clothes instead of educational, inspirational, and nifty shirts like *moi*?"

"What's that have to do with Dixie posting names of each of her…plant things?"

"Same answer to each question. Because she wants to."

"That helps."

He rolled his eyes, again. "Can I get back to what I was saying?"

"Please do."

"Martha and Dixie are widows. Kind of quiet, don't think they get out much. I occasionally see Martha walking around carrying a cane." He waved his handmade wooden cane in the air. "Not nice like this, one of those silver ones they sell at Harris Teeter. Enough about them, learn anything new about Joy?"

I told him no, and he was interrupted from asking me why not when Burl approached and said that he, Lottie, Joy, Bernard, and Dude were heading to Loggerhead's for lunch, and wondered if we would like to join them. The invitation was kind, participation by Dude unusual, and the chance for Charles to grill Joy about her past impossible to turn down. He answered yes for both of us.

Loggerhead's was on West Arctic Avenue, four blocks from First Light's foul-weather sanctuary, and across the street from Barb's condo in the Oceanfront Villas. Burl had removed his robe/sheet, so he didn't look like a ghost as we followed him to the restaurant. Charles spent the entire walk talking to Joy, not surprising knowing how curious—nosy—he was. In better weather, the large outside bar and dining area would have been packed. Today we were forced to move inside. Burl must have used his heavenly influence since there was a table available large enough to accommodate our group.

Yvonne, one of the owners, greeted us and said that Joe would be taking care of us. Joe, a long-tenured employee I'd known for a few years, was close behind Yvonne and took our drink orders. Five of us said water would be fine while Burl and Lottie ordered Diet Pepsi.

We were seated at a large, bar-height, rectangular table with Burl at the head and three of us seated on each of its long sides. Various NFL games were on televisions strategically located throughout the room.

"Thank you for breaking bread with me this lovely sabbath," Burl said, sounding more like a prayer than something you would normally hear in a bar.

Lottie was closest to Burl and patted him on the arm. "Preacher, we're delighted to join you."

Joy and Dude were seated next to Lottie and across from Bernard, Charles, and me. Bernard spoke next, but it was so loud in the room that I couldn't hear what he was saying. Joy and Burl laughed, so it must've been humorous. It was good seeing Joy fitting in.

Our drinks arrived, and Dude stood, raised his glass and said, "Toast. Boss preacher."

Dude wore one of his many tie-dyed shirts, was in his mid-sixties and looked like the stereotype of an aging hippie, which he happened to be. He also had a way with words, a way to mangle them.

The rest of us raised our glasses to toast while Joy looked at the lifelong surfer like he was speaking Tigrinya. I told Joy that Dude owned the surf shop and had been on Folly many years. I failed to mention that despite his appearance, and extensive vocabulary that may exceed fifty words, that he was one of the island's most successful businesspeople and well-respected by both its bohemian residents and city fathers.

Joe returned and took our orders, and Bernard leaned across the table and asked Joy how she enjoyed the service. I thought it was an awkward question with the preacher in hearing range.

"Bernard," Joy said, "I thought it was inspiring."

Dude leaned toward Joy. "Be good as other preachin' you been to?"

I realized that Dude didn't know anything about Joy and the reason she was staying at Hope House. I wanted to tell him what'd happened but didn't want her story and whereabouts known outside a limited group of people.

Charles decided that Dude was someone we could trust, and said, "Dude, Joy has amnesia and can't remember much about her past."

Dude tapped Joy on the arm and said, "Cool. You be lucky, bad history gone."

Joy's eyes darted around the table, most likely, hoping someone would comment. No one did, and she said, "Thanks, Dude. I think. I wish it was a cool thing. All it makes me think is that I'm an outcast here."

"Cool," Dude said, repeating one of his favorite words.

I was pleased when Joy said, "Why?"

He pointed to each person at the table. "We all outcasts. You be in good company. Cool."

I wouldn't have put it like that, but the truth was that each of us were either outsiders to Folly, or in the cases of Charles and Dude who'd been here many years, were considered left of quirky, even by Folly standards.

Our commends appeared to put Joy at ease and she asked Lottie what'd brought her to Folly. Lottie hesitated before sharing her story, a story involving physical and emotional abuse, and homelessness. Bernard jumped in the conversation and talked about his experiences in Afghanistan, and how he'd been homeless.

Dude had never been homeless or abused, yet felt he needed to add something and said, "Me have Pluto."

As farfetched as it may seem, Joy didn't understand what he was talking about, and said, "You have a planet?"

Dude shook his head and pointed to the ceiling. "Pluto up there be dwarf planet, not planet."

"Oh," Joy said in response to Dude, as many others had said before her.

He pointed to his chest. "Australian Terrier be my Pluto."

Joy grinned. "Oh, they're so cute."

I wondered how she knew that. Clearly, there was much I could learn about amnesia.

Food arrived, and Burl asked for a moment of silence while he offered a prayer. The noise was getting louder in the crowded restaurant and our table was the only island of silence. The comforting aroma of lunch permeated the area. Burl finished the prayer, and Joy looked at her plate and slowly turned back to Dude, and said, "Dude, what if I have a dog? If I do, who's taking care of it?"

Dude swallowed his first bite of food, and said, "Me be flummoxed."

Charles said, "I'm sure that if you have a dog, it's being taken care of."

I wondered why he was sure.

The conversation turned to what everyone was doing between now and Christmas and Burl shared stories about his younger days growing up on a cattle ranch in southern Illinois. Joy appeared to drift in and out of the conversation and I wondered how difficult it must be for her listening to stories about past Christmases.

Most of us were laughing at something Bernard had said when I noticed Joy staring at the bar along the side of the restaurant. I said, "Joy, what are you thinking?"

She shook her head like she was trying to move back to the present and nodded toward the bar. "Chris, that looks so familiar."

"Like you've been in here before?"

She closed her eyes and said, "Maybe."

10

It turned out to be a pleasant Sunday afternoon. Puffy white clouds dotted the blue sky, and the temperature hovered in the low-fifties. Instead of heading home, I turned on Center Street and started toward Barb's Books, when I noticed Joy hurrying to catch up with me. I made a benign comment about how nice the weather was. She asked where I was going, and I told her the bookstore.

"Would you mind if I tag along? I haven't seen Barb since, umm, you know."

"Sure," I said, not waiting for her to relive the traumatic event in the surf.

"Everyone at the house is so nice. Preacher Burl and Adrienne found me some clothes, and, well, they're kind." We walked a few more steps, and she added, "You know what they can't do?"

"What?"

"Give me my memories. I need to get out and get some fresh air to clear my head, at least the little that's in it."

Two men wearing shorts were leaving the bookstore as we

approached. They turned our direction, pivoted, and walked the other way.

Joy shivered and said, "Aren't those guys freezing?"

"I'd be if I had on shorts," I said, and held the door open for Joy.

Barb saw us and smiled. "Hey, Joyce, it's great to see you. Who's that old geezer with you?"

Joy laughed, louder than I thought necessary, and said, "Picked him up on the street. You know him?"

Barb said, "Seen him around. He's not important, how are you?"

"Physically, I'm okay except for a couple of bruises. Can't say the same about my memory."

Barb nodded. "Nothing coming back?"

Joy shook her head.

"Can I offer you something to drink? Coffee, soft drink, water?"

"Coffee would be nice. I'm not as warm blooded as those guys in shorts."

Barb led us to the tiny office behind the showroom. "Oh, did you meet Troy and Nate?"

"No," I said. "They went the other direction."

Barb said, "They're from Canada, Ottawa, I believe. They think it's hot here."

The names sounded familiar. "Are they your next-door renters?"

"Good memory, Chris." Barb turned to Joy. "Joyce, they're staying next to me in my condo building. They're here for a month."

Joy returned the smile and said, "Preacher Burl started calling me Joy instead of Joyce. I sort of like it."

"Then Joy it is."

Joy's smile faded. "Those guys are here for a month. I wonder how long I'll be here?"

Barb inserted a K-cup pod in her Keurig coffeemaker and turned to Joy. "It'll work out."

Joy turned from looking at the coffeemaker to staring at Barb. "What makes you so certain?"

"From what I've heard, you're surrounded by good people at Hope House, and this is a loving community. It may not be quick, but your memory will start returning and everyone will help you with whatever is needed."

"I hope so."

I told Barb who we had lunch with.

She turned to Joy and said Dude was her half brother.

Joy stared at her and said, "You're kidding."

Barb laughed and gave Joy an abridged version of their relationship.

All Joy said was, "Hmm, half brother. Guess that's why he only got half of your vocabulary."

Barb laughed again and said, "Joy, Chris may not have told you, I practiced law for many years before opening the bookstore. I even had a client with the same kind of amnesia you have. I've avoided doing legal work since opening the store, but I'll be glad to help you in any legal entanglements you may encounter."

Barb handed Joy a mug of coffee and inserted another pod in the Keurig.

Joy took a sip, and said, "Barb, I don't have any money. I can't—"

"Joy, we'll deal with that when the time comes. Heck, you may be a billionaire and will want to pay me more than I'm worth."

"Or, I could be broke."

Barb smiled. "Then we'll deal with it later."

My phone rang, I answered and instead of Charles saying anything normal like *hi* or *hello*, he screamed, "Where are you?"

I told him.

"We've gotta go. I'll be out front in five minutes."

"Where?"

The word was wasted. He'd hung up.

I returned the phone to my pocket and Barb said, "What?"

"It was Charles."

"I know that. I heard him yelling."

"He wants me to meet him out front."

Barb shook her head. "Then go?"

"Joy, Charles wants me to go somewhere with him."

Barb answered for her. "Go. Joy and I have some catching up to do. I want to tell her more about Dude and the geezer she came in with. We'll be fine."

I opened the door and Charles's Toyota Venza was already in front of the store and blocking the driving lane. Two cars behind him were patiently waiting for him to move. A third vehicle wasn't as patient and tapped the horn twice. I slid in the passenger seat before road rage commenced, and Charles turned right at the next intersection.

"Would it be too much to ask where we're going and why the hurry?"

"Nope," he said and kept his eye on the narrow road.

Two blocks later, my question about our destination was answered. Charles pulled in Dude's front yard and parked beside his rusting, green Chevrolet El Camino. The front of the pre-Hugo, elevated, wood-frame house had old-fashioned, multi-colored Christmas lights strung around the front door, up the corners of the house and across the roofline. Straggly shrubs on each side of the steps were covered with more of the near-antique lights.

Before getting out, Charles smacked the steering wheel and said, "Pluto's vamoosed."

Dude must've seen us arrive. He scampered out the front

door, down the steps, and was standing at the driver's window motioning for Charles to get out.

"He be gone!" Dude shouted as we exited the car.

Charles put his arm around the distressed, aging hippie. "Let's go in and you can tell us about it."

"What's to tell. He be gone!"

Charles nudged Dude up the steps, and I followed.

This was the second time I'd been in Dude's abode, so I'd gotten over the surprise of seeing wall-to-wall, bright-green shag carpet and the three colorful beanbag chairs arranged in a triangle. Charles helped lower Dude into the green one. Dude slumped down and stared at a lower half of what appeared to be a rubber Santa Claus the size of a large dog bone on the floor beside the red chair.

"Dude, I know Pluto's gone," I said. "What happened."

Dude turned to the back door and said, "Me be at Logger's. Church lunch."

Charles said, "We were with you, remember?"

I wanted to say, "Charles, shut up, and let him finish." Instead, I said. "Let Dude tell us what happened."

"Me skip home from Logger's. See back door cracked open. Pluto gone … gone."

Charles said, "Do you think someone broke in and took him?"

"You be detective. That's why I call you."

With an effort I wouldn't have needed twenty years ago, I pushed out of the beanbag chair, and walked to the back door. The lock didn't appear tampered with and there was no evidence of a break in. I looked at Charles and shook my head.

He nodded, and said, "Dude, did you go out the back door when you left for church?"

"Exit front. Ride be parked in front." He rubbed his unshaven face. "Woe, today backwards. Took trash out back, then boogied to church."

"Is it possible that the door didn't close all the way when you left?"

He again rubbed his face. "Possible, affirmative. Likely, not." He shrugged.

"Has Pluto gotten out before?"

Dude stood and started pacing the living room floor. "Never."

I said, "Don't you think he'll come home when he gets hungry?"

"What me think, don't mean what he do. Australian Terriers be bred to boogie after rodents and snakes. Me never be lettin' him out without leash. Never," Dude said and went through the kitchen, grabbed his jacket off a chair, and exited to the large patio.

Charles and I followed and watched Dude as he stared at the back yard. He turned to Charles and said, "Woe, plum forgot. You be detective. Here be clue." He picked up a red rhinestone-studded collar that usually adorned Pluto's neck and handed it to Charles. "Stuck to branch behind *hacienda*."

The collar was fastened. I said, "Dude, was it loose on his neck?"

"Loose enough that he could have snagged it on a branch and pulled it off?" Charles added.

"Could be. Me no want to hurt cute little neck. Kept it loose."

Charles ran his hands around the collar, and said, "So, Pluto could have escaped if the door wasn't closed tight enough, got his collar caught on the branch, and ran away."

Dude stared at Charles. "You be detective. You tell me."

Dude then said he was going to drive around and look for the missing member of his family. Charles and I said we'd do the same. I wasn't nearly as worried about Pluto. I figured when he got hungry, he'd find his way back.

An hour later, we'd driven every road on Folly, had seen several dogs walked by their masters, and stopped to ask each person if he or she had seen Pluto. All, to no avail. My optimism faded.

Charles dropped me at the house and said he was going to ride around longer. I didn't think his luck would change. I called Barb to see how her time with Joy went. She had three customers and said she'd call later. I settled in the recliner in my living room and alternated between rehashing the busy day and snoozing. Snoozing ruled.

11

It wasn't yet six-thirty and the sun had faded behind the marsh. Early sunsets were my least-favorite features of December. I sighed as it departed and realized that I hadn't had anything to eat since lunch at Loggerhead's. I also realized that my cupboard was bare, its normal condition, and I didn't want to eat another meal today at a restaurant. I walked next door to Bert's Market, Folly's iconic, eclectic grocery that prides itself on never closing and was the island's go-to place for everything from beer to Band-Aids. Included in that mix was a deli where I ordered a five-cheese panini and was killing time waiting for the sandwich when Chief Cindy LaMond moved behind me and said, "You're not ordering something healthy, are you?"

I smiled and said, "I plead the fifth."

"That answers my question," she said, and looked around to see if anyone was close enough to hear us. No one was, and she continued, "I'm glad I ran into you. I was going to call after I got home, and despite being pooped from an exhausting day at work, I'm going to fix a fine five-course gourmet meal for hubby."

"Picking up a pizza from Woody's?" I said.

Woody's pizza was an institution on Folly and had been feeding visitors and locals for years.

Cindy smiled.

"You were going to call me?" I said to move her past the dinner menu.

"Two reasons. Our search for anything, I mean anything, about Joyce Doe, or Jane Joyce, has come up with a big, fat zero. If I hadn't seen her in person, I'd swear she doesn't exist. Her prints aren't on file anywhere. Unless she lost 127 pounds in the last week and changed her skin color, she's not the 215-pound mother of three who's been reported missing in Moncks Corner. The TV stations ran her photo and we've received zero calls from anyone who has an inkling of who she is."

"Cindy, a few of us had lunch at Loggerhead's after church this morning. Joy came with Burl."

"Good," Cindy interrupted. "Burl will be a good influence. Better than some people I know."

I let her comment go. "While we were there, she stopped paying attention to what was being said and looked at the bar. I asked her what was on her mind and she said that it looked familiar."

"Familiar like she'd been there?"

"That's what I asked. She said maybe."

"Or it could be that any bar may look familiar, and it had nothing to do with Loggerhead's."

"Yes," I said.

"So, it doesn't tell us more than she's seen a bar."

"I agree. From what you said about not finding anything about a missing person fitting her description, or anyone calling about her photo on television, do you think she's from outside the area?"

Cindy shook her head. "Either that or she's from another planet. And, speaking of being from another planet, that leads me to the second thing I wanted to talk to you about, your buddy Dude."

The deli clerk handed me my panini, I paid, and followed Cindy outside to her city-owned truck. Charles had often joked that Dude emigrated to earth from another planet, a planet where complete sentences were frowned upon and had a different meaning than they do on earth. This was one of the few times Cindy agreed with Charles.

"What about him?"

"He began calling and pestering me this afternoon about the shorter, more articulate version of him that's missing."

"Dude called you about Pluto?"

"Eventually. Dude first called Mayor Newman, Councilmember Salmon, the preacher at the Baptist Church, Preacher Burl, and then me about his missing canine. Mayor Newman called me and rearranged the priorities of my department from catching bad guys, stopping speeders, and ticketing those law-breaking vacationers who have the audacity to park with a tire or two touching the pavement on our streets. My priority now is finding one lost Australian Terrier. To paraphrase the words of our fine citizen, *Dude be full o clout*."

I smiled and asked if she's had any luck.

"As much as we've had at learning Joy's identity. Dude told me that you and Charles were the first on the scene of the canine escape. I was going to call to ask if Dude said anything that made you think that Pluto's disappearance was anything other than the critter wanting to get away from Dude to maintain his sanity. Believe it or not, there are times that I don't fully understand what Dude's talking about. You spend more time with him and other oddball characters than I do, so I figured you might understand him better."

I understood Dude better than I understood thermodynamics although not much better.

"Cindy, Dude's upset."

"Duh."

"Pluto means everything to him. Dude doesn't have many close friends and Pluto is probably his best. He was clueless about how Pluto escaped. I didn't see anything that made me think it was anything other than the dog scampering out the back door that was left ajar. Dude had taken the trash out that way before going to church. Most of the time he leaves by the front door since his car's parked in the front yard. He was carrying trash, so it would've been easy for him to not shut the door all the way."

"That's what I thought but wanted your take. When I was there, the poor boy was near tears. My experience with dogs, and with Larry, is that once hunger sets in, they find their way home. Worry not, all my patrol vehicles are out scouring the island for one missing Australian Terrier. If they happen to stumble across a murder in progress, they may stop, unless they're chasing Pluto. And speaking of dogs, Larry, and hunger, I'd better get home with a pizza before he calls the mayor on me."

I wished her luck, headed home, used my one culinary skill, and microwaved the panini that'd turned cold while I was talking to Cindy. I also poured a glass of Cabernet, and wondered who Joy was, and to a lesser extent, where Pluto was.

1 2

Christmas was less than a week away although you could hardly tell it from looking at my house, inside or out. I had hooked a ten-year-old, dusty artificial wreath I bought at a yard sale for seventy-five cents on the front door and inside my decorating was a ceramic Dickens Village Victoria Station setting on a table in the living room. Other than the wreath, the Station was the only item I brought from Kentucky that I associated with Christmas. I'd thought of adding more but rationalized that there was no need since I seldom had anyone to the house and considered the party at Cal's Country Bar and Burgers my prime event on Christmas Day. Looking at the Victoria Station reminded me that it'd been a couple of weeks since I'd talked to Cal, besides a burger sounded good. During the off-season, there was less than a fifty-fifty chance that Cal's would be open for lunch or early beer drinking. I had nothing better to do, so I took a chance and drove the short distance since the outside temperature was near freezing.

The front door was locked. If I wanted food my gamble hadn't paid off, but there was still a chance Cal was inside. I went to the side door and had better luck. The jukebox was playing a Hank Williams Sr. classic, and Cal, who could double as an older, much older, version of Hank, was singing along and sliding a table to the center of the room. My friend was seventy-three-years-old, six-foot-three, razor thin with a spine that curved forward from leaning down to a microphone and living for decades out of the back seat of his car. His long, gray hair inched out from around a Stetson that had travelled with him for forty plus years. I smiled when I saw a strand of battery-operated LED lights strung around the crown, his seasonal addition to the hat. Cal wore a black T-shirt instead of his rhinestone covered white coat he wore when performing. *Ho, Ho, Ho!* was in glittery, silver paint on the front of the T-shirt. His holiday-inspired attire also included bright-red slacks and red tennis shoes. The bar, like Cal, was in a marginal state of repair, yet with its beat-up tables and chairs, indoor/outdoor carpet covered floor, and antique Wurlitzer jukebox, the owner swore it was "the perfect country music bar." Cal would know since he travelled the South for more than four decades singing at any venue that would have him.

Cal saw me in the doorway. He tipped his Stetson my direction, and said, "Halleluiah! My Christmas wish is answered. An elf has come to help this old codger."

And, all I wanted was a hamburger.

"Help with what?"

He waved his hand around the room. "I'm running late finishing party decorations. It's getting harder and harder each year for me to get everything done. My energy level ain't what it used to be."

I followed his gaze and saw three—yes, three—seven-foot-tall artificial Christmas trees in the room. Their multiple strands of colorful lights matched the strands Cal had attached to each non-moving vertical surface, and more were hanging from the ceiling. Unless Santa was shoveling snow in front of the room while Mrs. Claus was feeding the reindeer, I couldn't imagine how much more could be done to make the bar Christmas-party ready.

"What can I do?"

He pointed to the corner near the front door. "Look over there. There's a wide-open space begging for a Christmas tree."

The corner's apparent cry for help was lost on the man who had a grand total of zero Christmas trees in his house. What wasn't lost on me was Cal's childlike enthusiasm for the holiday and his desire to make his bar reflect his glee.

"Do you have a tree?"

His smile was as wide as his face. "Sure do, and now I have an elf to help put it up."

Not only did he have a tree, he had a six-foot ladder, and enough strands of lights to humiliate the tree in Times Square. As if on cue, Gene Autry's version of "Frosty the Snowman" began on the jukebox. "Frosty" was one of many Christmas songs Cal added each December.

During the lull between Gene Autry's singing and Burl Ives, the singer, not the preacher, telling us about "Rudolph the Red-Nosed Reindeer," Cal said, "Have you and Charles found Pluto?"

"How do you know about Pluto?"

He handed me the strand of lights to hang around the back of the tree. "Let's see. It could've been when Officer Spencer came in last night and said he'd driven around the island 739 times looking for the dog or could've been when Councilmember Salmon stopped by for a brew and said that his wife made him ride around looking. No, I got it, it was when the Dudester charged in the door whistling and yelling, 'Yo, Pluto, you be here?'"

I laughed, and said, "The word's out."

"A woeful understatement, my friend," Cal said, and pulled a chair to the front of the tree and lowered his body in it.

"What makes you think Charles or I may've found Pluto?"

He pointed to a nearby chair. "Take a load off."

We weren't finished with the tree, but Cal was breathing heavily and needed to rest. I pulled the chair close to his and sat.

"Dude said the police would do their best to find the missing family member, but he had more confidence that you and especially Charles would find him since your buddy was a professional detective."

"He said all that?"

"Not those words, but that's my interpretation of what he was trying to say."

"To my knowledge, neither Charles nor anyone else has found Pluto. I haven't talked to Dude today, so the pup might be safe and cuddled up to his master."

Cal removed his Stetson and set it on the floor beside the chair. "Then let me ask you this," he said. "Figured out who that Joy gal is that you and Miss Barb found surfin' at the County Park?"

"How do you know about Joy?"

"I hope you don't want me to name everyone who told me about her? There've been a dozen or so guys and gals in here talking about it."

"What've you heard?"

"About you finding her? About where she's staying? Or, about what happened to her memory?"

"All of them."

He told me what he knew about Barb and me finding her, and where she was staying. He was one-hundred percent accurate. When it came to what happened to her memory, the percent dropped drastically. The consensus was that she'd been clobbered with a steel pipe and left on the beach. Theories about who clobbered her included her husband, someone robbing her, the jealous wife of someone who was cheating with Joy, and an alien who'd parked his/her/it's spaceship in the County Park because of its wide-open space. Cal said he didn't put much faith in the alien option. Unfortunately, the accuracy of where she was staying was dead on. That shoots the idea that if someone is after her, the fewer people who knew where she was the better.

He exhausted everything he knew about Joy and was rejuvenated and anxious to finish decorating the tree. Frank Sinatra was singing "Jingle Bells," as Cal pushed himself out of the chair and pointed for me to get back on the ladder so he could give me the final strand of lights.

"Chris," he said as I wrapped the lights around the top of the tree, "remember when I told you why my Christmas party was so important?"

"Wasn't it three years ago when you had the first one?"

"Four."

"Time flies. You said it was because you'd spent many Christmases on the road and most of those years you didn't have anywhere to go to celebrate the holiday. You'd met others in the same boat."

"Yeah, I told myself that if I ever had a place where I could throw a party for everyone who wanted to come, regardless if they had a family, were homeless, had any money, whatever, that I'd do it." He smiled and pointed to each tree. "Being able to do this makes me happier than anything I do all year. People are saying this'll be the biggest."

I'd been to most of his Christmas parties and the number attending had increased dramatically.

The sound of Bing Crosby singing "White Christmas" filled the room.

Cal hooked a large ornament on the tree and pointed to the jukebox. "My favorite Christmas song."

He'd told me that last year. I was thinking how strange it was that I'd remembered that bit of trivia when I couldn't remember what I had for lunch two days ago.

He interrupted my thought when he said, "I have three versions on the jukebox: Bing, Eddy Arnold, and Loretta Lynn."

He hesitated, glanced at the new tree, and then at the jukebox, and joined Bing singing, "I'm dreaming of a white Christmas, just like the ones I used to know." He turned to me. "Chris, think about how bad it'll be for poor Joy on Sunday. She won't be able to remember anything about the ones she used to know. Christmases with friends, with families, maybe with children. How lonely and sad must that be?"

I'd thought about her lack of memory about family and friends but hadn't thought of it in relation to Christmas. "You're right."

"Chris, ain't nothing I can do about her past and those memories. If you can get her to the party, we'll give her a Christmas she'll remember for a long time."

"I'll see what I can do."

13

I left my car at Cal's and walked two blocks to the surf shop to see if Dude's wayward child had returned. The surf shop, with its name in all lower case for reasons known only to Dude, was a goldmine during vacation season. In the winter, its owner spent days in the Lost Dog Cafe drinking tea and bemoaning how bad business was. He seldom got sympathy from the less-successful business owners.

To my chagrin, I was met by Stephon instead of Dude. Stephon was rude and snarky. I'd learned to tolerate his condescending attitude, and he tolerated me to the point that he didn't become hostile when he saw me. Dude kept him on the payroll because he was a surfer and magically meshed with the store's more offbeat customers.

"Good afternoon, Stephon," I said in the most civil tone I could muster. "Is Dude around?"

The clerk was rearranging a rack of wetsuits and wasn't going to let my arrival distract him. "No."

"Is he at the Lost Dog Cafe?"

"No."

"Do you know where he is?"

"No."

This was one of my more civil conversations with Stephon, so I decided to quit while I was ahead.

"Thanks."

I turned to leave, and was surprised to hear, "He's looking for Pluto."

I stopped and looked at the employee who'd turned from the wetsuits and was staring at me. I motioned for him to continue.

"I've never seen boss man so upset. I don't know why, but he likes you. Maybe you can try to find him and help him search. Don't tell him I said this." He looked around and lowered his voice like he was about to tell me the combination to Dude's safe. "You could put your arm around the boss man and say it'll be okay. I would, except you may not know this, but I'm not much at warm and fuzzy. When you asked if I knew where he was, I said no because I don't. Oh yeah, one more thing, when you find him, don't say anything about the Lost Dog Cafe. He might start whimpering if he hears the words lost dog. He's walking the streets. Please help him."

Where was my recorder when I needed it? I said I would and heard two words I didn't know were in Stephon's vocabulary. "Thank you."

The odds on me finding Dude if I walked would be near zero and the temperature felt nearly that cold, so I returned to Cal's and got the car and started my canvas of the island. I was surprised that Pluto hadn't ventured home on his own. I started on Dude's street and drove a grid for fifteen minutes. I saw two couples walking dogs and stopped to ask if they'd seen Dude or a lost Australian Terrier. Each said they hadn't seen Pluto but had talked to Dude who stopped them and asked if they'd seen his missing buddy.

I was about to give up my search when I spotted the surf shop owner in front of Hope House talking with Preacher Burl. I stopped and joined them. Dude wore a stoplight-red unzipped parka revealing his tie-dye T-shirt with a peace symbol on the front, jeans with a rip in each knee, red driving gloves, and hiking boots. He held the leash with the rhinestone-studded collar dangling Pluto-less. He looked more like he was hiking the Appalachian Trail than looking for his pet. He also wore a frown.

"No luck," I said.

Dude shook his head and Burl patted him on the back and said, "We're putting together a search party to help Brother Dude. Brother Bernard and Sister Joy are robing themselves in heavier clothing and Sister Rebekah should arrive any minute. She had to wait for someone to relieve her at Black Magic." Burl held up his phone. "I'm coordinating the search."

"Chrisster, my poor baby could be frozen like a popsicle."

The temperature was well above freezing although it didn't feel it, so I doubted Pluto could have frozen, but it wouldn't do any good to share that observation.

Joy and Bernard joined us, and Burl asked if I was going to help search. Dude looked at me with sad eyes, so I said, "Of course."

Burl said, "Okay, here's the plan. Brother Bernard, you know the island pretty well." Burl pointed east. "Why don't you head off that way? Brother Dude, why don't you go toward town and check behind shops and restaurants? Pluto should be hungry and there are plenty of places where he could root in the trash for food."

Bernard said, "Dude, if you want, I can tell you the best trash cans for food."

Bernard was talking from experience after having been homeless for many months and searching for food and warmth wherever possible.

Dude said, "Okeydokey."

"Sister Joy, you're new here so why don't you go with

Brother Chris? That way you'll learn more about the island and will help Chris look while he focuses on driving."

Joy glanced at me, and I said, "Good idea."

"Good," Burl said. "When Sister Rebekah gets here, I'll recommend that she looks west of Center Street."

Joy was quiet the first few minutes or our search. The coat Burl found for her was several sizes too large and she had a challenging time getting comfortable in the seat with the seatbelt and bulky overgarment. She finally took it off and threw it in the backseat. I carried the conversation and tried to point out some sites and homes where I knew the residents.

"Chris," she finally said, "I don't know who my friends were before, well, you know."

"Yes."

She shook her head. "I don't know if I have a family."

"I understand."

"Let me tell you what I do know. Preacher Burl and the others in the house have been fantastic. They're from diverse backgrounds. They've had ups and downs, mostly downs, I'm saddened to learn. Despite that, they've been wonderful. They seem to truly care. I hope that if, no, when, I regain my memory, my past has that many good people in it."

"I do too."

The heater was pumping out hot air full-blast, but she was shivering. I didn't think it was because she was cold since she'd removed the coat.

I said, "Want some coffee?"

She smiled. "That sounds good."

I pulled in a parallel parking space at the side of Bert's Market and asked if she wanted to go in with me. She said sure, grabbed the coat from the back seat, and followed me to the coffee urn. Two men were putting sugar in cups. I didn't recognize them at first, and then it hit me. They were Barb's temporary neighbors. One of them noticed me standing behind them and said, "Oh, sorry. Let us get out of your way."

He stepped aside and pulled the other man with him.

"Hi," I said, "I'm Chris, and this is my friend, Joy. Aren't you Barb Deanelli's new neighbors?"

"Yes," the taller of the two said. "How'd you know?"

I explained that I'd seen them coming out of Barb's Books and she told me who they were.

"Oh. I'm Troy and this is Nate."

Troy shook my hand and nodded to Joy. Nate stood back and didn't seem interested in talking to us.

"You're from Canada," I said, to end the awkward silence.

"Yes," Troy said.

"Troy, we'd better get going," Nate said and took a step toward the door.

Troy shook his head. "Nate's always in a hurry. Nice meeting you Chris. You too, Joy. Pretty name."

She mumbled, "Thank you."

Barb's neighbors were gone, we got our coffee, and I asked Joy if she wanted anything to eat. She said no, and we continued our search. Over the next hour we saw dogs of assorted sizes, breeds, and colors. Not one was named Pluto.

"Joy, Sunday when we were eating at Loggerhead's, you said the bar looked familiar. Did anything else about it come back to you?"

"I thought about it all night. Nothing. You asked if I'd been there before. I still don't know. Sorry."

"That's okay."

I drove out East Ashley Avenue to Thirteenth Street. I didn't think Pluto would have wandered that far but had an idea. I turned on Tabby Drive and past the house with *Caulder* painted in script on a piece of driftwood on the wall beside the front door. The driveway was empty, so I figured no one was home. I asked Joy to follow me to the back yard. She gave me a strange look but followed me to the walking pier that led to the eighteen-foot-long runabout that had been returned to its owners.

"Chris, did you see Pluto?"

I walked to the end of the pier and put my hand on the Tahoe's stern. "No. I was wondering if this boat means anything to you?"

She looked at it and at me. "No, why should … oh, is this the one that was stolen, the one you think I was on?"

I nodded.

She pulled her coat tighter and returned her gaze to the water-craft. She leaned over and looked in the boat and stepped back and looked at its side.

"I know it would be good if I recognized it, but I don't."

It was worth a try. "Ready to get back on Pluto patrol?"

She nodded, and we headed to the car. Before she stepped off the pier, she looked back at the boat, stopped, slowly shook her head, and whispered, "Sorry."

Forty-five minutes later, we'd covered most every street on the island, some more than once, and decided that if Pluto was wandering around, one of the many searchers would have found him. I was beginning to think that the poor dog had suffered a fate that none of us had imagined, a fate that would devastate Dude. I didn't share that thought with Joy or Burl who was waiting for us. Bernard had already returned and was in the living room sipping on a mug of coffee. Burl offered cups to Joy and me which we quickly accepted. He said that Rebekah was in her room resting after working all morning at Black Magic and traipsing around looking for Pluto. Dude had phoned Burl and said he wasn't stopping until sunset and thanked us for our efforts. Burl went to the kitchen to get more coffee.

"Chris," Joy said during a break in the conversation about Pluto, "who again were those men you talked to in Bart's?"

"Bert's," I corrected, sounding like Charles. "They're Barb's neighbors. She told us about them when we were in the bookstore the other day?"

"I remember. It's just, I wondered if you knew anything else about them."

"No, why?"

"Nothing specific. It's like how the bar in Loggerhead's looking familiar. They're vaguely familiar. I've probably seen them around town, that's all."

Burl returned to the living room and said, "Chris, will you be joining us for our Christmas Eve service?"

"I plan to, why?"

"Curious. What about Christmas Day?"

"Of course."

"Good."

Then I remembered what Cal had said about Joy coming to his party. "Preacher, will you be at Cal's Christmas party? I remember you had an enjoyable time there last year."

Burl smiled, "Brother Chris, I had a wonderful time until Brother Cal dragged me on stage and made me sing a duet with him. I could've crawled under a table."

"Preacher, you were good. Joy, our friend Cal has a big party each Christmas. I know he'd love for you to come."

"I don't know. Everyone will be a stranger, and—"

Bernard interrupted, "Bologna, Joy. You'll be among friends, lots of them. You'll see. Last year was the first time I went. That's when I talked to Preacher Burl and he helped me, helped me a bunch."

She smiled. "Maybe I'll give it a try."

That would do for now.

14

The weather gurus predicted Tuesday would be the best day of the week, so I took advantage of the warm, dry morning and walked two blocks to Rita's Seaside Grille at the corner of Center Street and East Arctic Avenue. The restaurant was on its third name since I'd moved to Folly and was conveniently located across the street from the Folly Pier, catty-corner from the nine-story, oceanfront Tides Hotel, and across Center Street from the iconic Sand Dollar Social Club. The lunch-hour was a few minutes away, and I had the choice of a table or a booth. My preference would have been a table on the patio, but even though today was to be the pick of the week, it was too cool to sit outside. I chose a booth along the sidewalk side of the colorful restaurant and quickly drew the attention of Samantha, a server who'd waited on me several times over the years. She asked if I wanted a menu and I told her I knew what I wanted.

She grinned and said, "Cheeseburger, medium rare?"

I smiled and nodded.

"One of these days you're going to order something different and I'll have to call the *Folly Current,* so they can do a story on the alien who invaded Chris Landrum's body." She turned and headed toward the kitchen.

While I waited for my predictable cheeseburger to arrive, I wondered if Dude had found Pluto. I started to dial his number when Charles bounded through the entry and headed my way.

"Thought that was your bald head shining in the window." He slid into the seat opposite me. "You already ordered your cheeseburger?"

"Good morning, Charles."

"There you go. Trying to introduce civility. When are you going to give up and start talking like your friends?"

I was beginning to wonder that myself when Samantha reappeared with my lunch and asked Charles if he wanted anything.

"Sam, I'm glad you asked. All morning I've had a hankering for world peace, a cure for the common cold, and a grouper sandwich."

"We can't fry up the first two, Charles, but the grouper sandwich is a no-brainer for the chef."

"I'll settle for that."

"So," Charles said as Samantha went in search of a grouper sandwich, "what's the latest on Pluto?"

"I was going to call Dude when you invited yourself to lunch."

Charles nodded toward my phone on the corner of the table. "What's stopping you?"

You, I wanted to say. Instead, I tapped the speaker icon, so Charles could listen, and then tapped on Dude's number and waited through six rings before his voicemail message said, "Be lookin' for pup Pluto. Unless you know where he be, don't waste time leavin' words."

I didn't know where Pluto was, so I didn't leave a message.

Charles stared at the phone. "Dude says more words on his voicemail message than he uses in person."

I shared how I, and several others, had spent hours yesterday looking for the lost canine. Charles said he knew because he ran into Dude snooping around Charles's apartment building looking for you know what. Charles then spent an hour walking the streets in his part of the island, to no avail.

Samantha told Charles his food would be out shortly, before she leaned over the table and said, "Any word on Dude's dog?"

"No," Charles said. "How did you hear about Pluto?"

She shook her head. "Do I look deaf and blind?"

"No," Charles said, in an astute observation.

"Everybody knows about Pluto. Dude was in here twice last night asking if anyone had seen an Australian Terrier hanging around. Those weren't his exact words. A couple from New Jersey looked at him funny, but most of us knew what he was talking about and said we hadn't seen the poor creature." She then said she'd better get Charles's lunch and headed to the kitchen.

Charles shared a couple of stories he'd heard about a restaurant closing on Folly Road and about a book he'd been reading about Herbert Hoover. I covered my mouth, so he wouldn't see my yawn of boredom. I said, "Interesting."

He detected my level of disinterest in his choice of books, and said, "Chris, I'm beginning to think something bad happened to Pluto. If he'd hopped, skipped, and jumped away on his own, don't you think he would've found his way home or some of us would have seen him?"

I nodded, and Samantha set Charles's lunch in front of him and moved to the next booth to see if a father and his two young kids were ready to order.

Charles took a bite and mumbled, "Think he's dead?"

"I'm not ready to go there. Someone could've taken him in and planned to keep him. He's cute and friendly."

"Yes, but he's Dude's."

"We know that. He didn't have a collar, so he could've been mistaken for a stray."

Charles took another bite, nodded left and then right, and said, "Think we should start knocking on doors and asking if anyone has a new pet?"

"I don't know."

"We need to do something, if we—"

I interrupted Charles and stood to greet Joy who was headed our way.

"I thought it was you, Chris," she said and smiled.

"You saw his bald head in the window, didn't you?" Charles said and scooted over and offered her a seat.

"No, I recognized him." She looked at the spot Charles had vacated for her, hesitated, and said, "Do you mind if I join you?"

I was pleased that she asked even after Charles moved over. I said, "We'd be honored."

Samantha returned and asking the newcomer if she wanted something to eat or drink.

Joy looked at Charles's plate, then at mine, and said, "I don't have any… I don't think—"

Charles interrupted and said, "Go ahead and get something. It's on Chris."

Thanks, Charles.

She looked at me and I smiled. "Maybe I'll have what Chris has."

Samantha said it was an excellent choice and once again headed to the kitchen.

Charles said, "Out for a walk?"

"Sort of. Still looking for Pluto. Dude came by early this morning and asked if we could help him look. The poor man was near tears. That dog means a lot to him."

"It's his family," Charles said.

I chose not to mention that Pluto wasn't Dude's entire family since Barb was his half sister.

Joy looked out the window and at the bartender pulling a beer out of the cooler behind the bar along the other side of the room. "Wonder if I have pets."

I said, "Do pets sound familiar? Is anything coming back?"

She continued to look at the bar and instead of answering my question, said, "Pets, no." She rubbed her eyes and continued to look at the bar. "Chris, why does that look familiar?"

I looked at the bar. "The bar, the bartender, or what?"

"The bar."

This was the second bar that she'd said looked familiar. "Does it look more familiar than the one in Loggerhead's?"

"I don't know." She shook her head. "There's something about it." She exhaled and said. "Don't you think I want to know what it is?"

Charles patted her arm. "It's okay, Joy. We'll figure it out. Won't we, Chris?"

Thanks again, Charles. "We'll do what we can."

She attempted a smile and failed.

Samantha returned with a real smile and Joy's cheeseburger. She asked if we needed anything else. I was tempted to say a memory for Joy. I resisted and thanked her.

Joy took a large bite, and I wondered if it was the first thing she'd had to eat today. Charles asked how she liked staying at Hope House.

"It's okay. Everyone is nice."

"How's your room?" Charles asked, mainly to get her mind off worrying about the past.

"Great. Preacher Burl says I have the best room in the house."

"That's great," Charles said. "The preacher is a great person."

Joy started to put a fry in her mouth, hesitated, and returned it to the plate. "Chris, I don't have a right to, but could I ask a big favor?"

"Sure."

"Would you take me back to that boat you said I was on?"

"Of course, we will," Charles answered for me.

We, I thought. "Joy, do you remember something about the boat?"

"I might. I woke up in the middle of the night thinking about it. I was half dreaming, half awake, so I'm not sure what was what. If I see it when I'm awake, something might click."

"If you want, we can go after we finish here."

"Good idea," Charles said, answering for Joy.

It could have been my imagination, but Joy finished lunch quicker than she'd started. Charles was waving for Samantha to bring me the check before any of us had finished our sandwiches.

15

We walked to my house with Charles stopping every few steps to holler Pluto and look for the elusive canine behind every structure. It took nearly as long to walk the short distance as it did to eat lunch.

"I like where you live," Joy said, as we approached my car in the drive. "It's cute. Lived here long?"

"Almost as long as I've been on Folly."

"Could use more Christmas decorations," Charles said as he pointed to the lonely wreath on the door.

We piled in the car before Charles, the man who had no Christmas decorations on his apartment, could tell me how to exterior decorate my cottage. The two-mile ride out East Ashley Avenue took longer than man's first flight to the moon. Charles had me pull over at each beach access walkway, so he could get out and yell for Pluto. We also had to stop at each house that had more Christmas decorations than my wreath, so Charles could show me how I could decorate my humble abode. I could tell that Joy was getting inpatient, but since we were doing her a favor, she held her annoyance. I wasn't as accommodating and ignored

Charles last five requests to stop. Our next stop was in front of the Caulder residence.

Fortunately, the house didn't have as much Christmas decorations as did mine, nor were there any vehicles in the drive. Charles was quick to exit and was nearly to the boat before Joy and I got out. The only witnesses to our trespassing were a dozen pelicans perched on a pier two houses away. Joy was staring at the boat through the window and didn't appear like she wanted to get closer.

"Are you okay, Joy?"

She jerked back from the window.

"Sorry to startle you, you okay?"

She whispered, "I don't know."

"Want to go home?"

She said something I couldn't understand. I leaned closer and asked her to repeat it.

"I think so."

"I'll get Charles."

I walked halfway to the pier and called for Charles who was leaning over the boat looking like he was about to climb aboard. I waved for him to return to the car until I noticed Joy opening the door and walking my way.

She was tiptoeing like she was on broken glass, and said, "You brought me out here and I need to look in the boat. Honest, I do."

Charles shrugged, pointed to the boat, and then at the car.

I put my arm around Joy and led her toward Charles. The temperature was mild, the sun was out in all its glory, and she had on her oversized coat, yet was shivering.

Charles moved away from the craft and let Joy look over the gunwale. She continued to shiver, and I kept my arm around her waist. She stared for just shy of an eternity, before saying, "I was back there."

Charles moved up beside us and looked in the back of the boat. "In the back seat?"

Joy nodded.

I tightened my grip on her, and said, "What do you remember?"

She closed her eyes, and said, "The boat moving fast. Bouncing in the waves. I'm on my stomach on that seat. My head hit the seat every wave. It hurt." She opened her eyes and pointed at the white with blue trim, fold-down back seat. She looked at her left wrist and massaged it with her right hand. "Tied with a rope. Got it loose. Untied my feet. He didn't look back." She continued to look at her wrist.

I waited for her to continue. Charles, who hadn't perfected the art of patience, said, "You were tied up and on the back seat. Then what?"

She looked at him like it was the first time she noticed him standing beside us. "Then nothing." She shook her head. "Nothing."

Charles said, "Are you sure that—"

Joy interrupted, "Can we leave?"

I said yes and moved beside her as she walked off the pier. We got in the car and slowly turned around at the end of the dead-end street and headed to town. Joy remained silent until we were in front of Hope House.

"Thank you for taking me. Sorry I couldn't remember more."

"That's okay. It's coming back."

"Joy," Charles said, "when you were talking about being on the boat, you said, 'He didn't look back.' Do you remember anything about him?"

"No."

I said, "Was there only one person?"

"There could've been more. I only remember the one sitting behind the wheel in front of me."

"And you can't remember anything about him?" Charles

said. "What he was wearing. If he had a hat on, or if you could you see the color of his hair. Did he say anything?"

"I don't remember."

"You're doing fine, Joy," I said. "Tell you what, if you remember more about being on the boat or the man, or if there was someone with him, would you give me a call? I can let the police know so they can follow up."

"Okay," she said, and thanked us again for lunch and for taking her to see the boat.

I pulled in Charles's gravel parking lot and waited for him to say something about Joy. He'd been unusually silent since we'd left her.

"Chris," he finally spoke, "I don't know what to make of it. I don't understand amnesia. How could she have been in that boat and then get off the boat and float to shore on a surfboard without remembering anything about it?"

I was no expert on retrograde amnesia but knew it was real. Joy had no reason to fake it. Slices of her memory are coming back, and if Barb was correct, most, if not all, will eventually return.

I shared my limited knowledge with Charles, and added, "I'm more worried about her safety. Whether it be one, two, or more people who took her out on the boat, it was against her will and I can only imagine what he, or they, had intended."

Charles added, "Dump her in the ocean, never to be seen again, alive, that is."

I nodded.

"You're afraid whoever it was will try again?"

"Yes. Despite the best efforts to keep her whereabouts secret, too many people know where she's living."

"That's why we have to figure out who and stop them from causing more harm."

I rolled my eyes. "That's why the *police* need to solve it— emphasis on police."

"Whatever. That's why you're going to pick up your phone and call Chief LaMond and tell her what we heard about Joy and the boat."

I thought about waiting until I got in the comfort of my home before calling and being the recipient of her wrath about me nosing in police business. Why not let Charles suffer with me? I called the Chief's cell phone and hit the speaker icon.

Cindy answered with, "Happy almost Christmas, Mr. Landrum."

Her pleasant comment threw me, and Charles stared at the phone like it was a scorpion.

"You're in a good mood," I said.

"Aren't I always?"

"No."

"Well, aren't you a damn Debbie downer? Get in the Christmas spirit. Take me, for example. I'm standing in this hoity-toity jewelry store in downtown Charleston with my lovey-dovey hubby and trying on an antique gold ring with a beryl stone and a cute little diamond on each side of it."

"Beryl?" I said.

"Light-blue gemstone, my jewelry-challenged friend. Enough about the exquisite ring lovey-dovey is getting me for Christmas. Why have you called to ruin my perfectly wonderful, and I might add, historic, day when hubby takes me jewelry shopping?"

"Charles and I were having lunch with Joy and she asked us to take her to the boat on Tabby Drive."

"Why?" she interrupted.

Charles leaned close to the phone and said, "Because we were hungry."

"Why'd she ask you to take her to the boat, Chris, who now sounds a lot like Charles, that moronic friend of yours?"

Enough foolishness, I thought. "She hoped it would bring back memories."

Cindy sighed. "Did it?"

I shared what Joy had remembered. Cindy asked twice if she said anything about the man in the boat other than he was sitting behind the wheel. Twice, I answered she hadn't.

"What am I supposed to do with that modicum of near-worthless information?"

"Modicum?" Charles said.

"Itsy, teeny-weeny bit," she said.

I was ready to hang up on the chief and throw Charles out of the car, when Cindy added, "Thanks, Chris. It's not much but it confirms that Joy was on the boat, and most likely, in the ocean. The who, what, and why are yet to be determined. Any word on Pluto?"

That kind of abrupt transition was a hallmark of Charles, but not foreign to several of my friends.

"Not that I've heard."

"Me either," Charles added to not be left out.

"Larry has another gem for me to try on. Better go. He only gets in this generous mood every… umm, never."

She ended the call after agreeing to let me know if she learned anything or if Pluto was found. And, at her urging, I agreed to let her know before I got killed playing cop.

16

I walked to Bert's to get prepackaged doughnuts for breakfast. It was four days until Christmas and Bert's employees' shirts reflected the holiday. Two guys hard at work behind the deli counter wore red T-shirts, one with a picture of Santa on the front and the other with the head of a smiling reindeer. Mary Ewing was stocking a shelf near the back of the store and smiled when she saw me. She had on a red and white Santa's hat and a green sweatshirt with *Merry Christmas* on the front. When I met Mary a year ago, she was anorexic thin with dirty blond hair. Since then, she'd added twenty pounds to her five-foot-five frame and her hair was clean and pulled in a ponytail. She looked fresh and younger than her mid-twenties.

Her smile lit up the room. "Good morning, Mr. Landrum."

"Mary, you know to call me Chris. Ready for the big day?"

She gave me a hug, stepped back, and continued to smile. "I'd better be. Jewel and Joanie are counting the hours until Santa arrives."

The single mother and high-school dropout was struggling last Christmas to find somewhere warm to spend the nights with her girls. Preacher Burl heard of their situation, found them a place to live, got Mary the job at Bert's, and gave them hope. He also got her enrolled in a GED program where she could work toward her high-school equivalency diploma.

I remembered how excited Joanie and Jewel were last Christmas to get something as simple as new clothes for the holiday. "I bet they're excited."

A customer interrupted our conversation to ask Mary where to find ketchup. Mary smiled and walked the woman to the condiments and returned to where I was looking at the packaged sweets, a.k.a. breakfast.

"They're super excited. This'll be the first Christmas for Jewel in a house where we're actually living."

"That's wonderful."

"I almost forgot," Mary said and tapped the side of her head. "I met someone you know."

"Who?"

"Joy. She said you and your lady friend saved her life."

"Barb and I were in the right place at the right time. Where did you meet her?"

"Yesterday, after work, Joanie, Jewel, and I were walking along the beach. It was windy and cold, but when my gals want to walk on the beach, nothing can stop them. We were bundled up and saw Joy walking toward us. She was wrapped-up in a big coat and looking at the pier. You know Joanie's never met a stranger, so she went over to Joy." Mary laughed and shook her head. "Joanie said, 'I'm excited about Christmas. How about you?'"

That sounded like Joanie. I smiled, and said, "What did Joy say?"

"She knelt and smiled at Joanie. I didn't think there was much happiness behind her smile, anyway, she said she was excited and asked Joanie her name. You know, that's all it took. Joanie not only told the stranger her name but pointed to Jewel and me and shared our names, where we lived, and how much we were looking forward to Christmas. She finally got around to asking the lady who she was. She told us she was Joy." Mary chuckled. "Joanie is obsessed with words, something she's getting from school, I suppose. She pointed to her sister, at Joy, and then at herself, and said, 'That's funny. All our names start with *J*.' That got an honest smile from Joy."

"How'd you learn that Joy knew me?"

"My busybody seven-year-old. After she figured out the *J* names, she asked Joy if she lived on Folly. Joy said she guessed she did. That did it. Joanie asked what Joy meant by guessed she lived here. Joanie said something like, 'Don't you know where you live?' Joy told her it was hard to understand, but that you and Barbara found her, and she was now staying at Hope House. Joanie knows about the house and that it was started by that wonderful man, Preacher Burl. I interrupted Joanie's interrogation of the poor lady who'd been minding her business and walking on the beach. I told Joanie we needed to get going and to let the lady continue her walk."

"That was nice of Joanie to talk to Joy."

"Yes. Joy said it was nice meeting us and that she looked forward to seeing us again. I told her that you and I were friends. I hope that was okay."

I told her it was. Mary said she didn't know anything about Joy but that she was going to stop by to visit her. I said it was a good idea. Another customer asked Mary a question, and I told her that I didn't want to keep her from work.

I grabbed some coffee, paid for breakfast, headed home, and thought how it would be good for both Mary and Joy to get better acquainted, or, knowing as little as I did about Joy, thought it would be good.

I tore open the package of doughnuts and started breakfast when the phone rang.

"I was thinking," Charles said to open the conversation.

"Might I ask what?" I said before stuffing one of the treats in my mouth.

"You might," Charles said, and smiled.

I waited for him to tell me instead of asking again.

"You're no fun. Why don't you come pick me up and I'll not only tell you, I'd do a show-and-tell, and we can see if I'm right."

The logical thing to do would be to ask what he might be right about, or moving past that, suggest that he pick me up. He had a car, and it was his idea. Logical and Charles seldom coexisted. I told him I'd be at his place in fifteen minutes.

"Where are we going?" I asked as he got in the car. I thought it was an appropriate question since all Charles had said was for me to pick him up.

"East Arctic, three-hundred block."

"Why?"

"To visit Martha."

"Martha?"

"Martha Wright. Remember, you asked about her after church?"

"One of the older ladies you were talking to?"

"Ah, ye of declining brain cells, you remember."

I'd turned left on East Arctic Avenue in front of the Tides Hotel.

"Now that we've determined the who, how about why?"

"Martha loves animals. I've never been there but have heard she has bunch of pets. She puts food out every night for hungry, homeless critters. I was told that if you walked by her house around sunset, you could see animals of all sizes, shapes, and kinds. The Ark would've been too small to hold them all."

The purpose of our trip finally dawned on me. "You think Martha has Pluto?"

"It's possible. Martha's house is close to Dude's if you go as the crow flies, or as the Pluto trots. He didn't have a collar and he's adorable. He could've been tempted by the food and as friendly as he is, I can see Martha taking him in. I don't know why I didn't think of it before." He pointed to a large, two-story, new, sky-blue house on our right that backed up to the beach.

I said, "Looks like Martha can afford plenty of pet food."

"I hear she's worth millions. She plops a couple of C-notes in the collection basket each week. Her husband died a few years ago, and she moved here from Atlanta. Rumor is hubby hated the beach and wouldn't leave the Peachtree State. He didn't have to. Now he's planted there, and Martha has her beach. A best-of-both-worlds' marriage."

"What's your plan? Knock on the door and ask if she's stolen any dogs?"

"Doubt that'll work. I'll start with my charming smile, then step aside, and you can ask if she heisted the little fellow."

We climbed what seemed like a hundred steps to the front door, and Charles, good to his word, rang the bell, and moved back. It must've sounded like the dinner bell. There were barks ranging from high-pitched yelps that sounded more like squeaks, to Barry White rumbles. None of the noises sounded like someone answering the door. Charles rang again, again receiving a cacophony of animal utterances.

Charles leaned closer to the door and said, "Hear Pluto in there?"

I looked at him and shook my head.

"I don't either," he said. "Pluto's not a big talker, takes after Dude."

Still no answer.

The garage door was closed so we couldn't tell if a vehicle was inside. Charles suggested we walk around back and see if Martha was in the yard. The back yard consisted of a thirty-foot deep patch of perfectly manicured grass, before steps that led to the beach. There must have been two dozen stainless-steel bowls along the rear of the house, with half of them overflowing with dog food. It was no wonder that canines, and I suspected a few cats, racoons, and an occasional opossum chose this restaurant for their evening meal. What wasn't in back was Martha Wright.

"Now what?" I said.

"Other than breaking in?"

"That's not an option."

"You're right," Charles said and looked at the back door. "Some of those dogs sound like they could have us for dessert."

That wasn't my reason for not committing a crime, but if it stopped Charles, I'd agree with him.

"Let's see if the neighbors know anything," he said, and looked to either side of Martha's house.

No one was in the yard, and for as far as we could see, the beach was deserted. We returned to the car and Charles looked across the street.

"Wonder if Dixie's home?" Charles said and started across the street.

Charles had already started up the steps of the house directly across from Martha's, so I assumed it was Dixie's. All I knew about her was that she attended First Light Church, and according to Charles was an uber-gardener and Martha's close friend.

We had better luck at Dixie's door. I recognized the woman who answered from church. She was in her late seventies, tall, at roughly five-foot-nine, thin, with hair so white that I suspected it might glow in the dark. Her face was tanned and leathery. She smiled at Charles and her teeth matched the color of her hair. She had on a white, long-sleeve men's dress shirts and jeans with mud caked on each knee.

"Charles, my oh my, what a pleasant surprise. Who's your friend?"

Charles nodded in my direction. "Dixie, this is my best friend, Chris Landrum. Chris, meet Dixie Thompson."

We exchanged pleasantries and Dixie invited us in, something I'm not sure I'd do if I found two guys who looked like us at the door.

"I wasn't expecting company, so things are a mess. I just came from the garden. Would either of you like a drink?"

"Water would be nice," Charles said.

She winked at me and said, "I've got bourbon."

"Water's fine," I said.

Charles and I sat on a burgundy sofa. Dixie was gone several minutes before returning with water in plastic glasses for Charles and me. She went back to the kitchen and returned carrying what I'd always heard referred to as a rocks glass filled with ice cubes and an amber-colored liquid. The odds on it being tea were slim. Her house wasn't nearly as new as Martha's and the living room furniture had been new in the 1950s. Dixie sat across from us in a white-on-khaki medallion patterned chair. She didn't seem worried that her muddy jeans would hurt it.

"Don't get me wrong, I love company, but what brings you gentlemen out today? Surely it's not to visit an old lady."

"Now Dixie," Charles said, "you're not old."

"Charles, you're a dear. You may not know this, but I pride myself in being able to spot bull dung a block away." She gave Charles a smile incongruous with her words.

Charles smiled. "You caught us, Dixie. We were at Martha's and it doesn't appear she's home. You know everything that goes on around here, so I figured you'd know where she is."

Martha smiled and wiggled her forefinger at Charles. "Did you forget what I said about my bull dung meter. I don't know everything, but I know Martha's whereabouts."

Charles smiled and said, "Where?"

"Dayton, Ohio. She's visiting a cousin who had a stroke."

I asked, "When's she coming back?"

"Christmas Eve, if the danged airlines don't mess up her flights. They're getting worse every day. You wouldn't catch me dead flying anywhere." She hesitated and bit her lower lip. "I do worry about Martha."

Charles asked, "Why?"

She frowned and shook her head. "The dear lady would slap me senseless if she knew I was telling you this. Her memory's slipping. She says she's fine, but she's fibbin'. If you ask me, she's on the road to Alzheimer's."

I said, "I'm sorry to hear it."

Charles jumped in with, "Who's taking care of her pets?"

"I offered to. She said don't be silly that it wasn't safe for me to be crossing the street to her house." She shook her head. "Charles, I've crossed that street for thirty-five years. Haven't been flattened yet. She hired a pet sitter; can you believe that? I'd never heard of such until Martha told me about it. The sitter, a sweet little thing, can't be over twenty, comes twice a day to feed and walk Martha's dogs. Didn't have jobs like that when I was a youngster. They sure didn't."

Charles said, "What time does the pet sitter come?"

"Lordy, young man. Do you think I sit here and keep tabs on what happens across the street? I have no idea when the sweet little thing shows up."

"Dixie," Charles said, "do you know if Martha took in any new pets in the last few days? Maybe an Australian Terrier?"

"Now that's one strange question, Charles. I don't have the vaguest idea." She took a sip, set her glass on the table beside her chair, and said, "You missing one?"

Charles told her about Dude and Pluto.

"Oh, dear. I can't imagine Martha stealing someone's pet. No, I can't. Don't get me wrong, my good friend loves, really loves, dogs and cats. I don't understand why she takes so fondly to them, but she does."

Charles leaned forward on the sofa. "Harry Truman once said, 'If you want a friend in Washington, get a dog.'"

Dixie looked at him like he sprouted a second head. "What's that have to do with Martha?"

Excellent question, I thought. "Charles likes to quote US presidents."

Charles glanced at me and back to Dixie. "It means that I understand how your friend can love dogs. Where did she get the ones she has over there?"

"Don't know about all of them. I know she's taken in strays over the years. One look at them and you can tell they were strays. Your friend's dog didn't look like a stray, did it?"

Dude looks like a stray and Pluto takes after his owner, so I wasn't ready to say no.

Charles didn't have my reservation and said, "Absolutely not."

"There you go," Dixie said.

"You're sure you don't know when the pet sitter will be back?" Charles said.

Her hand balled into a fist and she glared at Charles. "I told you I don't know."

She was getting annoyed, and I didn't blame her.

"Dixie, I hear you have one of the nicest gardens on Folly," I said to lower her level if irritation, or so I hoped.

A smile returned to her face. "I like to think so. Would you like to see it?"

Not really, I thought. "I'd love to."

She finished her liquid relaxer and led us through the kitchen to a deck, and down the steps. I knew as much about gardens as I did about the flora and fauna on Iceland but could tell that Dixie's was special. There were fifteen, four-foot-by-six-foot raised cedar rectangular boxes, each a foot high. Three rows of low shrubs and a row of ornamental grasses were behind the beds.

Dixie started telling us what each thing was and pointing out the name holders beside each item. Most of the flowers weren't in bloom, but it didn't stop her from telling us about them. It wasn't long before I zoned out when she was giving us the Latin name of the flowers and described the lasagna method of layering the mulch that works best for each variety of whatever those things were that were planted in each box. Charles, being Charles, was taking in everything the tour guide said. I started paying more attention, particularly where I was walking, when she mentioned having to occasionally "scat" a snake out of the garden. Dixie was in her element and her mood improved with each description, or it could have been heightened by the drink she had before giving us the tour. Charles wisely didn't ask her anything else about Martha or the pet sitter, and I fended interest until I'd reached my limit and said that we needed to be going.

"You can have another drink before you leave."

I said we'd love to, but I had somewhere I had to be. Charles continued to be wise by not asking me where. He wrote his phone number on a piece of paper he found in his back pocket and gave to Dixie and asked her to call if she learned anything about Pluto.

1 7

Confucius said, "A ringing phone after midnight seldom brings glee." Okay, he didn't say it, but should have.

"Brother Chris, this is Preacher Burl. I apologize for waking you."

He knew me enough to know that if I wasn't asleep by ten o'clock, it was a bad night.

"That's okay," I lied. "What is it?"

"Something happened, and I wonder if I could inconvenience you to delay sleep and come over."

The clock read 12:15.

"Now?"

"The police just left and—"

That was all it took. I interrupted and told him I'd be there as soon as I got dressed.

Every light in Hope House was on as I pulled in the parking area. Shadows from the live oak beside the house snaked across the side of the parking lot, giving the house an ominous feel.

Burl was standing at the open front door waiting for me. His eyes were bloodshot and his shirttail untucked. "Please come in."

I followed him to the living room to find Bernard, Adrienne, Rebekah, and Joy seated on the sofa and two of the chairs. The Christmas lights were off and the presents under the tree looked forlorn.

Joy jumped up when she saw me and gave me a hug. She had on a heavy, brown bathrobe and was barefoot. "Thank you for coming. I asked Preacher Burl to call you. I was scared and feel close to you since you saved me."

"I'm glad he called. Is everyone okay? What happened?"

"Brother Chris, would you like something to drink? I have coffee brewing."

"I'm fine, Preacher."

Burl nodded and turned to Joy who'd returned to the sofa. "Sister Joy, would you like to start?"

"I don't know much," she said and pulled her knees up and wrapped her arms around them. "I was falling asleep, maybe already asleep. I heard a noise at my door like someone fiddling with the knob."

Burl added, "The knobs are old and make a lot of noise when they're turning. Sorry, Sister Joy, go on."

"Everyone here respects each other's privacy, so I was surprised that someone was trying to get in without knocking. I sat up and said, 'Who is it?' The noise stopped, and I heard what sounded like someone walking away."

"The old floors squeak a lot," Burl interrupted.

Joy continued, "I rushed to the door to see who was there." She turned to Bernard who was in the chair beside her. "I must've been loud when I asked who it was."

Bernard said, "You weren't that loud, Sister Joy. I was awake."

Burl said, "Bernard's room is beside Joy's."

"Preacher Burl," Bernard interrupted, "may I continue?"

"Of course."

"I heard Sister Joy and opened my door to see what was

going on. The hall was dark, but I saw the outline of a guy rushing toward the steps. I started after him, and—"

Adrienne said, "Bernard nearly knocked me down. I stepped out of my room on the other side of Joy's to see what the commotion was about, and Bernard tried to run over me."

"Adrienne, I apologized. You came out so fast I didn't see you."

Adrienne pulled her robe tight and smiled. "Apology accepted."

I said, "Then what happened?"

Bernard looked at his fellow housemates to see who was going to interrupt him next. Everyone remained silent, so he continued, "After Adrienne tried to tackle me, I yelled for the intruder to stop. He didn't. I followed him down the stairs and out the back door. I was barefoot and not quite as fleet as I was in my younger days when I was traipsing around Afghanistan. The troublemaker was out of the yard in a flash. Gone, poof." He held out his hands, palms up. "That's about it."

"Brother Chris," Burl said, "I heard Brother Bernard yell and came out of my room to see what was going on. He told me about the outsider, so I called the police and asked the residents to join me in here.

Rebekah yawned and spoke for the first time. "I slept through the whole thing. Preacher Burl woke me up and asked that I go to the living room. I have to be at work at six and was asleep before everyone else."

"Sister Rebekah, I'm sorry to have disturbed you."

"That's okay, Preacher. I was sharing so Chris would know where I was during it all."

"Did anyone get a clear look at the man?" I asked, again, to get the conversation back on track.

Burl said, "Brother Chris, I don't believe so."

"No, sir," Bernard added.

Joy and Adrienne shook their head.

"I was asleep and didn't see anything," Rebekah said.

"Preacher," I said, "you once mentioned that you lock the exterior doors after everyone is in for the night. How'd he get in?"

"Brother Chris, the doors were locked, but as you can imagine, the locks are old and Officer Spencer, who responded to my call, said the back door looks like it was jimmied allowing access."

I remembered the first time I visited, a broken lock on the front door was being repaired. Burl tried to keep the house as secure as possible, but I could see how someone could get in without much trouble.

"Preacher, why would someone would want to break in?"

"I can only speculate. It should be obvious to everyone that there are no great riches here, no valuable jewelry, little cash. If a burglar sought to steal something of value, he would've been better off breaking in any other house on the island."

Bernard raised his hand.

Burl said, "Yes, Brother Bernard?"

"From my way of thinking, he was after Joy. He was trying to get in her room. Someone took her before. Tied her up, put her on a boat, took her out in the ocean, and probably planned to throw her overboard. Yes sir, he was after her."

Burl said, "Now, Bernard, we don't know that."

"Preacher," Rebekah said, "can I go? I've got to get some sleep before my shift."

"Of course, Rebekah. Bernard, Adrienne, why don't you head upstairs and get some sleep."

The three of them slowly walked upstairs. Joy and Burl remained seated and watched the others go.

"Chris," Joy said, "I'm scared. I don't remember everything, but bits and pieces are coming back. That man was after me."

Burl moved beside Joy on the sofa and put his hand over her

hand. "Sister Joy, go ahead and tell Brother Chris what you told me before you went to your room."

"I think I was a bartender, and that's why the bars over here looked familiar. I didn't work in those places, but watching their bartenders struck me as familiar."

"Do you know where you worked?"

"Not exactly. I remember it was smaller than the ones I've been in on Folly. Darker, too. I remember overhearing two guys talking. I wouldn't swear to it, but it seems like they were talking about a robbery."

"Like they were planning one or talking about one that'd already happened?" I asked.

"I'm not certain, I'm really not."

"Sister Joy, you told me that they didn't know you overheard what they were saying."

"Yes, Preacher, that's what I said." She looked at the floor and then at me. "What if I'm wrong?"

I nodded. "And they saw you and figured you were a threat."

"Then caught me, took me out to sea, and wanted to drown me."

I nodded. "Joy, can you remember anything else about where you worked, or about the two men?"

"The bar was dark, really dark. It's small. Most of its customers were dressed like they did physical labor. Muddy boots, yes, I remember several of them wearing muddy boots."

"Anything else?" I said.

"No, sorry. Chris, if that guy who broke in here was one of the men who took me, they know where I live. I'm scared."

"Sister Joy," Burl said, "I'm going to call Larry at Pewter Hardware as soon as it opens and have him install better locks on our doors. I should've done it long ago."

I hoped that would be enough.

1 8

It was two in the morning before I got home, and another hour before I fell asleep. I don't normally watch the morning news, but it took all my energy to get out of bed after the early morning trip, so sitting in front of the television was all I had energy to do. I wasn't paying attention until the anchor mentioned an overnight break-in at Grogan's Fine Jewelry in Mt. Pleasant and threw the broadcast to a reporter standing in front of the store.

The reporter looked like he was ten-years-old pretending to be an adult dressed in his light-gray suit, red and green Christmas tie, and a white shirt that was loose around his neck. He was standing in front of the strip center that housed Grogan's. Yellow crime-scene tape stretched across the front of the building and provided a visual loved by television cameras. The reporter held the mic in front of an older gentleman with curly white hair, and wearing a black suit, a conservative burgundy and gray rep tie, and an expression that reminded me of an undertaker.

"Mr. Grogan," the reporter said, "how did the burglars get in? Also, can you tell us what was taken?"

"The lock on the back door was picked, and the thief somehow

657

disarmed the alarm. Our most precious items were in the safe and undisturbed. Unfortunately, being three days before Christmas, our inventory was much larger than any other time of the year. Space was tight in the safe and we left several pieces in the display cases that weren't visible from the windows." Mr. Grogan smiled. "Many of our gentlemen customers wait until the last minute to shop for their wives or lady friends, so we're always prepared for the last-minute Christmas rush from procrastinators. As you know, we're known for our high-end jewelry and luxury watches."

"I must confess, I'm one of those procrastinators," the reporter said, and smiled. "One last question, Mr. Grogan. What would you estimate to be the worth of what was taken?"

"We've not had time to do a complete inventory, but I'd guess it was in the one-fifty to two-hundred-thousand-dollar range."

I patiently waited through three commercials to hear the weather. An un-seasonable warm front was pushing thought the area, and the temperatures were projected to soar into the lower seventies. Barb called while a sports reporter was raving about the good season the College of Charleston Cougars were having and his prediction about tonight's game again Coastal Carolina. I answered the phone and missed the prediction.

"Any news about Pluto?" she said, instead of hello. She had become acclimated to Folly phone etiquette.

"None that I've heard."

"Why not? What have you been doing all morning?"

She knew I normally would've been up for a couple of hours and I told her it was a long story and I'd tell her later. She said she was walking to the bookstore and if I wanted, she'd fix me a cup of coffee on the condition that I stop at Bert's and get her something for breakfast. I told her it was the best offer I'd had all day. She suggested that it was the only offer I'd had all day.

"Guilty as charged. I'll be there in a half hour."

Denise, one of the personable clerks, welcomed me with a smile and the question that I hear way too often. "Any word on Pluto?"

I told her no.

She said, "Poor Dude. I hope the pup comes home soon. I can't imagine how sad Christmas will be for him if Pluto's not there."

Denise went to wait on a customer, and I headed to the case where there were two cinnamon rolls begging for me to take them with me. I gave in to their wishes and headed to the cash register.

"It's about time you got here," Barb said, her smile indicating that she was kidding. "I'm starved."

We went to the office in the back of the store where she fixed two cups of coffee and I pulled two paper plates out of the drawer and adorned each with a cinnamon roll.

She looked at her watch. "I can't believe you've gone this long in the day without checking with Dude to see about Pluto. You're slipping."

I told her about my late-night call from Burl and what'd happened at Hope House.

"Do you think someone was there to harm Joy?"

"I don't know. The residents are convinced that's the case."

Barb sipped her coffee and set the mug on the glass-top table. "Speaking of Joy, let me tell you something that happened yesterday after work."

I took a bite of roll and nodded for her to continue.

"You know my vacationing neighbors."

"Troy and Nate," I said and figuratively patted myself on my back for remembering their names.

"Yes. I was in the elevator going to my condo, and before the door closed, Troy came around the corner and asked me to hold it open. He was pushing one of those big luggage carts. It was empty, and I teased him about having such a light load. He chuckled and said that they were checking out."

"Aren't they supposed to be here a couple more weeks?"

"They were. I asked if the weather was too hot for them. He laughed and said no that something came up and they had to leave early."

"That's unusual. All he said was something came up?"

Barb nodded. "I wouldn't have thought much of it until I remembered something, I believe it was Nate who said it the night before. We were in the parking lot talking about the weather, our usual conversation when we couldn't think of anything else to say. Nate asked how Joy was doing. It threw me a little until I remembered that he'd met her. I was vague and said as far as I knew, she's fine. Nate was silent for a few seconds and then asked if her memory was returning."

"Is that all he said?"

"I didn't want to answer yet didn't want to be rude. I said I didn't know. He didn't say anything else."

I watched her take a bite of roll, and said, "Are you thinking that they may be the men who took Joy?"

She swallowed and sipped her coffee before shrugging. "I have no reason to believe that they are. It simply struck me as strange that they were asking about someone they'd only met once, and that they were leaving two weeks early."

"Leaving early because Joy's memory might return, and she'd remember that they took her?"

"You said it, not me."

"You have good instincts about stuff like this. What's your gut tell you?"

Barb smiled. "Good instincts because I spent years defending white-collar crooks?"

I returned her smile. "Could be."

"Okay, here goes. My gut tells me that I don't know. Their actions struck me as strange."

"Strange enough for me to share with Chief LaMond?"

"You know her better than I do. What would she do with the information?"

"First, she'll give me a lecture about nosing in her business. Let's see, second, she'll repeat the lecture adding a few East Tennessee phrases that mean I'm a jackass." I paused and thought about previous times I'd shared none-of-my-business thoughts with Cindy.

Barb said, "Third?"

"She'll hang up on me or say something like, 'Okay, buttin-sky, tell me again who these guys are, what they said about Joy, and when they checked out?'"

She took another sip of coffee, looked at my phone I'd set on her desk, and said, "What are you waiting for?"

Two rings later, Chief Cindy LaMond answered with, "This better be important. I have a meeting in five minutes with the mayor and rumor is that he's spittin' nails about how one of my brilliant officers shared his displeasure with a vacationer from Vermont about the speed in which he was traversing East Erie Avenue."

"I wouldn't want you to be late for your pleasant conversation with His Honor. Call me when you get a chance."

I told Barb that by hanging up on me, the chief meant that she'd love to call me.

Neither of us believed it.

19

One thing I've learned over the years is if I'm walking on Center Street, there's a good chance I'll see someone I know. The appropriately named street is only five blocks long, yet most all the island's restaurants and retail establishments are either on it or within a block.

Since the weather was picture-perfect, I left Barb's books and turned right and ran into Cal, more accurately, he ran into me. He was walking with his head down and humming "White Christmas." I put my hand out to keep him from stepping on my foot.

"Oh, sorry. Guess I was daydreaming." He tipped his Stetson in my direction.

"Are you ready for your party?"

"Yes, umm, no, well maybe."

"Glad you clarified that," I said and smiled at the crooner.

"That's where my mind was wandering when I plum near ran you down. Trying to figure out what else I need to do."

"While I'm thinking of it, I talked to Joy, and she's planning on being there."

"How's her memory?"

"A few are coming back."

"She know who she is, other than Joy?"

"Not yet."

"I remember how screwed up I was after getting conked on my noggin. It's harder for her." He shook his head. "Not even knowing any of the who, what, where, and whys of her life."

"True."

Cal said, "Heard more about Pluto?"

"I haven't talked to Dude today, so I don't know if the pup's still missing."

"That'll be a mighty big Christmas double-downer. No memory and no Pluto."

I agreed and told him that if he needed help to get ready for his party to give me a call.

"Much obliged, pard."

He tipped his Stetson again and moseyed on.

I walked two more blocks to the Folly River Park, the site of several oversized Christmas decorations and the official city Christmas tree. The lights were on, but the cloudless day made it difficult to appreciate the illuminated displays. Regardless, there were two young mothers holding toddlers and pointing to the outline of Santa's sleigh and then at the tree.

At the edge of the park a foot pier crossed a portion of marsh and jutted over the Folly River. Leaning on the wood railing at the far end of the pier was a familiar, bright red University of Arizona Wildcats sweatshirt wrapped around Charles Fowler. He appeared in deep-thought as he stared at the water and didn't notice me walking toward him until I was within a few yards.

"Hi, Chris. Nice day, isn't it?"

I said, "What's wrong?"

"Why think something's wrong?"

I shrugged. *Hi, Chris. Nice day.* Charles, that's something a normal person would say."

He shook his head and returned to gazing at the water. "Sorry I didn't insult you."

I stood close to him and waited for him to continue.

We watched several cars cross the bridge to the island and Charles finally said, "It seems that this year's been mired in deep manure. Poor Heather was thrown in jail and accused of killing her manager and then tried to kill herself. Now she's gone." He continued to stare at the slow-moving water.

Charles and Heather had dated a few years. She was a country music singer and had convinced Charles to move to Nashville with her at the urging of an unscrupulous manager who took her hard-earned money along with her hopes of a singing career. They returned to Folly six months ago with Heather's dream crushed. She left the island, and left Charles a farewell note, hours before he'd planned to propose marriage.

I was tempted to say that everything would be okay. Not knowing if it would be, I didn't say anything.

Several minutes passed before he said, "Now add to Heather leaving, poor Joy doesn't know who she is, and may be in danger. And, that's not even mentioning Dude missing his best buddy." He looked at me. "Chris, this is a seriously sucky year, and Christmas is almost here."

I remained silent.

He finally said, "Know where I was for two hours this morning?"

"Malibu," I said. An absurd answer to a question I couldn't know the answer to, usually got a smile from my friend. Not this December 22.

"No," he said, expressionless.

"Where?"

"Sitting outside Martha Wright's house."

"Waiting for the dog sitter?"

He nodded.

"Did she show up?"

He shook his head and said, "Guess."

"No."

"No, you're not going to guess? No, you think she didn't show up, or no to Pluto being there?"

I should have stuck with Malibu.

"Did she show up?"

"No."

"Sorry. Want to go back?"

"Thought you'd never ask."

He'd walked to the River Park, so I suggested we go to my house and take my car.

We ran into Bernard in front of Mr. John's Beach Store.

"Y'all looking for Pluto?" he asked to begin the conversation.

I told him we were and asked if that's what he was doing.

"Yes, sir. Dude woke Preacher Burl and me up when he pounded on the door as soon as the sun stuck its head over the ocean. Scared the shi… umm, crap out of me until I saw it was Dude. He said Pluto was still AWOL and wanted to know how long it'd be before we started looking."

Charles said, "What'd you tell him?"

Bernard smiled. "Well, I bit my tongue, so I wouldn't say I hadn't planned on looking. The poor little hippie looked so sad. I told him I'd be out as soon as I got dressed." He pointed to his jacket and slacks. "And, here I am?"

I said, "I know Dude appreciates it."

Bernard started to leave, turned, and said, "Chris, have you talked to Joy this morning?"

"No, why?"

"I was heading out and only saw her a second. She's going to call to tell you she remembered something that could be important."

"Thanks, Bernard. I'll give her a call."

He gave me a quick salute and headed the other direction.

Charles moved to the edge of the sidewalk, leaned against the fence in front of Mr. John's, and pointed to the pocket that held my phone.

Message received. I started to call Hope House.

He grabbed my hand. "Wait. Got a better idea. We need to go see her. That way, both of us can help her remember."

I didn't know if a visit would help her remember better, but the best way to improve Charles's mood was to give him a purpose.

"Good idea."

A block from Hope House, Charles yelled for me to pull over. I pulled between a rusting motorhome and a pile of broken tree limbs. Charles was out of the car before I put it in park. I waited to see where he was going before I opened the door. I didn't have to go far. Charles jogged between two houses and was returning before I saw what had drawn his attention.

He said, "Thought I saw him."

I waited for his findings.

"It was a little dog the same color as Pluto." He pointed between the two houses. "The guy back there was calling Lulu." Charles sighed. "Not Pluto."

I said, "Sorry," and followed my dejected friend to the car.

"Thought for sure it was him," Charles mumbled.

He appeared sadder now than he'd been when I found him on the walking pier. I pulled in Burl's parking area and was afraid Charles was going to stay in the car. I was beginning to agree with him that this year was mired in deep manure.

2 0

Preacher Burl waved us in. He said Joy and Adrienne were in the living room watching television. Joy smiled when she saw us, and Adrienne looked like she would have been as well off if we weren't there. Burl asked if we wanted coffee. I told him that would be nice, and Charles showed as much enthusiasm as Adrienne had shown seeing us.

"Joy," I said, "Bernard said you had something to tell me."

Burl returned and handed us mugs of steaming hot coffee. He asked the ladies if they wanted more. They declined, and Burl returned to the kitchen to refill his mug.

Joy watched me take a sip, and said, "Yes, but you didn't have to come over. I was going to call."

I told her we were in the area and thought it would be better to stop.

"Thank you. Don't know if this means anything. I woke up around one remembering being in a little apartment. It had a green blanket on the bed and a kitchen so tiny that the table was up against the wall and there was barely room to walk past it. Funny that I would remember those things."

"Were you there with the man from the boat?" Charles asked, showing more life than he had all morning.

She closed her eyes and turned her head from side to side. "I don't think so. I had the impression it's where I lived."

Charles said, "Remember anything else?"

"The whole place was small, not much more than a bedroom, a kitchen, and a bathroom."

I said, "Were there windows?"

Her eyes widened. "I didn't think of it until you asked. I don't remember one in the bedroom, just the ugly green blanket. There was a window over the kitchen sink."

I leaned closer. "Good, you're doing great. Let's say you're standing at the sink. Can you see anything out the window?"

She closed her eyes again. "Not really—no, wait, there's a gravel drive between my building and a long, narrow brick building. There's a *No Parking* sign on the building."

"Is that all?" interrupted Charles, who has the patience of a puppy.

"I think so."

I said, "Joy, let's try one more thing. Is there a door leading outside from the kitchen?"

"Chris, I can't remember." She lowered her head and repeated, "I can't remember."

"That's okay, Sister Joy," Burl said. "You're doing good, isn't she, Chris?"

"Yes, Joy, you are."

Adrienne appeared bored with our conversation and stared at the television. I glanced up to see what was so fascinating and saw a newscaster with a photo of the jewelry store on the monitor behind her. She was talking about the burglary that I'd seen reported on the earlier newscast.

Burl looked at the screen. "Why is it that such a glorious Christian holiday brings out the worst in people?"

"Preacher," Adrienne said, "places get broken in all the time. I don't think it has anything to do with Christmas."

"I suppose you're right, Sister Adrienne. It's just that—"

Joy interrupted, "Turn up the sound."

Joy's tone startled Adrienne. She dropped the remote, uttered a profanity, apologized to Burl, and grabbed the device off the floor.

All of us were now staring at the television. The story concluded with the newscaster telling her viewers to call the police if they knew anything about the burglary. An auto dealership ad promoting it's *gigantic Christmas sale* blared from the screen. Adrienne muted the sound, and Joy continued to stare at the silent screen, and Charles asked who buys someone a car for Christmas?

I waved for him to stop talking and turned to Joy. "What are you thinking, Joy?"

She turned away from the television, glanced at Preacher Burl, and then at me. "Chris," she said, no more than a whisper. "The bar was dark. I had to get a case of beer out of the store-room. Budweiser. The sound system, actually it wasn't more than a cheap, grease-covered CD player, was blasting a Bob Segar song." She hesitated and looked at the floor. "Two men at the end of the bar were huddled together, and..."

"And what?" Charles asked.

She looked at him, looked back at the floor, and gazed at the television. "I don't know."

"Joy," I said, "why did that jewelry store burglary remind you of being in a bar?"

"I'm not certain. It must've had to do with the men."

"That's good, Joy," I said. "Two men were huddled together. Did you hear something they were saying?"

She glanced back at the television like it would miraculously give her the answer. "Seger's 'Old Time Rock-and-Roll' was playing. Was loud. Then it stopped." She jerked her head in my direction. "I heard one of the guys say the name of that store that was on TV."

"Grogan's Fine Jewelry," Charles said.

Joy continued to look at me, and said, "Yes."

I nodded. "Joy, I know this is hard. Why don't you close your eyes and try to remember back? You were in a bar, a dark bar. You went to get a case of beer, so do you think that's where you worked?"

She didn't answer but nodded.

"Okay, good. The two men were talking but you couldn't hear them because of the loud music."

She nodded again.

"The music stopped, and you heard one of the men say Grogan's Fine Jewelry."

"Said Grogan's, don't think he said the rest of the name."

"Okay, good. Did you get a good look at the men?"

She closed her eyes. Charles started to speak. I put my forefinger to my lips. He remained silent.

"Chris, I'm sorry. No. They faced the other direction. It was dark, so dark."

"You don't remember anything else they said?"

She shook her head.

"Joy," Charles said, "did the men see you listening?"

Good question, I thought.

Burl leaned forward and nearly fell out of the chair. He caught his balance, and said, "Do you think they thought Sister Joy heard them planning to rob the jewelry store?"

Charles tilted his head to the side. "Yes."

"And took her so she couldn't tell anyone?" Burl said.

"There's a good chance that's what happened," I added.

Adrienne finally stopped looking at the television and twisted around on the sofa toward us. "Joy," she said, "do you remember the name of the bar?"

An even better question.

"No," Joy said. She returned to looking at the floor. Her left hand balled in a fist, her right hand trembled.

"Joy," I said. "You've done great. I know this is rough. Why don't we stop pestering you and let you rest?"

Charles glared at me.

Burl stood and said, "Sister Joy, let me get you more coffee."

"Thank you, Preacher," she whispered.

"Brother Chris, Brother Charles, would you like more?"

"No thanks, Preacher Burl, we need to be going."

Charles continued to glare at me. He wasn't ready to leave.

"Brother Burl," Adrienne said, "do you think we, umm, Joy is safe here? What if they come after her again?"

"Sister Adrienne, the man from Pewter Hardware is coming this afternoon to put on the new locks."

"What about the locks to our rooms—to Joy's door?"

Burl smiled. "All the doors will get new locks."

"Thank you, Preacher Burl," Joy said, and made a valiant effort to smile.

"Joy," I said, "Is it okay if I tell the Chief what you shared?"

"If it'll help."

"It will, thanks. Please call if you remember anything else."

Charles and I stood to leave, and Joy jumped up and gave each of us a hug. Adrienne surprised me when she moved behind Joy and when Joy stepped back, she stepped forward and hugged Charles and me, and whispered, "Thank you for caring."

"Why'd you want to hightail it out of there?" Charles groused as soon as we were in the car. "Joy was figuring out what happened."

"She was struggling. She couldn't remember anything else. I was afraid it'd hurt more than help if we pushed her, besides, she said she'd call if she remembered more."

He sighed. "She's close to remembering what happened. The quicker she does, the safer she'll be. You don't really think new locks will keep them safe, do you? The burglars broke in a jewelry store. That store's locks had to be better than whatever Larry installs, and the store had a security system."

Charles had a good point. Regardless, Joy will remember when she remembers. We can't push her. I was going to share that morsel of wisdom with him when the phone rang.

"Okay," Cindy LaMond said, "what was so all-fired important for you to call?"

"Hello, Chief, how was the meeting with the mayor?"

Charles was flailing his arm around to get me to put the phone on speaker. I did, and he gave a thumb's up.

"The bad news is despite the best efforts of one of my officers to get me fired, I'm still chief."

I pulled in the drive of a house that appeared vacant, so I could focus on the call instead of driving.

Charles leaned closer to the phone, and said, "What's the good news?"

"Chris, you got a Charles stuck in your throat?"

"Got a Charles stuck in my car," I said.

"Poor boy," Cindy said.

I assumed she meant me instead of Charles.

Not to be deterred, Charles said, "The good news?"

"I'm still getting a paycheck and get to drive around in a nifty vehicle with a siren and I don't have to pay for it."

"Congratulations," Charles said.

"Enough about my wonderful life. Why'd you call?"

I told her what Barb had said about the Canadians checking out of their condo two weeks early.

"Holy moly Chris, you know how many people check out early from rentals, hotels, condos, and tree houses?"

"How many?" Charles butted in.

"First, Charles, I asked Chris, not you. Second, I don't have a flippin' clue. It's got to be several. Things happen that we didn't count on. Plans change."

"True," I said. "There's more. Barb also said the guys were asking if Joy's memory was returning."

"I want to know that myself. So what?"

"So, they're two men from outside the area with no reason to care about Joy or her memory. I know it's a weak link, but don't you find it interesting that they're interested in her memory, and then leave Folly when her memory starts returning?"

"Weak link," Cindy said, "It's a feeble, puny, scrawny link, and that's giving it too much credit."

"I know. Regardless, Barb said she had an uneasy feeling when the guys were talking about Joy."

I heard Cindy sigh. "Suppose it's better than no link. Barb didn't happen to know what the guys drove, their license plate number, or their home addresses, did she?"

"No. She said they rented through Avocet. I suspect a police chief who still has a job and a vehicle with a siren could wrangle that information out of the rental agency."

"Okay, I'll do it for Barb. We chicks need to stick together. Anything else you want to share while you have my less than undivided attention?"

"Yes," Charles said, "we just—"

"Charles, I was talking to Chris."

"In fact, yes," I said. I told her about our visit to Hope House and Joy's vague memories of an apartment, most likely hers, and seeing two men in the bar and their mention of the jewelry store that was burglarized. She stopped me and said she needed to get something to write on. I heard her rustling papers, and she asked me to repeat everything.

I did, and Charles added, "Larry's going to replace the locks at Hope House this afternoon."

"That I knew," she said. "That's the advantage of sleeping with a hardware store owner."

"Ewe," Charles said.

"Chris, and I mean Chris, did Joy happen to remember the name of the bar or the location of the apartment?"

"Afraid not."

"Anything else, *Chris*."

"No, sorry."

Charles said, "That's it, Chief."

Charles pointed at the next cross street. "Next stop, Martha Wright's house."

I turned right and back toward town, so I could get on East Arctic Avenue, the one-way street headed toward Martha's. Her drive was empty.

"Crap," Charles said. "How can the danged pet sitter sit if she's never here?"

Add that to the lengthy list of questions to which I had no answer. I pulled in the drive and didn't know if Charles thought the pet sitter walked to the house or someone dropped her off. He bounded up the steps and rang the bell and received the same response that he'd received the last time he tried. Barks in several octaves reverberated through the house, and the door remained closed. We headed to the back yard where we found more of the bowls had food in them then during our last visit. Someone had been here.

Charles shook his head, and said, "Want to wait for the sitter to come back?"

"That could be hours."

"Or minutes," he said, with more optimism than I could muster.

"I don't think it'll do any good to wait. Besides, we don't know that Pluto is still missing."

Charles pulled his phone out his pocket and tapped in a number. "Yo, Dude. This is Charles. Is—" His head bobbed from side to side. "Oh." The head bobbed some more. "I'll keep looking."

He ended the call. "Pluto still 'be bye-bye.'"

"Sorry."

"Me too. Why don't you go on home? I want to stay and wait for the sitter. I'll walk home."

"You sure?"

He said he was, and I left him on Martha's front steps.

I took an extra-long route home in the unlikely event I'd see Pluto hitching a ride, and to think through what Joy had said about an apartment and overhearing two men talking about the jewelry store that happened to be burglarized overnight. I couldn't shake the fear that she was in danger and that I couldn't do anything to lessen that chance.

2 2

I awoke early the next morning and realized that I hadn't had anything substantial for supper. I checked the weather on my phone and saw that it was already in the low-fifties; a glance out the window revealed that it was sunny. A walk to the Dog would be good for me even if French toast wouldn't.

I stepped through the entry and was greeted by Amber.

"Merry Christmas Eve, Eve," she said and pointed to my favorite table, which was empty and waiting for me.

I thanked her for holding the table for me.

"You're not that important," she said with a smile. "Nobody else wanted it."

With my ego sufficiently deflated, I slid in the booth and she said coffee and water would arrive shortly. I thanked her and looked around the near-empty restaurant. Marc Salmon was at his usual table near the center of the room. He nodded my direction and said he was waiting for Houston. I smiled and nodded, acknowledging his comment.

Amber returned with my water, a cup of coffee, and a question. "Has Pluto returned?"

I told her I didn't know, but as of yesterday afternoon, he hadn't.

"Nope," Marc said from the center of the room. "I saw Dude on my way here. He was looking for his little buddy."

"That's too bad," Amber said. "Hope the little fellow's okay."

"And, hope Pluto is too," Marc teased.

Amber and I smiled but didn't comment on the councilmember's joke.

Bernard stuck his head in the door and headed my way.

"Would it be possible for me to join you?"

"Sure," I said, like I had a choice with him standing in front of the table eying the seat across from me.

"Thanks, Broth—umm, I mean, Chris. Sorry, sir, Preacher Burl's got me talking like that." He sat and unbuttoning his faded army jacket.

"Chris, do you know what the word mistletoe means?"

That was a question I'd never been asked. "No, what?"

"Get this," he said and smiled. "It's derived from two old-time words that mean poop on a stick. Can you believe that?"

"You made that up."

"No, sir. Saw it on TV this morning. It seems that mistletoe seeds are eaten by birds, and then pooped on tree branches, and the seeds grow into mistletoe. Ain't that a hoot?"

Now there was a Christmas story I hadn't heard before, and doubt Preacher Burl had ever shared from the pulpit.

"Bernard, that's interesting. Do me a favor and don't tell Charles."

"Poop on a stick is safe with me," he said. "Knew you'd be interested."

He didn't know me as well as he thought he did. "What brings you out so early?"

"Thought I'd walk around a while and look for Pluto. Besides, the kitchen was getting a little too uncomfortable for my liking. Joy, Rebekah, and Adrienne were gathered around drinking coffee and complaining about men. I felt like I was the enemy, being of the male species."

I was tempted to laugh, but saw that Bernard was serious. "What were they saying?"

"Not exactly sure. I walked in on the conversation. Joy was saying something about men and escaping off the boat. Adrienne were saying that they knew what Joy was talking about and that she was at the house after being deserted by an abusive husband who left her for his massage therapist. I didn't hear Rebekah's problem with guys, but from the look on her face, it must've been bad."

Burl had shared the information about Adrienne, but I didn't know anything about Rebekah other than she worked at Black Magic. I was curious about Joy and asked Bernard if she'd said anything more about being on the boat since she'd been unclear about what had happened when she talked to me.

Before he answered, Amber was at the table asking what we wanted to eat. I said French toast. Amber acted shocked.

Bernard said, "That sounds mighty good, ma'am. I'll try some."

Amber smiled and said she thought she'd be able to find him French toast.

She left, and Bernard said, "Nice lady."

I agreed, and he asked what my question was again. I asked if he remembered anything new that Joy had said.

"Not that I heard, other than she was on the boat and was tied up by two men."

"She said two men?"

"Yes, sir. I remember because it was the first time I'd heard her talking about being on the boat. It got my attention because there was only one guy who tried to break in her room. Why?"

"She'd only mentioned one man when she talked to me."

Bernard scratched his head. "Wait, there's something else.

Some of us were talking last night about how we got around on Folly. Rebekah and I don't have wheels and hoof it. Adrienne has an old Chevy pickup truck. Smokes like a pile of damp logs on a fire. Joy said she didn't have a car or a truck and had to walk from her apartment to work."

That was new, and I asked him if she knew where her apartment was.

"No, sir. All she said was that she had to walk."

"She say anything else?"

"Nothing she hadn't said before."

"How well do you think she's adjusting to Hope House?"

"Better than I'd be doing if I didn't have a memory and didn't know why someone took me on a boat to do whatever they planned to do. I can't see how it could've been anything good. It's fortunate that she managed to slip out of the ropes that were on her ankles and wrists. She said the next thing she remembered was how the storm was flinging water over the bow and how the guys in front were fighting to keep it from overturning. Then she was in the water, clinging to a surfboard."

Some of that was news to me. "Did she tell you that or are you guessing about what happened?"

"She said it last night, sir. I couldn't have thought that up on my own."

Our breakfast arrived, and Bernard stuffed three bites in his mouth like he hadn't eaten in days.

He took another bite and pointed his fork at me. "Got a question for you, Chris. We live in a big place, the biggest house on the street, with lots of bedrooms. How do you think the man trying to break in Joy's room knew what room was hers? I'm thinking that someone living there must've told him."

"Any idea who?"

"It wasn't me, and I'd wager it wasn't Preacher Burl." He chuckled. "I don't have anything to wager, but you get my drift."

"I understand. What about the others?"

"That only leaves Rebekah and Adrienne. I know Adrienne better than I know Rebekah. She doesn't strike me as someone who would do something bad like that. She's a loner so I don't know who she could tell. Rebekah, come to think of it, has been seeing someone, or that's what she says. None of us have seen him."

"What do you know about him?"

"Near nothing. It's someone she met at Black Magic."

"Customer or employee?"

"Sir, that's more intel than I have access to."

"How do Joy and Rebekah get along?"

"I haven't seen them conversing much. The most I'd ever seen them talking was on Woody's Wednesday."

"Woody's Wednesday?"

"Burl picks up two large pizzas from Woody's each Wednesday. I think he pays for them some weeks and other times they're donated. Other restaurants occasionally kick us a few meals, but Wednesdays are my favorite."

"That's nice of the restaurants."

"Preacher has made a lot of friends since opening First Light. It makes us feel like we're part of the community."

"Back to Joy and Rebekah. Do you remember them saying anything about what happened to Joy?"

"Nah. It was more girly stuff, you know, like makeup, hair, and how stupid men are."

"Nothing else about the men who took Joy?"

"No, more than anything, I think we're all nervous about somebody sneaking around the house and talk to each other to keep our minds off it. We'll rest easier after the hardware store man gets the locks changed. Hope he doesn't charge too much. Money's in short supply. If it wasn't for the donated food, I don't know what Preacher would do."

"I know Larry LaMond, the man who owns the hardware store. He'll give Preacher Burl a good deal."

Bernard nodded. "Good. Money don't grow on trees, you know."

"Bernard, you said you thought it may've been someone living there who told the intruder which room was Joy's."

"Yes."

"What about someone who used to live there?"

"Chris, there've been a bunch of people since I moved in. I don't remember some of them. How could we figure out which one?"

"Most of them wouldn't know which room was Joy's. What about people who recently moved?"

"If they moved before Joy moved in, how would they know which room was hers?"

"Process of elimination."

"Chris, you're going to have to dumb that down for me."

"They'd know which room you, Adrienne, and Rebekah were in, and where Preacher Burl lives. They'd know that Joy was in one of the other rooms."

"Got it. Let's see, there's Al. No, he moved a few weeks before Adrienne moved in. Besides, he moved to California. Scratch him." He took another bite of breakfast and rubbed his chin. "Okay, in the last couple of weeks before Joy arrived, two guys left. There's Alex and Taylor."

"Tell me about them."

"Let's see, Taylor left after Preacher Burl found him a job in North Charleston. Lucky man. And, there's Alex Rockford. Never did trust him and was glad to see him go."

"Where'd he go?"

"Don't know. He was there for supper one evening and gone by the time breakfast was served. I don't like spreading rumors, but I heard he'd been in jail for burglary. Don't know if it's true."

"When did he leave?"

"Give me a minute. Oh yeah, it was the day the faucet in one of the bathrooms broke and water spewed all over the room. Had to get a plumber. I'll tell you, it was a mess."

"Bernard, when?"

"Oh, two days before Joy showed up."

"Would Taylor and Alex have known which rooms would've been vacant when Joy moved in?"

"I would think they'd know that their rooms would be empty."

"Anyone else?"

"Not that I recall."

Bernard took the last bite of breakfast, wiped his mouth with a napkin, and said, "Chris, I sure appreciate you letting me break bread with you." He smiled. "Preacher Burl says break bread a lot. It's rubbing off on me."

I returned his smile and said, "Worse things could rub off on you."

"One more thing. Could I impose on you to lend me a few dollars to cover my breakfast. My inheritance hasn't come through yet, and you wouldn't believe how difficult it is to pull money out of a stock portfolio."

I smiled and told him I'd take care of the breakfast. "Under one condition," I added, "you call me if you hear Joy say anything new about her ordeal."

He saluted, said, "Deal, sir," and left the restaurant with a full stomach and a smile.

I had nowhere else to be, and the Dog had several vacant tables, so I asked Amber for a more coffee. She returned with the coffee and asked if I'd run Bernard off with my boring conversation. I told her no, and that I reserved boring conversations for Charles since he doesn't listen to anything I say.

She patted me on the arm and said, "Don't be too hard on yourself, I'm certain that in the decade you've known him, he must've heard something you said."

I thanked her for the vote of confidence, and she smiled and headed to a table in the center of the room to spread more holiday cheer.

I took a sip of the refreshed mug of coffee and tried to recall everything Bernard said that Joy shared, especially anything new.

Joy seemed more certain that there were two men on the boat instead of only one as she previously mentioned. Also, one of the things that I couldn't previously figure out was how she'd untied herself, grabbed a surfboard, and get off the eighteen-foot-long boat without the men knowing. I hadn't thought about how horrific the storm had been the day before we found her. If the men were struggling to keep the boat from capsizing, it was possible that she could've slipped overboard before they noticed her missing. They probably figured she drowned with the storm so intense, which was probably their intent from the beginning.

Joy also told Bernard and the others that she didn't own a vehicle and that she walked from her apartment to the bar where she worked. It could've been a bar on Folly since they are all within easy walking distance of most buildings with apartments, yet, her description of the bar didn't fit any that I was aware of.

Then, what about Bernard's theory that one of the current residents told the man who was trying to get in Joy's door which one was hers? Even if he was right, how could anyone prove it. Even if you add residents who recently moved, you have the same problem.

I left the Dog with a full stomach, a lighter wallet, and more unanswered questions than I had entered with. At least, I knew the origin of the word mistletoe.

It was turning out to be one of the warmest late-December days I could remember, so I headed to the far end of the Folly Pier to walk off a few of the hundreds, okay, thousands, of calories I'd devoured with my French toast. The Pier, like much of downtown Folly two days before Christmas, was nearly deserted. A handful of diners were enjoying an early lunch in Pier 101, but there couldn't have been more than ten people strolling along the thousand-plus-foot-long fishing pier. From the end of the structure, I had a view of much of the island's Atlantic shoreline and in the distance a glimpse of the County Park where I first met Joy. With a little imagination, I pictured the area of the ocean where she bailed from the boat. It was a miracle that the surfboard carried her to safety.

The phone rang as I was climbing the steps to the second level of the Pier.

"Mr. Landrum, this is Joyce, I mean Joy."

I asked how she was doing.

"Okay. I just saw Bernard, and he said he had breakfast with you. Are you still at the Lost Dog Cafe?"

I told her no, where I was, and asked why.

"I remembered a few more things overnight, and you told me to let you know so you could tell the police. I could call them but feel more comfortable talking to you."

"Want me to come by the house?"

"I'd like to get out of here. If you're going to be there for a while, I could walk over and meet you."

Thirty minutes later, I saw her heading my way. I waved from the upper deck and she smiled and returned my wave. Her hair was pulled in a neat ponytail and she had on jeans, a white blouse, and a gray jacket.

She said, "Thanks for waiting."

I motioned for her to join me on the bench. I didn't tell her I had nowhere else to be.

She looked toward shore, and said, "This is my second time out here. It's relaxing."

I agreed and waited for her to get to the reason for the visit. If the walk to the end of the pier relaxed her, I'd hate to see her when she wasn't. Her hand moved from her lap to pushing an errant strand of hair behind her ear, back to her lap, and then zipped and unzipped her jacket.

"Joy, are you okay?"

She continued to look at the hotel, and said, "How would I know if I'm okay? I don't know who I am, where I should be, who I should be with, and what'll happen next."

I understood that, yet she appeared more anxious than the last two times I'd been with her. "I don't know how I'd handle it either."

She slowly turned my direction. "Have you heard of a bar called something like Blackbeard's?"

"I don't think so. Why?"

"It came to me during the night. It may be where I worked."

"Have you asked anyone else?"

"No. I'm not sure who I can trust. I know I'm being paranoid, but the guy trying to get in my door freaked me out. I think I can trust you."

I told her she could. I also knew that anyone could say that and saying it didn't make it true.

"Joy, is that all you remembered?"

"I don't think I worked there long."

"Why do you say that?"

"It didn't seem that familiar, like I couldn't find the clean bar towels. I know it sounds silly, and I could've remembered it wrong. It's vague."

I took out my phone and searched for Blackbeard's Bar in the Charleston area. There were numerous references to the notorious pirate called Blackbeard, most of them talked about his terrorizing merchant ships along the coast in the early 1700s. There were nearly as many pirate tales in the Lowcountry as there were ghost stories, and those were in the too-many-to-count range. There was only one bar with Blackbeard in the name.

"Joy, does Blackbeard's Hangout Bar sound familiar?"

"Vaguely. Is that a bar over here?"

I showed her a photo of the front of the bar from its website. "Look familiar?"

"I'd love to say yes. Honestly, I can't tell. Where is it?"

"About seven miles up Folly Road. Would you like to go there?"

She jerked her head in my direction. "When?"

"We could go now."

"Like, right now?"

"Now or later today. It's up to you."

"I don't think … okay. Would you mind?"

"Gosh, Joy, it'll take valuable time away from me sitting here wasting the day away."

She smiled. "I might learn who I am." She closed her eyes and was silent for the longest time. Finally, she said, "Let's go before I chicken out."

We were leaving my drive ten minutes later. I didn't tell Joy, but I started to question what we might face. What if she worked at the bar and someone there was the person who'd abducted her? We pulled off the island, and I wondered if I should've asked Charles to go. What if we're headed into danger?

Joy didn't help when she said, "I'm scared. I want to know who I am, yet, what if I don't like me?" She turned in the seat and faced me. "What if the men who took me are there? I might not know who they are."

I'd driven this stretch of Folly Road numerous times, in fact, one of my favorite restaurants, the Charleston Crab House, was less than a half-mile from Blackbeard's Hangout Bar, yet I couldn't recall ever seeing our destination. When the street numbers indicated we were there, I understood my confusion. There was a deteriorating strip center on the left and at the far end of it was a narrow storefront with a faded-black awning and the words Blackbeard's Hangout Bar in Old English script. If I hadn't been looking for it, I wouldn't have noticed the sign. Several cars were parked at the other end of the shopping center in front of a dollar store and a nail salon. No vehicles were in front of the bar and the plate-glass windows were painted black, so I couldn't tell if anyone was behind them.

"Joy, does anything look familiar?" I said and parked in front of the black awning.

She stared at the door, gripped the center console, and whispered, "That's where I work, where I worked."

Joy's paranoia was rubbing off on me and I thought the smart thing for me to do was to call Cindy LaMond and see if she could "visit" the venue with us. We were out of her jurisdiction, but I would've felt safer visiting with someone carrying a weapon.

"Let's get this over," Joy said before I could make the call.

"Are you sure?"

She nodded and opened the door.

For better or worse, here we go.

24

Compared to Blackbeard's Hangout Bar, the darkest bar I'd ever been in looked as bright as a polar bear in a snowstorm. We stepped into the darkness to the blaring sounds of "Dark Necessities" by the Red Hot Chili Peppers. There was a dim, red light over the exit door at the rear of the building, and I thought I saw movement from the right side of the room.

The song ended and someone with a deep, gruff voice said, "Well, look what the cat dragged in."

Whoever it was must have been wearing night-vision goggles or was a bat with a bass voice. I couldn't see anyone. Joy walked in the direction of the sound. I followed and hoped I wouldn't trip over a chair, table, or vampire.

"Kevin's going to have a cow when he sees you," said the voice. "You sure you want to be here?"

A refrigerator door opened, and its light illuminated the face of the man who pulled it open, and the person, I assumed, who'd been talking. I wasn't old enough by a couple of hundred years to have seen Blackbeard, but imagined the man standing in front of us shared a striking resemblance. He was at least six-foot-five, weighed two-seventy, with black, stringy hair that reached his shoulders and a beard that reached low on his chest.

My eyes were beginning to adjust to the near darkness, and I glanced around. The room was empty except for Joy, Mr. Blackbeard, and me.

"Do I know you?" Joy said to the unsmiling bartender.

"Crap, kiddo, did you crack your skull and forget the only friend you had here?"

He wasn't far off.

She smiled. "Something like that. What's your name?"

"You're serious, ain't you?"

I stepped closer to the man dressed in black. He could've been one of those creepy creatures in a Halloween haunted house.

"Hi, I'm Chris. My friend Joy's suffering from amnesia. Did she work here?"

"Joy," the man said. "You mean Joyce?"

"Yes, and you are?"

"I'm Darryl. Joyce and I worked two shifts together, and then she disappeared. Thought Kevin was going to blow a gasket when she didn't show her next shift." He turned to Joy. "What happened, sweetie?"

"I don't know. Who's Kevin?"

Darryl waved his hand around the room. "Kevin Beard, owner of this dump."

With no music playing, I heard traffic on Folly Road, and a door slamming in back of the building.

Following closely behind the slamming door, came a higher-pitched voice that said, "Joyce Tolliver, if you think you're going to slink in here and get a check for the two days you worked, you're out of your freakin' gourd."

I stepped between the new voice and Joy. "Hi, I'm Chris Landrum, a friend of Joyce. Are you Kevin Beard?"

The room was still dark, but I thought I saw him nod.

"Is there somewhere the three of us can talk?" I asked and looked around for an office, hopefully with lights.

He headed to the far side of the room, and I followed. Darryl whispered to Joy, "Good luck. He's pissed."

Kevin ushered us into a small office that doubled as a storeroom. I thought Darryl's beard was long until I saw Kevin's. If it didn't reach his belt, it didn't lack much. He wore black slacks, black tennis shoes, and a white T-shirt. Cases of beer were stacked six high on one side, and three cases of liquor were on the floor beside two chairs with rips in their vinyl seats. They'd probably been taken out of service from the bar. Kevin pointed to the chairs, and we sat. He had a chair behind the makeshift desk but sat on the edge of the desk.

"What happened, Joyce? I thought you were going to be reliable. You gave me a song and dance about how you never missed work and had bartending experience. You said you lived in walking distance, so you could be here whenever I needed you."

"Mr. Beard, Joy, umm, Joyce, had a traumatic event that caused amnesia. She—"

"Mister, was I talking to you? I asked Joyce a question. What are you anyway, her doctor?"

"Mister Beard, Chris is a friend who saved my life. He's right about my amnesia so we'd appreciate it if you could tell us what you know about me."

"Joyce, I told you when I hired you to call me Kevin. You serious about losing your memory?"

"Yes. How long did I work here?"

"Two nights. A Friday and Saturday. You were scheduled to be off Sunday and come in Monday. The last I saw you was when you left that Saturday."

"They've shown my photo on television. Didn't you see me there?"

"Joyce, guess you don't remember me telling you this when you hired on. This is probably the only bar in Charleston without televisions. My customers are here to grab a drink and don't want to be caught up in sports and politics, stuff that dominates the danged TV. I don't even have a television in my house, although it wouldn't matter, I'm never there. This place is my life."

"Kevin," I said, and hoped he would allow me in the conversation. "Joyce really has amnesia. What can you tell us about her?"

He glared at me and I was afraid he wasn't going to say anything, at least nothing pleasant. He slid off the desk, moved behind it, opened a drawer, and pulled out a manila folder that had scribbling on the front and a tab that was peeling off the top. I couldn't read what was on the paper he pulled out of the folder, but it looked like a job application.

He looked at the document and up at Joyce. "Your application says that you're Joyce E. Tolliver, age forty-seven. Born in Kansas City, Kansas, and ain't got any living relatives." He looked down at the paper and flipped it over to the other side. "Any of this coming back to you?"

She shook her head.

"You have a management degree from Kansas State University. It's not on the application, but you told me that you'd been married to an eye doctor, an optometrist. Something about him leaving you for one of his patients." Darryl smiled, something I didn't think was in his repertoire. "I remember why you told me someone with a job in management wanted to tend bar. Said you were bored working in an office and took part-time bartending jobs." He glanced at me and turned to Joy. "You remember any of this?"

"Afraid not, Kevin. Did I tell you what brought me to Charleston?"

"Nothing other than you said you moved around a lot. Spent time in Texas, Oklahoma, and I think Georgia. That's all you said."

"Were you here the second night she worked?"

"I'm here every Saturday night. I done told you that's the last time I saw her."

"Do you remember if there was a crowd?"

"Good, but not one of my best. Why?"

I didn't want to tell him too much about what'd happened. For all I knew, he could've been one of the abductors. "Just curious. Something may have happened to Joyce after she left here."

"Like what?"

"We're not certain."

"Joyce, you remember telling me how you walked home after work and I said I'd get you a ride if you wanted? It's not good having an attractive lady like you walking around at two in the morning."

"I don't remember that."

"Sorry," he said. "Of course, you don't."

"Kevin, do you remember Joyce talking to a couple of men more than others that night?"

"Chris, that's your name, right?"

I nodded.

"You saw how dark it was out there. If my hands weren't connected, I'd have trouble knowing where they were most of the time."

I assumed that meant no. "Didn't you wonder what happened to Joyce when she didn't return?"

"Sure. She didn't have a phone, so I couldn't call. Besides, she's not the first person I hired who skipped out after a few days. This isn't the most fun work, and I struggle to get good help. Getting any help. I figured you'd moved on to another job or skipped town."

"Kevin, this may sound like a strange question, where does it say I live?"

He was looking down at the application and slowly raised his head and looked at her. "You really don't remember anything?"

"No."

"Wow," he said and shook his head. He gave her the name of the apartment complex off the application. He told her it was three blocks behind the bar and that it'd been there forever. I asked if an apartment number was listed. He glanced at the application and wrinkled his nose. "Nope. Wonder why I didn't catch that?"

"What about the other paperwork you need on a new employee," I said.

He glanced over at Joy and returned his gaze to me. "I was desperate to fill the bartender's job. The last one walked out on me with the weekend around the corner. Joyce said she had bartending experience. That was enough for me. I told her that we would get all that done the next week when things slowed down." He looked at her again. "You didn't come back to do it."

He was getting either nervous about not filling out the required paperwork, or angry that we were pestering him. We thanked him for the information and stood to leave.

"Joyce, if you get your memory back and want to come back to work, I could find a place for you. Sorry about whatever happened."

Kevin stood in the office's doorway as we weaved our way through the dark room.

I nearly bumped into Darryl who was standing by the front door. He gave Joy a hug and said he was sorry she wasn't still working there. She thanked him, and he glanced back at his boss who was still standing in his office doorway. Joy opened the front door and Darryl slipped me a folded piece of paper, patted me on the back, and said, "Take good care of Joyce. She's a nice lady."

We left on much better terms than when we'd arrived, as Coldplay filled the air with "A Sky Full of Stars."

I didn't know if I should look at the paper in front of Joy, so I slipped it in my pocket and headed to the car.

Joy stopped me. "Can we walk to where I lived, umm, live?"

"Do you remember the way?"

"Not really. Didn't Darryl say it was three blocks that way?" She pointed behind the bar.

We walked three blocks in the direction Darryl had indicated and found two apartment buildings. They were decades from being new and backed up to each other with a gravel alley separating the structures. There were no signs listing the name of the complex or anything indicating there was an office. The apartment numbers were the same style, so I assumed they were part of the same development. *Now what*, I wondered. "Anything look familiar?"

Joy looked at the building on our side of the alley and then at the one on the other side. "Not really."

I jotted the street name and address on a card from my pocket and said that I'd call Chief LaMond and see if she could find out anything about the apartments and the company that managed them, and with luck, which apartment had been rented by Joyce Tolliver. She agreed and said she'd like to get back to people she knew.

Joy was exhausted by the time I pulled in her parking area. She had her hand on the car's door handle. Instead of getting out she said, "The rain was blowing sideways. Ocean water lapped over the side of the boat and my head kept bouncing off the wooden arm rest each time we hit a wave. I was soaked, and I twisted my arms until the rope I was tied with loosened enough for me to pull my hand free." She closed her eyes, gave an abbreviated nod, and continued, "The man in the seat in front of me cussed the weather and kept saying the boat was going to sink. I managed to untie my feet and grabbed the surfboard and slipped over the side. I didn't know where we were but knew the farther away from the boat I could get, the safer I'd be." She stared at the house and then said. "Chris, the next thing I remember was you and Barb looking down at me on the beach."

25

I returned home, poured a glass of Cabernet, and plopped down in the living room. I would have bet money on Charles's reaction to my trip to Joy's former place of employment and would've won.

"You did what?" he blurted before I got to the part about meeting the Blackbeard lookalike.

"Charles, why don't you let me finish and you'll know what I did."

"You wouldn't have to tell me if you'd let me go," he said, in a voice that would make a sniveling, ten-year-old, with hurt feelings, throwing a tantrum sound like Gandhi.

I continued sharing what we learned at Blackbeard's Hangout Bar, and from the unsuccessful visit to the apartment complex Joy listed on her employment application.

"Joyce Tolliver, Joyce Tolliver. I like Joy Doe better. How did she take it?"

"As well as you can imagine. I was going to call Cindy and tell her but wanted to call you first." I hoped to get a glimmer of appreciation from him.

"You wouldn't have had to call me at all if you'd taken me with you."

"Are you finished reminding me?"

"Not sure. What happens now?"

"I end this cheerful discussion and call Cindy."

"You could've already called her. You wouldn't have had to call me if you'd taken me."

I did what some of my friends had done to me on more than one occasion. I hung up on him.

The next call also went off the tracks before I got it headed the direction I'd desired.

"Glad you called," Cindy said instead of hello, reinforcing my dislike of caller ID. "Let me tell you about our two friends from north of the border."

"The Canadians?"

Cindy made an audible sigh. "No, Santa and Mrs. Claus."

I smiled and asked what she'd learned.

"I got a call this afternoon from Staff Sergeant Major Urton from the Royal Canadian Mounted Police. I'm a lowly ole cop in this humble burg, so I haven't the foggiest how high or low a staff sergeant major is in the RCMP pecking order, but he seemed nice, although a bit stuffy when I asked if her rode a horse to work and wore a red coat and one of those funny wide-brimmed hats."

"Cindy, what'd he say?"

"Patience, Charles in waiting. He was reporting on what he'd learned about Troy Ellis and Nate Cook's early departure from our slice of heaven. It seems that Nate's mother was in an auto accident near Ottawa. A lumber truck driver decided that one of those pesky stop signs wasn't applicable to him and poor Mrs. Cook made the mistake of being in the intersection at the time. She's in critical condition, and Nate's father called and asked him to come home."

"You don't think he had anything to do with Joy's abduction?"

"Unlikely. There goes your number one and number two suspect. Any other brilliant ideas?"

It wasn't brilliant, but I reminded her that I was the one who initiated the call, and shared what Joy and I'd learned from our trip to Joy's former place of employment. Cindy scolded me for not letting her know where we were going. She added that I was too old, or in her words, "Way too fossilized to be gallivanting around where angels fear to tread." I reminded her that Joy and I had simply visited a bar where she may've been employed and not barging in on a gang of thieves, abductors, and other mischief-makers.

"How'd you know that before you got there?"

She was right although I wasn't going to give her the satisfaction of agreeing. I asked if she could use her official resources to learn about the apartment complex where Joy allegedly lived and find the landlord to get a key to her apartment.

"Chris, you know I'm at your beck and call, whatever that means, and live and breathe to seek answers to your countless questions."

She then did what I did moments earlier to Charles. The phone went dead.

It was two more sips of wine before I remembered the note that Darryl had handed me.

It read: *Call me. I know the guys you asked Kevin about.* He added a phone number.

I punched in the numbers and four rings later was afraid no one was going to answer. Finally, I heard a rock song in the background that I didn't recognize, and a voice that I did. "Yeah."

"Darryl, this is Chris, the guy with Joyce earlier today."

"Listen, I can't talk now. Can I call you at this number in about an hour?"

I said he could.

The next hour lasted about a week, or so it seemed, until the phone rang, and Darryl said, "This Chris?"

I said it was.

"Listen, I'm on a break and can't talk long. I overheard you talking to Kevin. It's amazing what you can hear in here when the music's not vibrating the walls. You asked about two guys who Joyce was talking to during her last shift. Kevin's protective of his customers and flat-out lied when he said he didn't know anything about it. He says many customers have been hassled by cops. He wants this to be a, how does he put it? Oh yeah, a hassle-free zone."

That was way more than I wanted to know. "Darryl, the guys?"

"Yeah, them. Listen, I've seen them in here a few times, didn't know them well. I don't know what their deal was, but the last two times they talked all hush-hush like. Looking around like they were planning to overthrow the government and not wanting anyone to hear."

"Did you ever hear what they were talking about?"

"No, but I think Joyce did."

"Why do you say that?"

"The last day she was here, I was getting off shift and grabbing my coat from the back room. Joyce was with me and started to go behind the bar near where the two guys were sitting. She stopped in the doorway for a long time. I couldn't tell what she was doing. I headed out and didn't think anything else of it until I heard you talking to Kevin. I figured it could've been important and had something to do with Joyce losing her memory. Am I right?"

"I think so. Did Joyce say anything to you about it?"

"No. I waved bye when I left and didn't say another word to her until she showed up today."

"Do you know who the guys are?"

"Only their first names. Raymond and Taylor."

"Know anything else about them."

"Raymond's fond of Miller High Life; Taylor's a Bud guy. That's it. Sorry."

"What do they look like?"

"White dudes. Looked like most of our other customers. Jeans, casual clothes. Average height. Raymond's a couple of inches taller than Taylor. Not fat, not thin."

"Age?"

"I'd guess late thirties, could be off several years. I'm not good with ages."

"Have you seen them since that night?"

"I was off a couple of days. They weren't in after that while I was here."

"Anything else?"

"Not that I remember. You really think they had something to do with what happened to Joyce?"

"There's a good chance. I'm going to have the let the police know what you've said, so you might get a visit from someone from Folly Beach or the county Sheriff's Office."

"I'm not a fan of cops. There's a history there." After a long pause, he sighed. "If it can help Joyce, I'll talk to them. She seems like a nice lady."

"She is. I appreciate you telling me about the men."

"No problem," he ended, with one of my least favorite sayings.

26

I've known a few Raymonds. Taylor was a more unusual and memorable name, and if I'm right, was the name of one of Burl's recent residents. A phone call to the preacher should verify it.

"Ah, Brother Chris, it's good to hear from you," he said, although he hadn't heard anything from me yet, and was responding to my name appearing on his phone.

"Good evening, Preacher. I hope I'm not interrupting anything."

"In fact, you are. We're having a Christmas party. Why don't you hop on your sled and have the reindeer bring you over and join us? Sister Joy was getting ready to tell me about your afternoon adventure. I know she'd love for you to be here."

I remembered how down she was when she got out of the car after our visit to Blackbeard's, but I also knew it was a Hope House party and didn't want to butt in. I thanked Burl for the invitation and shared my reluctance to crash the party.

"Nonsense. You wouldn't be crashing, I invited you. Besides, Sister Joy was saying how much she enjoyed spending time with you, and Brother Bernard was recounting how you and Charles had invited him to last year's party at Cal's. Remember how you encouraged him to speak with me about being homeless and the tough time he'd had finding a homeless shelter? It meant the world to him. He'd like to see you."

I wasn't keen on the idea of going out again. I was more reluctant to turn down a generous offer from a minister this close to Christmas. Besides, I wanted to ask him about Taylor. I said I'd head over.

The seasonal lights around the front door and along the roofline were in full holiday splendor. The house looked in much better repair in the dark than during daylight. Bernard greeted me wearing a stop-light red shirt and black jeans. He also greeted me with a smile, a firm handshake, and, "Welcome to the first annual Hope House Christmas party." He leaned close and whispered. "Alcohol's prohibited. Thought I'd warn you."

I thanked him for the welcome and the warning. He pointed to the living room where from the sounds of multiple voices I assumed everyone was gathered. Burl was standing on a two-step ladder by the tree and fiddling with a strand of lights that weren't working and Rebekah was putting a CD in a portable player on the table in another corner. Adrienne was sitting in the chair farthest from the action and looking either tired or bored.

Joy saw me in the doorway and jumped up from the sofa and rushed over and gave me a robust hug. She looked more refreshed than when I let her off earlier today but wore the same clothes.

"Preacher said you were coming. It's nice of you to join us."

Burl saw me and thanked me for coming while he was holding the unlit lights. He had on a red sweatshirt with a reindeer on the front, gray slacks, red house slippers, and a Santa hat. I asked if there was anything I could do to help, and he said he knew what the problem was and would soon have the lights burning brightly. He asked Bernard if he would take me to the kitchen to get something to eat and drink.

Elvis's version of "Santa Claus is Back in Town" began playing from the CD player and Bernard told me the drink menu included soft drinks and a fruit punch that he whispered was yucky. I selected Diet Coke before Bernard showed me the platter of peanut-butter sandwiches cut in half, and another platter of sliced celery, carrots, and for a reason I wouldn't attempt to guess, dried okra. Apparently, Bernard couldn't guess either. He shrugged.

I filled a paper plate with portions of everything except okra and followed Bernard back to the party.

Elvis was singing "White Christmas," Burl had managed to get the lights working and was sitting on the sofa between Joy and Rebekah, and Adrienne was still in her chair expressionless. Bernard motioned me to sit in the remaining chair and lowered himself to a sitting position on the floor. I felt bad taking his seat, but not bad enough to stand and try to balance my food and drink while eating.

"Here Comes Santa Claus," started playing and Burl said, "*Elvis' Christmas Album*. My favorite."

I knew who it was since at one time I had the same album. Adrienne didn't appear to share Burl's appreciation for the King. She rolled her eyes.

Joy said, "I was getting ready to tell Preacher Burl about our trip to the bar when you called."

"That can wait," Burl said. "Wouldn't want to spoil the party. Chris, this is my first Christmas in here. I've been blessed this year."

Bernard said, "And we're blessed you chose to share the house with us, Preacher."

Rebekah added, "Bernard's right. We are blessed, Preacher."

Adrienne remained silent.

Joy didn't say anything. She was staring at the tree and I couldn't imagine what must be going through her mind. For me, Christmas has always been a time of reflection. It's been a time to look back, think about Christmases past, Christmases with family and friends, and while most people take New Year's Eve and Day to think about the future, I found it more meaningful to focus those thoughts at Christmas. Joy can't see back much more than a week. And, without that perspective, she wouldn't be able to see, predict, or even hope for things to come. I looked over and gave her a smile, hopefully received as one of love, trust, and hope.

She returned the smile, and Burl stood and said, "Brother Chris, we were getting ready to sing some Christmas carols. Now that you're here, we can add another voice to our group. Sister Rebekah, would you ask Elvis to take a break until we get finished caroling?"

Burl knew from listening to me in church that I had a terrible singing voice, so he clearly must be under the influence of Coke, the cola kind.

"That's okay, Preacher. I'd rather listen to your outstanding voices."

I had no idea how outstanding the others would be. All I knew was that compared to me, Alvin and the Chipmunks sounded operatic.

"As you wish, Brother Chris. It's not actually a carol, but let's begin with 'A Holly Jolly Christmas,' a ditty made famous by Burl Ives, a man named after me." The preacher chuckled at his joke; a joke that I was probably the only person in the room to catch. Preacher Burl was named after the singer Burl Ives because his father was a fan of the singing actor.

Burl raised his arms like he was going to direct a choir and began singing, "Have a holly, jolly Christmas; it's the best time of the year."

Few would argue with that sentiment. Many could argue that the sounds of this group singing couldn't make this the best time of the evening. That didn't stop the enthusiastic choir director from smiling and bouncing on the balls of his feet as he led the vocally challenged group through the song. Burl was the only person who knew the words past the first three lines, so he increased his volume to cover up the random words the remainder of the group were spewing. The sounds were sad, the intent uplifting.

The song came to a merciful end and Burl beamed like he'd been conducting the Mormon Tabernacle Choir. "Joyous," he said.

Not the word I would have chosen; regardless, the group was having an enjoyable time. Even Adrienne smiled.

"Great start," Burl continued. "Brother Bernard, what's your favorite Christmas carol?"

Bernard turned and looked behind him like it was another Bernard the preacher was talking to. He then glanced at the Christmas tree and said, "Preacher Burl, I must say I've never given that much thought. I'll go with 'Away in a Manger.'"

"Then let's give it a go. Folks, let's make a joyful noise unto the Lord." He returned to his conducting stance and sang, "Away in a manger, no crib for His bed. The little…"

It may have been my imagination, but the singing sounded nearly on key. I mouthed the words and enjoyed the fellowship. After Bernard's favorite finished, the preacher asked Rebekah the same question, and she didn't hesitate when she said, "O Holy Night." We—they—muddled through it, when Burl turned to Adrienne and repeated his question.

"Preacher Burl, if I had to choose one, it'd be 'Pretty Paper.'"

Burl smiled and didn't tell her that the Willie Nelson penned song wasn't a carol. "Good choice," he said, and the group began singing Adrienne's selection.

It was heartwarming to see how not only the preacher, but everyone, embraced Adrienne's song. I also wondered what he would say to the newcomer who had no memory of the past. Would he ask about her favorite carol, or would he acknowledge her lack of memory?

We finished Willie's "carol," and Burl said, "Wonderful job."

I glanced at Joy who was staring at the floor like she was wishing to be somewhere else. I empathized with her.

Burl moved closer to Joy and said, "Sister Joy, instead of asking you about your favorite carol, let me say that when I look at you, I can't help but think about the beautiful carol 'Joy to the World.' Would you mind if I chose it as your song?"

Joy smiled and nodded.

That level of sensitivity was one more reason Preacher Burl was a godsend to Folly Beach and its residents without traditional church homes.

Burl returned to his role of conductor and led the group in Joy's song. With the final "And wonders of His love," Burl put his arm around Joy and said, "Thank you for being with us."

She mumbled, "You're welcome," and Burl turned to me. "Now Brother Chris, I don't have to ask your favorite. Last Christmas you told me it was 'Silent Night.' Folks, shall we sing the marvelous hymn to the man who's been pretending to sing with us?"

They did, and I was touched.

"I don't know about you," Burl said, "my throat is parched. Shall we take a break and refresh our drinks?"

No one protested and everyone except Burl and I moved to the kitchen.

Burl watched everyone leave, and said, "It wasn't lost on me that you called for a reason. Care to share it was while the others are imbibing?"

"Preacher, didn't you have a resident named Taylor?"

Burl nodded. "That wasn't a question I'd anticipated. Yes. You saw him the day I was in the Lost Dog Cafe. Remember, I told you I was looking for someone about a job."

"I remember, although I didn't catch his name."

"He's Taylor Strong. He moved out the night before we were blessed by the appearance of Joy. Why?"

"Preacher, what can you tell me about him?"

"I assume you will answer my question at the appropriate time."

I nodded.

"Brother Taylor was only here a few weeks. He was quiet, not as quiet as Sister Adrienne, but quieter than the rest. He shared that he was originally from North Carolina, never said what town. Getting him to talk was a challenge. I managed to get that he'd had various jobs over the years. He said he'd been an armored car driver, and a clerk in a convenience store. He also shared that a few years ago he went to school to learn how to be a locksmith. In fact, the day you saw me looking for him, I was there to tell him about a vacant position in a locksmith company in North Charleston."

"Did he get the job?"

"He didn't tell me directly, but I gathered that he did and would be earning enough to move."

"You don't know for certain?"

"No." The preacher smiled. "It was fortunate that he left because that freed up the best room in the house for Joy."

Bernard and Rebekah returned and moved back to their previous locations. Adrienne came back and asked if she could get Burl and me something else to drink. The caroling must have put her in a better, if not more generous, mood. Burl said that another Coke would be great, and I said I'd go with her to get the drinks.

"Brother Chris," Adrienne said as she poured the Preacher's Coke, "this is one of the nicest nights I can remember. I love it here."

I was surprised since she looked bored most of the evening. Once again, I was reminded not to judge others by appearances.

We returned, and Burl led us in a few more Christmas songs, more secular than religious, and I told him I needed to be going. He walked me to the door.

"Preacher, would you do me a favor?"

"If I can."

"Call the locksmith shop and see if Taylor took the job?"

"I'll try, but tomorrow is Christmas Eve. I don't know if it'll be open."

I said I understood and asked him to try.

"You think he was one of the men who abducted Joy?"

I nodded.

"I pray not," he said.

"I'll be calling Chief LaMond in the morning. She'll probably be contacting you to learn everything you know about him. Do you know what kind of car he drives?"

"I'm horrible with stuff like that. I know it's a few years old and black. I doubt that helps."

We shook hands, and he told me to have a pleasant rest of the evening.

Christmas Eve began as another beautiful day. The sun rose over the ocean a little after seven and was escorted on its upwards path by wispy cirrus clouds. The temperature was already in the low-forties, ten degrees above average. I decided that this would be a good morning to walk to the Lost Dog Cafe for breakfast. It appeared that I wasn't the only person to have that thought. Amber saw me enter and pointed to the only two empty tables. I chose the smaller of the two, and she had a mug of coffee in front of me before I'd wiggled out of my jacket.

"Merry Christmas Eve," she said and followed up by leaning over and hugging me around the neck.

"And the same to you. What are you and Jason doing tomorrow?"

She glanced around the room to see if her services were needed elsewhere. They weren't, and she turned back to me. "We're going to First Light's service and then to Samuel and Jacob's house for lunch."

Samuel was a good friend of Amber's son, Jason. Jacob,

Samuel's dad, and Amber had been dating a year. Their first date was last Christmas at Burl's Christmas Eve service.

"Great. Is Jacob fixing lunch?"

Amber chuckled. "Jacob's a guy; Samuel's a guy. The best they can muster is burning toast. I'll do everything."

Jacob and Samuel's culinary skills had me beat, but I didn't remind Amber of my shortcomings. "It's great you'll get a chance to be together."

"I think so. Changing the subject, have you heard anything about Pluto? Dude was in for lunch yesterday and I thought he was going to cry when I asked him if his pup had turned up."

"I haven't heard anything."

"Don't know what'd happen to Dude if something happened to his short look-alike."

"I agree."

"Any news about Joy?"

Amber had earned her reputation of knowing all the gossip worth repeating.

I told her about going to Burl's party and how well Joy appeared to be adjusting to her new home. I then added, "Do you know Taylor Strong?"

"Name's not familiar. Why?"

I shared what Joy and I'd learned about her job at Blackbeard's and overhearing something that possibly resulted in her abduction.

"Want me to ask around?"

"Yes, if you limit it to people you can trust. I don't want Taylor hearing about it."

"Have you told the police any of this?"

"Some of it. I need to talk to Chief LaMond."

She pointed at me and frowned. "Yes, you do."

She took my order and headed to the kitchen.

My phone rang while I was waiting for food to arrive. I didn't recognize the number and nearly didn't answer. There are only so many "free" vacations I can win, or "opportunities" I must learn about the latest-greatest Medicare supplemental insurance.

"Chris, Chris Landrum," said the voice on the other end. It was familiar, but I couldn't place it.

"Yes."

"Oh good. This is Bernard, you know, the one at Hope House."

"Sure, Bernard. How are you?" I said, although I was more wanting to know why he was calling rather than how he was.

"I'm fine, sir. I was talking to Preacher Burl after you left last night. He told me you were asking about Taylor Strong. The preacher said you asked what Taylor drove, and Preacher didn't know. He's mighty good about knowing the scriptures; he's short on knowledge about some things in this here world. Cars are one of them."

"Do you know what Taylor drives?"

"Yes, sir. A black, 2013 Ford Focus. Got itself a dent in the front bumper. The rear tires have too much mileage on them and are nearly bald."

"Thanks. That may help the police find him."

"There's more, sir. It has South Carolina plates; the first three numbers are 339. I hate to say, I don't recall the last three."

"How do you know that?"

"That's the kind of unimportant stuff I remember."

"Bernard, that'll be helpful. It's not unimportant. Do you know anything else about Taylor, other than he was a locksmith and moved out the night before Joy arrived?"

"I don't know the best way to put it, but he acted like he was in a box and no one could find a way in. Don't get me wrong, he was friendly enough. It's like he had secrets and didn't want anyone to get close enough to figure them out. Does that make sense?"

"Yes. Do you know if he had friends on Folly other than

people in Hope House? Anyone ever come to visit him or to pick him up?"

"It wasn't at the house. I saw him on West Ashley talking to a man. They were huddled up against the wall at St. James Gate, near the opening to the outdoor patio. Know where I mean?"

I told him I did.

"I couldn't tell what they were talking about because I was on the sidewalk at the stoplight. It looked sort of sketchy, sir."

"Can you describe the other man?"

"Not really. He looked taller than Taylor and heavier. Sorry, that's the best I can do."

"That's fine, Bernard. Anything else?"

"Nothing about anything I know about Taylor. I know Preacher Burl tried to call the locksmith where Taylor was supposed to go to work. I think the place is closed until after Christmas. He left a message on the machine. I won't take up more of your time. Will I see you at tonight's service?"

I said I'd be there.

"Then, *adios*, sir."

Amber had slid my breakfast in front of me while I was talking to Bernard. I was on my second bite when Chief LaMond came in the restaurant, looked around, and headed to my table.

"Merry Christmas Eve, Cindy. Care to join me?"

"You buying?"

"Wouldn't that be bribing a law-enforcement official?"

"Not unless you plan to ask me to do something illegal, immoral, or considering the season, un-Christian."

"None of the above. Have a seat."

Amber must have figured that the Chief would be joining me. She had a mug of coffee for Cindy before she had time to remove her jacket, and said, "Something to eat, Chief?"

"Anything expensive and put it on his tab." Needless to say, she pointed at me.

Cindy took a sip of coffee, and I said, "Dude find Pluto?"

She shook her head.

"Too bad. You working or taking today off?"

"What do you think? Dear sweet hubby's chained to the cash register at the hardware store and won't get home until every Tom, Dick, and Harriet buy every battery, extension cord, and those cheap, chintzy, *hecho en Mexico* Christmas ornaments that hang on the tree, spin, and play 'Jingle Bells.'"

"Sorry."

"I'm not. That's what makes him enough money to spoil me and allows me to live like a queen."

"A queen?"

"Whoops, I drifted into my fantasy world for a moment. Enough about my phantasmagorias life. Yes, I'm working. In fact, I'm waiting for a call from the landlord at the apartment where Joy lives, or where the owner of that bar thinks she lives. What other trouble have you been sticking your nose in?"

Cindy's expensive breakfast arrived, and I told her what Bernard had shared. She jotted down the vehicle information and said she'd see what she could find out, although she wasn't optimistic since, in her words, without the last three numbers of the license, there were "three billion combinations." I was certain that was a tad high but didn't get in an argument about math. I'd exhausted my latest information, and our conversation drifted to what she was doing Christmas Day—attending Cal's party, going to Planet Follywood's annual Christmas pot-luck dinner later in the day, and acting like a queen. I shared my plans.

I waited for her to finish eating, paid the tab, and walked with her to the door. In a moment totally out of character, she hugged me and said, "Merry Christmas, and thanks for being such a good friend."

She slid back to her normal self when she said, "You tell anyone I did that, and I'll have you arrested for embarrassing a public official."

I told her that the act of kindness was safe with me.

I was headed home after leaving the Dog when the phone rang again. This time, I knew who it was.

"Merry Christmas Eve, Charles."

"Yeah, yeah. Where are you?"

"In front of City Hall."

"Park your butt on the nearest bench. I'll pick you up in ten minutes."

"Where are we going?" I asked, wasting words since he'd already hung up.

It couldn't have been more than five minutes before Charles' Toyota pulled to the curb and he waved me in.

"Could you tell me where we're going?" I asked, thinking it was not too much to ask.

He turned left on East Arctic Avenue, and said, "Dixie called and said Martha was home."

"Your plan is to barge in on Martha on Christmas Eve?"

"Nope. Figured you'd ring the doorbell and flash your old-man charm. How could she resist inviting us in?"

I could think of several ways and rolled my eyes.

I rang the doorbell and the sounds of her menagerie filled the house. Unlike our earlier visit, the door opened, and Martha said, "Hold on a second, Teri, I'll get your … Whoa, you're not Teri."

Charles stepped in front of me. "Hi, Martha, I'm Charles from church. This is my friend, Chris."

Martha wore gray sweatshirt and sweatpants. She leaned on her cane and looked from Charles to me. "Where's Teri?"

Charles looked down the steps and toward the street. "Who's Teri?"

"The child watching my family while I was away. She's supposed to stop by this morning to get her money." She stepped on the porch, closed the door, probably to keep her herd of family members inside, and looked up and down the street. "If you're not Teri, why are you here?"

"Chris and I stopped by the other day to see you. Your neighbor, Dixie, said you were out of town."

"Yes, I was up in Dayton visiting, poor Tommy. He had a stroke, you know. Got back last night. Flight was three hours late. Can you believe that?"

Charles said that he could.

"Oh, I'm being inconsiderate. Would you like a cup of coffee?" She hesitated and winked at Charles. "Or a hot toddy? I've got some good whiskey to spike it with."

Charles said, "Coffee would be fine."

"Give me a minute to herd my family into another room. Otherwise they'd lick the livin' tar out of you."

She opened the door enough to slip back in the house and Charles turned to me and whispered, "Wonder how long it'll be before we're begging for the hot toddy?"

The animals quietened to a low roar, and Martha opened the door and invited us in and led us to what she referred to as the "sitting room." I would've called it an animal play house. In one corner there was a three-foot-high, triple deck, carpeted cat tower. Beside the tower was a large wicker basket filled with rubber balls, a tennis ball that looked like it'd rolled under a running lawnmower, and a hard-rubber thing shaped like a five-pound weight. Other toys were located on the brown pile carpet.

She told us to sit anywhere we liked while she got the coffee and asked again if we were sure we didn't want a toddy. I declined, although I was getting closer to saying yes. We each chose one of the three wingback chairs and lowered our bodies in the dog and cat hair infested seats. I noticed an end table beside my chair holding a large aquarium. It wasn't more than a foot away, so I saw there was no water in it. What it was filled with was a boa constructor that was a mile long, or so it seemed. It stared at me and I knew what a mouse must feel like on its way to supper—the boa's supper.

Martha returned to the room carrying two, white china cups of coffee. "Oh," she said, "I see you've met Squeezy. Would you like to hold him?"

Where was the hot toddy when I needed it? "That's okay, Martha. Not today." *Not tomorrow, not ever*, I thought.

"Martha," Charles said, "You have a lovely house."

"Thank you. It's comfortable, and wonderful for my pets."

Charles asked, "How many pets do you have?"

"It varies. Most of the time, there're a dozen of God's wonderful creatures living with me."

That probably meant there were more until Squeezy got hungry. "How many dogs?" I asked, hoping to move the conversation closer to the reason for our visit.

She bit her lower lip, held out her hand and raised her fingers, one at a time. "Let's see, Bruce, Ink Spot, Little Dog, Pooch, Gink, and Lady. That's six today. Now don't neglect asking about my other lovely creatures."

"What're their names?" Mr. Nosy asked.

She pointed her cane at the boa. "You already met Squeezy. There are three cats, Cat One, Cat Two, and Crazy. My poor little parrot, Jolly Roger, must stay upstairs. He doesn't get along with the cats, and his vocabulary is, well let's say, his mouth needs to be washed out with soap more often than I would like. We celebrated his ninth birthday before I went to visit poor Tommy."

Charles wiggled his fingers like he was counting. "Martha, if my ciphering is right, that's only eleven pets. Didn't you say twelve?"

"Oh, you're right. I keep forgetting Davy Crockett." She looked around like Davy was loose in the room. I hoped Mr. Crockett wasn't another snake.

"Davy Crockett?" Charles said.

"A raccoon. He's my indoor/outdoor pet." She put her finger to her lips, and whispered, "It's illegal to have a raccoon as a pet. You won't turn me in to the pet police, will you?"

We assured her we wouldn't although turning her in to a mental institution was becoming a tempting option.

"Martha," I said. "Are any of your dogs Australian Terriers?"

"What a queer question, young man. Gink is."

Charles said, "Gink?"

"The word Gink means 'a peculiar fellow,' in Australian. That's why Vincent and I named our little fellow that. That little bugger, Gink, not Vincent, was as strange as any dog we ever had."

Pot calling a kettle black came to mind.

"Vincent's not here is he?" Charles said.

"Heavens no. I dumped him back in Atlanta eons ago. Can you believe he hated the beach?"

"No, ma'am," Charles said.

"Now young men, don't get me wrong. Vincent was a wonderful husband, and we had some great times. I remember back when we got married in '58, and he bought the prettiest blue, 1957 Chevy. For our honeymoon, we drove all the way to the Grand Canyon, soaking in the air from the open windows. Gink would stick his head out the window and gobble up the breeze like he was lapping water. Ah, the good old days."

Now to get back to the not-so-good current days. "Martha, I'm confused. Gink was your Australian Terrier when you were in Atlanta?"

She nodded.

"Yet, when you were naming your dogs, didn't you say Gink?"

"Yes, so?"

"Gink is an Australian Terrier, right?"

She nodded again.

"And he's in the other room with your other dogs?"

Another nod.

"I see," I said, although I didn't. "How long have you had Gink?"

"Let's see. It was a few days before I left to visit poor Tommy. He had a stroke, you know?"

She had my attention. I leaned forward in the chair and motioned for her to continue.

"I was out back filling the food bowls. I put food out for the poor strays. Terrible how some people just throw their pets out to fend for themselves. Terrible. I was filling the bowls when the cutest little Australian Terrier peeked around the corner of the house. He saw the food and zip, he was eating out of the bowl. He was a spittin' image of Gink. Lo-and-behold, the poor thing didn't have a collar and licked my hand just like Gink used to do. Oh, the memories the cute thing brought back. Did I ever tell you about Vincent, Gink, and me going to the Grand Canyon?"

"Yes," I said.

She continued, "I simply had to bring him in, feed him, and give him a warm home to live in." She closed her eyes and slowly shook her head. "I had to."

I didn't know who I felt sorrier for, Martha or Dude. Martha was reliving her past through Gink, umm, Pluto, and we were here to shatter her memories. And, I can't imagine how much anguish Dude has been going though without Pluto. I also realized that Martha hadn't asked why two near strangers appeared at her door.

I was trying to figure out how to broach the subject of her taking Dude's dog. Charles, didn't share my dilemma.

He nodded toward the door separating us from the rest of her family. "Martha, what if I told you that Gink belongs to our friend, Dude Sloan?"

Her hand jerked up to cover her mouth. I would have sworn that Squeezy hissed at Charles. Martha exhaled and said, "Oh my heavens. That's not possible. Gink didn't have a collar. He came to me and begged me to take him in." She lowered her head. "Who's this Dude fellow?"

I explained who he was and how Pluto had escaped, caught his collar on something in the yard, and how Dude and several others had been looking for him for days. She appeared to be shrinking in her chair. It may have been the light, but I thought I saw tears in her eyes. Charles and I remained silent. That was the least we could do after ruining her day.

She pushed herself out of the chair and walked to the door where the dogs had been herded. She opened the door a few inches, bent down, and said, "Here, Gink."

Dude's look-alike inched his way through the door, saw Charles, jumped in his lap, and licked his face. Charles returned Pluto's "kisses" and said something to him in dog-speak.

Martha returned to her chair, and whispered, "What's his name?"

Charles gave his lap mate another kiss, and said, "Dude Sloan."

"No, what's Gink's name?"

"Pluto," I said.

"That's a funny name," said the person who has a snake named Squeezy, and cats named Cat One and Cat Two.

I explained how Dude was an astronomy buff and named his dog after the dwarf planet.

"He must be heartbroken," she said after a long, uncomfortable silence.

I said, "He is."

She stared at Pluto, and said, "You should call him and let him know his pup's safe. He can come get him."

"That's a good idea, Martha," I said.

"Won't you call him now? I feel horrible that I stole someone's family member. Horrible."

I punched in Dude's number in my phone, and was rewarded with, "Unless you know where Pluto is, I don't want to talk to you."

I smiled, told him who I was, and broke the news. Good news for Dude, not so good for Martha.

He screamed so loud that I moved the phone a foot away from my ear. He screamed a second time before I had the nerve to return the phone close enough to tell him where we were.

I heard Dude's 1970 Chevrolet El Camino a block before it pulled in Martha's drive. I opened the front door before he knocked it off the hinges. I'd never seen Dude move so quickly. Pluto ran a close second as he charged out of Charles's lap and met his master in the center of the room.

Watching Dude reunite with Pluto was a sight that would soften the hardest heart. I wouldn't call it a Christmas miracle, but it was close. Even Martha, who'd moments earlier been tearing up about losing Gink, and feeling badly about taking in someone else's dog, broke into a smile.

Charles had tears in his eyes.

I wasn't far behind.

Charles and I left Martha, Dude, and Pluto/Gink after Martha apologized profusely for taking the surf shop owner's dog, and Dude told her, "Me be giggly getting' Pluto back." He also told her that he wanted to meet all of Pluto's new four-, two-, and zero-legged friends. We would've stayed longer, but Dude told Martha that it'd "be cool" to wrap Squeezy around his neck. That was our cue to exit.

Charles dropped me at the house after saying he'd had enough excitement for one morning and wanted to take a nap to get ready for First Light's Christmas Eve service. A cold wave was pushing through the area since my early morning walk to the Dog. The sky morphed from chamber of commerce blue to threatening rain. I didn't need a nap yet thought spending several hours inside was becoming a better idea. I knew Dude would be so excited about getting Pluto back that he wouldn't think to let anyone know his dog had been found.

I called the Chief who answered with, "Ho, Ho, Ho! Merry Christmas Eve. If you say anything to stomp on my feelings of great joy, you won't live long enough to wish anyone Merry Christmas tomorrow."

"Cindy, I'm about to make your day of feeling great joy even better."

"You and Charles are moving to Tibet."

"Guess again."

"You and Charles are moving to Tibet and taking my husband with you."

"What if I told you that Pluto has been reunited with Dude?"

"Has he?"

"Yes," I said, through a smile.

"Oh, my God. That's incredible. How, when, where?"

I filled her in on some details, leaving out the names of Martha's animals, my near snake-handling experience, and Martha's honeymoon trip to the Grand Canyon.

"Chris, that's the best news you could've given me. Thanks for letting me know."

"You're the first person I've called. I'll let you get back to whatever police chiefs do on Christmas Eve."

"Don't go so fast, bearer of great news. I have a kernel of news for you although it's not as great as Pluto's return. I talked to the landlord where Joy lives or lived before she moved here. The guy who sounds about as smart as a corkscrew, but not as useful, is on vacation in some town in Maryland I've never heard of. He thought it was a brilliant idea to leave his tenants in a lurch while he's frolicking with some floozy near our nation's capital."

"Did he tell you that's what he's doing?"

"Nah, he sounded like someone who'd be frolicking with a floozy. He remembered Joyce Tolliver, called her a 'hot chick' and said if he was twenty years older, or she was twenty years younger, he'd be camped out on her curb hoping she'd pick him up. Honest to God that's what he said. Yuck. I told him I wasn't a hot chick, but was a police chief and carried a gun, and if he didn't want me camped on his curb, he'd call the second he got back to the complex and let me in her apartment."

"What'd he say?"

"Yes, sir, Chief, ma'am."

"When's he coming back?"

"Day after Christmas."

"You'll call me when he gets back?"

"Nope. I'll be calling the tenant who's paid rent for that apartment. If she wants to let you know that's her business."

"Fair enough. Anything on the whereabouts of Taylor Strong?"

"Chris, you sure know how to drag a girl down after cheering her up about Pluto."

"Sorry."

"Our Mr. Strong has a rap sheet. If Preacher Burl was correct about his former resident attending school to learn locksmithing, either the school specialized in training burglars, or didn't check his background before letting him in."

"Is that what he'd been arrested for?"

"Yep, his career of crime had been given three years off when he was taking advantage of an all-expense paid vacation in Arkansas."

"Any idea where he is?"

"Nary a clue. I'm going to swing by the house this afternoon to see if the driver's license photo that was on record matches the Taylor Strong who stayed there. I'm fairly certain it will, but there's always the chance it's another guy with the same name."

"Anything more on his car?"

"Negative. If I learn anything, you might be one of the first I'll let know."

I knew not to push. "That'd be great, Cindy."

"Of course, it would."

My next call was to Preacher Burl.

"Brother Chris," he said, based on my name appearing on his phone, since I hadn't said anything.

"Yes, Preacher."

"Are you psychic?"

"Preacher, I've been accused of many things. That's not one of them. Why?"

"I was reaching for the phone to call you."

"Why were you going to call?"

"You called first. What do I owe the pleasure of this call?"

I shared the news about Pluto's reappearance, and Burl responded with "Halleluiah," and a prayer. I then told him that he would be receiving a visit from Chief LaMond and the reason for her visit.

"Ah, Brother Chris, perhaps you are psychic after all."

Burl was beginning to sound more and more like some of my other friends with disjointed comments, thoughts, and occasionally, actions. I asked what he meant.

"Brother Lawrence from Holy City Locksmiths returned my call less than an hour ago. That's the company I'd told Brother Taylor about. The store was closed today, but out of habit, Brother Lawrence checks his messages when the store's closed. He said that around Christmas it's not uncommon for people to get locked out of their home or vehicle. Mine happened to be the fifth message left for—"

"That's interesting, Preacher," I interrupted. "What did he say about Taylor?"

"He had little to share. It seems that Brother Taylor never showed for the interview. Can I surmise that Sister Cindy's visit is related to Brother Taylor's past?"

I told him what I knew about his former resident and the reason for Cindy's visit.

It took him a long time to say, "Brother Chris, I have a confession to make, and a dilemma that I face in my profession."

"What?"

"First, the dilemma. Faith is the foundation of my being. I, by personality and profession, seek the good in everyone. Over the years, I have seen firsthand how even the most horrid person can, as we preachers are prone to say, see the light. Men and women of all ilk can turn their lives around. I truly believe that miracles occur." He was silent for a moment, before repeating, "Miracles occur."

"That's wonderful, Preacher."

"There's a downside, which leads to my confession. When I opened Hope House, I did so with much trepidation. It was created as a place where those with little hope could find not only the necessities of a warm bed and a warm meal, but where they could find, as its name says, hope. From hopeless to hope requires change, a change in the residents. It's not up to me, nor is it in me to control the changes. That is up to a much higher power than in this humble, lowly, preacher man. Not everyone is ready or willing to make the necessary changes, hence the reason for my trepidation, and something that has kept me awake many a night with worry." He paused again. I started to ask him to elaborate, when he said, "I have no application for admittance. I have no way to determine where the potential resident is with his or her life; what black holes have existed in the past; and, what evil thoughts may be present. Brother Chris, I continually am in fear of introducing someone to the house who has evil intent. How, pray tell, is it fair to the others if I subject them to such a person?"

"Preacher, I've known you long enough to know that you'd do everything possible to prevent that from happening and look how much good Hope House has done. I know what Bernard was experiencing before you gave him a chance and hope. And look at Joy, she had no hope, nowhere to go. I don't know as much about Adrienne or Rebekah, but from what I see, you've helped them immensely."

"That may be true, Brother Chris. While it's taken me a long time to get to it, my confession is that I never had a good feeling about Brother Taylor."

"What about him?"

"I may not be all-knowing," he laughed. "Heavens, at times I'm not even part-knowing, but what I am decent at is detecting when someone is not being truthful. Brother Taylor often fit in that group. I should never have let him move in. I knew he was lying about previous jobs. That's one reason I was intent on him attending the job interview at Holy City Locksmiths. I figured if they liked him, they would check his background. If there was nothing in it to raise red flags, he'd get the job and be on the road to a productive life. Most everyone lies about something. I told myself that his could be minor and Hope House was giving him the break he needed."

"Preacher, you had no way of knowing. You shouldn't beat yourself up. You do wonderful work."

"Perhaps. I can only pray that by letting Brother Taylor reside here, it didn't contribute to what he did to Sister Joy."

"Preacher, he didn't meet her there. Whatever happened took place before she knew about your ministry."

"I suppose you're right. I must focus on tonight's message and not let this interfere with how I interact with those loyal members of my flock who will be celebrating Christmas Eve with fellow believers. You will be there tonight, won't you?"

"Of course," I said, like there could be any other option.

3 0

The weather continued to deteriorate, so First Light's Christmas Eve service will be in the storefront location. Last Christmas, the service was in a tent on the beach, but the tent wasn't available this year.

Joy met me at the door and asked if we could talk after the service. I told her yes, and she joined Mary and her two girls in the second pew. I smiled as I remembered watching Mary, Joanie, and Jewel enter last year's Christmas Eve service. The girls had been wearing new clothes and entered the tent with their heads held high, radiating pride in their appearance.

Charles was in the third pew waving for me to join him. I passed Amber and her son, Jason, seated with Samuel and his dad. Amber nodded to me as I passed. I slid in beside Charles and watched Joy, Joanie and Jewel laughing. Mary hushed them.

Preacher Burl waved his hands for latecomers and those who wanted to continue their conversations to take their seats, and he began with, "Please silence thy portable communication devices." Tonight, it was followed by him encouraging us to make a joyful noise unto the Lord by singing "O Come All Ye Faithful."

We tried to sound joyful, but William Hansel had the lone true singing voice. Burl thanked us for coming and began his traditional Christmas Eve sermon. I had to give him credit, he'd overcome his earlier feelings of trepidation and guilt for allowing Taylor to stay in Hope House. His message was inspirational, heartwarming, and had the rapt attention of everyone present. He followed it with another carol, a reminder of tomorrow morning's regular Sunday service, before asking William to end the service with a solo of "Silent Night."

We slowly wandered out of the sanctuary into a light rain. Joanie asked her mom if the rain was going to turn to snow for Christmas. I didn't hear Mary's answer, but knew it would disappoint her daughter. Joy moved beside Charles and me. I asked if it was okay if Charles joined us. She said sure, and I suggested we make the short walk to the Crab Shack where we could stay dry and talk. Charles was leading the group, followed by Joy and me. As we got to the restaurant, I noticed a black car slowly pass us on Center Street and then turn on East Erie Avenue just past the restaurant. In the glow of the streetlight, it looked like it had a dent in the front bumper. Hadn't Bernard mentioned that Taylor's Ford Focus had a dent? Was the car that passed us a Focus or was I being paranoid? No way to know now.

The restaurant, normally crowded on Saturday nights, was near empty. A couple of others from the church service were seated near the bar, and a half-dozen patrons were scattered throughout the dining room. We were told to sit anywhere, and I suggested a table by the wall and away from others. The server appeared and asked what we wanted to drink. Joy asked what imported beers they had, the server told her, and Joy said Heineken. Charles said Bud, and I ordered the house wine.

"I remembered this morning that I preferred imported beer," Joy said, explaining her order.

"That's great," I said. "Anything else new?"

"That's what I wanted to talk about. Yesterday afternoon, your Police Chief came to talk to Preacher Burl. I didn't know the Chief was there and walked in the kitchen where they were talking. I apologized and Chief LaMond said I wasn't interrupting. She had a driver's license photo and asked if I recognized the person."

"Did you?" Charles blurted, before Joy could finish talking.

She put both palms on the table and leaned forward. "It was him."

Charles said, "Who?"

"The man in the boat."

"You're certain?" I said.

She nodded, and said, "I remember walking home from work and the next thing I remember was laying on the back seat of the boat with my hands and feet tied. My head hurt so much that I figured I must still be alive. There was a dim light by the boat's steering wheel, and I recognized that man Taylor in the front seat. No doubt, it was him. It was dark in the rest of the boat and I never got a good look at the other guy. I already told you what happened next."

Drinks arrived, and the server asked if we wanted something to eat. Charles and I declined, and Joy asked me if she could borrow a few dollars. Charles said that she couldn't borrow anything and that he would pay. A Christmas miracle was in the making. She told the server that she wanted a cup of she crab soup and the house salad.

The server left, and I said, "Joy, do you remember anything else?"

"Not about them taking me out to dump me in the ocean. I remember my apartment in that building that you and I walked around. It came furnished, and I was travelling light. The only thing I had in there was a large suitcase and some hang-up clothes. Nothing more."

"Joy," I said, "did you tell Chief LaMond everything you remembered?"

She smiled for the first time since the service ended. "Everything but liking imported beer."

Charles said, "It sounds like a lot of your memory's back. Had you made friends in your apartment building or from the job at the bar?"

"Not really. I only worked at Blackbeard's two nights, and I hadn't lived much longer than that in the apartment. I nodded at a couple of other ladies who lived at the complex. I already have more friends here than over there or anywhere else I've lived."

Charles patted her on the arm, and said, "Folly folks are addictive."

I added, "You looked like you were enjoying sitting with Mary and her girls."

She smiled and sipped her beer. "The kids are adorable, and Mary actually stopped by yesterday to visit, to visit me. Can you believe that? She could be the daughter I never had." She hesitated, and turned to me, "Chris, Mary tells me that you helped her find a place to live after you discovered that she and her gals were sneaking in vacant rental houses to have somewhere to sleep."

"Several people helped Mary and her children. I didn't do more than anyone else."

Joy smiled. "That's not Mary's version."

I was embarrassed and changed the subject. "Will you be attending Cal's party tomorrow afternoon?"

"Preacher Burl said that it was an event I couldn't miss."

"More than going to church tomorrow morning?" Charles said.

She took another sip, smiled, and said, "Nope, he said the party was the second-best event happening on Folly tomorrow."

We watched Joy enjoying the soup and salad and talked more about what she remembered about the apartment and previously living in Atlanta. Her mood improved the more she recalled and recounted the past. She'd finished her meal and thanked Charles and me for an entertaining and happy evening. From our vantage point, it looked like the rain had stopped, and I suggested that it may be a good time for her to walk home.

Charles's home was the opposite direction, so I told him to head to his apartment and I'd escort Joy home.

Joy was euphoric on the way home. She hooked her arm in mine and kept talking about how much she enjoyed spending time with the others in Hope House. It was as if an anvil had been lifted off her shoulders. We were two houses from her place when a light drizzle filled the air. The house next to Hope had strands of multi-colored lights on large shrubs beside the drive. If I hadn't been looking at the Christmas lights, I would've missed a car backed to the rear of the neighbor's house—the same car that I would've sworn I'd seen on Center Street when Charles, Joy, and I were entering the Crab Shack. I was even more certain it was the same vehicle when the red and green Christmas lights reflected off a dented bumper.

I couldn't tell if anyone was in it without walking up the drive. Joy's safety was my main concern, so I pretended to not see the vehicle and continued walking her home. We started up the steps and she asked if I wanted to come in.

"Preacher Burl always had coffee brewing if you want some."

I opened the door and said, "That's a kind offer, but it's been a long day and I need to rest up for tomorrow's church service and Cal's party."

"I should do the same."

I told her to lock the door behind her. She said she would, and good to her word, I heard the tumbler secure the entry.

The rain had increased, and I wondered what to do. Should I approach the vehicle? Should I call the police? If the car belonged to the neighbor and had been there all night, I'd look foolish. I slowed as I crossed the drive where the car was parked. The lights reflected off the vehicle, but the rain-covered wind-shield, kept me from seeing if it was occupied. I decided to keep walking and regardless how foolish it may make me look, call the police as soon as I was out of sight from the suspicious vehicle.

I was startled to hear the car door slam shut and turned to see what was going on. A man wearing a black, hooded raincoat was heading toward me. My first thought was that it was Taylor Strong although I wasn't certain since the Christmas lights were the only illumination, and I'd only seen him twice. What I did know was that whoever it was gripped a baseball bat, and from his body language, knew how to use it.

Now what? Running wasn't an option. The man was three decades younger than me, and even when I was younger, I wasn't that fast. I probably outweighed him by thirty pounds and would have a chance, although slight, to subdue him in a fair fight. The bat and my age eliminated a fight being fair. It's amazing how much goes through your mind in a split second. My best option was to wait for him to swing at me and try to grab the bat's barrel before it contacted my body. With luck, it would throw him off balance and I might be able to wrestle him down or get the bat. *Might* being the key word.

I didn't have to put my feeble plan into action. I caught a glimpse of someone darting from beside the house and lunge at the bat-wielding assailant. The latest addition to the fray blindsided my attacker and collided with such force that both men were knocked to the concrete driveway. The bat flew in the opposite direction. I grabbed the weapon and stepped back from the men. I then recognized it was Bernard who'd saved me from being a baseball. The man who was coming after me hadn't moved since he'd smacked into the drive. Bernard slowly pushed himself up and rubbed his elbow that had been under the other man when he struck the drive. The rain intensified, Bernard's hair was plastered to his head, and a wide smile was plastered to his face.

I stared at the assailant. He hadn't moved and must've been knocked out when his head hit the pavement. I reached for my phone to call the police and then heard the siren from a Folly Beach police cruiser less than a block away. The car stopped in front of the drive and Officer Allen Spencer rushed to the three of us.

Spencer glanced at Bernard, felt the unmoving person's neck for a pulse, and called for an ambulance. He then turned to me. "Mr. Landrum, I should have known. What's going on?"

"I walked Joy Tolliver to Hope House after supper." I pointed to the car. "I saw that car and was afraid it belonged to Taylor Strong, the man suspected of abducting Joy. I was going to call the police when a man—"

Bernard interrupted, "It's Taylor Strong, sir."

"Thank you," Spencer said, and turned back to me.

I continued with the story up to when Bernard jumped out of nowhere and collided with Taylor.

The rain continued to fall, and Spencer turned to Bernard. "Why were out in this lousy weather and able to see what was happening?"

A fire engine arrived before Bernard could share his version of the event. One of Folly's EMT firefighters knelt beside Taylor. The other firefighter opened a large umbrella over his colleague and Taylor.

I said, "Officer Spencer, before Bernard answers, could we take this conversation inside? We'd be more comfortable out of the rain."

A second patrol car arrived, and Spencer told the new arrival to keep watch on the unconscious man.

Bernard led us to the door which was opened by Adrienne wearing a long, white robe and house slippers. She waved us in, hugged Bernard, and whispered to him, "Are you okay, hero?"

He told her that other than a sore elbow, he was fine, and followed the rest of us to the living room. Burl met us and asked if we wanted coffee. He acted like it was nothing unusual to entertain three soaked men, including a police officer and a man carrying a baseball bat. I said coffee sounded good, and Bernard and Spencer agreed. Joy had slipped in behind Burl and had a confused look on her face. I didn't blame her.

Spencer took a notebook from his jacket, wiped water off the cover, flipped through a few pages, and said, "Bernard, let's start again, why were you out there?"

"Sir, folks living here are a family, not by blood, but still a family. Families stick together." He pointed to Joy who had taken a seat on the sofa. "Joy is the latest member. I knew you all were looking for Taylor Strong for what you thought he did to Joy."

Burl returned with a tray carrying three coffee mugs and Adrienne handed them to Bernard, Allen, and me.

Allen thanked her and asked Bernard to continue.

"You see, I knew what Taylor drove and thought I saw it cruisin' past the house a couple of times earlier tonight. I wasn't sure it was him, so I didn't say anything. I took a little walk before it started to rain hard and saw the car back in the drive where it is now. It didn't belong to the owner of that house. Sir, that made me more than a mite suspicious. I went around the house and sneaked behind those shrubs out there. The driver was still in the car and not moving. I figured he was waiting to see where Joy was and maybe try to take or kill her." He stopped and caught his breath.

"How long were you there?" Spencer asked.

"I don't have a watch. I'd guess a half hour or so. I also don't have a phone, so I couldn't call for you to come check it out. Sir, I was afraid to leave and not see what the man in the car, umm, Taylor, was going to do. The rain got harder and harder."

"You had to be miserable," Burl added.

"Nah," Bernard said, "I did a lot of recon in Afghanistan, like hours at a time. A half hour in the rain was nothing."

Spencer said, "Then what happened?"

"I saw Mr. Landrum, umm, Chris, walking Joy to the house. I was afraid Taylor was going to try to get her before she got in. He didn't, so I figured he was going to wait until everyone was asleep and do something then. I was surprised when Chris left, and Taylor went after him with a bat."

Spencer smiled for the first time, and said, "So, you took a football tackle to a baseball game."

Laughter, probably fueled by the release of tension more than Spencer's joke, filled the room.

Bernard added to the laughter, and then said, "Couldn't have said it better, sir."

"Allen," I said, "Were you headed here?"

Adrienne answered for the officer. "I called the police. Bernard thought he was hiding, maybe he was from Taylor, but I saw him behind the shrubs from my second-floor window. I remembered what he'd said about Taylor's car so when I saw it parked out there, I called the police. Bernard's right, we're a family, and I didn't want to see Joy, Bernard, or any of us hurt."

I heard the siren from an ambulance approaching and Allen jotted down Adrienne and Bernard's full name and asked Bernard if he wanted the EMTs to check his arm. Bernard said it was fine, and Allen asked if anyone had anything to add. None of us did.

3 2

After last night's events, I was tempted to skip First Light's Christmas service. I'd told Preacher Burl and Joy that I'd be there, so I resisted temptation and walked to church. The rain that'd made last night more miserable than it had already been, was gone and nary a cloud could be seen.

I arrived fifteen minutes before I knew Preacher Burl would repeat his "Please silence thy portable communication devices" opening. A familiar group of people were gathered around the coffee urn at the front of the room. Charles was talking with Bernard. Joy, Adrienne, and Rebekah were huddled together in deep conversation, and William was talking with Dixie and Martha.

Charles spotted me at the entry and pointed to his wrist, his way of telling me that I was late. I shook my head, and he mouthed, "Just kidding."

The Christmas spirit had taken hold of my friend. I nodded to Lottie who was helping Burl with his robe. Everyone wore their Christmas best, even Charles, who wore a solid red, long-sleeve sweatshirt instead of one featuring college logos. Burl headed to the lectern and Mary, Joanie, and Jewel entered and looked around. Joy spotted them and asked if they wanted to sit with her. In unison, Joanie and Jewel said, "Yes, oh yes." Mary ceded to their wishes, and the four moved to the second pew.

Barb entered as Burl was beginning his opening. She tiptoed to the back pew where I was sitting with Charles and squeezed my hand as she sat. "Sorry I'm late. I was at the store straightening up after being busy yesterday and lost track of time."

I SAW fatigue in Burl's eyes, but he didn't let it show. His message was uplifting, his enthusiasm for, and telling about, the birth of Jesus was contagious, and miracle of miracles, the congregations singing of traditional Christmas carols, sounded good—okay, passable.

Before the closing song, Charles leaned my way and whispered, "Whenever I have a problem, I sing. Then I realize my singing is a lot worse than my problem."

"Did a President say that?"

"No, I did. Didn't you just hear me?"

William Hansel singing "What Child is This" drowned out more silliness from Charles.

Most of those in attendance appeared to want to linger in the sanctuary after the service. Burl said there was more coffee and a few of us took advantage of it.

Charles took me by the arm and moved to a corner of the room, and in a muffled voice, said, "Why did I hear about last night from Bernard and not from my best friend?"

"Charles, I was exhausted and the only thing I wanted to do was go to sleep. Sorry."

Instead of berating me, he said, "Are you okay?"

The phone rang before I could assure him that I was. The screen read Cindy.

"Merry Christmas, Chief."

"Caller ID strikes again. Can you talk?"

I said for her to give me a second and walked outside where I'd have more privacy. Charles followed me. To keep him for flailing his arms and pointing to the phone, I put it on speaker and told Cindy to go ahead.

"Figured you'd want to know. Your new friend, the baseball batter, ain't what crooks call a stand-up guy. My guys turned him over to the Sheriff's Office when they got to the hospital. The detective called me a little while ago and said that it wasn't fifteen minutes after he started interrogating Taylor before he blamed everything on Raymond Tilford, his partner in crime. According to Taylor, it was Tilford's idea to burglarize the jewelry store, abduct Joy, steal the boat, take her out and dump her in the ocean. He didn't say it, but I suspect if given a chance, he'd blame Raymond for global warming, fighting in the Middle East, and shingles."

"Did he say why he attacked me?"

Cindy chuckled. "It appears that your surveillance skills aren't as good as your detective friend Charles."

Charles smiled, but kept his mouth shut. For once.

"And?" I said.

"Taylor thought he saw you looking at his car when you walked by with Joy, and when you were leaving, he said you slowed down and gazed his way. He figured he had to stop you before you did something stupid like calling the cops. Your reputation for nosing in my business, has spread to the criminal element. Tell Charles he needs to give you some lessons in surveilling."

"Never," I said.

Cindy laughed, and Charles stuck his lower lip out and pouted.

I asked, "Did Taylor tell them where to find Tilford?"

"Yep, and before you ask, they picked him up late last night and found some pretty earrings, necklaces, and watches in his car. Funny how they all were in in boxes with Grogan's Fine Jewelry on the top."

"Cindy, thanks for letting me know. You still plan to go to Cal's party this afternoon?"

"Only if Charles, that idiotic, moronic, weird friend of yours isn't there." She then laughed.

"I'm not those things," Charles said.

Cindy said, "I know, you're not idiotic and moronic. Merry Christmas, Charles."

Charles said, "I'll admit to weird. How'd you know I was listening?"

"Charles, I'm the Chief. I know everything. Besides, do you think I don't know when a phone's on speaker? The only person Chris puts the phone on speaker for is his nosy friend. Merry Christmas to both of you, and bye."

CAL HAD SAID that this party would be bigger and better than ever. From the sounds coming from the room as I opened the door, he was right. Loud conversations mixed with laughter were coming from all corners. Christmas lights twinkled from the bar, the front of the stage, and from four trees.

Cal was in the center of the room standing beside a table holding bowls of salsa, avocado dip, and something with lettuce, tomatoes, and onions in it. Two bowls overflowed with chips. The smiling host wore his much-travelled, rhinestone-covered coat, red jeans, and his Stetson with twinkling lights around the crown. He was talking with Amber and her son while Samuel and his dad were scooping dip on a paper plate full of chips.

Gene Autry's 1950 version of "Frosty the Snowman" was playing on the Wurlitzer.

Charles leaned on the bar and was talking with Joy, Mary and her girls. Joy saw me at the door and waved for me to join her. I did, and Charles said that he was telling the ladies about the police catching the second person responsible for Joy's abduction. Bernard joined us, and Charles started the story over again. He was swinging his arm around. I was afraid he was going to slosh beer on Bernard from the bottle in his hand.

Adrienne and Rebekah had been standing in a corner by themselves, but slowly came our way after they saw that Bernard had joined the group. They each put an arm around Bernard and called him their hero. He turned three shades of red and looked at the floor. That made the ladies squeeze harder. Jim Reeves was singing "Silver Bells" and Adrienne hummed along while she was squeezing their embarrassed housemate.

Speaking of squeezing, Dixie and Martha peeked in the door, and hesitated before getting enough courage to enter. I nodded to Charles and then at the ladies. Charles took the hint and moved to greet them. I saw him get each a beer from the tub next to the appetizer table and they moved to the far side of the room.

Joy watched them go, and leaned close to me and said, "You won't believe this. Preacher Burl talked to Cal about me. Cal told him he had a powerful need for another bartender, that's how he said it, *powerful need*. Cal hired me, and Preacher Burl said I could stay at Hope House as long as I want to. Isn't that wonderful?"

It was, and I told her so.

Dude was next to stick his head in the door. Correction, Pluto stuck his head in and then Dude. Pluto sniffed the air like he knew there must be a hamburger nearby with his name on it. Martha saw Pluto and left Dixie and Charles standing before she scooped up the canine and gave it a series of kisses.

I excused myself from Joy and moved toward Pluto, hopefully to prevent a war over the canine suffering an identity crisis. I hadn't needed to. Dude stood back, smiled, and told Martha that she could visit Pluto any time.

She thanked him, and added, "Can I call him Gink?"

"That be cool. His official name now be Pluto Gink Sloan."

Barb entered wearing a red sweater without any Christmas message adoring it, and came over to me and kissed my cheek and said, "Want to hunt shark teeth in the morning?"

"No," I said, so loud that two people standing nearby stopped talking and stared at me.

Burl was next to arrive. He wore a Santa hat and a sweater that would win any ugly Christmas sweater contest. He made his way around the room patting people on the back, kissing ladies on the cheek, and lifting and hugging Joanie and Jewel.

Cal saw Burl and moved close and whispered something to him. Burl shook his head so hard that the Santa hat nearly fell off. Cal smiled, patted the preacher on the back, and moved to the stage in front of the room. He waited for Brenda Lee to finish "Rockin' Around the Christmas Tree," and unplugged the jukebox.

He clinked two beer bottles together close to the antique mic that he's sung approximately a trillion songs in over the years. "Yo! How about lending me an ear?"

All but Dixie and Martha stopped talking. Cal tried again and this time they stopped and turned to the country singer.

Cal tipped his Stetson to the group. "Merry Christmas. This is our biggest Christmas shindig ever. Thanks for coming and joining this old crooner on his favorite day of the year. Now, I've got a question. How many of you'd like to hear Preacher Burl and me sing a duet?"

All but Burl responded by either clapping or saying, "Yes." Burl stared at the floor and shook his head.

"That's what I thought," Cal said. "If you were here last Christmas, I bet you remember the preacher and me singing, 'Silent Night.' I know I do. Come on up, Preacher."

Burl glanced at the door leading outside. I suspected that's where he'd rather be, but in the spirit of Christmas, he slowly moved to the stage while Cal grabbed his guitar. Burl faked a smile and moved to the mic like he would approach a rattlesnake. Cal whispered something to Burl and Burl responded.

Cal stepped to the mic and pulled Burl closer. "Gals and guys," the singer said, "I can't think of a better song to sing that this one. Here's to you, Joy, my newest bartender, and another fine addition to our community."

They began singing "Joy to the World," and two minutes later ended with,

"He rules the world with truth and grace,
And makes the nations prove
The glories of His righteousness,
And wonders of his love,
And wonders of his love."

ABOUT THE AUTHOR

Bill Noel is the best-selling author of fifteen novels in the popular Folly Beach Mystery series. Besides being an award-winning novelist, Noel is a fine arts photographer and lives in Louisville, Kentucky, with his wife, Susan, and his off-kilter imagination. Learn more about the series, and the author by visiting www.billnoel.com

1

———

Greny Scylax resolved to dump his boots as soon as he escaped the sewers. And his clothes. The perfumed ointment he had rubbed under his nostrils couldn't protect him from the stench of the city's bowels. Greny feared no amount of washing could ever remove that stink.

Beside him, Ecethor Orom stalked, oblivious to the fetor, the filth bespattering the hem of her glossy black dress, and the foul drips from the arched ceiling pattering her increasingly mussed platinum bouffant. The meritocrat's attire was more suited to a ball than a trip down here. Typical of her to overdress.

She came to an abrupt halt and, wrinkling her nose, brushed away a black spatter from its tip with a black lace handkerchief. "Your servants must find it homey down here."

Greny glanced at the half-dozen ratchers tramping behind them with primed springbows. Obscured by their colleagues from the light of the lampstones Greny and Ecethor carried, the rearmost two were barely visible, aside from their eyes which shone like pairs of persistent sparks. "They might superficially look like rat-headed men, but that doesn't mean this environment is to their liking. On the contrary, the sewers are an affront to their powerful sense of smell.

Under different circumstances, I'd have used cordents, but a situation like this demands ... discretion."

Ecethor burnished the gold disc on her forehead, her emblem of merit, a whorl-shelled wyrm. Finishing, she contemplated the handkerchief, then threw it away. "I appreciate your tact on this matter. Thank you."

"Thank me when your daughter's safe," Greny muttered. If Ecethor had kept her daughter in line, none of this might have been necessary.

Ecethor strode on, forcing Greny and the others to hurry after her.

"Cibiela has always been such a strong-willed child," Ecethor said. "I can't believe she fell under the spell of a Gadfly mage."

Greny's previous encounter with Holver Dronan suggested the only magic the Rhumgadian wielded was a modestly handsome face and an oily charisma, but now was not the time to dispel Ecethor's delusion.

"I suppose you must think me a terrible mother. If I had more sons than Rosel and Thenem, I'd have sent them down here to deal with Dronan and his cronies. Courtesars are supposed to defend family honor, after all. Perhaps I should have brought them to bolster our number, but ... I'm simply too embarrassed."

"Courtesars aren't suited to something like this. They are too honorable, too bound to their code to deal with rogues like Dronan."

"Cibiela's a good girl, unlike that *Thean Rerato*." Ecethor whispered the name. "That one was a traitor to the core."

Greny inhaled to contradict her, thought better of it. Thean's treason was undeniable. Duty came before his personal feelings for the girl.

"Of course, you know the Rerato girl best," Ecethor said with a wincing smile. "Not, of course, implying—"

"Let's stick to the matter at hand." Greny checked the marker on the wall of the tunnel against his map. "This is far as we dare go. You'll have to meet Dronan by yourself. Promise him anything to secure Cibiela's release. Offer him the Ducalion's head, if you must.